The

or,

The Monks of Monk Hall

Patience,

This is an amazing read. I could not put it down. In fact I read it for hours at a time.

CEW

GREATEST AMERICAN ROMANCE EVER PUBLISHED.

COMPLETE IN TWO VOLUMES.

THE QUAKER CITY.

PHILADELPHIA

THE AUTHOR'S REVISED EDITION

Philadelphia:

T. B. PETERSON & BROTHERS, 306 CHESTNUT STREET.

VOLUME ONE. PRICE FIFTY CENTS.

WE ADVISE ALL PERSONS TO READ CAREFULLY THE THREE OTHER PAGES OF

Wood engraved bastard title page from George Lippard, *The Quaker City; or The Monks of Monk Hall: A Romance of Philadelphia Life, Mystery, and Crime* (Philadelphia: T. B. Peterson and Brothers, [1845]).
Courtesy, the American Antiquarian Society.

THE QUAKER CITY;

or,

The Monks of Monk Hall.

A ROMANCE OF PHILADELPHIA LIFE,
MYSTERY, AND CRIME

George Lippard

Edited with introduction and notes
by David S. Reynolds

University of Massachusetts Press
Amherst

This edition published by arrangement with Macmillan Publishing Company from *The Monks of Monk Hall*, by George Lippard, Odyssey Press edition,
Printed in the United States of America
LC 94-44599
ISBN 0-87023-971-6

Library of Congress Cataloging-in-Publication Data

Lippard, George, 1822-1854.
[Quaker City]
The Quaker City, or, The monks of Monk Hall : a romance of Philadephia life, mystery, and crime / George Lippard ; edited, with introduction and notes by David S. Reynolds.
p. cm.
Includes bibliographical references.
ISBN 0-87023-971-6 (paperback)
1. Philadelphia (Pa.)—Social life and customs—Fiction. 2. City and town life—Pennsylvania—Philadelphia—Fiction. 3. Crime—Pennsylvania—Philadelphia—Fiction. I. Reynolds, David S., 1948– II. Title. III. Title: Quaker City. IV. Title: Monks of Monk Hall.
PS2246.L8Q3 1995
813'.3—dc20 94-44599
CIP

British Library Cataloguing in Publication data are available.

This book is published with the support and cooperation of the University of Massachusetts Boston.

Contents

Introduction

George Lippard's *The Quaker City* is one of the most important popular novels in American history. The fact that it was long forgotten, surviving only as an underground classic, in no way diminishes its significance. Today, with noncanonical literature and "bottom-up" history attracting widespread attention, we have a fresh opportunity to appreciate the many facets of Lippard's powerful, disturbing novel.

The publication of *The Quaker City* was a landmark event in popular culture. When it appeared in 1845, it sold 60,000 copies in its first year and 10,000 copies annually during the next decade. The most popular American novel before the appearance of *Uncle Tom's Cabin* (1852), it went through some twenty-seven American printings in four years and was pirated in Germany and England, where it appeared under different titles. Its fierce social satire and suggestive eroticism made it an instant *succes de scandale*. It became, as Lippard boasted, "more attacked, and more read, than any work of American fiction ever published."[1] By 1848 *Godey's Lady's Book* could say of Lippard: "This author has struck out on an entirely new path, and stands isolated on a point inaccessible to the mass of writers of the present day. He is unquestionably the most popular writer of the day, and his books are sold, edition after edition, thousand after thousand, while those of others accumulate, like useless lumber, on the shelves of the publishers."[2]

Like certain other best-sellers of the period, such as Harriet Beecher

Stowe's *Uncle Tom's Cabin* and Susan Warner's *The Wide, Wide World,* Lippard's novel crystallizes nineteenth-century social issues with a directness unseen in more familiar writers like Melville and Hawthorne. If Stowe's cultural work was to unmask the slave system and Warner's to trace the travails and triumphs of middle-class women, Lippard's was to reveal the underside of capitalism and urbanization. *The Quaker City* is the quintessential example of what I have elsewhere called the city-mysteries novel, which delved into the dark, unsettling aspects of urban life.[3] Although anticipated in some ways by Eugene Sue's *The Mysteries of Paris* and imitated in a host of novels about American cities from New York to San Francisco, *The Quaker City* stands out for its demonic energy, its soaring imaginativeness, and its revolutionary political themes.

Lippard is significant as both a product and a mover of his times. A pioneering critic of institutions, he forged a social theory in several ways analogous to that of his German contemporary Karl Marx (whose works he never read) and founded a nationwide labor organization to put this theory into action. A man with feminist leanings, he supported women's self-organization, believing that the woman's lot was as bad as the slave's. A harbinger of reformers and revolutionists to come, he brandished his literary sword against what he perceived to be capitalist oppression with a militancy unprecedented in his country. Although he stressed peaceful social change, he warned that if the demands of workers were not met, they would be forced "to go to War in any and all forms—War with the Rifle, Sword, and Knife."[4]

In a day when few American authors paid attention to the working class, he declared that "a literature which does not work practically for the advancement of social reform, or which is too good or too dignified to picture the wrongs of the great mass of humanity, is just good for nothing at all."[5] Again and again he railed against the prevailing bourgeois literature of his time, which he considered a false literature of "twaddle-dom" and "lollypopitude" characterized by a "syllabub insipidity." Despite its anticapitalist motivation, his work does not reflect what would later be known as socialist realism. Lippard sought to expose the grim side of life in America undergoing rapid urbanization, not through objective sociological analysis or sober representation but rather through passionate, often unbridled, poetic expression. In the implacable extremism of his radical imagination—in his constant recourse to the marvelous, black humor, eroticism, and violence—Lippard arrived at the threshold of modern surrealism.

"George Lippard." S. F. Earl, oil on canvas, 1846.
Courtesy, Historical Society of Pennsylvania.

George Lippard emerged out of a background of private pain and social turmoil. Descended from Palatines who had come to the Philadelphia area to escape religious persecution in their native Germany, he was born on April 10, 1822, on a farm in West Nantmeal Township, Chester County, Pennsylvania, the fourth of six children of Daniel and Jemima Lippard. His father, an erstwhile teacher who had served for three years as the treasurer of Philadelphia County, had bought the fertile ninety-two-acre farm in 1820 but put it up for sale shortly after George was born. Two years later, after Daniel had suffered a crippling carriage accident while delivering farm goods to market, the family moved to the old Lippard homestead in Germantown, where George's German-speaking grandfather Michael was still living. By 1825 George's parents, both of whom had become physically incapable of raising a large family, had moved to Philadelphia, leaving George and his sisters in Germantown in the care of their grandfather and their two maiden aunts, Catherine and Mary.

George's years in Germantown nurtured several of the anxieties and loyalties that would be revealed in his adult writings. A sickly and intense youth who wore his black hair long in back-country German fashion, George was thought to be a "queer" fellow "of no account" by some of his mates at the old Concord School across from his home.[6] He liked to play hooky and fish or hunt for birds by the Wissahickon, the lovely winding creek that would be the setting of several of his romances. An important feature of the Germantown period was the steady sale of the family property, which had been owned by Lippards since 1784. To make ends meet, George's aunts sold first the orchard and garden and finally the house itself to a local tanner. Later on, George bitterly wondered why "this old house, this bit of land could not have been spared from the land sharper and mortgage hunter," whom Lippard had come to view as the murderous "destroyer of the homestead."[7]

A contemporary biographer of Lippard portrayed him as a Dantesque youth "perpetually haunted by a sense of his own mortality," which is not surprising because between 1830 and 1843 he was to lose his grandfather, his mother, an infant brother, his father, and two of his sisters.[8] Shortly after the death of his mother in 1831, George moved with his aunts and sisters to Philadelphia. George's father, who ran a grocery store and served as a constable, remarried in 1833. George never went to live with his father and stepmother. The frail, feverishly imaginative boy found refuge from misfortune in religion, incessantly reading the Bible and holding religious services in the woods with friends. In August 1837 Cornelia Bayard, a Philadelphia woman who thought George showed academic promise, persuaded him, against the wishes of his aunts and sisters, to go to Catherine Livingston Garretson's Classical School in Rhinebeck, New York, with the aim of eventually studying for the Methodist ministry at Middletown College. This experience brought more disillusionment. Upset by the uncharitable behavior of the school's clergyman director, the fifteen-year-old Lippard left the school in disgust—the first act of open rebellion against established religion by one who would later become a trenchant critic of hypocritical preachers.

Lippard returned to Philadelphia to witness his father's death in October 1837. He soon learned that his father, with whom he had never been close, had left him no share of an estate worth about $2,000. Distraught and penniless, Lippard took on a couple of law-assistant jobs that paid little. For a while he lived like a homeless bohemian, wandering the Philadelphia streets and sleeping in abandoned buildings and artists' studios. While his law jobs exposed him to "social life, hidden sins, and iniquities covered with the cloak of authority," his walks about Philadelphia gave him firsthand knowledge of the terrible effects of the great depression of 1837–44.[9] This was a time of bank closings, unemployment, strikes, and widespread starvation. Especially wretched were the city's tailors and seamstresses, who led squalid, desperate lives in crowded tenements.

Alarmed by this social misery, Lippard decided to become a writer for the masses. Apparently his original impulse was to entertain rather than save these masses, for one of the first products of his pen, *The Ladye Annabel,* was a traditional Gothic romance involving medieval torture, alchemy, social revolution, live burial, and necrophilia. Nevertheless, the novel was sufficiently powerful to draw an accolade from his friend Poe, who called it "richly inventive and imaginative—indicative of *genius* in its author."[10]

While he was writing *The Ladye Annabel,* Lippard worked as a rewrite man and then as a city news reporter for the *Spirit of the Times,* a lively Philadelphia penny newspaper edited by John S. DuSolle. The volatile Lippard was well suited to the paper, whose motto was "Democratic and Fearless: Devoted to No Clique and Bound to No Master." His crowd-pleasing satirical columns, "The Sanguine Poetaster" and "Our Talisman," which attacked literary sentimentalists and the idle rich, caused a dramatic rise in the paper's circulation. After five months with the *Spirit of the Times,* Lippard quit to write for and then edit the *Citizen Soldier,* another Philadelphia paper. Among his most popular *Citizen Soldier* pieces was "The Spermaceti Papers," which cleverly caricatured the writers and editors associated with George R. Graham and Co., publisher of *Graham's Magazine,* the *Saturday Evening Post,* and other popular periodicals.

While he presented most of those in the Graham group as mawkish and venal, he singled Edgar Allan Poe out for praise. He had met Poe, presumably in 1842 while he was working with the *Spirit of the Times,* whose offices were near those of *Graham's Magazine,* where Poe was working at the time. He wrote of Poe: "He is, perhaps, the most original writer that ever existed in America. Delighting in the wild and visionary, his mind penetrates the inmost recesses of the human soul, creating vast and magnificent dreams, eloquent fancies, and terrible mysteries."[11]

Lippard's early newspaper writings initiated a period of remarkable productivity and popularity for him. Between 1842 and 1852 he produced an average of a million words annually in novels, essays, and lectures. He was a literary volcano constantly erupting with hot rage against America's ruling class. In his city novels he portrayed licentiousness and hypocrisy among urban aristocrats. In his semi-fanciful "legends" about early Christian and American history, he romanticized history's humanitarian heroes, from Jesus to George Washington. In a day when Thoreau's social criticism went virtually unnoticed, Lippard's took the nation by storm, provoking constant controversy and causing unprecedented sales of his fiction.

None of his writings were as controversial as *The Quaker City; or, The Monks of Monk Hall. A Romance of Philadelphia Life, Mystery and Crime.* For all its racy scandal sheets, sensational penny papers, and imported French novels, Philadelphia had never seen the likes of *The Quaker City.* The novel's main plot was familiar to many, for it was based on a famous case of 1843 in which a Philadelphian named Singleton Mercer was acquitted after killing Mahlon Heberton, who had enticed Mercer's sister into a house of assignation and allegedly seduced her on a promise of marriage. Onto this real-life scandal Lippard added several other plots as well as various elements—the violent grotesquerie of the Gothic novel, the democratic antielitism of the penny press and French fiction, colorful Dickensian satire—to produce a serial novel with instant appeal for the mass audience. The ten paper-covered installments of the novel appearing between the fall of 1844 and the spring of 1845 sold at a record-breaking pace. When the first two-thirds of the novel were bound together after six months, 48,000 copies were bought. When in May 1845 the whole expanded version appeared, with a dedication to Charles Brockden Brown and engravings by DeWitt C. Hitchcock and F. O. C. Darley, the publishers claimed that more than 60,000 copies had been sold within a year.

The Quaker City reportedly divided Philadelphia into two camps, with poor workers taking Lippard's side. The city was buzzing with guesses about which local celebrities Lippard was trying to expose in his various subplots. In November 1844, when only a few of the ten serial segments had appeared, a local paper was running ads for "The Monk Hall Cigars . . . Fresh from Monk Hall."

Also in November Lippard signed a contract with Francis C. Wemyss, the manager of the Chesnut Street Theater, to furnish a dramatized version of *The Quaker City.* Lippard wrote a play, which went into rehearsal and was scheduled for performance on November 11. When the playbills were put up, however, Singleton Mercer, displeased by Lippard's notably qualified portrayal of him as Byrnewood Arlington, defaced a bill that was posted outside the theater while a jeering crowd gathered to watch. Mercer then applied for two hundred tickets "for the purpose of a grand row" and threats were heard that the theater would be sacked or burned.[12] Alarmed by the growing agitation, Wemyss, after consulting with the mayor of Philadelphia and the state deputy attorney-general, decided to cancel the play. On November 11 an unruly crowd, angry about the cancellation, gathered outside the theater, with the whole city police force trying to keep order. Lippard, who later said he was armed with a sword-cane and pistols to repel assaults, helped pacify the crowd by giving a speech. When a substitute play was proposed, the mob finally dispersed.

The theater affair was wonderful publicity and encouraged the first publisher of *The Quaker City,* George B. Zieber, to sign a new contract giving Lippard a salary of five dollars a week for three months plus half of the publisher's profits from a greatly expanded version of the novel which Lippard completed early in 1845.

Critical response to the novel was mixed. The local press generally praised it. The *Philadelphia Home Journal* called it "the first American work which, written with the intention of illustrating the secrets of life in our large cities, has met with the decided approval of the public."[13] The *Saturday Courier* lauded Lippard's insights into the human soul. In Boston Theodore Parker found "scenes of great power and unexceptionable excellence" in the novel. Lippard received ambiguous plaudits from as far away as England, where in London the *New Monthly Magazine* called his novel "one of the most remarkable that has emanated from the new world."[14]

These voices, however, were drowned out by the protest against what was called the novel's obscenity and libelous intent. John S. DuSolle, Lippard's former employer at the *Spirit of the Times,* charged Lippard with writing "a disgusting mass of filth" and with trying to blackmail prominent Philadelphians.[15] The *United States Saturday Post* lambasted him as a "pernicious" writer of "the French school," arguing that as the chief of "*the raw head and bloody bones school*" of literature he aroused "the wanton devil that lies sleeping in every human heart" and gilded "robust licentiousness" with "namby-pamby sentimentalities about the beauty of virtue, and heaven and hell."[16] In London the *Athenaeum* declared that Lippard dealt with "atrocities too horrid for belief."[17] Responding to charges that he had written "the most immoral work of the age," Lippard insisted that he was a moral crusader who depicted sex and violence only to expose them.[18]

The critical debate over Lippard's "immorality" raged for years, stimulating sales and keeping alive curiosity about the book. In 1846 the popular German novelist Friedrich Gerstäcker claimed authorship of *Die Quackserstadt und ihre Geheiminisse,* a translation of Lippard's novel that passed through three editions in as many months. Two years later another pirated version of *The Quaker City* was printed in London under the title of *Dora Livingstone, the Adulteress; or, The Quaker City.*

In America the success of Lippard's work and of Eugene Sue's *The Mysteries of Paris* gave impetus to a whole school of popular fiction about the "mysteries and miseries" of American cities. Some fifty American novels of city life, most of which exaggerated Lippard's sensationalism while leaving out his reformist purpose and psychological themes, appeared between 1844 and 1860; Ned Buntline, Henri Foster, and George Thompson established themselves as the most prolific and opportunistic authors in the field. The corrupt aristocracy and squalid poverty of New York, Boston, and Philadelphia were the most popular topics, though the city novelists investigated a remarkable array of other American cities, including Rochester, Lowell, Nashua, St. Louis, New Orleans, and San Francisco. One of these novels, A. J. H. Duganne's *Mysteries of Three Cities* (1845), included a plot about "George Davenant" (Lippard), a poor long-haired Philadelphian who worked for "Stephen Soleill's *Eau de Temps*" (DuSolle's *Spirit of the Times*) and then went on to "rail at the world" in his exposé of Philadelphia.[19] Henri Foster's *Ellen Grafton. The Den of Crime* (1850) was one of several obvious imitations of *The Quaker City,* and other city novels either directly quoted Lippard's work or blatantly lifted devices from it.

After the initial furor over *The Quaker City* had died down, Lippard turned his attention to writing "legends" of the American Revolution. On the surface, these patriotic stories, which presented the founding fathers as virtual demigods, seem distant from his blood-curdling city novels. But they were the product of a radical-democrat sensibility that simultaneously idealized America's republican ideals and found these ideals unrealized in an urban world of class divisions and widespread corruption. In novels like *Blanche of Brandywine* and story collections like *Washington and His Generals,* Lippard re-created history in such a way as to accentuate the courage, magnanimity, and democratic sympathies of bygone heroes.

His legends had widespread cultural impact. The millions of Americans today who think that on July 4, 1776, the Liberty Bell was rung to proclaim freedom throughout the land, after fifty-six founding fathers had communally signed the Declaration of Independence, are indebted to Lippard, who fabricated the myth in one of his legends for the *Saturday Courier.* The facts about the Declaration are not nearly as dramatic as Lippard led many Americans to believe. In reality, the Declaration was adopted on July 2, 1776. The preamble was adopted on July 4, but the signing did not begin until August 2, and the list of signers as it now stands was not completed until January 18, 1777. There was no public celebration the day the preamble was adopted. The Declaration was proclaimed and read in public by the city sheriff at noon on July 8, in the State House Square, and reportedly there were bonfires and a general ringing of bells.

In Lippard's version, on July 4 an old man climbs to the State House bell tower, telling a blue-eyed boy below to yell "Ring!" as soon as he hears from the recently convened Continental Congress that the Declaration has been signed. After a long description of the fifty-six signers inside Independence Hall, Lippard has John Hancock emerge to speak with the boy, who runs to the State House with the glorious message of liberty. The Liberty Bell tolls triumphantly and there is a mass celebration. The perpetuation of Lippard's myth resulted not only from its powerful jingoistic appeal but also from its being presented as fact in several important history books, including Benson J. Lossing's *The Pictorial Field Book of the Revolution* (1850), John Franklin Jameson's famous *Dictionary of United States History* (1894), and, most remarkable of all, John H. Hazleton's exhaustively documented *The Declaration of Independence* (1906). Although more recent scholars have confirmed

Hazleton's remark that the story might be apocryphal, the Liberty Bell has become a sacred relic venerated by thousands of visitors to Philadelphia and widely exploited by politicians and advertising people—all a direct result of Lippard's sky-scraping fancy.

Predictably, the popularity of Lippard's legends made them subject to pirating and plagiarism. When Joel Tyler Headley's *Washington and His Generals* appeared shortly after Lippard's work of the same name, Lippard, in a series of newspaper articles, accused Headley of plagiarism. Lippard declared that he had been "the victim of such petty larcenies for years" and that "the very men who have clamored loudest about my immorality, have manifested their sincerity by appropriating whole pages from my books."[20] He documented his claim against Headley and against three other "pilferers" as well. When Headley failed to reply to his charges, he turned on another plagiarist, Friedrich Gerstäcker, the translator of *The Quaker City* of whom Lippard said: "Here is a Dutch Headley, with a vengeance, who takes not only part of my book, but takes it all, and put his [name] on the cover."

Lippard looked and lived like a rebel. Sporting unfashionably long hair that fell in curls to his shoulders, he often wore a blue velvet coat, with a white vest that buttoned tightly at his slim waist. A billowing cravat and black cloak added Byronic flourish to his appearance. His defiance of custom was also manifested by his unusual wedding ceremony. He had courted Rose Newman for three years; in May 1847 they were married by moonlight on a high rock overlooking the Wissahickon in Germantown. This odd ceremony provoked embellished newspaper reports that Rose and George, dressed in buckskin, had exchanged a corncob and a pipe in weird imitation of Indian ritual.

But far more shocking to Lippard's contemporaries than his looks or behavior was the radicalism of his fiction. In his city novels he angrily attacked nearly every type of "respectable" Philadelphian: capitalists, clergymen, lawyers, politicians, bankers, editors, and merchants. He depicted such pillars of society as guilty of the most heinous sins—including incest, rape, and murder—and portrayed their crimes with brutal detail in his books. As a result, he was variously dubbed a "licentious popinjay," a "redhot locofoco," and a "political pothouse brawler."

Although Lippard's works were pilloried and pirated, they had an increasing appeal for those who viewed Lippard as a champion of the poor and a foe of the hypocritical elite. Chief among his defenders was his friend Charles Chauncey Burr, a liberal Philadelphia clergyman who in 1847 wrote a long article praising him as a genius on the level of Dante or Shakespeare and as the age's leading defender of the oppressed and the neglected.

Whatever we make of Burr's characterization of his friend as a modern-day Shakespeare, the sincerity of Lippard's radical social views is beyond question. In the late 1840s he became actively involved in politics. After losing a race for the office of district commissioner of Philadelphia in 1848, he took the initiative and founded first a reform newspaper and then a radical labor organization. The newspaper that he edited for nearly two years, the *Quaker City* weekly, reached a circulation of over fifteen thousand. The paper was designed, in his words, to advance "social reform through the medium of popular literature."[21] For the paper he wrote five novels and many original essays advocating land reform and militant labor combination.

Although committed to transforming society, he was not above helping out an old friend. On July 12, 1849, the impoverished Poe, having wandered for two weeks seeking monetary assistance from old literary associates, came to Lippard's newspaper office begging for help. Lippard later recalled that Poe, hungry and hung-over, told him: "You are my last hope. If you fail me, I can do nothing but die."[22] The next day Lippard went around the hot, cholera-ridden city collecting some eleven dollars from various authors and publishers. This money helped save Poe from starvation, and Charles Chauncey Burr bought a train ticket that enabled the poet to reach Baltimore, where he took a boat to Richmond, arriving there on July 14 with two dollars to spare. In a letter to his mother Poe wrote, "To L[ippard] and C[hauncey] B[urr] . . . I am indebted for more than life."[23] When Lippard got the news of Poe's death on October 7, he wrote a moving eulogy of this wronged "man of genius," correctly predicting, "As an author, his name will live, while three-fourths of the bastard critics and mongrel authors of the present day go down to nothingness and night."[24]

About the same time that he was helping out Poe, Lippard announced in his newspaper the formation of his new labor organization, the Brotherhood of the Union. The first order of its kind in America, the Brotherhood was designed to supplant the capitalist system, which Lippard viewed as exploitative and corrupt, with a nationwide network of consumers' and producers' cooperatives, by which workers would enjoy the fruits of their own labor through self-employment and profit-sharing. Combining secrecy and ritual with radical anticapitalism, the Brotherhood adopted symbols from the American Revolution in its officer titles.

At the group's first annual convention in October 1850, Lippard was elected the "Supreme Washington" of the order, a post he held until his death. Within four years of the founding of the Brotherhood, some 150 branches, called "circles," had been formed in twenty-four states, most notably Pennsylvania but also other Eastern states and as far away as Florida, Alabama, Minnesota, and Texas. Lippard wished to replace "partial" reform groups with a universal Brotherhood, so that the "hundred thousand Arms" of American workers would "form one Great Arm, their hundred thousand separate Dollars, one Great Purse." No race, creed, sex, or trade, he emphasized, would be excluded from the Brotherhood. As a committed feminist, he was among the few in his day who made ardent pleas for women's economic independence. He declared in 1850: "Let the women from work-shops in which every woman is a worker and proprietor.—If they establish stores, let the stores be governed in such a manner that every woman concerned therein—every woman whose savings or labor is deposited there—shall have a direct 'say' in the managing of said store or work-shop."[25]

Lippard devoted his last years mainly to supervising the Brotherhood, traveling hundreds of miles lecturing on its behalf and collecting his labor writings in a volume titled *The White Banner.* Although exuberant over the growth of the Brotherhood, he suffered several personal tragedies. Between 1848 and 1851 he witnessed the deaths by tuberculosis of his beloved sister Harriet and his two young children, Mima and Paul. The hardest blow came when his twenty-six-year-old wife, Rose, died in 1851. Rose's death made him wretched and suicidal. He tried to leap into Niagara Falls but was saved when a friend pulled him back just in time. A devotee of spiritualism, he had constant visions of deceased friends and family. He once interrupted a conversation by leaping from his chair, pointing into the air, and exclaiming, "There is a figure in a shroud there! It is always behind me."[26]

Lippard came to believe he was doomed to succumb to the disease that had killed most of his immediate family. He predicted in June 1853 that tuberculosis would claim him within a year—a prediction that proved accurate. But he remained energetic and active almost to the moment of his death. After publishing a long novel in 1853, he spent the summer lecturing and returned in October to Philadelphia to supervise the annual convocation of the Brotherhood. By December his health had become so poor that he was confined to his house, but he spent the next two months writing a long newspaper story protesting against the Fugitive Slave Law. When his doctor told him he was too ill to write, he sketched some twenty stories in pictures. He was still at his desk scribbling on February 9, 1854, but weakened and died the next morning, about a month before his thirty-second birthday.

Lippard did not lack eulogists after his death. At a meeting of a Philadelphia labor organization he was hailed as "one of the shining lights in the firmament of the Nineteenth Century—one whose mind and pen has given the initiative to future stateswomen and men, so to legislate as to remove the degradation and subserviency of labor to capital, that now oppress the human race."[27] One newspaper lamented the loss of the author "whose works have been read probably as extensively as those of any other writer in the country."[28] Another prophesied that "his memory will live, his genius will live, and future ages will recognize his works while here, as a bright and good inheritance."[29]

To some degree, this prediction was right. Although Lippard's novels fell into obscurity within half a century after his death, his name was revered by members of the Brotherhood of the Union (later renamed the Brotherhood of America). Unlike most labor unions formed before the Civil War, which were snuffed out by economic depressions or internal problems, Lippard's order enjoyed a long life. It reached a peak membership of 30,000 in 1917. Although it had lost its revolutionary fervor and had become little more than a mutual aid society, it honored the name of its founder. In 1886 members of the Brotherhood erected a large monument to Lippard's memory in Philadelphia's Odd Fellows' Cemetery. Over the years Brotherhood members made mass pilgrimages to his monument. One such pilgrimage took place in 1922, the centennial of his birth. At the grave site, passages from his novels were read aloud and he was hailed as a "writer for the poor, defender of the oppressed, enemy of the tyrant, and ever tireless in doing good."[30] Subsequently, the Brotherhood dwindled, becoming a tiny insurance group in Pennsylvania and New Jersey. It ceased to exist in 1994.

While Lippard's Brotherhood shrank, his reputation among literary and cultural historians steadily increased. In 1917 the Philadelphia writer Albert Mordell noted that "George Lippard, the most interesting man of letters here in the first half of the last century, is practically unknown."[31] Lippard was long excluded altogether from official histories or mentioned only passing as a picturesque eccentric. The neglect of him was curious, especially in light of the fact that everything American critics found intriguing in Poe—his use of horror, verbal delirium, irrationalism, his preoccupation with evil, his passion for mad love, his attraction to the occult, his weird humor—appear, even more intensely, in Lippard. New Critics and other formalists evidently felt more at home with Poe's artistic sculpting of these themes than with Lippard's imaginative fusion of them with revolutionary socialist commentary in fervent novels and manifestos that are light years distant from Poe's self-consciously apolitical, autonomous tales.

Only within the past two decades, with the rise of cultural studies and historicist criticism, has the situation begun to change. Some of Lippard's writings have been reprinted, and a number of articles and book chapters on aspects of his work have appeared. More and more commentators concede that Lippard deserves recognition as a significant popular novelist. His most important novel, however, has been until now virtually inaccessible. The current republication of *The Quaker City* allows today's readers to enjoy and ponder this energetic, intricate novel.

The Quaker City has three main plots, loosely connected. First is the seduction of the merchant's daughter, Mary Arlington, by the rake, Gustavus Lorrimer, and the subsequent murder of the seducer by the woman's vindictive brother, Byrnewood Arlington. Second is the attempt of Dora Livingstone, reared in poverty and now married to the wealthy Albert Livingstone, to rise even higher socially by taking up with Algernon Fitz-Cowles, who pretends he is an English lord who will give her royal rank. Dora's husband, alerted to her infidelity by her old lover, Luke Harvey, vows revenge, finally poisoning her in his country estate and then dying there in a fire. The third plot revolves around a young woman, Mabel, who was the illegitimate daughter of the monstrous pimp Devil-Bug but who was raised by the Rev. F. A. T. Pyne (originally Dick Baltzar). The lecherous, hypocritical Pyne drugs Mabel in an effort to rape her, but she is rescued by Devil-Bug, who wants to present her to the world as the daughter of the rich Livingstone, so that she will gain wealth and status. Mabel is temporarily inveigled into becoming the principle "priestess" of a cult led by a mad sorcerer,

Ravoni, but Devil-Bug kills Ravoni and frees her; she becomes known to the world as the rich Izole Livingstone, and she marries Luke Harvey.

Interwoven into these plots are others: the murders of the seducer Paul Western and the wealthy widow Becky Smolby by Devil-Bug, who ultimately dies for his crimes; a forgery scheme involving the con-artist Fitz-Cowles, the businessman Livingstone, and a Jew named Gabriel Von Pelt; and the establishment of a new religion of humanism and brotherhood by the magnetic cult leader Ravoni. Much of the action takes place in Monk Hall, Devil-Bug's huge, multitiered den of iniquity where Philadelphia's social rulers gather nightly to enjoy brandy, women, and opium.

Although these plots sometimes have the feverish, heightened quality of melodrama, they are handled with a certain dexterity. At one point in the novel Lippard pauses to praise the artistic handling of plot by the popular British novelist William Harrison Ainsworth. Often abused by "starch-and-buckram critics," writes Lippard, "Ainsworth understands the art and theory of the *plot* of a story better than any living artist."[32] In *The Quaker City* Lippard seems to be trying to outdo Ainsworth, Dickens, and other plot fabricators in the complexity of his palimpsestic plots. Compressing complicated narratives into a short time span, he isolates the three days leading up to Christmas 1842 and traces the tangled activities of his characters. Like today's soap operas, the novel proceeds by episodes, with rapid shifts in time and perspective, creating a disorienting effect for the reader.

Because Lippard's overriding goal is to replicate in fiction a society he regards as nightmarish and depraved, he creates an entire nightmare world that is always threatening to destroy ordinary perceptions of objective surroundings. The novel itself is like Monk Hall, a labyrinthine structure riddled with trap doors that are always opening beneath the reader's feet and leading to another dimension.

There has been so much concern lately with nineteenth-century sentimental-domestic writing that a somewhat lopsided view of antebellum popular culture has emerged. In surveying the total range of American fiction volumes published between 1789 and 1860, I have found that although sentimental-domestic writing was popular, sensational or adventurous fiction was even more so. *The Quaker City,* the quintessential sensational novel, determinedly undercut and ironized the sentimental-domestic genre. It drew from the mass-oriented sensationalism which had arisen in opposition to the powerful cult of domesticity, purveyed in ladies' magazines and domestic novels. American penny newspapers, which arose in the early 1830s, were known worldwide as crime ridden, scandal mongering, and profit mad. Lippard not only exploits the sensational but also directs it against the values of home, church, family, and purity that were central to the sentimental-domestic sphere.

He encodes the conflict between the sensational and the sentimental by portraying two characters from the popular press: Buzby Poodle, editor of the scandalous penny paper *The Daily Black Mail,* and Sylvester Petriken, editor of the cloyingly sentimental *Ladies Western Hemisphere.* Poodle represents sensational reportage, always featuring a "mysterious disappearance" or "terrible outrage" in a manner anticipatory of tabloid journalism. Petriken represents the bourgeois world of trite morality, filling his magazine with saccharine poetry and tepid prose.

Lippard satirizes the sentimental and, more significantly, suggests that, at bottom, the sensational and the sentimental are conjoined in the commercialized environment of urban America. The images of domesticity and religion offered by Petriken are finally as manipulated and constructed as are the sensational ones of Poodle. That the antebellum public was hungry for sentimentalism is proven by the success of *Godey's Lady's Book,* religious tracts, and domestic novels. That it was equally voracious for horror and tales of illicit sex is demonstrated by the popularity of penny papers, crime pamphlets, and yellow-covered novels. In *The Quaker City* sentimentalism and sensationalism come together in a swirling, demonic center.

Lippard relentlessly parodies the sentimental-domestic ethos. Whereas the sentimental-domestic novelists dramatize a heroine's steady progress toward domestic harmony through piety and virtue, Lippard pictures the shattering of homes as the result of obsession, betrayal, lust, and greed. Mary Arlington, the character who most closely resembles the conventional heroine, willingly leaves her quiet family circle to satisfy her naive craving for her beloved "Lorraine" (Gus Lorrimer), who uses promises of a pastoral home as an instrument of seduction. The wedding, which in domestic novels is the ultimate reward for probity, is in *The Quaker City* a sham ceremony conducted by charlatans intent on bringing about Mary's ruin. Dora Livingstone, the principal wife figure in the novel, abandons domestic virtue in her deluded quest for aristocratic status, for which she willingly gives herself to illicit sex and murderous schemes. Mockery of domesticity is equally visible in the plight of Mabel, who is led to the brink of apparent incest when her "father," F. A. T. Pyne, uses parental words of love in his attempt to seduce her. Among other things, Lippard is showing how women, in a twisted society driven by lust and money, become victims of a massive male power struggle, falling prey to male-constructed images of romance and social advancement.

Whereas most popular novelists rely chiefly upon either the sentimental or the sensational, Lippard shows how the two realms interpenetrate, creating multiple ironies. Irony controls the story of Byrnewood Arlington, who, despite his eventual disgust over the seduction of his sister, had actually facilitated that seduction by encouraging and laying a bet on Lorrimer's plans for a sexual escapade. Also ironic is the fact that Byrnewood is a seducer in his own right; Annie, the young servant he has impregnated, haunts his mind even as he tracks down and kills his sister's seducer. This sister, Mary, seems like the conventional heroine but comes close to being the obverse of one: she lies to her parents, gullibly swallows Lorrimer's talk about a Wyoming home, and at the end croons longingly for her lost "Lorraine," even after he has been exposed as a fraud.

Parody of the sentimental-domestic genre operates on many levels. Devil-Bug, the keeper of Monk Hall, uses all the terminology of domesticity. He talks of his "purty quiet" life in "the comfortable retiracy o' domestic fellicity" (221). He holds what he calls "a werry respectable family party" in his basement (503). He arranges a room in Monk Hall like a middle-class parlor, with bookcases and a fireplace "as housewives use for domestic purposes," so that the room seems to tell "a pleasant tale of fireside joys and comforts" (109, 120). His commands to others have all the unction of doting parenthood: "By-a-baby, go to sleep—that's a good feller—," or "You better go home. Your mammy's a waitin' tea for you" (120, 115). Such language is savagely parodic, since Devil-Bug is perhaps the most gleefully evil, sadistic character in American literature. His "respectable family party" is a convocation of gangsters in the underground Dead Vault of Monk Hall. His parlorlike room is a torture chamber, and his command about going to sleep is directed toward a man he has drugged with charcoal and opium.

Devil-Bug's female cohorts, the procurers Mother Nancy and Long-haired Bess, are also walking parodies of domesticity. "Mother Nancy," Lippard writes, "looked, for all the world, like a quiet old body, whose only delight was to scatter blessings around her, give large alms to the poor, and bestow unlimited amounts of tracts among the vicious" (76). This "good, dear, old body," who occupies "a fine old room" in Monk Hall with "a cheerful wood fire blazing on the spacious hearth," arranges a quiet tea party for Mary Arlington (76). But the tea party, like Mother Nancy, is a charade designed to undermine female virtue; Lippard tells us that hundreds of women have been driven to prostitution and suicide by the wily, pleasant-seeming Nancy.

One of her early victims, Emily Walraven, is now living with her in Monk Hall as Long-haired Bess, vindictively dedicated to luring other women into crime and illicit sex. Bess also uses the appurtenances of domesticity to entrap her victims. Posing as a kindly older lady, she escorts Mary to what she calls Lorrimer's family mansion. She is so convincing in her role that Mary calls her "my dear good friend" and compares the wedding Bess has arranged for her to "the stories we read in a book" (86). But the wedding, which in domestic novels is the crowning blissful ritual, is the main instrument of ruin, a mock ceremony in which various depraved characters (Poodle, Petriken, Nancy, and Bess) pose as religious or domestic types.

While Lippard repeatedly parodies the sentimental-domestic novel, he reveals his exasperation as well with the opposing genre of the sensational penny newspaper. Penny papers, replacing the stodgy sixpennies of the past, arose in the 1830s due to changes in print technology and distribution. The penny press made shock and gore, perennially sources of human interest, suddenly available to the masses. Papers like the *New York Sun,* the *New York Herald,* and the *Philadelphia Public Ledger* purveyed shocking stories in daily issues that cost just one or two pennies. In a day before strong governmental regulation, newspaper editors became notorious for their exploitative sensationalism and questionable tactics. When Walt Whitman labeled the *Herald* editor James Gordon Bennett "a reptile marking his path wherever he goes," "a midnight ghoul preying on rottenness and repulsive filth," he was airing a common attitude toward the penny press.[33] Editors were known to report crimes and disasters with more concern for profit making and excitement than for objectivity, and many accepted bribes or favors in exchange for puffing plays, books, or individuals.

Lippard was thoroughly aware of the opportunism and moral laxness of the penny editors. Buzby Poodle, editor of the aptly named *Daily Black Mail,* seems polite and domesticated—he talks in what he calls

"Domestic French"—but is in fact amoral and degraded. His one concern is with the outrage of the moment. "Do I want cash?" he asks. "I stick in an article charging some well-known citizen with theft, or seduction, or some more delightful crime. Citizen comes down in a rage—wants the article contradicted in next day's paper. He *pays* for the contradiction, of course. I have known a mere *on dit* that so-and-so had committed a hideous crime, to bring me in as much as a cool hundred at a 'lick'—" (163). Known as Count Common Sewer, Poodle feasts on the nefarious activities in Monk Hall like a vulture on decaying flesh.

Given the immense cultural influence of the penny papers, it is fitting that the whole novel resolves itself into a series of sensational headlines and news reports. "The seduction of Mary Arlington with a portr-a-i-t! Daily Black Mail—only one cent!" scream newsboys toward the end of the novel (562). Lippard invites us to "glance at the contents of a newspaper" to learn the fates of the other characters (571). The news reports he gives us are confusingly mixed: Fitz-Cowles, for instance, is pronounced innocent in one column and damned as a villain in another, and F. A. T. Pyne is congratulated in one report for saving Mabel and excoriated in another for trying to seduce her (571–72). Such contradictions, in Lippard's eyes, reflect a journalistic world in which distortion reigns and sensation is valued more than truth.

Lippard is not only commenting on popular sensational writing; he is writing a mass-oriented sensational text as well. His novel runs with blood and reeks of murder and madness. It is filled with freakish characters who swing between cold sarcasm and crazed terror. Even as it parodies the penny papers, it is itself a kind of massive penny paper, piling hair-raising events on top of each other with dizzying speed. It is of a piece with the commercialized freaks and overall violence of antebellum life. Three years before the novel was published, P. T. Barnum had opened his famous museum featuring a calf with two heads, a bearded lady, dwarves, giants, and a host of other oddities. When Lippard has Dr. McTourniquet take Livingstone into his "museum" whose displays include jars containing body parts and a two-headed black child, he is reflecting on the Barnumesque taste for the freakish (210). In a larger sense, almost every character in the novel is in some way a freak—most obviously the grotesque Devil-Bug, but also the shape-shifting Fitz-Cowles, the cackling widow Becky Smolby, the oily F. A. T. Pyne, and many others.

The sensationalism of *The Quaker City* mirrored the actual violence of rapidly urbanizing America. American cities grew at a remarkable pace between 1800 and 1840, resulting in extreme dislocation and new forms of mass violence. "The turbulent era" is the name some have assigned to the Jacksonian period, a time of race riots, theater riots, church burnings, and gang warfare that accompanied urbanization. Lippard felt he lived in an age when, as he writes in the novel, "riot after riot went howling through the town" (206). "I have stood in the streets of the Quaker City," he tells us, "while a fierce mob, hungry for blood, howled onward, their ten thousand faces glaring in the light of a burning church, whose dome went up to Heaven in clouds of smoke and waves of fire" (524). The outrages reported in the popular papers reflected a reality that was increasingly violent. *The Quaker City* enacted the turbulence of a culture in which crime rates soared and the line between mass celebrations and riots was perilously thin.

Lippard's style, likewise, reflects the zest and creativity of American street life. The term "slang" was first used around 1850 to mean common language. During the thirties and forties American urban culture had generated many slang words—"done brown," "chum," "swell," "kick the bucket," for instance—that were destined to have a long life. Whitman called slang "the lawless germinal element" behind literature, showing that language "has its bases broad and low to the ground."[34] Emerson and Thoreau were also intrigued by this "lawless" form of speech, and Melville incorporated slang into his major writings.

No antebellum writer, however, used slang as extensively and variously as Lippard. Mikhail Bakhtin's notion of polyvocality—the integration of different levels of discourse into the literary text—is exemplified by Lippard's style. The so-called flash language of sports (urban men who boasted of their sexual exploits) is used liberally by Gus Lorrimer and Byrnewood Arlington. Gutter slang is spouted by Luke Harvey in his Brick-Top phase and by the gangsters who gather in the cellar of Monk Hall. The linguistic gimmicks of evangelical preaching appear parodically in the mock sermons of F. A. T. Pyne. Southern dialect is humorously exaggerated when Easy Larkspur disguises himself as the South Carolina plantation owner Major Rappahanock Mulhill. The infusion into American language of foreign idioms that took place with rising immigration is registered in the Irish brogue of the servant Peggy Grud and the bootmaker Michael O'Flanagan, in the butchered French of Buzby Poodle, and in the Hebrew inflections of the Jewish Gabriel Von Pelt. African American dialect is used by Devil-Bug's black helpers, Musquito and Glow-worm, and, differently, by Fitz-Cowles's servant Endymion. Devil-Bug has a bizarre language of his own that seems to couple street slang with foreign inflections, as in "I vonders how *that*'ll vork!"

By absorbing extreme sensationalism and lively slang into the fabric of his novel, Lippard often reaches a stylistic level of premodern distortion and oddity. It is small wonder that he has been a cult figure among certain surrealists, because he repeatedly uses the kind of bizarre, oneiric images and blackly humorous effects that surrealism prizes. He frequently juxtaposes wildly disparate images in presurrealistic fashion. The opening chapter of *The Quaker City,* in which several men reel through the Philadelphia streets in drunken revelry, is full of time-space distortion. The inebriated Lorrimer describes a watchbox walking across the street and blacking the eyes of a lamppost that had made a face at it. One of Lorrimer's companions rides a fireplug as though it were a galloping horse, and another has a face like "a dissipated full-moon, with a large red pear stuck in the centre for a nose, while two small black beads, placed in corresponding circles of crimson tape, supply the place of eyes" (7). Such dreamlike distortion and grotesquerie enliven many other scenes in the novel, as when Dr. McTourniquet boasts of his stallion Harry Clay's simultaneous talents in horse races and politics, or when Devil-Bug dreams of "coffins floating slowly past, and the stars shining through the eyes of skulls, and the sun pouring his livid light straight downward into a wilderness of new-made graves which extended yawning and dismal over the surface of a boundless plain" (370).

To praise Lippard's style is to flout canonical wisdom, according to which Lippard is an undisciplined stylist who simply catered to popular taste. It is easy enough to spot his flaws: his penchant for archaisms like "sate" (for "sat") and "corse" (for "corpse"); his repetitions, especially when describing "voluptuous" women whose "snowy globes" and small feet fascinate him; his unrelievedly feverish tone and unlikely plot twists, such as Livingstone's last-minute revelation of his royal lineage to his dying wife; his sometimes faulty grammar, evidently the product of speedy composition and poor copyediting. Still, finish and precision are not always key ingredients in imaginative writing: witness Emily Dickinson's countless violations of grammatical rules or Whitman's loosely constructed prose-poetry. Lippard was writing for the masses at a white heat, and we can forgive his crudities in light of his overall imaginativeness and boldness.

Links can be made between Lippard and the major writers of the period. Like his close friend Poe, he combined an interest in horror and diseased psychology with a rationalist regard for the minutiae of mechanical contrivances and plot construction. There appear to be particular connections between certain scenes in *The Quaker City* and "The Cask of Amontillado," the horror tale Poe wrote shortly after Lippard's novel appeared. The Dead Vault below Monk Hall, dripping with moisture and filled with skeletons, wine casks, and hidden niches, is much like the skeleton-filled, dripping wine cellar into which Montresor lures Fortunato. The portait of Devil-Bug, spade in hand, preparing to bury alive Byrnewood Arlington and taunting him with black jokes and screeching laughter looks forward to that of Montresor, spade in hand, burying alive Fortunato while torturing him psychologically with jokes and screams.

Like Hawthorne, Lippard often emphasized multiple perspectives: for example, the many rumors about the background of Monk Hall anticipate the dark legends surrounding the House of the Seven Gables, just as the questions about Devil-Bug's lineage presage the mystery of Miriam Schaefer in *The Marble Faun*. Lippard also shared with Hawthorne certain character types, such as the fallen minister (F. A. T. Pyne and Dimmesdale) and the mad sorcerer-pseudoscientist (Ravoni and Chillingworth or Westervelt).

There are several Melvillian elements in *The Quaker City*. The dark-temperance scene in Smokey Chiffin's oyster cellar, where a "Giant of a Decanter" [10] destroys hope and wealth, looks forward to the Spouter Inn's barroom in *Moby-Dick*, where "deliriums and death" are served in "abominable" tumblers filled with the "poison" alcohol.[35] The astrologer who forewarns Lorrimer and Arlington about their grim destiny is similar to Melville's prophetic Elijah, who cautions Ishmael and Queequeg about the *Pequod* and its captain. Ahab's dark pronouncements about all-controlling fate are anticipated in Lippard's interjection about his characters: "Fools that they were! To think that Fate which drives its iron heels over hearts and thrones and graves, would turn aside its career for them!" (366)

To describe a world they viewed as fundamentally skewed, both Lippard and Melville fixed on the word "queer." "Queer world this!" exclaims Luke Harvey. "Don't know much about other worlds, but it strikes me that if a prize were offered somewhere by somebody, for the queerest world a-going, this world of ours might be rigged up nice, and sent in like a bit of show-beef, as the premium queer world" (34). In a letter to Hawthorne, Melville imagined sitting together in heaven and singing about "that queer little hole called the world," and he featured the word in *Moby-Dick,* especially in the language of the humorous mate Stubb, who typically says: "It's very queer. . . . It's queer; very queer; and [Ahab's] queer too: aye, take him fore and aft, he's about the queerest old man Stubb ever sailed with. . . . Damn me, but all things are queer, come to think of 'em."[36]

Other pre-Melvillian images are scattered throughout *The Quaker City.* The partially veiled Skeleton Monk that hangs in Monk Hall, symbolizing the depravity of Philadelphia's rulers, anticipates the veiled skeleton on the ship in "Benito Cereno" which stands for, among other things, the oppressiveness of slaveholding Western imperialists. Lippard's interpolated story of a sailor wrongly accused and then hanged for killing his captain, after which spectators take pieces of wood from his gibbet as relics of the execution, presages the climax and denouement of *Billy Budd.* Both Lippard and Melville were profoundly disturbed by the distance between surface appearances and reality. Just as Lippard calls high society "a specimen of paste-board statuary, giving but a grotesque outline, of the reality which it is intended to represent" (182), so Melville has Ahab call reality a "pasteboard mask" he wants to pierce.[37]

Both writers found the confidence man an appropriate character for expressing the illusory nature of appearances. In *The Quaker City* Lippard portrays an urban world of mass deceit. His primary confidence man, Algernon Fitz-Cowles, has so many disguises that when he asks his servant, "*Who are we?*" the reply is, "We are so many tings, dat de debbil hisself could'nt count 'em—" (155). Actually, though, virtually every character in the novel is a confidence man or woman, often using a phony name and almost always presenting a false front. Reality itself seems elusive and impenetrable, as is suggested by Lorrimer's summary of life: "Every thing fleeting and nothing stable, every thing shifting and changing, and nothing substantial! A bundle of hopes and fears, deceits and confidences, joys and miseries, strapped to a fellow's back like Pedlar's wares" (23). A dozen years later, Melville in *The Confidence-Man* would similarly conjure up a world of fleeting, deceptive appearances, particularly in his depiction of the title character, who in many avatars embodies a quicksandlike vision of things.

To mention such analogies between Lippard and the major writers is to bring up the question of literary influence. Since none of the above writers, except Poe, mentioned Lippard in his writings, it is difficult to declare with certainty that *The Quaker City* influenced other works. Suffice it to say that Lippard was drawing from the same repository of cultural images as the other writers and that his dramatization of these images frequently paralleled theirs.

In the case of Mark Twain and Walt Whitman, the issue of influence becomes especially tantalizing, since they *did* mention him. In 1853 Mark Twain wrote: "Geo. Lippard in his *Legends of Washington and His Generals* has rendered the Wissahickon sacred in my eyes, and I shall make that trip, as well as one to Germantown, soon."[38] Did Lippard's romantic portrayal of the Wissahickon River influence Twain's later romanticization of the Mississippi? Even more significant, did Twain read not only Lippard's Revolutionary legends but also *The Quaker City*? It is perhaps significant that he used *The Quaker City* as the name for his ship of fools in *Innocents Abroad.* If he did read Lippard's best-selling novel, he may have noticed several things that piqued his imagination: the use of vernacular language; the depiction of human savagery in Devil-Bug (who anticipates the cruel Pap in *Huckleberry Finn*); the cynical view of conventional society; and the parody on sentimental literature, to be perfected by Twain in the portrait of the lachrymose poetess Emmeline Grangerford.

Also intriguing is the possible influence of Lippard on Whitman. In 1860 Whitman discussed the novelist in Pfaff's restaurant with the Philadelphia author Charles D. Gardette. Whitman jotted this note about the conversation:

> Nov. 26, '60—Lippard
> Gardette's account to me, (in Pfaff's) of George Lippards life,—was handsome, Byronic,—commenced at 18—wrote sensation novels—drank—drank—drank—died mysteriously either of suicide or mania a potu at 25—or 6—a perfect wreck—was ragged, drunk, beggarly—[39]

Gardette, of course, had some things wrong: Lippard, unlike Poe, did not have a drinking problem; nor was he ragged, beggarly, or a suicide. Still, the fact that Whitman was discussing Lippard six years after his death suggests his interest in the popular novelist. Had this been a longstanding interest? Had Whitman known Lippard's works in the 1840s, before the first edition of *Leaves of Grass*?

There are strong indications he had. There was a close parallel between Lippard's indictment of capital punishment in *The Quaker City* and three Whitman articles published shortly after the novel appeared. Appalled by the incongruity of Christian ministers endorsing death by hanging, Lippard sprinkled ironic comments on the cruel "gibbet" throughout the novel and had the blackly humorous Devil-Bug cheer at the sight of the gallows: "Hurrah! The gallows is livin' yet! Hurrah!" (375). Whitman picked up Lippard's wording in his 1846 newspaper articles "Hurrah for Hanging!" and "Hurrah for the Choking of Human Lives!"[40] In an 1845 article he made the Lippardian comment that every time he passed a church he saw a gallows frame and heard the words "Strangle and kill in the name of God!" Several of Whitman's scribblings in his early notebooks also bear the impress of Lippard. Devil-Bug's outlandish vision of a skeleton-filled coffin propelled on the Schuylkill seems to be echoed in Whitman's equally strange notebook entry: "A coffin swimming buoyantly on the swift flowing current of the river."[41]

There is compelling evidence that Whitman's radical, subversive spirit in his major poetry was influenced by Lippard. A tame writer of conventional verse early in his career, Whitman made a notable change toward radicalism in his political-protest poems of the early 1850s, including two, "Resurgemus" and "A Boston Ballad," that were later incorporated into *Leaves of Grass*. Both poems contain the combined social radicalism and Gothic imagery that was Lippard's special contribution to American popular discourse. Just as Lippard portrayed workers as "slaves" victimized by lying, cheating upper-class figures, Whitman in "Resurgemus" indicted social rulers as "liars" who have been inflicting "numberless agonies, murders, lusts" on the people and have been "worming from his simplicity the poor man's wages."[42] Just as Lippard imagined a time when the shapes of the murdered, oppressed classes would rise in an eerie procession behind the upper classes, so Whitman describes ruling-class exploiters and then sees "behind all, lo, a Shape/Vague as the night, draped interminably," with a finger pointed high in terrible warning.

Whitman resorted again to blackly humorous Gothic imagery in "A Boston Ballad," his 1854 poem protesting the retrieval by Boston authorities of the fugitive slave Anthony Burns. The bizarre procession in Devil-Bug's dream, in which haughty rulers lead chained black and white slaves through the city until the phantoms of the oppressed rise up behind them, finds an echo in Whitman's poem, in which the government procession leading the chained Burns is surrounded by the phantoms of old patriots who are shocked by the betrayal of American ideals in the arrest of Burns.

In a larger sense, the bracingly rebellious spirit of *Leaves of Grass* participates in the zestful defiance popularized by Lippard. If Lippard used words as weapons to attack social conventions, Whitman declared, "I think agitation is the most important factor of all—the most deeply important. To stir, to question, to suspect, to examine, to denounce!"[43] This Lippardian tone resonates in key lines in his poems: "I am he who walks the States with a barb'd tongue, questioning every one I meet"; "Let others praise eminent men and hold up peace, I hold up agitation and conflict."[44] He sounded much like Lippard when he denounced the "vast ganglions of bankers and merchant princes," or when he characterized the grotesque rich: "I see an aristocrat/I see a smoucher grabbing the good dishes exclusively to himself and grinning at the starvation of others as if it were funny,/I gaze on the greedy hog."[45]

Although we cannot go so far as to say of *The Quaker City* what Hemingway said of *Huckleberry Finn*—that all American literature came from it—it is useful to note such continuities between Lippard and the others. At the same time, however, Lippard is not to be confused with anyone else. He has a style and vision all his own, rooted deeply in his powerfully felt political views.

If *The Quaker City* has the atmosphere of a nightmare, it is largely because Lippard regarded American society as a nightmarish realm of class divisions, economic uncertainty, and widespread corruption. Lippard was not a city novelist in the way the realists or naturalists would be. He described the city not mimetically but impressionistically. In the 1830s and 1840s the American city became in several senses a strange, overwhelming place. In a time before effective sanitation, cities were squalid and disease prone. Garbage was heaped on unpaved streets that rapidly turned to mud or dust. The tenement areas where the poor lived were filled with overcrowded, ramshackle houses. Lippard places Monk Hall in an area where "a mass of miserable frame houses seemed about to commit suicide and fling themselves madly into the gutter, and in the distance a long line of dwellings, offices, and factories, looming in broken perspective, looked as if they wanted to shake hands across the narrow street" (48). Huge hotels, department stores, and mansions stood in stark contrast to the humble homes of the poor. Lippard captures the architectural inequality of the city when he pictures "a row of massive buildings, dwellings and warehouses, with a small frame house, arising near the centre of the square, like an image of starvation in the midst of plenty" (403).

The inequality Lippard perceived in the city's physical landscape reflected the widening gap between the rich and the poor. The dramatic upward redistribution of wealth in Philadelphia between 1800 and 1860 was typical of what was happening in many American cities. According to some historians, during this period the share of Philadelphia's wealth controlled by the richest 10 percent of the city's population nearly doubled, increasing from 50 to 90 percent.[46] Even more remarkably, the share controlled by the wealthiest 1 percent ballooned from less than a quarter to a half, while that owned by the poorest 75 percent sank from 30 to less than 3 percent. Urbanization and industrialization brought about a wholesale shift in the social structure toward a large wage-earning, poor and near-poor work force. There was justification for Lippard's indictments of the wealthy class, which, he writes, attends church and supports foreign missions "while it has not one single throb of pity, for the poor, who starve, rot and die, within its very eyesight!" (224).

The urban rich lived in conspicuous opulence, trying to create a surrogate aristocracy in a supposedly democratic nation. Lippard's notion of a huge Monk Hall where the wealthy gathered to revel was by no means a complete fabrication. Very exclusive social clubs for the wealthy were formed during this period. The Philadelphia Club, founded in 1834, had 160 members by the mid-1840s. In New York, the Bread and Cheese Club, the Century Club, the St. Nicholas Society, and the Hone Club were all established before 1840. These clubs represented a highly visible, arrogant display of status on the part of the urban elite. The main pastimes at the clubs were card playing, smoking, chatting, and wine drinking. From Lippard's working-class perspective, the clubs seemed nothing less than demonic. Monk Hall is called a place "where the very devil is played under a cloak, and sin grows fat within the shelter of quiet rooms and impenetrable walls" (23), a place where lawyers, merchants, parsons, editors, and others drink themselves into oblivion while mouthing moral platitudes.

Lippard was painfully aware of rising evidence of upper-class corruption. As Mark Summers has shown, during this period corruption infested the legislative and judicial branches of American city governments up and down the eastern seaboard. Vote fraud, graft, and money skimming were common among the aldermen and judges who wielded power in the cities.[47] Whitman in the 1855 preface to *Leaves of Grass* would indict the "swarms of cringers, suckers, doughfaces, lice of politics, planners of sly involutions for their own preferment to city offices or state legislatures or the judiciary or congress or the presidency." In this protest, Lippard anticipated him by a decade.

Many times in *The Quaker City,* ruling-class exploitativeness or corruption is targeted. Lippard describes one judge with "his pocket-book crammed full of bribes" and another fingering "the hard gold which buys the life of some wealthy murderer from the gallows, or the liberty of some gilded robber from the jail" (372, 347). Vote fraud, especially common among city politicians who purchased the votes of immigrants and poor natives, is exposed through the portrayal of the criminal Rusty Jake, "a small politician" who had been "an influential party man, on a limited scale." "In procuring forged naturalization papers for verdant foreigners," Lippard writes, "or in swearing native paupers and thieves into the inestimable knowledge of voting, he was alike efficient and skillful" (482). Almost every facet of American official life is said to be subject to bribery. Fitz-Cowles boasts that he has the prices of seven judges, ten juries, and a score of lawyers in his pocket, explaining, "These things are all for sale—" (174).

Bankers were particularly guilty in Lippard's eyes because they seemed to conspire against the poor. In 1837 most of the nation's banks suspended specie payment, refusing any longer to redeem their paper notes in hard money. The great depression of 1837–44 put nearly a third of Americans out of work at a time when hundreds of banks were failing and when some leading bankers were being tried for criminal activity. In 1842 the prominent banker Nicholas Biddle and several associates were brought to trial in a two-million-dollar fraud case. The trial provoked a storm of protest against Biddle. Even one of Biddle's wealthy friends, Sidney George Fisher, admitted of the "Bank of United States frauds": "Indeed it is villainy on a most enormous scale. . . . I believe there has been more corruption and fraud in this country for the last five years than in all England for the last five hundred."[48]

The Quaker City directs many barbs at bankers, as when Byrnewood Arlington sees "old Grab-and-Snatch, the President of the——Bank, which every body says is on the eve of a grand blow-up!" or when Devil-Bug says that America's aristocrats "aint nothin' but a pack o' swindlin'

Bank d'rectors" (25, 374). Most memorable is the portrait of the bank director Job Joneson—"one of your good citizens, who subscribe large sums to tract societies, and sport velvet-cushioned pews in the church"—who refuses to give a cent to the indigent John Davis, who had deposited a small sum in Joneson's bank before it had failed (406). Davis returns home only to find his wife and daughter dead of starvation, at which point the poor man kills himself.

Lippard held Nicholas Biddle's United States Bank especially reprobate because of its mishandling of the legacy of Stephen Girard, the Philadelphia philanthropist who at his death in 1831 had left some six million dollars to fund a college for white male orphans. Due to Biddle's indifference to the poor, Girard's money languished in the bank until 1848, when the college was finally built. Lippard often lamented the plight of Philadelphia orphans who, deprived of an education because of the postponement of the college's construction, were doomed by illiteracy to lives of poverty and crime. "Come into court, old Stephen Girard," he has Luke Harvey exclaim; "come into court with your will in hand. . . . What say you of Quaker City justice? Is your College built? Has a single orphan been fed, clothed, or educated at your expense, or with your money?" (205–6). Later in the novel Lippard refers again to "Girard College—that unfinished Monument of a foul wrong, done to ten thousand orphans . . . in order that a Corporation might feast and riot upon old Stephen's money" (269).

In addition to political and corporate malfeasance, hypocrisy among America's religious and moral spokespersons was a major issue with Lippard. He wrote *The Quaker City* in the wake of the Washingtonian temperance movement, which after 1840 had spread among the working class but which had soon fallen into disrepute because of its sensational tactics and noted instances of backsliding among its leaders, especially John Bartholomew Gough. Lippard notes the "imposture and trickery" of "intemperate temperance lecturers," and he has the preacher-reformer F. A. T. Pyne say as he takes opium: "We temperance folks must have some little excitement after we have forsworn intemperance. When we leave off Alcohol, we indulge our systems with a little Opium" (291).

Pyne is not only an immoral reformer; he is also a nativist Catholic baiter, a fire-and-brimstone evangelist, and an unblushing sensualist. He embodies the intolerance and hypocrisy Lippard associated with organized religion. One of the most daring scenes in *The Quaker City,* in which Pyne attempts to rape his "daughter" Mabel, can be placed against the background of notorious instances of sexual misconduct among antebellum preachers. The reverend rake, one of the foremost characters in sensational writings of the period, was based on real-life ministers, including Ephraim K. Avery, the Methodist preacher who in 1833 was tried for seducing and murdering a sluttish woman in his charge; Charles L. Cook, removed from two pulpits for his homosexual activities; Samuel F. Jarvis, a leading Episcopalian priest who in 1839 was sued by his wife for ignoring her sexually while sleeping with a German governess; and John N. Maffitt, the immensely successful itinerant who was regularly reported as having illicit sexual affairs. For Lippard, the most shocking case involved the New York Episcopalian bishop Benjamin T. Onderdonk, who in 1844 was brought to trial and then defrocked for seducing several of his female parishioners. In Lippard's eyes, Onderdonk was "a wine-bibber, a sensualist, an adulterer."[49]

Lippard knew that Onderdonk was hardly alone. Just as scandal sheets of the day ran articles with headlines like "The Reverend Seducer" and "Incest by a Clergyman of Three Daughters," so Lippard has Devil-Bug tell Pyne, "I know you preachers are awful sly with the women; and the pulpit is rather celebrated for its taste in that line" (341). Pyne's sexual advances toward Mabel, then, were intended by Lippard to be representative of ministerial behavior.

Because Lippard found no exemplars among his nation's rulers, he sought exemplars elsewhere. He confronted a problem like the one that would face Whitman in the 1850s: when social institutions and rulers seem hopelessly flawed, where can redemption be found? For Whitman, it could be located amidst average Americans, whose intrinsic, democratic nobility forms the humanistic core of *Leaves of Grass.* Lippard sometimes takes a Whitmanesque tack, as when he has Dora exclaim, "Give me the honest Mechanic at the bench if we must have a nobility, for your true nobleman; not the dishonest Bank-director at the desk!" (184). But Lippard's vision of American society was too bleak to permit him to dwell long on humanistic alternatives to institutionalized corruption. His self-appointed mission was to dramatize this corruption, even exaggerate it, and to suggest its dire consequences. At moments, he gives predictions, similar to Marx's, that capitalism's flaws would be rooted out only through working-class revolution. He warns of "the vengeance of the People, which shall one day hurl the lordly minister of the law from his proud position; already he beholds written on the walls of his chamber, in letters of flame, that black and staring word—'CORRUPTION'" (347). He imagines a time when "the God of the Poor would arise in his might, and crush the lordlings under the heel of his power!" (383).

But the eventual overthrow of capitalism is just a dream in *The Quaker City,* which focuses instead on the all-grasping nature of capitalism in urban America. When Fitz-Cowles says that political and judicial favors are "all for sale," he is bringing attention to the inescapable power of money in the new market economy. Capitalism, in Lippard's view, governs not only politics, justice, religion, and the press; it also controls the deepest aspects of human relations, most notably sex. Framing the novel's relationships in monetary terms, Lippard explores sex as a capitalist commodity. Lorrimer and Arlington not only lay bets on the planned seduction but also raise a toast to women in an oyster cellar whose owner is secretly calculating the profits he is making from their revel. Later in the novel, Fitz-Cowles offers Pyne money for Mabel. Epitomizing the sex-as-commodity spirit, Pyne replies, "Fitz, I've sold the girl to you for one hundred dollars, and you shall have her" (348). The social-climbing Dora sells herself for dreamed-of wealth, muttering in her sleep, "Algernon—a coronet—wealth and power—" (135). The conflation of sex and money is vivified in the episode in which Devil-Bug does a favor for Dora and demands to be rewarded not with cash but with "go-o-old," meaning sex.

Because capitalism seemed to Lippard deeply entrenched in the American consciousness, he resorted to verbal violence to expose what he considered its shortcomings. Some contemporary reviewers took him to task for his forceful, sometimes frenzied style. One remarked that "the Lippard style . . . requires the writer to be born with St. Vitus's dance, to be inoculated with the Delirium Tremens, take the nightmare in the natural way, get badly frightened at a collection of snakes, and write under the combined influence of these manifold causes of inspiration."[50] Similarly flippant criticism would later be aimed at the writings of the surrealists. Unrestrained fantasy, verbal excess, lyrical exuberance, and revolutionary fervor are frequently disturbing to the defenders of moderation. "One of the chief properties of poetry," wrote the surrealist Paul Eluard in a polemical spirit close to Lippard's, "is to inspire in humbugs a grimace which unmasks them and allows them to be judged."[51] Lippard used style as an unmasking device, to assault and punish his enemies.

Among the main weapons in his literary arsenal were role reversal and black humor. By role reversal, I refer to his practice of investing oppressed or marginalized types—including fallen women, African Americans, and criminals—with retributive, even socially redemptive qualities. The women characters who stand out in this regard are Dora and Bess, who embody the problems and potentialities of women in a male-dominated, capitalistic society. Antebellum reformers who claimed that most American women were doomed to prostitution, in marriage or out of it, were lamenting the cultural conditions that produced women like Dora and Bess. Both moved from indigent backgrounds into different kinds of prostitution—Dora within marriage and Bess without. But both of these fallen women gain great power in the novel. Whereas the conventional heroine, Mary Arlington, is weak and passive, Dora and Bess are spirited and forceful. Dora, at once intellectual and sexually adventurous, several times stands up to men with great verve. When she dresses as a man and enters Monk Hall, she exhibits what Devil-Bug calls "Pluck, reg'lar pluck!" by threatening him with pistols (361). A feminist criminal who plans the murder of two men, she also becomes an agent for social criticism. Her tirade against "this magnificent Pretension—the Aristocracy of the Quaker City" is one of the most powerful critiques of the upper class in the novel (183).

Bess also shows surprising strength and, unlike Dora, works actively for good. At the beginning of the novel, she is a figure of vindictive rage against the patriarchal system. Having abandoned virtue after being victimized by a man, she dedicates herself to destroying the virtue of others. But her principal crime in the novel, facilitating Mary's ruin, becomes a stepping-stone to her moral recovery. Pitying the helpless Mary, she draws upon her intrinsic shrewdness and sturdiness to assist people in danger. She tries to rescue Byrnewood Arlington, confronts and taunts Devil-Bug several times, and, in a climactic scene, spirits Mary and Mabel out of Monk Hall. The depiction of Bess—"her heart filled with one fixed purpose, and her very soul nerved for the effort"—supporting the "half-fainting" girls and leading them away from pursuing men is a portrait of grit and female bonding in the face of patriarchal oppression (343). Fittingly, Bess at the end exposes the misogynist Lorrimer to the Arlington family.

African Americans appear, at first glance, to receive a harsher treatment than women in *The Quaker City.* Devil-Bug's helpers Musquito and Glow-worm seem the stereotypically brutish, comical blacks characteristic of antebellum popular culture. Actually, though, they are no more inhuman than the other freakish characters in Lippard's world. In their roles as "slaves" to Devil-Bug they enact the degrading subservience that blacks suffered at the hands of whites. Moreover, their honest brutishness is found to be preferable to the cloaked brutishness of most of the white characters. They are the herculean police of Monk Hall, the enforcers who punish bourgeois hypocrites. They forcibly prevent F. A. T. Pyne from raping Mabel, and they become "a couple o' first rate lawyers" by pinning down the hypocritical preacher as Devil-Bug tickle-tortures him (326). In the end, they participate in a kind of unwitting slave revolt when their master has them topple a boulder on himself.

Role reversal among blacks is also visible in Fitz-Cowles's servant Endymion. Lippard's portrayal of the Creole mulatto shows his daring capacity, predictive of Stowe, for rising above a merely stereotypical view of blacks. Endymion, Lippard tells us, is "eminently handsome, . . . altogether one of the most beautiful things, ever fashioned by the hand of Nature" (152). Sufficiently witty and spunky to spar verbally with the clever Fitz-Cowles, he also has notably rebellious moments, as when he imagines firing his boss. "Tink I shall hab to discharge Massa," he says. "Debbil of a flare-up 'tween me and him some day when I tells him; 'I don't want you any more, you sah!—you kin take dem wages and go!' " (153). Here again, Lippard gives a veiled, indirect prophecy of slave revolt.

Like many northern Democrats, including Whitman and the Bowery politician Mike Walsh, Lippard hated abolitionists because he feared their disunionist appeals for the separation of the North and South. Still, he never became a defender of the South, as did some Democrats, because he could not tolerate slavery in any form. He grouped black chattel slaves with white "wage slaves" in an especially moving moment in Devil-Bug's dream: "Here they were, the slaves of the cotton Lord and the factory Prince; above their heads a loom of iron, rising like a gibbet in the air, and by their sides the grim overseer" (389).

Nowhere does role reversal come more dramatically into play than in the characterization of Devil-Bug. On the one hand, he is one of the most despicable characters in American literature. He gets the same pleasure from acts of special cruelty that others get from ones of special benevolence. He loves not so much to murder as to watch a victim's blood ooze drop by drop. He is no mere criminal; he is an "Outlaw of hell," a "deplorable moral monstrosity," "a wild beast, a snake, a reptile, or a devil incarnate—any thing but a man" (106–7).

But, as with Musquito and Glow-worm, Devil-Bug's cruelty is at least open and direct, as opposed to the disguised cruelty of most characters in the novel. Unlike the hypocrites in mainstream society, Devil-Bug does not wear a false face. As Luke Harvey says after reviewing Devil-Bug's crimes, "But he's an honest rogue for all that" (237). Also, he becomes a vehicle for many of Lippard's social arguments. An orphan who emerged from a poor, lowly background, he is a living exemplum on the vicious results of economic deprivation. He illustrates the claim of antebellum criminal reformers that crime results largely from adverse social conditions. In his role as the master of Musquito and Glow-worm, he is initially analogous to a harsh slaveowner, barking commands to them in racist terms, but ultimately becomes a kind of emancipator, assigning them punitive power and freeing them by letting them participate in his suicide. Like Bess, he at first appears to be thoroughly degraded but in the course of the novel becomes a remorseful figure who is actually capable of doing good. Haunted by visions of his murdered victims, he eventually dedicates himself to saving his daughter, Mabel, first from Pyne and then from Ravoni. His actions on behalf of Mabel permit him to have one of the few genuinely religious experiences in the novel. As he thinks of his family and God, "For a moment the soul of Devil-Bug was *beautiful*. . . . He felt that he, Devil-Bug, the outcast of the earth, the incarnate outlaw of hell, had one friend in the wide universe; that friend his Creator" (339).

Devil-Bug is an updated version of the Puritan Calvinist belief that salvation results from a total awareness of depravity. The main change Lippard makes in the Puritan paradigm is that the depravity Devil-Bug witnesses has a profoundly social dimension reflective of Lippard's radical views. Devil-Bug speaks in a disturbingly sarcastic, darkly humorous way, but more often than not his sarcasm is, like Lippard's style in general, an unmasking device that awakens the reader to social ills. This unmasking humor governs Devil-Bug's dystopic dream of Philadelphia in 1950. Devil-Bug cheers gleefully at several social horrors: the destruction of Independence Hall and Girard College, with royal palaces raised on their ruins; the spectacle of titled aristocrats controlling the city; the continued use of the gallows in punishing criminals; and the apocalyptic collapse of this aristocratic civilization, with "WO UNTO SODOM" blazing luridly in the sky.

The fact that Devil-Bug laughs infernally throughout this horrid scene reflects Lippard's belief that modern money changers can be most effectively combatted through black humor. Few novels are as full of blackly humorous effects as *The Quaker City.* Typical is the moment when Luke Harvey wonders how full the town would be if "all who have sold their God for gold would hang themselves," following Judas Iscariot's example. His laconic answer: "Hooks in the market house would rise" (35). Black jokes surround the wealthy Livingstones. Albert Livingstone asks Luke Harvey if he sees "our position," referring to a business problem, at which Luke says that he sees "a fine branching pair" of horns on Albert's head that will impede his entering his aristocratic church (41). Albert himself becomes a main source of black jokes, as when he answers his adulterous wife's talk about a coronet by promising her a coronet of worms, or when he has a carriage carrying her inscribed coffin follow them on their ostensibly happy jaunt to their country estate. But to isolate such moments is deceptive, since virtually every page of the novel contains odd puns, surprises, or ironic situations that have the effect of black humor.

For the modern reader, the unmasking force of *The Quaker City* can be exhilarating and thought provoking. Although some of the social problems Lippard lashed out against have been rectified, many have not, and some have worsened. One can almost hear Devil-Bug's shrieking laughter echoing along the corridors of time.

David S. Reynolds

Notes

1. Lippard, preface to 1849 edition of *The Quaker City; or, the Monks of Monk Hall* (1849; reprint, Amherst, 1995), 2.
2. In the *Philadelphia Quaker City* weekly, May 12, 1849. Hereafter cited as *QCW*.
3. See David S. Reynolds, *Beneath the American Renaissance: The Subversive Imagination in the Age of Emerson and Melville* (New York, 1988), 82–87.
4. *QCW*, September 29, 1849.
5. *QCW*, February 10, 1849.
6. Edwin C. Jellet Ms., 1902, Germantown Historical Society.
7. Lippard, "The Destroyer of the Homestead" (1849), in *The White Banner* (Philadelphia) 1 (1851): 107.
8. Charles Chauncey Burr, introductory essay to Lippard, *Washington and His Generals; or, Legends of the American Revolution* (Philadelphia, 1847), p. iv.
9. James B. Elliott, "Biographical Sketch of George Lippard," introduction to Lippard, *Thomas Paine, Author-Soldier of the American Revolution* (Philadelphia, 1894), 15.
10. Poe to Lippard, letter of February 18, 1844; for this and other primary documents on the Lippard-Poe relationship, see David S. Reynolds, ed., *George Lippard, Prophet of Protest: Writings of an American Radical, 1822–1854* (New York, 1986), 256–67.
11. *Philadelphia Citizen Soldier*, November 15, 1843; in Reynolds, *Prophet of Protest*, 258.
12. Francis C. Weymyss, *Twenty-Six Years of the Life of an Actor and Manager* (New York, 1847), 19.
13. Quoted in Joseph Jackson, "George Lippard: Poet of the Proletariat" (ca. 1930), manuscript in Historical Society of Pennsylvania, chap. 8, p. 31.
14. *Massachusetts Quarterly* 1 (December 1847): 125; *New Monthly Magazine*, 74 (1845): 238.
15. *Philadelphia Spirit of the Times*, January 17, 1845.

16. *United States Saturday Post,* September 25, 1845.
17. Quoted in Joseph Jackson, "A Bibliography of the Works of George Lippard," *Pennsylvania Magazine of History and Biography* 54 (April 1930): 134.
18. *The Quaker City,* preface, 1.
19. A. J. H. Duganne, *The Knights of the Seal; or, the Mysteries of the Three Cities* (Philadelphia, 1845), 26.
20. *Philadelphia Saturday Courier,* May 15, 1847. The quotation at the end of this paragraph about "a Dutch Headley" is from the *Courier,* November 27, 1847.
21. *QCW,* June 23, 1849.
22. In Reynolds, *Prophet of Protest,* 264.
23. Quoted in Arthur Hobson Quinn, *Edgar Allan Poe: A Critical Biography* (New York, 1941), 621.
24. In Reynolds, *Prophet of Protest,* 262.
25. In Reynolds, *Prophet of Protest,* 212, 216.
26. In Reynolds, *Prophet of Protest,* 8.
27. Association of the Daughters and Sons of Toil, *Monthly Jubilee* (March 1854): 87.
28. *Philadelphia Public Ledger,* February 10, 1854.
29. *Philadelphia Sunday Mercury,* March 5, 1854.
30. *Camden Post-Telegraph,* April 15, 1922.
31. Albert Mordell, "A Forgotten Novelist," *Philadelphia Press Magazine,* September 16, 1917.
32. *The Quaker City,* 260. Hereafter, page numbers from the present edition of *The Quaker City* are cited parenthetically in the text.
33. *Walt Whitman of the New York Aurora: Editor at Twenty-Two,* ed. Joseph J. Rubin and Charles J. Brown (Westport, Conn., 1950), p. 115.
34. Whitman, *Prose Works, 1892,* ed. Floyd Stovall, 2 vols. (New York, 1963–64), 2: 572–73.
35. Melville, *Moby-Dick; or, The Whale,* ed. Harrison Hayford and Hershel Parker (1851; reprint, New York, 1967), 21, 23.
36. Melville to Hawthorne, letter of ca. June 1, 1851, cited Hayford and Parker, afterword to *Moby-Dick,* 558; *Moby-Dick,* 113.
37. Melville, *Moby-Dick,* 144.
38. Samuel Langhorne Clemens to his brother Orion, letter of October 26, 1853, in Albert B. Paine, *Mark Twain: A Biography,* 4 vols. (New York, 1912), 1: 100.
39. Whitman, *Notebooks and Unpublished Prose Manuscripts,* ed. Edward F. Grier, 6 vols. (New York, 1984), 1: 434.
40. *The Uncollected Poetry and Prose of Walt Whitman,* ed. Emory Holloway, 2 vols. (Gloucester, Mass., 1972), 1: 97, 116. The quotation in the following sentence is in 1: 103.
41. Whitman, *Notebooks and Unpublished Prose Manuscripts,* 1: 131.
42. Quotations from "Resurgemus" are from Whitman, *The Early Poems and the Fiction,* ed. Thomas L. Brasher (New York, 1963), 38–40.
43. Horace Traubel, *With Walt Whitman in Camden,* 7 vols. to date (Carbondale, Ill., 1964–), 5: 529.
44. Whitman, *Leaves of Grass, Comprehensive Reader's Edition,* ed. Harold Blodgett and Sculley Bradley (New York, 1965), 342, 237.

45. *Walt Whitman's Workshop: A Collection of Unpublished Prose Manuscripts,* ed. Clifton Joseph Furness (New York, 1964), 57; and *Leaves of Grass, Comprehensive Reader's Edition,* 696.
46. See Edward Pessen, *Riches, Class, and Power before the Civil War* (Lexington, Mass., 1973), chap. 3.
47. Mark Summers, *The Plundering Generation: Corruption and the Crisis of the Union* (New York, 1987).
48. *A Philadelphia Perspective: The Diary of Sidney George Fisher Covering the Years 1834–1871,* ed. Nicholas B. Wainwright (Philadelphia, 1967), 120.
49. *QCW,* December 30, 1848.
50. This comment by Jane Grey Swisshelm was quoted by Lippard in *QCW,* August 18, 1849.
51. Quoted in André Breton, *What Is Surrealism? Selected Writings,* ed. Franklin Rosemont (New York, 1978), 86.

The Quaker City;

or,

The Monks of Monk Hall

Frontispiece wood engraving, F. O. C. Darley, delineator, from George Lippard, *The Quaker City; or The Monks of Monk Hall: A Romance of Philadelphia Life, Mystery, and Crime* (Philadelphia: T. B. Peterson and Brothers, [1845]). Courtesy, the American Antiquarian Society.

Preface to this Edition

My Publishers ask me to write a Preface for this new Edition of the Quaker City. What shall I say? Shall I at this time enter into a full explanation of the motives which induced me to write this Work? Shall I tell how it has been praised—how abused—how it has on the one hand been cited as a Work of great merit, and on the other, how it has been denounced as the most immoral work of the age?

The reader will spare me the task. The Quaker City has passed through many Editions in America, as well as in London. It has also been translated and numerous editions of it have been published in Germany, and a beautiful edition in four volumes, is now before me, bearing the imprint of Otto Wigand, Leipsic, as Publisher, and the name of Frederick Gerstaker, as the Author.

Taking all these facts into consideration, it seems but just that I should say a word for myself on this occasion.

The motive which impelled me to write this Work may be stated in a few words.

I was the only Protector of an Orphan Sister. I was fearful that I might be taken away by death, leaving her alone in the world. I knew too well that law of society which makes a virtue of the dishonor of a poor girl, while it justly holds the seduction of a rich man's child as an infamous crime. These thoughts impressed me deeply. I determined to write a book, founded upon the following idea:

That the seduction of a poor and innocent girl, is a deed altogether as criminal as deliberate murder. It is worse than the murder of the body, for it is the assassination of the soul. If the murderer deserves death by the gallows, then the assassin of chastity and maidenhood is worthy of death by the hands of any man, and in any place.

This was the first idea of the Work. It embodies a sophism, but it is a sophism that errs on the right side. But as I progressed in my task, other ideas were added to the original thought. Secluded in my room, having no familiarity with the vices of a large city, save from my studentship in the office of an Attorney-General—the Confessional of our Protestant communities—I determined to write a book which should describe all the phases of a corrupt social system, as manifested in the city of Philadelphia. The results of my labors was this book, which has been more attacked, and more read, than any work of American fiction ever published.

And now, I can say with truth, that whatever faults may be discovered in this Work, that my motive in its composition was honest, was pure, was as destitute of any idea of sensualism, as certain of the persons who have attacked it without reading a single page, are of candor, of a moral life, or a heart capable of generous emotions.

To the young man and young woman who may read this book when I am dead, I have a word to say:

Would to God that the evils recorded in these pages, were not based upon facts. Would to God that the experience of my life had not impressed me so vividly with the colossal vices and the terrible deformities, presented in the social system of this Large City, in the Nineteenth Century. You will read this work when the hand which pens this line is dust. If you discover one word in its pages, that has a tendency to develop one impure thought, I beseech you reject that word. If you discover a chapter, a page, or a line, that conflicts with the great idea of Human Brotherhood, promulgated by the Redeemer, I ask you with all my soul, reject that chapter, that passage, that line. At the same time remember the idea which impelled me to produce the book. Remember that my life from the age of sixteen up to twenty-five was one perpetual battle with hardship and difficulty, such as do not often fall to the lot of a young man—such as rarely is recorded in the experience of childhood or manhood. Take the book with all its faults and all its virtues. Judge it as you yourself would wish to be judged. Do not wrest a line from these pages, for the encouragement of a bad thought or a bad deed.

GEORGE LIPPARD

[1849]

INSCRIBED TO THE MEMORY OF CHARLES BROCKDEN BROWN

The Origin and Object of this Book

One winter night I was called to the bedside of a dying friend. I found him sitting up in his death-couch, pale and trembling yet unawed by the gathering shadows of the tomb. His white hairs fell over his clammy brow, his dark grey eye, glared with the unnatural light, which, heralds the approach of death. Old K——— had been a singular man. He had been a profound lawyer, without fame or judgeship. In quiet he pursued his dreamy way, deriving sufficient from his profession, to support him in decency and honor. In a city, where no man has a friend, that has not money to back him, the good old lawyer had been my friend. He was one of those old-fashioned lawyers who delight to bury themselves among their books, who love the law for its theory, and not for its trick and craft and despicable chicanery. Old K——— had been my friend, and now I sat by his bedside in his last hour.

"Death is coming," he said with a calm smile, "but I dread him not. My accounts with God are settled; my face is clammy with the death-sweat, but I have no fear. When I am gone, you will find in yonder desk, a large pacquet, inscribed with your name. This pacquet, contains the records of my experience as a private counsellor and a lawyer, for the last thirty years. You are young and friendless, but you have a pen, which will prove your best friend. I bequeath these Papers to you; they may be made serviceable to yourself and to the world———"

In a faint voice, I asked the good old lawyer, concerning the nature of these records.

"They contain a full and terrible development of the Secret Life of Philadelphia. In that pacquet, you will find, records of crimes, that never came to trial, murders that have never been divulged; there you will discover the results of secret examinations, held by official personages, in relation to atrocities almost too horrible for belief———"

"Then," said I, "Philadelphia is not so pure as it looks?"

"Alas, alas, that I should have to say it," said the old man with an expression of deep sorrow, "But whenever I behold its regular streets and formal look, I think of The Whited Sepulchre, without all purity, within, all rottenness and dead men's bones. Have you courage, to write a book from those papers?"

"Courage?"

"Aye, courage, for the day has come, when a man dare not speak a plain truth, without all the pitiful things of this world, rising up against him, with adder's tongues and treacherous hands. Write a book, with all your heart bent on some good object, and for every word you write, you will find a low-bred calumniator, eager to befoul you with his slanders. Have you courage, to write a book from the materials, which I leave you, which shall be devoted to these objects: To defend the sanctity of female honor; to show how miserable and corrupt is that Pseudo-Christianity which tramples on every principle ever preached or practised by the Saviour Jesus; to lay bare vice in high places, and strip gilded crimes of their tinsel. Have you courage for this?"

I could only take the old man's hand, within my own, and murmur faintly, "I'll try!"

"Have you courage, to lift the cover from the Whited Sepulchre, and while the world is crying honor to its outward purity, to show the festering corruption that rankles in its depths? Then those records are yours!"

I sat beside the deathbed of the old man all night long. His last hours were past in calm converse, full of hope and trust in God. Near the break of day, he died. God bless him! He was my friend, when I had nothing but an orphan's gratitude, to tender in return for his friendship. He was a lawyer, and *honest;* a Christian and yet no bigot; a philosopher and yet no sceptic.

After his funeral, I received the pacquet of papers, inscribed with my name, and endorsed, REVELATIONS OF THE SECRET LIFE OF PHILADELPHIA, *being the records of thirty years practice as a councillor, by* * * * K———.

The present book is founded upon those portions of the Revelations, more intimately connected with the present day.

With the same sincerity with which I have written this Book of the Quaker City, I now give it to my countrymen, as an illustration of the life, mystery and crime of Philadelphia.

BOOK THE FIRST

THE FIRST NIGHT

Mary, the Merchant's Daughter

CHAPTER FIRST

THE WAGER IN THE OYSTER-CELLAR

"I say, gentlemen, shall we make a night of it? That's the question gents. Shall we elevate the—the devil along Chesnut street, or shall we subside quietly to our homes? Let's toss up for it—which shall have the night—brandy and oysters, or quilts and feather-beds?" And as he spoke, the little man broke loose from the grasp of his friends, and retiring to the shelter of an awning-post, flung his cloak over his shoulder with a vast deal of drunken dignity, while his vacant eyes were fixed upon the convivial group scattered along the pavement.

"Brandy"—cried a gentleman distinguished by a very pursy figure, enveloped in a snow-white overcoat, and a very round face, illuminated by a pear-shaped nose—"Brandy is a gentleman—a per—perfect gentleman. He leaves no head-ache next morning by way of a card. Champagne's a sucker—a hypocritical scoundrel, who first goes down your throat, smooth as oil, and then—a—a—very much so—how d———d irregular these bricks are—puts a powder-mill in your head and blows it up—dam 'im!—Mem:—Byrnewood—d'ye hear? write to the corporation to-morrow, about these curst mountainous pavements—" And having thus said, the pursy gentleman retreated to the shelter of another awning-post, leaving the two remaining members of the conviveal party, in full possession of the pavement, which they laid out in any given number of garden-plots without delay.

"Byrnewood—d'ye hear?" exclaimed the tallest gentleman of the twain, gathering his frogged overcoat closer around him, while his mustachioed lip was wreathed in a drunken smile—"Look yonder at the statehouse—sing—singular phenomenon! There's the original steeple and a duplicate. Two steeples, by Jupiter! Remarkable effect of moonlight! Very—Doesn't it strike you, Byrnewood, that yonder watch-box is walking across the street, to black the lamp-post's eyes—for—for—making a face at him?"

The gentleman thus addressed, instead of replying to the sagacious query of his friend, occupied a small portion of his leisure time in performing an irregular Spanish dance along the pavement, terminating in a pleasant combination of the cachuca, with a genuine New Jersey double-shuffle. This accomplished, he drew his well proportioned figure to its full height, cast back his cloak from his shoulders, and turned his face to the moonlit sky. As he gazed upon the heavens, clear, cold, and serene as death, the moonlight falling over his features, disclosed a handsome tho' pallid face, relieved by long curling locks of jet black hair. For a moment he seemed intensely absorbed amid the intricacies of a philosophical reverie, for he frequently put his thumb to his nose, and described circles in the air with his outspread fingers. At last tottering to a seat on a fire-plug, he delivered himself of this remarkable expression of opinion—

"Miller the Prophet's right! Right I say! The world—d———n the plug, how it shakes—the world is coming to an end for certain—for, d'ye see boys—there's *two* moons shining up yonder this blessed night sure as fate—"

The scene would have furnished a tolerable good subject for an effective convivial picture.

There, seated on the door-way step of a four storied dwelling, his arms crossed over his muscular chest, his right hand grasping a massive gold-headed cane, Mr. Gustavus Lorrimer, commonly styled the handsome Gus Lorrimer, in especial reference to his well-known favor among the ladies, presented to the full glare of the moonbeams, a fine manly countenance, marked by a brilliant dark eye, a nose slightly aquiline, a firm lip clothed with a mustache, while his hat tossed slightly to one side, disclosed a bold and prominent forehead, relieved by thick clusters of rich brown hair. His dark eye at all times full of fire, shone with a glance of unmistakeable humor, as he regarded his friend seated on the fire-plug directly opposite the doorway steps.

This friend—Mr. Byrnewood, as he had been introduced to Lorrimer—was engaged in performing an extemporaneous musical entertainment on the top of the fire-plug with his fingers, while his legs were entwined around it, as though the gentleman was urging a first-rate courser at the top of his speed.

His cloak thrown back from his shoulders, his slight though well-proportioned and muscular form, was revealed to the eye, enveloped in a closely fitting black frock-coat. His face was very pale, and his long hair, which swept in thick ringlets to his shoulders, was dark as a ravens wing, yet his forehead was high and massive, his features regular, and his jet-black eye, bright as a flame-coal. His lips, now wreathing in the very silly smile peculiar to all worshippers of the bottle-god, were, it is true, somewhat slight and thin, and when in repose inclining to severity in expression; yet the general effect of his countenance was highly interesting, and his figure manly and graceful in its outlines, although not so tall by half-a-head as the magnificent Gus Lorrimer.

While he is beating a tattoo on the fire-plug, let us not forget our other friends, Col. Mutchins, in his snow-white overcoat and shiny hat; and Mr. Sylvester J. Petriken, in his glazed cap and long cloak, as leaning against opposite awning posts, they gaze in each others faces and afford a beautiful contrast for the pencil of our friend Darley.

Col. Mutchins' face, you will observe, is very much like a picture of a dissipated full-moon, with a large red pear stuck in the centre for a nose, while two small black beads, placed in corresponding circles of crimson tape, supply the place of eyes. The Colonel's figure is short, thick-set, and corpulent; he is very broad across the shoulders, broader across the waist, and very well developed in the region of the hands and boots. The gentleman, clinging nervously to the opposite awning post, is remarkable for three things—smallness of stature, slightness of figure, and slimness of legs. His head is very large, his face remarkable for its pallor, is long and square—looking as though it had been laid out with a rule and compass—with a straight formal nose, placed some distance above a wide mouth marked by two parallel lines, in the way of lips. His protuberant brow, faintly relieved by irregular locks of mole-skin colored hair, surmounted by a high glazed cap, overarches two large, oyster-like eyes, that roll about in their orbits with the regularity of machinery. These eyes remind you of nothing more, than those glassy things which, in obedience to a wire, give animation to the expressive face of a Dresden wax-doll.

And over this scene of quadruple convivialism, shone the midnight moon, her full glory beaming from a serene winter sky, upon the roofs and steeples of the Quaker City. The long shadows of the houses on the opposite side of the way, fell darkly along the street, while in the distance, terminating the dim perspective, arose the State-House buildings, with the steeple shooting upward into the clear blue sky.

"That champagne—" hiccuped Mr. Petriken, clinging to the awning-post, under a painful impression that it was endeavoring to throw him down—"That champagne was very strong—and the oysters—Oh my ———"

"As mortal beings we are subject to sud—sudden sickness—" observed the sententious Mutchins, gathering his awning-post in a fonder embrace.

"I say, Byrnewood—how shall we terminate the night? Did I understand you that the d———l was to be raised? If so, let's start. Think how many bells are to be pulled, how many watch-boxes to be attacked, how many—curse the thing, I believe I'm toddied—watchmen to be licked. Come on boys?"

"Hist! Gus! You'll scare the fire-plug. He's trying to run off with me—the scoundrel. Wait till I put the spurs to him, I say!"

"Come on boys. Let's go round to Smokey Chiffin's oyster cellar and have a cozy supper. Come on I say. Take my arm, Byrnewood—there, steady—here Petriken, never mind the awning-post, take this other arm—now Mutchins hook Silly's arm and let's travel ———"

But Mutchins—who, by the way, had been out in a buffaloe hunt the year before—was now engaged in an imaginary, though desperate fight with a Sioux warrior, whom he belabored with terrific shrieks and yells.

"D———n the fool—he'll have us all in the watch house—" exclaimed Lorrimer, who appeared to be the soberest of the party by several bottles—"Fun is fun, but this thing of cutting up shines in Chesnut street, after twelve, when it—keep steady Silly—amounts to yelling like a devil in harness is—un-un-der-stand me, no fun. Come along, Mutchy my boy!"

And arm in arm, linked four abreast, like horses very tastelessly matched, the boon companions tottered along Chesnut street, toward Smokey Chiffin's oyster cellar, where they arrived, with but a single interruption.

"*Hao-pao-twel-o-glor-a-a-damuley-mor!*"

This mysterious combination of sounds emanated from a stout gentleman in a slouching hat, and four or five overcoats, who, with a small piece of cord-wood in his hand met our party breast to breast, as they were speeding onward in full career.

"I say stranger—do that over again—will yo'?" shrieked Petriken, turning his square face over his shoulder and gazing at the retreating figure with the cord-stick and the overcoats—"Jist do that again if you please. Let me go I tell you, Gus. Don't you see, this is some—dis-distinguished vocal-ist from London? What a pathos there is in his voice—

so deep—so full—why Brough is nothing to him! Knock Wood, and Seg-Seguin—and Shrival—and a dozen more into a musical cocked-hat, and they can't equal our mys-mysterious friend—"

"I say you'd better tortle on my coveys—" cried he of the great coats and cord stick, in a subterranean voice—"Or p'r'aps, my fellers, ye'd like to tend Mayor Scott's tea-party—would ye?"

"Thank you kindly—" exclaimed Gus Lorrimer in an insinuating tone, "otherwise engaged. But my friend—if you will allow me to ask —what *do* you mean by that infernal noise you produced just now? Let us into the lark?"

The gentleman of the cord stick and overcoats, was however beyond hearing by this time, and our friends moved on their way. Byrnewood observing in an under tone, somewhat roughened by hiccups, that on his soul, he believed that queer old cove, in the slouched hat, meant by his mysterious noise to impart the important truth that *it was half-past twelve o'clock and a moonlight morning*.

Descending into Smokey Chiffin's subterranean retreat, our friends were waited upon by a very small man, with a sharp face and a white apron, and a figure so lank and slender, that the idea involuntarily arose to the spectators mind, of whole days and nights of severe training, having been bestowed upon a human frame, in order to reduce it to a degree of thinness quite visionary.

"Come my 'Virginia abstraction'—" exclaimed Lorrimer—"Show us into a private room, and tell us what yov've got for supper—"

"This way sir—this way gents—" cried Smokey Chiffin, as the thin gentleman was rather familiarly styled—"What got for supper? Woodcock sir? excellent sir. Venison sir; excellent sir. Oysters sir, stewed, sir, fried sir, roasted sir, or in the shell sir. Excellent sir. Some right fresh, fed on corn-meal sir. What have sir? Excellent sir. This way gents—"

And as he thus delivered his bill of fare, the host, attended by his customers, disappeared from the refrectory proper, through an obscure door into the private room.

There may be some of our readers who have never been within the confines of one of those oyster-caverns which abound in the Quaker City. For their especial benefit, we will endeavor to pencil forth a few of the most prominent characteristics of the "Oyster Saloon by Mr. Samuel Chiffin."

Lighted by flaring gas-pipes, it was divided into two sections by a blazing hot coal stove. The section beyond the stove, wrapt in comparative obscurity, was occupied by two opposing rows of 'boxes,' looking very much like conventual stalls, ranged side by side, for the accommodation of the brothers of some old-time monastery. The other section, all light, and glitter, and show, was ornamented at its extreme end, by a tremendous mirror, in which a toper might look, time after time, in order to note the various degrees of drunkenness through which he passed. An oyster-box, embellished by a glorious display of tin signs with gilt letters, holding out inviting manifestations of "oysters stewed fried or in the shell," occupied one entire side of this section, gazing directly in the face of the liquor bar placed opposite, garnished with an imposing array of decanters, paint gilding, and glasses.

And the company gathered here? Not very select you may be sure. Four or five gentlemen with seedy coats and effloresent noses were warming themselves around the stove, and discussing the leading questions of the day; two individuals whose visits to the bar had been rather frequent, were kneeling in one corner, swearing at a very ragged dog, whom they could'nt persuade to try a glass of 'Imperial Elevator,' and seated astride of a chair, silent and alone, a young man whose rakish look and ruffled attire betrayed the medical student on his first 'spree' was endeavouring to hold himself steady, and look uncommonly sober; which endeavour always produces, as every body knows, the most riduculous phase of drunkenness.

These Oyster Cellers are queer things. Like the caverns of old story, in which the Giants, those ante-diluvian rowdies, used to sit all day long, and use the most disreputable arts to inveigle lonely travellers into their clutches, so these modern dens, are occupied by a jolly old Giant of a decanter, who too often lures the unsuspecting into his embrace. A strange tale might be told, could the stairway leading down into the Oyster Celler be gifted with the power of speech. Here Youth has gone down laughing merrily, and here Youth has come up, his ruddy cheek wrinkled and his voice quavering with premature age. Here Wealth has gone down, and kept going down until at last he came up with his empty pocket, turned inside out, and the gripe of grim starvation on his shoulder. Here Hope, so young, so gay, so light-hearted has gone down, and came up transformed into a very devil with sunken cheeks, bleared eyes, and a cankered heart. Oh merry cavern of the Oyster Celler, nestling under the ground so close to Independence Hall, how great the wonders, how mighty the doings, how surprising the changes accomplished in your pleasant den, by your jolly old Giant of a Decanter!

It is here in this Oyster Celler, that we open the fearful tragedy which it is the painful object of our narrative, to tell. Here amid paint, and glitter and gilding, amid the clink of glasses and the roar of drinking songs, occurred a scene, which trifling and insipid as it may appear to the casual observer, was but the initial letter to a long and dreary alphabet of crime, mystery and bloodshed.

In a room, small and comfortable, lighted by gas and warmed by a cheerful coal-fire, around a table furnished with various luxuries, and garnished with an array of long necked bottles, we find our friends of the convivial party. Their revel had swelled to the highest, glass clinked against glass, bottle after bottle had been exhausted, voices began to mingle together, the drinking song and the prurient story began to pass from lip to lip, while our sedate friend, Smokey Chiffin, sate silently on the sofa, regarding the drunken bout with a glance of quiet satisfaction.

"Let me see—let me see"—he murmured quietly to himself—"Four bottles o' Cham. at two dollars a bottle—four times two is eight. Hum—hum. They'll drink six more. Let's call it twelve altogether. Say twenty-four shiners for supper and all. Hum—hum—Gus pays for all. That fellow Petriken's a sponge. Wonder when Col. Mutchins will call for the cards? Don't know who this fellow Byrnewood is? New face—may be he's a *roper** too? We'll see—we'll see."

"Give us your hand, Gus"—cried Byrnewood, rising from his seat and flinging his hand unsteadily across the table—"Damme, I like you old fellow. Never—never—knew until to-night—met you at Mutchin's room—wish I'd known you all my life—Give us your hand, my boy!"

Calm and magnificent, Gustavus extended his hand, and exclaimed, in a voice, which champagne could not deprive of its sweetness, that it gave him pleasure to know such a regular bird as Mister Byrnewood; great pleasure; extraordinary pleasure.

"You see, fellows, I believe I'll take a spree for three days—wont go home, or to the store in Front street. Mean to keep it up until after Christmas. Wants three days o' Christmas—mean to jolly—ha—ha—how the room reels."

"Gentle-men—I don't know what is the matter with me—" observed Petriken, who rested his elbows helplessly on the table, as he looked around with his square face, lengthened into a vacant stare—"There's somethin' queer a-goin' on with my eyes. I seem to see spiders—lots o' 'em—playin' corner-ball with roaches. See anything o' the kind, Mutchins?"

* This genteel term is applied to a well dressed edition of the vulgar stool-pigeon, used by gamblers, to decoy the unwary into their dens. The stool-pigeon is the loafer decoy, the roper is very aristocratic, prevails in the large hotel and is called a—gentleman.

"Why—why—" replied that sententious gentleman as his red round face was overspread by a commiserating smile—"Why the fact is—Silly—you've been drinkin'. By the bye does'nt it strike you that there's something queer going on with that gas light. I say, Smokey, is'nt there a beetle tryin' to mash his brains out against that gas-pipe?"

"Gentlemen—I will give you a toast!" exclaimed Lorrimer, as he stood erect, the bold outline of his manly form, his handsome face, the high forehead relieved by thick masses of brown hair, the aquiline nose, the rounded chin, and the curving lip darkened by a mustache, all shown to advantage in the glowing light—"Gentlemen fill your glasses—no heeltaps! WOMAN!"

"WOMAN!" shrieked the other three, springing unsteadily to their feet, and raising their glasses on high—"WOMAN! Three times three—hip-hip-hurrah!"

"Women!" muttered Sylvester Petriken—"Women for ever! when we're babies she nusses us, when we're boys she lathers us, when we're men she bedevils and bewitches us!"

"Woman—" muttered Colonel Mutchins—"without her what 'ud life be? A dickey without a 'plete,' a collar without starch!"

"We can't help it if we fascinate 'em?" exclaimed Byrnewood—"Can we Gus?"

"All fate, my boy—all fate. By the bye—set down boys. I've got a nice little adventure of my own to tell. Smokey—bring us some soda to sober off with—"

"Gentlemen—" cried Petriken, sinking heavily in his chair—"Did any of you see the last number of my magazine? 'The Ladies' Western Hemisphere and Continental Organ.' Offers the following inducements to sub—subscribers—one fashion-plate and two steel engravings per number—48 pages, octavo—Sylvester J. Petriken, Editor and Proprietor, office 209 Drayman's alley, up stairs. Damme, Mutchins, what's your idea of fleas?"

There was not, it is true, the most visible connexion between the Ladies Continental Organ and the peculiar insect, so troublesome to young puppies and very small kittens, yet as Mr. Petriken was not exactly sober, and Col. Mutchins very far from the temperance pledge, the idea seemed to tickle them both immensely and they joined in a hearty laugh, which terminated in another glass from a fresh bottle of champagne.

"Let's have your story, Gus!" shouted Byrnewood—"Let's have your story! Damme—life's but a porcelain cup—to-day we have it, to-morrow we hav'nt—why not fill it with sweetness?"

As he said this, in tones indistinct with liquor he flung his long curling hair back from his brow, and tossed his glass unsteadily on high.

Life a porcelain cup, why not fill it with sweetness? Great God of Mercy! Could the terrible future, which was to break, in a few brief hours, with all its horrors, on the head of this young man, who now sat unconsciously at the drinking board, have at that moment assumed a tangible form, it would have stood like an incarnate devil at his shoulder, its outstretched hand, pouring the very gall of despair into the cup of his life, crowding it to the brim with the wormwood of death.

"Well boys for my story. It's a story of a sweet girl, my boys—a sweet girl about sixteen, with a large blue eye, a cheek like a ripe peach, and a lip like a rose-bud cleft in two—"

"Honor bright Gus. Damme, that's a quotation from my last Ladies' Western Hem. Damme Gus———"

"Byrnewood do hold poor Silly down. There's this material difference, boys, between a ripe peach or a cleft rose-bud, and a dear little woman's lips or cheek. A ripe peach won't throb and grow warm if you lay your cheek against it, and I never yet heard of a rose-bud that kissed back again. She's as lovely a girl as ever trod the streets of the Quaker City. Noble bust—slender waist—small feet and delicate hands. Her hair? damme, Byrnewood, you'd give your eyes for the privilege of twining your hands through the rich locks of her dark brown hair ———"

"Well, well, go on. Who is this girl; uncover the mystery!"

"Patience, my boy, patience. A little of that soda if you please. Now, gentlemen, I want you to listen attentively, for let me tell you, you don't hear a story like mine every day in the year."

Half sobered by the combined influences of the soda water and the interest of Lorrimer's story, Byrnewood leaned forward, fixing his full dark eyes intently upon the face of Gus, who was seated opposite; while Col. Mutchins straightened himself in his chair, and even Petriken's vacant face glowed with a momentary aspect of sobriety.

"I see, boys, that you expect something nice. (Smokey put some more coal on the fire.) Well Byrnewood, you must know I'm a devil of a fellow among the girls—and—and—d———n the thing, I don't know how to get at it. Well, here goes. About two weeks ago I was strolling along Chesnut street towards evening, with Boney (that's my big wolf dog, you know?) at my heels. I was just wondering where I should spend the evening; whether I should go to see Forrest at the Walnut, or take a turn round town; when who should I see walking ahead of me, but one of the prettiest figures in the world, in a black silk mantilla, with one of these saucy kiss-me-if-you-dare bonnets on her head. The walk of the creature, and a little glimpse of her ankle excited my curiosity, and I pushed ahead to get a view of her face. By Jupiter, you never saw such a face! so soft, so melting, and—damme—so innocent. She looked positively bewitching in that saucy bonnet, with her hair parted over her forehead, and resting each cheek in a mass of the richest curls, that ever hung from the brow of mortal woman———"

"Well, Gus, we'll imagine all this. She was beautiful as a houri, and priceless as the philosopher's stone———"

"Byrnewood you are too impatient. A pretty woman in a black silk mantilla, with a lovely face peeping from a provoking bonnet, may seem nothing to you, but the strangest part of the adventure is yet to come. As I looked in the face of this lovely girl, she, to my utter astonishment addressed me in the softest voice in the world, and ———"

"Called you by name?"

"No. Not precisely. It seems she mistook me for some gentleman whom she had seen at a country boarding-school. I took advantage of her mistake, walked by her side for some squares along Chesnut street, and———"

"Became thoroughly acquainted with her, I suppose?" suggested Byrnewood.

"Well, you may judge so, when I mention one trifling fact for your consideration. This night, at three o'clock, this innocent girl, the flower of one of the first families in the city, forsaking home and friends, and all that these sweet girls are wont to hold dear, will seek repose in my arms—"

"She can't be *much*—" exclaimed Byrnewood, over whose face a look of scornful incredulity had been gathering for some few moments past—"Pass that champagne, Petriken my boy. Gus, I don't mean to offend you, but I rather think you've been humbugged by some 'slewer?' "*

A frown darkened over Lorrimer's brow, and even as he sate, you might see his chest heave and his form dilate.

"Do you mean to doubt my word—*Sir?*"

"Not at all, not at all. But you must confess, the thing looks rather improbable. (Will you smoke, Col.?) May I ask whether there was any one in company with the lady when first you met her?

"A Miss something or other—I forget her name. A very passable beauty of twenty and upwards, and I may add, a very convenient one,

* A cant term used by profligates for female servants of indifferent character.

for she carried my letters, and otherwise favored my cause with the sweet girl."

"And this 'sweet girl' is the flower of one of the first families in the city?" asked Byrnewood with a half formed sneer on his upper lip.

"She is—" answered Lorrimer, lighting a cigar.

"And this girl, to-night, leaves home and friends for you, and three hours hence will repose in your arms?"

"She will—" and Lorrimer vacantly eyed a column of smoke winding upward to the ceiling.

"You will not marry her?"

"Ha-ha-ha! You're ahead of me now. Only a pretended marriage, my boy. As for this 'life interest' in a woman, it don't suite my taste. A nice little sham marriage, my boy, is better than ten real ones———"

"You would be a d———d fool to marry a woman who flung herself in your power in this manner. How do you know she is respectable? Did you ever visit her at her father's house? What is her name? Do enlighten us a little———"

"You're 'cute, my boy, mighty 'cute, as the Yankees says, but not so 'cute as you think. Her name? D'ye think I'm so particularly verdant as to tell it? I know her name, could tell you the figure of her fathers wealth, but have never been inside of the threshold of her home. Secret meetings, secret walks and even an assumed name, are oftentimes wonderfully convenient."

"Gus, here is a hundred dollar bill on the Bank of North America. I am, as you see, somewhat interested in your story. I will stake this hundred dollars that the girl who seeks your arms to-night, is not respectable, is not connected with one of the first families in the city, and more than all has never been any better than a common lady of the sidewalk—"

"Book that bet, Mutchins. You heard it, Silly. And now, Byrnewood, here is another hundred, which I will deposit with yours in Mutchins' hands until the bet is decided. Come with me and I'll prove to you that you've lost. You shall witness the wedding—ha, ha—and to your own sense of honor will I confide the secret of the lady's name and position—"

"The bet is booked and the money is safe"—murmured the sententious Mutchins, enclosing the notes in the leaves of his pocket-book—"I've heard of many rum go's but *this is* the rummest go of all."

"If I may be allowed to use the expression, this question involves a mystery. A decided mystery. For instance, what's the ladys name? There is a point from which Hypothesis may derive some labor. 'What's in a name'—as Shakespeare says. I say, gents, let's pick out a dozen names, and toss up which shall have it?''

This rather profound remark of Mr. Petriken's was received with unanimous neglect.

It was observable that during this conversation, both Lorrimer and Byrnewood had been gradually recovering from the effects of their debauch. Lorrimer seemed somewhat offended at the distrust manifested by Byrnewood; who, in his turn, appeared to believe the adventure just related with very many doubts and modifications.

Lorrimer leaned over the table and whispered in Sylvester's ear.

''Damme—damme my fellow''—murmured Sylvester, apparently in reply to the whispered remark of his friend—''It cannot be done. Why man its a penitentiary offence.''

Lorrimer again hissed a meaning whisper in the ear of the little man.

''Well, well, as it is your wish I'll do it. A cool fifty, did you say? You think a devlish sight of the girl—do you then? I must provide myself with a gown and prayer book? I flatter myself I'll rather become them—three o'clock, did you say?''

''Aye—aye—'' answered Lorrimer, turning to the rubicund face of Col. Mutchins and whispering hurriedly in his ear.

A pleasant smile overspread the face of the benevolent man, and his pear-shaped nose seemed to grow expressive for a single moment.

''D———d good idea? I'll be your too-confiding uncle? Eh? Stern but relenting? I'll bless the union with my benediction—*I'll give the bride away?''*

''Come along Byrnewood. Here Smokey is the money for our supper. Mark you gentlemen, Mr. Petriken and Col. Mutchins—the hour is three o'clock. Don't fail me, if the d———l himself stands in the way. Take my arm Byrnewood and let's travel—''

''Then 'hey for the wedding.' Daylight will tell who wins!''

And as they left the room arm in arm, bound on the adventure so suddenly undertaken, and so full of interest and romance, Petriken looked vacantly in Mutchins face, and Mutchins returned the look with a steady gaze that seemed to say—'How much did he give you, old boy?'

Whether Sylvester translated the look in this manner, it is difficult to tell, but certain it is, that as he poured a bumper from a fresh bottle of champagne, he motioned the Colonel to do the same, and murmured in an absent manner, or perhaps by way of a sentiment, the remarkable words—

''Fify dollars! Egad that 'ill buy two steel engravings and three fashion plates for the next number of the Ladies' Western Hemisphere. 'Economy is wealth,' and the best way to learn to fly is to creep—creep very low, remarkably low, d———d low—*always creep!*''

CHAPTER SECOND

MARY, THE MERCHANT'S DAUGHTER

Leaning gently forward, her shawl falling carelessly from her shoulders, and her bonnet thrown back from her brow, the fair girl impressed a kiss on the cheek of her father, while the glossy ringlets of her hair mingled their luxuriant brown with the white locks of the kind old man.

The father seated on the sofa, his hands clasping her slight and delicate fingers, looked up into her beaming face with a look of unspeakable affection, while a warm glow of feeling flushed over the pale face of the mother, a fine matronly dame of some forty-five, who stood gazing on her daughter, with one hand resting on the husband's shoulder.

The mild beams of an astral lamp diffused a softened and pleasing light through the parlor. The large mirror glittering over the mantle, the curtains of crimson silk depending along the windows, the sofa on which the old man was seated, the carpet of the finest texture, the costly chairs, the paintings that hung along the walls, and in fine all the appointments of the parlor, designated the abode of luxury and affluence.

The father, who sate on the sofa gazing in the face of his child, was a man of some sixty years, with a fine venerable countenance, wrinkled by care and time, with thin locks of snow-white hair falling along his high pale forehead. In his calm blue eye, looking forth from the shadow of a thick grey eyebrow, and in the general contour of his face, you might trace as forcible a resemblance to his daughter, as ever was witnessed between an old man just passing away from life, and a fair young girl, blooming and blushing on the very threshold of womanhood. The old man was clad in glossy black, and his entire appearance, marked the respectable merchant, who, retiring from active business, sought in the quietude of his own home, all the joys, that life, wealth or affection united and linked in blessings, have in their power to bestow.

The mother, who stood resting her hand on her husband's shoulder, was, we have said, a fine matronly dame of forty-five. A mild pale face, a deep black eye, and masses of raven hair, slightly sprinkled with the silver threads of age, parted over a calm forehead, and tastefully disposed beneath a plain cap of lace, gave the mother an appearance of sweetness and dignity combined, that was eminently effective in winning the respect and love of all who looked upon her.

"Mary—my child—how lovely you have grown!" exclaimed the Merchant, in a deep quiet tone, as he pressed her fair hands within his own, and looked up in her face.

"Nonsense! You will make the child vain—" whispered the wife playfully, yet her face flushed with affection, and her eyes shone an answer to her husband's praise.

The girl was indeed beautiful.

As she stood there, in that quiet parlor, gazing in her father's face, she looked like a breathing picture of youth, girlhood and innocence, painted by the finger of God. Her face was very beautiful. The small bonnet thrown back from her forehead, suffered the rich curls of her brown hair to escape, and they fell twining and glossy along each swelling cheek, as though they loved to rest upon the velvet skin. The features were regular, her lips were full red and ripe, her round chin varied by a bewitching dimple, and her eyes were large, blue and eloquent, with long and trembling lashes. You looked in those eyes, and felt that all the sunlight of a woman's soul was shining on you. The face was lovely, most lovely, the skin, soft, velvety, blooming and transparent, the eyes full of soul, the lips sweet with the ripeness of maidenhood, and the brow calm and white as alabaster, yet was there no remarkable manifestation of thought, or mind, or intellect visible in the lines of that fair countenance. It was the face of a woman formed to lean, to cling, to love, and never to lean on but one arm, never to cling but to one bosom, never to love but once, and that till death and forever.

The fair round neck, and well-developed bust, shown to advantage in the close fitting dress of black silk, the slender waist, and the ripening proportions of her figure, terminated by slight ancles and delicate feet, all gave you the idea of a bud breaking into bloom, a blossom ripening into fruit, or what is higher and holier, a pure and happy soul manifesting itself to the world, through the rounded outlines of a woman's form.

"Come, come father, you must not detain me any longer—" exclaimed the daughter in a sweet and low-toned voice—"You know aunt Emily has been teasing me these two weeks, ever since I returned from boarding-school, to come and stay with her all night. You know I was always a favorite with the dear old soul. She wants to contrive some agreeable surprise for my birth-day, I believe. I'm sixteen next Christmas, and that is three days off. Do let me go, that's a good father———"

"Had'nt you better put on your cloak, my love?" interrupted the

Mother, regarding the daughter with a look of fond affection—"The night is very cold, and you may suffer from exposure to the winter air—"

"Oh no, no, no mother—" replied the fair girl, laughingly—"I *do* so hate these cloaks—they're so bungling and so heavy! I'll just fling my shawl across my shoulders, and run all the way to Aunt Emily's. You know it's only two squares distant in Third Street—"

"And then old Lewey will see you safe to the door?" exclaimed the Mother—"Well, well, go along my dear child, take good care of yourself, and give my love to your Aunt—"

"These old maids are queer things"—said the Merchant with a smile—"Take care Mary or Aunt Emily will find out all your secrets—"

And the old man smiled pleasantly to himself, for the idea of a girl, so young, so innocent, having any secrets to be found out, was too amusing to be entertained without a smile.

A shade fell over the daughters face so sudden and melancholy that her parents started with surprise.

"Why do you look so sad, my child!" exclaimed the Father, looking up in his daughter's face. "What is there in the world to sadden *you*, my Mary?"

"Nothing, father, nothing—" murmured Mary, flinging her form on her fathers bosom and twining her arms round his neck as she kissed him again and again—"Only I was thinking—just thinking of Christmas, and———"

The fair girl rose suddenly from her fathers bosom, and flung her arms hurriedly around her mother's neck, imprinting kiss after kiss on her lips.

"Good bye mother—I'll be back—I'll be back—to-morrow."

And in an instant she glided hastily to the door and left the room.

"Lewey is'nt it very cold to night!" she asked as she observed the white-haired negro-servant waiting in the hall, wrapped up in an enormous overcoat, with a comforter around his neck and a close fur cap surmounting his grey wool and chubby round face—"I'm sorry to take you out in the cold, Lewey."

"Bress de baby's soul—" murmured the old negro opening the door —"Habbent I nuss you in dese arms when you warnt so high? Lewey take cold? Debbil a cold dis nigger take for no price when a-waitin' on missa Mary—"

Mary stood upon the threshold of her home looking out into the cold starlit night. Her face was for a moment overshadowed by an expression of the deepest melancholy, and her small foot trembled as it stepped over the threshold. She looked hurriedly along the gloomy street, then cast her glance backwards into the entry, and then with a wild bound she retraced her steps, and stood beside her father and her mother.

Again she kissed them, again flung her arms round their necks, and again bounded along the entry crying laughingly to her parents—"Good night—good night—I'll be back to-morrow."

Again she stood upon the threshold, but all traces of laughter had vanished from her face. She was sad and silent, and there were tears in her eyes. At least the old negro said so afterwards, and also that her tiny foot, when resting on the door-sill, trembled like any leaf.

Why should her eye grow dim with tears and her foot tremble? Would not that tiny foot, when next it crossed the threshold, bound forward with a gladsome movement, as the bride sprung to meet her father and her mother once again? Would not that calm blue eye, now filled with tears, grow bright with a joy before unknown, when it glanced over the husbands form, as for the first time he stood in the fathers presence? Would not Christmas Eve be a merry night for the bride and all her friends as they went shouting merrily through the luxuriantly furnished chambers of her fathers mansion? Why should *she* fear to cross the threshold of her home, when her coming back was to be heralded with blessings and crowned with love?

How will the future answer these trembling questions of that stainless heart?

She crossed the threshold, and not daring to look back, hurried along the gloomy street. It was clear, cold, starlight, and the pathways were comparatively deserted. The keen winter wind nipped her cheek, and chilled her form, but above her, the stars seemed smiling her 'onward,' and she fancied the good angels, that ever watch over woman's first and world-trusting love, looking kindly upon her from the skies.

After traversing Third street for some two squares, she stood before an ancient three-storied dwelling, at the corner of Third and ——— streets, with the name of 'Miss. E. Graham,' on the door plate.

"Lewey you need'nt wait—" she said kindly—yet not without a deeper motive than kindness—to the aged Negro who had attended her thus far—"I'll ring the bell myself. You had better hurry home and warm yourself—and remember, Lewey, tell father and mother that they need not expect me home before to-morrow at noon. Good night, Lewey."

"Good night, Missa Mary, Lor' Moses lub your soul—" muttered the honest old Negro, as, pulling his fur cap over his eyes, he strode homeward—"Dat ar babby's a angel, dat is widout de wings. De Lor grant when dis here ole nigger gets to yander firmey-ment—dat is if niggers gets dar at all—he may be 'pinted to one ob de benches near Missa Mary, so he can wait on her, handy as nuffin—dats all. She's a angel, and dis here night, is a leetle colder dan any night in de memory ob dat genel'man de Fine Col'ector nebber finds—de berry oldest inhabitant."

Thus murmuring, Lewey trudged on his way, leaving Mary standing in front of Aunt Emily's door. Did she pull the bell? I trow not, for no sooner was the negro out of sight, than the tall figure of a woman, dressed in black, with a long veil drooping over her face, glided round the corner and stood by her side.

"Oh—Bessie—is that you?" cried Mary, in a trembling voice—"I'm so frightened I don't know what to do—Oh Bessie—Bessie don't you think I had better turn back—"

"*He* waits for you—" said the strange woman, in a husky voice.

Mary hurriedly laid her hand on the stranger's arm. Her face was overspread with a sudden expression of feeling, like a gleam of sunshine, seen through a broken cloud on a stormy day, and in a moment, they were speeding down Third street toward the southern districts of the Quaker City. Another moment, and the eye might look for them in vain.

And as they disappeared the State House clock rung out the hour of nine. This, as the reader will perceive, was just four hours previous to the time when Byrnewood and Lorrimer closed their wager in the subterranean establishment along Chesnut street. To the wager and its result we now turn our attention and the readers interest.

CHAPTER THIRD

BYRNEWOOD AND LORRIMER

The harsh sound of their footsteps, resounding along the frozen pavement, awoke the echoes of the State House buildings, as linked arm in arm, Byrnewood and Lorrimer hurried along Chesnut street, their figures thrown in lengthened shadow by the beams of the setting moon.

The tall, manly and muscular figure of Lorrimer, attired in a close-fitting black overcoat, presented a fine contrast to the slight yet well-proportioned form of Byrnewood, which now and then became visible as the wind flung his voluminous cloak back from his shoulders. The firm and measured stride of Lorrimer, the light and agile footsteps of Byrnewood, the glowing countenance of the magnificent Gus, the pale solemn face of the young Merchant, the rich brown hair which hung in clustering masses around the brow of the first, and the long dark hair which fell sweeping to the very shoulders of his companion, all furnished the details of a vivid contrast, worthy the effective portraiture of a master in our sister-art.

"Almost as cold as charity, Byrnewood my boy—" exclaimed Lorrimer, as he gathered Byrnewood's arm more closely within his own—"Do you know, my fellow, that I believe vastly in faces?"

"How so?"

"I can tell a man's character from his face, the moment I clap my eye on him. I like or dislike at first sight. Now there's Silly Petriken's face—how do you translate it?"

"The fact is, Lorrimer, I know very little about him. I was introduced to him, for the first time, at a party, where he was enrapturing some sentimental old maids, with a few quires of sonnets on every thing in general. Since that occasion I have never met him, until tonight, when he hailed me in Chesnut street, and forced me into Mutchins room at the United States Hotel. You know the rest—"

"Well, well, with regard to Petriken, a single word. Clever fellow, clever, but like Mutchins, he sells for a reasonable price. I buy them both. By Jupiter! the town swarms with such fellows, who will sell themselves to any master for a trifle. Petriken—poor fellow—his face indicates his character—a solemn pimp, a sententious parasite. Mutchins is just the other way—an agreeable jolly old-dog of a pander. They hire themselves to me for the season—I use and, of course, despise them—"

"You're remarks are truly flattering to these worthy gentlemen!" said Byrnewood, drily.

"And now my fellow, you may think me insincere, but I tell you frankly, that the moment I first saw your face, I liked you, and resolved you should be my friend. For your sake I am about to do a thing which I would do for no living man, and possibly no dead one———"

"And that is—" interrupted Byrnewood.

"Just listen my fellow. Did you ever hear any rumors of a queer old house down town, kept by a reputable old lady, and supported by the purses of goodly citizens, whose names you never hear without the addition of 'respectable,' 'celebrated,' or—ha—ha—'pious'—*most* 'pious?' A queer old house my good fellow, where, during the long hours of the winter nights, your husband, so kind and good, forgets his wife, your merchant his ledger, your lawyer his quibbles, your parson his prayers? A queer old house, my good fellow, where wine and women mingle their attractions, where at once you sip the honey from a red-lip, and a sparkling bubble from the champagne? Where luxuriantly-furnished chambers resound all night long with the rustling of cards, or the clink of glasses, or—it may be—the gentle ripple of voices, murmuring in a kiss? A queer old house, my dear fellow, in short, where the very devil is played under a cloak, and sin grows fat within the shelter of quiet rooms and impenetrable walls—"

"Ha—ha—Lorrimer you are eloquent! Faith, I've heard some rumors of such a queer old house, but always deemed them fabulous—"

"The old house is a fact, my boy, a fact. Within its walls this night I will wed my pretty bride, and within its walls, my fellow, despite the pains and penalties of our Club, you shall enter—"

"I should like it of all things in the world. How is your club styled?"

"All in good time, my friend. Each member, you see, once a week, has the privilege of introducing a friend. The same friend must never enter the Club House twice. Now I have rather overstepped the rules of the Club in other respects—it will require all my tact to pass you in to-night. It shall be done, however—and mark me—you will obtain a few fresh ideas of the nature of the *secret life* of this good Quaker City—"

"Why Lorrimer—" exclaimed Byrnewood, as they approached the corner of Eighth and Chesnut—"You seem to have a pretty good idea of life in general—"

"Life?" echoed the magnificent Gus, in that tone of enthusiasm peculiar to the convivialist when recovering from the first excitement of the bottle—"Life? What is it? As brilliant and as brief as a champagne bubble! To day a jolly carouse in an oyster cellar, to-morrow a nice little pic nic party in a grave-yard. One moment you gather the apple, the next it is ashes. Every thing fleeting and nothing stable, every thing shifting and changing, and nothing substantial! A bundle of hopes and fears, deceits and confidences, joys and miseries, strapped to a fellow's back like Pedlar's wares—"

"Huzza! Bravo—the *Reverend* Gus Lorrimer preaches. And what moral does your reverence deduce from all this!"

"One word, my fellow—ENJOY! Enjoy till the last nerve loses its delicacy of sense; enjoy till the last sinew is unstrung; enjoy till the eye flings out its last glance, till the voice cracks and the blood stagnates; *enjoy*, always *enjoy*, and at last———"

"Aye, aye—that terrible *at last*———"

"At last, when you can enjoy no longer, creep into a nice cozy house, some eight feet deep, by six long and two wide, wrap yourself up in a comfortable quilt of white, and tell the worms—those jolly gleaners of the scraps of the feast of life—that they may fall to and be d———d to 'em—"

"Ha—ha—Lorrimer! Who would have thought this of you?"

"Tell me, my fellow, what business do you follow?"

"Rather an abrupt question. However, I'm the junior partner in the importing house of Livingston, Harvey, & Co., along Front street—"

"And I—" replied Gustavus slowly and with deliberation—"And I am junior and senior partner in a snug little wholesale business of my own. The firm is Lorrimer, & Co.—the place of business is everywhere about town—and the business itself is enjoyment, nothing but enjoyment; wine and woman forever! And as for the capital—I've an unassuming sum of one hundred thousand dollars, am independent of all relations, and bid fair to live at least a score of years longer. Now my fellow, you know me—come, spice us up a few of your own secrets. Have you no interesting little *amour* for my private ear?"

"By Heaven, I'd forgotten all about it!" cried Byrnewood starting aside from his companion as they stood in the full glare of the gas-lamp at the corner of Eighth and Chesnut street—"I'd forgotten all about the letter!"

"The letter? What letter?"

"Why just before Petriken hailed me in Chesnut street this evening—or rather *last* evening—a letter was placed in my hands, which I neglected to read. I know the hand-writing on the direction, however. It's from a dear little love of a girl, who, some six months ago, was a servant in my father's house. A sweet girl, Lorrimer—and—you know how these things work—she was lovely, innocent and too confiding, and I was but a—man—"

"And she a 'slewer.' Rather a low walk of business for *you*, my boy. However, let's read the letter by lamplight—"

"Here it is—'Dear Byrnewood—I would like very much to see you to-night. I am in great distress. Meet me at the corner of Fourth and Chesnut streets at nine o'clock or you will regret it to the day of your death. Oh for God's sake do meet me—Annie.' What a pretty hand she writes—Eh! Lorrimer! That '*for God's sake*' is rather cramped—and —egad! there's the stain of a tear—"

"These things are quite customary. These letters and these tears. The dear little women can only use these arguments when they yield too much to our persuasions—"

"And yet—d———n the thing—how unfortunate for the girl my acquaintance has proved! She had to leave my father's house on account of—of—the *circumstance* becoming too apparent, and her parents are very poor. I should have liked to have seen her to-night. However, it will do in the morning. And now, Lorrimer, which way?"

"To the 'queer old house' down town. By the bye, there goes the State House—one o'clock, by Jupiter! We've two good hours yet to decide the wager. Let's spend half an hour in a visit to a certain friend of mine. Here, Byrnewood, let me instruct you in the mysteries of the 'lark'—"

And, leaning aside, the magnificent Gus whispered in the ear of his friend, with as great an appearance of mystery as the most profound secret might be supposed to demand.

"Do you take, my fellow?"

"Capital, capital—" replied Byrnewood, crushing the letter into his pocket—"We shall crowd this night with adventures—that's certain!"

The dawn of daylight—it is true—closed the accounts of a night somewhat crowded with incidents. Did these merry gentlemen who stood laughing so cheerily at the corner of Eighth and Chesnut streets, at the hour of one, their faces glowing in the light of the midnight moon, did they guess the nature of the incidents which five o'clock in the morning could disclose? God of Heaven—might no angel of mercy drop from the skies and warn them back in their career?

No warning came, no omen scared them back. Passing down Eighth street, they turned up Walnut, which they left at Thirteenth. Turning down Thirteenth they presently stood before a small old fashioned two storied building, with a green door and a bull window, that occupied nearly the entire width of the front, protruding in the light. A tin sign, placed between the door and window, bore the inscription, "*. *****, ASTROLOGER."

"Wonder if the old cove's in bed—" exclaimed Lorrimer, and as he spoke the green door opened, as if in answer to his question, and the figure of a man, muffled up in the thick folds of a cloak with his hat drawn over his eyes, glided out of the Astrologer's house, and hurried down Thirteenth street.

"Ha—ha—devilish cunning, but not so cunning as he thinks!" laughed Byrnewood—"I saw his face—it's old Grab-and-Snatch, the President of the ——— Bank, which every body says is on the eve of a grand blow-up!"

"The respectable old gentleman has been consulting the stars with regard to the prospects of his bank—ha—ha! However, my boy, the door is open—let's enter! Let's consult this familiar of the fates, this intimate acquaintance of the Future!"

CHAPTER FOURTH

THE ASTROLOGER

In a small room, remarkable for the air of comfort imparted by the combined effects of the neatly white-washed walls, the floor, plainly carpeted, and the snug little wood-stove roaring in front of the hearth, sat a man of some forty-five winters, bending over the table in the corner, covered with strange-looking books and loose manuscripts.

The light of the iron lamp which stood in the centre of the table, resting on a copy of Cornelius Agrippa, fell full and strongly over the face and form of the Astrologer, disclosing every line of his countenance, and illumining the corner where he sat, while the more distant parts of the room were comparatively dim and shadowy.

As he sat in the large old-fashioned arm-chair, bending down earnestly over a massive manuscript, covered with strange characters and crossed by intricate lines, the lampbeams disclosed a face, which somewhat plain and unmeaning in repose, was now agitated by an expression of the deepest interest. The brow, neither very high nor very low, shaded by tangled locks of thin brown hair, was corrugated with deep furrows, the eyebrows were firmly set together, the nostrils dilated, and the lips tightly compressed, while the full grey eyes, staring vacantly on the manuscript, indicated by the glassy film spread over each pupil, that the mind of the Astrologer, instead of being occupied with outward objects, was buried within itself, in the contemplation of some intricate subject of thought.

There was nothing in the dress of the man, or in the appearance of his room, that might realize the ideas commonly attached to the Astrologer and his den. Here were no melodramatic curtains swinging solemnly to and fro, brilliant and terrible with the emblazoned death's-head and cross-bones. Here were no blue lights imparting a lurid radiance to a row of grinning skeletons, here were no ghostly forms standing pale and erect, their glassy eyes freezing the spectator's blood with horror, here was neither goblin, devil, or mischievous ape, which, as every romance reader knows, have been the companions of the Astrologer from time immemorial; here was nothing but a plain man, seated in an old-fashioned arm chair, within the walls of a comfortable room, warmed by a roaring little stove.

No cap of sable relieved the Astrologer's brow, no gown of black velvet, tricked out with mysterious emblems in gold and precious stones, fell in sweeping folds around the outlines of his spare figure.

A plain white overcoat, much worn and out at the elbows, a striped vest not remarkable for its shape or fashion, a cross-barred neckerchief, and a simple linen shirt collar completed the attire of the astrologer who sat reading at the table.

The walls of the room were hung with the Horoscopes of illustrious men, Washington, Byron, and Napoleon, delineated on large sheets of paper, and surrounded by plain frames of black wood; the table was piled with the works of Sibly, Lilly, Cornelius Agrippa and other masters in the mystic art; while at the feet of the Astrologer nestled a fine black cat, whose large whiskers and glossy fur, would seem to afford no arguments in favor of the supposition entertained by the neighbors, that she was a devil in disguise, a sort of familiar spirit on leave of absence from the infernal regions.

"I'm but a poor man—" said the Astrologer, turning one of the leaves of the massive volume in manuscript which he held in his hand—"I'm but a poor man, and the lawyer, and the doctor, and the parson all despise me, and yet—" his lip wreathed with a sneering smile—"this little room has seen them all within its walls, begging from the humble man some knowledge of the future! Here they come—one and all—the fools, pretending to despise my science, and yet willing to place themselves in my power, while they affect to doubt. Ha-ha—here are their Nativities one and all—That" he continued, turning over a leaf—"is the Horoscope of a clergyman—Holy man of God! —He wanted to know whether he could ruin an innocent girl in his congregation without discovery. And that is the Horoscope of a lawyer, who takes fees from both sides. His desire is to know, whether he can perjure himself in a case now in court without detection. Noble counsellor! This Doctor—" and he turned over another leaf—"told me that he had a delicate case in hand. A pretty girl had been ruined and so on—the seducer wants to destroy the fruit of his crime and desires the doctor to undertake the job. Doctor wants to know what moment will be auspicious—ha-ha!"

And thus turning from page to page, he disclosed the remarkable fact, that the great, the good, and the wise of the Quaker City, who met the mere name of astrology, when uttered in public, with a most withering sneer, still under the cover of night, were happy to steal to the astrologer's room, and obtain some glimpses of their future destiny through the oracle of the stars.

"A black-eyed woman—lusty and amorous—wants to know whether she can present her husband with a pair of horns on a certain night? I warned her not to proceed in her course of guilt. She does proceed—and will be exposed to her husband's hate and public scorn—"

And thus murmuring, the Astrologer turned to another leaf.

"The Horoscope of a puppy-faced editor! A spaniel, a snake, and an ape—he is a combination of the three. Wants to know when he can run off with a lady of the *ballet* at the theatre, without being caught by his creditors? Also, whether next Thursday is an auspicious day for a little piece of roguery he has in view? The penitentiary looms darkly in the distance—let the editor of the 'Daily Black Mail' beware—"

Another leaf inscribed with a distinguished name, arrested the Astrologers attention.

"Ha—ha! This fellow is a man of fashion, a buck of Chesnut street, and—and a Colonel! He lives—*I* know *how*—the fashionables who follow in his wake don't *dream* of his means of livelihood. He has committed a crime—an astounding crime—wants to know whether his associate will betray him! I told him *he* would. The Colonel laughed at me, although he paid for the knowledge. In a week the fine, sweet, perfumed gentleman will be lodged at public expense—"

The Astrologer laid down the volume, and in a moment seemed to have fallen into the same train of thought, marked by the corrugated brow and glassy eye, that occupied his mind at the commencement of this scene. His lips moved tremulously, and his hands ever and anon were pressed against his wrinkled brow. Every moment his eye grew more glassy, and his mouth more fixedly compressed, and at last, leaning his elbows on the table with his hands nervously clasped, his gaze was fixed on the blank wall opposite, in a wild and vacant stare that betrayed the painful abstraction of his mind from all visible objects.

And as he sat there enwrapt in thought, a footstep, inaudible to his ear, creaked on the stairway that ascended into the Astrologer's chamber from the room below, and in a moment, silent and unperceived, Gus Lorrimer stood behind his chair, looking over his head, his very breath hushed and his hands upraised.

"In all my history I remember nothing half so strange. All is full of light except one point of the future, and that is dark as death!" Thus ran the murmured soliloquy of the Astrologer—"And yet they will be here to-night—here—here both of them, or there's no truth in the stars. Lorrimer must beware———"

"Ha—ha—ha—" laughed a bold and manly voice—"An old stage trick, that. You didn't hear my footsteps on the stairs—did you? Oh no—oh no. Of course you didn't. Come—come, my old boy, that claptrap mention of my name, is rather too stale, even for a three-fipenny-bit melo-drama—"

The sudden start which the Astrologer gave, the unaffected look of surprise which flashed over his features at the sight of the gentleman of pleasure, convinced Lorrimer that he had done him rank injustice.

"Sit down, sir—I have much to say to you—" said the Astrologer, in a voice strikingly contrasted with his usual tone, it was so deep, so full and so calmly deliberate—"Last Thursday morning at this hour you gave me the day and hour of your birth. You wished me to cast your horoscope. You wished to know whether you would be successful in an enterprise which you meditated. Am I correct in this?"

"You are, my old humbug—that is my *friend*—" replied Lorrimer, flinging himself into a seat.

"Humbug?" cried the other with a quiet sneer—"You may alter your opinion after a-while, my young friend. Since last Thursday morning I have given the most careful attention to your horoscope. It is one of the most startling that ever I beheld. You were born under one of the most favorable aspects of the heavens, born, it would seem, but to succeed in all your wishes; and yet your future fate is wrapt in some terrible mystery—"

"Like a kitten in a wet blanket, for instance?" said Lorrimer, in the vain endeavor, to shake off a strange feeling of awe, produced by the manner of the Astrologer.

"This night I was occupied with your horoscope when a strange circumstance attracted my attention. Even while I was examining book after book, in the effort to see more clearly into your future, I discovered that you were making a new acquaintance at some festival, some wine-drinking or other affair of the kind. This new acquaintance is a man with a pale face, long dark hair and dark eyes. So the stars tell me. Your fate and the fate of this young man are linked together till death. So the heavens tell me, and the heavens never lie."

"Yes—yes—my friend, very good—" replied Gustavus with a smile—"Very good, my dear sir. Your conclusions are perfect—your prophetic gift without reproach. But you forget one slight circumstance:—I have made no new acquaintance to-night! I have been at no wine-drinking! I have seen no interesting young man with a pale face and long dark hair—"

"Then my science is a lie!" exclaimed the Astrologer, with a puzzled look—"The stars declare that this very night, you first came in contact with the man, whose fate henceforth is linked with your own. The future has a doom in store for one of ye. The stars do not tell me which shall feel the terror of the doom, but that it will be inflicted by one of ye upon the other, is certain—"

"Well, let us suppose, for the sake of argument, that I did meet this mysterious young man with long black hair. What follows?"

"Three days ago, a young man, whose appearance corresponds with the indication given by the stars of the new acquaintance you were to make this very night, came to me and desired me to cast his horoscope. The future of this young man, is as like yours as night is to-night. He too is threatened with a doom—either to be suffered or inflicted. This doom will lower over his head within three days. At the hour of sunset on next Saturday—Christmas Eve—a terrible calamity will overtake him. At the same hour, and in the same manner, a terrible calamity will blacken your life forever. The same doubt prevails in both cases—whether you will endure this calamity in your own person, or be the means of inflicting its horrors on some other man, doomed and fated by the stars—"

"What connection has this young man with the 'new acquaintance' which you say I have formed to-night?"

"I suspect that this young man and your new acquaintance are *one*. If so, I warn you, by your soul, beware of him—this stranger to you!"

"And why *beware of me?*" said a calm and quiet voice at the shoulder of the Astrologer.

As though a shell had burst in the centre of that quiet room, he started, he trembled, and arose to his feet. Byrnewood, the young merchant, calm and silent, stood beside him.

"I warn ye." he shrieked in a tone of wild excitement, with his grey eyes dilating and flashing beneath the woven eyebrows—"I warn ye both—beware of each other! Let this meeting at my house be your last on earth, and ye are saved! Meet again, or pursue any adventure together, and ye are lost and lost forever! I tell ye, scornful men that ye are, that ask my science to aid you, and then mock its lessons, I tell ye, by the Living God who writes his will, in letters of fire on the wide scroll of the firmament, that in the hand of the dim Future is a Goblet steeped in the bitterness of death, and that goblet one or the other must drink, within three little days!"

And striding wildly along the room, while Byrnewood stood awed, and even the cheek of Lorrimer grew pale, he gave free impulse to one of those wild deliriums of excitement peculiar to his long habits of abstraction and thought. The full truth, the terrible truth, seemed crowding on his brain, arrayed in various images of horror, and he shrieked forth his interpretation of the future, in wild and broken sentences.

"Young man, three days ago you sought to know the future. You had never spoken to the man who sits in yonder chair. I cast your horoscope—I found your destiny like the destiny of this man who affects to sneer at my science. My art availed me no further. I could not identify you with the man who first met Lorrimer this night, amid revelry and wine. Now I can supply the broken chain. You and his new-formed acquaintance are *one*. And now the light of the stars breaks more plainly on me—*within three days, one of you will die by the other's hand*———"

Lorrimer slowly arose to his feet, as though the effort gave him pain. His cheek was pale, and beaded drops of sweat stood on his brow. His parted lips, his upraised hands and flashing eyes attested his interest in the astrologer's words. Meanwhile, starting suddenly aside, Byrnewood veiled his face in his hands, as his breast swelled and quivered with sudden emotion.

Stern and erect, in his plain white overcoat, untricked with gold or gems, stood the Astrologer, his tangled brown hair flung back from his brow, while, with his outstretched hand and flashing eye, he spoke forth the fierce images of his brain.

"Three days from this, as the sun goes down, on Christmas eve, one of you will die by the other's hand. As sure as there is a God in Heaven, his stars have spoken, and it will be so!"

"What will be the manner of *the death*?" exclaimed Lorrimer, in a low-tuned voice, as he endeavored to subdue the sudden agitation inspired by the Astrologer's words, while Byrnewood raised his head and awaited the answer with evident interest.

"There is the cloud and the mystery—" exclaimed the Astrologer, fixing his eye on vacancy, while his outstretched hand trembled like a leaf in the wind—"The death will overtake the doomed man on a river, and yet it will not be by water; it will kill him by means of fire and yet he will not perish in the midst of flames—"

There was a dead pause for a single instant. There stood the Astrologer, his features working as with a convulsive spasm, the light falling boldly over his slight figure and homely attire, and there at his side, gazing in his face, stood Byrnewood, the young merchant, silent as if a spell had fallen on him, while on the other side, Gustavus Lorrimer, half recoiling, his brow woven in a frown, and his dark eyes flashing with a strange glance, seemed making a fearful effort to command his emotion, and dispel the gloom which the wierd prophecy had flung over his soul.

"Pah! What fools we are! To stand here listening to the ravings of a madman or a knave—" cried Byrnewood, with a forced laugh, as he shook off the spell that seemed to bind him—"What does he know of the future—more than we? Eh? Lorrimer? Perhaps, sir, since you are so familiar with fate, destiny and all that, you can tell us the nature of the adventure on which Lorrimer is bound to-night?"

The Astrologer turned and looked upon him. There was something so calmly scornful in his glance, that Byrnewood averted his eyes.

"The adventure is connected with the honor of an innocent woman —" said the Astrologer—"More than this I know not, save that a foul outrage will be done this very night. And—hark ye sir—either the heavens are false, or your future destiny hangs upon this adventure. Give up the adventure at once, go back in your course, part from one another, part this moment never to meet again, and you will be saved. Advance and you are lost!"

Lorrimer stood silent, thoughtful and pale as death. It becomes me not to look beyond the veil that hangs between the Visible and the Invisible, but it may be, that in the silent pause of thought which the libertine's face manifested, his soul received some indications of the future from the very throne of God. Men call these sudden shadows, presentiments; to the eyes of angels they may be, but messages of warning spoken to the soul, in the spirit-tongues of those awful beings whose habitation is beyond the threshold of time. What did Lorrimer behold that he stood so silent, so pale, so thoughtful? Did Christmas Eve, and the River, and the Death, come terrible and shadow-like to his soul?

"Pshaw! Lorrimer you are not frightened by the preachings of this fortune-teller?" cried Byrnewood with a laugh and a sneer—"You will not give up the girl? Ha—ha—scared by an owl! Ha—ha—What would Petriken say? Imagine the rich laugh of Mutchins—ha—ha—Gus Lorrimer scared by an owl!"

"Give up the girl?" cried Lorrimer, with a blasphemous oath, that profaned the name of the Saviour—"Give up the girl? Never! She shall repose in my arms before daylight! Heaven nor hell shall scare me back! There's your money Mister Fortune Teller—your croaking deserves the silver, the d———l knows! Come on Byrnewood—let us away."

"Wait till I pay the gentleman for our coffins—" laughed Byrnewood, flinging some silver on the table—"See that they're ready by Saturday night, old boy? D'ye mind? You are hand-in-glove with some respectable undertaker—no doubt—and can give him our measure. Good bye—old fellow—good bye! Now, Lorrimer, away—"

"Away, away to Monk-hall!"

And in a moment they had disappeared down the stairway, and were passing through the lower room toward the street.

"On Christmas Eve, at the hour of sunset—" shrieked the Astrologer, his features convulsed with anger, and his voice wild and piercing in its tones—"One of you will die by the other's hand! The winding sheet is woven, and the coffin made—you are rushing madly on your doom!"

CHAPTER FIFTH

DORA LIVINGSTONE

It was a nice cozy place, that old counting-house room, with its smoky walls, its cheerful coal-fire burning in the rusty grate, and its stained and blackened floor. A snug little room, illuminated by a gas-light, subdued to a shadowy and sleepy brilliancy, with the Merchant's Almanac and four or five old pictures scattered along the walls, an old oaken desk with immense legs, all carved and curled into a thousand shapes, standing in one corner, and a massive door, whose glass window opened a mysterious view into the regions of the warehouse, where casks of old cogniac lay, side by side, in lengthened rows, like jolly old fellows at a party, as they whisper quietly to one another on the leading questions of the day.

Seated in front of the coal fire, his legs elevated above his head, resting on the mantel-piece, a gentleman, of some twenty-five years, with his arms crossed and a pipe in his mouth, seemed engaged in an earnest endeavour to wrap himself up in a cloak of tobacco smoke, in order to prepare for a journey into the land of Nod, while the tumbler of punch standing on the small table at his elbow, showed that he was by no means opposed to that orthodox principle which recognizes the triple marriage of brandy, lemon and sugar, as a highly necessary addition to the creature comforts of the human being, in no way to be despised or neglected by thinking men.

You would not have called this gentleman well-proportioned, and yet his figure was long and slender, you could not have styled his dress eminently fashionable, and yet his frock coat was shaped of the finest black cloth, you would not have looked upon his face as the most handsome in the world, and yet it was a finely-marked countenance, with a decided, if not highly intellectual, expression. If the truth must be told, his coat, though fashioned of the finest cloth, was made a little too full in one place, a little too scant in another, and buttoned up somewhat too high in the throat, for a gentleman whose ambition it was to flourish on the southern side of Chesnut street, amid the animated cloths and silks of a fashionable promenade. And then the large black stock, encircling his neck, with the crumpled, though snow-white, shirt collar, gave a harsh relief to his countenance, while the carelessly-disposed wristbands, crushed back over the upturned cuffs of his coat, designated the man who went in for comfort, and flung fashion to the haberdashers and dry goods clerks.

As for his face, whenever the curtain of tobacco smoke rolled aside, you beheld, as I have said, a finely-marked countenance, with rather lank cheeks, a sharp aquiline nose, thin lips, biting and sarcastic in expression, a full square chin, and eyes of the peculiar class, intensely dark and piercing in their glance, that remind you of a flame without heat, cold, glittering and snake-like. His forehead was high and bold, with long and lanky black hair falling back from its outlines, and resting, without love-lock or curl, in straight masses behind each ear.

"Queer world this!" began our comfortable friend, falling into one of those broken soliloquies, generated by the pipe and the bowl, in which the stops are supplied by puffs of smoke, and the paragraph terminated by a sip of the punch—"Don't know much about other worlds, but it strikes me that if a prize were offered somewhere by somebody, for the queerest world a-going, this world of ours might be rigged up nice, and sent in like a bit of show beef, as the premium queer world. No man smokes a cigar that ever tried a pipe, but an ass. I was a small boy once—ragged little devil *that* Luke Harvey, who used to run about old Livingstone's importing warehouse. Indelicate little fellow: wore his ruffles out behind. Kicked and cuffed because he was poor—served him right—dammim. Old Liv. died—young Albert took the store—capital, cool one hundred thousand. Luke Harvey rose to a clerkship. Began to be a fine fellow—well-dressed, and of course virtuous. D———d queer fellow, Luke. Last year taken into partnership along with a young fellow whose daddy's worth at least one hun. thousand. Firm now—Livingstone, Harvey, & Co. Clever punch, that. Little too much lemon—d———d it, the sugar's out.

"Queer thing, that! Some weeks ago respectable old gentleman in white cravat and hump-back, came to counting house. Old fellow hailed from Charleston. Had rather a Jewish twang on his tongue. Presented Livingstone a letter of credit drawn by a Charleston house on our firm. Letter from Grayson, Ballenger, & Co., for a cool hundred thousand. Old white cravat got it. D———n that rat in the partition—why can't he eat his victuals in quiet? Two weeks since, news came that G. B. & Co. never gave such letter—a forgery, a complete swindle. Comfortable, that. Hot coals on one's bare skull, quite pleasant in comparison. Livingstone in New York—been trying for a week to track up the villain. Must get new pipe to-morrow. Mem. get one with

Judas Iscariot painted on the bowl. Honest rogue, that. Went and hanged himself after he sold his master. Wonder how full the town would be if all who have sold their God for gold would hang themselves? Hooks in market house would rise. Bear queer fruit—eh? D———d good tobacco. By the bye—must go home. Another sip of the punch and I'm off. Ha—ha—good idea that of the handsome Colonel! Great buck, man of fashion and long-haired Apollo. Called here this evening to see me—smelt like a civet cat. Must flourish his pocket-book before my eyes by way of a genteel brag. Dropped a letter from a bundle of notes. Valuable letter that. Wouldn't part with it for a cool thousand—rather think it will raise the devil—let me see—"

And laying down his pipe, Mr. Luke Harvey drew a neatly-folded billetdoux from an inside pocket of his coat, and holding it in the glare of the light perused its direction, which was written in a fair and delicate woman's hand.

" 'Col. Fitz-Cowles—United States Hotel' "—he murmured—"good idea, Colonel, to drop *such* a letter out of your pocket-book. Won't trouble you none? 'Spose not—ha, ha, ha—d———d good idea!"

The idea appeared to tickle him immensely, for he chuckled in a deep, self-satisfied tone as he drew on his bearskin overcoat, and even while he extinguished the gas-light, and covered up the fire, his chuckle grew into a laugh, which deepened into a hearty guffaw, as striding through the dark warehouse, he gained the front door, and looked out into the deserted street.

"Ha-ha-ha—to drop such a dear creature's letter!"—he laughed, locking the door of the warehouse—"Wonder if it won't raise h——l? I loved a woman once. Luke, you were a d———d fool *that* time. Jilted—yes jilted. That's the word I believe? Maybe I won't have my revenge? Perhaps not—very likely not—"

With this momentous letter, so carelessly dropped by the insinuating millionaire, Colonel Fitz-Cowles resting on his mind, and stirring his features with frequent spasmodic attacks of laughter, our friend, Mr. Harvey, pursued his way along Front street, and turning up Chesnut street, arrived at the corner of Third, where he halted for a few moments in order to ascertain the difference in time, between his gold-repeater and the State House clock, which had just struck one.

While thus engaged, intently perusing the face of his watch by the light of the moon, a stout middle-aged gentleman, wrapped up in a thick overcoat, with a carpet bag in his hand, came striding rapidly across the street, and for a moment stood silent and unperceived at his shoulder.

"Well Luke—is the repeater right and the State House wrong?" said a hearty cheerful voice, and the middle-aged gentleman laid his hand on Mr. Harvey's shoulder.

"Ah-ha! Mr. Livingstone! Is that you?" cried Luke, suddenly wheeling round, and gazing into the frank and manly countenance of the new-comer—"When did you get back from New York?"

"Just this moment arrived. I did not expect to return within a week from this time, and therefore come upon you by a little surprise. I wrote to Mrs. L. yesterday, telling her I would not be in town until the Christmas holidays were over. She'll be rather surprised to see me, I suppose?"

"Rather!" echoed Luke, drily.

"Come Luke, take my arm, and let's walk up toward my house. I have much to say to you. In the first place have you any thing new?"

While Mr. Harvey is imparting his budget of news to the senior partner of the firm of Livingstone, Harvey & Co., as they stroll slowly along Chesnut street, we will make some few notes of his present appearance.

Stout, muscular, and large-boned, with a figure slightly inclining towards corpulence, Mr. Livingstone strode along the pavement with a firm and measured step, that attested all the matured strength and vigor peculiar to robust middle age. He was six feet high, with broad shoulders and muscular chest. His face was full, bold, and massive, rather bronzed in hue, and bearing some slight traces of the ravages of small-pox. Once or twice as he walked along, he lifted his hat from his face, and his forehead, rendered more conspicuous by some slight baldness, was exposed to view. It was high, and wide, and massive, bulging outward prominently in the region of the reflective organs, and faintly relieved by his short brown hair. His eyes, bold and large, of a calm clear blue, were rendered strangely expressive by the contrast of the jet-black eyebrows. His nose was firm and Roman in contour, his mouth marked by full and determined lips, his chin square and prominent, while the lengthened outline of the lower jaw, from the chin to the ear, gave his countenance an expression of inflexible resolution. In short, it was the face of a man, whose mind, great in resources, had only found room for the display of its tamest powers, in enlarged mercantile operations, while its dark and desperate elements, from the want of adversity, revenge or hate to rouse them into action, had lain still and dormant for some twenty long years of active life. He never dreamed himself that he carried a hidden hell within his soul.

Had this man been born poor, it is probable that in his attempt to rise, the grim hand of want would have dragged from their lurking-places, these dark and fearful elements of his being. But wealth had lapped him at his birth, smiled on him in his youth, walked by him through life, and the moment for the trial of all his powers had never happened. He was a fine man, a noble merchant, and a good citizen—we but repeat the stereotyped phrases of the town—and yet, quiet and close, near the heart of this cheerful-faced man, lay a sleeping devil, who had been dozing away there all his life, and only waiting the call of destiny to spring into terrible action, and rend that manly bosom with his fangs.

"Have you heard any news of the—forger?" asked Luke Harvey, when he had delivered his budget of news—"Any intelligence of the respectable gentleman in the white cravat and hump-back?"

"He played the same game in New York that he played in our city. Wherever I went, I heard nothing but 'Mr. Ellis Mortimer, of Charleston, bought goods to a large amount here, on the strength of a letter of credit, drawn on your house by Grayson, Ballenger, & Co.,' or that 'Mr. Mortimer bought goods to a large amount in such-and-such a-store, backed by the same letter of credit—' No less than twelve wholesale houses gave him credit to an almost unlimited extent. In all cases the goods were despatched to the various auctions and sold at half-cost, while Mr. Ellis Mortimer pocketed the cash—"

"And you have no traces of this prince of swindlers?"

"None! all the police in New York have been raising heaven-and-earth to catch him for this week past, but without success. At last I have come to the conclusion that he is lurking about this city, with the respectable sum of two hundred thousand dollars in his possession. I am half-inclined to believe that he is not alone in this business—there may be a combination of scoundrels concerned in the affair. To-morrow the police shall ransack every hiding-hole and cranny in the city. My friend, Col. Fitz-Cowles gave me some valuable suggestions before I left for New York—I will ask his advice, in regard to the matter, the first thing in the morning—"

"Very fine man, that Col. Fitz-Cowles—" observed Luke, as they turned down Fourth street—"Splendid fellow. Dresses well—gives capital terrapin suppers at the United States—inoculates all the bucks about town with his style of hat. Capital fellow—Son of an English Earl—ain't he, Mr. Livingstone?"

"So I have understood—" replied Mr. Livingstone, not exactly liking the quiet sneer which lurked under the innocent manner of his partner—"at least so it is rumored—"

"Got lots of money—a millionaire—no end to his wealth. By the bye, where the d——l did he come from? isn't he a Southern planter with acres of niggers and prairies of cotton?"

"Luke, that's a very strange question to ask me. You just now asked me, whether he was the son of an English Earl—did'nt you?"

"Believe I did. To tell the truth, I've heard both stories about him, and some dozen more. An heir-apparent to an English Earldom, a rich planter from the South, the son of a Boston *magnifique*, the only child of a rich Mexican—these things you will see, don't mix well. Who the devil is our long-haired friend, anyhow?"

"Tut-tut—Luke this is all folly. You know that Col. Fitz-Cowles is received in the best society, mingles with the *ton* of the Quaker City, is 'squired about by our judges and lawyers, and can always find scores of friends to help him spend his fortune—"

"Fine man, that Col. Fitz-Cowles. Very," said the other in his dry and biting tone.

"Do you know, Luke, that I think the married men the happiest in the world?" said Livingstone, drawing the arm of his partner closely within his own—"Now look at my case for instance. A year ago I was a miserable bachelor. The loss of one hundred thousand dollars then, would have driven me frantic. Now I have a sweet young wife to cheer me, her smile welcomes me home; the first tone of her voice, and my loss is forgotten!"

The Merchant paused. His eye glistened with a tear, and he felt his heart grow warm in his bosom, as the vision of his sweet young wife, now so calmly sleeping on her solitary bed rose before him. He imagined her smile of welcome as she beheld him suddenly appear by her bedside; he felt her arms so full and round twining fondly round his neck, and he tried to fancy—but the attempt was vain—the luxury of a kiss from her red ripe lips.

"You may think me uxorious, Luke—" he resumed in his deep manly voice—"But I do think that God never made a nobler woman than my Dora! Look at the sacrifice she made for my sake? Young, blooming, and but twenty summers old, she forgot the disparity of my years, and consented to share my bachelor's-home—"

"She *is* a noble woman—" observed Luke, and then he looked at the moon and whistled an air from the very select operatic spectacle of 'Bone Squash.' "

"Noble in heart and soul!" exclaimed Livingstone—"confess, Luke that we married men live more in an hour than you dull bachelors in a year—"

"Oh—yes—certainly! You may well talk when you have such a handsome wife! Egad—if I was'nt afraid it would make you jealous—I would say that Mrs. Livingstone has the most splendid form I ever beheld—"

There was a slight contortion of Mr. Harvey's upper lip as he spoke, which looked very much like a sneer.

"And then her heart, Luke, her heart! So noble, so good, so affectionate! I wish you could have seen her, where first I beheld her—in a small and meanly furnished apartment, at the bed-side of a dying mother! They were in reduced circumstances, for her father had died insolvent. He had been my father's friend, and I thought it my duty to visit the widowed mother and the orphan daughter. By-the-bye, Luke, I now remember that I saw you at their house in Wood street once—did you know the family?"

"Miss Dora's father had been kind to me—" said Luke in a quiet tone. There was a strange light in his dark eye as he spoke, and a remarkable tremor on his lip.

"Well, well, Luke—here's my house—exclaimed Mr. Livingstone, as they arrived in front of a lofty four storied mansion, situated in the aristocratic square, as it is called, along south Fourth street. "It is lucky I have my dead-latch key. I can enter without disturbing the servants. Come up stairs, into the front parlor with me, Luke; I want to have a few more words with you about the forgery—"

They entered the door of the mansion, passed along a wide and roomy entry, ascended a richly carpeted staircase, and, traversing the entry in the second story, in a moment stood in the centre of the spacious parlor, fronting the street on the second floor. In another moment, Mr. Livingstone, by the aid of some Lucifer matches which he found on the mantle, lighted a small bed-lamp, standing amid the glittering volumes that were piled on the centre table. The dim light of the lamp flickering around the room, revealed the various characteristics of an apartment furnished in a style of lavish magnificence. Above the mantle flashed an enormous mirror, on one side of the parlor was an inviting sofa, on the other a piano; two splendid ottomans stood in front of the fireless hearth, and, curtains of splendid silk hung drooping heavily along the three lofty windows that looked into the street. In fine, the parlor was all that the upholsterer and cabinet maker combined could make it, a depository of luxurious appointments and costly furniture.

"Draw your seat near the centre table, Luke—" cried Mr. Livingstone, as he flung himself into a comfortable rocking chair, and gazed around the room with an expression of quiet satisfaction—"Don't speak too loud, Luke, for Dora is sleeping in the next room. You know I want to take her by a little surprise—eh, Luke? She doesn't expect me from New York for a week yet—I am the last person in the world she thinks to see to-night. Clearly so—ha—ha!"

And the merchant chuckled gaily, rubbed his hands together, glanced at the folding doors that opened into the bed-chamber, where slept his blooming wife, and then turning round, looked in the face of Luke Harvey with a smile, that seemed to say—'I can't help it if you bachelors are miserable—pity you, but can't help it.'

"It *would* be a pity to awaken Mrs. Livingstone—" said Luke fixing his brilliant dark eye on the face of the senior partner, with a look so meaning and yet mysterious, that Mr. Livingstone involuntarily averted his gaze—"A very great pity. By the bye, with regard to the forgery—"

"Let me recapitulate the facts. Some weeks ago we received a letter from the respectable house of Grayson, Ballenger, & Co., Charleston, stating that they had made a large purchase in cotton from a rich planter—Mr. Ellis Mortimer, who, in a week or so, would visit Philadelphia, with a letter of credit on our house for one hundred thousand dollars. They gave us this intimation in order that we might be prepared to cash the letter of credit at right. Well, in a week a gentleman of respectable exterior appeared, stated that he was Mr. Ellis Mortimer, presented his letter of credit; it was cashed and we wrote to Grayson, Ballenger, & Co., announcing the fact—"

"They returned the agreeable answer that Mr. Ellis Mortimer had not yet left Charleston for Philadelphia, but had altered his intention and was about to sail for London. That the gentleman in the white cravat and hump-back was an imposter, and the letter of credit a—forgery. There was considerable mystery in the affair; for instance, how did the imposter gain all the necessary information with regard to Mr. Mortimer's visit, how did he acquire a knowledge of the signature of the Charleston house?"

"Listen and I will tell you. Last week, in New York, I received a letter from the Charleston house announcing these additional facts. It appears that in the beginning of fall they received a letter from a Mr. Albert Hazelton Munroe, representing himself as a rich planter in Wainbridge, South Carolina. He had a large amount of cotton to sell, and would like to procure advances on it from the Charleston house. They wrote him an answer to his letter, asking the quality of the cotton, and so forth, and soliciting an interview with Mr. Munroe when he visited Charleston. In the beginning of November Mr. Munroe, a dark-complexioned man, dressed like a careless country squire, entered their store for the first time, and commenced a series of negotiations about his cotton, which had resulted in nothing, when another planter, Mr. Ellis Mortimer, appeared in the scene, sold his cotton, and requested the letter of credit on our house. Mr. Munroe was in the store every day—was a jolly unpretending fellow—familiar with all the clerks—and on intimate terms with Messrs. Grayson, Ballenger, & Co. The letter written to our house, intimating the intended visit of Mr. Mortimer to this city, had been very carelessly left open for a few moments on the counting house desk, and Mr. Munroe was observed glancing over its contents by one of the clerks. The day after that letter had been despatched to Philadelphia, Mr. Albert H. Munroe suddenly disappeared, and had not been heard of since. The Charleston house suspect him of the whole forgery in all its details—"

"Very likely. He saw the letter on the counter—forged the letter of credit—and despatched his accomplice to Philadelphia without delay—"

"Now for the consequences of this forgery. On Monday morning next we have an engagement of one hundred thousand dollars to meet, which, under present circumstances, may plunge our house into the vortex of bankruptcy. Unless this imposter is discovered, unless his connection with this Munroe is clearly ascertained before next Monday, I must look forward to that day as one of the greatest danger to our house. You see our position, Luke?"

"Yes, yes—" answered Luke, as he arose, and, advancing, gazed fixedly into the face of Mr. Livingstone—"I see *our* position, and I see *your* position in more respects than one—"

"Confound the thing, man, how you stare in my face. Do you see anything peculiar about my countenance, that you peruse it so attentively?"

"Ha—ha—" cried Luke, with a hysterical laugh—"Ha—ha! Nothing but—horns. Horns, sir, I say—horns. A fine branching pair! Ha—ha—Why damn it, Livingstone, you won't be able to enter the church door, next Sunday, without stooping—*those* horns are so d———d large!"

Livingstone looked at him with a face of blank wonder. He evidently supposed that Luke had been seized with sudden madness. To see a man who is your familiar friend and partner, abruptly break off a conversation on matters of the most importance, and stare vacantly in your face as he compliments you on some fancied resemblance which you bear to a full-grown stag, is, it must be confessed, a spectacle somewhat unfrequent in this world of ours, and rather adapted to excite a feeling of astonishment whenever it happens.

"Mr. Harvey—are—you—mad?" asked Livingstone, in a calm deliberate tone.

Harvey slowly leaned forward and brought his face so near Livingstone's that the latter could feel his breath on his cheek. He applied his mouth to the ear of the senior partner, and whispered a single word.

When a soldier, in battle, receives a bullet directly in the heart, he springs in the air with one convulsive spasm, flings his arms aloft and utters a groan that thrills the man who hears it with a horror never to be forgotten. With that same convulsive movement, with that same deep groan of horror and anguish Livingstone, the merchant, sprang to his feet, and confronted the utterer of that single word.

"Harvey—" he said, in a low tone, and with white and trembling lips, while his calm blue eye flashed with that deep glance of excitement, most terrible when visible in a calm blue eye—"Harvey, you had better never been born, than utter that word again. To trifle with a thing of this kind is worse than death. Harvey, I advise you to leave me—I am losing all command of myself—there is a voice within me tempting me to murder you—for God's sake quit my sight—"

Harvey looked in his face, fearless and undaunted, though his snake-like eye blazed like a coal of fire, and his thin lips quivered as with the death spasm.

"*Cuckold!*" he shrieked in a hissing voice, with a wild hysterical laugh.

Livingstone started back aghast. The purple veins stood out like cords on his bronzed forehead, and his right hand trembled like a leaf as it was thrust within the breast of his coat. His blue eye—great God! how glassy it had grown—was fixed upon the form of Luke Harvey as if meditating where to strike.

"To the bedchamber—" shrieked Luke. "If *she* is there, I am a liar and a dog, and deserve to die. *Cuckold*, I say, and will prove it—to the bedchamber!"

And to the bedchamber with an even stride, though his massive form quivered like an oak shaken by the hurricane, strode the merchant. The folding door slid back—he had disappeared into the bedchamber.

There was silence for a single instant, like the silence in the graveyard, between the last word of the prayer, and the first rattling sound of the clods upon the coffin.

In a moment Livingstone again strode into the parlor. His face was the hue of ashes. You could see that the struggle at work within his heart was like the agony of the strong man wrestling with death. *This* struggle was tenfold more terrible than death—death in its vilest form. It forced the big beaded drops of sweat out from the corded veins on his brow, it drove the blood from his face, leaving a black and discolored streak beneath each eye.

"She is not there—" he said, taking Luke by the hand, which he wrung with an iron grasp, and murmured again—"She is not there—"

"False to her husband's bed and honor—" exclaimed Luke, the agitation which had convulsed his face, subsiding into a look of heart-wrung compassion, as he looked upon the terrible results of his disclosure—"False as hell, and vile as false!"

An object on the centre table, half concealed by the bed-lamp arrested the husband's attention. He thrust aside the lamp and beheld a note, addressed to himself, in Mrs. Livingstone's hand.

With a trembling hand the merchant tore the note open, and while Luke stood fixedly regarding him, perused its contents.

And as he read, the blood came back to his cheeks, the glance to his eyes, and his brow reddened over with one burning flush of indignation.

"Liar and dog!" he shouted, in tones hoarse with rage, as he grasped Luke Harvey by the throat with a sudden movement—"Your lie was well coined, but look here! Ha—ha—" and he shook Luke to and fro like a broken reed—"Here is my wife's letter. Here, sir, look at it, and I'll force you to eat your own foul words. Here, expecting that I might suddenly return from New York, my wife has written down that she would be absent from home to-night. A sick friend, a school-day companion, now reduced to widowhood and penury, solicited her company by her dying bed, and my wife could not refuse. Read, sir—oh read!"

"Take your hand from my throat or I'll do you a mischief—" murmured Luke, in a choaking voice as he grew black in the face. "I will, by God—"

"Read—sir—oh read!" shouted Livingstone, as he force Luke into a chair and thrust the letter into his hands—"Read, sir, and then crawl from this room like a vile dog as you are. To-morrow I will settle with you—"

Luke sank in the chair, took the letter, and with a pale face, varied by a crimson spot on each cheek, he began to read, while Livingstone, towering and erect, stood regarding him with a look of incarnate scorn.

It was observable that while Luke perused the letter, his head dropped slowly down as though in the endeavor to see more clearly, and his unoccupied hand was suddenly thrust within the breast of his overcoat.

"That is a very good letter. Well written, and she minds her stops—" exclaimed Luke calmly, as he handed the letter back to Mr. Livingstone—"Quite an effort of composition. I didn't think Dora had so much tact—"

The merchant was thunderstruck with the composure exhibited by the slanderer and the liar. He glanced over Luke's features with a quick nervous glance, and then looked at the letter which he held in his hand.

"Ha! This is not the same letter!" he shouted, in tones of mingled rage and wonder—"This letter is addressed to Col.' Fitz-Cowles'—"

"It was dropped in the counting house by the Colonel this evening—" said Luke, with the air of a man who was prepared for any hazard—"The Colonel is a very fine man. A favorite with the fair sex. Read it—*Oh* read—"

With a look of wonder Mr. Livingstone opened the letter. There was a quivering start in his whole frame, when he first observed the handwriting.

But as he went on, drinking in word after word, his countenance, so full of meaning and expression, was like a mirror, in which different faces are seen, one after another, by sudden transition. At first his face grew crimson, then it was pale as death in an instant. Then his lips dropped apart, and his eyes were covered with a glassy film. Then a deep wrinkle shot upward between his brows, and then, black and ghastly, the circles of discolored flesh were visible beneath each eye. The quivering nostrils—the trembling hands—the heaving chest—did man ever die with a struggle terrible as this?

He sank heavily into a chair, and crushing the letter between his fingers, buried his face in his hands.

"Oh my God—" he groaned—"Oh my God—and I loved her so!"

And then between the very fingers convulsively clutching the fatal letter, there fell large and scalding tears, drop by drop, pouring heavily, like the first tokens of a coming thunderbolt, on a summer day.

Luke Harvey arose, and strode hurriedly along the floor. The sight was too much for him to bear. And yet as he turned away he heard the groans of the strong man in his agony, and the heart-wrung words came, like the voice of the dying, to his ear—

"Oh my God, oh my God, and I loved her so!"

When Luke again turned and gazed upon the betrayed husband, he beheld a sight that filled him with unutterable horror.

There, as he sat, his face buried in his hands, his head bowed on his breast, his brow was partly exposed to the glare of the lamp-beams, and all around that brow, amid the locks of his dark brown hair, were streaks of hoary white. The hair of the merchant had withered at the root. The blow was so sudden, so blighting, and so terrible, that even his strong mind reeled, his brain tottered, and in the effort to command his reason, his hair grew white with agony.*

* This is a fact, established by the evidence of a medical gentleman of the first reputation.

"Would to God I had not told him—" murmured Luke—"I knew not that he loved her so—I knew not—and yet—ha, ha, *I* loved her once—"

"Luke—my friend—" said Livingstone in a tremulous voice as he raised his face—"Know you anything of *the place*—named in—the letter?"

"I do—and will lead you there—" answered Luke, his face resuming its original expression of agitation—"Come!" he cried, in a husky voice, as olden-time memories seemed striving at his heart—"Come!"

"Can you gain me access to the house—to *the—the* room?"

"Did I not track them thither last night? *Come!*"

The merchant slowly rose and took a pair of pistols from his carpet bag. They were small and convenient travelling pistols, mounted in silver, with those noiseless 'patent' triggers that emit no clicking sound by way of warning. He inspected the percussion caps, and sounded each pistol barrel.

"Silent and sure—" muttered Luke—"They are each loaded with a single ball."

"Which way do you lead? To the southern part of the city?"

"To Southwark—" answered Luke, leading the way from the parlor—"To the rookery, to the den, to the pest-house—"

In a moment they stood upon the door step of the merchant's princely mansion, the vivid light of the December moon, imparting a ghastly hue to Livingstone's face, with the glassy eyes, rendered more fearful by the discolored circles of flesh beneath, the furrowed brow, and the white lips, all fixed in an expression stern and resolute as death.

Luke flung his hand to the south, and his dark impenetrable eyes shone with meaning. The merchant placed his partner's arm within his own, and they hurried down Fourth street with a single word from Luke—

"To Monk-hall!"

CHAPTER SIXTH

MONK-HALL*

Strange traditions have come down to our time, in relation to a massive edifice, which, long before the Revolution, stood in the centre of an extensive garden, surrounded by a brick wall, and encircled by a deep grove of horse-chesnut and beechen trees. This edifice was located on the out-skirts of the southern part of the city, and the garden overspread some acres, occupying a space full as large as a modern square.

This mansion, but rarely seen by intrusive eyes, had been originally erected by a wealthy foreigner, sometime previous to the Revolution. Who this foreigner was, his name or his history, has not been recorded by tradition; but his mansion, in its general construction and details, indicate a mind rendered whimsical and capricious by excessive wealth.

The front of the mansion, one plain mass of black and red brick, disposed like the alternate colors of a chessboard, looked towards the south. A massive hall-door, defended by heavy pillars, and surmounted by an intricate cornice, all carved and sculptured into hideous satyr-faces; three ranges of deep square windows, with cumbrous sash frames and small panes of glass; a deep and sloping roof, elaborate with ornaments of painted wood along the eaves, and rising into a gabled peak directly over the hall-door, while its outlines were varied by rows of substantial chimneys, fashioned into strange and uncouth shapes,—all combined, produced a general impression of ease and grandeur that was highly effective in awing the spirits of any of the simple citizens who might obtain a casual glance of the house through the long avenue of trees extending from the garden gate.

This impression of awe was somewhat deepened by various rumors that obtained through the southern part of the Quaker City. It was said that the wealthy proprietor, not satisfied with building a fine house with three stories above ground, had also constructed three stories of spacious chambers below the level of the earth. This was calculated to stir the curiosity and perhaps the scandal of the town, and as a matter of course strange rumors began to prevail about midnight orgies held by the godless proprietor in his subterranean apartments, where wine was drunken without stint, and beauty ruined with-

* *No reader who wishes to understand this story in all its details will fail to peruse this chapter.*

out remorse. Veiled figures had been seen passing through the garden gate after night, and men were not wanting to swear that these figures, in dark robes and sweeping veils, were pretty damsels with neat ankles and soft eyes.

As time passed on, the rumors grew and the mystery deepened. The neatly-constructed stable at the end of the garden was said to be connected with the house, some hundred yards distant, by a subterranean passage. The two wings, branching out at either extremity of the rear of the mansion, looked down upon a courtyard, separated by a light wicket fence from the garden walks. The court-yard, overarched by an awning in summer time, was said to be the scene of splendid festivals to which the grandees of the city were invited. From the western wing of the mansion arose a square lantern-like structure, which the gossips called a tower, and hinted sagely of witchcraft and devildom whenever it was named. They called the proprietor, a libertine, a gourmand, an astrologer and a wizard. He feasted in the day and he consulted his friend, the Devil, at night. He drank wine at all times, and betrayed innocence on every occasion. In short the seclusion of the mansion, its singular structure, its wall of brick and its grove of impenetrable trees, gave rise to all sorts of stories, and the proprietor has come down to our time with a decidedly bad character, although it is more than likely that he was nothing but a wealthy Englishman, whimsical and eccentric, the boon-companion and friend of Governor Evans, the rollicking Chief Magistrate of the Province.

Although tradition has not preserved the name of the mysterious individual yet the title of his singular mansion, is still on record.

It was called—Monk-hall.

There are conflicting traditions which assert that this title owed its origin to other sources. A Catholic Priest occupied the mansion after the original proprietor went home to his native land, or slid into his grave; it was occupied as a Nunnery, as a Monastery, or as a resort for the Sisters of Charity; the mass had been said within its walls, its subterranean chambers converted into cells, its tower transformed into an oratory of prayer—such are the dim legends which were rife some forty years ago, concerning Monk-hall, long after the city, in its southern march, had cut down the trees, overturned the wall, levelled the garden into building lots and divided it by streets and alleys into a dozen triangles and squares.

Some of these legends, so vague and so conflicting, are still preserved in the memories of aged men and white-haired matrons, who will sit by the hour and describe the gradual change which time and improvement, those twin desolators of the beautiful, had accomplished with

Monk-hall.

Soon after the Revolution, fine brick buildings began to spring up along the streets which surrounded the garden, while the alleys traversing its area, grew lively with long lines of frame houses, variously fashioned and painted, whose denizens awoke the echoes of the place with the sound of the hammer and the grating of the saw. Time passed on, and the distinctive features of the old mansion and garden were utterly changed. Could the old proprietor have risen from his grave, and desired to pay another visit to his friend, the Devil, in the subterranean chambers of his former home, he would have had, to say the least of it, a devil of a time in finding the way. Where the old brick wall had stood he would have found long rows of dwelling houses, some four storied, some three or one, some brick, some frame, a few pebble-dashed, and all alive with inhabitants.

In his attempt to find the Hall, he would have had to wind up a narrow alley, turn down a court, strike up an avenue, which it would take some knowledge of municipal geography to navigate. At last, emerging into a narrow street where four alleys crossed, he would behold his magnificent mansion of Monk-hall with a printing office on one side and a stereotype foundry on the other, while on the opposite side of the way, a mass of miserable frame houses seemed about to commit suicide and fling themselves madly into the gutter, and in the distance a long line of dwellings, offices, and factories, looming in broken perspective, looked as if they wanted to shake hands across the narrow street. The southern front of the house—alas, how changed—alone is visible. The shutters on one side of the hall-door are nailed up and hermetically closed, while, on the other, shutters within the glasses bar out the light of day. The semi-circular window in the centre of the gabled-peak has been built up with brick, yet our good friend would find the tower on the western wing in tolerable good preservation. The stable one hundred yards distant from Monk-hall—what has become of it? Perhaps it is pulled down, or it may be that a splendid dwelling towers in its place? It is still in existence, standing amid the edifices of a busy street, its walls old and tottering, its ancient stable-floor turned into a bulk window, surmounted by the golden balls of a Pawnbroker, while within its precincts, rooms furnished for household use supply the place of the stalls of the olden-time. Does the subterranean passage still exist? Future pages of our story may possibly answer that question.

Could our ancient and ghostly proprietor, glide into the tenements adjoining Monk-hall, and ask the mechanic or his wife, the printer or the factory man to tell him the story of the strange old building, he would find that the most remarkable ignorance prevailed in regard to the structure, its origin and history. One man might tell him that it had been a factory, or a convent, or the Lord knows what, another might intimate that it had been a church, a third (and he belonged to the most numerous class) would reply in a surly tone that he knew nothing about the old brick nuisance, while in the breasts of one or two aged men and matrons, yet living in Southwark, would be discovered the only chronicles of the ancient structure now extant, the only records of its history or name. Did our spirit-friend glide over the threshold and enter the chambers of his home, his eye would, perhaps, behold scenes that rivalled, in vice and magnificence, anything that legend chronicled of the olden-time of Monk-hall, although its exterior was so desolate, and its outside-door of green blinds varied by a big brass plate, bore the respectable and saintly name of "ABIJAH K. JONES," in immense letters, half indistinct with dirt and rust.

Who this Abijah K. Jones was, no one knew, although the owner of the house, a good christian, who had a pew in ——— church, where he took the sacrament at least once a month, might have been able to tell with very little research. Yet what of that? Abijah K. Jones might have nightly entertained the infernal regions in his house, and not a word been said about it; because, as the pious landlord would observe, when cramming Abijahs rent-money into the same pocket-book that contained some tract-society receipts,—"Good tenant that!—pays his rent with the regularity of clockwork!"

CHAPTER SEVENTH

THE MONKS OF MONK HALL

The moon was shining brightly over the face of the old mansion, while the opposite side of the alley lay in dim and heavy shadow. The light brown hue of the closed shutters afforded a vivid contrast to the surface of the front, which had the strikingly gloomy effect always produced by the intermixture of black and red brick, disposed like the colors of a chessboard, in the structure of a mansion. The massive cornice above the hall-door, the heavy eaves of the roof, the gabled peak rising in the centre, and the cumbrous frames of the many windows,—all stood out boldly in the moonlight, from the dismal relief of the building's front.

The numerous chimneys with their fantastic shapes rose grimly in the moonlight, like a strange band of goblin sentinels, perched of the roof to watch the mansion. The general effect was that of an ancient structure falling to decay, deserted by all inhabitants save the rats that gnawed the wainscot along the thick old walls. The door-plate that glittered on the faded door, half covered as it was with rust and verdigris, with its saintly name afforded the only signs of the actual occupation of Monk-hall by human beings: in all other respects it looked so desolate, so time-worn, so like a mausoleum for old furniture, and crumbling tapestry, for high-backed mahogany chairs, gigantic bedsteads, and strange looking mirrors, veiled in the thick folds of the spider's web.

Dim and indistinct, like the booming of a distant cannon, the sound of the State-House bell, thrilled along the intricate maze of streets and alleys. It struck the hour of two. The murmur of the last stroke of the bell, so dim and indistinct, was mingled with the echo of approaching footsteps, and in a moment two figures turned the corner of an alley that wound among the tangled labyrinth of avenues, and came hastening on toward the lonely mansion; lonely even amid tenements and houses, gathered as thickly together as the cells in a bee-hive.

"I say, Gus, what a devil of a way you've led me!" cried one of the strangers, with a thick cloak wrapped round his limbs—"up one alley and down another, around one street and through another, backwards and forwards, round this way and round that—damme if I can tell which is north or south except by the moon!"

"Hist! my fellow—don't mention names—cardinal doctrine that on an affair of this kind—" answered the tall figure, whose towering form was enveloped in a frogged overcoat—"Remember, you pass in as *my friend*. Wait a moment—we'll see whether old Devil-Bug is awake."

Ascending the granite steps of the mansion, he gave three distinct raps with his gold-headed cane, on the surface of the brass-plate. In a moment the rattling of a heavy chain, and the sound of a bolt, slowly withdrawn, was heard within, and the door of the mansion, beyond the outside door of green blinds, receded about the width of an inch.

"Who's there, a disturbin' honest folks this hour o' the night—" said a voice, that came grumbling through the blinds of the green door, like the sound of a grindstone that hasn't been oiled for some years—"What the devil you want? Go about your business—or I'll call the watch—"

"I say, Devil-Bug, what hour o' th' night is it?" exclaimed Lorrimer in a whispered tone.

" 'Dinner time'—" replied the grindstone voice slightly oiled—"Come in sir. Did'nt know 'twas you. How the devil should I? Come in—"

As the voice grunted this invitation, Lorrimer seized Byrnewood by the arm, and glided through the opened door.

Byrnewood looked around in wonder, as he discovered that the front door opened into a small closet or room, some ten feet square, the floor bare and uncarpeted, the ceiling darkened by smoke, while a large coal fire, burning in a rusty grate, afforded both light and heat to the apartment.

The heat was close and stifling, while the light, but dim and flickering, disclosed the form of the door-keeper of Monk-hall, as he stood directly in front of the grate, surrounded by the details of his den.

"This is *my friend*—" said Lorrimer in a meaning tone—"You understand, Devil-Bug?"

"Yes—" grunted the grindstone voice—"I understand. O'course. But my name is 'Bijah K. Jones, *if* you please, my pertikler friend. I never know'd sich a individooal as Devil-Bug—"

It requires no great stretch of fancy to imagine that his Satanic majesty, once on a time, in a merry mood, created a huge insect, in order to test his inventive powers. Certainly that insect—which it was quite natural to designate by the name of Devil-Bug—stood in the full light of the grate, gazing steadfastly in Byrnewood's face. It was a strange thickset specimen of flesh and blood, with a short body, marked by immensely broad shoulders, long arms and thin destorted legs. The head of the creature was ludicrously large in proportion to the body. Long masses of siff black hair fell tangled and matted over a forehead, protuberent to deformity. A flat nose with wide nostrils shooting out into each cheek like the smaller wings of an insect, an immense mouth whose heavy lips disclosed two long rows of bristling teeth, a pointed chin, blackened by a heavy beard, and massive eyebrows meeting over the nose, all furnished the details of a countenance, not exactly calculated to inspire the most pleasant feelings in the world. One eye, small black and shapen like a bead, stared steadily in Byrnewood's face, while the other socket was empty, shrivelled and orbless. The eyelids of the vacant socket were joined together like the opposing edges of a curtain, while the other eye gained additional brilliancy and effect from the loss of its fellow member.

The shoulders of the Devil-Bug, protruding in unsightly knobs, the wide chest, and the long arms with talon-like fingers, so vividly contrasted with the thin and distorted legs, all attested that the remarkable strength of the man was located in the upper part of his body.

"Well, Abijah, are you satisfied?" asked Lorrimer, as he perceived Byrnewood shrink back with disgust from the door-keeper's gaze—"*This* gentleman, I say, is *my* friend?"

"So I s'pose," grunted Abijah—"Here, Musquito, mark this man—here, Glow-worm, mark him, I say. This is Monk Gusty's friend. Can't you move quicker, you ugly devils?"

From either side of the fire-place, as he spoke, emerged a tall Herculean negro, with a form of strength and sinews of iron. Moving slowly along the floor, from the darkness which had enshrouded their massive outlines, they stood silent and motionless gazing with look of stolid indifference upon the face of the new-comer. Byrnewood had started aside in disgust from the Devil-Bug, as he was styled in the slang of Monk-hall, but certainly these additional insects, nestling in the den of the other, were rather singular specimens of the glow-worm and musquito. Their attire was plain and simple. Each negro was dressed in coarse corduroy trowsers, and a flaring red flannel shirt. The face of Glow-worm was marked by a hideous flat nose, a receding forehead, and a wide mouth with immense lips that buried all traces of a chin and disclosed two rows of teeth protruding like the tusks of a wild boar. Musquito had the same flat nose, the same receding forehead, but his thick lips, tightly compressed, were drawn down on either side towards his jaw, presenting an outline something like the two sides of a triangle, while his sharp and pointed chin was in direct contrast to the long chinless jaw of the other. Their eyes, large, rolling and vacant, stared from bulging eyelids, that protruded beyond the outline of the brows. Altogether, each negro presented as hideous a picture of mere brute strength, linked with a form scarcely human, as the imagination of man might well conceive.

"This is Monk Gusty's friend—" muttered Abijah, or Devil-Bug, as the reader likes—"Mark him, Musquito—Mark him, Glow-worm, I say. Mind ye now—this man don't leave the house except with Gusty? D'ye hear, ye black devils?"

Each negro growled assent.

"Queer specimens of a Musquito and a Glow-worm, I say—" laughed Byrnewood in the effort to smother his disgust—"Eh? Lorrimer?"

"This way, my fellow—" answered the magnificent Gus, gently leading his friend through a small door, which led from the door-keeper's closet—"This way. Now for the club—and then for the wager!"

Looking around in wonder, Byrnewood discovered that they had passed into the hall of an old-time mansion, with the beams of the moon, falling from a skylight in the roof far above, down over the windings of a massive staircase.

"This is rather a strange place—eh? Gus?" whispered Byrnewood, as he gazed around the hall, and marked the ancient look of the place—"why the d———l don't *they* have a light—those *insects*—ha-ha—whom we have just left?"

"Secrecy—my fellow—secrecy! Those are the 'police' of Monk-Hall, certain to be at hand in case of a row. You see, the entire arrangements of this place may be explained in one word—it is easy enough for a stranger—that's you, my boy—to find his way *in*, but it would puzzle him like the devil to find his way *out*. That is, without assistance. Take my arm Byrnewood—we must descend to the club room———"

"*Descend?*"

"Yes my fellow. *Descend*, for we hold our meetings one story under ground. Its likely all the fellows—or Monks, to speak in the slang of the club—are now most royally drunk, so I can slide you in among them, without much notice. You can remain there while I go and prepare the bride—ha—ha—ha! the *bride* for your visit—"

Meanwhile, grasping Byrnewood by the arm, he had led the way along the hall, beyond the staircase, into the thick darkness, which rested upon this part of the place, unillumined by a ray of light.

"Hold my arm, as tight as you can—" he whispered—"There is a staircase somewhere here. Softly—softly—now I have it. Tread with care, Byrnewood—In a moment we will be in the midst of the Monks of Monk-Hall—"

And as they descended the subterranean stairway, surrounded by the darkness of midnight, Byrnewood found it difficult to subdue a feeling of awe which began to spread like a shadow over his soul. This feeling it was not easy to analyze. It may have been a combination of feelings; the consideration of the darkness and loneliness of the place, his almost entire ignorance of the handsome libertine who was now leading him—he knew not where; or perhaps the earnest words of the Astrologer, fraught with doom and death, came home to his soul like a vivid presentiment, in that moment of uncertainty and gloom.

"Don't you hear their shouts, my boy—" whispered Lorrimer—"Faith, they must be *drunk* as judges, every man of them! Why Byrnewood, you're as still as death—"

"To tell you the truth, Lorrimer, this place looks like the den of some old wizard—it's so d———d gloomy—"

"Here we are at the door: Now mark me, Byrnewood—you must walk in the club-room, or Monk's room as they call it, directly at my back. While I salute the Monks of Monk-hall, you will slide into a vacant seat at the table, and mingle in the revelry of the place until I return—"

Stooping through a narrow door, whose receding panels flung a blaze of light along the darkness of the passage, Lorrimer, with Byrnewood at his back, descended three wooden steps, that led from the door-sill to the floor, and in a moment, stood amid the revellers of Monk-hall.

In a long, narrow room, lighted by the blaze of a large chandelier, with a low ceiling and a wide floor, covered with a double-range of carpets, around a table spread with the relics of their feast, were grouped the Monks of Monk-hall.

They hailed Lorrimer with a shout, and as they rose to greet him, Byrnewood glided into a vacant arm-chair near the head of the table, and in a moment his companion had disappeared.

"I'll be with you in a moment, Monks of Monk-hall—" he shouted as he glided through the narrow door—"A little affair to settle up stairs—you know me—nice little girl—ha-ha-ha—"

"Ha-ha-ha—" echoed the band of revellers, raising their glasses merrily on high.

Byrnewood glanced hurriedly around. The room, long and spacious as it was, the floor covered with the most gorgeous carpeting, and the low ceiling, embellished with a faded painting in fresco, still wore an antiquated, not to say, dark and gloomy appearance. The walls were concealed by huge panels of wainscot, intricate with uncouth sculpturings of fawns and satyrs, and other hideous creations of classic mythology. At one end of the room, reaching from floor to ceiling, glared an immense mirror, framed in massive walnut, its glittering surface, reflecting the long festal board, with its encircling band of revellers. Inserted in the corresponding panels of the wainscot, on either side of the small door, at the opposite end of the room, two large pictures, evidently the work of a master hand, indicated the mingled worship of the devotees of Monk-hall. In the picture on the right of the door, Bacchus, the jolly god of mirth and wine, was represented rising from a festal-board, his brow wreathed in clustering grapes, while his hand swung aloft, a goblet filled with the purple blood of the grape. In the other painting, along a couch as dark as night, with a softened radiance falling over her uncovered form, lay a sleeping Venus, her full arms, twining above her head, while her lips were dropped apart, as though she murmured in her slumber. Straight and erect, behind the chair of the President or Abbot of the board, arose the effigy of a monk, whose long black robes fell drooping to the floor, while his cowl hung heavily over his brow, and his right hand raised on high a goblet of gold.

From beneath the shadow of the falling cowl, glared a fleshless skeleton head, with the orbless eye-sockets, the cavity of the nose, and the long rows of grinning teeth, turned to a faint and ghastly crimson by the lampbeams. The hand that held the goblet on high, was a grisly skeleton hand; the long and thin fingers of bone, twining firmly around the glittering bowl.

And over this scene, over the paintings and the mirror, over the gloomy wainscot along the walls, and over the faces of the revellers with the Skeleton-Monk, grinning derision at their scene of bestial enjoyment, shone the red beams of the massive chandelier, the body and limbs of which were fashioned into the form of a grim Satyr, with a light flaring from his skull, a flame emerging from each eye, while his extended hands flung streams of fire on either side, and his knees were huddled up against his breast. The design was like a nightmare dream, so grotesque and terrible, and it completed the strange and ghostly appearance of the room.

Around the long and narrow board, strown with the relics of the feast, which had evidently been some hours in progress, sate the Monks of Monk-hall, some thirty in number, flinging their glasses on high, while the room echoed with their oaths and drunken shouts. Some lay with their heads thrown helplessly on the table, others were gazing round in sleepy drunkenness, others had fallen to the floor in a state of unconscious intoxication, while a few there were who still kept up the spirit of the feast, although their incoherent words and heavy eyes proclaimed that they too were fast advancing to that state of brutal inebriety, when strange-looking stars shine in the place of the lamps, when the bottles dance and even tables perform the cracovienne, while all sorts of beehives create a buzzing murmur in the air.

And the Monks of Monk-hall—who are they?

Grim-faced personages in long black robes and drooping cowls? Stern old men with beads around their necks and crucifix in hand? Blood-thirsty characters, perhaps, or black-browed ruffians, or wan-faced outcasts of society?

Ah no, ah no! From the eloquent, the learned, and—don't you laugh—from the pious of the Quaker City, the old Skeleton-Monk had selected the members of his band. Here were lawyers from the court, doctors from the school, and judges* from the bench. Here too, ruddy and round faced, sate a demure parson, whose white hands and soft words, had made him the idol of his wealthy congregation. Here was a puffy-faced Editor side by side with a Magazine Proprietor; here were

* This *of course* alludes to Judges of distant country courts.

sleek-visaged tradesmen, with round faces and gouty hands, whose voices, now shouting the drinking song had re-echoed the prayer and the psalm in the aristocratic church, not longer than a Sunday ago; here were solemn-faced merchants, whose names were wont to figure largely in the records of 'Bible Societies,' 'Tract Societies' and 'Send Flannel-to-the-South-Sea-Islanders Societies;' here were reputable married men, with grown up children at college, and trustful wives sleeping quietly in their dreamless beds at home; here were hopeful sons, clerks in wholesale stores, who raised the wine-glass on high with hands which, not three hours since, had been busy with the cash-book of the employer, here in fine were men of all classes,—poets, authors, lawyers, judges, doctors, merchants, gamblers, and—this is no libel I hope—*one* parson, a fine red-faced parson, whose glowing face would have warmed a poor man on a cold day. Moderately drunk, or deeply drunk, or vilely drunk, all the members of the board who still maintained their arm-chairs, kept up a running fire of oaths, disjointed remarks, mingled with small talk very much broken, and snatches of bacchanalian songs, slightly improved by a peculiar chorus of hiccups.

While Byrnewood, with a sleeping man on either side of him, gazed around in sober wonder, this was the fashion of the conversation among the Monks of Monk-hall.

"Judge—I say, judge—that last Charge o' yours was capital—" hiccupped a round-faced lawyer, leaning over the table—"Touched on the vices of the day—ha—ha! 'Dens of iniquity and holes of wickedness'—its very words!—'exist in city, which want the strong arm of the law to uproot and ex-ex—d———n the hard words—exterminate them!' "

"Good—my—very—words—" replied the Judge, who sat gazing around with a smile of imbecile fatuity—"Yet, Bellamy, not quite so good as your words, when your wife—how this d———d room swims —found out your *liason* with the Actress! Ha—ha, gents—too d———d good that—"

"Ha—ha—ha—" laughed some dozen of the company—"let's hear it—let's hear it—"

"Why—you—see—" replied the Judge—"Bellamy is *so* d———d fat, (just keep them bottles from dancing about the table!) so *very* fat, that the i-i-idea of his writing a love-letter is rath-rather improbable. Nevertheless—he did—to a pretty actress, Madame De Flum—and left it on his office table. His wife found it—oh Lord—what a scene! ranted—raved—tore her hair. 'My dear—' said our fat friend, 'do be calm—this is the copy of a letter in a breach of promise case, on which I am about to bring suit for a—lady—client. The mistake of the names is the fault of my clerk. Do—oh—*do* be calm.' His wife swallowed the story—clever story for a fat man—very!"

"Friends and Brethren, what shall ye do to be saved?" shouted the beefy-faced parson, in the long-drawn nasal tones peculiar to his pulpit or lecture-room—"When we con-consider the wickedness of the age, when we reflect tha-that there are thousands da-i-ly and hou-r-ly going down to per-per-dition, should we not cry from the depths of our souls, like Jonah from the depths of the sea—I say, give us the brandy, Mutchins!"

"Gentlemen, allow me to read you a poem—" muttered a personage, whose cheeks blushed from habitual kisses of the bottle, as he staggered from his chair, and endeavoured to stand erect—"It's a—poem—on (what an unsteady floor this is—hold it, Petriken, I say)—on the Ten Commandments. I've dedicated it to our Rev-Reverend friend yonder. There's a touch in it, gentlemen—if I may use the expression—above ordinary butter-milk. A sweetness, a path-pathos, a mildness, a-a-vein, gentlemen, of the strictest mo-ral-i-ty. I will read sonnet one—'Thou shalt not take the co-eternal name'—eh? Dammit! This is *a bill!* —I've left the sonnet at home—"

"Curse it—how I'll cut this fellow up in my next Black-Mail!" murmured the puffy-faced editor, in a tone which he deemed inaudible to the poet—"Unless he comes down handsome—I'll give him a stinger, a real scorcher—"

"Will you, though?" shouted the poet, turning round with a drunken stare, and aiming a blow at the half-stupid face of the editor—"Take that you fungus—you abortion—you d———d gleaner of a common sewer—you ———"

"Gentlemen, I con-consider myself grossly insulted—" muttered the editor, as the poet's blow took effect on his wig and sent it spinning to the other end of the table—"Is the *Daily Black Mail* come to this?"

Here he made a lunge at the author of the 'Ten Commandments, a Series of Sonnets,' and, joined in a fond embrace, they fell insensible to the floor.

"Take that wig out of my plate—" shouted a deep voice from the head of the table—"Wigs, as a general thing, are not very nice with oysters, but that fellow's wig—ugh! Faugh!"

Attracted by the sound of the voice, Byrnewood glanced towards the head of the table. There, straight and erect, sate the Abbot of the night, a gentleman elected by the fraternity to preside over their feasts. He was a man of some thirty odd years, dressed in a suit of glossy black, with a form remarkable for its combination of strength with symmetry. His face, long and dusky, lighted by the gleam of a dark eye, indicating the man whose whole life had been one series of plot, scheme, and intrigue, was relieved by heavy masses of long black hair—resembling, in its texture, the mane of a horse—which fell in curling locks to his shoulders. It needed not a second glance to inform Byrnewood that he beheld the hero of Chesnut street, the distinguished millionaire, Col. Fitz-Cowles. The elegant cut of his dark vest, which gathered over his prominent chest and around his slender waist, with the nicety of a glove, the plain black scarf, fastened by a breast-pin of solid gold, the glossy black of his dress-coat, shapen of the best French cloth, all disclosed the idol of the tailors, the dream of the fashionable belles, the envy of the dry goods clerks, Algernon Fitz-Cowles. He seemed, by far, the most sober man in the company. Every now and then Byrnewood beheld him glance anxiously toward the door as though he wished to escape from the room. And after every glance, as he beheld one Monk after another kissing the carpet, bottle in hand, the interesting Colonel would join heartily in the drunken bout, raising his voice with the loudest, and emptying his glass with the most drunken. Yet, to the eye of Byrnewood, this looked more like a mere counterfeit of a drunkard's manner than the thing itself. It was evident that the handsome millionaire emptied his glass under the table.

The revel now grew wild and furious. As bottle after bottle was consumed, so the actors in the scene began to appear, more and more, in their true characters. At last all disguise seemed thrown aside, and each voice, joining in the chorus of disjointed remarks, indicated that its owner imagined himself amid the scenes of his daily life.

"Gentlemen—allow—me—to read you a tale—a tale from the German on *Transcendental Essences*—" cried Petriken, rising, for he too was there, forgetful, like Mutchins, of his promise to Lorrimer—"This, gents, is a tale for my next Western Hem.:" here his oyster-like eyes rolled ghastily—"The Ladies Western Hem., forty-eight pages—monthly—offers following inducements—two dollars—" at this point of his handbill the gentleman staggered wofully—"Office No. 209 Drayman's Alley—hurrah Mutchins what's your idea of soft crabs?"

Here the literary gentleman fell heavily to the floor, mingled in the same heap that contained the poet and the wigless editor. In a moment he rose heavily to his feet, and staggered slowly to Mutchin's side.

"Gentlemen of the jury, I charge you—" began the Judge.

"Your honor, I beg leave to open this case—" interrupted the lawyer.

"My friends and brethren," cried the parson—"what shall ye do to be saved—oh—"

"Hand us the brandy—" shouted Mutchins.

"Mutchy—Mutchy—I say—" hiccupped Petriken—"Rem-Rem-ember the gown and the prayer book—"

"Silly—we must take a wash-off—" cried Mutchins, starting suddenly from his seat—"The thing—had slipped my memory—this way, my parson—ha, ha, ha—"

And taking Silly by the arm, he staggered from the room in company with the tow-haired gentleman.

"Lord look down upon these thy children, and—" continued the parson, who, like the others, appeared unconscious of the retreat of Petriken and his comrade.

"Hand the oysters this way—" remarked a mercantile gentleman, with a nose decorated by yellowish streaks from a mustard bottle.

"Boys I tell you the fire's up this alley—" cried another merchant—rather an amateur in fires when sober—"Here's the plug—now then—"

"Gentlemen of the Grand Jury, I beg leave to tell you that the amount of sin committed in this place in your very eyesight, cannot be tolerated by the court any longer. Dens of iniquity must be uprooted—who the h———ll flung that celery stalk in my eye?"

"Who soaked my cigar in champagne?"

"Somebody's lit another chandelier—"

"Hand us the brandy—"

"Did you say I didn't put down my name for 'one hundred,' to the Tract Society?"

"No I didn't, but I do now—"

"Say it again, and I'll tie you up in a meal bag—"

"My friends—" said the reverend gentleman, staggering to his feet—"What is this I see—confusion and drunkenness? Is this a scene for the house of God?" He glanced around with a look of sober reproof, and then suddenly exclaimed—"No heeltaps but show your bottoms—ha-ha-ha!"

There was another person who regarded this scene of bestial mirth with the same cool glance as Byrnewood. He was a young man with a massive face, and a deep piercing brown eye. His figure was somewhat stout, his attire careless, and his entire appearance disclosed the young Philadelphia lawyer. Changing his seat to Byrnewood's vicinity, he entered into conversation with the young merchant, and after making some pointed remarks in regard to the various members of the company, he stated that he had been lured thither by Mutchins, who had fancied he might cheat him out of a snug sum at the roulette table, or the faro-bank in the course of the night.

"Roulette-table—faro-bank?" muttered Byrnewood, incredulously.

"Why, my friend—" cried the young lawyer, who gave his name as Boyd Merivale—"Don't you know that this is one of the vilest rookeries in the world? It unites in all its details the house-of-ill-fame, the clubhouse, and the gambling hell. Egad! I well remember the first time I set my foot within its doors! What I beheld then, I can never forget—"

"You have been here before, then?"

"Yes have I! As I perceive you are unacquainted with the place, I will tell you my experience of

A NIGHT IN MONK-HALL*

Six years ago, in 1836, on a foggy night in spring, at the hour of one o'clock, I found myself reposing in one of the chambers of this mansion, on an old-fashioned bed, side by side with a girl, who, before her seduction, had resided in my native village. It was one o'clock when I was aroused by a hushed sound, like the noise of a distant struggle. I awoke, started up in bed, and looked round. The room was entirely without light, save from the fire-place, where a few pieces of half-burned wood, emitted a dim and uncertain flame. Now it flashed up brightly, giving a strange lustre to the old furniture of the room, the high-backed mahogany chairs, the antiquated bureau, and the low ceiling, with heavy cornices around the walls. Again the flame died away and all was darkness. I listened intently. I could hear no sound, save the breathing of the girl who slept by my side. And as I listened, a sudden awe came over me. True, I heard no noise, but that my sleep had been broken by a most appaling sound, I could not doubt. And the stories I had heard of Monk-hall came over me. Years before, in my native village, a wild rollicking fellow, Paul Western, Cashier of the County Bank, had indulged my fancy with strange stories of a brothel, situated in the outskirts of Philadelphia. Paul was a wild fellow, rather good looking, and went often to the city on business. He spoke of Monk-hall as a place hard to find, abounding in mysteries, and darkened by hideous crimes committed within its walls. It had three stories of chambers beneath the earth, as well as above. Each of these chambers was supplied with trapdoors, through the which the unsuspecting man might be flung by his murderer, without a moment's warning. There was but one range of rooms above the ground, where these trap-doors existed. From the garret to the first story, all in the same line, like the

* The reader will remember, that Merivale entered Monk-Hall *for no licentious object, but with the distinct purpose of discovering the retreat of Western*. This story, told in Merivale's own words, is strictly true.

hatchways in a storehouse, sank this range of trap-doors, all carefully concealed by the manner in which the carpets were fixed. A secret spring in the wall of any one of these chambers, communicated with the spring hidden beneath the carpet. The spring in the wall might be so arranged, that a single footstep pressed on the spring, under the carpet, would open the trap-door, and plunge the victim headlong through the aperture. In such cases no man could stride across the floor without peril of his life. Beneath the ground another range of trap-doors were placed in the same manner, in the floors of three stories of the subterranean chambers. They plunged the victim—God knows where! With such arrangements for murder above and beneath the earth, might there not exist hideous pits or deep wells, far below the third story under ground, where the body of the victim would rot in darkness forever? As I remembered these details, the connection between Paul Western, the cheerful bachelor, and Emily Walraven, the woman who was sleeping at my side, flashed over my mind. The child of one of the first men of B———, educated without regard to expense by the doating father, with a mind singularly masculine, and a tall queenly form, a face distinguished for its beauty and a manner remarkable for its ladylike elegance, poor Emily had been seduced, some three years before, and soon after disappeared from the town. Her seducer no one knew, though from some hints dropped casually by my friend Paul, I judged that he at least could tell. Rumors came to the place, from time to time in relation to the beautiful but fallen girl. One rumor stated that she was now living as the mistress of a wealthy planter, who made his residence at times in Philadelphia. Another declared that she had become a common creature of the town, and this —great God, how terrible!—killed her poor father. The rumor flew round the village to-day—next Sunday old Walraven was dead and buried. They say that in his dying hour he charged Paul Western with his daughter's shame, and shrieked a father's curse upon his head. He left no property, for his troubles had preyed on his mind until he neglected his affairs, and he died insolvent.

Well two years passed on, and no one heard a word more of poor Emily. Suddenly in the spring of 1836, when this town as well as the whole Union was convulsed with the fever of speculation, Paul Western, after a visit to Philadelphia, with some funds of the Bank, amounting to near thirty thousand dollars, in his possession, suddenly disappeared, no one knew whither. My father was largely interested in the bank. He despatched me to town, in order that I might make a desperate effort to track up the footsteps of Western. Some items in the papers stated that the Cashier had fled to Texas, others that he had been drowned by accident, others that he had been spirited away. I alone possessed a clue to the place of his concealment—thus ran my thoughts at all events—and that clue was locked in the bosom of Emily Walraven, the betrayed and deeply-injured girl. Sometime before his disappearance, and after the death of old Walraven, Paul disclosed to me, under a solemn pledge of secresy, the fact that Emily was living in Philadelphia, under his protection, supported by his money. He stated that he had furnished rooms at the brothel called Monk-hall. With this fact resting on my mind, I had hurried to Philadelphia. For days my search for Emily Walraven was in vain. One night, when about giving up the chase as hopeless, I strolled to the Chesnut Street Theatre. Forrest was playing Richelieu—there was a row in the third tier—a bully had offered violence to one of the ladies of the town. Attracted by the noise, I joined the throng rushing up stairs, and beheld the girl who had been stricken, standing pale and erect, a small poignard in her upraised hand, while her eyes flashed with rage as she dared the drunken 'buffer' to strike her again. I stood thunderstruck as I recognized Emily Walraven in the degraded yet beautiful woman who stood before me. Springing forward, with one blow I felled the bully to the floor, and in another moment, seizing Emily by the arm, I hurried down stairs, evaded the constables, who were about to arrest her, and gained the street. It was yet early in the evening—there were no cabs in the street—so I had to walk home with her.

All this I remembered well, as I sat listening in the lonely room.

I remembered the big tears that started from her eyes when she recognized me, her wild exclamations when I spoke of her course of life. "Don't talk to me—" she had almost shrieked as we hurried along the street—"it's too late for me to change now. For God's sake let me be happy in my degradation."

I remembered the warm flush of indignation that reddened over her face, as pointing carelessly to a figure which I observed through the fog, some distance ahead, I exclaimed—"Is not that Paul Western yonder?" Her voice was very deep and not at all natural in its tone as she replied, with assumed unconcern—"I know nothing about the man." At last, after threading a labyrinth of streets, compared to which the puzzling-garden was a mere frolic, we had gained Monk-hall, the place celebrated by the wonderful stories of my friend Western. Egad! As we neared the door I could have sworn that I beheld Western himself disappear in the door but this doubtless, I reasoned, had been a mere fancy.

Silence still prevailed in the room, still I heard but the sound of Emily breathing in her sleep, and yet my mind grew more and more heavy, with some unknown feeling of awe. I remembered with painful distinctness the hang-dog aspect of the door-keeper who had let us in, and the cut-throat visages of his two attendants seemed staring me visibly in the face. I grew quite nervous. Dark ideas of murder and the devil knows what, began to chill my very soul. I bitterly remembered that I had no arms. The only thing I carried with me was a slight cane, which had been lent me by the Landlord of the —— Hotel. It was a mere switch of a thing.

As these things came stealing over me, the strange connexion between the fate of Western and that of the beautiful woman who lay beside me, the sudden disappearance of the former, the mysterious character of Monk-hall, the startling sounds which had aroused me, the lonely appearance of the room, fitfully lighted by the glare on the hearth, all combined, deepened the impression of awe, which had gradually gained possession of my faculties. I feared to stir. You may have felt this feeling—this strange and incomprehensible feeling—but if you have not, just imagine a man seized with the night-mare when wide awake.

I was sitting upright in bed, chilled to the very heart, afraid to move an inch, almost afraid to breathe, when, far, far down through the chambers of the old mansion, I heard a faint hushed sound, like a man endeavouring to cry out when attacked by night-mare, and then—great God how distinct!—I heard the cry of 'Murder, murder, murder!' far, far, far below me.

The cry aroused Emily from her sleep. She started up in bed and whispered, in a voice without tremor—"What is the matter Boyd—"

"Listen—" I cried with chattering teeth, and again, up from the depths of the mansion welled that awful sound, *Murder!* MURDER! MURDER! growing louder every time. Then far, far, far down I could hear a gurgling sound. It grew fainter every moment. Fainter, fainter, fainter. All was still as death.

"What does this mean?" I whispered almost fiercely, turning to Emily by my side—"What does this mean?" And a dark suspicion flashed over my mind.

The flame shot upward in the fireplace, and revealed every line of her intellectual countenance.

Her dark eyes looked firmly in my face as she answered, "In God's name I know not!"

The manner of the answer satisfied me as to her firmness, if it did not convince me of her innocence. I sat silent and sullen, conjuring over the incidents of the night.

"Come, Boyd—" she cried, as she arose from the bed—"You must leave the house. I never entertain visitors after this hour. It is my custom. I thank you for your protection at the theatre, but you must go home—''

Her manner was calm and self-possessed. I turned to her in perfect amazement.

''I will not leave the house—'' I said, as a dim vision of being attacked by assassins on the stairway, arose to my mind.

''There is Devil-Bug and his cut-throat negroes—'' thought I—''nothing so easy as to give me a 'cliff' with a knife from some dark corner; nothing so secret as my burial-place in some dark hole in the cellar—''

''I won't go home—'' said I, aloud.

Emily looked at me in perfect wonder. It may have been affected, and it may have been real.

''Well then, I must go down stairs to get something to eat—'' she said, in the most natural manner in the world—''I usually eat something about this hour—''

''You may eat old Devil-Bug and his niggers, if you like—'' I replied laughing—''But out of this house my father's son don't stir till broad daylight.''

With a careless laugh, she wound her night gown around her, opened the door, and disappeared in the dark. Down, down, down, I could hear her go, her footsteps echoing along the stairway of the old mansion, down, down, down. In a few moments all was still.

Here I was, in a pretty 'fix.' In a lonely room at midnight, ignorant of the passages of the wizard's den, without arms, and with the pleasant prospect of the young lady coming back with Devil-Bug and his niggers to despatch me. I had heard the cry of 'Murder'—so ran my reasoning—they, that is the murderers—would suspect that I was a witness to their guilt, and, of course, would send me down some d———d trap-door on an especial message to the devil.

This was decidedly a bad case. I began to look around the room for some chance of escape, some arms to defend myself, or, perhaps from a motive of laudible curiosity, to know something more about the place where my death was to happen.

One moment, regular as the ticking of a clock, the room would be illuminated by a flash of red light from the fire-place, the next it would be dark as a grave. Seizing the opportunity afforded by the flash, I observed some of the details of the room. On the right side of the fire-place there was a closet: the door fastened to the post by a very singular button, shaped like a diamond; about as long as your little finger and twice as thick. On the other side of the fire-place, near the ceiling, was a small oblong window, about as large as two half sheets of writing paper, pasted together at the ends. Here let me explain the use of this window. The back part of Monk-hall is utterly destitute of windows. Light, faint and dim you may be sure, is admitted from the front by small windows, placed in the wall of each room. How many rooms there are on a floor, I know not, but, be they five or ten, or twenty, they are all lighted in this way.

Well, as I looked at this window, I perceived one corner of the curtain on the other side was turned up. This gave me very unpleasant ideas. I almost fancied I beheld a human face pressed against the glass, looking at me. Then the flash on the hearth died away, and all was dark. I heard a faint creaking noise—the light from the hearth again lighted the place—could I believe my eyes—the button on the closet-door turned slowly round!

Slowly—slowly—slowly it turned, making a slight grating noise. This circumstance, slight as it may appear to you, filled me with horror. What could turn the button, but a human hand? Slowly, slowly it turned, and the door sprung open with a whizzing sound. All was dark again. The cold sweat stood out on my forehead. Was my armed murderer waiting to spring at my throat? I passed a moment of intense horror. At last, springing hastily forward, I swung the door shut, and fastened the button. I can swear that I fastened it as tight as ever button was fastened. Regaining the bed I silently awaited the result. Another flash of light—Great God!—I could swear there was a face pressed against the oblong window! Another moment and it is darkness—creak, creak, creak—is that the sound of the button again? It was light again, and there, before my very eyes, the button moved slowly round! Slowly, slowly, slowly!

The door flew open again. I sat still as a statue. I felt it difficult to breathe. Was my enemy playing with me, like the cat ere she destroys her game!

I absently extended my hand. It touched the small black stick given me by the Landlord of the ——— Hotel in the beginning of the evening. I drew it to me, like a friend. Grasping it with both hands, I calculated the amount of service it might do me. And as I grasped it, the top seemed parting from the lower portion of the cane. Great God! It was a sword cane! Ha-ha! I could at least strike *one* blow! My murderers should not despatch me without an effort of resistance. You see my arm is none of the puniest in the world; I may say that there are worse men than Boyd Merivale for a fight.

Clutching the sword-cane, I rushed forward, and standing on the threshold of the opened door, I made a lunge with all my strength through the darkness of the recess. Though I extended my arm to its full length, and the sword was not less than eighteen inches long, yet to my utter astonishment, I struck but the empty air! Another lunge and the same result!

Things began to grow rather queer. I was decidedly beat out as they say. I shut the closet door again, retreated to the bed, sword in hand, and awaited the result. I heard a sound, but it was the footstep of poor Emily, who that moment returned with a bed-lamp in one hand, and a small waiter, supplied with a boiled chicken and a bottle of wine in the other. There was nothing remarkable in her look, her face was calm, and her boiled chicken and bottle of wine, decidedly common place.

"Great God—" she cried as she gazed in my countenance—"What is the matter with you? Your face is quite livid—and your eyes are fairly starting from their sockets—"

"Good reason—" said I, as I *felt* that my lips were clammy and white —"That d———d button has been going round ever since you left, and that d———d door has been springing open every time it was shut—"

"Ha-ha-ha—" she laughed—"Would it have sprung open if you had not shut it?"

This was a very clear question and easy to answer; but—

"Mark you, my lady—" said I—"Here am I in a lonely house, under peculiar circumstances. I am waked up by the cry of 'Murder'—a door springs open without a hand being visible—a face peers at me through a window. As a matter of course I suspect there has been foul work done here to-night. And through every room of this house, Emily you must lead the way, while I follow, this good sword in hand. If the light goes out, or if you blow it out, you are to be pitied, for in either case, I swear by Living God, I will run you through with this sword—"

"Ha-ha-ha—" she fairly screamed with laughter as she sprung to the closet-door—"Behold the mystery—"

And with her fair fingers she pointed to the socket of the button, and to the centre of the door. The door has been 'sprung,' as it is termed, by the weather. That is, the centre bulged inward, leaving the edge toward the door-post to press the contrary direction. The socket of the button, by continual wear, had been increased to twice its original size. Whenever the door was first buttoned, the head of the screw pressed against one of the edges of the socket. In a moment the pressure of the edge of the door, which you will remember was directed outward, dislodged the head of the screw and it sank, well-nigh half an inch into the worn socket of the button. Then the button, removed *farther* from the door than at first, would slowly turn, and the door spring open. All this was plain enough, and I smiled at my recent fright.

"Very good, Emily—" I laughed—"But the mystery of this sword—what of that? I made a lunge in the closet and it touched nothing—"

"You are suspicious, Boyd—" she answered with a laugh—"But the fact is, the closet is rather a deep one—"

"Rather—" said I—"and so are you, my dear—"

There may have been something very meaning in my manner, but certainly, although her full black eyes looked fixedly on me, yet I thought her face grew a shade paler as I spoke.

"And my dear—" I continued—"What do you make of the face peeping through the window:—"

"All fancy—all fancy—" she replied, but as she spoke I saw her eye glance hurriedly toward the very window. Did she *too* fear that she might behold a face?

"We will search the closet—" I remarked, throwing open the door—"What have we here? Nothing but an old cloak hanging to a hook—let's try it with my sword!"

Again I made a lunge with my sword: again I thrust at the empty air.

"Emily, there is a room beyond this cloak—you will enter first if you please. Remember my warning about the light if you please—"

"Oh now that I remember, this closet *does* open into the next room—" she said gaily, although her cheek—so it struck me—grew a little paler and her lip trembled slightly—"I had quite forgotten the circumstance—"

"Enter Emily, and don't forget the light—"

She flung the door aside and passed on with the light in her hand. I followed her. We stood in a small room, lighted like the other by an oblong window. There was no other window, no door, no outlet of any sort. Even a chimney-place was wanting. In one corner stood a massive bed—the quilt was unruffled. Two or three old fashioned chairs were scattered round the room, and from the spot where I stood looking over the foot of the bed, I could see the top of another chair, and nothing more, between the bed and the wall.

A trifling fact in Emily's behaviour may be remarked. The moment the light of the lamp which she held in her hand flashed round the room, she turned to me with a smile, and leading the way round the corner of the foot of the bed, asked me in a pleasant voice "Did I see any thing remarkable there?"

She shaded her eyes from the lamp as she spoke, and toyed me playfully under the chin. You will bear in mind that at this moment, I had turned my face toward the closet by which we had entered. My back was therefore toward the part of the room most remote from the closet.

It was a trifling fact, but I may as well tell you, that the manner in which Emily held the light, threw that portion of the room, between the foot of the bed and the wall in complete shadow, while the rest of the chamber was bright as day.

Smilingly Emily toyed me under the chin, and at that moment I thought she looked extremely beautiful.

By Jove! I wish you could have seen her eyes shine, and her cheek—Lord bless you—a full blown rose wasn't a circumstance to it. She looked so beautiful, in fact, as she came sideling up to me, that I stepped backward in order to have a full view of her before I pressed a kiss on her pouting lips. I did step back, and did kiss her. It wasn't singular, perhaps, but her lips were hot as a coal. Again she advanced to me, again chucked me under the chin. Again I stepped back to look at her, again I wished to taste her lips so pouting, but rather warm, when—

To tell you the truth, stranger, even at this late day the remembrance makes my blood run cold!

——— When I heard a sound like the sweeping of a tree-limb against a closed shutter, it was so faint and distant, and a stream of cold air came rushing up my back.

I turned around carelessly to ascertain the cause. I took but a single glance, and then—by G———d—I sprung at least ten feet from the place. There, at my very back, between the bed and the wall, opposite its foot, I beheld a carpeted space some three feet square, sinking slowly down, and separating itself from the floor. I had stepped my foot upon the spring—made ready for me, to be sure—and the trap-door sank below me.

You may suppose my feelings were somewhat excited. In truth, my heart, for a moment, felt as though it was turning to a ball of ice. First I looked at the trap-door and then at Emily. Her face was pale as ashes, and she leaned, trembling, against the bedpost. Advancing, sword in hand, I gazed down the trap-door. Great God! how dark and gloomy the pit looked! From room to room, from floor to floor, a succession of traps had fallen—far below—it looked like a mile, although that was but an exaggeration natural to a highly excited mind—far, far below gleamed a light, and a buzzing murmur came up this hatchway of death.

Stooping slowly down, sword in hand, my eye on the alert for Miss Emily, I disengaged a piece of linen, from a nail, near the edge of the trap-door. Where the linen—it was a shirt wristband—had been fastened, the carpet was slightly torn, as though a man in falling had grasped it with his finger ends.

The wristband was, in more correct language, a ruffle for the wrist. It came to my mind, in this moment, that I had often ridiculed Paul Western for his queer old bachelor ways. Among other odd notions, he had worn ruffles at his wrist. As I gathered this little piece of linen in my grasp, the trap-door slowly rose. I turned to look for Miss Emily, she had changed her position, and stood pressing her hand against the opposite wall.

"Now, Miss Emily, my dear—" I cried, advancing toward her—"Give me a plain answer to a plain question—and tell me—what in the devil do you think of yourself?"

Perfectly white in the face, she glided across the room and stood at the foot of the bed, in her former position leaning against the post for support. You will observe that her form concealed the chair, whose top I had only seen across the bed.

"Step aside, Miss Emily, my dear—" I said, in as quiet a tone as I could command—"Or you see, my lady, I'll have to use a little necessary force—"

Instead of stepping aside, as a peaceable woman would have done, she sits right down in the chair, fixing those full black eyes of her's on my face, with a glance that looked very much like madness.

Extending my hand, I raised her from the seat. She rested like a dead weight in my arms. She had fainted. Wrapped in her night-gown, I laid her on the bed, and then examined the chair in the corner. Something about this chair attracted my attention. A coat hung over the round—a blue coat with metal buttons. A buff vest hung under this coat; and a high stock, with a shirt collar.

I knew these things at once. They belonged to my friend, Paul Western.

"And so, my lady—" I cried, forgetting that she had fainted; "Mr. Western came home, from the theatre, to his rooms, arrived just before us, took off his coat and vest, and stock and collar—maybe was just about to take off his boots—when he stepped on the spring and in a moment was in—in h———ll—"

Taking the light in one hand, I dragged or carried her, into the other room and laid her on the bed. After half an hour or so, she came to her senses.

"You see—you see—" were her first words uttered, with her eyes flashing like live-coals, and her lips white as marble—"You see, I could not help it, for my father's curse was upon him!"

She laughed wildly, and lay in my arms a maniac.

Stranger, I'll make a short story of the thing now. How I watched her all night till broad day, how I escaped from the house—for Mr.

Devil-Bug, it seems, didn't suspect I knew anything—how I returned home without any news of Paul Western, are matters as easy to conceive as tell.

Why didn't I institute a search? Fiddle-faddle! Blazon my name to the world as a visiter to a Bagnio? Sensible thing, that! And then, although I was sure in my own soul, that the clothes which I had discovered belonged to Paul Western, it would have been most difficult to establish this fact in Court. One word more and I have done.

Never since that night has Paul Western been heard of by living man. Never since that night has Emily Walraven been seen in this breathing world. You start. Let me whisper a word in your ear. Suppose Emily joined in Western's murder from motives of revenge, what then were Devil-Bug's? (*He* of course was the real murderer.) Why the money to be sure. Why he troubled with Emily as a witness of his guilt, or a sharer of his money? This is rather a—a *dark house*, and it's my opinion, stranger, that *he murdered her too!*

Ha-ha—why here's all the room to ourselves! All the club have either disappeared, or lie drunk on the floor! I saw Fitz-Cowles—I know him—sneak off a few moments since—I could tell by his eye that he is after some devils-trick! The parson has gone, and the judge has gone, the lawyer has fallen among the slain, and so, wishing you good night, stranger, I'll vanish! Beware of the Monks of Monk-hall!"

Byrnewood was alone.

His head was depressed, his arms were folded, and his eye, gazing vacantly on the table, shone and glistened with the internal agitation of his brain. He sate there, silent, motionless, awed to the very soul. The story of the stranger had thrilled him to the heart, had aroused a strange train of thought, and now rested like an oppressive weight upon his brain.

Byrnewood gazed around. With a sudden effort he shook off the spell of absence which mingled with an incomprehensible feeling of awe, had enchained his faculties. He looked around the room. He was, indeed, alone. Above him, the hideous Satyr chandelier, still flared its red light over the table, over the mirror, and along the gloomy wainscot of the walls. Around the table, grouped in various attitudes of unconscious drunkenness, lay the members of the drinking party, the merry Monks of Monk-hall. There lay the poet, with his sanguine face shining redly in the light, while his hand rested on the bare scalp of the wigless editor, there snored some dozen merchants, all doubled up together, like the slain in battle, and there, a solitary doctor, who had fallen asleep on his knees, was dozing away with one eye wide open, while his right hand brushed away a solitary fly from his pimpled nose.

The scene was not calculated to produce the most serious feelings in the world. There was inebriety—as the refined phrase it—in every shape, inebriety on its face, inebriety with its mouth wide open, inebriety on its knees brushing a fly from its nose, inebriety groaning, grunting, or snoring, inebriety doubled up—mingled in a mass of limbs, heads and bodies, woven together—or flat inebriety simply straightened out on its back with its nose performing a select overture of snores. To be brief, there, scattered over the floor, lay drunkenness—as the vulgar will style it—in every shape, moddled after various patterns, and taken by that ingenious artist, the Bottle, fresh from real life.

Raising his eyes from the prostrate members of the club, Byrnewood started with involuntary surprise as he beheld, standing at the tables-head, the black-robed figure of the Skeleton-Monk, with his hand of bone flinging aloft the goblet, while his fleshless brow glared in the light, from the shadow of the falling cowl. As the light flickered to and fro, it gave the grinning teeth of the Skeleton the appearance of life and animation for a single moment. Byrnewood thought he beheld the teeth move in a ghastly smile; he even fancied that the orbless sockets, gleaming beneath the white brow, flashed with the glance of life, and gazed sneeringly in his face.

He started with involuntary horror, and then sate silent as before. And as you can feel cold or heat steal over you by slow degrees, so he felt that same strange feeling of awe, which he had known that night for the first time in his life, come slowly over him moving like a shadow over his soul, and stealing like a paralysis through his every limb. He sate like a man suddenly frozen.

"My God!" he murmured—and the sound of his voice frightened him—"How strange I feel! Can this be the first attack of some terrible disease—or—is it, but the effect of the horrible story related by the stranger? I have read in books that a feeling like this steals over a man, just before some terrible calamity breaks over his head—this is fearful as death itself!"

He was silent again, and then the exclamation broke from his lips—

"Lorrimer—why does he not return? He has been absent full an hour—what does it mean? Can the words of that—pshaw! that fortune teller have any truth in them? How can Lorrimer injure me—how can I injure him? Three days hence—Christmas—ha, ha—I believe I'm going mad—there's cold sweat on my forehead—"

As he spoke he raised his left hand to his brow, and in the action, the gleam of a plain ring on his finger met his eye. He kissed it suddenly, and kissed it again and again? Was it the gift of his ladye-love?

"God bless her—God bless her! Wo to the man who shall do *her* wrong—and yet poor Annie—"

He rose suddenly from his seat and strode towards the door.

"I know not why it is, but I feel as though an invisible hand, was urging me onward through the rooms of this house! And onward I will go, until I discover Lorrimer or solve the mystery of this den. God knows, I feel—pshaw! I'm only nervous—as though I was walking to my death."

Passing through the narrow door-way, he cautiously ascended the dark staircase, and in a moment stood on the first floor. The moon was still shining through the distant skylight, down over the windings of the massive stairway. All was silent as death within the mansion. Not a sound, not even the murmur of a voice or the hushed tread of a footstep could be heard. Winding his cloak tightly around his limbs, Byrnewood rushed up the staircase, traversing two steps at a time, and treading softly, for fear of discovery. He reached the second floor. Still the place was silent and dismal, still the column of moonlight pouring through the skylight, over the windings of the staircase only rendered the surrounding darkness more gloomy and indistinct. Up the winding staircase he again resumed his way, and in a moment stood upon the landing or hall of the third floor. This was an oblong space, with the doors of many rooms fashioned in its walls. Another stairway led upward from the floor, but the attention of Byrnewood was arrested by a single ray of light, that for a moment flickered along the thick darkness of the southern end of the hall. Stepping forward hastily, Byrnewood found all progress arrested by the opposing front of a solid wall. He gazed toward his left—it was so dark, that he could not see his hand before his eyes. Turning his glance to the right, as his vision became more accustomed to the darkness, he beheld the dim walls of a long corridor, at whose entrance he stood, and whose farther extreme was illumined by a light, that to all appearance, flashed from an open door. Without a moment's thought he strode along the thickly carpeted passage of the corridor; he stood in the full glow of the light flashing from the open door.

Looking through the doorway, he beheld a large chamber furnished in a style of lavish magnificence, and lighted by a splendid chandelier. It was silent and deserted. From the ceiling to the floor, along the wall opposite the doorway, hung a curtain of damask silk, trailing in heavy folds, along the gorgeous carpet. Impelled by the strange impulse, that had urged him thus far, Byrnewood entered the chamber, and without pausing to admire its gorgeous appointments, strode forward to the damask curtain.

He swung one of its hangings aside, expecting to behold the extreme wall of the chamber. To his entire wonder, another chamber, as spacious as the one in which he stood, lay open to his gaze. The walls were all one gorgeous picture, evidently painted by a master-hand. Blue skies, deep green forests, dashing waterfalls and a cool calm lake, in which fair women were laving their limbs, broke on the eyes of the intruder, as he turned his gaze from wall to wall. A curtain of azure, sprinkled with a border of golden leaves, hung along the farther extremity of the room. In one corner stood a massive bed, whose snow-white counterpane, fell smoothly and unruffled to the very floor, mingling with the long curtains, which pure and stainless as the counterpane, hung around the couch in graceful festoons, like the wings of a bird guarding its resting place.

"The bridal-bed!" murmured Byrnewood, as he flung the curtains of gold and azure, hurriedly aside.

A murmur of surprise, mingled with admiration, escaped from his lips, as he beheld the small closet, for it could scarcely be called a room, which the undrawn curtaining threw open to his gaze.

It was indeed a small and elegant room, lined along its four sides with drooping curtains of faint-hued crimson silk. The ceiling itself was but a continuation of these curtains, or hangings, for they were gathered in the centre, by a single star of gold. The carpet on the floor was of the same faint-crimson color, and the large sofa, placed along one side of the apartment, was covered with velvet, that harmonized in hue, with both carpet and hangings. On the snow-white cloth, of a small table placed in the centre of the room, stood a large wax candle, burning in a candlestick of silver, and flinging a subdued and mellow light around the plate. There was a neat little couch, standing in the corner, with a *toilette* at its foot. The quilt on the couch was ruffled, as though some one had lately risen from it, and the equipage of the *toilette* looked as though it had been recently used.

The faint light falling over the hangings, whose hue resembled the first flush of day, the luxurious sofa, the neat though diminutive couch, the small table in the centre, the carpet whose colors were in elegant harmony with the hue of the curtains, all combined, gave the place an air of splendid comfort—if we may join these incongruous words—that indicated the sleeping chamber of a lovely woman.

"This has been the resting place of the *bride*—" murmured Byrnewood, gazing in admiration around the room—"It looks elegant it is true, but if she is the innocent thing Lorrimer would have me believe, then better for her, to have slept in the foulest gutter of the streets, than to have lain for an instant in this woman-trap—"

There was a woman's dress—a frock of plain black silk—flung over one of the rounds of the sofa. Anxious to gather some idea of the form of the bride—oh foul prostitution of the name!—from the shape of the dress, Byrnewood raised the frock and examined its details. As he did this, the sound of voices came hushed and murmuring to his ear from a room, opposite the chamber which he had but a moment left. Half occupied in listening to these voices, Byrnewood glanced at the dress which he held in his hand, and as he took in its various details of style and shape, the pupil of his full black eye dilated, and his cheek became colorless as death.

Then the room seemed to swim around him, and he pressed his hand forcibly against his brow, as if to assure himself, that he was not entangled in the mazes of some hideous dream.

Then, letting his own cloak and the black silk dress fall on the floor at once, he walked with a measured step toward that side of the room opposite the Painted Chamber.

The voices grew louder in the next room. Byrnewood listened in silence. His face was even paler than before, and you could see how desperate was the effort which he made to suppress an involuntary cry of horror, that came rising to his lips. Extending his hand, he pushed the curtain slightly aside, and looked into the next room.

The extended hand fell like a dead weight to his side.

Over his entire countenance flashed a mingled expression of surprise, and horror, and woe, that convulsed every feature with a spasmodic movement, and forced his large black eyes from their very sockets. For a moment he looked as if about to fall lifeless on the floor, and then it was evident that he exerted all his energies to control this most fearful agitation. He pressed both hands nervously against his forehead, as though his brain was tortured by internal flame. Then he reared his form proudly erect, and stood apparently firm and self possessed, although his countenance looked more like the face of a corpse than the face of a living man.

And as he stood there, silent and firm, although his very reason tottered to its ruin, there glided to his back, like an omen of death, pursuing the footsteps of life, the distorted form of the Door-keeper of Monk-hall, his huge bony arms upraised, his hideous face convulsed in a loathsome grin, while his solitary eye glared out from its sunken socket, like a flame lighted in a skull, grotesque yet terrible.

In vain was the momentary firmness which Byrnewood had aroused to his aid! In vain was the effort that suppressed his breath, that clenched his hands, that forced the clammy sweat from his brow! He felt the awful agony that convulsed his soul rising to his lips—he would have given the world to stifle it—but in vain, in vain were all his superhuman efforts!

One terrific howl, like the yell of a man flung suddenly over a cataract, broke from his lips. He thrust aside the curtain, and strode madly through its folds into the next room.

CHAPTER EIGHTH

MOTHER NANCY AND LONG-HAIRED BESS

'So ye have lured the pretty dove into the cage, at last—" said the old lady, with a pleasant smile, as she poised a nice morsel of buttered toast between her fingers—"This tea is most too weak—a little more out of the caddy, Bessie, dear. Lord! who'd a-thought you'd a-caught the baby-face so easy! Does the kettle boil, my dear? I put it on the fire before you left, and you've been away near an hour, so it ought to be hissing hot by this time. Caught her at last! Hah-hah—hey? Bessie? You're a reg'lar keen one, I must say!"

And with the mild words the old lady arranged the tea things on the small table, covered with a neat white cloth, and pouring out a cup of 'Gunpowder,' chuckled pleasantly to herself, as though she and the buttered toast had a quiet little joke together.

"Spankin' cold night, I tell ye, Mother Nancy—" exclaimed the young lady in black, as she flung herself in a chair, and tossed her bonnet on the old sofa—"Precious time I've had with that little chit of a thing! Up one street and down another, I've been racing for this blessed hour! And the regular white and black 'uns I've been forced to tell! Oh crickery—don't mention 'em, I beg—"

"Sit down, Bess—sit down, Bessie, that's a dove—" said the delighted old lady, crunching the toast between her toothless gums—"and tell us all about it from the first! These things are quite refreshin' to us old stagers."

"What a perfect old d———l—" muttered Bessie, as she drew her seat near the supper table—"These oysters are quite delightful—stewed to a turn, I *do* declare—" she continued, aloud—"Got a little drop o' the 'lively'—hey, Mother?"

"Yes, dovey—here's the key of the closet. Get the bottle, my dear.

A leetle—jist a *leetle*—don't go ugly with one's tea—"

While the tall and queenly Bessie is engaged in securing a drop of the lively, we will take a passing glance at Mother Perkins, the respectable Lady Abbess of Monk-hall.

As she sate in that formal arm-chair, straight and erect, her portly form clad in sombre black, with a plain white collar around her neck and a bunch of keys at her girdle, Mother Nancy looked, for all the world, like a quiet old body, whose only delight was to scatter blessings around her, give large alms to the poor, and bestow unlimited amounts of tracts among the vicious. A good, dear, old body, was Mother Nancy, although her face was decidedly prepossessing. A low forehead, surmounted by a perfect tower-of-Babel of a cap, a little sharp nose looking out from two cheeks disposed in immense collops of yellowish flesh, two small grey eyes encircled by a wilderness of wrinkles, a deep indentation where a mouth should have been, and a sharp chin, ornamented with a slight 'imperial' of stiff grey beard; such were the details of a countenance, on which seventy years had showered their sins, and cares, and crimes, without making the dear old lady, for a moment, pause in her career.

And such a career! God of Heaven! did womanhood, which in its dawn, or bloom, or full maturity, is so beautiful, which even in its decline is lovely, which in trembling old age is venerable, did womanhood ever sink so low as this? How many of the graves in an hundred churchyards, graves of the fair and beautiful, had been dug by the gouty hands of the vile old hag, who sate chuckling in her quiet armchair? How many of the betrayed maidens, found rotting on the rivers waves, dangling from the garret rafter, starving in the streets, or resting, vile and loathsome, in the Greenhouse;* how many of these will, at the last day when the accounts of this lovely earth will be closed forever, rise up and curse the old hag with their ruin, with their shame, with their unwept death?

The details of the old lady's room by no means indicated her disposition, or the course of her life. It was a fine old room with walls neatly papered, all full of nooks and corners, and warmed by a cheerful wood fire blazing on the spacious hearth. One whole side of the room seemed to have been attacked with some strange eruptive disease, and broken out into an erysipelas of cupboards and closets. An old desk that might

* The house for the unknown dead.

have told a world of wonders of Noah's Ark from its own personal experience, could it have spoken, stood in one corner, and a large sideboard, on whose top a fat fellow of a decanter seemed drilling some raw recruits of bottles and glasses into military order, occupied one entire side of the room, or cell, of the Lady Abbess.

There are few persons in the world who have not a favourite of some kind, either a baby, or a parrot, or a canary, or a cat, or, in desperate cases, a pig. Mother Nancy had her favourite as well as less reputable people. A huge bull dog, with sore eyes and a ragged tail—that seemed to have been purchased at a second-had store during the hard times—lay nestling at the old lady's feet, looking very much like the candidate whom all the old and surly dogs would choose for Alderman, in case the canine race had the privilege of electing an officer of that honorable class, among themselves. This dog, so old bachelor-like and aldermanic in appearance, the old lady was wont to call by the name of 'Dolph,' being the short for 'Dolphin,' of which remarkable fish the animal was supposed to be a decided copy.

"Here's the 'lively,' Mother Nancy—" observed Miss Bessie, as she resumed her seat at the supper table—"It's the real hot stuff and *no* mistake. The oysters, if you please—a little o' that pepper. Any mustard there? Now then, Mother, let's be comfortable—"

"But" observed the old lady pouring a glass of the 'Lively' from a decanter labelled 'Brandy'—"But Bessie my love, I'm a-waitin' to hear all about this little dove whom you trapped to night—"

It may be as well to remark that Bessie, was a tall queenly girl of some twenty-five, with a form that had once been beautiful beyond description, and even now in its ruins, was lovely to look upon, while her faded face, marked by a high brow and raven-black hair, was still enlivened by the glance of two large dark eyes, that were susceptable of any expression, love or hate, revenge or jealousy; anything but fear. Her complexion was a very faint brown with a deep rose-tint on each cheek. She was still beautiful, although a long career of dissipation had given a faded look to the outlines of her face, indenting a slight wrinkle between her arching brows, and slightly discoloring the flesh beneath each eye.

"This here 'Lively' is first rate, after the tramp I've had—" said Bessie as her eyes grew brighter with the 'lively' effects of the bottle—" You know Mother Nancy its three weeks since Gus mentioned the *thing* to me—"

"What thing, my dear?"

"Why that he'd like to have a little dove for himself—something above the common run. Something from the aristocracy of the Quaker

City—you know?"

"Yes my dear. Here Dolph—here Dolph-ee—here's a nice bit for Dolph—"

"Gus agreed to give me something handsome if I could manage it for him, so I undertook the thing. The bread if you please, Mother. You know I'm rather expert in such matters?"

"There ain't you beat my dear. Be quiet Dolph—that's a nice Dolph-ee—"

"For a week all my efforts were in vain. I could'nt discover anything that was likely to suit the taste of Gus—At last he put me on the right track himself—"

"He did, did he? Ah deary me, but Gus is a regular lark. You can't perduce his ekle—"

"One day strolling up Third Street, Gus was attracted by the sight of a pretty girl, sitting at the window of a wealthy merchant, who has just retired from business. You've heard of old Arlington? Try the 'Lively' Mother. Gus made some enquiries; found that the young lady had just returned, from the Moravian boarding school at Bethlehem. She was innocent, inexperienced, and all that. Suited Lorrimers taste. He swore he'd have her."

"So you undertook to catch her, did ye? Butter my dear?"

"That did I. The way I managed it was a caution. Dressing myself in solemn black, I strolled along Third street, one mild winter evening, some two weeks since. Mary—that's her name—was standing at the front door, gazing carelessly down the street. I tripped up the steps and asked in my most winning tone———"

"You can act the lady when you like, Bess. That's a fact.—"

"Whether Mr. Elmwood lived there? Of course she answered 'No.' But in making an apology for my intrusion, I managed to state that Mr. Elmwood was my uncle, that I had just come to the city on a visit, and had left my aunt's in Spruce street, but a few moments ago, thinking to pay a nice little call on my dear old relative—"

"Just like you Bessie! So you scraped acquaintance with her?"

"Fresh from boarding school, as ignorant of the world as the babe unborn, the girl was interested in me, I suppose, and swallowed the white'uns I told her, without a single suspicion, The next day about noon, I met her as she was hurrying to see an old aunt, who lived two or three Squares below her father s house. She was all in a glow, for she had been hurrying along rather fast, anxious to reach her aunt's house, as soon as possible. I spoke to her—proposed a walk—she assented with a smile of pleasure. I told her a long story of my sorrows; how I had been engaged to be married, how my lover had died of consumption but a month ago; that he was such a nice young man, with curly hair, and hazel eyes, and that I was in black for his death. I put peach fur over her eyes, by whole hand's full I tell you. The girl was interested, and like all young girls, she was delighted to become the *confidante* of an amiable young lady, who had a little love-romance of real life, to disclose. Oysters, Mother Nancy—"

"The long and short of it was, that you wormed yourself into her confidence? That it my dear? Keep still Dolph or Dolph's mommy would drop little bit of hot tea on Dolph's head—"

"We walked out together for three days, just toward dark in the evening. You can fancy Mother, how I wound myself into the heart of this young girl. Closer and closer every day I tightened the cords that bound us, and on the third evening I believe she would have died for me.—"

"Well, well child, when did Gusty first speak to her? A little more of the "Gunpowder" my dear—"

"One evening I persuaded her to take a stroll along Chesnut Street with me. Gus was at our heels you may be sure. He passed on a little-a-head determining to speak to her, at all hazards. She saved him the trouble. Lord love you Mother Nancy, she spoke to him first—"

"Be still Dolph—be still Dolph-ee! Now Bessie that's a leetle too strong! Not the tea, but the story. She so innocent and baby-like speak first to a strange man? Ask me to believe in tea made out of turnip tops will ye?—"

"She mistook him for a Mr. Belmont whom she had seen at Bethlehem. He did not undeceive her, until she was completely in his power. He walked by her side that evening up and down Chesnut Street, for nearly an hour. I saw at once, that her girlish fancy was caught by his smooth tongue, and handsome form. The next night he met us again, and the next, and the next—Lord pity her—the poor child was *now* entirely at his mercy—"

"Ha—ha—Gusty is sich a devil. Put the kettle on the fire my dear. Let's try a little of the 'Lively.' And how did she—this baby-faced doll—keep these walks secret from the eyes of her folks? Eh? Bessie?"

"Easy as *that*—" replied Bessie gracefully snapping her fingers—"Every time she went out, she told father and mother' that she went to see her old Aunt. I hinted at first, that our friendship would be more romantic, if concealed from all intrusive eyes. The girl took the hint. Lorrimer with his smooth tongue, told her a long story about his eccentric uncle who had sworn he should not marry, for years to come; and therefore he was obliged to keep his attentions to her, hidden from both of their families. Gusty was dependent on this old uncle—you know? Once married, the old uncle would relent as he beheld the beauty and innocence of the young—*wife!* So Gusty made her believe. You can imagine the whole trap. We had her in our power. Last night she consented to leave her home for Lorrimer's *family* mansion. He was to marry her, the approval of his uncle—that imaginary old Gentleman—was to be obtained, and on Christmas Eve, Mr. and—ha, ha, ha—*Mistress* Lorrimer, were to rush into old Middleton's house, fall on their knees, invoke the old man's blessing; be forgiven and be happy! Hand us the toast Mother Nancy—"

"And to night the girl *did* leave the old folk's house? Entered the door of Monk-hall, thinking it was Lorrimer's *family* Mansion, and to-morrow morning at three o'clock will be married—eh? Bess?"

"Married, pshaw! *Over the left.* Lorrimer said he would get that fellow Petriken to personate the Parson—Mutchins the gambler, acts the old uncle; you, Mother Nancy must, dress up for the kind and amiable grandma—suit you to a T? Lorrimer pays high for his rooms you know?"

"'Spose it must be done. It's now after ten o'clock. You left the baby-face sleeping, eh? At half-past two you'll have to rouse her, to dress. Be quiet Dolph or I'll scald its head—that's a dear. Now Bessie tell me the truth, did you never regret that you had undertaken the job? The girl you say is so innocent?"

"Regret?" cried Bess with a flashing eye—"Why should I regret? Have I not as good a right to the comforts of a home, to the smile of a father, the love of a mother, as she? Have I not been robbed of all these? Of all that is most sacred to woman? Is this innocent Mary, a whit better than I *was* when the devil in human shape first dragged me from my home? I feel happy—aye happy—when I can drag another woman, into the same foul pit, where I am doomed to lie and rot—"

"Yet this thing was *so* innocent—" cried the good old lady patting Dolph on the head—" I confess I laugh at all qualms—all petty scruples, but you were so different when first I knew you—you *Emily*, you—"

"*Emily*—" shrieked the other as she sprung suddenly to her feet—"You hag of the devil—call me by that name again, and as God will judge at the last day, I'll throttle you!" She shook her clenched hand across the table, and her eyes were bloodshot with sudden rage—"*Emily!*" Your mother called you by that name when a little child—" She cried with a burst of feeling, most fearful to behold in one so fallen—"Your father blessed you by that name, the night before you fled from his roof!

'Emily!' Aye, *he*, the foul betrayer, whispered that name with a smile as he entered the Chamber, from which he never came forth again—You remember it old hell-cat, do ye?—"

"Not so loud, Good G———d, not so loud—" Cried the astonished Mother Nancy—" Abuse me Bessie dear—but not so loud; down Dolph don't mind the girl, she's mad—not so loud, I say—"

"I can see him now!" cried the fallen girl, as with her tall form raised to its full height, she fixed her flashing eye on vacancy—"He enters the room—that room with the—the trap-door you know? 'Good night, Emily,' he said, and smiled—'*Emily*,' and—my father had cursed him! I laid me down and rested by another man's side. *He* thought I slept. Slept! ha, ha! When, with my entire soul, I listened to the foot-steps in the next room—ha, ha—when I heard the creaking sound of the falling trap, when I drank in the cry of agony, when I heard that name 'Emily, oh Emily,' come shrieking up the pit of death! My father had cursed him, and he died! 'Emily'—oh my God—" and she wrung her hands in very agony—"Roll back the years of my life, blot out the foul record of my sins, let me, oh God—you are all powerful and can do it—let me be a child again, a little child, and though I crawl through life in the rags of a beggar, I will never cease to bless—oh God—to bless your name—"

She fell heavily to her seat, and, covering her face with her hands, wept the scalding tears of guilt and shame.

" 'Gal's been a-takin' opium—" said the old lady, calmly—"And the fit's come on her. 'Sarves her right. 'Told her never to mix her brandy with opium—"

"Did I regret having undertaken the ruin of the girl—" said Bess, in a whisper, that made even the old lady start with surprise—"Regret? I tell ye, old hell-dame as you are, that my very heart strings seemed breaking within me to-night, as I led her from her home—"

"What the d———l did you do it for, then? Here's a nice Dolph—eat a piece o' buttered toast—that's a good Dolph-ee—"

"When the seducer first assailed me—" continued Bess, in an absent tone—"He assailed a woman, with a mind stored with knowledge of the world's ways, a soul full as crafty as his own, a wit sharp and keen as ever dropped poison or sweetness from a woman's tongue! But this girl, so child-like, so unsuspecting, so innocent! my God! how it wrung my heart, when I first discovered that she *loved* Lorrimer, loved him without one shade of gross feeling, loved him without a doubt, warmly, devotedly, with all the trustfulness of an angel-soul, fresh from the hands of God! Never a bird fell more helplessly into the yawning jaws of the snake, that had charmed it to ruin, than poor Mary fell into the accursed wiles of Lorrimer! And yet I, *I* aided him—"

"So you did. The more shame for you to harm sich a dove. Go up stairs, my dear, and let her loose. We'll consent, won't we? Ha-ha! Why Bess, I thought you had more sense than to go on this way. What *will* become of you?"

"I suppose that I will die in the same ditch where the souls of so many of my vile sisterhood have crept forth from their leprous bodies? Eh, Mother Nance? Die in a ditch? '*Emily*' die in a ditch? And then in the next world—ha, ha, ha—I see a big lake of fire, on which souls are dancing like moths in a candle—ha, ha, ha!"

"Reely, gal, you must leave off that opium. Gus promised you some five or six hundred if you caught this gal, and you can't go back now—"

"Yes, yes, I know it! I know it! *Forward's* the word if the next stop plunges me in hell—"

And the girl buried her face in her hands, and was silent again. Let not the reader wonder at the mass of contradictions, heaped together in the character of this miserable wreck of a woman. One moment conversing in the slang of a brothel, like a thing lapped from her birth in pollution; the next, whispering forth her ravings in language indicative of the educated woman of her purer days; one instant glorying in her shame, the next recoiling in horror as she viewed the dark path which she had trodden, the darker path which she was yet to tread—these paradoxes are things of every day occurrence, only to be explained, when the mass of good and evil, found in every human heart, is divided into distinct parts, no more to mingle in one, no more to occasion an eternal contest in the self-warring heart of man.

"Well, well, Bessie—go to bed and sleep a little—that's a dear—" said the old lady, with a pleasing smile—"Opium isn't good for you, and you know it. A leetle nap 'ill do you good. Sleep a bit, and then you'll be right fresh for the wedding. Three o'clock you know—Come along, Dolph, mommy must go 'tend to some little things about the house—Come along, Dolph-*ee*—Sleep a leetle, Bessie, that's a dear!"

CHAPTER NINTH

THE BRIDE

A CHAPTER IN WHICH EVERY WOMAN MAY FIND SOME LEAVES OF HER OWN HEART, READ WITH THE EYES OF A HIGH AND HOLY LOVE

"Mary!"

Oh sweetest name of woman! name by which some of us may hail a wife, or a sister in heaven; name so soft, and rippling, and musical; name of the mother of Jesus, made holy by poetry and religion!—how foully were you profaned by the lips that whispered your sound of gentleness in the sleeper's ear!

"Mary!"

The fair girl stirred in her sleep, and her lips dropped gently apart as she whispered a single word—

"Lorraine!"

"The assumed name of Lorrimer—" exclaimed the woman, who stood by the bedside—"Gus has some taste, even in his vilest loves! But, with this girl—this child—good Heavens: how refined! He shrunk at the very idea of *her* voice whispering the name which had been shouted by his devil mates at a drinking bout! So he told the girl to call him—not Gusty, no, no, but something musical—*Lorraine!*"

And, stooping over the couch, the queenly woman, with her proud form arrayed in a dress of snow white silk, and her raven-black hair gathered in thick tresses along her neck, so full and round, applied her lips to the ear of the sleeper and whispered in a softened tone—

"Mary! Awake—it is your wedding night!"

The room was still as death. Not a sound save the faint breathing of the sleeper; all hushed and still. The light of the wax candle standing on the table in the centre of the Rose Chamber—as it was called—fell mild and softened over the hangings of faint crimson, with the effect of evening twilight.

The maiden—pure and without stain—lay sleeping on the small couch that occupied one corner of the closet. Her fair limbs were enshrouded in the light folds of a night-robe, and she lay in an attitude of perfect repose, one glowing cheek resting upon her uncovered arm, while over the other, waved the loosened curls of her glossy hair. The parting lips disclosed her teeth, white as ivory, while her youthful bosom came heaving up from the folds of her night-robe, like a billow that trembles for a moment in the moonlight, and then is suddenly lost to view. She lay there in all the ripening beauty of maidenhood, the light falling gently over her young limbs, their outlines marked by the easy folds of her robe, resembling in their roundness and richness of proportion, the swelling fulness of the rose-bud that needs but another beam of light, to open it into its perfect bloom.

The arching eyebrows, the closed lids, with the long lashes resting on the cheek, the parted lips, and the round chin, with its smiling dimple, all these were beautiful, but oh how fair and beautiful the maiden's dreams. Rosier than her cheeks, sweeter than her breath, lovelier than her kiss—lovely as her own stainless soul, on whose leaves was written but one motto of simple meaning—"*Love in life, in death, and for ever.*"

And in all her dreams she beheld but one form, heard the whisper of but one voice, shared the sympathies of but one heart! *He* was her dream, her life, her *God*—him had she trusted with her all, in earth or heaven, him did she love with the uncalculating abandonment of self, that marks the first passion of an innocent woman!

* And was there aught of *earth* in this love? Did the fever of sensual passion throb in the pulses of her virgin blood? Did she love Lorrimer because his eyes was bright, his form magnificent, his countenance full of healthy manliness? No, no, no! Shame on the fools of either sex, who read the first love of a stainless woman, with the eyes of Sense. She loved Lorrimer for a something which he did not possess, which vile worldlings of his class never will possess. For the magic with which her fancy had enshrouded his face and form, she loved him, for the wierd fascination which *her own soul* had flung around his very existence, for a dream of which *he* was the idol, for a waking trance in which *he* walked as her good Angel, for imagination, for fancy, for any thing but *sense*, she loved him.

It was her first love.

She knew not that this fluttering fascination, which bound her to his slightest look or tone—like the charmed bird to the lulling music which the snake is said to murmur, as he ensnares his prey—she knew not that this fluttering fascination, was but the blind admiration of the moth, as it floats in the light of the flame, which will at last consume it.

She knew not that in her own organization, were hidden the sympa-

* The reader who desires to understand thoroughly, the pure love of an innocent girl for a corrupt libertine, will not fail to peruse this passage.

thies of an animal as well as of an intellectual nature, that the blood in her veins only waited an opportunity to betray her, that in the very atmosphere of the holiest love of woman, crouched a sleeping fiend, who at the first whisperings of her Wronger, would arise with hot breath and blood shot eyes, to wreak enternal ruin on her, woman's-honor.

For this is the doctrine we deem it right to hold in regard to woman. Like man she is a combination of an animal, with an intellectual nature. Unlike man her animal nature is a *passive* thing, that must be roused ere it will develope itself in action. Let the intellectual nature of woman, be the only object of man's influence, and woman will love him most holily. But let him play with her animal nature as you would toy with the machinery of a watch, let him rouse the treacherous blood, let him fan the pulse into quick, feverish throbbings, let him warm the heart with convulsive beatings, and the woman becomes like himself, but a mere animal. *Sense* rises like a vapor, and utterly darkens *Soul.*

And shall we heap shame on woman, because man, neglecting her holiest nature, may devote all the energies which God has given him, to rouse her gross and earthy powers into action? On whose head is the shame, or whose the wrong? Oh, would man but learn the solemn truth—that no angel around God's throne is purer than Woman when her intellectual nature alone is stirred into development, that no devil crouching in the flames of hell is fouler than Woman, when her animal nature alone is roused into action—would man but learn and revere this fearful truth, would woman but treasure it in her inmost soul, then would never a shriek arise to heaven, heaping curses on the betrayer's head, then would never a wrong done to maiden virtue, give the suicide's grave its victim, then in truth, would woman walk the earth, the spirit of light that the holiest Lover ever deemed her!

And the maiden lay dreaming of her lover, while the form of the tall and stately woman, stood by the bedside, like her Evil Angel, as with a mingled smile and sneer, she bade the girl arise, for it was her wedding night. *Her wedding night!*

"Mary! Awake—it is your wedding night!"

Mary murmured in her sleep, and then opened her large blue eyes, and arose in the couch.

"Has—*he* come?" were the first words she murmured in her musical tones, that came low and softened to the listeners ear—"Has *he* come?"

"Not yet—not yet—my dear—" said long-haired Bess, assisting the young maiden to rise from the couch, with all imaginable tenderness of manner—" You see Mary love, it's half-past two o'clock and over, and of course, high time for you to dress. Throw back your night-gown my love, and let me arrange your hair. How soft and silky—it needs but little aid from my hands, to render each tress a perfect charm—"

"Is it not very strange Bessie—" said Mary opening her large blue eyes with a bewildered glance as she spoke.

"What is strange? I see nothing strange except the remarkable beauty of these curls—"

"That I should first meet him, in such a singular manner, that he should love me, that for his sake I should fly to his uncle's mansion and that you Bessie—my dear good friend—should consent from mere friendship to leave your home and bear me company. All this is very strange—how like the stories we read in a book! And his stern old uncle you say has relented?"

"Perfectly resigned to the match my dear. That's the way with all these relations—is not that curl perfect?—when they've made all the mischief they can, and find it amounts to nothing, at the last moment they roll up their eyes, and declare with a sigh—that they're *resigned* to the match. And his dear old grand-ma—She lives here you know? There that is right—your curls should fall in a shower over your snow-white neck—The dear old lady is in a perfect fever to see you! She helped me to get everything ready for the wedding—"

"Oh Bessie—Is it not most sad?" said Mary as her blue eyes shone with a glance of deep feeling—"To think that Albert and you should love one another, so fondly, and after all, that he should die, leaving you alone in this cheerless world! How terrible! *If* Lorraine should die —"

A deep shade of feeling passed over Mary's face, and her lip trembled. Bessie held her head down, for a moment, as her fair fingers, ran twining among the tresses of the Bride. Was it to conceal a tear, or a—smile?

"Alas! *He* is in his grave! Yet it is the *memory* of his love, that makes me take such a warm interest in your union with Lorraine. This plain fillet of silver, with its diamond star—how well it becomes your brow! You never yet found a woman, who knew what it was to love, that would not fight for two true-hearted lovers, against the world! Do you think Mary dear, that I could have sanctioned your flight to this house, if my very soul had not been interested in your happiness? Not I—not I. Now slip off your night-gown my dear—Have you seen the wedding dress?"

"It seems to me—" said Mary, whose thoughts dwelt solely on her love for Lorrimer—"That there is something deeply touching in a wedding that is held at this hour of the night! Every thing is calm and tranquil; the earth lies sleeping, while Heaven itself watches over the union of two hearts that are all in all to each other—"

The words look plain and simple, but the tone in which she spoke was one of the deepest feeling. Her very soul was in her words. Her blue eyes dilated with a sudden enthusiasm, and the color went and came along her glowing cheek, until it resembled a fair flower, one moment resting in the shade, the next bathing in the sunlight.

"Let me assist you to put on this wedding dress. Is it not beautiful? That boddice of white silk was Lorrimer's taste. To be sure I gave the dress-maker a few hints. Is it not perfect? How gently the folds of the skirt rest on your figure! It is a perfect fit, I do declare! Why Mary you are *too* beautiful! Well, well, handsome as he is, Lorrimer ought to be half crazy with vanity, when such a Bride is hanging on his arm!"

A few moments sufficed to array the maiden for the bridal.—

Mary stood erect on the floor, blush after blush coursing over her cheek, as she surveyed the folds of her gorgeous wedding dress.

It was in truth a dress most worthy of her face and form. From the shoulders to the waist her figure was enveloped in a boddice of snow-white satin, that gathered over her swelling bosom, with such gracefulness of shape that every beauty of her form,—the width of the shoulders, and the gradual falling off, of the outline of the waist,—was clearly perceptible.

Fitting closely around the bust, it gave to view her fair round neck, half-concealed by the drooping curls of glossy hair, and a glimpse of each shoulder, so delicate and white, swelling away into the fullness of the virgin bosom, that rose heaving above the border of lace. From the waist downward, in many a fold, but with perfect adaptation to her form, the gorgeous skirt of satin, fell sweeping to the floor, leaving one small and tiny foot, enclosed in a neat slipper, that clung to it as though it had grown there, exposed to the eye.

The softened light falling over the rose-hued hangings of the room, threw the figure of the maiden out from the dim back-ground, in gentle and effective prominence. Her brown tresses showering down over each cheek, and falling along her neck and shoulders, waved gently to and fro, and caught a glossy richness from the light. Her fair shoulders, her full bosom, her long but not too slender waist, the downward proportions of her figure, swelling with the full outlines of ripening maidenhood; all arrayed in the graceful dress of snow-white satin, stood out in the dim light, relieved most effectively by the rose-hued hangings, in the background.

As yet her arms, unhidden by sleeve or robe, gave their clear, transparent skin, their fullness of outline, their perfect loveliness of shape, all freely to the light.

"Is it not a gorgeous dress?" said long-haired Bess, as she gazed with unfeigned admiration upon the face and form of the beautiful maiden—"As gorgeous, dear Mary, as you are beautiful!"

"Oh it will be such a happy time!" cried Mary, in a tone that scarcely rose above a whisper, while her blue eyes flashed with a glance of deep emotion—"There will sit my father and there my mother, in the cheerful parlor on Christmas Eve! My father's grey hairs and my mother's kindly face, will be lighted up by the same glow of light. And their eyes will be heavy with tears—with weeping for me, Bessie, their 'lost child,' as they will call me. When behold! the door opens, Lorraine enters with me, his wife, yes, yes *his wife* by his side. We fling ourselves at the feet of our father and mother—for they will be *ours*, then! We crave their forgiveness! Lorraine calls me his wife—we beg their forgiveness and their blessing in the same breath! Oh it will be such a happy time! And my brother he will be there too—*he* will like Lorraine, for he has a noble heart! Don't you see the picture, Bessie? I see it as plainly as though it was this moment before me, and—my father—oh how he will weep when again he clasps his daughter in his arms!"

There she stood, her fair hands clasped trembling together, her eyes flashing in ecstacy, while her heart, throbbing and throbbing like some wild bird, endeavoring to burst the bars of its cage, sent her bosom heaving into view.

Bessie made no reply. True she attempted some common-place phrase, but the words died in her throat. She turned her head away, and—thank God, she was not *yet* fallen to the lowest deep of woman's degradation—a tear, big and scalding, came rolling down her cheek.

And while Mary stood with her eyes gazing on the vacant air, with the manner of one entranced, while Bess—poor and fallen woman!—turned away her face to hide the falling tear, the curtains that concealed the entrance to the Painted Chamber were suddenly thrust aside, and the figure of a man came stealing along with a noiseless footstep.

Gus Lorrimer, silent and unperceived, in all the splendor of his manly beauty, stood gazing upon the form of his victim, with a glance of deep and soul-felt admiration.

His tall form was shown to the utmost advantage, by a plain suit of black cloth. A dress coat of the most exquisite shape, black pantaloons that fitted neatly around his well-formed limbs, a vest of plain white Marseilles, gathering easily across the outlines of his massive chest, a snow-white shirt front, and a falling collar, confined by a simple black cravat; such were the brief details of his neat but effective costume. His manly face was all in a glow with health and excitement. Clustering curls of dark brown hair fell carelessly along his open brow. His clear, dark-hazel eye, gave forth a flashing glance, that failed to reveal anything but the frank and manly qualities of a generous heart. You did not read the villain, in his glance. The aquiline nose, the rounded chin, the curving lip, darkened by a graceful moustache, the arching eyebrows, which gave additional effect to the dark eyes; all formed the details of a countenance that ever struck the beholder with its beaming expression of health, soul, and manliness, combined.

And as Gus Lorrimer stood gazing in silent admiration upon his victim, few of his boon companions would have recognized, in his thoughtful countenance, the careless though handsome face of the reveller, who gave life and spirit to their drinking scenes.

The truth is, there were *two* Lorrimers in *one*. There was a careless, dashing, handsome fellow who could kill a basket of champagne with any body, drive the neatest 'turn out' in the way of horse flesh that the town ever saw, carry a 'frolic' so far that the watchman would feel bound to take it up and carry it a little farther—This was the magnificent Gus Lorrimer.

And then there was a tall, handsome man, with a thoughtful countenance, and a deep, dark hazel eye, who would sit down by the side of an innocent woman, and whisper in her ear, in a low-toned voice for hours together, with an earnestness of manner and an intensity of gaze, that failed in its effect, not once in a hundred times. Without any remarkable knowledge derived from education, this man knew every leaf of woman's many-leaved heart, and knew how to apply the revealings, which the fair book opened to his gaze. His gaze, in some cases, in itself was fascination; his low-toned voice, in too many instances, whispered its sentences of passion to ears, that heard it to their eternal sorrow. This man threw his whole soul, in his every passion. He plead with a woman, like a man under sentence of death pleading for his life. Is it a wonder that he was but rarely unsuccessful? This man, so deeply read in woman's heart, was the 'inner man' of the handsome fellow, with the dashing exterior. Assuming a name, never spoken to his ear, save in the soft whispers of one of his many victims, he styled himself Lorraine Lorrimer.

"Oh, Bessie, is not this Love—a strange mystery?" exclaimed Mary, as though communing with her own heart—"Before I loved, my soul was calm and quiet. I had no thought beyond my school-books—no deeper mystery than my embroidery-frame. *Now*—the very air is changed. The atmosphere in which I breathe is no longer the same. Wherever I move *his* face is before me. Whatever may be my thoughts, the thought of *him* is never absent for a moment. In my dreams I see him smile. When awake, his eyes, so deep, so burning in their gaze—even when he is absent—seem forever looking into mine. Oh, Bessie—tell me, tell me—is it given to man to adore his God? Is it not also given to woman to adore the *one* she loves? Woman's *religion* is her *love*—"

And as the beautiful enthusiast, *whose mind had been developed in utter seclusion from the world*, gave forth these revelations of her heart, in broken and abrupt sentences, Lorrimer drew a step nearer, and gazed upon her with a look in which passion rose predominant, even above admiration.

"Oh, Bessie, can it be that his love will ever grow cold? Will his voice ever lose its tones of gentleness, will his gaze ever cease to bind me to him, as it enchains me now?"

"Mary!" whispered a strange voice in a low and softened murmur.

She turned hastily round, she beheld the arms outspread to receive her, she saw the manly face of him she loved all a-glow with rapture, her fair blue eyes returned his gaze, "Lorraine," she murmured, in a faint whisper, and then her head rested upon his bosom, while her form trembled in his embrace.

"Oh, Lorraine—" she again murmured, as, with one fair hand resting upon each arm of her lover, she gazed upward in his face, while her blue eyes shone with all the feeling of her inmost soul. "Oh—Lorraine—will you love me ever?"

"Mary—" he answered, gazing down upon her blushing face, as he uttered her name in a prolonged whisper, that gave all its melody of sound to her ear—"Mary can you doubt me?"

And as there he stood gazing upon that youthful face, now flushed over with an expression of all-trusting love, as he drank in the glance of her large blue eyes, and felt her trembling form resting gently in his arms, the foul purpose of his heart was, for a moment, forgotten, for a moment his heart rose swelling within him, and the thought flashed over his soul, that for the fair creature, who hung fascinated on his every look, his life he could willingly lay down.

"Ha-ha—" muttered Bess, who stood regarding the pair with a glance of doubtful meaning—"I really believe that Lorrimer is quite as much in love, as the poor child! Good idea, that! A man, whose heart has been the highway of a thousand loves—a man like this, to fall in love with a mere baby-face! Mary, dear—" she continued aloud, too happy to break the reverie which enchained the seducer and his victim

—"Mary, dear, hadn't I better help you to put on your wedding robe?"

Lorrimer turned and looked at her with a sudden scowl of anger. In a moment his face resumed its smile—

"Mary—" he cried, laughingly—"let me be your costumer, for once. My hands must help you on with the wedding robe. Nay, nay, you must not deny me. Hand me the dress, Bessie—"

It was a splendid robe of the same satin, as the other part of her dress. Gathering tightly around her form, it was designed to remain open in front, while the skirt fell trailing along the floor. Falling aside from the bust, where outlines were so gracefully developed by the tight-fitting boddice of white satin, its opposite sides were connected by interlacing threads of silvercord, crossed and recrossed over the heaving bosom. Long and drooping sleeves, edged with silver lace, were designed to give bewitching glimpses of the maiden's full and rounded arms. In fine, the whole dress was in the style of some sixty years since, such as our grand-dames designated by the euphonious name of 'a gown and curricle.'

"How well the dress becomes you Mary!" exclaimed Lorrimer with a smile as he flung the robe over her shoulders—"How elegant the fall of that sleeve! Ha—ha—Mary, you *must* allow me to lace these silver cords in front. I'm afraid I would make but an awkward lady's-maid. What say you Bessie? Mary, your arms seem to love the light embrace of these drooping sleeves. You must forgive me, Mary, but I thought the style of the dress would please you, so I asked our good friend Bessie here to have it made. By my soul, you give additional beauty to the wedding dress. Is she not beautiful Bessie?"

"Most beautiful—" exclaimed Bess, as for the moment, her gaze of unfeigned admiration was fixed upon the Bride, arrayed in the full splendor of her wedding robes—"Most beautiful!"

"Mary, your hand—" whispered Lorrimer to the fair girl, who stood blushing at his side.

With a heaving bosom, and a flashing eye, Mary slowly reached forth her fair and delicate right hand. Lorrimer grasped the trembling fingers within his own, and winding his unoccupied arm around her waist he suffered her head, with all its shower of glossy tresses, to fall gently on his shoulders. A blush, warm and sudden, came over her face. He impressed one long and lingering kiss upon her lips. They returned the pressure, and clung to his lips as though they had grown there.

"Mary, my own sweet love—" he murmured in a low tone, that thrilled to her very heart—"Now I kiss you as the dearest thing to me in the wide world. Another moment, and from those same lips will I snatch the first kiss of my lovely bride! To the Wedding Room my love!"

Fair and blushing as the dawn, stainless as the new-fallen snow, loving as one of God's own cherubim, he led her gently from the place, motioning onward with his hand as again and again he whispered 'To the Wedding Room my love, to the Wedding Room!"

"To the Wedding Room—" echoed Bess who followed in her Bridesmaid robes—"To the Wedding Room—ha, ha, ha, say rather to h———ll!"

There was something most solemn, not to say thoughtful and melancholy, in the appearance of that lonely room. It was wide and spacious, and warmed by invisible means, with heated air. Huge panels of wainscotting covered the lofty walls, and even the ceiling was concealed by massive slabs of dark walnut. The floor was all one polished surface of mahogany, destitute of carpet or covering of any kind. A few high-backed mahogany chairs, standing along the walls, were the only furniture of the place. The entrance to the Rose Chamber, was concealed by a dark curtain, and in the western, and northern walls, were fashioned two massive doors, formed like the wainscotting, of dark and gloomy walnut.

In the centre of the glittering mahogany floor, arose a small table or altar, covered with a drooping cloth, white and stainless as the driven snow. Two massive wax candles, placed in candlesticks of silver, stood on the white cloth of the altar, imparting a dim and dusky light to the room. In that dim light the sombre panelling of the walls and the ceiling, the burnished floor of mahogany as dark as the walnut-wood that concealed the ceiling and the walls, looked heavy and gloomy, as though the place was a vault of death, instead of a cheerful Wedding Room.

As yet the place was silent and solitary. The light flickered dimly along the walls, and over the mahogany floor, which shone like a rippling lake in the moonlight. As you gazed upon the desolate appearance of that place, with the solitary wax lights burning like two watching souls, in the centre, you would have given the world, to have seen the room tenanted by living beings; in its present stillness and solitude, it looked so much like, one of those chambers in olden story, where the ghosts of a departed family, were wont to assemble once a year, in order to revive the memories of their lives on earth.

It might have been three o'clock, or even half an hour later, when the western door swung slowly open, and the Clergyman, who was to solemnize this marriage, came striding somewhat unsteadily along the floor. Clad in robes of flowing white—he had borrowed them from the

Theatre—with a Prayer Book in his hand, Petriken as he glanced uneasily around the room, did not look at all unlike a Minister of a particular class. His long, square, lugubrious face, slightly varied by red streaks around each eye, was tortured into an expression of the deepest solemnity. He took his position in silence, near the Altar.

Then came the relenting Uncle, striding heavily at the parson's heels—He was clad in a light blue coat with metal buttons, a buff vest, striped trowsers, and an enormous scarf, whose mingled colors of blue and gold, gathered closely around his short fat neck. His full-moon face—looking very much like the face of a relenting uncle, who is willing to bestow mercy upon a wild young dog of a nephew, to almost any extent—afforded a pleasing relief to his pear-shaped nose, which stood out in the light, like a piece of carved work from a crimson wall. Silently the relenting Uncle, took his position beside the venerable Clergyman.

Then dressed in solemn black, the respected Grand-ma of the Bridegroom, who was in *such* a fever to see the Bride, came stepping mincingly along the floor, glancing from side to side with an amiable look that ruffled the yellowish flesh of her colloped cheeks.

The 'imperial' on her chin had been softened down, and with the aid of a glossy dress of black silk, and a tower of Babel cap, she looked quite venerable. Had it not been for a certain twinkle in her eyes, you could have fallen in her arms and kissed her; she looked so much like one of those dear old souls, who make mischief in families and distribute tracts and cold victuals to the poor. The Grand-ma took her position on the left of the Clergyman.

And in this position, gathered around the Altar, they stood for some five minutes silently awaiting the appearance of the Bridegroom and the Bride.

CHAPTER TENTH

THE BRIDAL

"I say Mutchy, my boy—" said Petriken, in a tone that indicated some lingering effects of his late debauch—"How *do* I do it? Clever—hey? D'ye like this face? *Good*—is it? If my magazine fails, I think I'll enter the ministry for good. Why not start a Church of my own? When a man's fit for nothin' else, he can always find fools enough to build him a church, and glorify him into a saint—"

"Do you think I *do* the Uncle well?" whispered Mutchins, drawing his shirt collar up from the depths of his scarf, into which it had fallen —"Devilish lucky you gave me the hint in time. 'Been the d———l to pay if we'd a-disappointed Gus. What am I to say, Silly. 'Is *she* not *beautiful!*' in a sort of an *aside* tone, and then fall on her neck and kiss her? Eh, Silly?'

"That'ill be coming it a little *too* strong—" said Petriken, smoothing back his tow-colored hair—"You're merely to take her by the finger-tips, and start as if her beauty overcame you, then exclaim 'God bless you my love, God bless you—' as though your feelings were too strong for utterance—"

" 'God bless you, my love—' " echoed Mutchins—" 'God bless you'—that will do—hey, Silly? I feel quite an interest in her already. Now Aunty, my dear and kind-hearted old relative, what in the d———l are *you* to do?"

"Maybe I'll get up a convulsion or two—" said the dear old lady, as her colloped cheeks waggled heavily with a smile—her enemies would have called it a hideous grin—"Maybe I'll do a hysteric or so. Maybe I won't? Dear me, I'm in sich a fever to see my little pet of a grand-daughter! Ain't I?"

"Hist!" whispered Petriken—"There they are in the next room. I think I heard a kiss. Hush! Here they come—d———n it, I can't find the marriage ceremony—"

No sooner had the words passed his lips, than Lorrimer appeared in the small doorway opening into the Rose Chamber, and stepped softly along the floor of the Walnut Room. Mary in all her beauty hung on his arm. Her robe of satin wound round her limbs, and trailed along the floor as she walked. At her side came Long-haired Bess, glancing in the faces of the wedding guests with a meaning smile.

"Nephew, I forgive you. God bless you, my dear—I approve my nephew's choice—God bless you, my dear—"

And, as though his feelings overcame him, Mutchins veiled his face in a large red handkerchief; beneath whose capacious shelter he covertly supplied his mouth with a fresh morsel of tobacco.

"And is *this* 'my grandchild?' Is this the dear pet? How shall I love her? Shan't I, grandson? Oh my precious, how do you *do?*"

The clergyman saluted the bride with a low bow.

A deep blush came mantling over Mary's face as she received these words of affection and tokens of kindness from the Minister and the relatives of her husband, while a slight, yet meaning, expression of disgust flashed over Lorrimer's features, as he observed the manner in which his minions and panders performed their parts.

With a glance of fire, Lorrimer motioned the clergyman to proceed with the ceremony.

This was the manner of the marriage.

Hand joined in hand, Lorrimer and Mary stood before the altar. The bridesmaid stood near the trembling bride, whispering slight sentences of consolation in her ear. On the right hand of the clergyman, stood Mutchins, his red round face, subdued into an expression of the deepest solemnity; on the other side, the vile hag of Monk-hall, with folded arms, and grinning lips, calmly surveyed the face of the fair young bride.

In a deep-toned voice, Petriken began the sublime marriage ceremony of the Protestant Episcopal Church. There was no hope for the bride now. Trapped, decoyed, betrayed, she was about to be offered up, a terrible sacrifice, on that unhallowed altar. Her trembling tones, joined with the deep voice of Lorrimer in every response, and the marriage ceremony, drew near its completion. "There is no hope for her *now*"—muttered Bess, as her face shone with a glance of momentary compassion—"She is sold into the arms of shame!"

And at that moment, as the bride stood in all her beauty before the altar, her eyes downcast, her long hair showering down over her shoulders, her face warming with blush after blush, while her voice in low tones murmured each trembling response of the fatal ceremony, at the very moment when Lorrimer gazing upon her face with a look of the deepest satisfaction, fancied the fulfilment of the maiden's dishonour, there shrieked from the next chamber, a yell of such superhuman agony and horror, that the wedding guests were frozen with a sudden awe, and transfixed like figures of marble to the floor.

The book fell from Petriken's trembling hands; Mutchins turned pale, and the old hag started backward with sudden horror, while Bess stood as though stricken with the touch of death. Mary, poor Mary, grew white as the grave-cloth, in the face; her hand dropped stiffly to her side, and she felt her heart grow icy within her bosom.

Lorrimer alone, fearless and undaunted, turned in the direction from whence that fearful yell had shrieked, and as he turned he started back with evident surprise, mingled with some feelings of horror and alarm.

There, striding along the floor, came the figure of a young man, whose footsteps trembled as he walked, whose face was livid as the face of a corpse, whose long black hair waved wild and tangled, back from his pale forehead. His eye—Great God!—it shone as with a gleam from the flames of hell.

He moved his trembling lips, as he came striding on—for a moment the word, he essayed to speak, stuck in his throat.

At last with a wild movement of his arms, he shouted in a voice whose tones of horror, mingled with heart-rendering pathos, no man would like to hear twice in a life time, he shouted a single word—

"Mary!"

The bride turned slowly round. Her face was pale as death, and her blue eyes grew glassy as she turned. She beheld the form of the intruder. One glance was enough.

"My Brother!" she shrieked, and started forward as though about to spring in the strangers arms; but suddenly recoiling she fell heavily upon the breast of Lorrimer.

There was a moment of silence—all was hushed as the grave.

The stranger stood silent and motionless, regarding the awe-stricken bridal party, with one settled and burning gaze. One and all, they shrank back as if blasted by his look. Even Lorrimer turned his head aside and held his breath, for very awe.

The stranger advanced another step, and stood gazing in Lorrimer's face.

"*My Sister!*" he cried in a husky voice, and then as if all further words died in his throat, his face was convulsed by a spasmodic movement, and he shook his clenched hand madly in the seducer's face.

"Your name—" cried Lorrimer, as he laid the fainting form of the Bride in the arms of Long-haired Bess—"Your name is Byrnewood. This lady is named Mary Arlington. There is some mistake here. The lady is no sister of yours—"

"My name—" said the other, with a ghastly smile—"Ask this pale-faced craven what is my name! He introduced me to you, this night by my full name. You at once forgot, all but my first name. My name, sir, is *Byrnewood Arlington*. A name, sir, you will have cause to remember in this world and—devil that you are!—in the next if you harm the slightest hair on the head of this innocent girl—"

Lorrimer started back aghast. The full horror of his mistake rushed upon him. And in that moment, while the fainting girl lay insensible in Bessie's arms; while Petriken, and Mutchins, and the haggard old Abbess of the den, stood stricken dumb with astonishment, quailing beneath the glance of the stranger; a long and bony arm was thrust from behind the back of Byrnewood Arlington, the grim face Devil-Bug shone for a moment in the light, and then a massive hand with talon-fingers, fell like a weight upon the wick of each candle, and the room was wrapt in midnight blackness.

Then there was a trampling of feet to and fro, a gleam of light flashed for a moment, through the passage, opening into the Rose Chamber, and then all was dark again.

"They are bearing my sister away!" was the thought that flashed over the mind of the Brother, as he rushed toward the passage of the Rose Chamber—"I will rescue her from their grasp at the peril of my life!"

He rushed along, in the darkness, toward the curtain that concealed the entrance into the Rose Chamber. He attempted to pass beyond the curtain, but he was received in the embrace of two muscular arms, that raised him from his feet as though he had been a mere child, and then dashed him to the floor, with the impulse of a giant's strength.

"Ha-ha-ha!—" laughed a hoarse voice—"You don't pass here, Mister. Not while 'Bijah's about! No you don't, my feller—ha, ha, ha!"

"A light, Devil-Bug—" exclaimed a voice, that sounded from the centre of the darkened room.

In a moment a light, grasped in the talon-fingers of the Doorkeeper of Monk-Hall, flashed around the place. Silent and alone Gus Lorrimer, stood in the centre of the room, his arms folded across his breast, while the dark frown on his brow was the only outward manifestation of the violence of the struggle that had convulsed his very soul, during that solitary moment of utter darkness. Calling all the resources of his mind to his aid, he had resolved upon his course of action.

"*It is a fearful remedy, but a sure one*—" he muttered as he again faced Byrnewood, who had just risen from the floor, where he had been thrown by Mr. Abijah K. Jones—"Begone Devil-Bug—" he continued aloud—"But wait without and see that Glow-worm and Musquito are at hand," He added in a meaning whisper. "Now Sir, I have a word to say to *you*—" And as he spoke he confronted the Brother of the girl, whose ruin he had contrived with the ingenuity of an accomplished libertine, mingled with all the craft of an incarnate fiend.

Aching in every limb from his recent fall, Byrnewood stood pale and silent, regarding the libertine with a settled gaze. In the effort to command his feelings, he pressed his teeth against his lower lip, until a thin line of blood trickled down to his chin.

"You will allow that this, is a most peculiar case—" he exclaimed with a calm gaze, as he confronted Byrnewood—"One in fact, that demands some painful thought. Will you favor me with ten minutes private conversation?"

"You are very polite—" exclaimed Byrnewood with a withering sneer—"Here is a man, who commits a wrong for which h———ll itself has no name, and then—instead of shrinking from the sight of the man he has injured, beyond the power of words to tell—he cooly demands ten minutes private conversation!"

"It is your interest to grant my request—" replied Lorrimer, with a manner as collected as though he had merely said 'Pass the bottle, Byrnewood!'

"I presume I must submit—" replied Byrnewood—"But after the ten minutes are past—remember—that there is not a fiend in hell whom I would not sooner hug to my bosom, than grant one moment's conversation to—a—a—man—ha, ha—a *man* like you. My sister's honor may be in your power. But remember—that as surely as you wrong her, so surely you will pay for that wrong, with your life—"

"You then, grant me ten minutes conversation? You give me your word that during this period, you will keep your seat, and listen patiently to all, that I may have to say? You nod assent. Follow me, then. A footstep or so this way, will lead us to a pleasant room, the last of this range, where we can talk the matter over—"

He flung open the western door of the Walnut room, and led the way along a narrow entry, up a stairway with some five steps, and in a moment stood before a small doorway, closing the passage at the head of the stairs. At every footstep of the way, he held the light extended at arms length, and regarded Byrnewood with the cautious glance of a man who is not certain at what moment, a concealed enemy may strike him in the back.

"My Library Sir—" exclaimed Lorrimer as pushing open the door, he entered a small oblong room, some twenty-feet in length and about half that extent in width. "A quiet little place where I sometimes amuse myself with a book. There is a chair Sir—please be seated—"

Seating himself upon a small stool, that stood near the wall of the room, furthest from the door, Byrnewood with a single glance, took in all the details of the place, It was a small unpretending room, oblong in form, with rows of shelves along its longest walls, facing each other, supplied with books of all classes, and of every description, from the pondrous history to the trashy novel. The other walls at either end, were concealed by plain and neat paper, of a modern pattern, which by no means harmonized with the ancient style of the carpet, whose half-faded colors glowed dimly in the light. Along the wall of the chamber opposite Byrnewood, extended an old-fashioned sofa, wide and roomy as a small sleeping couch; and from the centre of the place, arose a massive table, fashioned like a chest, with substantial sides of carved oak, supplying the place of legs. To all appearance it was fixed and jointed, into the floor of the room.

Altogether the entire room, as its details were dimly revealed by the beams of the flickering lamp, wore a cheerless and desolate look, increased by the absence of windows from the walls, and the ancient and worn-out appearance which characterized the stool, the sofa and the table; the only furniture of the place. There was no visible hearth, and no sign of fire, while the air cold and chilling had a musty and unwholesome taint, as though the room had not been visited or opened for years.

Placing the lamp on the solitary table, Lorrimer flung himself carelessly on the sofa, and motioned Byrnewood, to draw his seat nearer to the light. As Byrnewood seated himself beside the chest-like table, with his cheek resting on his hand, the full details of his countenance, so pale, so colorless, so corpse-like, were disclosed to the keen gaze of Lorrimer. The face of the Brother, was perfectly calm, although the large black eyes, dilated with a glance that revealed the Soul, turning madly on itself and gnawing its own life, in very madness of thought, while from the lips tightly compressed, there still trickled down, the same thin line of blood, rendered even more crimson and distinct, by the extreme pallor of the countenance.

"You will at least admit, that *I have won the wager*—" said Lorrimer, in a meaning tone, as he fixed his gaze upon the death-like countenance of Byrnewood Arlington.

Byrnewood started, raised his hands suddenly, as if about to grasp the libertine by the throat, and then folding his arms tightly over his chest, he exclaimed in a voice marked by unatural calmness—

"For ten minutes, sir, I have promised to listen to all—*all* you may have to say. Go on, sir. But do not, I beseech you, tempt me too far—"

"Exactly half-past three by my repeater—" cooly replied Lorrimer, looking at his watch—"At twenty minutes of four, our conversations ends. Very good. Now, sir, listen to my proposition. Give me your word of honor, and your oath, that when you leave this house, you will preserve the most positive secrecy with regard to—to—*everything*— you may have witnessed within its walls; promise me this, under your word of honor and your solemn oath, and I will give you my word of honor, my oath, that, in one hour from daybreak, your sister shall be taken to her home, pure and stainless, as when first she left her father's threshold. Do you agree to this?"

"Do you see this hand?" answered Byrnewood, with a nervous tremour of his lips, that imparted an almost savage sneer to his countenance—"Do you see this flame? Sooner than agree to leave these walls, without—my—my—without Mary, pure and stainless, mark ye, I would hold this good right hand in the blaze of this lamp, until the flesh fell blackened and festering from the very bone. Are you answered?"

"Excuse me, sir—I was not speaking of any *anatomical experiments;* however interesting such little efforts in the surgical line, may be to you. I wished to make a compromise—"

"*A compromise!*" echoed Byrnewood.

"Yes, a compromise. That melodramatic sneer becomes you well, but it would suit the pantomimist at the Walnut street Theatre much better. What have I done with the girl, that you, or any other young blood about town, would *not do*, under similar circumstances. Who was it, that entered so heartily into the joke of the *sham* marriage, when it was named in the Oyster Cellar? Who was it called the astrologer a knave—a fortune teller—a catch-penny cheat, when he—simple man!—advised me to give up the girl? I perceive, sir, you are touched. I am glad to observe, that you appreciate the graphic truth of my remarks. You will not sneer at the word '*compromise*' again, will you?"

"Oh, Mary! oh, Mary!"—whispered Byrnewood, drawing his arms yet more closely over his breast, as though in the effort to command his agitation—"Mary! Was I placing your honor in the dice-box, when I made the wager with yonder—*man*? Was it your ruin the astrologer foretold, when he urged this *devil*—to turn back in his career? Was it my *voice* that cheered *him* onward in his work of infamy? Oh Mary, was it for *this*, for *this*, that I loved you as brother never loved sister? Was it for this, that I wound you close to my inmost heart, since first I could think or feel? Was it for *this*, that in the holiest of all my memories, all my hopes, your name was enshrined? Was it for this, that I pictured, again and again, every hour in the day, every moment of the night, the unclouded prospects of your future life? Oh Mary, oh Mary, I may be wrong, I may be vile, I may be sunken as low as the *man* before me, yet my love for you, has been without spot, and without limit! And now Mary—oh *now*—"

He paused. There was a husky sound in his throat, and the blood trickled faster from his tortured lip.

Lorrimer looked at him silently for a moment, and then, taking a small pen-knife from his pocket, began to pare his nails, with a quiet and absent air, as though he did'nt exactly know what to do with himself. He wore the careless and easy look of a gentleman, who having just dined, is wondering where in the deuce he shall spend the afternoon.

"I say, Byrnie my boy—" he cried suddenly, with his eyes fixed on the operations of the knife—"Devilish odd, ain't it? That little affair of yours, with *Annie*? Wonder if she has any *brother*? Keen cut *that*—"

Had Mr. Lorrimer intended the allusion, about the keenness of the 'cut,' for Byrnewood instead of his nail-paring knife, the remark would, perhaps, have been equally applicable. Byrnewood shivered at the name of Annie, as though an ague-fit had passed suddenly over him. The 'cut' was rather keen, and somewhat deep. This careless kind of intellectual surgery, sometimes makes ghastly wounds in the soul, which it so pleasantly dissects.

"May I ask what will be your course, in case you leave this place, without the lady? You are silent. I suppose there will be a suit instituted for '*abduction*,' and a thousand legal et ceteras? This place will be ransacked for the girl, and your humble servant will be threatened with the Penitentiary? A pleasant prospect, truly. Why do you look so earnestly at that hand?"

"You have your pleasant prospects—I have mine—" exclaimed Byrnewood with a convulsive smile—"You see that right hand, do you? I was just thinking, how long it might be, ere that hand would be reddened with your heart's blood—"

"Poh! poh! Such talk is d———d boyish. D'ye agree to my proposition? Yes or no?"

"You have had my answer—"

"In case I surrender the girl to you, will you then promise unbroken secrecy, with regard to the events of this night?"

"I will make no terms whatever with a *scoundrel* and a *coward!*" hissed Byrnewood, between his clenched teeth.

"Pshaw! It is high time this mask should be cast aside—" exclaimed Lorrimer, as his eye flashed with an expression of triumph, mingled with anger and scorn—"And do you suppose that on any condition, or for any consideration, I would leave this fair prize slip from my grasp? Why, innocent that you are, you might have piled oath on oath, until your very breath grew husky in the effort, and still—still—despite of all your oaths, the girl would remain mine!

"Know me as I am! Not the mere man-about-town, not the wine-drinking companion, not the fashionable addle-head you think me, but the *Man of Pleasure!* You will please observe, how much lies concealed in that title. You have talents—these talents have been from childhood, devoted to books, or mercantile pursuits. I have some talent—I flatter myself—and that talent, aided and strengthened in all its efforts, by wealth, from very boyhood, has been devoted to Pleasure, which, in plain English, means—Woman.

"Woman—the means of securing her affection, of compassing her ruin, of enjoying her beauty, has been my book, my study, my science, nay my *profession* from boyhood. And am I, to be foiled in one of the most intricate of all my adventures, by such a child—a mere boy like you? Are you to frighten me, to scare me back in the path I have chosen; to wrest this flower, to obtain which I have perilled so much, are *you* to wrest this flower from *my* grasp? You are *so* strong, *so* mighty, you talk of reddening your hand in my heart's blood—and all such silly vaporing, that would be hissed by the pit-boy's, if they but heard it, spouted forth by a fifth-rate hero of the green-room—and yet with all this—*you are my prisoner*—"

"*Your prisoner?*" echoed Byrnewood slowly rising to his feet.

"Keep cool Sir—" cried Lorrimer with a glance of scorn—"Two minutes of the ten, yet remain. I have your word of honor, you will remember. Yes—*my prisoner!* Why do you suppose for a moment, that I would let you go forth from this house, when you have it in your power to raise the whole city on my head? You know that I have placed myself under the ban of the laws by this adventure. You know that the Penitentiary would open its doors to enclose me, in case I was to be tried for this affair. You know that popular indignation, poverty and disgrace, stare me in the very eyes, the moment this adventure is published to the world, and yet—ha, ha, ha—you still think me, the egregious ass, to open the doors of Monk-Hall to you, and pleasantly bid you go forth, and ruin me forever! Sir, you are my prisoner."

"Ha—ha—ha! I will be even with you—" laughed Byrnewood—"You may murder me, in the act but I still have the power to arouse the neighbourhood. I can shriek for help. I can yell out the cry of Murder, from this foul den, until your doors are flung open by the police, and the secrets of your rookery laid bare to the public gaze—"

"Scream, yell, cry out, until your throat cracks! Who will hear you? Do you know how many feet, you are standing, above the level of the earth? Do you know the thickness of these walls? Do you know that you stand in the Tower-Room of Monk-Hall? Try your voice—by all means—I should like to hear you cry Murder or Fire, or even hurra for some political candidate, if the humor takes you—"

Byrnewood sank slowly in his seat, and rested his cheek upon his hand. His face was even paler than before—the consciousness that he was in the power of this libertine, for life or death, or any act of outrage, came stealing round his heart, like the probings of a surgeon's knife.

"Go on Sir—" he muttered biting his nether lip, until the blood once more came trickling down to his chin—"The hour is yours. *Mine will come*—"

"At my bidding; not a moment sooner—" laughed Lorrimer rising his feet—"Why man, death surrounds you in a thousand forms, and you know it not. You may walk on Death, you may breathe it, you may drink it, you may draw it to you with a fingers-touch, and yet be as unconscious of its presence, as a blind man is of a shadow in the night—"

Byrnewood slowly rose from his seat. He clasped his hands nervously together, and his lips muttered an incoherent sound as he endeavoured to speak.

"Do what you will with me—" he cried, in a husky voice—"But oh, for the sake of God, *do not wrong my sister!*"

"She is in *my* power!" whispered Lorrimer, with a smile, as he gazed upon the agitated countenance of the brother—"She is in *my* power!"

"Then by the eternal God, you are in mine!" shrieked Byrnewood, as with one wild bound, he sprung at the tall form of Lorrimer, and fixed both hands around his throat, with a grasp like that of the tigress when she fights for her young—"You are in my power! You cannot unloose my grasp! Ha—ha—you grow black in the face! Struggle!—struggle!—With all your strength you cannot tear my hands from your throat—you shall die like a felon, by the eternal God!"

Lorrimer was taken by complete surprise. The wild bound of Byrnewood had been so sudden, the grasp of his hands, was so much like the terrific clutch with which the drowning man makes a last struggle for life, that for a single moment, the handsome Gus Lorrimer reeled to and fro like a drunken man, while his manly features darkened over with a hue of livid blackness, as ghastly as it was instantaneous. The struggle lasted but a single moment. With the convulsive grasp tightening around his throat, Lorrimer sank suddenly on one knee, dragging his antagonist with him, and as he sank, extending his arm, with an effort as desperate as that which fixed the clinched fingers around his throat, he struck Byrnewood a violent blow with his fist, directly behind the ear. Byrnewood sank senseless to the floor, his fingers unclosing their grasp of Lorrimer's throat, as slowly and stiffly as though they were seized with a sudden cramp.

"Pretty devilish and d———d hasty!" muttered Lorrimer, arranging his cravat and vest—"Left the marks of his fingers on my throat, I'll be bound! Hallo—Musquito! Hallo, Glow-worm—here's work for you!"

The door of the room swung suddenly open, and the herculean negroes stood in the doorway, their sable faces, agitated by the same hideous grin, while the sleeves of the red flannel shirts, which formed their common costume, rolled up to the shoulders disclosed the iron-sinews of their jet-black arms.

"Mark this man, I say—"

"Yes—Massa—I doo-es—" chuckled Musquito, as his loathsome lips, inclining suddenly downward toward the jaw, on either side of his face, were convulsed by a brutal grin—"Dis nigger nebber mark a man yet, but dat *somefin'* cum ob it—"

"Massa Gusty no want de critter to go out ob dis 'ere door?" exclaimed Glow-worm, as the long rows of his teeth, bristling from his thick lips, shone in the light like the fangs of some strange beast—" 'Spose he go out ob dat door? 'Spose de nigger no mash him head, *bad?* Ain't Glow-worm got fist? Hah-hah! 'Sketo did you ebber see dis chile (child) knock an ox down? Hah-hah!"

"You are to watch outside the door all night—" exclaimed Lorrimer, as he stood upon the threshold—"Let him not leave the room on the peril of your lives. D'ye mark me, fellows?"

And as he spoke, motioning the negroes from the room, he closed the door and disappeared.

He had not gone a moment when Byrnewood, recovering from the stunning effect of the blow which had saved Lorrimer's life, slowly staggered to his feet, and gazing around with a bewildered glance.

" *'On Christmas Eve—'* " he murmured wildly, as though repeating words whispered to his ear in a dream—" *'On Christmas Eve, at the hour of sundown, one of ye will die by the other's hand—the winding sheet is woven and the coffin made!'* "

CHAPTER ELEVENTH

DEVIL-BUG

"It don't skeer me, I tell ye! For six long years, day and night, it has laid by my side, with its jaw broke and its tongue stickin' out, and yet I ain't a bit skeered! There it is now—on my left side, ye mind—in the light of the fire. Ain't it an ugly corpse? Hey? A reel nasty christian, I tell ye! Jist look at the knees, drawed up to the chin, jist look at the eyes, hanging out on the cheeks, jist look at the jaw all smashed and broke—look at the big, black tongue, stickin' from between the teeth —say it ain't an ugly corpse, will ye?

"Sometimes I can hear him groan—*only* sometimes! I've always noticed when anything bad is a-goin' to come across me, that critter groans and groans! Jist as I struck him down, he lays afore me now.

Whiz—wh-i-z he came down the hatchway—three stories, every bit of it! Curse it, why hadn't I the last trap-door open? He fell on the floor, pretty much mashed up, but—but he wasn't dead—

"He riz on his feet. Just as he lays on the floor—in his shirt sleeves, with his jaw broke and his tongue out—he riz on his feet. Didn't he groan? I put him down, I tell ye! Down—down! Ha! What was a sledge hammer to this fist, in that pertikler minnit? Crack, crack went the spring of the last trap-door—and the body fell—the devil knows where—I don't. I put it out o' my sight, and yet it came back to me, and crouched down at my side, the next minnit. It's been there ever since. If I sleep, or if I'm wide awake, it's there—*there*—always on my left side, where I hain't got no eye to see it, and yet I do—I *do* see it. What a cussed fool I was arter all! To kill him, and he not got a cent in his pockets! Bah! Whenever I think of it I grow feverish. And there he is now—With his d———d ugly jaw. How he lolls his tongue out—and his eyes! *Ugh!* But I ain't a bit skeered. No. Not me. I can bear wuss things than that 'are—"

The light from the blazing coal-fire, streamed around the Door-keeper's den. Seated close by the grate, in a crouching attitude, his feet drawn together, his big hands grasping each knee with a convulsive clutch, his head lowered on his breast, and his face, warmed to a crimson red by the glare of the flame, moistened with thick drops of perspiration; Devil-Bug turned the orbless eye-socket to the floor at his left side, as though it was gifted with full powers of sight, while his solitary eye, grew larger and more burning in its fixed gaze, until at last, it seemed to stand out, from his overhanging brow, like a separate flame.

The agitation of the man was at once singular and fearful. Oozing from his swarthy brow, the thick drops of sweat fell trickling over his hideous face, moistening his matted hair, until it hung, damp and heavy over his eyebrows. The lips of his wide mouth receding to his flat nose and pointed chin, disclosed the long rows of bristling teeth, fixed as closely together, as though the man, had been suddenly seized with lock-jaw. His face was all one loathsome grimace, as with his blazing eye, fixed upon the fire, he seemed gazing upon the floor at his left, with the shrunken and eyeless socket, of the other side of his face.

This creature, who sate crouching in the light of the fire, muttering words of strange meaning to himself, presented a fearful study for the Christian and Philanthropist. His Soul was like his body, a mass of hideous and distorted energy.

Born in a brothel, the offspring of foulest sin and pollution, he had grown from very childhood, in full and continual sight of scenes of vice, wretchedness and squalor.

From his very birth, he had breathed an atmosphere of infamy.

To him, there was no such thing as *good* in the world.

His world—his place of birth, his home in infancy, childhood and manhood, his only theatre of action—had been the common house of ill-fame. No mother had ever spoken words of kindness to him; no father had ever held him in his arms. Sister, brother, friends; he had none of these. He had come into the world without a name; his present one, being the standing designation of the successive Doorkeepers of Monk-hall, which he in vain endeavoured to assume, leaving the slang title bestowed on him in childhood, to die in forgetfulness.

Abijah K. Jones he might call himself, but he was Devil-Bug still.

His loathsome look, his distorted form, and hideous soul, all seemed to crowd on his memory, at the same moment, when the word 'Devil-Bug'—rang on his ear. That word uttered, and he stood apart from the human race; that word spoken, and he seemed to feel, that he was something distinct from the mass of men, a wild beast, a snake, a reptile, or a devil incarnate—any thing but a—man.

The same instinctive pleasure that other men, may feel in acts of benevolence, of compassion or love, warmed the breast of Devil-Bug, when enjoyed in any deed, marked by especial *cruelty*. This word will scarcely express the instinctive impulse of his soul, He loved not so much to kill, as to observe the blood of his victim, fall drop by drop, as to note the convulsive look of death, as to hear the last throttling rattle in the throat of the dying.

For years and years, the instinctive impulse, had worked in his own bosom, without vent. The murder which had dyed his hands, with human blood for the first time, some six years ago, opened wide to his soul, the pathway of crime, which it was his doom and his delight to tread. Ever since the night of the Murder, his victim, hideous and repulsive, had lain beside him, crushed and mangled, as he fell through the death-trap. The corpse was never absent from his fancy; which in this instance had assumed the place of eyesight. Did he sit—it was at his left side. Did he walk—crushed and mangled as it was, it glided with him. Did he sleep—it still was at his side, ever present with him, always staring him in the face, with all its loathsome details of horror and bloodshed.

Since the night of the Murder, a longing desire had grown up, within this creature, to lay another corpse beside his solitary victim. Were there he thought, two corpses, ever at his side, the terrible details of the mangled form and crushed countenance of the first, would lose half their horror, all their distinctness. He longed to surround himself with the Phantoms of new victims. In the *number* of his crimes, he even anticipated pleasure.

It was this man, this deplorable moral monstrosity, who knew no God, who feared no devil, whose existence was one instinctive impulse of cruelty and bloodshed, it was this Outlaw of heaven and earth and hell, who held the life of Byrnewood Arlington in his grasp.

"It's near about mornin' and that ere boy ought to have somethin' to eat. A leetle to drink—per'aps? Now *sup*-pose, I should take him up, a biled chicken and a bottle o' wine. He sits down by the table o' course to eat—I fix his plate on a pertikler side. As he planks down into the cheer, his foot touches a spring. What is the consekence? He git's a fall and hurts hisself. *Sup*-pose he drinks the wine? Three stories down the hatchway—reether an ugly tumble. He git's crazy, and wont know nothin' for days. Very pecooliar wine—got it from the Doctor who used to come here—dint kill a man, only makes him mad-like. The Man with th' Poker is n't nothin' to this stuff—Hallo! Who's there?"

"Only me, Bijah—" cried a woman's voice, and the queenly form of Long Haired Bess with a dark shawl thrown over her bridesmaid's dress advanced toward the light—"I've just left Lorrimer. He's with the girl you know? He sent me down here, to tell you to keep close watch on that young fellow—"

"Jist as if I couldn't do it mesself—" grunted Abijah in his grindstone voice—"Always a-orderin' a feller about? That's his way. Spose you cant make yourself useful? Kin you? Then take some biled chicken —and a bottle o' wine up to the younk chap. Guess he's most starved —"

"Shall I get the chicken and the wine?" asked Bess gazing steadily in Abijah's face.

"What the thunder you look in my face that way fur? No you shant git 'em. Git 'em mesself. Wait here till I come back. Do'nt let any one in without the pass word—'What hour of the night—' and the answer 'Dinner time—' you know?"

And as Devil-Bug strode heavily from the den, and was heard going down into the cellars of the mansion, Bess stood silent and erect before the fire, her face, shadowed by an expression of painful thought, while her dark eyes, shot a wild glance from beneath her arching brows, suddenly compressed in a frown.

"Some mischief at work I suppose—" she whispered in a hissing voice—"I've sold myself to shame, but not to Murder!"

A low knock resounded from the front door.

Suddenly undrawing the bolt and flinging the chain aside, Bess gazed through a crevice of the opened door, upon the new-comers, who stood beyond the out-side door of green blinds.

"Who's there?" she said in a low voice.

"Ha—ha—" laughed one of the strangers—"It's bonny Bess. 'What hour of the night' is it, my dear?"

" 'Dinner time', you fool—" replied the young lady opening the out-side door—"Come in Luke! Ha! There is a stranger with you! *Your friend* Luke?"

"Aye, aye, Bessie my love,—" answered Luke as he entered the den, with the stranger at his side—"Did ye hear the Devil-Bug say, whether there was fire in my room? all right—hey? And *cards* you know Bess—*cards*? This gentleman and I, want to amuse ourselves with a little game. Bye-the-bye—where's Fitz-Cowles? I should like him to join us. Seen him to night my dear?"

"Up stairs you know Luke—" answered Bess with a meaning smile—" '*Veiled figure*,' Luke you know? That's a game above your fancy I should suppose?"

And as she said this with an expressive glance of her dark eye, Bess observed that the stranger who accompanied Luke, was a very tall, stout man, wrapped up in a thick overcoat, whose upraised collar, concealed his face to the very eyes. His eyes were visible for a single moment, however as half-hidden by the shadow of Luke's figure, the stranger strode swiftly across the floor of the den. Bess started, with a feeling of terror, akin to the awe one experiences in the presence of a madman, as those eyes, so calm and yet so burning in their fixed gaze, flashed for a moment in the red light.

"Luke, I am—ready—" said the Stranger in a smothered voice—"To *the room* Luke—to *the Room!*"

Without a word Luke led the way from the den, and in a moment Bess heard the half-hushed sound of their footsteps, as they ascended the staircase of the mansion.

"That's a strange eye for a man who's only *a-goin'* to play cards—" muttered Bess as she stood by the fireplace—"Now it's more like the eye of a man, who's been playin' all night, and lost his very soul in a game with the D———l! Lord!—But that's a wicked eye for a dark night!"

"Here's the biled chicken and the wine—" grated the harsh voice of Devil-Bug, who approached the fire, with a large 'waiter' in his arms—"Take it up to the feller, Bess. He's hungry praps? And d'ye mind gal—

set his plate on the side of the table, furthest from the door?"

"Any particular reason for that, 'Bijah?"

"Cuss it gal, cant you do it, without axeing questions? It's only a whim o' mine. That bottle is worth its weight in red goold. Don't taste such Madeery every day I tell you. Poor fellow—guess he's a-most starved—"

"Well, well, I'll take him the chicken and the wine—" exclaimed Bess pleasantly as she took possession of the 'waiter' with its cold chicken and luscious wine—"Hang it though, when I come to think o' it, why couldn't you have taken it up yourself? 'Bijah you're growin' lazy—"

"Mind gal—" grunted Devil-Bug as the girl disappeared through the door—"Set his plate on the side of the table furthest from the door. D'ye hear? It's a whim o' mine—furthest from the door—d'ye hear"

" 'Furthest from the door'—" echoed Bess, and in a moment her footsteps resounded with a low pattering noise along the massive staircase.

"The *Spring*—and the *bottle*—" muttered Devil-Bug as he resumed his seat beside the fire—"It seems to me, I should like to creep up stairs, and listen at his door to see how them things work. The niggers is there: but no matter. May be he'll howl—or groan—or do all sorts of ravin's? Gusty did not exactly tell me to do all this—but I guess he'll grin as wide as any body, *when the thing is done*. It seems to me I should like, to see how them things works. It'ud be nice to listen a bit at his door. Wonder if that gal suspicions anything?"

He rubbed his hands earnestly together, as a man is want to do, under the influence of some pleasing idea, and his solitary eye, dilated and sparkled, with a glance of the most remarkable satisfaction. A slight chuckle shook his distorted frame, and his lips performed a succession of vivid spasms which an ignorant observer might have confounded under the general name of laughter.

"Poor feller—guess he's cold without a fire—" said complacent Devil-Bug as he rubbed his hands cheerfully together—"I might build him a little fire. I might—I might—ha! ha! ha!" he arose slowly to his feet, and laughed so loud, that the echoes of his voice resounded from the den, along the hall, and up the staircase of the mansion—"I might try *that*"—he cried with a hideous glow of exultation—"Wonder *how that* would *work?*"

Opening the door of a closet on one side of the fire-place, he drew from its depths, a small furnace of iron; such as housewives use for domestic purposes. He placed the furnace in the full light of the fire, surveyed it closely, rubbed his hands pleasantly together yet once more, while a deep chuckle shook his form, from head to foot. His face wore an expression of extreme good humor—the visage of a drunken loafer, as he flings a penny to a ragged sweep, was nothing in comparison.

"A leetle kindlin' wood—" he muttered, drawing to the fire an old sack that had lain concealed in the darkness—"And a leetle charcoal! Makes a *rougeing* hot fire! Fat pine and charcoal—ha, ha, ha! Rather guess the poor fellow's cold! Now for a light—Cuss it how the fat pin blazes!"

He waited but a single moment for the wood and charcoal to ignite. It flared up at first in a smoky blaze, and then subsided into a clear and brilliant flame. Seizing the iron handle of the furnace Devil-Bug suddenly raised it from the floor, and rushed from the den, and up the staircase of the mansion, as though his very life hung on his speed. And as he ascended the stairway, the light of the furnace gradually increasing to a vivid flame, was thrown upward over his hideous face, turning the beetling brow, the flat nose and the wide mouth with its bristling teeth, to a hue of dusky red. One moment as he swung the furnace from side to side, you beheld his face and form in a glow of blood red light, and the next it was suddenly lost to view, while the vessel of iron, with its burning coals, seemed gliding up the stairway, impelled by a single swarthy hand, with fingers like talons and sinews starting out from the skin like knotted cords.

"Halloo! I didn't know Monk Luke was in his room—" he muttered, as he paused for a moment before a massive door, opening into the hall, which extended along the mansion, above the first stairway—"There's a streak of light from the keyhole of his door! And voices inside the room—but no matter! The charcoal's a-burnin'—and—wonder how *that'ill work?*"

And up the staircase of the mansion he pursued his way, flinging the blazing furnace from side to side, while his face, grew like the visage of a very devil, as again the words rose to his lips—

"The charcoal's a-burnin'—wonder how *that*'ill work?"

The light still flickered through the keyhole of the massive door.

Within the sombre panels, it shone over the rich furniture of an apartment, long and wide, with high ceiling and wainscotted walls. There was a gorgeous carpet on the floor, a thickly curtained bed in one corner, a comfortable fire burning in the grate, and a large table standing near the center of the room, on which a plain lamp, darkened by a heavy shade, was burning. The shade flung the light of the lamp down over the table—it was covered with books, cards, and wine glasses—and around the carpet, for the space of a yard or more, while the other portions of the apartment, were enveloped in faint twilight.

And in that dim light, near the fire, stood two men, steadfastly regarding each other in the face. The snake-like eye of the tall and slender man, was fixed in keen gaze upon the bronzed face of his companion, whose stout and imposing form seemed yet more large and commanding in its proportions, as occasional flashes from the fireplace lighted up the dim twilight. It was a strange thing, to see those large blue eyes, gleaming from the bronzed face, with such a calm and yet burning lustre.

"Luke—to the—the—*room*—" whispered a voice, husky with suppressed agitation.

"He is calm—" muttered Luke to himself—"I led him a d———l of a way in order to give him time to command his feelings. He is calm now —and it's *too late to go back.*"

Extending his hand he reached a small dark lanthern from the mantel-piece, and walked softly across the floor. Opening the door of a wide closet, he motioned Livingstone to approach.

"You see, this is rather a spacious closet—" Luke whispered, as silently drawing Livingstone within the recess, he closed the door, leaving them enveloped in thick darkness—"The back wall of the closet, is nothing less than a portion of the wainscotting of the next room. Give me your hand—it is firm, by G———d!—Do you feel that bolt? It's a little one, but once withdrawn, the panelling swings away from the closet like a door, and—egad!—the next room lays before you!"

While Livingstone stood in the thick darkness of the closet, silent as death, Luke slowly drew the bolt. Another touch, and the door would swing open into the next room. Luke could hear the hard breathing of the Merchant, and the hand which he touched suddenly became cold as ice.

As though by mere accident, in that moment of suspense, when their joined fingers touched the bolt, Harvey allowed the door of the dark lanthern, to spring suddenly open. The face of Livingstone, every line and feature, was disclosed in the light, with appaling distinctness. Luke was prepared for a sight of some interest, but no sooner did the light fall on the Merchant's face, than he gave a start of involuntary horror. It was as though the face of a corpse, suddenly recalled to life, had risen before him. White and livid and ghastly, with the discolored circles of flesh deepening beneath each eye, and with the large blue eyes, steadily glaring from the dark eyebrows, it was a countenance to strike the very heart with fear and horror. The firm lips wore a blueish hue, as though the man had been dead for days, and corruption was eating its way through his vitals. Around his high and massive brow, hung his hair, in slight masses; fearful streaks of white resting like scattered ashes, among the locks of dark brown.

"Well, Luke—you see—I am calm—" whispered Livingstone, smiling, with his lips still compressed—"I—am—calm—"

Luke slowly withdrew the bolt, and closed the door of the lanthern. The secret door, of the wainscotting swung open with a faint noise.

"Listen!" he whispered to Livingstone, as the dark room lay before them—"Listen!"

And with his very breath hushed, Livingstone silently listened. A low sound like a woman breathing in her sleep, came faintly to his ear. Luke felt the Merchant start as though he was reeling beneath a sudden blow.

"Give me the dark lanthern—" whispered Livingstone—"*The pistols I have!*" he continued, hissing the words through his clinched teeth—"The room is dark, but I can discern the outlines of the bed—"

He pressed Luke by the hand with a firm grasp, took the lanthern, carefully closing its door, and strode with a noiseless footstep, into the dark room.

Luke remained in the closet, listening with hushed breath.

There was a pause for a moment. It seemed an age to the listener. Not a sound, not a footstep, not even the rustling of the bed-curtains. All was silent as the grave-vault, which has not been disturbed for years.

Luke listened. He leaned from the closet and gazed into the dark room. It was indeed dark. Not the outline of a chair, or a sofa, or the slightest piece of furniture could he discern. True, near the centre of the place, arose a towering object, whose outlines seemed a shade lighter than the rest of the room. This might be the bed, thought Luke, and again, holding his breath, he listened for the slightest sound.

All was dark and still.

Presently Luke heard a low gurgling noise, like the sound produced by a drowning man. Then all was silent as before.

In a moment the gurgling noise was heard again, and a sudden blaze of light streamed around the room.

CHAPTER TWELFTH

THE TOWER ROOM

"My sister is in his power, for any act of wrong, for any deed of outrage! And I cannot strike a blow in her defence! A solitary wall may separate us—in one room the sister pleads with the villain for mercy—in the other, trapped and imprisoned, the brother hears her cry of agony, and cannot—cannot raise a finger in her behalf! Ha! The door is fast—I hear the hushed breathing of negroes on the other side. I have read many legends of a place of torment in the other world, but what devil could contrive a hell like this?"

He flung himself on the sofa, and covered his face with his hands. The lamp burning dimly on the solitary table, flung a faint and dusky light around the walls of the Tower Room.

Byrnewood lay in dim shadow, with his limbs thrown carelessly along the sofa, his outspread hands covering his face, while the long curls of his raven-black hair, fell wild and tangled over his forehead. As he lay there, with his dress disordered and his form resting on the sofa, in an attitude which, careless as it was, resembled the crouching position of one who suffers from the cold chill succeeding fever, you might have taken him for an inanimate effigy, instead of a living and breathing man.

No heaving of the chest, no quick and gasping respiration, no convulsive movements of the fingers, indicated the agitation which shook his soul to its centre. He lay quiet and motionless, his white hands, concealing his livid face, while a single glimpse of his forehead was visible between the tangled locks of his raven hair.

The silence of the room was broken by the creaking of the door, as it swung slowly open.

Bess silently entered the room, holding the waiter with the cold chicken and bottle of Madeira in her hands. She hurriedly closed the door and advanced to the solitary table. Her face was very pale, and her long dark hair, hung in disordered tresses around her full voluptuous neck. The dark shawl which she had thrown over her bridesmaid's dress, had fallen from her shoulders and hung loosely from her arms as she walked. Her entire appearance betrayed agitation and haste.

"He sleeps!" she murmured, arranging the refreshments—provided by Devil-Bug—along the surface of the chest-like table—" 'Fix his plate on the side of the table furthest from the door'—what could the monster mean? Ha! There may be a secret spring on that side of the table, which the foot of the victim is designed to touch. I'll warn him of his danger—and then, the *bottle*—"

She said she would warn Byrnewood of his danger, and yet she lingered about the small table, her confused and hurried manner betraying her irresolution and changeability of purpose. Byrnewood still lay silent and motionless on the sofa. As far from slumber as the victim writhing on the rack, he was still unconscious of the presence of Long-haired Bess. His mind was utterly absorbed in the harrowing details of the mental struggle, that shook his soul to its foundations.

At first, arranging the knife and plate on one side of the table, and then on the other, now placing the bottle in one position and again in another, it was evident that Long-haired Bess was absent, confused and deeply agitated. The side-long glance, which every other instant, she threw over her shoulder at the reclining form of Byrnewood, was fraught with deep and painful meaning. At last, with a hurried footstep, she approached the sofa, and glancing cautiously at the door, which hung slightly ajar, she laid her hand lightly on Byrnewood's shoulder.

"I come to warn you of your danger—" she whispered in his ear.

Byrnewood looked up in wonder and then an expression of intolerable disgust impressed every line of his countenance.

"Your touch is pollution—" he said, shaking her hand from his shoulder—"You were one of the minions of the villain. You plotted my sister's dishonor—"

"I come to warn you of your danger!" whispered Bess, with a flashing eye—"You behold refreshments spread for you on yonder table. You see the bottle o' wine. On peril of your life don't drink anything—"

"But rale good brandy—" grated a harsh voice at her shoulder—"Liqu-ood hell-fire for ever! That's the stuff, my feller! Ha! ha! ha!"

With the same start of surprise, Byrnewood sprang to his feet, and Bess turned hurriedly around, while their eyes were fixed upon the face of the new-comer.

Devil-Bug, hideous and grinning, with the furnace of burning coals in his hand, stood before them. His solitary eye rested upon the face of Long-haired Bess with a meaning look, and his visage passed through the series of spasmodic contortions peculiar to his expressive features, as he stood swinging the furnace from side to side.

"You can go, Bessie, my duck—" he said, with a pleasant way of speaking, original with himself. "This 'ere party don't want you no more. You see, my feller citizen—" he continued, turning to Byrnewood—"yer humble servant thought you might be hungry, so he sent you suffin' to eat. Thought you might be cold; so he brung you some coals to warm yesself. You can *re*-tire, Bessie—"

He gently led her to the door, fixing his eye upon her face, with a look, as full of venom as a spiders sting.

"You'd a-spilt it all—would yo'?" he hissed the whisper in her ear as he pushed her from the room—"Good night my dear—" he continued aloud—"You better go home. Your mammy's a waitin' tea for you. Now I'll make you a little bit o' fire, Mister, if you please—"

"Fire?" echoed Byrnewood—"I see no fire-place—"

"That's all you know about it"—answered Devil-Bug swinging the furnace from side to side—"You think them 'are's books do you? Look a little closer, next time. The walls are only painted like books and shelves—false book-cases you see. And then there's glass doors, jist like real book-cases. They did it in the old times—them queer old chaps as used to keep house here, all alone to themselves. Nice fire-place—aint it?"

He opened two folding leaves of the false book-case near the centre of the wall opposite the door, and a small fire-place neatly white-washed and free from ashes or the remains of any former fire, became visible. Stooping on his knees, Devil-Bug proceeded to arrange the furnace in the hearth, while the half-closed folding leaves of the book-case, well-nigh concealed him from view.

"A false bookcase on either side of the room! Ha! Books of all classes, painted on the pannels, within the sashes, with inimitable skill! They deceived me, in the dim light of yonder lamp. What can this mean? By my life, I shrewdly suspect, that these bookcases, conceal secret passages, leading from this den—"

Byrnewood flung himself on the sofa, and again covered his face with his hands.

"Blazes up quite comfortable—" muttered Devil-Bug, as half concealed by the folding doors of the central part of the bookcase, he stooped over the furnace of blazing coal, warming his hands in the flame. "A nice fire, and a nice fire-place. But I'll have to discharge my bricklayer for one thing. Got him to fix up this harth not long ago. Scoundrel walled up the chimbley. Did ye ever hear of sich rascality? Konsekence is, this young gentleman will be rather uncomfortable a'cause, the charcoal smoke wont find no vent. If I should happen to shut the door right tight he might die. He might so. Things jist as bad have happened afore now. He *might* die. Ha—ha—ha—" he chuckled as he retired from the fire-place, screening the blazing furnace, with the half-closed doors of the book-case—"Wonder how *that* 'ill work!"

He approached the side of Byrnewood, with that same hideous grin distorting his features, but had not advanced two steps, when he started backward with a moment of involuntary horror.

"Look here you sir—" he whispered grasping Byrnewood by the arm—"Jist look here a minnit. You see the floor at my left side—do you? Now tell us the truth, aint there a dead man layin' there? His jaw broke and his tongue out? Not that I'm afeered, but I wants to satisfy my mind. Jist take a good look while I hold still—"

"I see nothing but the carpet—" answered Byrnewood with a look of loathing, as he observed this strange being, standing before him, motionless as a statue, while his left hand pointed to the floor—"I see nothing but the carpet."

"Don't see a dead man, with his knees drawed up to his breast, and his tongue stickin' out? Well that's queer. I'd take my book oath, that the feller was a layin' there, nasty as a snake—Hows'ever *re*-fresh yourself young man. There's plenty to eat and drink and—" he pointed to the hearth as he spoke—"There's a nice comfortable fire. Good charcoal—and—I wonder's how *that* 'ill *work*—"

Closing the door, he stood in the small recess, at the head of the stairs, leading to the Tower-Room. The huge forms of the negroes, Musquito and Glow-worm, were flung along the floor, while their hard breathing indicated that they slumbered on their watch. Listening intently for a single moment, at the door of the Tower-Room, Devil-Bug slowly turned the key in the lock, and then withdrawing it from the keyhole placed it in his pocket. He stepped carefully over the forms of the sleeping negroes, and passed his hands slowly along the panelling of the recess, opposite the door.

"The spring—ha, ha—I've found it—" he muttered in the darkness. —"The bookcases dont conceal no passage between the walls of this 'ere Tower, and the room itself—do they? O'course they do not. Quiet little places where a feller can say his prayers and eat ground-nuts. Ha! Ha! Ha! I must see how *that* 'ill work."

The panelling slid back as he touched the spring and Devil-Bug disappeared into the secret recess or passage, between the false bookcases and the massive walls of the Tower; as the solitary chamber, rising from the western wing of Monk-Hall, was termed in the legends of the place.

Meanwhile within the Tower-Room, Byrnewood Arlington paced slowly up and down the floor, his arms folded, and his face, impressed with a fixed expression, that forced his lips tightly together, darkened his brows in a settled frown and drove the blood from his entire visage, until it wore the livid hues of death.

"My sister in his power! Last night she was pure and stainless—to morrow morning dawns and she will be a thing stained with pollution, dishonored by a hideous crime! No lapse of time, no prayers to Heaven, no bitter tears of repentance can ever wash out the foul stains of her dishonor. And I am a prisoner, while she shrieks for help and shrieks in vain—"

As Byrnewood spoke, striding rapidly along the floor, a grateful warmth began to steal around the room, dispelling the chill and damp, which seemed to infect the very air, with an unwholesome taint.

"And we have been children together! I have held her in these arms, when she was but a babe—a smiling babe, with golden hair and laughing cheeks! And then when she left home for school, how it wrung my soul to part with her! So young, so lighthearted, so innocent! Three years pass—she returns grown up into a lovely girl—whose pure soul, a very devil would not dare to tarnish—she return to bless the sight of her father—her mother, with her laughing face and she is—*dishonored!* I never knew the meaning of the word till now—*dishonored* by a villain —"

He flung himself on the sofa, and covered his face with his hands.

"And yet I, I, wronged an innocent girl, because she was my father's servant! Great God! Can she, have a brother to feel for her ruin? My punishment is just, but Mary—Oh! whom did she ever harm, whom *could* she ever wrong?"

He was silent again. And while his brain was tortured by the fierce struggles of thought, while the memories of earlier days came thronging over his soul—the image of his sister, present in every thought, and shining brightest in each old-time memory—he could feel, the grateful heat which pervaded the atmosphere of the room, restoring warmth and comfort to his limbs, while his blood flowed more freely in his veins.

There was a long pause, in which his very soul was absorbed in a delirium of thought. It may have been the effect of internal agitation, or the result of his half-crazed intellect acting on his physical system, but after the lapse of some few minutes, he was aroused from his reverie, by a painful throbbing around his temples, which for a single moment destroyed all consciousness, and just as suddenly restored him to a keen and terrible sense of his appaling situation. Now his brain seemed to swim in a wild delirium, and in a single instant as the throbbing around his temples grew more violent, his mental vision, seemed clearer and more vigorous than ever.

"I can scarcely breathe!" he muttered, as he fell back on the sofa, after a vain attempt to rise—There is a hand grasping me by the throat

—I feel the fingers clutching the veins, with the grasp of a demon. My heart—ah!—it is turning to ice—to ice—and now it is fire! My heart is a ball of flame—the blood boils in my veins—"

He sprung to his feet, with a wild bound and his hands clutched madly at his throat, as though he would free the veins from the grasp of the invisible fingers, which were pressing through the very skin.

He staggered to and fro along the floor, with his arms flung overhead as if to ward off the attacks of some invisible foe.

His face was ghastly pale, one moment; the next it flushed with the hues of a crimson flame. His large black eyes dilated in their glance, and stood out from the lids as though they were about to fall from their sockets. His mouth distended with a convulsive grimace, while his teeth were firmly clenched together. One instant his brain would be perfectly conscious in all its operations, the next his senses would swim in a fearful delirium.

"My God—My God!" he shouted in one of those momentary intervals of consciousness, as he staggered wildly along the floor—"I am dying—I am dying! My breath comes thick and gaspingly—my veins are chilled—ha, ha—they are turned to fire again—"

Even in his delirium he was conscious of a singular circumstance. A portion of the panelling of the false bookcase, along the wall opposite the fire, receded suddenly, within the sash of the central glass-door, leaving a space of black and vacant darkness. The aperture was in the top of the bookcase, near the ceiling of the room.

Turning toward the hearth, Byrnewood endeavoured to regain the sofa, but the room seemed swimming around him, and with a wild movement, he again staggered toward the bookcase opposite the fire.

He started backward as a new horror met his gaze.

A hideous face glared upon him, from the aperture of the book-case, like some picture of a fiend's visage, suddenly thrust against the glass-door of the book-case.

A hideous face, with a single burning eye, with a wide mouth distending in a loathsome grin, with long rows of fang-like teeth, and a protuberent brow, overhung by thick masses of matted hair. This face alone was visible, surrounded by the darkness which marked the square outline of the aperture. It was, indeed, like a hideous picture framed in ebony, although you could see the muscles of the face in motion, while the flat nose was pressed againt the glass of the book-case, and the thick lips were now tightly closed, and again distending in hideous grin.

"Ho! ho! ho!" a laugh like the shout of a devil, came echoing through the glass, faint and subdued, yet wild and terrible to hear—

"The charcoal—the charcoal! Wonder how *that'ill work!*"

Byrnewood stood silent and erect, while the throbbing of his temples, the gasping of his breath, and the deadening sensation around his heart, subsided for a single moment.

The full horror of his situation rushed upon him. He was dying by the gas escaping from charcoal, in a room, rendered impervious to the air; closed and sealed for the purpose of this horrible death.

A brilliant idea flashed across his brain.

"I will overturn the furnace—" he muttered, rushing toward the hearth—"I will extinguish the flame!"

With a sudden bound he sprang forward, but in the very action, fell to the floor, like a drunken man.

His breath came in thick convulsive gasps, his heart grew like a mass of fire, while his brain was tortured by one intense and agonizing throb of pain, as though some invisible hand had wound a red hot wire round his forehead. He lay on the floor, with his outspread hands grasping the air in the effort to rise.

"It works, it works!" shouted the voice of Devil-Bug, as his loathsome countenance was pressed against the glass-door of the book-case—"Ha! ha! ha! He is on the floor—he cannot rise—he is in the clutch of death. How the poor feller kicks and scuffles!"

A wild, wild shriek echoing from a distant room came faintly to Byrnewood's ear. That sound of a woman's voice, shrieking for help, in an emphasis of despair, aroused the dying man from the spell which began to deaden his senses.

"It is my sister's voice!" he exclaimed, springing to his feet with a last effort of strength—"She is in the hands of the villain! I will save her—I will save her—"

"The sister outraged! The brother murdered!" shouted Devil-Bug, through the glass-door—"I wonder how *that'ill work!*"

Byrnewood rushed towards the door; it was locked and secured. All hope was in vain. He must die. Die, while his sister's shriek for aid rang on his ears, die, with the loathsome face of his murderer pressed against the glass, while his blazing eye feasted on his last convulsive agonies, die, with youth on his brow, with health in his heart! Die, with all purposed vengeance on his sister's wronger unfulfilled; die, by no sudden blow, by no dagger thrust, by no pistol shot, but by the most loathsome of all deaths, by suffocation.

"Ha! ha!" the thought flashed over his brain—"The hangman's rope were a priceless luxury to me in this dread hour!"

Staggering slowly along the floor, with footsteps as heavy as though he had leaden weights attached to his feet, he approached the chest-like table, and with a faint effort to recover his balance, sunk down on the floor, in a crouching position, while his outspread hands clutched faintly at the air.

In a moment he rolled slowly from side to side, and lay on his back with his face to the ceiling, and his arms extended on either side. His eyes were suddenly covered with a glassy film, his lower jaw separated from the upper, leaving his mouth wide open, while the room grew warmer, the air more dense and suffocating.

"Help—help!" murmured Byrnewood, in a smothered voice, like the sound produced by a man throttled by nightmare—"Help! help!"

" 'By-a-baby, go to sleep'—that's a good feller—" the voice of Devil-Bug came like a faint echo through the glass—"A drop from the bottle 'ud do you good, and—jist reach your right hand a leetle bit further! There ain't no spring there, I *sup*-pose? Ain't there? Ho-ho-ho!"

And Byrnewood could feel a delicious languor stealing over his frame, as he lay there on the floor, helpless and motionless, while the voice of Devil-Bug rang in his ears. The throbbing of his temples had subsided, he no more experienced the quick gasping struggle for breath, his heart no more passed through the quick transitions from cold to heat, from ice to fire, his veins no more felt like streams of molten lead. He was sinking quietly in a soft and pleasing slumber. The film grew more glassy in each eye, his jaws hung further apart, and the heaving of his chest subsided, until a faint and tremulous motion, was the only indication that life had not yet fled from his frame. His outspread arms seemed to grow stiffened and dead as he rested on the floor, while the joints of the fingers moved faintly to and fro, with a fluttering motion, that afforded a strange contrast to the complete repose of his body and limbs. His feet were pointed upward, like the feet of a corpse, arrayed for burial.

The dim light burning on the chest-like table, afforded a faint light to the ghastly scene. There were the untouched refreshments, the cold chicken and the bottle of wine, giving the place the air of a quiet supper-room, there were the false book-cases, indicating a resort for meditation and study, there was the cheerful furnace, its glowing flame flashing through the half-closed doors, speaking a pleasant tale of fireside joys and comforts, and there, along the carpet, stiffening and ghastly lay the form of Byrnewood Arlington, slowly and quietly yielding to the slumber of death, while a hideous face peered through the glass-door, all distorted by a sickening grimace, and a solitary eye, that gleamed like a live coal, drank in the tremulous agonies of the dying man.

"Reach his hand a leetle bit further—that's a good feller. Won't have no tumble down three stories, nor nothin', if his fingers touch the spring? Ho-ho! Quiet now, I guess. Jist look how his fingers tremble—He! he! he! Hallo! He's on his feet agin!"

With the last involuntary struggle of a strong man wrestling for his life, Byrnewood Arlington sprang to his feet, and reaching forth his hand with the same mechanical impulse that had raised him from the floor, he seized the bottle of wine; he raised it to his lips, and the wine poured gurgling down his throat.

"Hain't got no opium in, I *sup*-pose? Not the least mossel. Cuss it, how he staggers! Believe my soul he's comin' to life agin'—"

Byrnewood glanced around with a look of momentary consciousness. The drugged wine, for a single moment, created a violent reaction in his system, and he became fully sensible of the awful death that awaited him. He could feel the hot air, warming his cheek, he could see the visage of Devil-Bug peering at him thro' the glass-door, and the danger which menaced his sister, came home like some horrible phantom to his soul. He felt in his very soul that but a single moment more of consciousness, would be permitted him, for action. That moment past, and the death by charcoal, would be quietly and surely accomplished.

"Keep me, oh Heaven!" he whispered as his mind ran over various expedients for escape—"Aid me, in this, my last effort, that I may live to avenge my sister's dishonor!"

It was his design to make one sudden and desperate spring toward the glass-door, through which the hideous visage of Devil-Bug, glared in his face and as he madly dashed his hands through the glass, the room would be filled with a current of fresh air.

This was his resolve, but it came too late. As he turned, to make this desperate spring, his heel pressed against an object, rising from the floor, near a corner of the chest-like table. It was but a small object, resembling a nail or spike, which has not been driven to the head, in the planking of a floor, but suffered to remain half-exposed and open to the view.

And yet the very moment Byrnewood's heel, pressed againt the trifling object, the floor on which he stood gave way beneath him, with a low rustling sound, half of the Chamber was changed into one black and yawning chasm, and the lamp standing on the table suddenly disappeared, leaving the place wrapt in thick darkness.

Another moment passed, and while Byrnewood reeled in the darkness, on the verge of the sunken trap-door, a hushed and distant sound, echoed far below as from the depths of some deep and dismal well. The lamp had fallen in the chasm, and the faint sound heard far, far below was the only indication that it had reached the bottom of the gloomy void, sinking down like a well into the cellars of Monk-hall.

Byrnewood tottered on the verge of the chasm, while a current of cold air came sweeping upward from its depths. The foul atmosphere of the Tower Room, lost half its deadly qualities, in a single moment, as the cool air, came rushing from the chasm.

Byrnewood felt the effects of the charcoal rapidly passing from his system, and his mind regained its full consciousness as his hot brow, received the freshning blast of winter air, pouring over the parched and heated skin.

But the current of pure air, came too late for his salvation. Tottering in the darkness on the very verge of the sunken trap-door, he made one desperate struggle to preserve his balance, but in vain. For a moment his form swung to and fro, and then his feet slid from under him; and then with a maddening shriek, he fell.

"God save poor Mary!"

How that last cry of the doomed man shrieked around the panelled walls of the Tower Room!

"Wonder how *that*'ill *work!*" the hoarse voice of Devil-Bug, shrieked through the darkness—"Down—down—*down!* Ah-ha! Three stories—down—down—down! I wonders how that 'ill work!"

Separated from the Tower Room by the glass-door, Devil-Bug pressed his ear against the glass, and listened for the death-groans of the doomed man.

A low moaning sound, like the groan of a man, who trembles under the operations of a surgeon's knife, came faintly to his ear. In a moment, Devil-Bug, thought he heard a sound like a door suddenly opened, and then, the murmur of voices, whispering some quick and hurried words, resounded along the Tower Room. Then there was a subdued noise, like a man struggling on the brink of the chasm, and then a hushed sound, that might have been taken for the tread of a footstep mingled with the closing of a door, came faintly through the glass of the book-case.

Gliding silently from the secret recess, behind the panelling of the Tower Room, Devil-Bug stepped over the forms of the slumbering negroes and descended the stairway leading to the Walnut Room. The scene of the wedding was wrapt in midnight darkness. Passing softly along the floor, Devil-Bug, reached the entrance to the Rose Chamber, and flung the hangings aside, with a cautious movement of his talon-like fingers.

"I merely wanted a light—" exclaimed Devil-Bug, as he stood

gazing into the Rose Chamber—"But here's a candle, and a purty sight into the bargain!"

He disappeared through the doorway, and after the lapse of a few moments, again emerged into the Walnut Room, holding a lighted candle in his hand.

"Amazin' circumstance, *that*—" he chuckled, as he strode across the glittering floor—"The brother *fell* in that 'are room, and the sister *fell* in *that;* about the same time. They *fell* in different ways though. Strange world, this. Let's see what become of the brother—Charcoal and opium—ho! ho! ho!"

Before another moment had elapsed, he stood before the door of Tower Room. Musquito and Glow-worm still slumbered on their watch, their huge forms and hideous faces, dimly developed in the beams of the light, which the Doorkeeper carried in his hand. Devil-Bug listened intently for a single moment, but not the slightest sound disturbed the silence of the Tower room.

He opened the door, he strode along the carpet, he stood on the verge of the chasm, produced by the falling of the death-trap.

"Down—down! Three stories, and the pit below! Ha! Let me hold the light, a leetle nearer! Every trap-door is open—he is safe enough! Think I see suffin' white a-flutterin' a-way down there! Hollered pretty loud as he fell—devilish ugly tumble! Guess it 'ill work quite nice for Lorrimer!"

Stooping on his knees with the light extended in his right hand, he again gazed down the hatchway, his solitary eye flashing with excitement, as he endeavoured to pierce the gloom of the dark void beneath.

"He's gone to see his friends below! Sartin sure! No sound—no groan —not even a holler!"

Arising from his kneeling position, Devil-Bug approached the recess of the fire-place. On either side, a plain panell of oak, concealed the secret nook behind the false book-case. Placing his hand cautiously along the panell to the right, Devil-Bug examined the details of the carving in each corner, and along its side, with a careful eye.

"Hasn't been opened to-night—" he murmured—"Leads to the Walnut Room, by a round-a-bout way. Convenient little passage, if that fool had only knowed on it!"

In an instant he stood outside of the Tower Room door, holding the key in one hand, and the candlestick in the other.

"Git up you lazy d———l's!" he shouted, bestowing a few pointed kicks upon the carcases of the sleeping negroes—"Git up and mind your eyes, or else I'll pick 'em out o' your head to play marbles with—"

Glow-worm arose slowly from the floor, and Musquito, opening his eyes with a sleepy yawn, stared vacantly in the Doorkeeper's face.

"D'ye hear me? Watch this feller and see that he don't escape? He's a sleepin' now, but there's no knowin'—Watch! I say watch!'

He shuffled slowly along the narrow passage, looking over his shoulder at the grinning negroes, as he passed along, while his face wore its usual pleasant smile, as he again muttered in his hoarse tones —"Watch him ye dogs—I say watch him!"

Another moment, and he stood before the entrance of the Rose Chamber, holding the curtaining aside, while his eye blazed up with an expression of malignant joy. He raised the light on high, and stood gazing silently through the doorway, as though his eyes beheld a spectacle of strange and peculiar interest.

And while he stood there, chuckling pleasantly to himself, with the full light of the candle, flashing over his loathsome face, two figures, stood crouching in the darkness, along the opposite side of the room, and the eastern door hung slightly ajar, as though they had entered the place but a moment before.

Once or twice Devil-Bug turned, as though the sound of suppressed breathing struck his ear, but every time, the shadow of the candle fell along the opposite side of the room, and the crouching figures were concealed from view.

"Quite a pictur'—" chuckled Devil-Bug as he again gazed through the doorway of the Rose Chamber—"A nice little gal and a handsome feller! Ha! Ha! Ha!"

He disappeared through the curtaining, while his pleasant chuckle came echoing through the doorway, with a sound of continued glee, as though the gentleman was highly amused by the spectacle that broke on his gaze.

The silence of the Rose Chamber was broken by the tread of a footstep and the figure of a man, came stealing through the darkness, with the form of a queenly woman by his side.

"Advance—and save your sister's honor—" the deep-toned whisper broke thrillingly on the air.

The man advanced with a hurried step, flung the curtain hastily aside, and gazed within the Rose Chamber.

The horror of that silent gaze, would be ill-repayed by an Eternity of joy.

CHAPTER THIRTEENTH

THE CRIME WITHOUT A NAME

"My brother consents? Oh joy, Lorraine—he consents!"

"Your brother consents to our wedding, my love—"

"How did he first discover, that the wedding was to take place to night?"

"It seems that for several days, he has noticed you walking out with Bess. You see, Mary, this excited his suspicions. He watched you with all a brother's care, and to night, tracked Bess and you, to the doors of this mansion. He was not certain however, that it was *you*, whom he seen, enter my uncle's house—"

"And so he watched all night around the building? Oh Lorraine, *he* is a noble brother!"

"At last, grown feverish with his suspicions, he rung the bell, aroused the servant, and when the door was opened, rushed madly up stairs, and reached the Wedding Room. You know the rest. After the matter was explained to him, he consented to keep our marriage secret until Christmas Eve. He has left the house, satisfied that you are in the care of those who love you. To morrow, Mary, when you have recovered from the effects of the surprise,—which your brother's sudden entrance occasioned—to-morrow we will be married!"

"And on Christmas Eve, hand linked in hand, we will kneel before *our* father, and ask his blessing—"

"One kiss, Mary love, one kiss, and I will leave you for the night—"

And leaning fondly over the fair girl, who was seated on the sofa, her form enveloped in a flowing night-robe, Lorrimer wound his right arm gently around her neck, bending her head slowly backward in the action, and suffering her rich curls to fall showering on her shoulders, while her upturned face, all radiant with affection lay open to his burning gaze, and her ripe lips, dropped slightly apart, disclosing the ivory teeth, seemed to woo and invite the pressure of his kiss.

One kiss, silent and long, and the Lover and the fair girl, seemed to have grown to each others lips.

The wax-light standing on the small table of the Rose Chamber, fell mild and dimly over this living picture of youth and passion.

The tall form of Lorrimer, clad in solemn black, contrasting forcibly with the snow-white robes of the Maiden, his arm flung gently around her neck, her upturned face half-hidden by the falling locks of his dark brown hair, their lips joined and their eyes mingling in the same deep glance of passion, while her bosom rose heaving against his breast, and her arms half-upraised seemed about to entwine his form in their embrace—it was a moment of pure and hallowed love on the part of the fair girl, and even the libertine, for an instant forgot the vileness of his purpose, in that long and silent kiss of stainless passion.

"Mary!" cried Lorrimer, his handsome face flushing over with transport, as silently gliding from his standing position, he assumed his seat at her side—"Oh! would that you were mine! We would flee together from the heartless world—in some silent and shadowy valley, we would forget all, but the love which made us one.'

"We would seek a home, quiet and peaceful, as that which this book describes—" whispered Mary laying her hand on Bulwer's play of Claude Mellnotte—"I found the volume on the table, and was reading it, when you came in. Oh, it is all beauty and feeling. You have read it Lorraine?"

"Again and again and have seen it played a hundred times.—'The home, to which love could fulfil its prayers, this hand would lead thee'—" he murmured repeating the first lines of the celebrated description of the Lake of Como—"And yet Mary this is mere romance. A creation of the poets brain. A fiction as beautiful as a ray of light; and as fleeting. I might tell you a story of a real valley and a real lake,—which I beheld last summer—where love might dwell forever, and dwell in eternal youth and freshness.—"

"Oh tell me—tell me—" cried Mary, gazing in his face with a look of interest.

"Beyond the fair valley of Wyoming, of which so much has been said and sung, there is a high and extensive range of mountains, covered with thick and gloomy forests. One day last September when the summer was yet in its freshness and bloom, toward the hour of sunset, I found myself wandering through a thick wood, that covered the summit of one of the highest of these mountains. I had been engaged in a deer-hunt all day—had strayed from my comrades—and now as night was coming on, was wandering, along a winding path, that led to the top of the mountain—"

Lorrimer paused for a single instant, and gazed intently in Mary's face. Every feature was animated with sudden interest and a warm flush, hung freshly on each cheek.

And as Lorrimer gazed upon the animated face of the innocent girl, marking its rounded outlines, its hues of youth and loveliness, its large blue eyes beaming so gladly upon his countenance, the settled purpose of his soul, came to him, like a sudden shadow darkening over a landscape, after a single gleam of sunlight.

It was the purpose of this libertine to dishonor the stainless girl, before he left her presence.

Before day break she would be a polluted thing, whose name and virtue and soul, would be blasted forever.

In that silent gaze, which drank in the beauty of the maiden's face, Lorrimer arranged his plan of action. The book which he had left open the table, the story which he was about to tell, were the first intimations of his atrocious design. While enchaining the mind of the Maiden, with a story full of Romance, it was his intention to wake her animal nature into full action. And when her veins were all alive with fiery pulsations, when her heart grew animate with sensual life, when her eyes swam in the humid moisture of passion, then she would sink helplessly into his arms, and—like the bird to the snake,—flutter to her ruin.

" 'Force'—'violence!' These are but the tools of grown-up children, who know nothing of the mystery of woman's heart—" the thought flashed over Lorrimer's brain, as his lip, wore a very slight but meaning smile—"I have deeper means, than these! I employ neither force, nor threats, nor fraud, nor violence! My victim is the instrument of her own ruin—without one rude grasp from my hand, without one threatning word, she swims willingly to my arms!"

He took the hand of the fair girl within his own, and looking her steadily in the eye, with a deep gaze which every instant grew more vivid and burning, he went on with his story—and his design.

"The wood grew very dark. Around me, were massive trees with thick branches, and gnarled trunks, bearing witness of the storms of an hundred years. My way led over a path covered with soft forest-moss, and now and then, red gleams of sunlight shot like arrows of gold, between the overhanging leaves. Darker and darker, the twilight sank down upon the forest. At last missing the path, I knew not which way to tread. All was dark and indistinct. Now falling over a crumbling limb, which had been thrown down by a storm long before, now entangled by the wild vines, that overspread portions of the ground, and now missing my foothold in some hidden crevice of the earth, I wandered wearily on. At last climbing up a sudden elevation of the mountain, I stood upon a vast rock, that hung over the depths below, like an immense platform. On all sides, but one, this rock was encircled by a waving wall of forest-leaves. Green shrubs swept circling around, enclosing it like a fairy bower, while the eastern side, lay open to the beams of the moon, which now rose grandly in the vast horizon.

Far over wood, far over mountain, far over ravine and dell, this platform-rock, commanded a distant view of the valley of Wyoming.

"The moon was in the sky, Mary: the sky was one vast sheet of blue, undimmed by a single cloud; and beneath the moonbeams lay a sea of forest-leaves, while in the dim distance—like the shore of this leafy ocean—arose the roofs and steeples of a quiet town, with a broad river, rolling along the dark valley, like a banner of silver, flung over a sable-pall—"

"How beautiful!"

And as the murmur escaped Mary's lips, the hand of Lorrimer grew closer in its pressure, while his left arm, wound gently around her waist.

"I stood entranced by the sight. A cool breeze came up the mountain side, imparting a grateful freshness to my cheek. The view was indeed beautiful, but I suddenly remembered that I was without resting-place or shelter. Ignorant of the mountain paths, afar from any farm-house or village, I had still a faint of hope, of discovering the temporary habitation of some hunter, who had encamped in these forest-wilds.

"I turned from the magnificent prospect—I brushed aside the wall of leaves, I looked to the western sky. I shall never forget the view—which like a dream of fairy-land—burst on my sight, as pushing the shrubbery aside, I gazed from the western limits of the platform-rock.

"There, below me, imbedded in the very summit of the mountain, lay a calm lake, whose crystal-waters, gave back the reflection of forest and sky, like an immense mirror. It was but a mile in length, and half that distance in width. On all sides, sudden and steep, arose the encircling wall of forest trees. Like wine in a goblet, that calm sheet of water, lay in the embrace of the surrounding wall of foliage. The waters were clear, so tranquil, that I could see, down, down, far, far beneath, as if another world, was hidden in their depths. And then from the heights, the luxuriant foliage, as yet untouched by autumn, sank in waves of verdure to the very brink of the lake, the trembling leaves, dipping in the clear, cold waters, with a gentle motion. It was very beautiful Mary and—"

"Oh, most beautiful!"

The left hand of Lorrimer, gently stealing round her form, rested with a faint pressure upon the folds of the night-robe, over her bosom, which now came heaving tremulously into light.

"I looked upon this lovely lake with a keen delight. I gazed upon the tranquil waters, upon the steeps crowned with forest-trees—one side in heavy shadow, the other, gleaming in the advancing moonbeams—I seemed to inhale the quietness, the solitude of the place, as a holy influence, mingling with the very air, I breathed, and a wild transport aroused my soul into an outburst of enthusiasm.

"Here—I cried—is the home for Love! Love, pure and stainless, flying from the crowded city, here can repose, beneath the shadow of quiet rocks, beside the gleam of tranquil waters, within the solitudes of endless forests. Yon sky, so clear, so cloudless, has never beheld a sight of human misery or wo. Yon lake, sweeping beneath me, like another sky, has never been crimsoned by human blood. This quiet valley, hidden from the world now, as it has been hidden since the creation, is but another world where two hearts that love, that mingle in one, that throb but for each other's joy, can dwell forever, in the calm silence of unalloyed affection—"

"A home for love such as angels feel—"

Closer and more close, the hand of Lorrimer pressed against the heaving bosom, with but the slight folds of the night-robe between.

"Here, beside this calm lake, whenever the love of a true woman shall be mine, here, afar from the cares and realities of life, will I dwell! Here, with the means which the accident of fortune has bestowed, will I build, not a temple, not a mansion, not a palace! But a cottage, a quiet home, whose roof shall arise—like a dear hope in the wilderness—from amid the green leaves of embowering trees—"

"You spoke thus, Lorraine? Do I not love you as a true woman should love? Is not your love calm and stainless as the waters of the mountain lake? We will dwell there, Lorraine! Oh, how like romance will be the plain reality of our life!"

"Oh! Mary, my own true love, in that moment as I stood gazing upon the world-hidden lake, my heart all throbbing with strange impulses, my very soul steeped in a holy calm, your form seemed to glide between my eyes and the moonlight! The thought rushed like a prophecy over my soul, that one day, amid the barren wilderness of hearts, which crowd the world, I should fine *one*, *one* heart, whose impulses should be stainless, whose affection should be undying, whose love should be mine! Oh, Mary, in that moment, I felt that my life would, one day, be illumined by your love—"

"And then you knew me not? Oh, Lorraine, is there not a strange mystery in this affection, which makes the heart long for the love, which it shall one day experience, even before the eye has seen the beloved one?"

Brighter grew the glow on her cheek, closer pressed the hand on her bosom, warmer and higher arose that bosom in the light.

"And there, Mary, in that quiet mountain valley, we will seek a home, when we are married. As soon as summer comes, when the trees are green, and the flowers burst from among the moss along the wood-path, we will hasten to the mountain lake, and dwell within the walls of our quiet home. For a home shall be reared for us, Mary, on a green glade that slopes down to the water's brink, with the tall trees sweeping away on either side.

"A quiet little cottage, Mary, with a sloping roof and small windows, all fragrant with wild flowers and forest vines! A garden before the door, Mary, where, in the calm summer morning, you can inhale the sweetness of the flowers, as they breath forth in untamed luxuriance. And then, anchored by the shore, Mary, a light sail-boat will be ready for us ever; to bear us over the clear lake in the early dawn, when the mist winds up in fleecy columns to the sky, or in the twilight, when the red sun flings his last ray over the waters, or in the silent night, when the moon is up, and the stars look kindly on us from the cloudless sky—"

"Alas! Lorraine! Clouds may come and storms, and winter—"

"What care we for winter, when eternal spring is in our hearts! Let winter come with its chill, and its ice and its snows! Beside our cheerful fire, Mary, with our hands clasping some book, whose theme is the trials of two hearts that loved on through difficulty and danger or death, we will sit silently, our hearts throbbing with one delight, while the long hours of the winter evening glide quietly on. Do you see the fire, Mary? How cheerily its beams light our faces as we sit in its kindly light! My arm is round your waist, Mary, my cheek is laid next to yours, our hands are locked together and your heart, Mary, oh how softly its throbbings fall on my ear!"

"Oh, Lorraine! Why is there any care in the world, when two hearts can make such a heaven on earth, with the holy lessons of an all-trusting love—"

"Or it may be, Mary—" and his gaze grew deeper, while his voice sank to a low and thrilling whisper—"Or it may be, Mary, that while we sit beside our winter fire—a fair babe—do not blush, *my wife*—a fair babe will rest smiling on your bosom—"

"Oh, Lorraine—" she murmured, and hid her face upon his breast, her long brown tresses, covering her neck and shoulders like a veil, while Lorraine wound his arms closely round her form, and looked around with a glance full of meaning.

There was triumph in that glance. The libertine felt her heart throbbing against his breast as he held her in his arms, he felt her bosom panting and heaving, and quivering with a quick fluttering pulsation and as he swept the clustering curls aside from her half-hidden face, he saw that her cheek glowed like a new-lighted flame.

"She is mine!" he thought, and a smile of triumph gave a dark aspect to his handsome face.

In a moment Mary raised her glowing countenance from his breast. She gazed around, with a timid, frightened look. Her breath came thick and gaspingly. Her cheeks were all a-glow, her blue eyes swam in a hazy dimness. She felt as though she was about to fall swooning on the floor. For a moment all consciousness seemed to have failed her, while a delirious langor came stealing over her senses. Lorrimer's form seemed to swim in the air before her, and the dim light of the room gave place to a flood of radiance, which seemed all at once to pour on her eyesight from some invisible source. Soft murmurs, like voices heard in a pleasant dream, fell gently on her ears, the langor came deeper and more mellow over her limbs; her bosom rose no longer quick and gaspingly, but in long pulsations, that urged the full globes in all their virgin beauty, softly and slowly into view. Like billows they rose above the folds of the night robe, while the flush grew warmer on her cheek, and her parted lips deepened into a rich vermillion tint.

"She is mine!" and the same dark smile flushed over Lorraine's face. Silent and motionless he sat, regarding his victim with a steadfast glance.

"Oh, Lorraine—" she cried, in a gasping voice, as she felt a strange unconsciousness stealing over her senses—"Oh, Lorraine—save me—save me!"

She arose, tottering on her feet, flinging her hands aloft, as though she stood on the brink of some frightful steep, without the power to retreat from its crumbling edge.

"There is no danger for you, my Mary—" whispered Lorrimer, as he received her falling form in his outspread arms—"There is no danger for you, my Mary—"

He played with the glossy curls of her dark brown hair as he spoke, while his arms gathered her half-swooning form full against his heart.

"She is mine! Her blood is a-flame—her senses swim in a delirium of passion! While the story fell from my lips, I aroused her slumbering woman's nature. Talk of force—ha, ha—She rests on my bosom as though she would grow there—"

As these thoughts half escaped from his lips, in a muttered whisper, his face shone with the glow of sensual passion, while his hazel eye dilated, with a glance, whose intense lustre had but one meaning; dark and atrocious.

She lay on his breast, her senses wrapt in a feverish swoon, that laid her powerless in his arms, while it left her mind vividly sensible of the approaching danger.

"Mary, my love—no danger threatens you—" he whispered playing with her glossy curls—"Look up, my love—*I* am with you, and will shield you from harm!"

Gathering her form in his left arm, secure of his victim, he raised her from his breast, and fixing his gaze upon her blue eyes, humid with moisture, he slowly flung back the night robe from her shoulders. Her bosom, in all its richness of outline, heaving and throbbing with that long pulsation, which urged it upward like a billow, lay open to his gaze.

And at the very moment, that her fair breast was thrown open to his sensual gaze, she sprang from his embrace, with a wild shriek, and instinctively gathered her robe over her bosom, with a trembling movement of her fair white hands. The touch of the seducer's hand, polluting her stainless bosom, had restored her to sudden consciousness.

"Lorraine! Lorraine!" she shrieked, retreating to the farthest corner of the room—"Oh, save me—save me—"

"No danger threatens you, my Mary—"

He advanced, as he spoke, towards the trembling girl, who had shrunk into a corner of the room, crouching closely to the rose-hued hangings, while her head turned over her shoulder and her hands clasped across her bosom, she gazed around with a glance full of terror and alarm.

Lorrimer advanced toward the crouching girl. He had been sure of his victim; he did not dream of any sudden outburst of terror from the half swooning maiden as she lay, helpless on his breast. As he advanced, a change came over his appearance. His face grew purple, and the veins of his eyes filled with thick red blood. He trembled as he walked across the floor, and his chest heaved and throbbed beneath his white vest, as though he found it difficult to breathe.

God save poor Mary, now!

Looking over her shoulder, she caught a gleam of his blood-shot eye, and read her ruin there.

"Mary, there is no danger—" he muttered, in a husky voice, as she shrunk back from his touch—"Let me raise you from the floor—"

"Save me, oh Lorraine—Save me!" she cried, in a voice of terror, crouching closer to the hangings along the wall.

"From what shall I save you?" he whispered, in a voice unnaturally soft and gentle, as though he endeavoured to hide the rising anger which began to gleam from his eye, when he found himself foiled in the very moment of triumph—"From what shall I save you—"

"From yourself—" she shrieked, in a frightened tone—"Oh, Lorraine, you love me. You will not harm me. Oh, save me, save me from yourself!"

Playing with the animal nature of the stainless girl, Lorrimer had aroused the sensual volcano of his own base heart. While he pressed her hand, while he gazed in her eyes, while he wound his embrace around her form, he had anticipated a certain and grateful conquest. He had not dreamed that the humid eye, the heaving bosom, the burning cheek of Mary Arlington, were aught but the signs of his coming triumph. Resistance? Prayers? Tears? He had not anticipated these. The fiend was up in his soul. The libertine had gone too far to recede.

He stood before the crouching girl, a fearful picture of incarnate LUST. Sudden as the shadow after the light this change had passed over his soul. His form arose towering and erect, his chest throbbed with sensual excitement, his hands hung, madly clinched, by his side, while his curling hair fell wild and disordered over his brows, darkening in a hideous frown, and his mustachioed lip wore the expression of his fixed and unalterable purpose. His blood-shot eyes, flashed with the unholy light of passion, as he stood sternly surveying the form of his victim. There was something wild and brutal in their savage glare.

"This is all folly—" he said, in that low toned and husky voice—"Rise from the floor, Mary. You don't think I'd harm you?"

He stooped to raise her from the floor, but she shrank from his extended hands as though there was pollution in his slightest touch.

"Mary, I wish you to rise from the floor!"

His clenched hands trembled as he spoke, and the flush of mingled anger and sensual feeling, deepened over his face.

"Oh, Lorraine!" she cried, flinging herself on her knees before him—"Oh, Lorraine—you will not harm *me?* This is not *you*, Lorraine; it cannot be *you*. You would not look darkly on me, your voice would not grow harsh as it whispered my name—It is not Lorraine that I see—it is an evil spirit—"

It was an evil spirit, she said, and yet looked up into his blood-shot eyes for a gleam of mercy as she spoke, and with her trembling fingers, wrung his clinched right hand, and clasped it wildly to her bosom.

Pure, stainless, innocent, her heart a heaven of love, her mind child-like in its knowledge of the World, she knew not what she feared. She did not fear the shame which the good world would heap upon her, she did not fear the Dishonor, because it would be followed by such pollution that, no man in honor might call her—Wife—no child in innocence might whisper her name as—Mother—she did not fear the foul Wrong, as society with its million tongues and eyes, fears it, and holds it in abhorence, ever visiting the guilt of the man upon the head of his trembling victim.

Mary feared the Dishonor, because her soul, with some strange consciousness of approaching evil, deemed it, a foul Spirit, who had arisen, not so much to visit her with wrong as to destroy the Love, she felt for Lorrimer. Not for herself, but for *his* sake, she feared that nameless crime, which already glared upon her from the blood-shot eyes of her Lover. Her *Lover!*

"Oh, Lorraine, you will not harm me! For the sake of God, save me—save me!"

She clasped his hand with a closer grasp and gathered it tremblingly to her bosom, while her eyes dilating with a glance of terror, were fixed upon his face.

"Mary—this is madness—nothing but madness—" he said in that voice, grown hoarse with passion, and rudely tore his hand from her grasp.

Another instant, and stooping suddenly, he caught her form in his arms, and raised her struggling from her very feet.

"Mary—you—are—mine!" he hissed the whisper in her ear, and gathered her quivering form more closely to his heart.

There was a low-toned and hideous laugh, muttering or growling through the air as he spoke, and the form of Devil-Bug, stole with a hushed footstep from the entrance of the Walnut Chamber, and seizing the light in his talon-fingers, glided from the room, with the same hyena laugh which had announced his appearance.

"The trap—the bottle—the fire, for the *brother*—" he muttered as his solitary eye, glanced upon the Libertine and his struggling victim, neither of whom had marked his entrance—"For the *Sister*—ha! ha! ha! The '*handsome*' Devil-Bug—Monk Gusty—'tends to her! 'Bijah did'nt listen for nothin'—ha, ha! this beats the *charcoal*, quite hollow!"

He disappeared, and the Rose Chamber was wrapt in midnight darkness.

Darkness! There was a struggle, and a shriek and a prayer. Darkness! There was an oath and a groan, mingling in chorus. Darkness! A wild cry for mercy, a name madly shrieked, and a fierce execration. Darkness! Another struggle, a low moaning sound, and a stillness like that of the grave. Now darkness and silence mingle together and all is still.

In some old book of mysticism and superstition, I have read this wild legend, which mingling as it does the terrible with the grotesque, has still its meaning and its moral.

In the sky, far, far above the earth—so the legend runs—there hangs an Awful Bell, invisible to mortal eye, which angel hands alone may toll, which is never tolled save when the Unpardonable Sin is committed on earth, and then its judgment peal rings out like the blast of the archangel's trumpet, breaking on the ear of the Criminal, and on his ear alone, with a sound that freezes his blood with horror. The peal of the Bell, hung in the azure depths of space, announces to the Guilty one, that he is an outcast from God's mercy for ever, that his Crime can never be pardoned, while the throne of the Eternal endures; that in the hour of Death, his soul will be darkened by the hopeless prospect of an eternity of wo; wo without limit, despair without hope; the torture of the never-dying worm, and the unquenchable flame, forever and forever.

Reader! Did the sound of the Judgment Bell, pealing with one awful toll, from the invisible air, break over the soul of the Libertine, as in darkness and in silence, he stood shuddering over the victim of his Crime?

If in the books of the Last Day, there shall be found written down, but *One unpardonable* crime, that crime will be known as the foul wrong, accomplished in the gaudy Rose Chamber of Monk-hall, by the wretch, who now stood trembling in the darkness of the place, while his victim lay senseless at his feet.

There was darkness and silence for a few brief moments, and then a stream of light flashed around the Rose Chamber.

Like a fiend, returned to witness some appalling scene of guilt, which he had but a moment left, Devil-Bug stood in the doorway of the Walnut Chamber. He grimly smiled, as he surveyed the scene.

And then with a hurried gesture, a pallid face and blood-shot eyes, as though some Phantom tracked his footsteps, Lorrimer rushed madly by him, and disappeared into the Painted Chamber. At the very moment of his disappearance, Devil Bug raised the light on high, and started backward with a sudden impulse of surprise.

"*Dead—Dead* and come to life!" he shrieked, and then the gaze of his solitary eye was fixed upon the entrance to the Walnut Room. With a mechanical gesture, he placed the light upon the table and fled madly from the chamber, while the curtains opening into the Walnut Room rustled to and fro, for a single instant, and then a ghastly face, with livid cheeks and burning eyes, appeared between the crimson folds, gazing silently around the place, with a glance, that no living man would choose to encounter, for his weight in gold—it was so like the look of one arisen from the dead.

CHAPTER FOURTEENTH

THE GUILTY WIFE

The light of the dark-lanthern streamed around the spot, where the Merchant stood.

Behind him, all was darkness, while the lanthern, held extended in his left hand, flung a ruddy blaze of light, over the outlines of the massive bed. Long silk curtains, of rich azure, fell drooping in voluminous folds, to the very floor, concealing the bed from view, while from within the gorgeous curtaining, that low softened sound, like a woman breathing in her sleep, came faintly to the Merchant's ear.

Livingstone advanced. The manner in which he held the lanthern flung his face in shadow, but you could see that his form quivered with a tremulous motion, and in the attempt to smother a groan which arose to his lips, a thick gurgling sound like the death-rattle, was heard in his throat.

Gazing from the shadow that enveloped his face, Livingstone, with an involuntary glance took in the details of the gorgeous couch—the rich curtaining of light azure satin, closely drawn around the bed; the canopy overhead surmounted by a circle of glittering stars, arranged like a coronet; and the voluptuous shapes, assumed by the folds, as they fell drooping to the floor, all burst like a picture on his eye.

Beside the bed stood a small table—resembling a lady's work stand—covered with a plain white cloth. The silver sheath of a large Bowie knife, resting on the white cloth, shone glittering in the light, and attracted the Merchant's attention.

He laid the pistol which he held at his right side, upon the table and raised the Bowie knife to the light. The sheath was of massive silver, and the blade of the keenest steel. The handle fashioned like the sheath, of massive silver, bore a single name, engraved in large letters near the hilt. *Algernon Fitz-Cowles*, and on the blade of polished steel, amid a wreath of flowers glittered the motto in the expressive slang of southern braggarts—'Stranger avoid a snag.'

Silently Livingstone examined the blade of the murderous weapon. It was sharp as a razor, with the glittering point inclining from the edge, like a Turkish dagger. The merchant grasped the handle of this knife in his right hand, and holding the lanthern on high, advanced to the bedside.

"His own knife—" muttered Livingstone—"shall find its way to his cankered heart—"

With the point of the knife, he silently parted the hangings of the bed, and the red glare of the lanthern flashed within the azure folds, revealing a small portion of the sleeping couch.

A moment passed, and Livingstone seemed afraid to gaze within the hangings, for he turned his head aside, more than once, and the thick gurgling noise again was heard in his throat. At last, raising the lanthern gently overhead, so that its beams would fall along a small space of the couch, while the rest was left in darkness, and grasping the knife with a firmer hold he gazed upon the spectacle disclosed to his view.

Her head deep sunken in a downy pillow, a beautiful woman, lay wrapt in slumber. By the manner in which the silken folds of the coverlid were disposed, you might see that her form was full, large and voluptuous. Thick masses of jet-black hair fell, glossy and luxuriant, over her round neck and along her uncovered bosom, which swelling with the full ripeness of womanhood, rose gently in the light. She lay on her side, with her head resting easily on one large, round arm, half hidden by the masses of black hair, streaming over the snow white pillow, while the other arm was flung carelessly along her form, the light falling softly over the clear transparent skin, the full roundness of its shape, and the small and delicate hand, resting gently on the coverlid.

Her face, appearing amid the tresses of her jet-black hair, like a fair picture half-hidden in sable drapery, was marked by a perfect regularity of feature, a high forehead, arching eyebrows and long dark lashes, resting on the velvet skin of each glowing cheek. Her mouth was opened slightly as she slept, the ivory whiteness of her teeth, gleaming through the rich vermillion of her parted lips.

She lay on that gorgeous couch, in an attitude of voluptuous ease; a perfect incarnation of the Sensual Woman, who combines the beauty of a mere animal, with an intellect strong and resolute in its every purpose.

And over that full bosom, which rose and fell with the gentle impulse of slumber, over that womanly bosom, which should have been the home of pure thoughts and wifely affections, was laid a small and swarthy hand, whose fingers, heavy with rings, pressed against the ivory skin, all streaked with veins of delicate azure, and clung twiningly among the dark tresses that hung drooping over the breast, as its globes rose heaving into view, like worlds of purity and womanhood.

It was a strange sight for a man to see, whose only joy, in earth or heaven, was locked within that snowy bosom, and yet Livingstone, the husband, stood firm and silent, as he gazed upon that strange hand, half hidden by the drooping curls.

It required but a slight motion of his hand, and the glare of the light flashed over the other side of the couch. The flash of the lanthern, among the shadows of the bed, was but for a moment, and yet Livingstone beheld the face of a dark-hued man, whose long dark hair mingled its heavy curls with the glossy tresses of his wife, while his hand reaching over her shoulder, rested, like a thing of foul pollution upon her bosom.

They slumbered together, slumbered in their guilt, and the Avenger stood gazing upon their faces while their hearts were as unconscious of his glance, as they were of the death which glittered over them in the upraised knife.

"Wife of mine—your slumber shall be deep and long—"

And as the whisper hissed from between the clenched teeth of the husband, he raised the dagger suddenly aloft, and then brought it slowly down until its point quivered within a finger's width of the heaving bosom, while the light of the lanthern held above his head, streamed over his livid face, and over the blooming countenance of his fair young wife.

The dagger glittered over her bosom; lower and lower it sank until a deeper respiration, a single heartdrawn sigh, might have forced the silken skin upon the glittering point, when the guilty woman murmured in her sleep.

"Algernon—a coronet—wealth and power—" were the broken words that escaped from her lips.

Again the husband raised the knife but it was with the hand clenched, and the sinews stiffened for the work of death.

"Seek your Algernon in the grave—" he whispered, with a convulsive smile, as his blue eyes, all alive with a glance, like a madman's gaze, surveyed the guilty wife—"Let the coronet be hung around your fleshless skull—let your wealth be a coffin, and—ha! ha!—your power—corruption and decay—"

It may have been that some feeling of the olden-time, when the image of that fair young wife dwelt in the holiest temple of his heart, came suddenly to the mind of the avenger, in that moment of fearful suspense, for his hand trembled for an instant and he turned his gaze aside, while a single scalding tear rolled down his livid cheek.

"Algernon—" murmured the wife—"We will seek a home—"

"In the grave!"

And the dagger rose, and gleamed like a stream of flame overhead, and then sank down with a whirring sound.

Is the bosom red with the stain of blood?

Has the keen knife severed the veins and pierced the heart?

The blow of a strong arm, stricken over Livingstone's shoulder, dashed his hand suddenly aside, and the knife sank to the very hilt in the pillow, within a hair's breadth of Dora's face. The knife touched the side of her cheek, and a long and glossy curl, severed from her head by the blow, lay resting on the pillow.

Livingstone turned suddenly round, with a deep muttered oath, while his massive form rose towering to its full height. Luke Harvey stood before him, his cold and glittering eye, fixed upon his face, with an expression of the deepest agitation.

"Stand back Sir—" muttered Livingstone with a quivering lip—"This spot is sacred to me! I want no witness to my wrong—nor to my vengeance!"

"Ha—ha!" sneered Luke bending forward until his eyes glared fixedly in the face of the Husband—"Is this a vengeance for a man like you?"

"Luke—again I warn you—leave me to my shame, and its punishment—"

" 'Shame' 'Punishment!' Ha—ha! You have been wronged in secret, slowly and quietly wronged, and yet would punish that wrong, by a blow that brings but a single pang!"

"Luke—you are right—" whispered Livingstone, his agitated manner subsiding into a look of calm and fearful determination—"The wrong has been secret, long in progress, horrible in result. So let the punishment be. She shall see *the* Death—" and his eyes flashed with a maniac wildness—"She shall see the Death as it slowly approaches, she shall feel it as it winds its very fangs into her very heart, she shall know that all hope is in vain, while my voice will whisper in her freezing ear—'Dora, it is by my will that you die! Shriek—Dora—shriek for aid! Death is cold and icy—I can save you! I your—husband! I can save you, but will not! Die—Adultress—die—' "

"Algernon—" murmured Dora half-awakened from her sleep—

"There is a cold hand laid against my cheek—"

"She wakes!" whispered Luke—"The dagger—the lanthern—"

It required but a single moment for Livingstone to draw the knife, from the pillow, where it rested against the blooming cheek of the wife, while Luke, with a sudden moment grasped the lanthern, and closed its door, leaving the Chamber wrapt in midnight darkness.

The husband stood motionless as a stone, and Luke held his very breath, as the voice of Dora broke on their ears, in tones of alarm and terror.

"Algernon—" she whispered, as she started from her slumber—"Awake—Do you not hear the sound of voices, by the bedside? Hist! Could it have been *the* dream? Algernon—"

"Deuced uncomfortable to be waked-up this way—" murmured a sleepy voice—"What's the matter Dora? What about a dream?"

"I was awakened just now from my sleep by the sound of voices.—I thought a blaze of light flashed round the room, while my hus—that is, Livingstone stood at the bedstead. And then I felt a cold hand laid against my cheek—"

"Ha—ha! Rather good, *that!* D'ye know Dora that I had a dream too? I dreamt that I was in the front parlor, second story you know, in your house on Fourth street, when the old fellow came in, and read your note on the table. Ha—ha—and then—are you listening?—I thought that the old gentleman while he was reading, turned to a bright pea-green in the face, and—"

"Hist! Do you not hear some one breathing in the room?"

"Pshaw, Dora, you're nervous! Go to sleep my love. Don't loose your rest for all the dreams in the world. Good night, Dora!"

"A little touch of farce with our tragedy—" half-muttered Luke, as a quiet chuckle shook his frame—"Egad! If they talk in this strain much longer, I'll have to guffaw! It's rather too much for my risibles; this is! A husband standing in the dark by the bedside, while his wife and her paramour are telling their pleasant dreams, in which he figures as the hero—"

Whether a smile passed over Livingstone's face, or a frown, Luke could not tell, for the room was dark as a starlit night, yet the quick gasping sound of a man struggling for breath, heard through the darkness, seem to indicate any thing but the pleasant laugh or the jovial chuckle.

"They sleep again!" muttered Luke—"She has sunken into slumber while Death watches at the bedside. Curse it—how that fellow snores!"

There was a long pause of darkness and silence. No word escaped the Husband's lips, no groan convulsed his chest, no half-muttered cry of agony, indicated the struggle which was silently rending his soul, as with a viper's fangs.

"Livingstone—" whispered Luke after a long pause—"Where are you? Confound it man, I can't hear you breathe. I'm afraid to uncover the light—it may awaken them again. I say Livingstone—had n't we better leave these quarters—"

"I could have borne expressions of remorse from her lips—I could have listened to sudden outpourings of horror wrung from her soul by the very blackness of her guilt, but this grovelling familiarity with vice!"

"Matter-of-fact pollution, as you might observe—" whispered Luke.

"Luke, I tell you, the cup is full to overflowing—but I will drain it to the dregs!"

"Now's your time—" whispered Luke, as, swinging the curtain aside, he suffered the light of the lanthern to fall over the bed—"Dora looks quite pretty. Fitz-Cowles decidedly interesting—"

"And on that bosom have I slept!" exclaimed Livingstone, in a voice of agony, as he gazed upon his slumbering wife—"Those arms have clung round my neck—and *now!* Ha! Luke you may think me mad, but I tell ye man, that there is the spirit of a slow and silent revenge creeping through my veins. *She* has *dishonored* me! Do you read anything like *forgiveness* in my face?"

"Not much o' it I assure you. But come, Livingstone—let's be going. This is not the time nor place for your revenge. Let's travel."

Livingstone laid down the bowie knife, and with a smile of bitter mockery, seized a small pair of scissors from the work-basket which stood on the table.

"You smile, Luke?" he whispered, as, leaning over the bedside, he laid his hand upon the jet-black hair of the slumbering Fitz-Cowles;—"Ha-ha! I will leave the place, but d'ye see, Luke, I must take some slight keepsake, to remind me of the gallant Colonel. A lock of his hair, you know, Luke?"

"Egad! Livingstone, I believe you're going mad! A lock of his hair? Pshaw! You'll want a straight jacket soon—"

"And a lock of my Dora's hair—" whispered Livingstone, as his blue eyes flashed from beneath his dark eyebrows, while his lips wore that same mocking smile—"But you see the knife saved me all trouble. Here is a glossy tress severed by the Colonel's dagger. Now let me wind them together, Luke, let me lay them next to my heart, Luke—yes, smile my fellow—Ha! ha! ha!"

"Hist! Your wife stirs in her sleep—you will awaken them again."

"D'ye know, Luke—" cried Livingstone, drawing his partner close to his side, and looking in his face, with a vacant glance, that indicated a temporary derangement of intellect—"D'ye know, Luke, that I didn't do that, o' my own will? Hist! Luke—closer—closer—I'll tell you. The Devil was at the bedside, Luke; he whispered it in my ear, he bade me take these keepsakes—ha, ha, ha—what a jolly set of fellows we are! And then, Luke—" his voice sank to a thrilling whisper—"He pointed with his iron hand to *the last scene*, in which my vengeance shall be complete. She shall beg for mercy, Luke; aye, on her knees, but—ha, ha, ha—*kill—kill—kill!* is written in letters of blood before my eyes, every where, Luke, every where. Don't you see it?"

He pointed vacantly at the air as he spoke, and seized Luke by the shoulder, as though he would command his attention to the blood-red letters.

Luke was conscious that he stood in the presence of a madman.

Inflexible as he was in his own secret purpose of revenge, upon the woman who had trampled on his very heart, Luke still regarded the Merchant with a feeling akin to brotherhood. As the fearful fact impressed itself on his soul, that Livingstone stood before him, deprived of reason, an expression of the deepest feeling shadowed the countenance of Luke, and his voice was broken in its tones as he endeavoured to persuade the madman, to leave the scene of his dishonor and shame.

"Come! Livingstone! let us go—" said Luke, taking his partner by the arm, and leading him gently toward the closet.

"But I've got the keepsakes safe, Luke—" whispered Livingstone, as that wild light flashed from his large blue eyes—"D'ye see the words in the air, Luke? Now they change to her name—Dora, Dora, Dora! All in blood-red letters. I say Luke, let's have a quiet whist party—there's four of us—Dora and I; you and Fitz-Cowles—"

"I'm willing—" exclaimed Luke, as with a quick movement he seized the pistol—left by Livingstone on the table, and concealed it within the breast of his greatcoat—"Suppose we step into the next room, and get every thing ready for the party—"

"You're keen, Luke, keen, but I'm even with you—" whispered Livingstone as his livid face lighted up with a sudden gleam of intelligence—"Here we stand on the threshold of this closet—we are about to leave my wife's bed-room. You think I'm mad. Do I look like a madman? I know there is no whist-party to be held this night, I know that—Hist. Luke. Don't you see it, all pictured forth in the air? The scene of my vengeance? In colors of blood, painted by the Devil's hand? Yonder Luke—yonder! How red it grows—and then in letters of fire, every where, every where, is written—Dora—Dora—Dora—"

It was a fearful spectacle to see that strong man, with his imposing figure, raised to its full stature and his thoughtful brow, lit up with an expression of idiotic wonder, as standing on the verge of the secret door, he pointed wildly at the blood-red picture which his fancy had drawn in the vacant air while his blue eyes dilated with a maniac glance, and his face grew yet more livid and ghastly.

"Come, Livingstone—" cried Luke gently leading him through the closet—"You had better leave this place—"

"And yet Dora, is sleeping here? My young wife? 'The mother of my children?' Do'ye think Luke, that I'd have believed you last Thursday morning, if you had then told me this? 'Livingstone, this day-week, you will leave a chamber in a brothel, and leave your young wife, sleeping in another man's arms.' But never mind Luke—it will all be right. For I tell ye, it is there, there before me in colors of blood! That last scene of my vengeance! And there—there—in letters of flame—Dora!—Dora! Dora!"

And while the fair young wife slept quietly in the bed of guilt and shame, Luke led the Merchant from the room and from the house.

CHAPTER FIFTEENTH

THE DISHONOR

All was silent within the Rose Chamber. For a single moment that pale visage glared from the crimson hangings, concealing the entrance to the Walnut Room, and then with a measured footstep, Byrnewood Arlington advanced along the floor, his countenance ghastly as the face of Lazarus, at the very instant, when in obedience to the words of the Incarnate, life struggled with corruption and death, over his cheek and brow.

Bring home to your mind the scene, when Lazarus lay prostrate in the grave, a stiffened corse, his face all clammy with corruption, the closed eyes surrounded by loathsome circles of decay, the cheeks sunken, and the lips fallen in: let the words of Jesus ring in your ears, 'Lazarus, come forth!" And then as the blue eyelids slowly unclose, as the gleam of life shoots forth from the glassy eye, as the flush of health struggles with the yellowish hue of decay along each cheek, as life and death mingling in that face for a single moment, maintain a fearful combat for the mastery; then I pray you, gaze upon the visage of Byrnewood Arlington, and mark how like it is to the face of one arisen from the dead; a ghastly face, on whose fixed outline the finger-traces of corruption are yet visible, from whose eyes the film of the grave is not yet passed away.

The gaze of Byrnewood, as he strode from the entrance of the Walnut Chamber, was riveted to the floor. Had the eyes of the rattlesnake gleamed from the carpet, slowly drawing its victim to his ruin, Byrnewood could not have fixed his gaze upon the object in the centre of the floor, with a more fearful and absorbing intensity.

There, thrown prostrate on the gaudy carpet, insensible and motionless, the form of Mary Arlington lay at the brother's feet.

He sank silently on his knees.

He took her small white hand—now cold as marble—within his own, he swept the unbound tresses back from her palid brow. Her eyes were closed as in death, her lips hung apart, the lower one trembling with a scarcely perceptible movement, her cheek was pale as ashes, with a deep red tint in the centre.

Byrnewood uttered no sound, nor shrieked forth any wild exclamation of revenge, or wo, or despair. He silently drew the folds of the night-robe round her form, and veiled her bosom—but a moment agone warmed into a glow by the heart's fires, now paled by the fingers of the ravisher—he veiled her fair young bosom from the light.

It was a sad sight to look upon. That face, so fair and blooming, but a moment past, now pale as death, with spot of burning red on the centre of each cheek: that bosom, a moment since, heaving with passion, now still and motionless; those delicate hands with tiny fingers, which had bravely fought for honor, for virtue, for purity, an instant ago, now resting cold and stiffened by her side.

Thick tresses of dark brown hair, hung round her neck. With that same careful movement of his hand, Byrnewood swept them aside. Along the smooth surface of that fair neck like some noisome reptile, trailing over a lovely flower, a large vein, black and distorted, shot upward, darkening the glossy skin, while it told the story of the maiden's dishonor and shame.

"My sister!" was the solitary exclamation that broke from Byrnewood's lips as he gazed upon the form of the unconscious girl, and his large dark eye, dilating as he spoke, glanced around with an expression of strange meaning.

He raised her form in his arms, and kissed her cold lips again and again. No tear trickled from his eyelids; no sigh heaved his bosom; no deep muttered execration manifested the agitation of his soul.

"My sister!" he again whispered, and gathered her more close to his heart.

A slight flush deepening over her cheek, even while he spoke, gave signs of returning consciousness.

Mary slowly unclosed her eyes, and gazed with a wandering glance around the room. An instant passed ere she discovered that she lay in Byrnewood's arms.

"Oh, brother—" she exclaimed, not with a wild shriek, but in a low-toned voice, whose slightest accent quivered with an emphasis of despair—"Oh, brother! Leave me—leave me. I am not worthy of your touch. I am vile, brother, oh, most vile! Leave me—Leave me, for I am lost!"

"Mary!" whispered Byrnewood, resisting her attempt to unwind his arms from her form, while the blood, filling the veins of his throat, produced an effect like strangulation—"Mary! Do not—do not speak thus—I—I—"

He could say no more, but his face dropped on her cold bosom, and the tears, which he had silently prayed for, came at last.

He wept, while that low choaking noise, sounding in his throat, that involuntary heaving of the chest, that nervous quivering of the lip, all betokened the strong man wrestling with his agony.

"Do not weep for me, brother—" she said, in the same low-toned voice—"I am polluted, brother, and am not worthy of the slightest tear you shed for me. Unwind your arms—brother, do not resist me—for the strength of despair is in these hands—unwind your arms, and let me no longer pollute you by my touch—"

There was something fearful in the expression of her face as she spoke. She was no longer the trembling child whose young face, marked the inexperience of her stainless heart. A new world had broken upon her soul, not a world of green trees, silver streams and pleasant flowers, but a chaos of ashes, and mouldering flame; a lurid sky above, a blasted soil below, and one immense horizon of leaden clouds, hemming in the universe of desolation.

She had sprung from the maiden into the woman, but a blight was on her soul forever. The crime had not only stained her person with dishonor, but, like the sickening warmth of the hot-house, it had forced the flower of her soul, into sudden and unnatural maturity. It was the maturity of precocious experience. In her inmost soul, she felt that she was a dishonored thing, whose very touch was pollution, whose presence, among the pure and stainless, would be a bitter mockery and foul reproach. The guilt was not hers, but the Ruin blasted her purity forever.

"Unwind your arms, my brother—" she exclaimed, tearing herself from his embrace, with all a maniac's strength—"I am polluted. You are pure. Oh do not touch me—do not touch me. Leave me to my shame—oh, leave me—"

She unwound her form from his embrace, and sank crouching into a corner of the Rose Chamber, extending her hands with a frightened gesture, as though she feared his slightest touch.

"Mary" shrieked Byrnewood, flinging his arms on high, with a movement of sudden agitation—"Oh, do not look upon me thus! Come to me—oh, Mary—come to me, for I am your brother."

The words, the look and the trembling movement of his outspread arms, all combined, acted like a spell upon the intellect of the ruined girl. She rose wildly to her feet, as though impelled by some invisible influence, and fell tremblingly into her brother's arms.

While one dark and horrible thought, was working its way through the avenues of his soul, he gathered her to his breast again and again.

And in that moment of silence and unutterable thought, the curtains leading into the Painted Chamber were slowly thrust aside, and Lorrimer again appeared upon the scene. Stricken with remorse, he had fled with a madman's haste from the scene of his crime, and while his bosom was torn by a thousand opposing thoughts, he had endeavored to drown the voice within him, and crush the memory of the nameless wrong. It was all in vain. Impelled by an irresistible desire, to look again upon the victim of his crime, he re-entered the Rose Chamber. It was a strange sight, to see the Brother kneeling on the floor, as he gathered his sister's form in his arms, and yet the Seducer, gave no sign nor indication of surprise.

A fearful agitation was passing over the Libertine's soul, as unobserved by the brother or sister, he stood gazing upon them with a wandering glance. His face, so lately flushed with passion, in its vilest hues, was now palest and livid. His white lips, trembled with a nervous moment, and his hands, extended on either side, clutched vacantly at the air, as though he wrestled with an unseen foe.

While the thought of horror, was slowly darkening over Byrnewood's soul, a thought as dark and horrible gathered like a Phantom over the mind of Lorrimer.

A single word of explanation, will make the subsequent scene, clear and intelligible to the reader.

From generation to generation, the family of the Lorrimer's, had been subject to an aberration of intellect, as sudden as it was terrible; always resulting from any peculiar agitation of mind, which might convulse the soul, with an emotion remarkable for its power or energy. It was a hallucination, a temporary madness, a sudden derangement of intellect. It always succeeded an uncontrollable outburst of anger, or grief, or joy. From father to son, since the family had first come over to Pennsylvania, with the Proprietor and Peace-Maker William Penn, this temporary derangement of intellect, had descended as a fearful heritage.

Lorrimer had been subject to this madness, but once in his life, when his father's corse lay stiffened before his eyes. And now, as he stood gazing upon the form of the brother and sister, Lorrimer, felt this temporary madness stealing over his soul, in the form of a strange hallucination, while he became conscious, that in a single moment, the horror which shook his frame, would rise to his lips in words of agony and fear.

"Raise your hands with mine, to Heaven, Mary—" exclaimed Byrnewood as the Thought which had been working over his soul, manifested its intensity in words—"Raise your hands with mine, and curse the author of your ruin! Lift your voice with mine, up to the God, who beheld the wrong—who will visit the wronger with a doom meet, for his crime—lift your voice with mine, and curse him—"

"Oh Byrnewood, do not, do not curse *him*. The wrong has been done but do not, I beseech you, visit his head with a curse—"

"Hear me, oh God, before whom, I now raise my hands, in the vow of justice! In life I will be to this wretch, as a Fate, a Doom, a Curse!

"I am vile—oh God—steeped in the same vices, which blacken the heart of this man, cankered by the same corruption. But the office, which I now take on myself, raising this right hand to thee, in witness of my fixed purpose, would sanctify the darkest fiend in hell! I am the avenger of my sister's wrong! She was innocent, she was pure, she trusted and was betrayed! I will avenge her! Before thee, I swear to visit her wrong, upon the head of her betrayer, with a doom never to be forgotten in the memory of man. This right hand I dedicate to this solemn purpose—come what will, come what may, let danger threaten or death stand in my path, through sickness and health, through riches or poverty, I now swear, to hold my steady pathway onward, my only object in life—the avengement of my sister's wrong! He *shall* die by this hand—oh God—I swear it by thy name—I swear it by my soul—I swear it by the Fiend who impelled the villain to this deed of crime—"

As he whispered forth this oath, in a voice which speaking from the depths of his chest, had a hollow and sepulchral sound, the fair girl flung herself on his breast, and with a wild shriek essayed to delay the utterance of the curse, by gathering his face, to her bosom.

For a moment her efforts were successful. Lorrimer had stood silent and pale, while the deep-toned voice of Byrnewood Arlington, breaking in accents of doom upon his ear, had aided and strengthened the strange hallucination which was slowly gathering over his brain like a mighty spell.

"There is a wide river before me, its broad waves tinged with the last red rays of a winter sunset—" such were the words he murmured, extending his hand, as though pointing to the scene, which dawned upon his soul—"A wide river with its waves surging against the wharves of a mighty city. Afar I behold steeples and roofs and towers, all glowing in the beams of the setting sun. And as I gaze, the waves turn to blood, red and ghastly blood—and now the sky is a-flame, and the clouds sweep slowly past, bathed in the same crimson hue. All is blood—the river rushes before me, and the sky and the city—all pictured in colors of blood.

"An invisible hand is leading me to my doom. There is Death for me, in yonder river, and I know it, yet down, down to the rivers banks, down, down into the red waters, I must go. Ha! ha! 'Tis a merry death! The blood-red waves rise above me—higher, higher, higher! Yonder is the city, yonder the last rays of the setting sun, glitter on the roof and steeple, yonder is the blood-red sky—and ah! I tell ye I will not die—you shall not sink me beneath these gory waves! Devil! Is not your vengeance satisfied—must you feast your eyes with the sight of my closing agonies—must your hand grasp me by the throat, and your foot trample me beneath the waves? I tell you I will not, will not die—"

"Ha—ha—ha! Here's purty going's on—" laughed the hoarse voice of Devil-Bug, as his hideous form appeared in the doorway of the Walnut Chamber, with his attendant negroes at his back—"Seems the gal helped him off. There he sits—the ornery feller, with his sister in his arms—while Gusty, is a-doin' some ravin's on his own indivdooal hook. Come here Glow-worm—here Musquito—come here my pets, and 'tend to this leetle family party—"

In another instant the Rose Chamber became the scene of a strange picture.

Byrnewood had arisen to his feet, while Lorrimer stood spell-bound by the hallucination which possessed his brain. The handsome Libertine stood in the centre of the room, his form dilating to its full stature, his face the hue of ashes, while with his hazel eyes, glaring on vacancy, he clutched wildly at the air, starting backward at the same moment, as though some invisible hand, was silently impelling him to the brink of the blood-red river, which rolled tumultuously at his feet, which slowly gathered around him, which began to heave upward to his very lips.

On one side, in a half-kneeling position, crouched Mary Arlington, her large blue eyes, starting from her pallid face, as with her upraised hands, crossed over her bosom, she gazed upon the agitated countenance of the seducer, with a glance of mingled awe and wonder; while, on the other side, stern and erect, Byrnewood, with his pale visage darkening in a settled frown, with one foot advanced and his hand upraised, seemed about to strike the libertine to the floor.

In the background, rendered yet more hideous by the dimness of the scene, Devil-Bug stood grinning in derisive triumph as he motioned his attendants, the Herculean negroes, to advance and secure their prey.

There was silence for a single moment. Lorrimer still stood clutching at the vacant air, Mary still gazed upon this face in awe, Byrnewood yet paused in his meditated blow, while Devil-Bug, with Musquito and Glow-worm at his back, seemed quietly enjoying the entire scene, as he glanced from side to side with his solitary eye.

"Unhand me—I will not die—" shrieked Lorrimer, as he fancied that phantom hand, gathering tightly round his throat, while the red waters swept surging to his very lips—"I will not die—I defy—ah! ah! You strangle me—"

"The hour of your death has come! You have said it—and it shall be so!" whispered Byrnewood, advancing a single step, as his dark eye was fixed upon the face of Lorrimer—"While your own guilty heart spreads a blood-red river before your eyes, this hand—no phantom hand—shall work your death!"

He sprang forward, while a shriek arose from Mary's lips, he sprang forward with his eyes blazing with excitement, and his outspread hand ready for the work of vengeance, but as he sprang, the laugh of Devil-Bug echoed at his back, and the sinewy arms of the negroes gathered suddenly round his form and flung him as suddenly to the floor.

"Here's fine goin's on—" exclaimed Devil-Bug, as he glanced from face to face—"A feller who's been a leetle too kind to a gal, stands a-makin' speeches at nothin'. The gal kneels on the carpet as though she were a gettin' up a leetle prayer on her own account; and this 'ere onery feller—git a good grip o' him you bull-dogs—sets up a small shop o' cussin' and sells his cusses for nothin'! Here's a tea party for ye—"

"What does all this mean, Devil-Bug—" exclaimed Lorrimer, in his usual voice, as the hallucination passed from him like a dream, leaving him utterly unconscious of the strange vision which had a moment since absorbed his very soul—"What does all this mean? Ha! Byrnewood and Mary—I remember? *You* are *her* brother—are you not?"

'I am her avenger—" said Byrnewood, with a ghastly smile, as he endeavoured to free himself from the grasp of the negroes—"And your executioner! Within three days you shall die by this hand!"

"Ha-ha-ha!" laughed Devil-Bug—"There's more than one genelman as has got a say in that leetle matter! How d'ye feel, young man? Did you ever take opium afore? You won't go to sleep nor nothin'? We can't do what we like with you? Kin we? Ho-ho-ho! *I vonders how that'ill vork!*"

BOOK THE SECOND

THE DAY AFTER THE NIGHT

The Forger

CHAPTER FIRST

FITZ-COWLES AT HOME

The scene changes to a Chamber in the fourth story of the TON HOTEL, which arises along Chesnut street, a monster-building, with some hundred windows varying its red-brick face, in the way of eyes, covered with green-blind shutters, looking very much like so many goggles intended to preserve the sight of the visual organs aforesaid; while the verandah, on the ground floor, affording an entrance to the bar-room, might be likened to the mouth of the grand-edifice, always wide open and ready to swallow a customer.

The sunshine of a cold, clear winter morning was streaming dimly, between the half-closed inside shutters, of the small chamber on the fourth story. The faint light, pouring between the shutters, of the two windows, looking to the south, served to reveal, certain peculiar characteristics of the place.

There was a dressing bureau, surmounted by a hanging mirror, stand ing between the two windows of the chamber. Along the marble top of the bureau, were disposed various bottles of perfumes, whose strong scent impregnated the atmosphere with remarkable reminiscences of musk, and orange, and lemon, and *patchoully;* a pair of well-used kid gloves, which had been white yesterday; a rumpled black scarf; a Play bill figured off with intoxicated letters, displaying the entertainment at the Walnut Street Theatre the night before; and a glittering bowie knife, side by side with its silver sheath.

All over the carpet, were scattered Windsor Chairs, either grouped in circles, as though they were talking about the various gentry who had reposed on their well-cushioned seats; or fixed in strange positions along the walls, like waiters at a party, overburdened with coats and vests and stocks, and other articles of apparel, thrown carelessly over their rounds; or yet again flung down on the floor, with their heels in the air, as though they had taken a drop too much, and didn't know how to get up again.

There was a large sofa on one side of the room, a coal fire blazing in the grate opposite; while in the dim distance, you might perceive the outlines of a bed, and hear the deep bass of a heavy snore, which held a concert of its own, within the closely drawn curtains.

Altogether, that entire room, located in the fourth story of the Ton House, said as plainly as a room can say, that somebody had come home very late last night, or very early this morning, most probably in liquor; and called up as witnesses to this interesting assertion, the chairs thrown disorderly about the floor, the gloves and Bowie knife on the dressing bureau, the hat on the sofa, and the heavy snore within the bed.

Sitting in the blaze of light streaming between the aperture of the half-closed shutters, was a small Creole boy, whose slight yet perfectly proportioned form, was perched on the edge of a Windsor chair, as with his legs crossed and his hair flung back from his tawny face, the young gentleman was briskly engaged in elaborating a fashionable boot into the requisite degree of polish.

The Boy was eminently handsome. His face was a light brown in hue, yet perfectly regular in every feature; his complexion clear as a ripe Seckel pear; his lips red as May cherries; his eyebrows penciled and arching, and his eyes full, large, and black; brilliant as diamonds, and glittering as icicles. Long curling hair, marked by that peculiar jet black, tinged with a shade of deep blue, which designates the child of white and African parents, fell waving around his neck and face, in stiffened locks, resembling in their texture, the mane of a horse. His form, light, springy and agile, was the Ideal of a Creole Cupid. Not an outline too large or too small, not the slightest disproportion visible in a single limb; with small feet and delicate hands, a waist as lithe as a willow, and a hollow in the back like a bow gently bent, the Creole, was altogether one of the most beautiful things, ever fashioned by the hand of Nature.

He was a pretty child, and yet his large black eyes had something in their glance which spoke of a precocious intimacy with the vices and intrigues of manhood.

"Massa tole Dim to polish dat boot until he see his face in de morroccor—" muttered the young gentleman, brushing away at the glittering leather—"Dim can see his nose, and his two eyes in de boot, but the mouth aint not perfect. Stop a minnit, I bring dat feature out—ha, ha, hah!"

It was a pleasure to hear the little fellow talk, there was such a delicate accent lingering on his words; and his laugh, not at all similar to the usual African guffaw, was a quiet chuckle, which rolled lusciously in his mouth like a delicious morsel, whose sweetness he wished to enjoy at leisure.

"Tink I shall hab to discharge Massa. Debbil of a flare-up 'tween me and him some day when I tells him; 'I don't want you any more, you sah!—you kin take dem wages and go!' Kep Dim up till broke ob day. Say dat Morroccor don' shine? Break de lookin'-glasses heart—I tells you. Till broke ob day kep Dim a-waitin', and den tumbles into bed, widout so much as giving de chile a-quataw! Oh—de High-Golly!"

This appeal to Master Endymion's favorite Saint, the High-Golly, supposed to be some imaginary Deity, created by the fertile fancy of the young Creole, was occasioned by a sudden mishap with the boot, which resenting a vigorous push of the brush, slipped out of his hands, and went spinning across the room.

"Wonder if the debbil aint in dat Morroccor? I jis does. Nebber see sich a boot in all my born days. I lay a bran new brass dollar, dat if I was to set dat boot at de head of the stair, and no watch him, he'd streak it right off to de bar room, and call for a mint-julap, an' pull out his quartair to pay for it! I jis try him some day—Ha! Ha! Ha!"

"I say Dim!"

"Yes Massa—I'se about—"

"I say, Dim!" continued the voice which resounded from the interior of the bed-curtains, in the dark corner of the room, where the snore had been heard—"I say Dim, what kind of a day is it?"

"Bran new day Massa. Got it's new coat and trowse's on."

"I say Dim, what have we got to do to day?"

"Last night de Curnel, gib dis chile a kick, in order to mem'randum dese tings on Dim's memory. Dis mornin' you got to pay all your creditors. Dey comes in about an hour. High-Golly—aint dere a lot ob 'em? Den you got to see de Lady, who libs in Fourth street. Den you got to go, down town, to see if ole Devil-Bug, keeps dat *dere feller* safe. You knows who I means? Den you got to gib Dim, a qua-taw, and not to gib him no kick, by no means—"

"Dressing-gown Dim!"

"Yes, Massa—"

"Got any hot water, ready for me, Dim?"

"Biles like a steam ingine—"

"Light up the room, Dim!"

And in obedience to this request, Endymion flung back the shutters, and the full glare of the sunlight poured into the room. The owner of the voice and snore heard from within the curtains, sprang from the bed and assuming the dressing gown, advanced toward the windows.

Col. Fitz-Cowles, the handsome colonel Fitz-Cowles, stood revealed in the light, his dark-hued face looking somewhat worn and haggard, around the eyes, while his slender form, attired in the rainbow morning-gown and close fitting drawers, though well proportioned, and graceful in its outlines, by no means displayed that perfection of symmetry, which distinguished the person of the millionaire in broad daylight, along Chesnut street. For instance, the Colonel was thicker around the waist, thinner about the hips, smaller in the region of the calves, than was usual with him, when arrayed in full dress. His face was very pale and his cheeks lacked that deep vermillion tint, which gave such life to his dusky countenance at the evening party, or the afternoon parade.

"Dim you d———l—" exclaimed the Colonel, bestowing a gentle hint upon the gentleman of color, with the toe of his slipper—"Go down and get my breakfast. Tell, the cook to butter my toast, and broil my steak. Vanish!"

Dim vanished through the door at the extreme end of the apartment. Arranging his shaving materials on the marble top of the dressing bureau, Fitz-Cowles commenced the solemn ceremonies of the toillette.

"Good razor that! Keen! Bad soap this—must kick the barber who sold it to me. Just think of my ticklish position! In debt up to my ears, forced to leave the United States Hotel only a day since, in order to avoid my creditors: perched in the fourth story of the Ton House; and why? Because I can't use the solid stuff, locked up in that old hair trunk. *Can't* use it. Somebody might find out something if I did. Curse the thing but I think the old trunk's laughing at me—"

Razor in hand Fitz-Cowles stooped to the floor, and drew from beneath the sofa, an old hair trunk, which looked as if it had been through all Napoleon's campaigns, and suffered in the battle of Waterloo; it was so battered, and scarred and weather-beaten, with great wounds of uncovered leather visible among the worn-out hair, of its exterior.

"An hundred thousand locked up in that old ruffian of a trunk—" muttered Fitz-Cowles, gazing upon the object, with an angry scowl—"Half in sovereigns—half in notes! The d———l throttle the fool, why could'nt he get it all in American gold?"

"De toast is buttered and de steak is briled—" and as he spoke, Endymion entered the room, carrying the breakfast of his Master in his hands—"Muss discharge dat cook. She gits quite sassy—"

"Dim—" cried Fitz-Cowles, making a hideous face at the glass in the effort to shave his chin—"Set my breakfast down by the fire, and come here. Now, Dim, answer me, one question. *Who are we?*"

"Massa take de chile for a philly sofer? Dat berry cute question! Sometime we are a plantaw from the Souf—sometimes we are a son of Mexican Prince; oder time we come from Englan' and our fader is a Lord. De High-Golly! We are so many tings, dat de debbil hisself could'nt count 'em—"

"Where were we this time last month?"

"Charleston, Massa—"

"The month before?"

"New Orleans Massa—"

"Month afore, that, eh, Dim?"

"Bos'on Massa—"

"How long since we first fixed our quarters in this city?"

"Six months ago, and been a travellin' about eber since. Led dis chile a debbil ob a life—"

"What were we travelling about for—eh?"

"Axe de ole hair trunk. He tell you plain as pie-crust—"

"I'll tell you what it is, Dim—" exclaimed Fitz-Cowles laying down the razor, and turning to the handsome Creole boy—"If you ever whisper a word to any body, about any-thing you may have seen or heard, while you travelled about with me, these last six months, I'll just take this knife, and skin you, you black scoundrel, skin you—d'ye hear?"

Dim looked up into the scowling face of his master, with a glance of perfect calmness. The brow of Fitz-Cowles was disfigured by a hideous frown, and his entire countenance, wore an expression, characteristic of a low bully, who has been accustomed to the vilest haunts, in the most corrupt cities of the South. Dim was used to these sudden outbursts of passion, when his master, dropping his gentlemanly repose of manner, was wont to stand before him with his Bowie knife in hand, while with a threatening tongue and sullen brow, he bade him reveal the things he had seen and the words he had heard; if he dared.

"You black scoundrel, d'ye hear?"

"De High-Golly! Dim aint black and Dim aint no scoundrel. Yes Massa, I hears—"

"If you ever whisper a word, mind, a word, I'd just take this bowie knife, and cut your heart from your body! I'd do't I tell you—"

"What make you do dat for? Dim could'nt draw bref den—"

"Pshaw! You know better than to whisper a word! Here—help me to dress Dim. My corsets, Dim—"

"Here they are Massa—" cried Dim, throwing open, one of the drawers of the dressing bureau—"New pair Massa—"

"Lay that Morning gown on the chair. Now lace me. Tighter I say—that 'ill do. That's about the waist we want—is n't it Dim?"

"Yes Massa. Dat's de wasp *com*-plete!"

"Hips, Dim—"

"Which hip you want, Massa? Big hip or little hip?" cried Endymion, rummaging in the open drawer—"Dis pair do?"

"More subdued, Dim, more subdued. Just large enough to make my frock coat set out in the skirt. That's the idea—"

With a careful movement Endymion strapped certain detached portions of padding, around his master's form below the waist, and in a moment, this part of the ceremony was finished, giving quite a voluptuous swell to the outline of the Colonel's figure.

"Calves, Dim—"

"Which boots Massa wear to-day? Hab dis big calf or de toder one?"

"We want a good calf to-day, Dim. A large, fat calf. That pair will do. Tie it round the leg—there, there. Draw the stocking over it—gently—gent-ly! That's about the outline—eh?"

"Dicky or a shirt, to-day, eh, Dim?"

"Shirt, Massa, as you are goin' to hold your *Lebee!*"

"Ha! ha! Wont there be a lot o' 'em—the creditors? Black scarf—Dim?"

"Dar it is, Massa. Turn de collar down and tie up de scarf wid dis gole pin—dat's de ticket!"

"Now, Dim, my slippers. She worked them for me, *you know*, Dim? How many ladies are engaged to be married to us, if we will have them?"

"Dare's de soap biler's daughter, who spends her fader's fortin in perfumery. Dare's de rich grocery man's daughter, and de hardware merchant's daughter, and de wool merchant's only chile, and dare's—"

"Oh, d———d them; the *set* is cursed low. Black pants, Dim? Which is our principle ticket in the female line? Eh, Dim?"

"Ha, ha, ha! Down Fourth street, Massa. De old genelman in New York, and de lady at home by herself! De High-Golly!"

"Vest, Dim. The new black vest, which, last night, came home from the tailor. What hour will the creditors be here?"

"Dey comes in that ar door—" observed Endymion, pointing to the door on the right of the western window—"And, accordin' to your directions, dey is shown into dat door, which conducts 'em into de large saloon, where dere's fire to warm their hands, and cheers to rest their bodies—"

"Hallo, Dim, there's a tap at the door—" exclaimed Fitz-Cowles, as, arrayed in the full splendor of his morning costume, with a gaudy silk wrapper, all broken out into spots of green, blue, and red, thrown round his limbs, he resumed his seat in the easy chair, beside the breakfast table—"I know the knock. It is Count Common Sewer—show him in."

Opening the door near the western window, Dim made a profound bow, as he ushered the visitor into the presence of Col. Fitz-Cowles.

"De Editaw ob de Daily Black Mail. Mistaw Poodle, sah—Buzby Poodle—s-a-h!"

"Ha-ha! Curnel—*Bon jour*, as we say in French. Seen the Black Mail this morning. Capital *on dit* about your gold mines—quite the thing—*ensemble de chose*, as we say in domestic French—"

As he spoke, Buzby Poodle, Esq., stood bowing and scraping in the centre of the vacant space of carpet, extending before the breakfast table. Buzby Poodle wasn't handsome. Not precisely. He was a little thickset man, with a short heavy body, shaped something like a pine-knot, and irregular legs, fashioned like a pair of inverted parentheses, or like a pair of sickles with their backs placed together. It must be confessed that his legs were deplorably knock-kneed nearly acquainted with each other at the knees, and quite distant in their intercourse at the feet. Buzby's feet were not small; Douzzle the bootmaker has been heard to say, with evident pain, that he would just as soon make slippers for a young hippopotamus, as boots for Buzby. You could not positively say that Buzby's hands were small, or delicate, or decently aristocratic. Very short in the fingers, and very thick across the palm and back, Buzby's hands reminded you of a terrapin's fin; they were such peculiar hands.

Buzby's face wasn't handsome. It may have been expressive, or intellectual, but it was not handsome. Looking upon his countenance, you were aware of the presence of a saffron lump of flesh, with a small projection in the centre for a nose, a delicate gash below this projection for a mouth, and two faint stripes of whity-brown hair, in the way of eyebrows. His eyes, looking from beneath the brows, without the intervention of anything you might call an eyelid, had a deplorable half-cooked appearance, very much like the visual organs of a salt mackerel, roasting on the griddle. A delicate strand of forehead, about half an inch in width, was agreeably relieved by a dense thicket of curly brown hair. There were mysterious rumors about town with regard to this luxuriant hair. Several of Buzby's intimates had been observed to smile, when the ladies complimented him on his delightful curls; Pettitoes, the wig maker, always grew mysterious when Poodle's head of hair was called in question, and once—but that was on a drinking party, when Pettitoe's intellects were muddled—he had said, with a melo-dramatic scowl, that 'there was some people in this 'ere world as stuck 'emselves up mighty high, and yet wore dead people's—hum—he wouldn't say *what* they wore—but they wore dead people's—hum—he could tell *what*.'

The general contour of his face was so singular, and—to use a word which he delighted to repeat on every occasion—so *unique*, that Coddle St. Giles, the celebrated miniature painter, who, having been honored with the patronage of Queen Victoria, had painted the whole royal family from Her Majesty down to the lap-dog; said, with a painful grimace, that he had never experienced such extraordinary feelings as came over him, when pourtraying Buzby on costly ivory, but once before in his life, and that—to use Coddle's delicious cockney dialect—'wos when the Royal Menageries had visited my native town, and I 'ad the extr'onery honor to deplict the lineaments of the female Hourang-Houtang.'

Altogether, Buzby Poodle, Esq., was an extraordinary man; something out of the common run of men; a specimen of that high pressure style of editorial genius which the Quaker City admires and loves, to the bottom of its universal heart.

"Like that hint about your gold mines—eh, Curnel?" observed Buzby, flinging his cloak on a chair, and seating himself beside the breakfast table—"Nice steak for breakfast. Quite *recherché*—as we say in French. Don't care if I do take a pull with you. Get me a plate Dim—"

"Why Buzby, this will *do;* yes certainly—" observed Fitz-Cowles, stirring his spoon in the coffee, while he glanced over the pages of the Daily Black Mail—"But what a bad smell your paper has! Quite an odor. The *patchoully*, Dim. Now get a plate for Count Common Sewer—"

"You are *so* jocular—" exclaimed Buzby with a pleasant laugh—"You have such a quantity of fun about you! 'Count Common Sewer—' ha, ha, Good! You like that *on dit*, then?"

"Yes, Buzby, but you must touch 'em up to-morrow, about the mysterious stranger at the Ton House; supposed to be the son of an English Earl; *perhaps* a Prince. *You* know, my boy?"

"Don't I!" exclaimed Buzby taking up Fitz-Cowles's toast between his fingers—"It takes me—*Il pris moi*—as we say in Domestic French—"

"Now Buzby—" exclaimed Fitz-Cowles, fixing his dark eyes on the unmeaning face of the Editor, with a look, that made the little fellow tremble in his shoes—"You know I pay you, well, for these little advertisements. As a matter of course, you have some knowledge of my affairs, little knowledge, very little, but you might use it some day to my injury. What security have I that you will not do so?"

"What security! Good Heaven's, Curnel!" cried Buzby rising from his chair—"Can you suspect me? This is *too* much—" and Poodle's voice grew quite pathetic—"Why Curnel, to show what are my feelings toward you, I will now place myself completely in your power—"

"As how?"

Buzby made no reply, but striding with a cautious step, to every door in the room, he assured himself that they were fast locked and secured; and then with an air of the deepest mystery approached Fitz-Cowles, and gazed steadily in his face.

"What the d———l do you mean?" exclaimed Fitz-Cowles, as he observed the boiled mackerel eyes fixed upon his countenance.

"There, there, I'm in your power. The secret's out. Nobody knows it but myself and wife. Now you know it too. You can ruin me if you like—"

"What in the d———l do you mean?"

"Why, why—" exclaimed Buzby fingering away at his curly hair—"*I wear a wig!*"

"Ha! Ha! Ha! roared Fitz-Cowles, as Poodle stood before him, holding his head of hair in his hand—"Ha! Ha! Ha! Count Common Sewer you do look like old Jocko, the Wonderful Ape—whom they exhibited some time ago at the Masonic Hall! Oh, Jupiter—I shall die! Ha! Ha! Ha! *That* head—*that* head!"

It was not the most solemn sight in the world. There stood Buzby, calm and solemn, his luxuriant head of hair extended in his right hand, while the outline of his *real* head, clothed with a short, wiry stubble of *real* hair, became painfully distinct in the light of the morning sun.

"And how is this, to place you in my power?" asked Fitz-Cowles, after his laughter had subsided to a quiet chuckle—"Oh, Jupiter! *that* head! Buzby, do put on your wig, or you'll drive me into convulsions—"

"How is this to place me in your power?" exclaimed Poodle in a half-offended tone, as he resumed his curly head of hair—"Would I figure so largely behind the scenes of the Theatre, if the *ballet* girls knew I wore a wig? Curse it, the very *supes* would laugh at me, and the scene-shifters would not hesitate to jeer me! Fitz-Cowles, it may seem foolish to you, who have no such feelings of a tender nature, but—but —my whole existence is wound up in that head o' hair—"

"The deuce it is! Why, Poodle, you didn't know that it was flung into my plate last night at Monk-Hall—did you?"

"Was it, though? Then I must have been drunk—" exclaimed Buzby, with a look of the deepest mortification. "That accounts for the peculiar 'sticky' state of my hair this morning—You think any of the fellows, noticed it?"

"Too drunk for that, Buzby! By-the-bye, you must have had a great many 'tender adventures' in your time? Eh, Poodle—"

"Hallo, Massa, open dis here door—" the voice of Endymion, who had been down stairs in search of a plate for Buzby, was heard in the entry—'I hab got de plate for 'Common Sewer'—"

In a moment the door was opened, and Dim entered with a plate and some additional refreshments; which having been placed upon the table, Fitz-Cowles and Buzby resumed their breakfast.

" 'Tender adventures?' " cried Poodle, masticating a piece of toast as he dropped his knife and fork—"D'ye see that?"

He drew a small pocket Bible, from his bosom as he spoke, and displayed it complacently, before the eyes of the astonished Fitz-Cowles. It was corpulent with letters, inserted between the leaves, like so many anchovies, between various thin slices of bread-and-butter.

"This rather goes a-head of the wig! What may it mean, Buzby?"

"Don't you see, I keep all my love letters, in the Bible? Ah, me! If I wasn't married! Well, well, it can't be helped! But these letters might tell a strange tale—"

"Let them tell it by all means—" observed Fitz-Cowles; and Buzby pushing his chair back from the table, and displaying his legs very wide apart, laid the pocket Bible on one knee, and commenced a soliloquy something after the fashion.

"That's from a delightful creature, Curnel—" he observed, turning over one of the leaves of the Bible, and extracting a letter—"She loves me. Of course, I had to be complaisant. Faint heart never won fair lady—*Le cœur ennuyé ne jamais pas engagé la belle blanche*—as we say in French. That's from a vocalist—that from an actress—and that—ah! Curnel there's a mystery about it!"

"How so?"

"It's from an unknown lady. I've tried to find out her name through the clerks of the Post Office, but in vain. She's a Southern Planter's daughter, Curnel. Rich, beautiful, just seventeen. Offers me her hand—don't know I'm booked. Ah me! it would make the tears come into your eyes if I was to read this letter; there, Curnel, is a lock of her hair—"

And Buzby, with a look of subdued melancholy, slowly unfolded the letter, and held up in the sunlight a lock of reddish, brownish hair, which, long and slender, looked amazingly like a patent whip lash.

Fitz-Cowles preserved the gravity of his face with considerable difficulty, while the Creole, Endymion, who stood at Poodle's shoulder, placed his hands alternately to his mouth and the pit of his stomach, as though he was suffering under intermitting attacks of the cholera and toothache.

Buzby sate in the full light of the morning sun, holding the lock of hair, extended in his right hand, while his other hand absently grasped the pocket Bible.

"You see she is a noble girl—" he exclaimed, gazing fixedly upon the lock of hair, with a glance of painful melancholy—"Loves me. Spoke of my early struggles in her letter. Asked me if the world hadn't been hard with me—if the iron grasp of persecution hadn't been on my shoulder, ever since the days of slips and pap-spoons—if it didn't gall me considerable to think my genius wasn't appreciated—if———"

Buzby paused, and with a look of tender melancholy, jerked the pinkish lock of hair up and down, as a carter 'cracks' his whip.

The action was too much for Fitz-Cowles. He burst into a roar of laughter, while Dim, the Creole, went rolling over the floor, holding his hands to his side, as though he was laboring under an epileptic fit.

"Curse me if I see any reason for laughing in this manner—" exclaimed Buzby, rising angrily from his seat—"That's a very singular boy of yours, Curnel. D———n him, he lays there wriggling like a snake—"

"Ha! Ha! Ha! This is *too* good—" roared Fitz-Cowles—"Of course, I had no hand in writing that letter—" he muttered to himself—"Get up, Dim, and behave yourself!"

"Massa, dis quite convulses us—it does—he! he! he!" exclaimed Dim, rising to his feet—"Massa didn't send me to the barber, nor nothing, to buy dat hair?" he chuckled, in a whisper inaudible to Buzby's ears—"Dim didn't take de letter to de Pos'Offis? De High-Golly!"

"This is quite a tender affair—*Il est une affaire tendre*—as we say in domestic French—" exclaimed Buzby, resuming his seat, with this sentiment in his peculiarly detestable French—"'Pon honour, Curnel—it's a fact. The girl—the unknown—loves me devotedly. I should suppose that she read my—paper. How d'ye feel after the bruise last night?"

"Capital. I intend to have some fun this morning. You see my Governor hasn't sent me the usual quarterly remittance. My creditors have been hunting me down for the last fortnight. I have been attacked in the street, assaulted in the Theatre, beseiged in my Hotel. As a last resort, I appointed a day for each of them to call and see me; and even named the hour. Of course each creditor is ignorant of the fact, that I have made the same appointment, with every one of his fellow blood-suckers. It happens to-day at ten o'clock, in the next room—this glorious family party!"

"Ha! Ha! Ha!" laughed Buzby Poodle—"This beats some insolvent schedules quite hollow! I say *some*—because I've had a little business in that line myself. Out of curiosity—mind ye—only from curiosity, I have looked over some of the schedules in the court, devoted to such interesting affairs—"

"And you discovered something rich, I s'pose?"

"The old proverb says 'a man is known by the company he keeps'—*comprenez-vous un homme par ses compagnons du voyage*—as we say in domestic French. Now I'm of the opinion that a man is known by his insolvent schedule. There's a schedule filed in the proper court, under the delicate nose of their Honors, which says queer things for the character of its signer. One day he went round town—the jolly dog—getting seven coats—*on credit*, mind ye—from seven tailors; rings from this jeweller and breast-pins from that; boots by the quantity, and hats by the half-dozen; in short, there was scarcely a store in Chesnut street that he didn't *do;* not a credulous merchant—ha, ha, ha!—but was diddled by him, on this remarkable day—"

"Well, well, what was the result?"

"One day, like a clock, he went exclusively 'on tick:' the next day the clock stopped going. It was wound up to some considerable extent. The creditors look blue. Their 'friend and pitcher' *took the Bankrupt Law!*"

"De High-Golly! By de way dat chap tells de story, one 'ud think he did all dat his ownself! Ha—hah!"

"Buzby, your paper must take you some considerable amount of '*l'argent*.' How d'ye manage the 'Daily Black Mail?' "

This question appealed to the noblest sympathies of Poodle's heart. He rose slowly from his seat, he glanced round with an expression of condescending pride, and his face became radiant with a sudden enthusiasm.

"How do I manage the 'Daily Black Mail?' " he exclaimed, extending his right fin, in the manner of a stump-orator, who wishes to enrapture a mass meeting, consisting of a few dirty boys, one loafer, and two small dogs—"I do it a little in the footpad line. A big motto at the paper's head—'*Fiat justitia*'—you know the rest. Do I want the cash? I stick in an article charging some well-known citizen with theft, or seduction, or some more delightful crime. Citizen comes down in a rage—wants the article contradicted in next day's paper. He *pays* for the contradiction, of course. I have known a mere *on dit* that so-and-so, had committed a 'hideous crime,' to bring me in as much as a cool hundred at a 'lick—' "

"How do you manage to acquire so much favor with the 'sex?' "

"Take the Theatre, for instance. A new actress appears. Suppose her virtuous—or silly. I make advances. She foolishly repels me: very likely calls me a—puppy. Next day an *on dit* appears in 'Black Mail,' headed, 'Licentiousness of the stage,' and embracing some compassionate allusion to the lady aforesaid. You understand? I damage her reputation by a paragraphical slur—"

"And she capitulates?"

"Sometimes; and sometimes she don't. But I keep up this delightful fire of genteel insinuations, delicate allusions, and spicy *on dits*. If the girl's character is ruined, it isn't my fault, I'm sure—"

"It's quite refreshing to hear you talk in this way. Are not times pretty dull with you now?"

"Oh, Lord, yes! Hasn't been a suicide for a week. Not even a murder down town, nor a nigger baby killed. I do wish something lively would spring up for Christmas—now an 'abduction case' with the proper trimmings, would go it with a rush! *Allez avec une furie*—as we say in domestic French!"

"How d'ye stand with the other papers?"

"Guess—when I tell you one slight circumstance. They regard my paper as a sort of literary *galleys*, in which every aspirant for fame, must serve his time. An author, who has once been connected with my sheet, is regarded as a convict all his life, by the rest of the world newspaporial. Good phrase that!"

"D'ye edit your paper, by yourself?"

"Bless you, no! I know a trick worth two o' that—*Je comprend un artifice double-la*—as we say in domestic French. Whenever I find an author in extreme distress—rather out of pocket, you know?—I take him into my office; give him a dog's salary, and make him do a dog's work."

"Dog's work, indeed! If he assists in getting up your paper!" was the murmured remark of Fitz-Cowles.

"Should he leave me—and they always do leave me after a month or so—I libel him on every occasion, and talk about 'ingratitude'—ha, ha, ha! But the poor devil, can never get rid of the crime of having been connected with my paper! *That* sticks to him, like 'original sin' to a Puritan!"

"Well, Buzby, you have given me some fresh ideas about newspapers —" observed Fitz-Cowles—"I thought I knew them like a book! You have given me a new wrinkle!"

He said this and gazed silently into the saffron face of Buzby Poodle.

Oh, glorious Liberty of the Press, let us take the opportunity afforded by this quiet moment, and chaunt a psalm in your praise! Oh, glorious Press, what a comfort it must be to you, to think and feel in your inmost heart, that Buzby Poodle who sits smiling in yonder chair, is no reality, no fact; but a mere fictitious impersonation of all the evils, which spring around your life, and darken your existence!

Oh, magnificent Quaker City, with your warehouses, and your Churches, your Theatres and your Brothels, your Banks and your Insane Hospitals, your Loan Companies and your Alms Houses, how delightful to all your denizens, must be the reflection that Buzby Poodle is no living nuisance, but an airy, though loathsome creation of the author's brain!

Nursed from his very infancy in the purlieus of the dance-house; an associate of the ruffian and the courtezan, from his earliest childhood; crawling from the pages of his foul journal, over the fairest reputations in the community; sneering at the character of this man's virtuous wife; blasting with his leprous pen, that man's stainless child; in his person and soul, one hideous blot and breathing deformity: an ulcer cankering over the bosom of society; a bravo who stabs for his dollar; a hireling who without character, without reputation, without even a name, prowls abroad, selling his sheet, to any man that will buy it, for any purpose under heaven; a tolerated infamy; an uncaged jail-bird an unconvicted felon—oh, Glorious, Quaker City, does it not make your moral heart grow warm, when you remember that a creature, despicable as this, has no existence in fact, but is only a fancy of the author, a fiction of his brain!

Other cities may have their abominations in the shape of a licentious press, with marketable Editors, who have in their time, pursued every honest occupation, from body-snatching up to newspaper publishing; but the Quaker City, like the Ideal town of some far-off El Dorado, is so pure, so spotless, that an Author in search of a cut-throat Editor, by the portraiture of whose character, he means to throw a dark relief around the brighter portions of his pages, must set his wits to work, and *invent, a Buzby Poodle!*

Oh, rare invention—Buzby Poodle—long may it be, ere a thing like you shall start into tangible existence, and all be-wigged and sickle-legged, walk visibly along Chesnut Street; a diminutive incarnation of a most nauseous emetic.

"Go to the door, Dim! There's the first of the Creditors! Be quiet, Poodle, and enjoy the fun—"

"Yes Massa, I opens the door—" cried Endymion as the hoarse voice of Creditor One, was heard in the next room.

"Tell Col. Fitz-Cowles, that Mr. Bluffly Bulk want's to see him."

And as the hoarse voice echoed through the aperture, Mr. Bluffly Bulk, appeared in the doorway, driving an immense paunch before him, as he walked along. His small head overlooked his immense corporation, like a pea observing the circumference of a pumpkin.

"Well, Fitz-Cowles—" said Mr. Bulk—"I've called according to appointment. You owe me a fee in the case of 'Commonwealth vs. Fitz-Cowles'—charge, lathering a watchman. The fee is 'fifty.' Pay it, and let me go—"

"Do me the kindness to step this way—" exclaimed Fitz-Cowles with one of his best bows as he motioned Creditor One, toward the small door, opposite—"In a moment I'll see you; and settle this little matter."

Bluffly Bulk Esq., disappeared within the eastern door, muttering strange curses as he walked along.

"Dar goes ten o'Cloc' Massa—" exclaimed Dim listening at the key-hole of the western door—"De High-Golly! I hear more of 'em in the nex' room—"

"Show 'em in Dim! One at a time! Ha! Whom have we here! My friend Smith—John Smith the Upholster—"

A little thin man, with a narrow face, a starved nose, and a green overcoat, advanced and seized Fitz-Cowles earnestly by the hand.

"Note to pay to day Sir—" he said in a thrilling whisper—"Bill for the curtains, you got of me, when you was at the United States Hotel—Six hundred and fifty two dollars, twelve and a half cents. Tight times Sir. Money very scarce—shall I give you a receipt Sir?—"

"In the next room if you please—" observed Fitz-Cowles with a pleasant smile—"You see my old fellow, we'll fix that matter in a minute—"

"Bress your eyes, Massa, dey are a-growlin' like cat-an' dog in toder room!" observed Dim holding the door slightly open—"I hear's 'em a-comin' up de stairs; and I hear's de sarvant a-showin' 'em into the next room—"

"This grows quite refreshing! Almost equal to a Schedule at the Insolvent Court!"

"Is Misther Fitz-Cow-*how*les, in the house himself, jest? Be aisy thare ye nager, and let me come in. Dhrop a word into his private ear, that Michael O'Flannagan, French Boot Maker from Paris, is a wantin' to get the taste ov a sight ov him—"

And a large boned man, attired in a shabby white great coat, with an old fur cap drawn over his eyes, came rushing into the room. He stood full six feet in his stockings; and his red face, seen through the apertures of his hair and whiskers, all of the same burning red, looked very much like the countenance of a man who won't stand upon trifles; or occupy his time in breaking the hind legs of a flea.

"Oh—the blazes! But them sixteen pairs of stairs give me a pain in the side; the top o' th' marnin' to ye Colonel—its yerself that's lookin' like a canary bird the-day. Shall we fingher the pewther Curnel? Cinshider the seventeen pair o' boots, all done and complated by Michael O'Flannagan, French Boot Maker, from the City o' Pari-i-s, in the ould Counthry—"

"He's got the real Parisian accent!" exclaimed Buzby Poodle—"Talks like a native. Quite *au fait!*"

"The accshent? And who the divil should have the accshent, but me? Wasn't I brot up all my life, a giniwine Frenchman, and didn't my father fight with ould Boney, in the scrimmage of Watherloo?"

"You speak it like a native Mikey. This way; I'll talk to you in minute. Show 'em in, Dim."

"Mistaw Douzzle, de toder Boot Maker from Paris!"

A mouldy looking man, of short stature, and a heavy face, invested by a dampish beard of some indefinable color, was now shown into the room, with his arms hanging straight by his sides, like pendulums to some walking clock.

"Curnel, I ish in want fery mosh ov dat small bill for de French Boots. Times is hardt; mine wife is sick, and von childt has got de measles. Eight pair of fine French Boots—seven dollars a-pair—seven eight ish fordy-eight—"

"Next room Douzzle. See you in a minute. Keep on showin' 'em in Dim!"

"I 'ave the *h*onour, to present my small bill—" exclaimed a little man in a Cockney face, and brown sack coat—"To one portrait of Col. Fitz-Cowles, fifty dollars. Very much in want of money, to day Sir. Obliged to you for a little. Never since I 'ad the extron'ery honor, to paint Her Royal Majesty Victoria, and Prince *H*albert with the 'ouses o' Parliament and the lap-dog in the background, never since that 'ere blessed moment, 'ave I taken so much pains with a mini'ture as with yours! Out of wood sir—out of coal sir—out of ivory, Sir—"

"Not out of brass I hope? Ha! Ha! Ha! There I had you St. Giles! Walk into the next room if you please! Pass 'em this way, Dim!"

And Dim did pass them that way to some considerable extent. It should be borne in mind, that Col. Fitz-Cowles had been living for some time past in a style of princely splendor, kept up and supported by a numerous retinue of credulous tradesmen. The results of this princely style, now manifested themselves in the shape of some four-and-thirty creditors, who came pouring from the ante-room, one after another, in quick succession, with their bills in hand, and their demands ringing loudly on the air, like a delightful chorus to the grand drama of the Bankrupt law.

"A small bill for horse hire. To a chaise and four—" began a little thickset man, with brown whiskers, and a short bang-up, smelling strongly of the race-course—"To a chaise and four, seventeen times—"

"My little bill for ten coats, fifteen pair of pants—fourteen vests and a dickey—" interrupted a solemn looking-personage pressing hurriedly forward—"Firm of Flunk, Checkley and Co. Five hundred and fifty dol—"

"I ave furnish you with parfumerie, to dis amount—"

"Seventy one pair of gloves. White kid. Hoskin's—"

"To the use of my cab, Gineral Washington won-hunder' and fafty times—"

"*To*, the 'Genelman's Universal Wardrobe, an' Furnishin' store,' Col. Fitz-Cowle's, Debtor—Sixteen shirts and—"

"My bill for Dry Goods, sir—" said a pompous man, with a snub nose and immense ragged whiskers—"McWhiley Mumshell, sir. Two hundred and six—"

" 'Pothecary's bill for med'cine. Seven bottles Swain's Panacea—"

"Ha—ha! This beats the Insolvent Court! What a scene for the next Black Mail!"

"De High-Golly! Dey come wid a parfac looseness, dis time!"

"Gentlemen, gentle-*men*—" exclaimed Fitz-Cowles, looking from face to face with a pleasant smile—"You are really too impatient. To see you rushing forward in this style, one would think I had the wealth of Girard in my pockets. Step into the next room, gentlemen. All your demands shall be satisfied—"

A murmur of satisfaction burst from the contrasted throng, and in an instant they had all disappeared into the next room.

"Now, Buzby, let's wait a few minutes, until they begin to grow feverish. When I think they've worked themselves up into the proper humor, we'll step in, and take a look at them. I'll show you how to bluff off a creditor—"

"I thought I was rather *au fait* at that business myself. However—*onter noos*—as we say in domestic French."*

* The author does not hold himself responsible for Mr. Buzby Poodle's violent assaults on Louis Phillipe's French.

CHAPTER SECOND

FITZ-COWLES AND HIS CREDITORS

In a large saloon, furnished in a style of magnificence, popularly known as the gingerbread style, with immense red silk curtains along the windows, scattered patches of gilt, glittering around the cornices, and a colossal mirror above the mantle, sate the four-and-thirty creditors, waiting for the appearance of the *millionaire*.

The softened light which came through the drawn curtains, gave a mild and shadowy effect to the figures of the patient band, while it was quite delightful to witness the animated expression of their countenances, as gazing into each other's eyes, they seemed to wonder why in the deuce they were all penned up there together, like various kinds of cattle at an Agricultural fair.

Bluffy Bulk, Esq., the fat lawyer sat glaring upon the little bootmaker, Douzzle, as though he was wondering what kind of a 'fry' the fellow would make for his breakfast; Michael O'Flannagan, the Parisian bootmaker, was engaged in polishing his shoes on the handsome hearth-rug; Coddle St. Giles, gazed vacantly around with the look of a man who has been feloniously decoyed into a den of thieves, while the rest of the four-and-thirty creditors were occupied in examining their various bills, which they raised frequently in the light; and crushed between their fingers, as though the action was productive of great peace of mind and tranquility of spirit.

A buz-buz of satisfaction, resounded through the saloon.

Col. Fitz-Cowles appeared in the doorway with Buzby Poodle, and Endymion at his back.

"Gentlemen—" said the Colonel, placing one hand between his back and his flashy morning-robe, while he waved the other gently up and down—"I owe you money—"

"*That* you do—" muttered Bluffly Bulk, Esq., stamping his cane on the floor; and a buz-buz from the four-and-thirty creditors, confirmed the truth of the sentiment. It was quite pleasing to see how much unanimity of feeling existed on this point. Had there been only half the concurrence of opinion, visible in the doings of most of our religious conventions, synods and conferences, the world would have been Christianized long ago.

"I owe you money and I mean to pay it—"

"*He* manes to pay it! Hurra! Three times, hur-rah!"

"I mean to make your fortunes. I should suppose you all want money rather bad?"

"Deuced bad." "Cursed bad." "Och, don't I?" "Wife and children —one sick with the measles." "Starvation." "Go to jail." "Out of wood, out of coal, out of ivory."

"If I don't pay you this morning I suppose it will ruin you all?"

"Totally." "Have to leave the city." "Can't think on't." "Horrible." "Och whillaloo!" "Ruin me, root and branch!"

"Well, then, gentlemen, I *will* make your fortunes. You have a pleasing countenance, my friend Bluffly Bulk, a respectable person. You shall oversee the hands. Yes, yes. That 'ill just suit you. Mister Flannagan, imagine yourself perched on the edge of a well, some hundred fathoms deep, telling the laborers below to mind their eyes and be d———d to 'em. 'Hoist away my hearties'—d'ye take? Coddle St. Giles, your remarkable talents will here be called into requisition. You can take drawings of the mines—publish 'em when we all get back—splendid volume—letter press by Sylvester J. Petriken, of the Western Hem. Flunk, my dear friend Flunk, of the firm of Flunk, Checkley & Co., Merchant Tailors, you can make up a lot of clothes for the miners! 'Gad gents, I like the plan altogether; it will suit our various talents. It will make our fortunes—"

"Gintlemen, me name is Mikey O'Flannagan, Bootmaker, from Paris, and me father fought with ould Boney, and so ye see there's some larnin' in our family, but may the divil fly away wid me, if I can make out what the Curnel manes—By Julias Caysar, but we're all a-listenin to a gintleman from the Insane Hozpittal!"

"What in the d———l do you mean?" exclaimed Bluffly Bulk, growing like a turkey cock in the face as he fixed his eyes upon Fitz-Cowles, who stood in the centre of the saloon, in an attitude of deep abstraction—"Be *so* kind as to explain yourself!"

"Yes the plan is feasible—" exclaimed Colonel Fitz-Cowles elevating his eyebrows with an absent stare—"But there's a rough desert to pass through before we reach the mines. Plenty of Mexicans and Texans—not to mention the Indians and wild beasts. Still the mines are productive: on my father's estate you know? I'm *incog.* just now, but when the Company is in full operation, under the combined patronage of Santa Anna the Mexican government, and Sam Houston, I'll make known the old man's name—"

"Sir—" cried Bluffly Bulk in a voice of thunder—"Will you tell us what you mean?"

"Arrah, man, and be quick at it!"

"Oblige us with some slight knowledge—"

"Guess he wants a straight-jacket."

"Tell you what I mean?" exclaimed Fitz-Cowles, starting from his reverie—"With pleasure. You see gentlemen, I propose to make your fortunes, by allowing you to enter your names, as stockholders of 'the Grand Montezuma Gold-Mining Company of the gold mines of Huancatepapetel, district of Tolpcaptl, South Mexico—Algernon Fitz-Cowles, *President*, Bluffly Bulk, *Secretary*, Board of Directors as follows —' you can fill up the blank at your leisure you know? I will allow you, each to take ten shares of the capital stock at $100 per share; and we will say nothing about the small sums I owe you. Mere trifles you know. Bluffly, in consideration of the post of Secretary, being tendered you, one hundred shares, will be the smallest number, you can be permitted to take—"

Fitz-Cowles paused, and looked around to note the effects of his important proposition. There was a dead silence in the Saloon. You might have heard a pin drop. The four and thirty Creditors, looked into one another's faces, but said nothing. Buzby Poodle and Dim the Creole, concealed themselves among the window curtains, which quivered and shook, as with a sudden convulsion.

"Gentlemen d'ye like my proposition?" said Fitz-Cowles blandly—"Is it feasible? We can all go to Huancatepapetel together; times are *so* hard in this city. Those that are married can take their families with them; those that are single, will get families soon enough on their arrival at the mines. You are silent—it is with surprise I suppose? Or d'ye want to advance some small amount on your shares? No gentlemen, I can't think of *that!* The trifles I owe you one and all, will more than pay, for your shares—"

"Well, may I be rammed into a shot gun, and fired off at a nigger riot, if this is n't the coolest thing I've heard of for some time!" and as he spoke the fat lawyer started from his feet, and confronted Fitz-Cowles—"Zounds Sir, what do you take me for?"

"A fine fat old gentleman—" replied Fitz-Cowles bowing—"Who would make a Capital Superintendent of the mines. By Jupiter! Bluffly, that person of yours carries respectability in its every outline. It is worth at least a-thousand shares to the company—"

The storm, long-gathering and silent in its growth, burst suddenly over the head of Fitz-Cowles. One and all the four and thirty Creditors rose, one and all they poured forth their anger in broken words and bitter curses.

"J———s the villian!—" "The scoundrel—" "Swindler—" "This is

wot I gits for his mini'tur'!—" "I'm paid for the fifteen coats and—" "Here's the cash for my gloves!" "Tish is damdt pat—my wife sick and de shildren got de measles—" "Hurrah! Lets whack into 'im!"

"This beats an Insolvent Schedule all hollow!" laughed Buzby Poodle, peeping out from behind the curtains—" 'Gad! what a scene for the Black Mail! Four and thirty Creditors, of all shapes, sizes and patterns, surrounding Fitz-Cowles, who greets 'em with a commis-serating smile! Ha—ha! Capital!"

"De High-Golly!" shouted Dim thrusting his head from the other curtain "Dey look as if dey eat Massa up widout any pepper or salt!"

"Gentlemen—will you hear me!" shouted Fitz-Cowles in a voice of thunder, as he gazed upon the four and thirty threatening faces—"Will you or will you not? Am I to be insulted in my own house? Dim—go and call the servants, and have these fellows trundled down stairs—"

"Well Sir, what do you propose?" cried Bluffly Bulk, his voice rising above the tumult—"No more humbug Sir—"

"You then reject my offer, made with the best feelings in the world, to combine you, one and all, into the Grand Montezuma Gold-Mining Company of the Huancatepapetel—"

" 'Huancatty-kettle-polly' be d———d!" shouted Flunk the tailor pressing forward, as he shook his clenched hand in the air.

"Pitch 'Gwan-goett-polly' to the divil!" screamed O'Flannagan the Boot Maker.—

"Just as you like Gentlemen. Pitch Huancatepapetel to the devil, by all means. But I was about to observe that the various sums, which I owe you separately, taken in the lump, amount to something over three thousand dollars. You are interested. Well now, my fellows here's the difficulty. I've but a thousand dollars, cash in my possession. You can divide it among you, if you like—"

"Now you, *talk*—" observed Bluffly Bulk, with a pleasing smile as though the previous remarks of Fitz-Cowles had not risen even to the dignity of talk—"Of course my little fee of fifty dollars, will be satis-fied out of this sum, in precedence to all other claims—"

"Av course me little bill of thirty sivin dollars, sixty cents—" observed Mr. Flannagan, stepping briskly forward, as he thrust his hands, deep into the vacuum of his great coat pockets—"Will take the prisidence of your thrifling claims—"

"Of course, Curnel, my bill of two hundred and fifty, for Dry Goods —" mildly exclaimed McWhiley Mumshell, pulling his ragged whiskers, with a hand, all glittering with costly rings—"My little bill will be considered, first of all—"

"And is it the likes of ye, to stand afore me? The divil dhrag me under a harrow, but ould rat-face, ye've a dale of impedence in them same whiskers."

"Curnel, don't forgit the min'itur'—" "Nor the horse-hire—" "Remember the gloves—" "Ishn't I to be paidt for my poots?"" De parfumerie Monsieur Viz-Cowle—" "Jist stand back there, will ye—" "Devil take your impudence—I'm as good as you—" "Say that again —" "Youre another—" "My bill, Curnel—" "*Mine* I say—" "Wife and five children, won sick wid de measles—"

"Gentlemen—*do* be calm—" cried Fitz-Cowles as he viewed the gathering storm—"Remember gentlemen, that you *are* gentlemen. Be calm Flannagan—Quiet yourself Bluffly—Soothe your excited feelings Mumshell—"

"Will you settle my bill—" shrieked Bluffly Bulk, red in the face with anger—"Yes or no!"

"Botherashin! Stand back auld porpise—and let me give him a receipt—Or is it a row ye've a-wantin'—"

"D———d Irishman—" grated Bluffly between his teeth.

"D———d Irishman, am I? And me a Paryshian barn? For the sake of my ould man, who was an Irishman, and who fit wid Boney at Watherloo—take *that*."

And with his clenched hand, he aimed a blow, full at the immense corporation of the fat lawyer. The blow brushed Mumshell's whiskers and took effect on the person of the lawyer. The effect was terrific. In an instant the four and thirty Creditors, their bills in hand, were all mingled through each other, every man striking the man who stood next to him, without regard to consequences, while Bluffly and Flannagan, went at it, tooth and nail, exchanging fisticuffs with remarkable good will.

The scene was peculiar. A forest of fists, rising up and down, a mass of angry faces, all mingled together, some four and thirty bodies of all sizes and descriptions, twisting and winding about, with so much rapidity, that they all looked like the different limbs of some strange monster, undergoing a violent epipletic fit.

"Gentlemen *do* be calm—"

"Go your death—*Allez-vous votre mort!*"—as we say in domestic French! "Hit 'em again!—*frappez duex fois!* That's it! Give him another! —*donnez lui un autre!*"

"You scoundrel—I'll prosecute you for damages—"

"Damages, you ould porpise—then by my father's soul, I'll damage you a thrifle more!"

"This is shameful! Show me the man who struck me in the eye—"
"Bi Gott! I vill murder somebodys tirectly—"
"Let me up! It wasn't me that struck you!"
"I'll take the wo'th of my gloves out o' somebody—"
"Oh my *h*-eye! 'Ere's a purty minature for you!"
"Oh! whililoo! Any one here that'll say I wasn't a Paryshien born? Fight it out boys—lather it into one another! Whoop! Say that black mark under yer eye isn't a bit o' patchwork—will ye? Jest say it! Come on six ov ye—I ain't pertikler which! Hurrah! There goes the lookin' glass! Crack—smash—bang! Thry it agin—ould porpise! This bates Watherloo—hurray, hurray!"

CHAPTER THIRD

THE DEATH WARRANT

The mirror, which hung above the dressing bureau, reflected the handsome form of Col. Fitz-Cowles. It must be confessed that the Colonel looked decidedly interesting, as standing before the mirror, in the glare of the morning sun, he surveyed his form for the last time, ere he sallied forth on Chesnut street. His figure, with its broad chest and tapering waist, was enveloped in a close-fitting overcoat of dark cloth, which, falling open along the breast, disclosed his black scarf, gathered over his shirt front with a plain gold pin, and tastefully disposed within the collar of his glossy coat and satin vest, whose jet black hues were in harmony with the other portions of his attire.

The dark visage of the Colonel, relieved by long curling locks of jet-black hair, was surmounted by an elegant hat, remarkable for its conical crown and width of brim. This was the much admired and very aristocratic '*Fitz-Cowles' hat,*' worn by all the distinguished bloods of the Quaker City. Introduced by the gallant Colonel, it soon became the rage, and was at the time of which we write, the standing test of fashion and elegance among the exquisites of Chesnut street.

"Dim—" said the Colonel, gently waving the gold-headed cane, which he held within the white-kid glove of his right hand—"Are they *all* gone?"

"All turned out, Massa. De sarvants tumble 'em down stairs more an half-hour ago—"

"Dim—" continued the Colonel, impregnating his snow-white handkerchief with an additional scent of *patchoully**—"What's the damage?"

"De looking-glass 'bove de mantel broke in tousan' pieces—one ob de winder curtains torn down. De berry debbil kicked up all ober de room—"

"Buzby—" resumed the Colonel, passing a comb lightly through the locks of his jet-black hair—"How did you like it?"

"Quite *recherché*. But won't they sue you for their various debts?"

"Let them sue and be hanged! The amount I owe them, applied in the proper way, would command a great influence in Court. Why man I've got the price of seven judges, ten juries and some score of lawyers, in my pocket. These things are all for sale—"

"Ha! ha! This is libellous! Hello! There's a knock at the door—"

"See who it is, Dim—"

Dim opened the door at the extreme end of the bed-chamber. He gazed for an instant through the aperture, and then closing the door with a sudden movement, he came running to his Master's side, his eyes dilating with surprise and his tawny face, pale as Fitz-Cowles's white kid gloves.

"What in the deuce, is the matter Dim?"

"Oh, Golly Massa! Oh Lor! Oh de debbil!" cried the Creole, dancing about the room.

"Shall I knock you down with the chair you scoundrel? Or would you like to be held out of a fourth-story window, by the heels, again?"

Dim approached his master's side, and whispered in his ear.

The Colonel's face grew suddenly pale, and a blasphemous oath escaped from his lips.

"Buzby, go into the next room—" he cried harshly, with the same tone, he would use, in getting rid of a troublesome dog—"Be quick. I have a visiter, whom I must see alone. Why do you stand there, staring in my face like an idiot? Begone I say—I must be alone—"

Buzby Poodle, disappeared through the Saloon door, with a look of malignant anger, that boded no good to his friend, Colonel Fitz-Cowles.

"Open the door. D'ye hear Dim?" shouted the Colonel, as his face grew paler, and his dark eye, emitted a clear flashing glance, that

* A perfume, once the 'rage' among the fashionables of our city. To the uninitiated it smells like a composition of Musk, cast-iron filings and bad rain water.

betokened powerful though suppressed emotion. "Show our visiter in—"

Dim opened the door, at the end of the bed-chamber, farthest from the windows, and the visiter entered. It must be confessed that the surprise which the mere utterance of his name occasioned, might be easily explained, when the singular appearance of the newcomer, was taken into consideration.

A short, thickset, little man, dressed in a suit of glossy black cloth, advanced from the open door. His face, which from its remarkable length, gave you the idea of a horse's head, affixed to the remnant of a human body, seemed to lay upon his heart, while his shoulders arose on either side, as high as his ears, and his back protruding in a shapeless hump, was visible above the outline of his head.

His face, it is true, from its extreme length, and the peculiar manner, in which it seemed to lay on his breast, might have appeared distorted and deformed, yet were the features perfectly regular, the nose a decided acquiline, the mouth well-proportioned and indicative of firmness, the chin, full and round, while the high forehead, with the dark eyebrows, over-arched two large and brilliant eyes, whose intense lustre beaming from a face, marked by a clear, healthy complexion, gave the beholder the idea, that he beheld a supernatural, rather than a human being.

Should the latter portion of this description, appear overstrained, the reader will remember, that the diminutive stature of the strange visiter, the hump on his back, and the manner in which his face, seemed to rest on his chest, all gave additional effect to the expression of his face and eyes. '*Jew*', was written on his face clearly and distinctly as though he had fallen asleep at the building of the Temple at Jerusalem, in the days of Solomon, the rake and moralist; and after a nap of three thousand years, had waked up in the Quaker City, in a state of perfect and Hebraic preservation.

"You are, here, are you?" whispered Fitz-Cowles in a tone of ungovernable rage—"Why is this? Why leave your hiding place in broad daylight?"

"I'ave comsh bekos I vanted to comsh—" said the Jew, calmly, as he folded his hands across his breast.

"You have, have you?" whispered Fitz-Cowles, as the gleam of rage, brightened in his dark eyes—"Do you know—you dog, you miserable dog—that I've a great notion to give you a taste of *this*—"

And as he spoke, quick as thought, he flung open the breast of his overcoat, and drawing the Bowie knife, from a secret pocket, he brandished it above the head of the Jew, with a look of ungovernable hatred.

"Puts away te carving-knifes—Puts away te carving-knifes—" said the humpback, with a bitter, though scarcely perceptable sneer—"You vill not hurts noboty."

"Perhaps you will tell me, why you have left your hiding place! In broad day, with all the police at your heels? Ha! Ha! This is delightful! Curse *that* Devil-Bug—" he muttered as he strode to the window—"How could he have let this dog escape?"

"I tells you vy I'ave left dat nashty plashe—" said the Hebrew in the coolest manner imaginable—"Bekos it vos a nashty plashe! Bekos dese leetle hand do all te vorks—andt maybe after all, you reaps te profit. I mosh hide in dat hole—viles you valksh Cheshnut Streets? Vos dat de kontraksh? You keep your pargain, vill yous?"

"And what was that bargain?" exclaimed Fitz-Cowles again facing the Jew.

"Ven te tings vos done, you vos to gif me ten tousand tollars in goldt. I vos to sail for Europes. Vot have you done? Left me to rots among roppers and tiefs, viles you walksh Cheshnut Streets! Got-tam!"

The Jew sate down, or rather fixed himself on the sofa, and looked up calmly into the flushed countenance of Fitz-Cowles.

"Well, well, Von Gelt, lets shake hands, and talk the matter over—"

"We may talksh as mosh as we pleashes, but we tont shake handts—"

"Just as you like. Well, Judos—is that your first name Von Gelt?"

"Supposh it vos my naturs? Vonder how long afore the handsome Curnels would be—Father Moses—I know veres—"

"So you threaten, me, do you Gabriel? Ha!-ha! This is amusing. May I ask what you propose to do?"

"To morrow mornings I vill take te carsh for New Yorksh. Nex tay I vill sail for Europes. To tay, you will gif me, ten tousandt tollars—"

"But Judas—that is Gabriel—Judas for short, you know? You must remember that I have not ten thousand dollars in my possession—"

"Veres is te ole hair trunksh?"

"But Gabriel—" exclaimed Fitz-Cowles in a conciliating tone, as he seated himself, beside the table opposite the Jew—"But Gabriel you know, that it is impossible for us to have this money, for months to come. The sovreigns and the notes, might be recognized at once. It is better to wait a little while and make sure of the whole sum beyond a chance of detection. Pen and ink, Dim."

"Meanviles te poleesh ranshack Monks-halls, andt fint me, hit avay among tiefs and roppers. No—No! I vill bear tish no longers. Tish tay I mosh ave ten tousandt tollars, or—or—"

"Or—or—" echoed Fitz-Cowles as he scrawled a few words on a sheet of gilt-edged note paper—"Or—or—You was about to observe —"

"May be I can git ten tousandt tollars, someveres else—" said the Jew with a meaning look.

"Ah—ha! You grow humorous, Gabriel—" observed Fitz-Cowles with a smile—"Please deliver this little note to Devil-Bug if you should chance to see him again, before you start for Europe. Will you Gabby?"

"Ha! vot is tish!" exclaimed the hump-backed Jew, as his eye glanced over the note, which read as follows:

> 'Devil-Bug—Our friend leaves us to-morrow. It is all right. Aid him as far as you can, in anything that concerns his departure.
>
> THE ABBOT.'

"Den you conshents?" exclaimed Gabriel, with a smile of triumph—"You vill gif me te monish?"

"Of course, *of course*. You know I would never refuse you anything, Gabriel. You must be careful though, Gabriel, with the money. Mighty careful—"

"Vot a fool I vos, ever to part mit it!" muttered Gabriel—"I hadt it all in mine own handts won time—"

"Excuse me one moment, Gabriel, while I write a note to my jeweller—" said Fitz-Cowles, with a pleasant smile. "Here, Dim—take this ring and this note down to Melchoir, the Jeweller, in Fourth street near Chesnut. Hurry back, d'ye hear?"

As he seized the note and folded it, Fitz-Cowles gazed smilingly in the face of the Hebrew. But when he took the diamond ring from his finger, and handed it to Dim, with one quick flashing glance of his dark eyes, the smile deepened into an agreeable laugh, and Fitz-Cowles looked, for all the world, like a man whose mind is unburdened by a single care. And this, while his life and fortune hung upon the note which he handed to the Creole!

"Dim—you understand? This ring and note are for the Jeweller in Fourth below Chesnut?"

"Yes, Massa—" answered Dim, with a stolid and imperturable expression of countenance. "I'll be back d'rectly."

That note was the Death Warrant of the Jew.

Thus it read:

'Devil-Bug———When the Jew comes back to Monk-hall he will have about his person ten thousand dollars. You can pay yourself for the care and trouble you have had with him. The ring will tell you what I mean.

THE ABBOT.

"Now, Gabby—" exclaimed Fitz-Cowles, as Dim hastened from the room—"You can amuse yourself by looking out of the window, while I get you the money."

As the handsome Algernon, stooping to the floor, drew the hair trunk from beneath the sofa, Gabriel, the Jew, rose from his seat and advanced toward the window.

"Dere's noting like improvin' vons times—" he muttered, as he seized an object, which lay exposed on the top of the dressing bureau. "Father Moses! He vill swear ven he mishes dis ting—"

"Ten notes of a thousand dollars each—" murmured Fitz-Cowles, locking the trunk again—"Much good will they do him! Devil-Bug is such an amiable man!"

"Now I vill pegone!" exclaimed Gabriel, hastily concealing the notes within the breast of his overcoat. "Dish countries is too hot to holdt me."

He strode to the door, and looked back at Fitz-Cowles, as he uttered this pleasant good-bye.

"Farewells! Ven ve meetsh agin may ve pe in betterish spiritsh—Goot byesh!"

He disappeared, and in a moment was heard passing hurriedly along the entry, without the bedchamber.

"Go!" shrieked Fitz-Cowles, the moment he had disappeared—"Go, and to your DEATH!"

He paced hurriedly along the room, his brow darkening over with a heavy frown, and his eye blazing with excitement.

"Ha! The door leading into the saloon is ajar—could any one have listened to our conversation?"—he pushed the door open and glanced around the spacious apartment as he spoke—"Ha, ha! There is no one in this room! What a fool I am to fancy a listener near. And yet that fellow, Buzby—but he's too cowardly to betray a *man*. He might muster courage to betray a lame nigger woman, or a sick rag picker—but *a man*—never!"

He closed the door, leading into the saloon, as he spoke.

And as the door was closed, the form of a man stole softly from the folds of the silken window curtains, and Buzby Poodle stood disclosed in the light. His face was very pale, and his hands trembled like pendulums, very much out of order.

"Here's a secret worth a fortune—" he exclaimed, as he passed through the saloon door, into the winding entry of the fourth story—"Betray a rag picker, indeed! Ho! Ho! What if I betray a forger?"

Meanwhile Fitz-Cowles strode swiftly along the floor of his bed-chamber, his face and manner, betraying the wild excitement which possessed his soul.

"If I manage my cards right I am safe! Ha! ha! That Jew got up some very neat letters from my father—the Earl of Lyneswold, Lincon-shire, England! To give the d——l his due, the Jew managed these letters with a masterly hand. English post marks and all! I showed them to Dora, together with a parchment containing our pedigree—the Lyndeswolds of Lyndeswold! I have used the Jew, and now—egad!—he must *retire* from the scene! By next Monday morning I can arrange every thing! And then, as from the decks of a steamer bound for England, I gaze upon the receding shores of America, while Dora smiles in my face, and the cash rattles in my pocket, then—ha, ha, ha! —how I shall laugh at these fools of the Quaker City!"

CHAPTER FOURTH

DORA LIVINGSTONE AT HOME

The *boudoir* was lighted by two long and narrow windows looking to the south. The morning sunshine shone mildly round the place, through the folds of the thick curtains of light silk, which hung droop-ing along the windows.

In shape, the room was sexagonal, with pedestals of dark marble, standing along four of the six walls. On the top of one pedestal stood an alabaster vase, containing flowers of the choicest hues and fragrance, gathered from the conservatory—which was visible through the small door, on the summit of the second, was placed a statue of the Venus de Medici, sculptured by a master hand, in snow-white marble; the third supported another vase, also filled with flowers, while the top of the fourth was occupied by an image of the Virgin Mary, her eyes raised upward to heaven, and her hands clasped over the crucifix, resting upon her bosom.

The small door leading into the adjoining conservatory, located in the second story of the western wing of Livingstone's princely mansion, hung slightly ajar. A delightful fragrance, the breath and sweetness of many flowers, pervaded the atmosphere. The perfume of the full-blown rose, the penetrating scent of the heliotrope, the delightful odor of the arbor vitœ, mingling with the fragrance of a thousand other plants and flowers, created an air of delicious and intoxicating sweetness.

The appointments of the *boudoir*—or, perhaps, closet would be the more correct designation—were neat and classic. Four handsome gothic chairs, with worked-cloth seats, disposed along the walls, an elegant sofa, placed between two of the pedestals, a severely-classic table of snow-white marble standing opposite, all burdened with books in costly binding, strewn over its surface; and a gorgeous Turkey carpet, whose deep rich colors were in effective contrast to the light and delicate papering of the walls; all combined produced an effect of elegance and taste, heightened and refined by the vases of flowers, and the marble statues presenting beauty in the contrasted forms of Religion and Love.

The heat of the conservatory, mingling with the sweetness of its flowers, imparted a fragrant warmth to the *boudoir*. No stove, nor grate, with glaring coal or crackling wood, was therefore needed to render the place comfortable.

Altogether the entire room was imbued with an air of spiritual repose of dreamy languor, which would have been very etherial indeed, if it had not been for the presence of the small breakfast table which stood in the centre of the carpet, like a plain and stubborn earthly fact, with its silver coffee-pot, porcelain cup, and buttered toast, disposed along the surface of a snow-white cloth. However, the coffee was cold, and the toast untasted. This was something in favor of the spirituality of the *boudoir*.

Through the dim light which imparted a twilight effect to the room, you might discern the outlines of a woman's form, as she lay reclining on the sofa. Her form, full, large and voluptuous, was enveloped in the folds of a snow-white morning gown, which gathering lightly around her queenly figure, displayed the symmetry of her rounded arms, the fulness of her bust, and the swelling outlines of her person, in the richest varieties of light and shade. A single red gleam of sun light, escaping through the folds of the window-curtain streamed over the whiteness of her snowy neck.

Her head resting on the sofa cushion, with the dark hair falling carelessly around, her eyes were half-closed in dreamy reverie and the brightness of her glance, subdued to a hazy dimness, which attested the absence of her thoughts from all outward things, stole mildly from the shadow of the long and trembling lashes.

Her entire attitude was that of a person, absorbed in some delightful reverie. Her hands were gently clasped in front of her form, her limbs, as you might see by the folds of her dress, were carelessly crossed, one over the other, while one small and delicate foot, with the slender ancle, encased in the snow-white stocking, was visible, as she lay with her voluptuous person, thrown lightly along the sofa.

She was indeed a beautiful and voluptuous woman. The deep vermillion of her lips, the burning flush crimsoning each cheek, the blackness of her eyelashes and pencilled brows, the long dark hair which when all unbound, fell in thick and glossy tresses, below her waist, the fullness of her bosom, the swelling roundness of her limbs, the smallness of her feet, and the delicacy of her hands, with long and tapering fingers, all attested her loveliness and beauty; while the swimming glance of her large eyes, indicates the innate voluptuousness of her nature.

Her eyes, were of that deep and well-like brightness, which seems to throw open to the vision of the gazer, not only their mellowed glance and dazzling radiance, but the entire prospect of the hidden soul. You gazed not upon, but into, those eyes, and felt that you were in the presence of a mighty intellect and a sensual organization.

As she lay reclining on the sofa, a low murmur of delight escaped from her lips, and a flush, like the sunnyside of a ripening peach, blightened over her face and neck. Her eyelids slowly unclosing revealed her large dark eyes, animate with an expression of sudden delight, and beaming with a swimming brightness that finds no parallel, save in the glance of a lovely and voluptuous woman.

Dora rose slowly to her feet, and stood erect upon the floor.

"That were a boon, worth the peril of a soul to win!" she whispered in a low and softened tone, as her hands absently toyed with the rose, which rested upon her bosom—"A coronet, yes, yes, a coronet! This is a fair brow they tell me—how well the glittering circlet of diamonds, would become its beauty! A coronet! But one short year ago, a poor girl, clad in the threadbare costume, which seems to belong by right, to poverty-stricken gentility, watched by the bedside of a dying mother, in a meanly-furnished apartment, faintly illumined by the beams of a flickering lamp. *Now* that poor girl, is the wife of one of the merchant-princes of the city, rolls in wealth, almost without limit, and of course moves among the first circles of the Aristocracy of this good city! Such Aristocracy ha, ha! Like a specimen of paste-board statuary, giving but a grotesque outline, of the reality which it is intended to represent. Another year! Ha, ha! My brain grows wild! Another year and this same poor girl, may, no, no, *will* stand among the glittering circles of a royal Court, with the blaze of rank and beauty flashing all around her, with the smile of a Queen, beaming upon her face, while a coronet, that tells the ancestral glories of a thousand years, rests brightly upon her brow!—

" 'Dora Livingstone, wife of Livingstone, the Merchant-Prince'—that sounds well, though 'prince' that word 'merchant' as you may, it still retains—ha, ha! a wonderful taint of the Shop! But there is a title, written on the very clouds which darken over my Future, which would sound much better, and that title—but hold my brain grows dizzy; I seem to glide on air—that title is—"

"Dora Lyndeswold, Countess of Lyndeswold!" said a deep voice at the shoulder of the beautiful woman.—

She turned hastily round, gazing upon the intruder, with a glance of mingled surprise and anger.

Fitz-Cowles, in all the elegance of his fashionable attire, stood before her, with his conical hat in one hand, his gold-headed cane in the other, while a smile of peculiar meaning lighted up his dusky countenance.

"Ha, ha! Dora, you are surprised to see me! The truth is, old Artichoke your gardener, attracted my eyes as I passed through the hall. He wanted me to examine, some of his favorite plants. While his attention was turned another way, I stole up the back staircase, reached the conservatory, and here I am! Yes—yes—Dora, notwithstanding your incredulous smile, it is in your power, to be Countess of Lyndeswold—"

"Algernon, it can never be—" exclaimed Dora, fixing the gaze of her brilliant eyes, upon his countenance, with a glance of strange meaning.

"But it can be, Dora, and it must be—" answered Fitz-Cowles, in a careless tone, as he gently balanced his gold-headed cane, on the palm of his right hand, with a see-saw motion.

Dora silently laid her hand on his shoulder, and gazed into his eyes, with a glance of deep interest.

"By what means, you would ask? By flight! Yes, by flight! Next Tuesday the Great Western, sails from New York. Let us arrange all our matters, take passage on board the steamer, and in fifteen days we will be in London. It is but a day's ride from London to Lyndeswold—"

" 'Lyndeswold'—" echoed Dora, and the name seemed to act like a spell upon her—"Ah, ha! England boasts an Aristocracy, founded on high deeds whose records we trace, in the history of a thousand years. The Aristocracy of this land, and ha, ha, this *city*, is founded on—what? Can you tell Algernon?"

"I've been trying to find out for the last three months. I flatter myself that I know something about the peculiar merits and glories of Quaker City, aristocracy—"

"An Aristocracy founded on the high deeds of dentists, tape-sellers, quacks, pettifoggers, and bank directors, all jumbled together in a ridiculous mass of absurdities. Your dentist, whose proper court of arms should be a 'tooth and pincers on a field gules', sends to the Herald's College, in London, and asks the Herald's to trace back his pedigree to the conquest! And so with all the classes of the Philadelphia *ton*. Now could we establish a Herald's college, in the State House, I would make the profession of every man, the rule by which to fashion his crest or coat of arms! To the Quack—a pill-box! To the petifogger, three links of a convicts chain, with the Penitentiary in the distance! To the Bank Director a Widow's Coffin, with a weeping Orphan on either side by way of heraldic supporters! Pah! There is no single word of contempt in the whole language, too bitter, to express my opinion of this magnificent Pretension—the Aristocracy of the Quaker City!"

"You are quite animated, Dora! I never trouble myself about such small matters!"

"Do you know, what was the profession of my grandfather?" exclaimed Dora, as with a smile of bitter sarcasm playing on her proud lip, she again confronted Fitz-Cowles—"Why, ha, ha, ha! He was—guess what?"

"A merchant perhaps? or a 'member of one of the oldest families of Pennsylvania' to use the slang of the day, or—or———

"*A Shoemaker!*" shrieked Dora, with a burst of laughter, as she strode hurriedly up and down the room—"Yes, yes a shoemaker!"

"A cobbler!" muttered Fitz-Cowles starting with a look of silent disgust.

"Yes, yes, a toil-begrim'd cobbler, who sate working all day long on an old bench, mending other peoples' old shoes? And I ashamed of this? Ha, ha! Not in the least! The cobbler's grand-daughter moves in the first circles of the Aristocracy of Philadelphia! And what is something to her credit, she is not ashamed of her ancestry! She does not conceal it with some sounding pretension to high birth, but at once, and without reserve, horrifies, the tape-and bobbin nobility of the Quaker City, with the plain declaration, that Dora Livingstone wife of the Merchant Prince, is a Cobbler's grand-daughter!"

"Deuce take me, if I can understand you Dora! You are not ashamed of having a shoemaker for your grand-father, and yet you reverence the spirit of ancestral pride!"

"You have given my opinions with remarkable precision! I tell you, Algernon, that I respect, the Mechanic, at his bench, though his hands be rough, his face begrimed with toil, his manners uncouth and destitute of polish! But for the petty Aristocrat; the Duke Thimble-and-thread, the Count Soap-and-candle, the Baron Peddle-and-cheat, for all these, I *do* entertain the most sovereign contempt! Give me the honest Mechanic at the bench if we must have a nobility, for your true republican nobleman: not the dishonest Bank-Director at the desk! But if you pass the Mechanic aside—whose honest vote, sustains your republic—if you pass him aside, when you form your Aristocracy, then I say, give us the Titles and the Trappings of an English nobility! Let us at once have a Throne and a Count, a King and Courtiers!"

"Ha, ha, ha! Dora—you grow philosophical! Decidedly so! But you have quite forgotten my proposition. Flight, Dora, sudden and successful flight!"

"And do you think Fitz-Cowles, that I would fly with you as an—it is a sweet word and a true one—as an Adultress! As an Adultress forsaking her husband? No—No! By my life; no!"

"Once in England, we could be united in marriage, without the slightest difficulty. You would become the Countess of Lyndeswood on the death of my father, when I would succeed to the Earldom. During his life, our title would merely be, my Lord and Lady Dalveny of Lyndeswold—"

"Countess of Lyndeswold, and my husband living in America! Ha, ha, ha! This is like some probable history in the Arabian Nights!"

"And how do you propose to overcome the—the *difficulty*—"

"Which is but another name for a—husband, after all—" muttered Dora in a tone, inaudible to Fitz-Cowles.

"You know, Dora, that we must arrange our plan of action without delay. A solitary word of suspicion, whispered in your husband's ears by some officious friend, and our schemes are blown to the—gentleman in black."

Dora approached Fitz-Cowles and laid her hand on his shoulder, while her dark eyes, flashing with a deep and meaning glance, were fixed upon his countenance.

"Suppose Livingstone should *die*—" she said, in a low whisper, while her eyes became intensely brilliant and her face grew suddenly pale.

"Why—" replied Fitz-Cowles, with a slight start—"Why, you would then be the widow Livingstone, with a fortune of some two hundred thousand in your possession. But you know, Dora, Livingstone bids fair to live at least half a century from the present moment—"

"*Livingstone may die, and that suddenly*—" said Dora, in that same low tone, while the hand, resting on Fitz-Cowles shoulder, trembled like a leaf.

"Egad! Dora, you're white as snow in the face! One would think you meant—*something*—by the glance of your eyes. Do speak out and let us hear the news—"

"Listen, Algernon, and I will tell you a secret. Strong and vigorous man as he looks, Livingstone has been for years the victim of a secret and insidious disease. It is that disease which slowly and quietly, almost without pain, ossifies the main arteries of the heart. The victim may live for years, with the flush of health on his cheek and brow, while this insidious disease is closing up the avenues of his life. He may live for years with all the outward signs of health and vigor, when a sudden excitement of mind would lay him down a lifeless corse; aye, in an instant, without a single pain to warn him of his danger, he would fall a lifeless corse—"

"Yes, yes, I remember. McTorniquet—the queer doctor, who talks of Henry Clay, the statesman, and Henry Clay, his blood horse, all in the same breath—took the trouble, one day last week, to explain this disease to me. However, he did not tell me that Livingstone was its victim—"

"This doctor, who is our family physician, called here but an hour ago, and asked me when I expected Mr. Livingstone back from New York. I answered, of course, next week. He then told me that the main arteries of *my husband's* heart were now almost entirely ossified; that I must take every care in the world of him, for any sudden excitement, *would kill him in an instant*—"*

* In the course of a series of lectures, delivered last winter by the gifted Dr. Mitchell, celebrated no less for his medical attainments than his political genius, the learned gentleman described the disease of the heart in detail. From his lecture I derived a knowledge of the various phenomena of the disease, which I have used in this portion of my narrative. The learned Doctor described, in eloquent terms, the insidious manner in which this disease, through a long course of years, gradually ossified the avenues to the heart of its victim, until at last, his life would hang suspended by a hair. The victim might live for years

"What a pity! Poor fellow! To think of a man going about with such a *bad heart* in his bosom!"

"You understand me, then? Livingstone may live for twenty, nay, for thirty years longer, and he may die in a year, a month, a day, or—it may be—in an hour."

"I appreciate his position, Dora. To say the least, its a very ticklish one. Jove! The idea of a man having red cheeks, bright eyes, and a firm step, while his heart is turning to bone—the idea of such a state of affairs, I say!"

Dora drew nearer to Algernon's side, and suddenly grasped him by the wrist. There was a wild light gleaming from her dark eyes as she gazed fixedly in his face, and a slight wrinkle indented the surface of her fair forehead, between the eyebrows. Her voice was utterly changed in its tones, when she whispered these words to the listener's ear.

"Algernon, give me your advice on a point of the deepest interest. When my husband returns from New York, I will seize the earliest opportunity to press upon his attention the importance of having his Will prepared without delay. Poor man! His life hangs by a slender thread—the most trifling chance may sever that thread, and precipitate him into eternity. It is important, therefore, that he should hold himself prepared for death. Justice to his wife demands that his Will, making a final disposition of his fortune, should be executed with all possible haste—"

"By Jove, Dora, you look quite wild. To what tends all this? Hush! Did you not hear a footstep in the conservatory?"

"Suppose, Algernon, that my husband should make his Will. Suppose he leaves his fortune to his wife. These suppositions made, I wish you to imagine a scene. Livingstone and myself are seated in the parlor, on a winter's evening, beside the cheerful fire. His face is lighted up with a pleasant smile, as, displaying the unfolded Will in his hands, he gazes upon the beaming countenance of his wife. And that wife—mark you, Algernon—at the very moment when the husband reaches forth his arms to clasp her to his bosom, falls on her knees at his feet, and, in broken words, shrieks forth the story of her guilt, and his dishonor! Yes, yes, to his ear, to the ear of the man who loves his wife as

---

—if I do not mis-quote the Doctor—with the main arteries of the heart most entirely ossified, but a sudden and violent excitement would result in instantaneous death. Since the lectures of the Doctor, I have seen the truth of his remarks confirmed, in the death of a man, whose cheeks were glowing with apparent health at the very moment when he fell a lifeless corse.

man never loved wife before, that young and *innocent* wife, tells the dark story of her shame! Even while his face beams with affection, she tells him that he is *dishonored*, aye, *dishonored!* That she has been false to his bed, recreant to her plighted faith! That she is polluted in person, corrupt in soul! That this young wife, whom he loved so well, is—ha, ha—an *Adultress!* This she tells him with tears of repentence, with prayers for mercy, with groans of anguish! And *he*—how think ye Livingstone would hear this confession from the wife whose very image he now worships? Ha! Algernon! Think ye not, it would kill him, even before his *frantic* wife had done with her tale of guilt? Even as he sate, without a moments delay, he would fall from his chair, a stiffened corse? Would he not, Algernon?"

A blasphemous oath escaped from Fitz-Cowles' lips, and in a sudden start, which shook his frame, he suffered his hat and cane to fall on the floor.

"By G———d, Dora, I don't think you're a human being!"

He said this in a low-toned voice, and turned away from the Merchant's wife, as she stood in the centre of the room, her statue dilating to its full heighth, while, with a panting bosom and a flashing eye, she awaited his answer to her momentous question.

"And *this*," she cried, gazing upon Fitz-Cowles, who stood near the window with his face averted from her glance—"And this, after I have sacrificed all I possess on earth, all I hope in heaven; and sacrificed for *you!*"

"Hush! Did'nt you hear a footstep in the conservatory? Really, Dora, you are very imprudent—" exclaimed Fitz-Cowles, in a sullen tone, as he gazed vacantly through the window-curtains.

"Would to God, there had been a footstep in the conservatory when I first resigned myself to shame!" said Dora, in a tone of keen and biting sarcasm.

"When a lady agrees, makes up her mind to part with her virtue, and a gentleman makes up his mind to accept the gift, all is fair and satisfactory, and nobody, but an injured husband has a right to complain. But, Murder, Dora—*Murder*—"

"Murder! Madman that you are, who spoke of murder? Fitz-Cowles, I beseech you do not force me to change my opinion, with regard to you. I thought you were a man; one of that class, in fact, who look rather to the end that is to be accomplished than to the delicacy of the means—"

"But Dora, this *experiment* of yours has ten chances of failure, to one of success. Livingstone might recover from the shock, occasioned by your confession—"

"Then it is the chance of failure, not the experiment itself, which turns your face to the hue of ashes—"

"D———n the thing, Dora, Livingstone never wronged me. And I can't see that he had done you any injury sufficient to warrant such a return—"

"I perceive Algernon—" said Dora, crossing her arms, with a calm gesture—"You do not understand me. Livingstone, never did me a wrong: on the contrary, he has bestowed wealth upon me, almost without bound, and lavished affection upon me, until it amounts to idolatry. You never gave me wealth, you never gave me love. Then what is the tie that binds me to you? You have it in your power to grace the—the—ha, ha! The Cobbler's grand-daughter with a *title!* Livingstone is the 'bar sinister', ha, ha, between me and hereditary rank! Who spoke of murder? Not I, by my life! Livingstone may die, he *may* die. That, was all I said—"

"He *may* die, that is true—" said Fitz-Cowles, turning away from the window—"By-the-bye, Dora, you are remarkably ambitious, for a sensible woman. Your very soul, seems absorbed in this ambition to rise—"

"There is a leaf of my heart, Fitz-Cowles, which you never yet, have read. I loved once; loved with all the intensity of my nature, and sacrificed my plighted love, for wealth and Livingstone. Did you never read in books, that the first love of a strong minded woman, when divested from its proper source, turns to the gall and bitterness of worldly ambition? I feel in my inmost soul, that I was destined from my birth to rank and station, to the sway of hearts and the rule of power.—In my early childhood, when forced by penury, my mother, a widowed and a friendless woman, sought a home, in the outskirts of the city, the prophecy was whispered in my ears, that one day, I should wear a coronet, and walk a titled lady among the grandees of a royal court—"

"And some old crone, I suppose, with a cup sprinkled with tea-grounds in her hand, was the Oracle?"

"It matters not, for the prophecy, come it from whom it might, found its echo in my own heart. Does it not often chance, that a casual word, uttered by an ignorant mechanic, strikes a mighty chord in some Statesman's heart, and originates a new and magnificent scheme of state policy? So a chance word, from vulgar lips, may arouse a prophecy which has been hidden in our souls, since the hour of our birth. Why did the Creole, Josephine, credit the withered hag, who foretold that her brow, would one day be encircled with the Crown of France? Because the old crone, was gifted by heaven with especial power? No—

no—no! She might have foretold a thousand incidents, and not one would have impressed the heart of Josephine, with even a passing sensation.

"On the heart of this same Creole, Josephine, from the hour of her birth, had been written down by God's own hand, the high destiny for which she had been born, and the chance words of the old crone, aroused the prophecy into life!"

"Hush! Dora, there is a footstep on the stairs—" exclaimed Fitz-Cowles with a sudden start.

"My God! It is Livingstone's footstep!" and as she spoke, Dora's face grew suddenly pale—"Ha! The note, which I left last night on the centre table, was gone, when I looked for it this morning. Could he have returned in the night?"

The door leading into the main building of the mansion, was suddenly opened, and a red-faced servant in grey livery, turned up with velvet, entered the *boudoir*.

"Mister Livingstone, ma'am!"

And in an instant Livingstone appeared in the doorway, and entered the room.

"Ah—ha! My dear—I've stole a march on you, have I? Back from New York sooner than I expected, you see! Ah—ah! Colonel, is that you? How *do* you do!"

"My God! Livingstone! How pale you are!" was the involuntary exclamation of the wife, as her eyes, were riveted to his countenance—"Have you been ill?"

"Egad! You look as if you been sick a-month!" exclaimed Fitz-Cowles—"Why Livingstone positively you're turning grey!"

Calm and smiling Livingstone advanced, and gathered his right arm round the waist of his beautiful wife. His face was very pale, and his blue eyes, had an unnatural brilliancy in their glance, which in the mind of an acute observer might have aroused a suspicion as to the sanity of the Merchant.

"One kiss my love!" exclaimed Livingstone, as he pressed his lips to the full and pouting lips of his wife, while his face, brightened with a look of pleasure—"You must excuse, these little matrimonial attentions Fitz-Cowles. We married men, are very apt to be fond of our wives; especially after a long absence. And how's your poor sick friend my dear!"

"You have my note, then?" exclaimed Dora, as a slight tremor was visible on her lip.

"To be sure, my dear, to be sure. I returned from New York in the night, found your note on the centre-table, and having read its con-

contents, I retired from the house without alarming the servants. I spent the night at the counting-house, examining my books and papers. How did you say your poor sick friend was, Dora?"

"Alas! She is—dead!" and Dora turned away as if to conceal her agitation.

"Well, well, it can't be helped. 'Debt we've all got to pay'—as the old women at a funeral, have it. By-the-bye, Fitz-Cowles I've got some traces of the Forger at last!"

The Merchant laid his hand playfully on Fitz-Cowles shoulder and gazed smilingly in his eyes, while his unoccupied hand, toyed with his watch-seals, in a careless manner.

"The deuce, you have?" answered Fitz-Cowles with a stare of surprise—"By Jove!" he muttered to himself—"There is a strange look, about Livingstone's eyes, that does'nt exactly please me!"

"I tell you how it was, my boy—" continued Livingstone, still toying with his watch-seals—"While I was in New York, the head clerk of the Charleston House, arrived in town. He recognized the Forger, one day in Broadway, strutting it, among the finest bucks of the city—"

"And you arrested him?"

"Not exactly. We had evidence enough for suspicion; but 'conviction' you know is a different thing. You'll laugh when I tell you how I managed it with the fellow. He was one of my most intimate friends in New York, and was wont to frequent my rooms, very much during the day, manifesting his familiarity by calling me 'a jolly old fellow'—'Old Lin.' and all that kind of thing, you understand? Before the head clerk arrived from the South, I did not ever dream of suspecting this perfumed gentleman of the forgery. Why Colonel do you know, that I'd just as soon suspected you, as him?"

"Curse me Livingstone these kind of comparisons, are deuced unpleasant—" observed Fitz-Cowles growing very uneasy under the Merchant's gaze.

"What do you think we did when we found that we had'nt evidence sufficient for conviction? Why—ha, ha! It's two good! We dressed up a decayed police officer, like a Southern planter, and introduced him to the Forger, as a gentleman of immense fortune from the South. The forger, promenades New York, with the disguised Police Officer at his elbow, showing the pseudo-planter all the 'lions' of the town, and making himself agreeable in a general way. Now the joke of the thing.

"Yes—" echoed Fitz-Cowles—"The joke of the thing—"

"Is simply this. The 'Southern Planter' has a warrant in his pocket, for the arrest of the Forger, the moment he shall attempt to leave the City! Ha—Ha Ha! Capital!"

"Capital! Capital! Ha, ha, ha!" roared Fitz-Cowles.

"Is'nt it too good?"

"Ha, ha, ha! It *is* too good! A warrant in his pocket, for the arrest of the Forger, all the while—did ye say! Capital—ha, ha, ha! Capital!"

"Why Fitz-Cowles, your ladye-love, has been making free with a lock of your hair!" exclaimed Livingstone playfully—"Look here, Dora, what space there is, near Fitz-Cowles' right temple! A large lock severed close to the skin—why Dora, I declare you too, have been making somebody a present of a lock of your hair! A large tress severed from the hair, near your right temple too! Singular coincidence —oh, Fitz-Cowles?"

With the same involuntary gesture, Fitz-Cowles and Dora, both raised their hands to their right temples, and both discovered that a large tress was missing, from among the clustering locks of their raven-black hair.

"Curse that barber! I shall have to flog him!" muttered Fitz-Cowles —"How deuced careless in him!"

"Positively Albert, I can't tell how this occurred—" said Dora approaching her husband—"I must have cut it off in my sleep. How extremely odd—" "Or somebody may have cut it off, to save you the trouble, while you were asleep!" said Livingstone with a kindly smile, as turning from his wife he approached one of the windows, and looked out upon the sky.

Meanwhile Dora stood silent and thoughtful, her bosom heaving upward with sudden pulsations, clashed for a moment, convulsively together, trembled with the agitation that quivered through her whole frame.

"*Now,*" she murmured as a slight pallor overspread her beautiful countenance—"*Now*, is the moment of my fate! The disease, gathering round his heart, manifests its progress already, in his countenance! I will confess all, ha, ha, I will throw myself at his feet and beseech his pardon!"

"Fitz-Cowles turned pale as ashes. He did not hear the whispered words of Dora, but he read her fixed and desperate purpose in the lines of her countenance, now moulded into an expression, as unrelenting as Death. While his brain whirled round in wild confusion, he resolved to delay or at least to thwart the accomplishment of her purpose.

"Aid me now, Great Father, before whom, I shall so soon appear!" were the murmured words that broke from the white lips of Livingstone, as with his face turned from his wife and her paramour, he made a pretence of gazing upon the clear and blue winter's sky—"I feel that fit of madness coming over me again. Oh, for a little strength to go through the mockery! To pretend affection to the wife; friendship to the paramour! There is frenzy in my veins; I know it; I feel it; but I will, I will command my soul!"

And yet as the words escaped from his lips, he felt that same feeling of mocking frenzy, which had given its impulse to his actions, in Monk-Hall, the night before, rushing like a torrent through his veins. Conscious that he was acting like a madman, he drew a pistol from his bosom, and making one stride across the floor, held it to the heart of Fitz-Cowles.

"*A* handsome pistol Colonel! Silver mounted with a hair trigger! One touch of my finger and you're a dead man! Ha—ha! How you step backward, how you recede to the wall. Zounds, man, but I believe you're afraid!"

"For Heaven's sake, Livingstone, put the thing away—" cried Fitz-Cowles as with the pistol at his heart, step by step he retreated to the wall—"You might, you know, pull the trigger by chance! It's loaded you say and—"

"The ball might lodge in your heart! Ha! ha! ha! So it might! Suppose we try!"

As he spoke he pulled the trigger, Dora uttered an involuntary shriek as the 'clinking' of the pistol broke on the air, and then covered her face with her hands. When she again looked around the room, she beheld Fitz-Cowles standing in one corner, pale as ashes, while Livingstone, with a bitter smile wreathing his white lips, still held the pistol presented at his breast.

"Confound those 'caps'—not worth the having!" exclaimed Livingstone, with a pleasant smile—"Why, Colonel, ha, ha, ha! You look as frightened as if, ha, ha, ha! I had intended to shoot you!"

"The pistol was loaded—" hesitated Fitz-Cowles, as he averted his eyes from Livingstone's flashing glance.

"Loaded? Nonsense man—I was merely trying some new percussion caps."

"The disease has affected his reason—" muttered Dora, as she advanced to her husband's side—"Now for the confession and the—*result!*"

"You dropped your handkerchief, Mrs. Livingstone—" exclaimed Fitz-Cowles, as starting hastily forward he presented the snow-white '*mouchoir*,' with a low bow—"*Not on the peril of your soul!*" he hissed the whisper between his set teeth, as his dark eyes were fixed upon her face with a malignant yet frightened glance.

She returned his glance with a look of scorn.

She advanced to her husband's side, she seized his arm with a convulsive grasp, while her dark eyes flashed with an expression of the deepest emotion.

"Livingstone—" she shrieked, with all the pathos of voice and gesture at her control—"I have much to tell you—"

In another instant she lay panting upon his breast, with her arms flung round his neck, while the convulsive sobs, which heaved her bosom, broke wildly on her husband's ear.

Fitz-Cowles saw that his fate hung in a balance, which the weight of a feather might turn.

"Ha!" cried Livingstone, with the same strange glance which marked his wandering intellect, flashing from his clear blue eye—"Ha! what means this agitation—this sudden emotion—these sobs and tears?"

"Why the fact is, Livingstone—your wife is anxious—that is to say —deuce take the thing! Dr. McTorniquet was here this morning, and— and—dropped some strange hints about a disease to which you are subject—and—and—your wife is alarmed for your health—"

"Fools! They think to deceive me!" thought Livingstone, as his wife lay sobbing in his arms—"They do not dream that I overheard their ingenious plans, as I stood in the conservatory, not five minutes past! Ha, ha! I will be even with them! Oh, with regard to the disease of the heart—" he continued, aloud—"Which has threatened me for so many years, I forgot to mention a slight circumstance—McTorniquet, this morning assured me that he had long mistaken my symptoms. I am no more in danger, from any malady of this kind than you are, my dear. There, Dora, don't weep—I can well appreciate this affectionate regard for my health, but you mus'n't weep—"

As Dora lay with her head buried in his bosom, a quick and sudden tremor shook her frame from head to foot. She was deceived for once in her life, and after having betrayed her husband—in the very hour of his madness—became his willing dupe. With one start she raised her head, and her face, pale and ghastly, from the effect of the sudden revulsion of feeling, was disclosed in the morning sunlight.

"Oh Livingstone—" she said in a voice tremulous with emotion,— "I am so glad to discover that all my apprehensions, are groundless!"

She walked to the window, as if to hide the agitation, the joyful agitation which Livingstone's unexpected disclosure, had aroused in her soul. As she passed Fitz-Cowles, she darted a look in his face, full of dark and fearful meaning. For a moment her countenance was convulsed by an expression, hideous as it was resolute, and then, like a sunbeam gleaming from a cloud, all was calm and smiling again.

"By-the-bye, Dora, I had nearly forgotten, an important circumstance, connected with our celebration of the Christmas holidays. You know, my country seat of Hawkwood in Jersey, some * * * * * * miles from Camden? It is the old family mansion of the Livingstone's—was built in fact long before the revolution. Full of secret passages, solemn old rooms with wide fireplaces, lofty halls, and wainscotting without limit—you know?"

"I have often heard of this strange old family seat—" replied Dora, without turning from the window, "And have as often felt a desire to see the place—"

"You shall see it, my dear, within two days. I have this morning despatched servants to the place, in order to arrange the old hall for the celebration of Christmas in the old English style. To morrow morning we will start for Hawkwood and spend the holiday's there. Fitz-Cowles, I hope you will favor us with your company? You nod assent. Well, that is settled; and now I must away to the warehouse. You will excuse me, Fitz-Cowles? I'll be home to dinner my dear—"

Livingstone left the *boudoir* as he spoke.

Dora turned from the window and faced Fitz-Cowles. Their eyes met in one deep and meaning glance.

"Well,—" said Fitz-Cowles drawing a long breath—"We're out of that d———d scrape, any how!"

Dora smiled, but did not speak. Her attention was attracted by a loose slip of letter paper, which lay on the carpet, near her feet. With a manner of easy *nonchalance*, she picked this paper from the floor, and examined it with a careless glance.

In a moment, quick as a lightning flash, her dark eyes shone with sudden fire, her stature dilated to its full height, and her bosom, rose and fell, beneath the folds of her morning gown, with an impulse of the deepest agitation. She stood in the centre of the room, in all her beauty and loveliness, regarding the paper which she held in her trembling hand, with one intense and flashing glance, while her face, was crimsoned over by a sudden flush of excitement. There was an expression of scorn mingled with triumph on her curving lip; and her high forehead, was impressed with a slight yet meaning frown.

"Why Dora—you are agitated—" exclaimed Fitz-Cowles advancing —"What can there be, in that slip of paper to move you thus?"

Her eyes gleamed like flame-coals as the answer broke from her lips in a slow and deliberate whisper, rendered most wild and thrilling, by the sudden huskiness of her voice:

"Leave that to me, and to *the Future!*"

CHAPTER FIFTH

THE GOLD WATCH

"Luke, you know how liable we are to accident and sudden death? If I should die suddenly, I wish you to open this packet and execute the commission which it names. Consider this request, Luke, as the last request of a dying man. Will you promise me?"

"I will, and do promise you—" Luke replied, grasping the hand of Livingstone—"As soon as you are dead, I will open this packet, and at every peril, at all hazards execute the commission which it names. Egad!" he muttered to himself—"he seems to have recovered from his mad fit! A precious tramp I've had, up and down this beautiful city ever since day break, in order to cool him off!"

"Now, Luke, I must go home to my family," said Livingstone, with a faint smile as they emerged from the Exchange—"Here we part, Luke, at least for a little while. It is now nine o'clock. At noon, I will meet you at my house on especial business. Good morning!"

They parted. Livingstone pursued his way up Walnut street, while Luke Harvey remained standing at the corner of Walnut and Third.

"I don't suppose anything *peculiar* will take place between this and sundown—do I? Very likely I don't. Possibly I do! Well, well, let matters take their course. When a woman adorns her husband's forehead with horns she ought to remember that these ornamental *branches* may be turned into dangerous weapons! Stags *gore* people sometimes! W-h-ew! There's that tooth again! I must to some tooth-butcher, right off!"

With great deliberation, Luke took his black silk cravat from around his neck, and investing his mouth and jaws with its folds, fastened it over the top of his head, with an ornamental knot. He presented rather a singular picture. His long and slim figure was enveloped in a tight overcoat, his hat was drawn down over his brows, while his face was nearly concealed by the folds of the black cravat, which left a glimpse of his eyes, the top of his nose, and a small portion of each cheek exposed to view.

"I'll swear that tooth of mine must have joined a Fire Company, by the way it goes on! W-h-ew!"

Passing the various good citizens who were pursuing their way along Walnut street, Luke, after a-half-an-hour's brisk walking, with his hand pressed against his jaw all the while, arrived before a splendid mansion, with a great big silver plate affixed to the door. "PILPETTE—SURGEON DENTIST," was blazoned on the plate, in immense letters. Luke rung the bell, and was swearing quietly at his tooth, when a liveried servant appeared and showed him into a large room, furnished in a style of lavish and auction-store splendor, where Mr. Auguste Pilpette, stood surrounded by the materials of his elegant profession.

Mr. Auguste Pilpette was a stout little man, with a high forehead and a nose which would have been Roman if it hadn't been shaped like a pear. Mr. Pilpette prided himself on his resemblance to Louis Phillipe, and his acquaintance with the literature of the day. Mr. Pilpette had been a bricklayer the year before, and his name had been Jonas Pulp, which by the same lively exertion of imagination that transformed the layer of bricks into the puller of teeth, had been changed into Auguste Pilpette.

"Pilpette, this tooth's agoin' on as tho' it would break my jaw, and blow my brains out! Pull it!"

"We will soon arrange this little matter—" said Auguste Pilpette, seating Mr. Harvey in a chair, which looked as though it had been made for an Alderman, in the days when Aldermen averaged three hundred pounds a-piece—"We'll soon arrange this little matter. A bad tooth. Shocking. What's your opinion of Bulwer?"

"Bulwer be d———d! Pulp, pull my tooth!"

'Pulp, did not please Mr. Auguste Pilpette. On the contrary, Mr. Pilpette was chafed.

"Pulp, indeed!" he muttered—"I'll give him a wrench for that!"

And, accordingly, throwing Luke's head so far back that his upturned eyes commanded a view of the vane surmounting a distant steeple, which was visible through the lofty window, Mr. Pilpette proceeded to give Mr. Harvey a wrench.

It was decidedly a wrench. Luke sprang from the chair with a tremendous bound and an oath.

"D———n———n!" he muttered or hissed, (and the man who objects to the oath never had the toothache.) "D———n———n! Why Pulp, you were born two centuries too late! The Inquisition ought to have had you!"

"Don't you think Dickens excels in the quiet touches?" said Mr.

Pilpette, with great suavity, as Luke performed an irregular Polka over the room—"It seems to me, there's a feeling and a finish in Dickens.

"Pulp you are an ass—" replied Luke, rather harshly, as well-nigh convulsed with the pain of his 'unworthy member,' the half-drawn tooth, he dashed into Mr. Pilpette's window curtains, and looked out upon the street—"It's my opinion, Pulp, that in you the Inquisition would have experienced a great acquisition. Hollo, who's that!"

Pulp, Pilpette, Inquisition, toothache, and all were forgotten as Luke gazed out in the street, with a stare of vacant wonder lengthening his visage.

"I'll soothe him by a criticism—" thought Pilpette—"Do you think, Mr. Harvey, that the beauties of Shelly are appreciated by the mass?"

"What!" shouted Luke, gazing into the street—"In the street at broad daylight! I'd swear it's him! Ha! Ellis Mortimer! He turns the corner! Now or never!"

While Mr. Pilpette stood stricken dumb with astonishment, Luke flung up the window-sash and sprang out upon the pavement, before Mr. Pilpette could say 'Jonas Pulp.' Rising from the pavement, for he had fallen in the spring, Luke rushed down Walnut street at the top of his speed, while his long black hair, and the flaps of his overcoat streamed carelessly in the wind.

The spectacle of a hatless man traversing Walnut street at the top of his speed, in a cold winters day, had rather a maniac wildness in it, and accordingly, two ladies with sharp faces and blue nose-tips, stopped somewhat suddenly in their course and gazed after the retreating form of Luke. A very ragged newsboy, with whom the sharp-nosed ladies, has just been endeavoring to trade two pious tracts headed "*Bad Children in Hell*," for one 'extrey Ledgey' containing accounts of a steamboat accident on the Mississippi, also turned round and looked after Luke, with an emphatic adjuration to his whiskers.

"Oh! You bad youth!" said the sharpest of the sharp-faced tract distributors—"Don't you know where little boys that say bad words will go to?"

"Can't say I do. House o' Refuge m'am?"

"Oh! You ignorant and deplorably-neglected youth!" said the other lady, whose nose was tipped with the faintest shade of blue—"Give me that Extra Ledger and I'll give you this tract, which tells you all about the bad place."

"I'd rather not. A-cause ven the bad place comes it comes, and vots the use of a feller riling his system with it aforehand?"

With these words the unrepentant youth strode away, making the air vocal with 'Extrey Ledgey—steamboat blowed up on Massesappy! Ten hunder' lives lost—all for two cents!'

Meanwhile, dashing along Walnut street, Luke Harvey pursued the distant form of a little hump-backed man, who, all unconscious of the danger at his back, was quietly wending his onward way. It was not long, however, before he became cognizant of his pursuer. While Luke was half-a-square distant, he suddenly slipped into an alley and was lost to view. Luke turned into the alley, emerged into an adjoining street, but no signs could he discern of Mr. Ellis Mortimer.

"I would have sworn it was the Jew!" he muttered, gazing hurriedly up and down the street—"The very look and dress of the man!"

"Here's a remarkable state of affairs! One of the first merchants in town 'digging' along Walnut street on a cold winters day, without his hat! Ha, ha! Quite *unique* in the way of *le grand spectacle*—as we say in domestic French! Eh, Harvey?"

"Harvey!" echoed Luke, turning round to greet the new-comer—"Why, damme, it's Poodle, Poodle of the Black Mail. Go way—fellow! I hav'n't got any *bribe* for you!"

"He, he, he, how jocular!" replied Buzby Poodle, rubbing his hands pleasantly together—"I know what you're after. *The Jew*—ha, ha, ha—I've been watching him. Yonder he goes! Harvey—I say I might tell you something if I liked! I might! I've been watching the *Jew!*"

"Pooh! The Jew has no *bribe* to give you!" exclaimed Luke, with the most emphatic disgust—"Hallo! There he is; far down Seventh street I'll have him yet!"

And down Seventh street Luke started, with as much speed as though he had a match against time, his hair and coat-flaps streaming in the wind, while Buzby Poodle watched his progress with quiet wonder.

"Ha, ha! There he goes like mad! He's a-diggin' down Seventh street—he nears the Jew! Two to one on Harvey—anybody take that bet? Ha! The Jew turns round—bravo! Now the race becomes exciting! Some little boys join the pursuit—a coal heaver flings down his shovel, and pelts after 'em! The Jew's ahead! Go it, hump-back! Go it, Harvey! Hullo! He's got him—no! He's clear! He turns down an alley—they're gone! I'd like to bet a considerable amount on the Jew yet. Hum-hum! Harvey wouldn't buy me. Bad, that, for Harvey. I can guess that he entertains some suspicions with regard to Fitz-Cowles; else why does he pursue the hump-backed gentleman, whom I tracked from the rooms of the 'millionaire?' I think we must sell Harvey to Fitz-Cowles. Damme, I'll cut up that fellow Harvey in to-morrow's Black Mail. I'll be bitter—d———d bitter!"

The State House struck eleven. His face, all crimson with excitement, his brow streaming with thick drops of perspiration, his long hair flying wildly in the wind, from under the shadow of a very bad hat, which he had borrowed from a friend, Luke Harvey came slowly round the corner of certain prominent streets in a remote district of the city, his entire appearance betraying great exhaustion of body, mingled with considerable depression of spirits.

"Nearly two hours passed in chasing that cursed Jew! Poh! Pretty figure I cut. The Jew ahead—a long tail of boys, sweeps and coal heavers behind me. Wild chorus of yells rending the air. People flinging up their windows—ha! ha! 'Twig that man without a hat!' All humbug! Hullo! Here's the old woman's house! Damme, I'll go in and see her!"

Luke stood in front of a three storied dwelling, which, remarkable for its old and desolate appearance, stood among a cluster of Pawnbroker shops, like a decayed gentleman surrounded by pickpockets and thieves. Thick masses of rank green moss grew over the steep roof, and the garret window was stuffed with an old straw hat and bundles of rags. The shutters on the first story were entirely closed, through the windows of the second floor, faded green blinds of a damp and mouldy aspect were visible, while the glasses of the remaining windows, in the third story, were concealed by rough boards, nailed loosely to the window-frame on the outside. The solitary front door, was one of your old fashioned front doors, with massive posts, and heavy cornices. The old brass knocker was covered with a thick crust of verdigris, and all along the door and frame some industrious hand had driven innumerable nails, and spikes of every size and pattern, as though a hardware merchant had been seized with an original fancy, and wished to turn the whole concern into a business card.

In fact, it looked just like the house which all the restless spirits in the city, gentlemen and lady ghosts, who frequent graveyards nightly, and prevail very numerously in Christmas-time, about the halls of old mansions, would choose for their scene of assemblage, in case the spiritual fraternity, determined upon a National Convention of all the ghosts in the union; a sort of death's head festival, with the Skeleton-God himself in the chair.

Becky Smolby lived in this ancient house. Becky Smolby and an Irish female servant were the only tenants of the old time mansion. Who Becky Smolby was, or what were her sources of livelihood, was a question often asked, but by no means frequently answered. Becky was old, penurious and avaricious; every body knew that. Didn't she keep the female servant for one entire week on stale gingerbread and sassafras beer? Becky was queer and whimsical; this point was never doubted. Did she not keep candles burning all the day long in the old mansion, even when she was starving herself for the want of generous onion-soups and broiled steaks! Becky was rich—aye, aye, old rooms lumbered with antique but costly furniture, mysterious caskets standing upon picturesque sideboards of black mahogany, great monsters of chests, stowed away beneath canopied bedsteads, ribbed with brass hands, and corded with thick ropes, all bore witness of Becky's hidden plate and doubloons. Becky was capricious to a fault; had she been a little younger, and worn blue stockings, and talked dictionary, she would have been termed a genius, and her whims would have assumed the shape of amiable eccentricities, peculiar to a gifted mind. Becky had four cats and a parrot, by way of agreeable companions, on whom she was wont to bestow her daily investments of good humor, which, as the reader may judge, were sometimes remarkably limited in their nature; while she kept her Irish female servant as a sort of safety valve for all her vapors, spites, animosities, and what was worse than all, her reminiscences of her five husbands, Buddy, Crank, Dulpins, Smolby and Tuppick.

How Becky made all her money was a mystery. The Tariff, Free Trade, or even the grand question, 'what ever became of the funds of the United States Bank,' were nothing to it. Some said she had saved it in the course of matrimonial experience, by stinting her five husbands; some averred she had made it by trading at sea, to Europe and the Indies; others stated that it had been slowly gathered at home, in the legitimate exercise of a profession, which may be dignified by the name of the Mum-Mum trade.

For instance, a gentleman on whose back a seedy coat hung very lightly, in comparison with the firm grasp of Hard-times (a modern deity) which was ever on his shoulder, pressing him steadily down, some day or other became possessed of a watch, or a few dozen spoons, or a piece of gold plate, all in a sudden and mysterious manner. These costly articles, the gentleman aforesaid, being modest in his disposition, and not disposed to aristocratic ostentation, would transfer to Becky, for a few hard dollars, or perhaps a gold eagle or two. While the transfer was going on, the gentleman placing his finger to his lips, would whisper mysteriously the monosyllable, Mum, to which Becky would reply with equal brevity and point—Mum—wherefore the transfer was known as the Mum-Mum trade.

By some means or other, either by the sea trade, or the Mum-Mum trade, or by stinting her five husbands, Becky Smolby had acquired various stores of gold and silver plate, great chests full of every thing valuable, together with four or five houses, and a small court, located in one of the purlieus of Southwark. Becky was rich, crusty and ancient; and Becky, in her old age, had joined a conventicle, which flourished under the pastoral care of the Rev. Dr. F. Altamont T. Pyne, one of those independent gentlemen who saving souls on their own particular hook, acquire their degrees from some unknown college, and hold forth in some dark alley, two stories up stairs, where they preach brimstone, turpentine and Millerism, in large instalments, according to the taste of their hearers.*

"Well, well," cried Luke, as he gazed upon the front of the old house. "The old lady has always passed for my aunt—the man in the moon knows whether I'm related to her at all! At all events I'll go in and see her."

He gave a slight tap with the knocker.

In a large room, furnished in an old fashioned style, sate the ancient lady, bending over a small table, on which was placed two lighted candles, flinging their glaring light full in her withered face.

Opposite the old lady, sate a gentleman of some forty-five, resting in a capacious arm-chair, his corpulent form clad in glossy broadcloth, while his round face, of oily sweetness, was strikingly relieved by the snow-white cravat encircling his neck. The sharp features of the old lady, all their harshness of outline, thrown out into the light by the tight-fitting black silk cap which covered her head, were impressed with peculiar and distinctive characteristics. A long aquiline nose, hooked like an eagle's beak, thick grey eyebrows meeting together and shooting up into the forehead at either extremity like two sides of a triangle; small dark eyes, quick, piercing and brilliant in their glance; a wide mouth with thin lips, much sunken from the absence of teeth; a pointed chin and high cheekbones; all gave a stern and decided expression to the countenance of the aged dame, which was in strong contrast with the oily sweetness of the round face, whose large grey eyes were gazing in her own.

* For the religion of Jesus Christ, our Savior and Intercessor, the author of this work has a fixed love and reverential awe. For the imposture and trickery of the various modern copies of Simon Magus, (who went about casting out devils in the name of the Lord, all for hire,) whether they take the shape of ranting Millerites, intemperate Temperance lecturers, or Reverend politicians, the author does entertain the most intolerable disgust and loathing. The first make maniacs, the second make drunkards, the last make infidels.

The Reverend Dr. Pyne, who sate opposite—commonly called Fat Pyne, from the initials of his name, or his peculiar disposition to blaze up in his sermons—was a fine specimen of a well-preserved dealer in popular credulity. A red, round face, with thick lips, watery grey eyes, and lanky hair, of a doubtful color, mingling white and brown, and hanging in uneven masses around the outline of his visage, formed the details of a countenance very sanctimonious and somewhat sensual in its slightest expression.

"Trouble brother Pyne, nothin' but trouble in this blessed world," said the widow Smolby, bending over the small work-stand which separated the parties. "Only to think o' it! This very mornin' I was sittin' up stairs in the back room, with Wes on one side and Nappy on t'other, when I heard a knock at the front door. D'ye mind? Ike was a sittin' in one corner; Washy was cardin' wool near the fire; Abe was hanging up against the winder, when I hears a knock at the front door—"

"I didn't know that the old lady's family was so extensive!" muttered the Rev. Dr. Pyne—"Ike, Washy, Nappy, Wes and Abe! Hired men I suppose—"

"Peggy Grud—that's the young woman who lives with me, you know? She goes to the front door and lets in a little hump-backed Jew, who wanted to sell me a gold watch. Ike was a spinnin' near the fire, as I heered the Jew's voice below, and Abe was a-hollerin' murder with all his might, when I comes down stairs—Now you know, Brother Pyne, that a poor lone widow woman like me, ought to turn an honest penny whenever she can, and so, 'cordingly, I buys watches whenever opport*oo*nity offers—"

"He that provideth not for his own house is worse than an infidel—" said Brother Pyne, with great oilyness of manner.

"Considerable. Well, the Jew hands me the gold watch and I goes up stairs to compare it with some timepieces I has on hand. Abe was a-hollerin' murder all the while, and Washington carded wool with all his might. Napoleon looked in my face as I compared the watch with another one, jist as if he'd say'd 'take care old woman, somethin's wrong about this house, I *do* say.' Down stairs I comes, considerin' the price o' th' watch over in my mind, when I diskivered that the Jew was gone! I say—" she cried, elevating her voice into a shriek—"I diskivered that the Jew was gone!"

"And left his watch with you? Surely, Sister, this was not the act of a Jew—"

"D'ye see that little drawer, in the old sideboard yonder? D'ye see the keys a-hanging in the keyhole? When I went up stairs I left the keys in the keyhole, jist as they are now—when I came down, the keys was jist the same as ever, but five thousand dollars in gold, which I, a poor lone woman, had saved up from five husbands, was—gone! The Jew took 'em! I'm ruined! I'm ruined! Oh, Lor'! Oh, Lor'! And Abe a hollerin' murder all the while—"

"He cried murder, did he? What could have induced Abel—"

"It ain't Abel—" said the old woman, sharply—"It's Abraham. I named him arter the First Patriarch. Washy I named arter Washington; Nappy, after Napoleon; Ike, arter Isaac son o' Abraham, which was the son of Heber; and Wes, arter the great and good, Wesley—"

"Bless me Sister, what a numerous family! Your grand-children I perceive?"

"Grand-children! Och, pelt me to pieces wid thimbles! They ain't no grand-childer; only four cats an' a parrit—"

"Now Peggy Grund, who told you to put in your sixpence?" said the old woman, turning sharply round to the new-comer, who stood in the doorway—"Bless my soul, if you ain't more pervokin' nor bad bank-stock!"

"Put in my sixpence, indade! And you sellin' your soul to the devil for yer cats and yer parrit! Twist the necks ov 'em! Wouldn't I, if I had my will o' th' creeturs!"

Peggy Grud, who had suddenly appeared in the doorway of the room, was a tall, stout Irishwoman, coarsely clad, with large hands, and a withered face—looking as though it had been scorched in some fire and hardened to the dryness of an Egyptian mummy—surrounded by an immense cotton night-cap, adorned with colossial ruffles.

"And Abe was a-hollerin' murder all the while—"

"Excuse me, Sister," said the Rev. Dr. Pyne, arising; "If I name the object which brought me here. I came on an errand of mercy. I have noticed you, sister, again and again, mingling with the crowd which weekly fills my church; the Church of True Believers and Free Repenters, conducted by Providence's blissful permission, by the Rev. Dr. Pyne, up Dorkley's court, second story, brick building to the right. Sister, is it not a comfort for you to think, that however hard the times may be, there is one thing cheap—very cheap—"

"And that's mackerel!" said the widow Smolby, with a delighted smile—"Mackerel *is* cheap! I'll stick to that—two small 'uns for a fip! Yes, yes, mackerel is cheap—"

"No, sister, you mistake me. I meant grace, sister, grace. And talking of grace, sister, if you have any small sum about you, which you would like to invest in a Heavenly Bank, here is an opportunity which should not be slighted. A poor man, sister, with a wife and seven small children to support, has met with a sad accident. Ascending a scaffold with a hod on his shoulder, he fell from the height of five stories, laming a negro sweep who was passing at the time, and injuring a school boy for life. He fell upon them both, sister—"

"I say Aunty, let's have a look, at that watch—" said a voice proceeding from the doorway, occupied by the form of Peggy Grud— "Let's see the trinket any how."

Luke Harvey advanced toward the light, his jaws enveloped in a kerchief of burning red, which gave a singular and flaming effect, to his entire appearance.

"My nevey, Brother Pyne—"

"Bah!" ejaculated Luke in a whisper intended for the reverend gentleman's ears—"You can't come it, Fat Pyne."

"Have you a small sum about you, say five dollars or ten, which you would like to invest in a Heavenly Bank?" said the Rev. Dr. in a remarkably bland whisper.

"Heavenly Bank!" echoed Luke—"Mônk-Hall for instance!"

"Monk Luke!"

The reverend gentleman turned aside, and spiritualized a whistle; or in plainer English, puckered up his mouth, as though he was about to perform a lively air, while a faint sound, like a sigh, was all that escaped his lips.

"I say Aunt," exclaimed Luke—"This Jew must have had some accomplice in the house. Otherwise how could he know, that you had five thousand dollars in yonder drawer?"

"Troth and so he must!" said Peggy Grud—"He must have had an accomplish—shure!"

"That's jist what I was a-goin' to tell Brother Pyne," exclaimed the old lady rising to her feet—"Three days ago, there comes, to my house a poor girl, without cloak, bonnet or shoes, a-beggin' me to take her in for God's sake, for somebody was pursuin' her, and a-goin' to murder her, an' what not! I took her in; though she would not tell me her name; I took her in, gave her bread to eat, and a bed to sleep on—here's my thanks I say, here's my thanks!"

"Ha! This is singular!" exclaimed Dr. Pyne, his red face turning suddenly pale—"Has the girl dark, very dark hair, and dark eyes? I merely ask from curiosity?"

"Black as your hat!" vociferated the Widow Smolby with vehemence—"Black as your hat—"

"Very pale in the face?" said the worthy Dr. in a suggestive tone.

"A freshly white-washed wall ain't no paler!" responded the Widow Smolby.

"And you suspect that this girl, was a spy, introduced into your house by the Jew in order to accomplish the robbery of your five thousand dollars?" asked Luke, in a quiet tone.

"Don't I? Ain't I a-goin' to give her up to justice in an hour? Haven't I penned her up, in the room, which has'nt been opened for these seventeen years? The Ghost-Room as Peggy Grud calls it! To think that I should outlive five husbands, Buddy, Crank, Dul—Dul—I say Peg, what was my third husband's name?"

"Dulphins av'it plase ye ma'am!"

"Ye see Brother Pyne, I hadn't that one more than three months, so I sometimes forgits his name. Buddy, Crank, Dulphins, Tuppick, and Smolby; five husbands in all. To think that I—I—should—What was I goin' to say Peg?"

"To think that you should outlive five husband's, and be robbed afther all in this murtherin' manner!"

"Jist so. And afore an hour goes over my head, this girl, shall be placed in the keer of Alderman Tallowdocket, that she shall. I'll have justice!"

"*Justice*, and in the Quaker City!" said Luke, with a quiet sneer, as folding his arms across his breast, he gazed from face to face—"Justice and in the Quaker City! A Strange Monster I trow! One moment it unbolts the doors of the prison, and bids the Bank-Director, who boasts his ten thousand victims, whose ears ring forever with the curses of the Widow and the Orphan, it bids the *honest* Bank-Director, go forth! The next moment it bolts and seals those very prison doors, upon the poor devil, who has stolen a loaf of bread to save himself from starvation! One day it stands grimly smiling while a mob fires a Church or sacks a Hall, the next, ha, ha, ha, it hurries from its impartial throne, and pastes its placards over the walls of a Theatre, stating in pompous words, and big capitals, that THE TRUTH *must not be told in Philadelphia!*"

"My friend, you are severe upon the 'proper authorities,' " exclaimed F. Altamont T. Pyne, (Pastor of the church of True Believers and Free Repenters,) with great suavity of manner.—"Take care? There are muzzles, and prisons, and fines, for those who speak thus!"

"Justice in the Quaker City! Suppose the Almighty God, should hold a Court one day, and try the Justice of the Quaker City, by his impartial law! Ha, ha, ha! What a band of witnesses would come thronging to that solemn bar, 'Come into court, old Stephen Girard; come into court with your will in hand—that will which bequeathed your enormous wealth to the white mail orphans of the past, the present, of generations yet unborn; come into court, and testify! What say you of Quaker City justice? Is your College built? Has a single orphan been fed, clothed, or educated at your expense, or with your money? Come into court, widows and orphans beggared by the frauds of bank directors, come into court, in your rags and misery; come, and testify: what thinks you of Justice, as she holds the scales in Philadelphia? Come into court, Religion, and point to your churches in ruins! Come into court, Humanity, and point to the blackened ashes of the Asylum, the School House, and the Hall! Come into court, one and all! What think ye of Quaker City Justice? 'Quaker City justice!' cries old Stephen Girard. 'Where is my College? A generation has past away since my death; where is my College, where is my money?' 'Quaker City Justice!' shout the widows and the orphans. 'By its decision we walk in penury and rags, while the bank director, who robbed us, rides in his coach-and-four.' 'Then, in God's name, what has this solemn mockery, Justice in the Quaker City, ever accomplished?' It has laughed pleasantly while riot after riot, went howling through the town; it has chuckled gaily as it bade assassin after assassin, go scatheless from its bar; it has grown violent in glee, as it beheld its judical halls, soiled by the footsteps of corruption; and, now and then, it has crept from off its lazar-throne, and arrested an editor who raised his voice for the right; or stopped a play, that dared speak out for the truth!"*

"Well, well, Luke, ain't you most out o' breath?" said the Widow Smolby, rubbing her hands together. "But that ain't nayther here nor

* Luke Harvey, in his usual sneering style, deals not only in gross anachronisms but in arrant falsehoods. In order that the readers of this book, at a distance from Philadelphia, may not be deceived by Luke's anti-Philadelphia tirade, we deem it proper to state a few facts.—Girard College has been built for years, and has been the home of some thousand orphans, who have been fed, clothed, and educated, at the expense of good old Stephen. Every body knows this to be true. Bank directors are always convicted in Philadelphia, when tried for robbing widows and orphans. Widows and orphans, plundered by bank directors, never starve in Philadelphia. The Quaker city is too charitable for that. Churches have *never* been burned in Philadelphia. Nor halls fired, nor orphans' asylums sacked, nor school houses, given up to a mob. Not in the least. The play of an author, who dared speak out for the truth, has never been *ukase*-d in this city. Never. *A contemptible coalition of charlatans, have never resorted to threats of assassination in order to put down a work, which held them up to public scorn*. Never, never!

This is a great city, and its dignitaries are great men, worthy of all respect.

Pity for them that their rule is so brief! Why not have an ordinance passed by the Councils, to make the dog days last all the year, and forever!

there. Afore an hour goes over my head, this gal, who is now up stairs, in the Ghost Room, shall be tuk to Alderman Tallowdocket's, and bound over for this 'ere robbery.' "

"Could I see the young lady for a few moments, alone?" said Dr. Pyne, with his usual bland smile. "It would be such a comfort to tell her, that in the next world, she'll be burned up forever and ever. It would, indeed."

"I 'spect you *can't* see her, brother. I'd rather not. Come this way, Luke, and I'll show you the watch."

The old lady led the way up two pair of dark stairs, followed by Luke. In a few moments, they stood in a large room, on the third floor, whose outlines, Luke might dimly discern by the glimmer of the candle, which the old lady grasped in her hand. It was wide and spacious, the floor covered with carpet of an ancient though costly pattern, while the ceiling was emblazoned with a picture in fresco, whose gorgeous hues had been softened down by time. Massive velvet curtains hung along the three windows, which, facing the street, were hermetically closed, by the boards outside the sashes. A bed with a lofty canopy, was in one corner; an antique dressing bureau, surmounted by a circular mirror, stood in the space between two of the windows; a wide hearth, with ashes and loose pieces of half burned wood scattered over the bricks, extended along one entire end of the chamber, while the wall above the mantel, was concealed by a large picture, set in a gorgeous frame. It was the picture of a fair and lovely girl, remarkable for the brilliancy of her eyes, and the midnight blackness of her hair.

It was a singular circumstance, which did not escape the notice of Luke, that the carpet was covered with thick dust, as though it had not been open for years, while the velvet of the window curtains, the gilt of the massive portrait frame, and the hangings of the bed, were all obscured by the same thick, grey dust, and hung with heavy spider webs.

"Ghost Room, indeed!" muttered Luke; "why look here, aunt, the carpet is covered with dust, and the air is damp and unwholesome as a grave vault. What's the meaning of all this, any how?"

"It has not been opened since she died, until this day!" said the Widow Smolby, as her features, withered and wrinkled as they were, glowed with an expression of strange feeling.—"She died in yonder bed. I held her in my arms. Her child lay dead upon her bosom. Yon hearth—d'ye see it, Luke? The fire went out when she died—it has never been lighted since!"

"What mean you?" cried Luke, amazed at the agitation of the old woman. "Ha!" he shouted, ere she could answer his question. "Here is the watch on the dressing bureau! It is Fitz-Cowles', by my life! The Jew must have stolen it from him! Fitz-Cowles once told me, that his name was inscribed within the case. Hold the light while I open it, Aunt. Ha! What is this! A memorandum on a slip of paper, in Fitz-Cowles' hand, inserted between the case and the body of the watch! '*In Charleston*,' on such a date—'*Must be in Philadelphia*,' on another date. '*Ellis Mortimer*,' ho, ho, ho! We've tracked the fox at last! Ellis Mortimer, and the hump-backed Jew are one! Fitz-Cowles is the master villain! Before to-morrow night, I'll have him, ha, ha, ha, where *patchoully* can't sweeten him!"

"Why, Luke, what in the world's the matter with you!" cried the Widow Smolby, in utter wonder. "You go on like mad. Howsomever, here's the Jew's accomplice, sleeping in the bed! Don't she sleep sound, for such a guilty thief?"

Leading the way along the floor, the old lady pushed aside the cob-web-hung curtains, and gazed upon the sleeper's form.

"Ha! The dead have come to life!" She shrieked, starting backward. —"It is not the stranger; it is my daughter, just as she looked nineteen years ago, when she was pure and innocent! Look, Luke; look, I say! That pale face, that long dark hair, that lily white hand! I'd swear it was my daughter come to life!"

Advancing to the bedside, Luke gazed upon the sleeper's form, as it lay dimly disclosed by the light of the flickering candle.

The face of a fair young girl, relieved by long tresses of jet-black hair, broke like a dream upon his gaze. True it was, the young form, thrown along the bed, in an attitude of slumber, was clad in a dress of tattered rags, yet the outline of a figure ripening from the bud of maidenhood into the bloom of beauty and womanhood, might be discerned, beneath the disguise of mean apparel; true it was, the face, pale as death, bore the traces of a long life of sorrow, yet were the features regular, the dark eyebrows, penciled and arching, the brow was calm and white, full of the silent grandeur of intellect, while the rounded outline of the cheeks, the fulness of the pouting lips, and the dimple of the chin, all bespoke the youth and loveliness of the sleeper.

"Thus nineteen years ago, she lay upon that bed! My only daughter! Seventeen years ago, upon that bed, she breathed her last! Since that hour, the light of day has not shown within the walls of this house! Since that hour I have not stepped beyond the threshold of my home! And now—now—she has arisen from the dead!"

"And this," cried Luke, gazing in silent wonder upon the pale yet beautiful face of the sleeper, "this is the accomplice of the Jew!"

Luke's exclamation aroused the old woman from her waking dream. Her daughter, for whom she had mourned so long, was forgotten when she remembered the five thousand dollars stolen from her house that very morning by the Jew, whose accomplice lay sleeping on the bed.

"The huzzy!" she cried, shaking her fist at the form of the unconscious girl—"To steal my hard earnings, and arter I'd given her a home and a bed, without so much as axing her name? But I'll have justice! That I will, Luke! To jail with the trollop!"

"I tell you what it is Aunt—" exclaimed Luke, with his gaze rivetted to the face of the lovely girl—"Promise me that you will not consign this child to the care of the Police until to-morrow morning, and I give you my word, that before sunrise your five thousand dollars shall be safe in your hands again!"

"You never yet broke your word to me, Luke! You're got my promise. But mind you keep yours! Hush! She wakes!"

The lids of the sleeper, fringed with long dark lashes, slowly unclosed, and her eyes, large, dark and brilliant, gazed wonderingly around. In a moment the glance of wonder changed to one of the deepest terror.

"MY FATHER!" she shrieked, starting up in the bed and gazing fixedly over Luke's shoulder.

Luke turned hastily around. The Rev. Dr. Pyne stood by his side with his smooth face all radiant with an expression whose doubtful meaning of malignancy and triumph Luke found it difficult to fathom.

"MY FATHER!" again shrieked the girl, crouching up in the bed, with her limbs all huddled together as though she anticipated a violent blow.

"My child, you please me—" said Brother Pyne, mildly. "You recognize your parent. You repent your late flight from his roof? You will return to your home?"

"To the prison!" shrieked the girl; "to the cell, to the gibbet, anywhere you please, but not to *him!* For God's sake, good woman, do with me what you will, but save me from *his* power! He is my father, but sooner than return to his roof again, I would drag out the life of a convict within a dungeon's walls, I would beg my bread on the highway, I would—I would—Stand back from the bedside! Back! Back, I say, or you will drive me mad! Ah! Ah! I see it all again! That scene—the night I fled from your roof! Oh God, oh God!"

She fell prostrate on the bed, her limbs writhing in a convulsive spasm, while her cheek grew like death, and the white foam hung on her vivid lips.

CHAPTER SIXTH

THE POISON OF CATHARINE DE MEDICIS

"This, you see, is my Museum. My Museum, Livingstone! A little of every thing from all parts of the world. In that jar a negro child with two heads. Preserved in spirits. Capital specimen of a double-headed negro. Ought to have been at Hall this morning; cut off a poor fellows arm. Took it quite lively. Henry Clay—seen my blood horse, Henry Clay? Splendid creature, capital action, glorious gait. Paid eight hundred for him. Make a good President; in favor of the Tariff; chivalrous fellow. Got a soul, Livingstone, a soul, I say, and a big soul it is, too!"

"Which do you mean, McTorniquet—the blood-horse or the statesman?"

"Ah! Hum! You're disposed to be jocular! Why the fact is, I'm such an admirer of the statesman, that whenever I begin with praising the horse I'm sure to slide into an expression of feeling with regard to the man. Singular specimen of an arm, that. In that long jar. Took it off the body of a man who was hung for robbing the mail. Hand had seven fingers. By-the-bye, did you hear that Henry Clay won the purse at the last races? He didn't run—he *flew!* All stuff about that duel with Randolph! Randolph came on the field in a morning-gown! Who the d———l ever heard of fighting a duel in that way? Pshaw!"

"By-the-bye, Doctor, what erroneous notions have come down to our time, with regard to Poisons! Now, some credulous historians would have us believe that in the time of Catharine De Medicis the art of poisoning was carried to such perfection that a feather, a glove, or a perfume, impregnated with a chemical preparation, would send the victim quietly to his long home. All fudge—isn't it Doctor?"

"Fudge?" echoed Doctor McTorniquet, raising his tall form to its extreme heighth, while his long black morning gown floated loosely round his spare limbs—"Fudge! Let me tell you, Livingstone, that I have devoted some small portion of my time to the study of Chemistry. Its very well to encourage the idea that these legends about Catharine De Medicis' poisons are all—fudge—for, were the truth known, there would be an end of all civilized society. Do you know that there are poisons so stealthy and subtle in their operations, that the minutest particle infused into a drink, mingled with food, laid gently on the victims lips, will produce instantaneous death?"

"But such a death will be attended with marks of violence?"

"Not a bit of it, Livingstone! No mark of violence, no sign of murder attests the manner of the death. The victim lays as though he (or she) had but fallen asleep. What d'ye suppose would be the consequences, were these chemical secrets made known?"

"Very disastrous, I presume—"

"Just fancy what a world it would make! A lawyer picks a quarrel with a judge, and sends him to Heaven with a whiff of a perfume. Two clergymen disagree on matters of controversial divinity—one makes the other a present of a pair of gloves! W-h-ew! He's gone! A lady jilts her lover—he sends her a magnificent Bird of Paradise, tipped with poison! The lady jilts no more lovers! Two candidates are running for office—one puts a pill in t'other's brandy, and kills him off, on the eve of th' 'lection. Delightful world it would make! Tom poisons Dick; Dick poisons Harry; Harry poisons his wife, and his wife poisons—the d———l knows who!"

"You've a very poor opinion of human nature, McTorniquet?"

"You've hit it! It's a way we doctors have. God Almighty trusts us with very little knowledge of the grand mysteries of nature, for fear we'll abuse our gift. Why Livingstone, d'ye know that were this secret and most subtle poison generally known, half the men in town would give their wives an eternal leave of absence? And *vice versa*. Precious world we'd have!"

"Ha, ha, ha, Doctor! You take such an original view of things! By-the-bye, have you seen my wife this morning! Did she expect me back from New York so soon?"

"Saw Mrs. Livingstone this morning, and cautioned her about your disease. Egad Albert, you must be very careful! Ticklish disease *that!* One moment lively as a bird; the next, stiff as a poker! Have you seen Harry Clay lately? Grand speech that: his farewell to the Senate! Wait a moment and I'll go round to the stable and order the servant to trot him out. Would you like to see a manuscript volume of mine, on the Theory of Poisons? Here it is in this Cabinet. Just take a peep at it while I run round and have Henry Clay brought to the front door. Put it back in the Cabinet when you've gratified your curiosity. Back in a minute, Livingstone!"

Livingstone took the small volume of manuscript in his hand and eagerly turned over the leaves. He was alone. He stood in McTorniquet's Museum, surrounded by shelves piled with surgical curiosities, preserved in jars, or hanging by parti-colored strings, or, yet again, huddled carelessly together. The very air was reminiscent of the scalpel and the torniquet. Dead men in fragments, in great pieces and little, in all shapes and every form, were scattered around. In the full light of the window, fashioned in the ceiling of the room, stood a grisly skeleton, one hand placed on his thigh-bone while the other, with the fingers stuck in the cavity of the nose, seemed performing the stale jest, common with the boys along the street. "You can't come it Mister, by no manner o' means!" that gesture said, as plainly as a skeleton's gesture can say.

" 'In the days of Catharine De Medicis' "—murmured Livingstone, reading from the manuscript volume—" 'There was prepared by her command, a poison, combining in its nature, the most deadly chemical attributes. This poison laid its victim down in the sleep of death without a mark of violence, without the slightest sign of murder, to tell the tale of an untimely death. Subtle and penetrating in its nature, most fearfully opposed to the Principle of life, in its mildest form; this poison was prepared by the Alchemist Ellarbin D'Zoisboigné, after the study of years passed in searching for the Grand Secret, the Water of Life. The Alchemist sold the poison to the Queen, for the price of one of her royal jewels. Secure of the deadly preparation, and aware of the manner in which it was to be used, the Queen determined that the secret of its composition should rest with her alone. The Alchemist was her first victim. Among various strange legends of medical lore, the poison, its various qualities, and the secret of its preparation, have descended to modern times. It is prepared thus—' "

Livingstone paused. The terrible idea which had rested upon his brain, since the scene of the past night, now began to take form and shape. He saw the horrible path which he was doomed to tread, more clearly and distinctly in its minutest windings.

He listened intently for a single moment. There was no sound of the Doctor's returning footstep. The Museum was still as the grave. And yet, as the fatal idea rose blackening Livingstone's brain, with all its details of horror, the very air of the room grew stifling, and he could distinctly hear the beatings of his own heart.

Ere another moment passed, seizing a lancet which lay on an adjoining shelf, with a calm and cautious movement, Livingstone severed the leaf, which he had just read, from the manuscript volume, and folding it in letter form, placed it within the breast of his overcoat.

"Close to the keepsakes—next to my heart!" he grimly smiled, as he placed the manuscript volume in the cabinet again—"Three days ago, I little dreamed that Catharine De Medicis would become serviceable to me!"

He quietly passed from the room and from the house. Hurrying along the crowded street, in the course of fifteen minutes he arrived before his stately mansion. At the very door he was met by Luke Harvey, who had just returned from his visit to the widow Smolby's house.

"Is it noon—" exclaimed Luke, with a quiet smile—"Here are the fruits of my morning's labors!"

He placed in the Merchant's hands the memorandum which he had taken from the stolen watch.

Livingstone started, but in an instant recovered the fearful composure which had marked his demeanor since the fatal scene at Monk-Hall.

"I bear it well? Do I not, Luke?" he calmly exclaimed. "So, so! He is not only the—the Adulterer, but the Swindler and Forger! We can settle both accounts at once!"

"There is enough in that slight memorandum to excite suspicion," exclaimed Luke, "but not enough to produce conviction. Leave the matter in my hands, and before Friday night—that's to-morrow—the fellow will be in the hands of the police."

"To-morrow morning Dora and I start for Hawkwood—" replied Livingstone, with a slight smile—"By-the-bye, while you are procuring the necessary documents for the conviction of the forger, we must be sure that he does not leave the city. Ha, ha! I have it! Let us walk down the street while I let you into my plans."

They were walking down the street, whispering earnestly together, when a hand was laid upon Livingstone's shoulder.

"Look here, Curnel—you don't forgit old friends, do you?" said a bluff voice, which sounded very much like the deep bass of an oyster-man.

"Why, Larkspur, is that you? I'd scarcely have known you! Why, what's the matter with you?"

"Nothin' much. Only there was a change in the admineystration.—Easy Larkspur was turned out. Konsekence is, he persents a pictur' for the portrait painter, and the daily papers. Does not he?"

Easy Larkspur, as the new comer was styled, certainly presented a picture, and a very remarkable picture it was, too. He was a short, stout man, with broad shoulders, and a tolerably corpulent person. His face was remarkable for its crimson hue, and its immensity of jaw or cheek, as the reader pleases. His costume was at once picturesque and simple. A short gray roundabout, exhibiting glimpses of a saffron shirt, at the elbows, and buttoned up to the neck across his muscular chest; corduroy trowsers, reaching to the calf, agreeably variegated with patches of various colors, and a pair of shoes, rather the worse for the wear, with the heels worn away all at one side, and picturesque crevices near the toes. Easy Larkspur wore no stockings. Such things as stockings had been invented long after man had departed from his primitive simplicity of manners; Easy Larkspur was above wearing stockings. The hat which surmounted Mr. Larkspur's broad face, was quite a curiosity in its way. In material it was rather flimsy, being fashioned of common straw; in shape it was singular, bearing a strong resemblance, to nothing in heaven above, or on earth beneath, or in the waters under the earth. Speculative people would have called it a shocking bad hat. You might have fallen down and worshipped it, without any violation of the commandment. The picturesque appearance of the hat was rather increased by a glimpse of a dingy red handkerchief, which peeped from the crevices of the crown, like a quiet observer, taking a view of the world, from a favorable elevation.

"Why, Larkspur, where have you been all this while?"

"Two years ago, I was turned out of the Police. Since that time I've been perambulating the continent. Part of the time, as a Tuppygraphical ingineer; I carried the chain on the railroad. Part of the time, I was ingaged in the mercantile marine service: drove the horse on the canawl. I attributes the present depression of my funds to the cursed Whig tariff of '42. It must be that; for, deuce take me, if I know what else it can be!"

"Larkspur, would you like to earn a hundred dollars?"

"Jist try me. I'm putty desp'rate now, I tell you. I might accept."

"Could you assume the manners of a Southern planter?"

"What d'ye mean? Swear a few big oaths, carry a Bowie knife, and talk about my niggers? I jist could do that, and nothing else."

"Go down to my store, in Front street, Larkspur, and wait for me," said Livingstone, turning toward his mansion again. "Luke, attend to the accomplice of the Forger, in the den of Monk-Hall. I'll see that the Forger himself does not leave the city."

It was in this state of mind, with his plans of vengeance fully matured, and his soul determined upon the prosecution of those plans, that Livingstone sought the presence of his wife, and passed through the scene in her boudoir, which we have already described.*

"The girl is beautiful"—Luke soliloquized as Livingstone and Larkspur passed on their separate ways, leaving him alone in the street. "Beautiful as a dream! Pshaw, Luke, this folly ought not to move you again! Jilted once, and again in love! and with whom? A nobody, who, coming from nowhere, knocks at old Widow Smolby's door, and begs admittance, but won't give her name! Fat Pyne, her father too—hum—that's suspicious, to say the least! Aunt Smolby,

* See Chapter Fourth—Dora Livingstone at Home.

promised that the girl should not leave her roof, until she heard from me.—There's mystery about the thing, take it as you will, and so—as I said last night—when hurrying down this very street—I say now! To Monk-Hall!"

CHAPTER SEVENTH

THE COUNCIL OF WAR

"I have gathered the fruit, and it is ashes!"

Lorrimer was alone in the Rose Chamber. The light of the candle, fast waning to the socket, streamed in fitful flashes over his wan and pallid face. Thus had he sate for hours, his arms crossed over his breast, his face drooped low on his clasped hands, while his hazel eyes glanced vacantly in the flickering light form beneath the shadow of his corrugated brows. Thus had he sate, while the morning dawned over river, and steeple, and roof; and as the day wore on, filling the darkest nooks and avenues of the old city with the noonday beams of the winter sun, he remained silent and alone, stricken with a strange apathy his very soul impressed with a fear, whose nature he might not analyze, and his heart imbued with a terrible remorse for the irreparable wrong.

"I have gathered the fruit and it is ashes!" he murmured—"Oh, would to heaven, that before the commission of this wrong, I had known my heart! Would that I had felt, twelve hours ago, how dear this girl would have been to me as a wife! How she would have wound herself into my heart, and grown into my very existence; the life of my life, and of my soul, a better and a purer soul! Curses, eternal curses upon the creed of the heart-cankered worldling which has dragged Mary to ruin, and which will—ha, ha, ha—within a few brief days, hasten her wronger to an untimely and unwept death!"

"Death?" echoed a hoarse voice—"Short word that, but good as a med'cin' to cure some disorders! I say Monk Gusty, what shall we do with the feller?"

"With Byrnewood—" muttered Lorrimer, turning his head slowly round and gazing upon the form of Devil Bug, who stood at his side, with his usual hideous grin—"With Byrnewood, you mean?"

"With Byrnewood or the feller, jist as you like! About these times I konsiders him a putty disagreeable feller, I does that! He's a-layin' on the floor of the Walnut Room, half dead with opium, and all sorts o' drugs! He won't come to his senses for hours yet.—But Gusty, what shall we do with him, when he does come to his senses. That's the pint which I wants to argur!"

"And the gal, what shall we do with the gal?" interrupted a voice proceeding from the other side of the room—"She's been sleepin' in the Painted Chamber ever since daylight. At fust she took on considerable, but a drop o' laud'num in her coffee settled that business! What shall I tell her ven she vakes?"

Mother Nancy, with her sharp features and colloped cheeks twisted into an expression of sneering malignity, approached Lorrimer, and laid her withered hand upon his shoulder.

"Tell her what you please, but leave me to myself!" and as Lorrimer spoke, his brow darkened with a frown, "and Devil-Bug, mark me—I would be alone!

"Very well, ve-r-y well! When the feller gits over the opium, I'll axe him down stairs very perlitely, and tell him to dig off! Vonder how that 'll vork? He won't come back with the poleese—o'course not. Monk Gusty won't be jugged up for makin' too free, with another man's darter? The feller's a nateral born fool what thinks it!"

"Come, come, young man," cried Mother Nancy, squaring her elbows, "it may suit you to sit here mopin' and mopin', over spilt milk, but it don't suit me, I tell you! Suppose this young chap, Byrnewood, or Byrnecoal, or whatever his name is, leaves Monk-Hall, what 'll be the konsekence? Monk-Hall will be torn up, root and branch, and—"

"Our leetle family joys walked into like bricks!" suggested Devil-Bug.—"Cuss that light, how it flares!"

"And what remedy do you propose?" exclaimed Lorrimer, as his face changed to a death-like pallor, was illumined by a sudden glare of light.

"I perpose to keep a tight hold on the gal!" said Mother Nancy, with a pleasant smile. "Nothin' like bein' on the safe side! And then, Gusty, you can have a little bird to yerself, all in this old cage of Monk-Hall, and no body be the wiser!"

"And as for Byrnewood," suggested Lorrimer, turning to Devil-Bug.

"I perpose to keep a tight hold on *him*, too!"

The face of the doorkeeper of Monk-Hall, was crossed by a hideous smile. His solitary eye glared with sudden intensity, and the muscles of his countenance were agitated for a single moment, by a violent and convulsive movement.

"What mean you?" exclaimed Lorrimer, starting with involuntary terror, as he beheld the purpose of Devil-Bug's soul, gleaming from his loathsome face.

"Cuss it, how that light flickers in the socket!" Devil-Bug calmly answered, raising his hand to his protuberant brow, and smoothing the matted hair to one side.—"What do I mean?" he continued gazing at Lorrimer through the outspread fingers of his hand—"Nothin' o' konsekence! Only the young feller will not come to his senses, till long arter dark, and then—and then—cuss the light, it's gone out!"

The libertine and his minions were enveloped in sudden darkness.

CHAPTER EIGHTH

MAJOR RAPPAHANNOCK MULHILL

Arrayed in all the paraphernalia of his walking costume, Fitz-Cowles was threading his way among the crowd of loiterers, who daily occupy the pavement in front of Independence Hall. His brow was clouded by a frown, and once or twice, as he walked along, he allowed his gold-headed cane to fall on the hard bricks, with a ringing sound. It was evident that the gallant Colonel, in all the glory of his original hat, his tight-fitting overcoat, his long dark hair, his white kid gloves, and gold-headed cane, was still somewhat ruffled in temper, and disturbed in soul.

"This woman!" he muttered, " 'Gad I never knew her match! Bold, reckless, and dangerous! I must take care! Dora, with her imprudence, may frustrate all my schemes, and scatter my fortunes to the wind! I stand upon a dangerous height! A step higher, and I arrive at the object of all my desires, unlimited wealth and safety! A step lower, a single misplaced movement, and—ugh! The prison, the convict's cell, and—it makes my flesh creep—the lash, are mine!"

"Ah, ha! Fitz-Cowles! I've just been seeking for you!"

"Is that you, Livingstone! Which way are you bound? Up Chesnut street or down?"

"Colonel Fitz-Cowles, allow me, to make you acquainted with Major Rappanhannock Mulhill, of Mulhill Plantation, South Carolina. A planter from the South, Colonel," suggested Livingstone, in a whisper; "rich as Girard. Lands without limit, and a gold mine!"

"I am proud of your acquaintance, sir," replied Fitz-Cowles, graciously extending his hand to the stranger. "Queer specimen of a planter," he muttered to himself.—"Wonder if he's keen at the cards? I must try him at Faro!"

"Sur! Happy of the honor! I like you—you're of the right stripe—'the real pig,' as we say at Mulhill," observed the Southern planter, clapping Fitz-Cowles on the back.—"May I be cussed, Curnel, if I don't think you're got the real allegator eye, which give sich wiwacity to the phizzes of us bloods, from down South!"

Col. Fitz-Cowles had seen many queer specimens of the Southern planter, but this gentleman was decidedly the queerest of all. Rappahannock Mulhill, was a stout, thickset gentleman, with a round, red face, and a corpulent paunch. His dress was at once singular and effective, as the playbills have it. A broad-brimmed hat, of raw felt, with a round crown, and a long blue cord, to which was appended a tassel, that hung drooping to the Major's shoulders. A deep crimson velvet waistcoat, double-breasted, and buttoned up to the throat. Pants made very full and wide, and striped like fancy bed-ticking; a sky blue coat with glaring metal buttons; yellow buckskin gloves; tight boots of patent French leather, and a check neckerchief, tied in an enormous bow, and affording free play to the colossal shirt collar, which rose to the Major's ears. Had you seen the Major, thus attired, walking along Chesnut street, you would have said, that there was only one thing wanting to complete the general finish of his appearance; a cane of the proper style and dimensions. This want was supplied, by an enormous stick or club, which the Major grasped in his right hand. Bending in a dozen ways, all twisted, and curled, and knotted, it looked as though it might have been, the root of the Tariff, which politicians have been endeavoring to find for years.

"How did you leave all the folks down South, Major?"

"Lively"—replied the Major, pulling up his shirt collar—"Lively! Roasted an Abolitionist the day afore I left, for tryin' to steal my niggers. Lynched a Yankee, the day afore that, for sellin' me some Jersey cider for sham-pane! Things is werry lively in our diggins, jist now—"

"I suppose you've been in a few knock-downs in your time?" observed Fitz-Cowles condescendingly.

"Can't say much for my skill in that line, Curnel—" replied the Major, still tugging away at his shirt collar, while he grew suddenly red in the face—"Killed four or five fellers in a duel. Took 'em one after another. Had to pay their funeral expenses. Very low business. The Sheriff had the imp*oo*dence to get a warrant out, for me. There it is—I've preserved it to this day as a coorosity!"

"Why it looks quite fresh—" observed Fitz-Cowles, looking at the document which Mulhill held in his extended hand—"Very fresh, indeed—"

"Oh, that's because I have kept it in spirits: a warrant's sich a c*oo*rosity down South—"

"Colonel, if you'll excuse me, I wish to speak a word with the Major before I resign him to your care. Major will you walk this way a moment—"

He led the Major beyond the hearing of Fitz-Cowles, and glanced quietly over his shoulder at the millionaire as he spoke.

"Larkspur, how can you be so hazardous!" exclaimed Livingstone—"His name on that very warrant, and the signature of the Mayor at the bottom!"

"Werry true—" replied Easy Larkspur, *alias* Rappahannock Mulhill, "werry true. The Ma'or swore me in as Deppity Poleesman. He, he! The idea-r! My comin' the Southern planter over him, when I've got a warrant in my pocket for his arrest! I say, Livingstone, you're a perfect Ericcson Perpellar for fun, you are!"

"Remember, Larkspur!" whispered Livingstone, in a deep and hurried tone—"Remember the injunctions which Mr. Harvey gave you. At three o'clock you are to leave this civet cat, and with a dozen policemen at your back hasten down town to *the house*—you know the rest? After that business has been settled, you are to hang on to Fitz-Cowles, until all our plans are matured; you understand?"

"Don't I? Good mornin' Livingstone—" he added aloud, as strutting to Fitz-Cowles' side, he waved his hand to the Merchant—"Call and see us at the Ton House when you've time."

"What a monster!" muttered Fitz-Cowles—"Red vest and blue coat! However, there's money to be made by cultivating this creature. Walk up to the Ton House, Major, and smoke a cigar—" he added aloud, in the most insinuating tone imaginable.

"I always carries my appeyratus with me," said the Major, taking a box of Lucifer matches from one pocket, and a large German pipe from the other—"Nothin' like bein' pervided with these things in case of accident. 'Tain't fashionable to smoke a pipe in Chesnut street, is it Curnel? Never mind—we're the rale alleygaters—we are."

And taking the Colonel's arm within his own, the Major strutted down Chesnut street, his immense pipe attracting the attention of all bystanders, while Fitz-Cowles regarded both pipe and planter with a look of smothered disgust.

"Ha, ha, ha!" chuckled Livingstone, as he gazed after the retreating pair—"The handsome millionaire arm in arm with a police officer!"

CHAPTER NINTH

THE DEAD-VAULT OF MONK-HALL

The beams of the lanthern flashed over a wide cellar, whose arched roof was supported by massive pillars of unplastered brick. Here and there, as the flickering light glanced fitfully along the dark recesses of the place, fragments of wood might be discovered, scattered carelessly around the pillars, or thrown over the floor in crumbling heaps.

Every moment, as the light of the lanthern shifted from side to side, some new wonder was discovered. Now the solid plastering of the ceiling, now the massive oak of the floor, now the uncouth forms of the pillars with loose bricks and crumbling pieces of wood scattered around, and now, as a gleam of light shot suddenly into the distant recesses of the cellar, a long row of coffins might be discovered, with the lids broken off and the bones of the dead thrown rudely from their last resting place.

The extent of the cellar might not be ascertained by the uncertain light of the lanthern. It may have been a hundred feet in extent, or even two hundred, but whenever the light flared up it disclosed some dark recess, filled with crumbling coffins, or laid bare some obscure nook, where ghastly skulls and fragments of the human skeleton, were thrown together like old lumber in a storehouse.

Even where the lanthern stood, in a square, described by four massive pillars which, arising from the oaken floor, supported the arching ceiling, its light gleamed over a skeleton, with the various bones separated by time, and the jaw, with its bristling teeth, falling apart from the blackened skull.

The sound of a footstep rung echoing among the arches of the cellar with a hollow sound; and in a moment, ere the figure of the intruder might be seen, the murmur of a human voice mingled with the echo of the footstep.

"Ha, ha, ha! While the broadcloth gentry of the Quaker City guzzle their champaigne two stories above, here, in these cozy cellars of Monk-Hall, old Devil-Bug entertains the thieves and cut-throats of the town with scorchin' Jamakey spirits and raw Moneygehaley! Hark how the fellers laugh and shout in the next cellar!"

And the chorus of a rude drinking song, chaunted first by a single voice, then echoed by a score, came faint and murmuring through the thick walls of the adjoining cellar.

"Let the Bank D'rector swill his sham-pane,
It's pisen'd with orphan's tears—
Raw Jamakey we'll drink and drink again,
For d———l a beak we fears!"

"That's what I likes—" said Devil-Bug, as he came shuffling onward into the light of the lanthern—"I usually wisits my private 'partments 'bout once a day, just to see how the boys gets on! This place is what I calls my study—he, he, he! The Pawnbroker in the next street ain't in partnership with me? There ain't no secret passage under ground from his shop to my cellars? We don't kontract to supply so many thieves an' cut-throats with vittels, lodgin' and viskey? Them ques'ins is better with corks on—it don't do for sich likker to spill out, I tell you!"

He disappeared for a moment behind one of the brick pillars, and in an instant emerged into the light again, dragging the remnant of a coffin at his heels.

"The genelman as used to inhabit this konwenient winter and summer residence, has softened into dust. His coffin 'ill sarve me for a seat. Turn it over—that's right—now let me think. Hum-hum! Musketer, I say—"

"Yes massa—" muttered the voice of the negro, from a distant part of the cellar.

"If any one wants to see me, tell Glow-worm to show 'em down, and —d'ye hear, you brute? Do you show 'em in when they are down Devil-Bug's at home for wisiters."

"Yes massa!" muttered the negro, from the darkness of the cellar; and then all was silent again.

Devil-Bug was seated upon the coffin, with his elbows supported by his knees, and his swarthy cheeks resting on his thick and heavy fingers. The full beams of the lanthern glared in his face, with the matted hair hanging over the protuberant forehead, while each hideous feature, the flat nose with the wing-like nostrils, the wide mouth with the rows of bristling teeth, the pointed chin, rough with a short and stubble-like beard, the eyeless socket and the solitary eye, all were disclosed in strong and glaring light, as the shadow of his figure was flung like a belt of darkness along the floor. As he sate there, with his face agitated, by various expressions, all mingled with his habitual sneer and scowl, he looked like the tutelar Demon of that vault of Death.

"My life's been a purty quiet one," he soliloquized. "Not many incidents to tell; passed my years in the comfortible retiracy o' domestic fellicity, as Parson Pyne would say! Yet there was one advent*oore* in my life: queer one, that. One stormy night, 'bout seventeen year ago, there comes to Monk-Hall, a rale bully of a feller, with a purty gal on his arm. He struck her a blow with his fist: I knocked him down. Gal liked me from that hour—ha, ha, ha—the thing makes me smile! A purty gal in love with a *han'some* man like Devil-Bug! And yit, and yit, many's the night I've laid at her door, a watchin' her—and a-keepin' harm from her, and—ho! ho! ho! She used to say she loved me 'cause I did'nt deceive my looks! For one year, me and that gal was man an' wife! The year passed—one night she quit Monk-Hall—I ain't never heerd on her since! And, what is a werry rimarkible circumstance, I never think o' that gal, without my heart gettin' soft, and the water comin' in my eyes! If any other man would say that o' me, I'd sue him for libel!—Hallo! who's there?"

"Monk Baltzar, massa," answered the voice of Musquito, from a distant recess of the cellar.

"That's Parson Pyne's slang name!" muttered Devil-Bug.—"Show him in, Musketer!"

And in a moment, there came hurrying from the darkness which enveloped the distant portions of the cellar, the figure of a man wrapped up in a long and drooping black cloak.

"I say, Abijah, what are you doing down here?" he muttered in a surly tone, from the folds of his cloak, as he approached Devil-Bug's lanthern. "Very odd taste, this!"

"Draw a cheer, Parson," exclaimed Devil-Bug, smiling blandly; "or, now, that I think o' it, there ain't no cheers. Draw a coffin, Parson, and let's have a talk!"

"I've no time to stay," muttered the new-comer, as he allowed the folds of his cloak to fall from his face, and discovered the full and beaming visage of the Rev. Dr. Pyne. "One word, and I'm gone."

"And that word about the gal you've been seekin' for three days?"

"At last I've lured her to Monk-Hall! This morning I discovered her hiding place; and, notwithstanding her tears and cries, forced her in a carriage, quieted her with threats, and but five minutes since, smuggled her into Monk-Hall."

"More work for me, I see! What was the kontract?"

"You were to give her a potion in her drink, in order———"

"That she might be prepared for your wishes?"

"See that it's done, before ten o'clock to-night, and the hundred dollars are yours?"

"I say, Brother Pyne," said Devil-Bug, with a pleasant smile—. "When do you preach again? I reely must come and hear you! Is the old ladies werry much melted when you gives it to the sinners?"

"Pshaw!" muttered Brother Pyne, moving toward the darkness of the cellar. "You will always have your joke. Remember, Abijah, the potion before ten to-night?"

He disappeared in the darkness, and Devil-Bug was alone, once more.

"Wonder if there's many more sich parsons in the world? Fine fat-faced fellers, with round paunches, and watery eyes? Seems to me, human natur' is wery much like a piece of putty in a baby's fingers! The baby can twist that piece of putty into any shape he likes, and the more the leetle crittur twists it, the more twist-able it becomes! The idee-ar of full grown human bein's listenin' to a steam ingine like that, with his mouth belching out smoke and blazes, all the while! Yes—yes—" he muttered, falling into the same soliloquizing mood which had come over his soul, before the entrance of the Rev. Mr. F. A. T. Pyne,—"Yes—yes—she was a purty gal, an' I sometimes thinks she's a livin' yit! She never told me nothin' but her first name, an' that's on the goold bracelet which she gave me. I've got it—fast—fast—under lock and key!"

Devil-Bug was silent. The shouts of the revellers in the adjoining cellar, grew more loud and uproarious, yet he heeded them not. Deep in the heart of this monster, like a withered flower blooming from the very corruption of the grave, the memory of that fair young girl, who, eighteen years ago, had sought the shelter of Monk-Hall, lay hidden, fast entwined around the life-cords of his deformed soul.

Oh, tell us, ye who in the hours of infancy, have laid upon a mother's bosom, who have basked in a father's smile, who have had wealth to bring you comfort, luxury, and a home, who have sunned in the light of religion as you grew toward manhood, and been warmed into intellectual life by the blessing of education; Oh, tell us, ye who with all these gifts and mercies, flung around you by the hand of God, have, after all, spurned his laws, and rotted in your very lives, with the foul pollution of libertinism and lust; tell us, who shall find most mercy at the bar of Avenging Justice—you, with your prostituted talents, gathering round your guilty souls, so many witnesses of your utter degradation, or Devil-Bug, the doorkeeper of Monk-Hall, in all his monstrous deformity of body and intellect, yet with *one* redeeming memory, gleaming like a star, from the chaos of his sins?

For him there had never been a church, a Bible, or a God! No ardent messenger of Jesus had ever spoken to his ears of the God who hung upon the cross, for all men's sins, and all mankind's salvation. Never, never!

And in this great city, there are thousands upon thousands hidden in the nooks and dens of vice, who, like Devil-Bug of Monk-Hall, have never heard that there is a Bible, a Savior, or a God! True, when dragged before the bar of Justice (as by a lively stretch of fancy the mockery is called) for the commission of crimes, to which the very evils of this most Christian community had driven them, hungry and starving as they were, these wretches have seen that Bible lifted up in Court, heard that Savior's name lipped over by some official, anxious for his dinner, or heard the name of that God profaned by some witness, greedy to sell his soul for the price of a hat! This one point stated, and you have comprised in a focus, all their knowledge of a Bible, a Savior, or a God!

And this, in that great Quaker City, which every Sunday lifts its demure face to Heaven, and, with Church-burning, Girard College, and Bank-robbery, hanging around its skirts, tells the Almighty God that it has sent missionaries to the Isles of the sea, to the Hindoo, the Turk, and the Hottentot; that it feels for the spiritual wants of the far-off nations, to an extent that cannot be measured by words, while it has not one single throb of pity, for the poor, who starve, rot and die, within its very eyesight!

"She wos a purty gal, and whenever I think of her, as I said afore, my eyes grow watery! I struck the feller who had laid his hands upon her—I struck him to the floor. I b'lieve my soul she liked me from that hour! Hullo—who's there?"

"A little nigga, massa—" replied the voice of Musquito, still speaking from the distant nook of the cellar.

"Fitz-Cowles' niggar!" muttered Devil-Bug—"Wonder what he can be wanting with me?"

"De High Golly!" cried a voice echoing from the darkness of the vault—"Dis de debbil's own den, and dare's de debbil hisself!"

Dim, the Creole, in his neat blue round-jacket and trowsers, came stealing cautiously toward the lanthern.

"You're a purty boy—ain't you? What d'ye want down here—hey?"

"Dare's a lettaw from Massa Fitz-Cowles—" observed Dim, approaching Devil-Bug with a cautious glance—"De High Golly! I wonder if dat ting hab got a tail!"

"Here, young indoovidooal, read this letter. There wasn't no Free Schools when I was young. Konsekence was, my eddycàtion was neglected."

"And he hab got *two* feet!" muttered Dim—"Bress my soul, I t'ought one foot was a hoof! Oh, massa, you can't read dat letter—may be you kin read dis ring!"

"Hullo! the ring!" cried Devil-Bug, with a start—"I remember well, that when Fitz-Cowles first rikvested me to hide the Jew, he told me to mark this ring. 'Mark it,' ses he, 'and whenever I send this ring to you, cause the Jew to *retire!*' Ho, ho, that's what's in the wind—is it? Hurray, Charcoal, an' read that letter!"

Bending slowly over the light, Dim read the letter which we have already laid before the reader.

"To think a nigger like that should read, and my eddycation neglected! Ten thousand dollars about his person! Recompense meself for the keer and trouble I've had with him! Won't I? You can go, young genelman—yet hold up a minnit! Why didn't you bring this ring and letter sooner than this? You've been playin' pitch-penny with some other nigger, I'll be bound?"

"Ha, yah!" laughed Dim, to himself—"Dat mus' be de debbil, sure 'nuf! I say, massa, how did yer know dat! I jis was doin' dat same t'ing! A part of us young bloods went down to see de Navy Yard and den we tuk a shine roun' town!"

"Re-tire young genelman!" said Devil-Bug, severely—"Re-tire and *re*-port yesself to head-quarters, forthwith!'

"Ha-yah!" laughed Dim, as he hurried from the cellar—"Dis chile know a little more dan mos' folk! He seen de debbil—ha, yah—once in his life, anyhow!"

Devil-Bug was alone again. Shifting the lanthern from its position, he carefully examined the oaken planks of the floor. The outlines of a large trap-door were discernible, with the bolt, which held it to the floor, inserted in the worn and rusted socket.

"Trap-door 'bout ten feet square! There's a well below it—a deep well, a dark well; the d———l knows how deep! Any individooal gettin' a fall through that trap-door, might stand in danger of bein' eat up by rats and all sorts o' wermin, in case the fall didn't hurt him! Ten thousand dollars! Buy a snug little farm out West, or, ha, ha, ha, if there wos a good tariff passed by some o' these cussed Congressmen, Devil-Bug might go into the iron-works!"

"Massa," exclaimed the voice of Musquito, from the darkness, "Dat ar Jew is a-comin' down stairs."

"Let him come," answered Devil-Bug.—"It don't cost nothing'. And, hark ye, the minnit he passes the cellar door, do you dig off!"

Having thus spoken, Devil-Bug hastily took the lamp from within the lanthern, and poured some oil over the rusted bolt of the trap door. In an instant the bolt yielded to the impulse of his hand, and moved quietly along the socket.

"All right! I'll jist leave the bolt a-clingin' to the socket, by its end!

The slightest touch from my hand, won't unloose it? Redikulus! I must get a cheer for my friend—taint nice to give a party without cheers!"

Disappearing behind a brick pillar, he drew the fragment of another coffin, from its resting place, and laid it down on the floor, some six feet from the spot where the lanthern stood.

"Any genelman a-sittin' on that cheer, will have the hinges o' the trap door directly at his back, with some six feet o' the trap a-twixt me and him! The bolt will be right under my foot, so it will! Suppose I was to git thinkin' on some subject, and forgit myself? My foot might unlodge the bolt from its socket in the trap door. K-u-sh-ew-*bang*!" he continued, producing a strange hissing sound, by suddenly forcing his breath through his clenched teeth. "K-u-sh-ew-*bang!* The trap door 'ud fall, and—'melancholy to *re*-late,' as the newspaper ses—some body 'ud git their brains knocked into shad-roe right off!"

"Massa Von Gelt, am here, massa 'Bijah," cried Musquito, from the distant extreme of the vault.

"Show the genelman in, and tell him to walk mighty keerful, or else he might fall through some o' them cussed holes in the floor!"

In a moment, a cautious footstep was heard, and the dim outline of the Jew's figure, became visible, as he advanced along the vault.

"Goot eveningsh!" was his salutation, as he approached the lanthern "—Fader Abraham! vot you dosh in dis place?"

"Good arternoon—" exclaimed Devil-Bug grinning hideously—"Sit down, an' take a cheer!"

With a slight shrug of disgust, the hump-back, seated himself upon the coffin opposite Devil-Bug, and quietly folding his arms over his fragment of a body, gazed fixedly into the hideous face of the Doorkeeper.

"I say old feller, will you smoke?" exclaimed Devil-Bug, taking some segars from the breast of his coarse outer garment, which neither frock-coat, over-coat nor dress-coat, was fashioned of dingy canvass, with great horn buttons, running up in front, while the wide sleeves, hung loosely round his muscular arms—"I say old feller will you smoke? Here's yer reglar Pax'on cannon smokers—" and he displayed a number of segars in the bony palm of his broad hand—"or here's yer baby-suckers wot ain't got no strength in them at all. Take a smoke, Gabr'el?"

"I vill take won baby-sucker, wot ish not doo sthrong—" replied Gabriel as reaching forth his hands, he seemed about advancing toward Devil-Bug—"Dis plashe is very dampish—"

"Beg you wont take the trouble to git up—" exclaimed Devil-Bug as hastily rising he removed the lanthern, from its location at his feet, to the immediate vicinity of the Jew—"Jist keep the lanthern there. I likes to *kon*-template beauty, in a strong light!"

The two figures, would have made an effective picture. The lanthern placed at the feet of the Jew, threw a strong light over his person, while the form of Devil-Bug, was wrapt in a sort of lively twilight. The calm visage of the Jew, rendered even more quiet and contemplative by the segar which he smoked, the unnatural length of his face, and the absurd disproportion of his small and hump-backed body, which looked more like a shapeless lump, dressed up in man's attire, than the frame of a human being, all presented a vivid contrast to the visage of Devil-Bug, its solitary eye, glaring through the obscurity of the vault, like a flame coal, while his short, but stout and muscular frame, with the heavy body, knotted into uncouth knobs at the shoulders, with the long arms and bony fists, the slim legs and massive feet, all gave you the idea, of a Sampson, stunted in his growth; a giant whom nature had dwarfed from the regular proportion of manly beauty, down into an uncouth image of hideous strength.

Around the twain, extended the death-vault of Monk-Hall, its distant recesses, wrapt in heavy shadow, while the arched ceiling directly overhead, the oaken floor around, and the four pillars of massive brick, were now disclosed in strong light, as a sudden gust of wind, agitated the lanthern-flame, or yet again veiled in a dim shadow, which gave a dark and dreary appearance to the place.

"I say Gabr'el, wot a pitty, it is; is'nt it?" exclaimed Devil-Bug, as he looked forth from the cloud of tobacco-smoke, which half-concealed his hideous countenance.

"Vot ish a bitty?"

"That me and you, was'nt jined together, with a cord, a-passin' through our witals! Would'nt we have made a specymen of Siamese twins! Ho, ho! What a pair of beauties!"

"What wos dish plashe made fur?" asked Gabriel knocking the ashes from his segar—"It looksh like won devil's counting-housh, Bi-Gott!"

"Why, ye see, Gabr'el—" said Devil-Bug in a cheerful way—"From all that I ever heered, them fellers as used to hold out in these diggins, the Monkses and Priestses, and Nunses, in the time of the Revvy-lushun, made a practice o' buryin' their dead in this 'ere cellar; and a lively practice it was too! They do say there was fine goin's-on in the old times, in these parts! I ought to 've been about in those days! I was born arter my time—"

"Vas you porn at all?" enquired Gabriel with a look of quiet sarcasm.

"Now d'ye know, Gabr'el, that I sometimes think, I was never born at all? very pecooliar that you should jist think as I do, on that pint. Suppose I was a devil, would'nt it be a lively thing for me, to chaw you up, without pepper or salt! Lord! How I should like to gouge out one of your eyes! Ha, ha! Nother segar, Gabr'el?"

"I wash to see Vitz-Cowle dis morningsh—" exclaimed Gabriel, with a calm decision of manner, that indicated the man of business.

"You wos, wos ye?" answered Devil-Bug, playing carelessly with the bolt of the trap-door—"And arter you'd seen him, what happened?"

"You knowsh de Widow Smolpy? She has de goldt plate, and de monish!"

"Know *her*?" cried Devil-Bug, still playing with the bolt—"The old woman's as rich as Geerard! You wos to see her, wos you, Gabr'el?"

"I vos, and soldt her a goldt watch. Dat ish to say, I made her a presentsh ov de watch—"

"Do I look like a werry young infant?" exclaimed Devil-Bug, as bending his face down between his knees, he passed his fingers along the floor, with a quick movement—"A Jew give any body a watch! I'll go an' jine the Free Repenters arter that!"

"Vot you scratch your fingersh on te floor? Hey? I doesh not like dat noise! I am so nervous! I gives te watch to her, but I takes five thousandt dollars in goldt, from the house, for my watch!"

"Five thousand dollars in gold, where is it, Gabr'el, where is it?"

"Up stairsh, in your room. I put it in te closetsh, near te firesh. Vot you scratch your fingers on te floor?"

"Gabr'el, are you good at 'rithmetic? How much is five thousand dollars and ten thousand dollars?'

"Fifteen tousandt tollars. Vot you asksh for?"

"Why—" replied Devil-Bug, as with his face still bent down between his knees, he played with the bolt of the trap-door—"Why—why—in fact, Gabr'el, you can *re*-tire!"

The word has not passed his lips before the bolt flew back from its socket; there was a creaking noise, succeeded by a crash—and the whirring sound produced by the falling trap-door, echoed around the death-vault. Devil-Bug listened. All was darkness and silence. With the last gleam of light he had beheld the Jew tottering on the brink of the chasm, and now he listened for the sound produced by the mangled body, as it went sweeping through the air, to the bottom of the well. Another moment passed. A sound arose from the depths of the well. It was the sound of the lanthern as it struck against the sides of the chasm. Bending over the well, on hands and knees, Devil-Bug listened with an intensity that forced the cold sweat out from his forehead. No sound came echoing up the chasm, not even a murmur or a groan.

"He's gone home to his daddy—" muttered Devil-Bug, as rising on his feet again, he turned, in the darkness, from the edge of the trap door—"He'll never refuse fat pork agin'. I warrant ye!"

"I say, vot te teffil you cuts dem capersh for?" said a clear bold voice, resounding through the darkness of the vault—"Got-tam! I might have fell town and hurtsh mesself! Vot for you actsh like a crashy man?"

Devil-Bug started. So certain had he been of the Jew's death, that when he heard his voice echoing through the darkness, it struck him with a feeling of supernatural awe. In a moment, however, he recovered himself and began to crawl around the edge of the trap-door, in the direction from whence the voice had issued.

"He got off, did he?" he muttered to himself—"Ha! I won't seize him by the throat, and pitch him into the well? Jist trust me with him, a minnit, somebody!—Why you see, Gabr'el," he added aloud, in his blandest tone—"I happened to put my foot on the bolt o' that cussed hatchway and it come loose! Where are you, Gabr'el? I'm got somethin' pertikler to say to you—"

"No toudt, no toudt," responded Gabriel—"Put I vill keepsh my dishtance! Fader Abraham! vot a man it ish!"

Creeping along the floor, on hands and feet, Devil-Bug approached the pillar from whence the voice proceeded.

"To sarve me sich a trick!" he muttered—"But I'll bruise him for it, I'll bruise him!"

"I vos a-goin' to tellsh you dat I drop mine pocketsh-book in de woman Smolpy's house. Ten tousandt tollars in it, too!"

"What's that you say?" grunted Devil-Bug—"Dropped your pocket-book in widow Smolby's house? You *are* a precious pork-hater, to give ten thousand dollars for five!"

A shrill whistle echoed round the vault, ringing through nook and crevice, with a piercing sound, like the winter wind shrieking down a chimney.

"What are ye up to?" growled Devil-Bug, as his outspread hands grasped the brick pillar—"Jist let me have a feel of your hand, Gabr'el—"

As he spoke the glare of a lamp flashed over the vault. Devil-Bug beheld the face of the Jew thrust from the opposite side of the pillar, with the keen and piercing eyes fixed upon his countenance.

"Where did that light come from?" he shouted—"Hey, Gabr'el?"

Turning suddenly, he beheld the form of a stranger, advancing from the distant door of the vault with a lighted candle in his hand.

"I vos jist a-goin' to tell you—" exclaimed Gabriel, as Devil-Bug was occupied in watching the stranger, who came hastening over the floor of the vault—"Tat we can rop te widow Smolpy's house. Dosh dat pleash you? I can git into te house tish very afternoon—"

"Now mister, may I axe, who *you* are, and what the d———l you want here?" cried Devil-Bug, as the newcomer, light in hand, stood in front of the pillar which separated the Doorkeeper from the Jew—"What's yer name, anyhow?"

"Brick-Top," responded the stranger in a snuffling voice, "Brick-Top, at your service, sir. My daddy was a scavenger, and my mammy sold rags. Now you know all about me, and my family into the bargain. How d'ye feel, old cove?"

"You're werry familiar, young man; you are!" exclaimed Devil-Bug as he gazed upon the new comer, with a suspicious glance.

Brick-Top, was a tall, thin personage, clad from head to foot in rags; not ragged clothes, nor damaged clothes, nor shabby genteel clothes; but absolute and unconditional rags. His thin face, with its aquiline nose, was spotted all over with large freckles, and a great bunch of fiery red hair hung over his forehead, down to the very eyes. The lower part of his face was hedged in by a thick beard, of the same fiery red as his matted hair; while his eyes, keen, dark, and brilliant, presented a strange contrast to the vacant and unmeaning expression of his freckled countenance.

"Yer daddy was a scavenger, and yer mammy sold rags? It's my opinion, young man, that yer mammy must a-dressed you up in her rag shop, and that yer daddy got mad with you won day, and cleaned some werry dirty alley with yer carcase! Wot a jail bird! It *must* a-been a dirty alley, any how! Who is the chap, hey, Gabriel?"

"A person I got dis mornin' to help us to rob te Widow Smolby's house. He can git into te house, easy as nothinsh! Dish young man vill help!"

"The Widow Smolby's house?" exclaimed Devil-Bug. "Stores o' plate, chests o' yaller boys, closets full o' walleyables? We kin git into the house easy as nothin', kin we? That 'ud be a haul; the Widder Smolby's jewelry! Why didn't ye say this at fust, Gabr'el? I wouldn't a-played any jokes on you then: no more I wouldn't!"

"Tem jokes ish very tampdt' fat," said Gabriel quietly; he little dreamed that this pleasant joke had been prepared by Fitz-Cowles, for his especial benefit.

"Vot a set o' wretches ye are," exclaimed Brick-top, snuffing the candle with his fingers—"To stand here gabblin' about nothin', ven the old Widdey's house is a-waitin' to be robbed. Didn't that servant wots a-goin' to betray her Missus, tell us to be on hand afore three in the arternoon!"

"So we kin git in that way, kin we?" exclaimed Devil-Bug, with his accustomed delightful chuckle; "Come along, Pork-hater, come along, Bundle o' Rags; this is *kon*-siderable better than 'Nited States Bank stock!"

And the three plesant companions hastened from the Death-vault of Monk-Hall; Devil-Bug and Gabriel Von Gelt, conversing together in subdued tones while, Brick-Top, following at their heels, manifested his exuberance of spirit, by various strange gestures and mysterious expressions.

"Can we trust that are loafer? Werry low feller, he is!" exclaimed Devil-Bug in a whisper.

"Very desperit fellersh!" replied Gabriel. "Toes not care for tanger, and ish goot mit a knifesh!"

"Hurray for Tippeycanoe!" shouted Brick-Top, cutting a caper in the air; "the lots o' gold and walleyables we're a-goin' to lay hold of! All in the arternoon, ven the Quaker City 'as had its dinner, and all the Aldermon is a-strugglin' with boat loads o' terripin and basket of oysters! Hurray for Tippeycanoe!"

CHAPTER TENTH

THE GHOST ROOM

"Now, Peggy Grud, did I ketch ye, that time? Fill the hopper to the brim with coffee, that cost me nine cents a pound! Hey! hey! Here's waste for you—here's comin' to want in my old age! Sit down, Ike, near the fire, Ike—don't mind that woman, Peggy Grud! *She* can't help it, if she's crazy! Here, Wessy, here Naphy, Wshy, Washy, I say—come an' sit near the fire, my dears! You Peggy Grud, where did ye put Abe, I say?"

"Murder—mur-*der!*" cried a shrill voice from the cage, above the mantel.

"Oh, yer there, are ye? Why jist look at that, Peggy Grud, the werry parrot cries out, 'Murder!' when he sees you wastin' the coffee in that style. Now, *what did* possess you, Peggy Grud, to fill that hopper brimful with that roast coffee, which cost me nine cents a pound?"

"Troth, Missus Smolby, an' its yerself that's hard to the poor! Did the divvil himself ever hear tell o' the likes o' this? A hopper full o' nine cent coffee ind*aa*de! D'ye think me bones is made o' broomsticks, and me blood o' turpentine an' melasses, that ye f-*aa*-de me, on' such likker as this?"

"Don't shake yer coffee mill under my nose! It costs nine cents a pound."

"Murder, mur-*der!*" screamed the parrot.

"Troth the parrot's a-laffin' at ye! No wondher! Didn't he, himself, wid his own eyes, see me the 'tother day, a-tryin' to make some o' this coffee run down the kitchen stairs—and all I could do, it wouldn't for the life o' me, stir a step! mair be, token it was very wake!"

"Git out o' my sight, Peggy Grud, git out o' my sight, and don't come near me to-day a n!"

"Ochone! We're got our dander riz, have we?" cried Peggy Grud, bouncing out of the room. "It's mighty crazy we're a-getting' in our old age," she shrieked, from the entry without the door. "An' it 'ud take a dozen divvils to manage us, it would!" She added, by way of a parting salute, as she was heard descending the stairs.

"It's about seventeen years this day!" muttered the old woman, quietly seating herself in the capacious armchair, placed in front of the fire place! "Seventeen years since *she* died—seventeen years since I have had a fire made in this room! Hum-hum! So Brother Pyne was that gal's father! The trollop, to run away from her own father's house! Howsomever, he tuk her home agin, this mornin'! Wonder if Luke won't swear when he hears it? To think I should outlive five husbands, Buddy, Crank, and Dul—Dul—Peg, I say, what was my third husband's name? Oh, she aint here. Dulcombe—or Dulman, or, yes that's it, Dulpins, and———what was I a-goin' to say?"

The old lady glanced around the room, with a puzzled look. The Ghost-Room was perfectly still and quiet. The faint wood fire, flickering over the hearth, every now and then, flared up in a sudden flash, dispelling the dim shadows which rested upon the corners of the chamber. As the fire died away, the light of the solitary candle, standing upon the work table, at the old lady's side, fell with glaring lustre, around its immediate vicinity, while the farther extremes of the room were wrapt in dusky shadow. The massive bed, with its heavy curtains, rose in the obscure air, like a mausoleum for the dead; the circular mirror, standing on the antique dressing bureau, as ever and anon, it received a gleam of light on its polished surface, looked like one of those mirrors, in which you are afraid to gaze, when alone in the silence of night, for fear a ghostly face may peer over your shoulder in the glass; and the thick hangings depending from the windows, waved slowly to and fro, as occasional gusts of wind came moaning through the crevices of the chamber door.

The picture above the mantel, as the light trembled over its surface, assumed the appearance of reality, and for a moment, ever and anon, it would seem animate with a sudden life. The deep, lustrous dark eyes, the pale face, blooming with a rose-bud freshness in the centre of either cheek, and strikingly relieved by the long black hair, twining around the neck, and falling over the bosom in glossy curls, seemed warming into life, while it gazed with a sad and melancholy gaze, upon the wrinkled visage of the old woman seated by the fireside.

"Murder—mur-der!" screamed the parrot, from his cage, which was hung beside the portrait. "Murder—Fi-er!"

"Now, Abe," cried the Widow Smolby, starting from her reverie,—"That's a lie! I was not a-goin' to say murder nor fi-er! But I was a-goin' to say that it was a strange thing that I should outlive five husbands, Buddy, and Crank, and Smolby, and Tuppick, an' one whose name I dis-remember; and be robbed, arter all, by a plunderin' Jew; not at all mentionin' Peggy Grud's filling the hopper brimfull o' nine cent coffee!"

The old lady gazed fondly into the faces of her four cats, grouped around the fire place, like pieces of Dutch statuary, as though she awaited their answer to her lamentations.

"Ike-y" she exclaimed, gazing in the countenance of a very vicious tortoise-shelled cat,—"You wos very naughty to *per*-voke that Abe this mornin'! You was so! Wesley, that's a good Wesley," and she patted the back of a cat, whose coat displayed an uniform of sky-blue and white. "To sit cardin' wool there all alone, by yerself! Washy didn't ketch any mice to-day." This was addressed in a tone of mock severity, to a large and lubberly white cat. "And, as for you, Nappy," —Nappy was a small black cat, with spiteful green eyes—"And, as for you, Nappy, you don't do nothin' but spin from mornin' till night!"

Attracted by the sound of the old woman's voice, the four cats, arose from their sleeping postures, and began to rub their sleek fur against her dress, while they exhibited their delight by purring to a lively tune.

"Ikey spins werry coarse—" soliloquize the old woman—"I feel very heavy, now that I come to think of it. I b'lieve I'll lay down a bit."

She moved toward the bed, with the cats following at her heels, and in a moment disappeared within the curtains.

"I've never laid in this bed—" her voice resounded from within the hangings—"Since the day afore *she* died! Be still Ike—don't stick yer claws into me, in that way! Down Wesley, I say get off my 'head—Wesley how dare you! Tear my cap to pieces in that way! Nappy, ye black snake ye, will you be quiet?"

"Abe wants a pe-ta-ter!" screamed the Parrot bustling about in his cage—"Abe wants a hot pe-ta-ter! Fi-er! Murder—Mur-*der!*"

"I'll get up and choke you, Abe! I will!" screamed the old woman turning over in bed—"Yer a perfec' pack o' wretches! To think that I should outlive five husbands, Buddy, Crank, Dul—Dul—I say Peg what's that one's name? Dul—Dul—'

The old lady was asleep. The parrot in a fit of violent misanthropy laid his head between his wings and muffled himself up in those very wings, like a traveller in his cloak. The room was perfectly quiet; the silence unbroken by a sound save the purring noise made by the cats, as they clustered round the sleeping widow.

This entire quietude continued for the space of ten minutes or more, when it was disturbed by the opening of the chamber-door.

The withered face of Peggy Grud was thrust through the aperture.

"Aslaape, is she? An' cut me aff wid a shillin'? The likes on her to thry that game wid me, a'ter my long sarvice! Wait till three o'clock, comes; jest wait!"

Closing the door, Peggy hurried down the dark stairway. Instead of making her way to the basement kitchen, her usual resort, she entered the front room on the first floor, and sate down by the table, on which a light was burning.

"The laud'num in the coffee, settled her hash!" she muttered squaring her elbows, as her withered face, was wrinkled by a sickly smile—"The front door aint on the jar? Divvil the taste! I'll jist cr*aa*pe down to my karner be the kitchen fire! 'Five hunder' dollars the Jew promished; and two hunder' he's give me, alreadhy! Faix I'll put 'em in the Loan Company!"

Peggy rose from her seat, and moved toward the door of the room.

"Troth it plashes me! Cut me a-ff wid a shillin' indaade!" she exclaimed as she closed the door and disappeared—"Faix she may be cut a-ff wid something besides a shillin'; sorrow to her sowl!"

The room was not long left to silence and solitude. Peggy had not disappeared more than five minutes, when the front door of the mansion, creaked harshly on its rusty hinges, footsteps were heard in the entry, and the door leading from the entry into the front room, swung slowly open.

"Dish is de plashe!" exclaimed a voice in a deep whisper, and the diminutive form of a hump-backed man, clad in a threadbare cloak, with an immense white hat concealing his face from view, strode softly into the room—"Dish is de plashe! Now for mine pockets-booksh, vich—" he added in a tone of quiet glee—"Vich I nefer did lost!"

Ere another moment passed, two other figures, wrapped in threadbare cloaks, like the first, stole cautiously into the room, and approached the light, which burned dimly on the small table in the centre.

"I say Gabr'el bolt the door—" said the stoutest figure of the three—"Let's have a quiet time to ourselves! Ho! Ho! Ho! Robbin' a house in broad daylight! It tickles me, it does! Now genelmen to your posts—two on us must go up stairs, while the 'tother one, watches below. Will you watch in this 'ere room Gabr'el?"

"Fader Abraham! Viles you has te priviliges of looking over te oldt lady's cash-pooks up stairsh! Not I, py no meansh!"

"What d'ye say Brick-Top? Will ye keep watch down stairs?"

"Jist as this 'ere convention of the Sovreign People, may decide—" replied the gentleman addressed, quietly taking his seat by the table—"But fair play ye mind? 'I'm to have my thirds out o' this estate' as the Irish widder said, when she fit with fourteen children for thirteen potatoes, and a salt mackerel! Go up stairs boys, and Remove the Deposits! We're the rale Dimmycrats—we are!"

"Gabr'el, they're a-waitin' prayer for us!" exclaimed Devil-Bug, as his solitary eye, twinkled from beneath the shadow of his ponderous hat—"Up stairs Gabr'el, up stairs and jine in prayer for the health o' the old lady—"

They hastened from the room, and in a moment were heard ascending the stairs, while their companion, the contemplative Brick-Top, remained seated beside the table in the front room.

"This is lively! They go up stairs; they commence rummaging the front room. Meanwhile, there is no one on the look out for them? Oh, no: don't think of such a thing. Having plundered the front room, on the third story, they try the back room door, and find it locked. This excites their curiosity. They break open the door and—*find themselves in the arms of Easy Larkspur and twelve police officers!*"

It was singular to note the change which came over Brick-Top's voice and manner, as he sate by the table muttering mysterious words to himself, in a tone of quiet satisfaction. His voice, suddenly lost all its vagabond-hoarsness, and his manner was utterly unlike the manner of the devil-may-care loafer, whom Devil-Bug and Von Gelt had left in the front room as their sentinel.

Suddenly rising from his seat, Brick-Top turned his face from the light, as he bent over a small washstand in an obscure corner of the room. It was very singular that a gentleman of his free-and-easy habits should take the trouble to wash his face, but judging from the gestures of Brick-Top, as he stood with his back to the light, he was certainly occupied in this vital act of Turkish devotion.

In a moment he turned toward the light again, and as a farmer strips a stalk of corn of all superfluous leaves, so Brick-Top, passing his hands rapidly up and down his person, stripped his costume of manifold rags, entirely from his tall figure, and lo! he stood disclosed in the beams of the candle, a very respectable gentleman, attired in a frock coat and pants of glossy broadcloth. His uncouth red hair, hanging over his very eyes, still gave him a most villianous air of decayed loaferism, but this he treated with the same disrespect as his costume of rags.

"Faugh! How that red wig stinks!" cried Brick-Top, flinging his head of hair to the other side of the room—"I flatter myself I did the 'loafer' rather genteely! Ha, ha, Luke, it wasn't so bad for you! 'My name is Brick-Top, gemmen, my daddy wos a scavenger, and my mommy sold rags!' Ha, ha, ha!"

Luke Harvey, dressed in his usual costume, with the paint and freckles washed from his face, stood disclosed in the light.

"Dressed myself in a small rag-shop this morning and prowled about the avenues leading to Monk-Hall. Met the Jew—introduced myself as a ruffian out of business—closed the bargain with him to help rob this house. Went to the Police office, engaged twelve fellows with red noses and agreeable complexions. Gave their leader, Easy Larkspur, the pass-key to the small door at the back of this house, which opens into the private staircase, leading up into the back room on the third story! The old lady sleeps there in the afternoon. The police were to warn her of her danger. And the old lady and the girl, I suppose, are safe in the garret, while Devil-Bug and Von Gelt are being trapped in the midst of their plunder. At all events, the police are close at hand! They are there at this moment waiting for their prey! Ha! Let me listen!"

Advancing to the foot of the stairs, he listened with silent intensity for a single moment. Not a sound came echoing down the dark staircase. All was silent as though no robber's foot pressed the floors of the old mansion.

"Let me once have the Jew in my power, and then Fitz-Cowles is a doomed man! Was not that a shriek? I will buy the documents by offering the Jew his liberty and all his share of the ill-gotten money into the bargain! Ha! the police are upon them! I hear them fighting up stairs! As for Devil-Bug, it rather pains me to bring the old fellow to harm's door! Egad, but they're at it up stairs! No doubt he has committed crimes enough to sink a ship, even if each separate crime weighed no more than a pebble on the seashore! But he's an honest old rogue for all that, and—the Oath of our Club prevented me from betraying the haunts of Monk-Hall to the police, so I had to lure the Jew from its cozy old nooks and cells! Pity that Devil-Bug came with him! Ha! Was not that a shriek? Another shriek—a groan—and the tramp of footsteps! Devil-Bug fights hard! He is scuffling with the police—I'll hurry up stairs and see the fun!

A piercing shriek, followed by a deep-toned shout, echoed through the chambers of the old mansion. Luke rushed up stairs. The noise grew louder in the third story, the hurried tramp of footsteps resounded through the mansion, and then all was silent again. Luke gained the head of the stairway; all was dark as the tomb. No light glaring from an open door served to illumine his way. Standing at the head of the topmost stair, Luke held his very breath as he listened. A dark fear and a horrible suspicion flashed over his soul. Not a sound struck his ear, not even the breathing of a man, or the rustling of a passing footstep.

"This is strange—" muttered Luke—"but a moment ago the house rung with shouts and shrieks, and *now*—Ha! This must be the door of the Ghost-Room—"

He entered the dark chamber, his hands outspread, while he listened with painful intensity for the slightest sound. He passed over the carpet, he was moving in the direction where he supposed the bed was fixed, when his foot slipped from under him, and he fell to the floor.

"The floor is wet—" he muttered, with an oath, as he endeavored to regain the floor—"Curse the thing, who has been flinging the furniture about the room?" he continued, as an object—a piece of furniture, or perhaps a chest, or a bundle of clothes—arrested his progress and flung him headlong to the carpet. "The police must have had a d——l of a schuffle! But what's become of the old woman and the girl?"

Arising hastily to his feet, he rushed down stairs, in order to procure a light. Entering the front room once more, he extended his hands to grasp the candlestick, and in the very action started back with a feeling of horror, that chilled him to the inmost heart.

His hands, which he raised in the glare of the light, were crimsoned with thick red blood.

CHAPTER ELEVENTH

DEVIL-BUG IN THE GHOST-ROOM

"Cuss the stairs—they creak as if they had the roomatiz! Keep close to my heels, Gabr'el!"

"Yes—I dosh!" whispered the Jew, in reply—"There ish a light—take keer now, take very goot keer—"

Ascending the dark staircase with a hushed and cautious footstep, Devil-Bug stood on the landing which gave entrance to the back and front rooms of the third story. A ruddy gleam of light flared out upon the passage, from within the Ghost-Room, as the door hung slightly ajar. Devil-Bug advanced a step and listened. All was silent. He pushed the door wide open, and with Gabriel following at his heels, stood within the confines of the ancient chamber. The candle was still burning upon the table, and the wood fire flickered fitfully on the hearth.

The old woman's a-sleepin' on that bed—" muttered Devil-Bug—"She snores like a trumpet! We must be keerful! Have you got the keys—them false keys—"

"Vich I took from wax impressions, preparedt by Peggy Grud? Here tey ish—te trunksh under te foots of the te bedt—"

Devil-Bug took the keys in one hand, the candle in the other and advanced to the foot of the bed. In a moment, placing the candle upon the carpet, he swept the bed-hangings aside, and drew from under the couch, with a slow and careful movement, a small chest of dark wood, with a keyhole of peculiar shape.

"Bi-Gott!" cried the Hebrew, who ever made use of this favorite oath when very much excited—"I smellsh te gooldt already!"

"H-u-sh!" whispered Devil-Bug, fixing one of the keys, which he grasped in his hand, in the keyhole of the chest—"Be still, or I'll damage you so the d———l won't know you! Ha, ha—there's the yeller boys! The rale giniwine mulatters!"

"Fader Abraham!" cried the Jew, rubbing his hands with glee.

With the light extended in one hand, Devil-Bug, bent slowly down, and as his every feature was thrown out in strong relief, he surveyed the prospect disclosed by the opened chest, with a glance of the deepest satisfaction. By his side, knelt the Jew, his dark eyes sparkling with delight, as he gazed upon the treasures of the opened chest. The light flared over their faces, and over the rich stores of coin, which peeped out from among musty parchments, and dingy rolls of time-eaten manuscript. The long face of the Jew, with its regularity of feature, its healthy hues, and its deep and brilliant eyes, was in vivid contrast with the hideous countenance of his companion, the eyeless socket and the solitary blazing eye, the wide mouth and the pointed chin, yet in that moment of intense gratification, their visages, so widely different in detail, were glowing with the same grinning expression of delight, and agitated by the same grasping lust for gold.

"Gott! Toubloonsh! Toubloonsh!" muttered the Jew, thrusting his hands eagerly into the chest.

"Are ye a nateral born fool?" muttered Devil-Bug in a surly tone—"The clink of the pewter 'ill wake up the old woman. Be quiet while I konsiders the pecooliar circumstances, under which we are placed—"

And as they bent lowly over the chest, their eyes feasting on the rich store of doubloons, the bed hangings, were agitated by a slight movement, and in an instant, a worn and withered face, whose sharp features, were rendered painfully distinct, by the tight-fitting cap of black silk, was thrust between the purple folds, within striking distance of the robbers' heads.

It was the face of the old woman, aroused from her sleep, by the clinking of her gold. With presence of mind, that would have done honor to a General in a battle-field, she noticed the movements of the robbers, without so much as a start or a cry of surprise, and in that instant of silent observation, she resolved upon her plan of action. Beneath the side of the bed, nearest the wall, was a small chest, in which a pair of pistols, had been always kept by her last husband. Could she, slowly drag her form along the massive couch, to the opposite side of the bed, and extending her hands, raise the lid of the chest, and seize the pistols, she had no fears for the result. While the robbers bent over the chest, whispering to one another in hushed tones, she withdrew within the curtains, and commenced dragging herself, slowly and cautiously along the bed.

"I tells you vat it ish—" whispered the Jew—"Dish is too mosh monish to take away leetle by leetle! Somepody may come, and take it afore we come agin. Let ush, put down the lid, and carry off te chest at wonsh!"

"Was that the old 'oman moanin' in her sleep?" whispered Devil-Bug, holding his breath to listen—"Hush! The bed's a creakin' like blazes. Let me go round an' take a look at the old lady—"

Arising from the chest, he strode cautiously around the bed, and gazed within the curtains. All was dark as midnight. He could hear a sound like the hissing of an enraged cat, mingled with a slight creaking noise.

"The light Gabr'el!" he whispered.

"I'll give it to you, you ornery scoundr'l—to rob a poor live woman, in this 'ere vay—" screamed a woman's voice, from within the curtains, and the light of a pistol, caused by the powder flashing in the pan, flared up in Devil-Bug's face. By that momentary gleam of light, he beheld the form of the old woman, crouching on the bed, in the attitude of an enraged tigress preparing to spring, a pistol extended in each outstretched hand, while a gleam of superhuman malignity shot from her small grey eyes.

"Rob a poor lone woman, will ye? Take that!" she cried, pulling the trigger of the remaining pistol. It flashed in the pan, but missed fire.

"Them pistols is old fashioned, like yerself—ought to have the rale percushions, ha, ha, ha!" laughed Devil Bug, but his laughter was of brief duration.

With a wild yell, gathering all her strength for a desperate effort, the old woman, bounded from the bed, and in an instant, came plunging at the throat of Devil-Bug, her arms outstretched, and her long skinny fingers, clutching him by the face and hair. She hung upon him, like a living Night-mare, her arms gathering convulsively round his neck, while her long nails, dug into his cheeks, like the talons of a vulture.

"Help me, Gabr'el—" muttered Devil-Bug, struggling fiercely with the old woman—"Give me a lift, and I'll choke her in a minnit—"

Gabriel looked up in surprise, mingled with terror. His course was taken in a moment. Closing the lid of the small chest, heaped with dubloons, he gathered it, in the embrace of his long arms, and winding this dingy cloak round his shoulders, made towards the door.

"Down the back staircase," he muttered, hurrying through the door. "I vill make my tracks!"

The old widow still clung to the robber's neck, gathering him to her withered form in an embrace, more pressing than maternal. With a violent effort Devil-Bug raised his arms, and poising her a moment in the air, dashed her to the floor. In an instant she was on her feet again; in another instant her arms were round his neck, with one hand gathered in his hair, and the other clutching him by the face.

"What an old crittur! Not to pare her nails!" muttered Devil-Bug, as his face, and hands were wet with his blood. I'll give ye a lesson, ye'll never forgit, I will!

"I'll larn ye to rob a poor lone woman," shrieked the widow.

Then commenced a contest, which but a minute or two in duration, was characterized on both sides by all the malignant energy of wild beasts, fighting for their prey. Again and again, Devil-Bug, raised her in his arms and dashed her to the floor; again and again, she sprung to her feet, and with the bound of a rattlesnake darting on its victim, gathered her hands round his throat. Along the floor, Devil-Bug dragged her, upsetting chairs and tables in the struggle; from one end of the room to the other, with the celerity of lightning, the combatants passed, the old woman muttering a suppressed shriek all the while, as the hand of the robber was pressed upon her mouth. Now around the bed, now along the hearth, scattering ashes and firebrands in the air, now against the wall, this desperate fight was continued, the old woman struggling with supernatural strength for her life and her gold, while Devil-Bug, with all his muscular vigor, his arms of iron sinew, and his fingers, whose grasp was like the shutting of a vice, found, for once, he had encountered an antagonist as determined as himself.

"Murder—Mur-*der!*" shrieked the parrot, aroused from his nap, by the sound of the contest.

"Ye'll cry murder, will ye!" cried Devil-Bug, mistaking the cry of the parrot, for a shriek of the old woman. "I'll settle that business for you, I will!"

His teeth were fixedly compressed, as with one desperate effort he unloosed the arms of the old woman from his throat, and grasped her firmly by the middle of the body. He fixed his eye upon a massive knob surmounting one of the brass andirons before the fire, and, as a blacksmith raises a hammer in his arms, he swung the body of the old woman suddenly on high. She uttered a loud and piercing shriek—it was her last! As the blacksmith with his muscular arms, braced for the blow, brings the hammer, whirling down upon the anvil, so Devil-Bug, with his hideous face, all a-flame with rage, swung the body of the old woman wildly over his shoulder, and with the every impulse of his strength, gathered for the effort, struck her head—her long grey hairs streaming wildly all the time—full against the knob of the brass andiron.

He raised her body in the air again to repeat the blow, but the effort was needless. The brains of the old woman lay scattered over the hearth, and the body which Devil-Bug raised in the air, was a headless trunk, with the bleeding fragments of a face and skull, clinging to the quivering neck.

"B'lieve me soul, the old 'ooman's hurt," muttered Devil-Bug, with a ghastly smile, as he flung the body, yet trembling with life, to the floor—"Ha! ha!" he shouted, standing as still as though suddenly frozen to stone. "There's that feller at my side with the jaw bruk and the tongue stickin' out! There is, just as he fell through the trap, and there, by his side, is the old woman, with the brains a-pourin' out from the empty skull! There's two on 'em now—and they'll always be with me—ah! ah! I'll not stand this: I won't! Why can't a feller kill his man or woman and have done with 'em? But to have 'em this way, always with you.—He, he, he! *I begin to b'lieve in hell now, I do!*"

He stood before the fireplace, with his back to the portrait. The corse of the old woman, the mangled fragments of a face and skull, resting in a pool of blood, lay at his very heels along the hearth. In front of him, at some distance along the floor, beside the bed, stood the candle, now flickering in its socket, and flinging a waning light around the room. The face of Devil-Bug was pale as ashes. His lips were tightly compressed, and his solitary eye glared out from the shadow of the overhanging brow, like the eye of a war-horse, with the death-arrow in his heart. His hands hung stiffened by his side. His entire appearance, was that of a man whom some wierd enchantment is transforming to lifeless stone. The cold sweat in big and clammy drops, streamed over his tawny visage, and his eye grew more vivid and intense in its burning gaze.

"I hear the critter groan—" he muttered, without moving the fraction of an inch from his statue-like position—"Somethin' evil is goin' to happen to me! Just as he fell through the hatchway, his jaw broke and his tongue out—he lays afore me! And he moves his blood-shot eyes and waggles his tongue, and groans an' groans! And the old woman's there too! She's layin' at my back, I know, but there she is, at my side—the brains oozing out from the hollow skull!"

For a moment the murderer trembled from head to foot.

"By God!" he muttered the oath with deep emphasis—and this was a singular thing for Devil-Bug to do, for he scarcely ever swore by the name of the Almighty—"By God! I do—*I do begin to b'lieve that there is a hell!*"

And around his feet and over the heart, silently and slowly the blood of the murdered woman began to flow and spread, while the ghastly corse, with the hollow skull oozing with clotted flesh and brains, lay huddled in a shapeless heap, the hand contorted with the spasm of death, and the stiffened limbs flung along the bricks, in the crouching position peculiar to a violent and a bloody death.

Murder was in that room in its most awful form. Like a terrible Presence, it seemed to darken the very air of the room, and chill the strong heart of the murderer. The light flickered dimly in the socket, and then sank down, after sudden glare, and all was dark as midnight.

"It's gone out—" muttered Devil-Bug, as his heart gathered a strange courage from the darkness, which took the sight of all outward objects from his view—"It's gone out! Why shouldn't I fill my pockets with some o' the old woman's plunder? Ha, ha, ha! Why not? Devil-Bug ain't so easily skeered, I tell ye—"

He turned toward the fire-place as he spoke. He was about to prosecute his researches in the darkness when the light, which he had fancied extinguished, flared up from its socket, and lit the room with a sudden glare. That glare was but for an instant, and yet by its red light Devil-Bug, with his face turned to the hearth, beheld the dark eyes of the portrait gazing fixedly upon him. He had not observed this portrait before. But now, as the pale cheeks glowed in the momentary glare of the dying candle, as the dark eyes grew suddenly brilliant, and the hair seemed to wave and float in the ruddy light, while the background of this picture, the frame and all its minor details were wrapt in thick darkness, Devil-Bug thought he beheld, not a portrait or a mere piece of inanimate canvass, but a breathing and living woman, whose look was fixed upon his face in terrible reproof.

"Nell!" he shrieked—"The gal come to life agin', jist as she was seventeen years ago! Ho, ho, ho! *I do believe there is—a God—that's a fact!*"

The light went out and all was darkness. Devil-Bug, with a wild yell, fled from the room, his footsteps echoed through the next chamber, and in a moment resounded from the private stairway leading into the yard. Again and again that wild yell, mingled with a woman's name, broke upon the air, and then all was still.

Silence, and darkness, and murder, were only the tenants of the Ghost-Room, while the oozing blood began to harden over the cold bricks of the fire-place.

BOOK THE THIRD

THE SECOND NIGHT

Mabel

CHAPTER FIRST

LUKE HARVEY IN THE GHOST-ROOM

Luke raised his blood-stained hands in the light, and stood chained to the spot with horror. In a moment he mastered the dead and icy feeling of awe which began to change his very heart to stone. He seized the candle, he rushed up the stairway, and stood before the door of the Ghost-Room. The light which he grasped flashed through the open door of the back-room. It was silent and untenanted by human being. The door, opening on the private staircase, hung slightly open. Luke gazed through the doorway of the back-room again and again, but his gaze, never for a single instant, wandered into the Ghost-Room, whose opened door laid its Secret bare to his glance.

He stood at the door with the light in his hand, trembling with a strange fear, but he dared not enter the room.

Even as he stood, footsteps, hushed and softened, came echoing faintly from the private staircase, and in a moment, through the doorway at its head, there stole the figure of a stout man, wrapped in a thick overcoat, with a pistol in one hand and a thick knotted mace in the other. One by one, at his heels, there followed twelve muscular men, dressed and armed like their leader. Luke neither heard nor saw them, but stood as if frozen to the floor, with his head turned away from the door of the Ghost-Room.

"Why Harvey—is that you?" cried the leader of the band of twelve

—"Has them fellers been here—hey? Or am I too early? Easy Larkspur is generally too early. Why what's the matter with you, man? Where's the old woman, and the gal? Strike me stoopid, if you haint struck dumb!"

Luke silently pointed to the Ghost-Room.

Larkspur seized the candle and, followed by the twelve police officers, hurriedly rushed into the chamber.

There was a pause for a single moment, and then from every man there yelled one involuntary and awful shriek of horror.

"By G———d we're too late!" muttered Larkspur, in a voice whose emphasis of horror was in fearful contrast with his usual devil-may-care tones—"The party has been here afore us, and finished their job!"

"Didn't I tell you—" cried a Police Officer—"That the feller, whom we saw shinnin' it down the alley, as we came in the gate, was one of the party from this house?"

"May I be hung for stealin' a toothpick from a match boy, if this aint a leetle a-head of my time!" exclaimed Larkspur, and Luke could hear him, walking hurriedly up and down the room—"Too late, boys, too late, by G———d!"

Luke gathered nerve for a sight of horror, and slowly advancing into the room, pushed through the band of police officers, and gazed upon the mangled corse—"Here's some of the fruits of my d———d plot to catch the thieves—" he said in a husky voice, as he gazed upon the shapeless mass, which but five minutes before, had been a living and breathing creature—"Larkspur I thought that you were hidden in the backroom, when I first entered the house: but no matter. It's all over now—"

His face was white as the death-shroud, and his upper lip trembled with an involuntary movement.

"Larkspur—" he said in a voice which did not rise above a whisper —"Search this room, and see—and—see—if there is not another—another—corpse!"

"Och, Whilaloo! Ochone! Ochone! Murtherin' th-a-aves in the house ov me misthress! Ochone!" a voice came echoing from the main stairway of the mansion—"Ochone! We're ruinated and kilt intirely! Heard ye iver the likes o' this?"

Peggy Grud came rushing into the room, her hair flying about her head in wild disorder, while with her clasped hands upraised, she rent the air with a succession of vivid shrieks. The Police officers were between her and the fireplace, and the fearful object, laid along the floor, did not meet her eyesight.

"Will ye git out o' this, ye murtherin' blaggards? Where's my misthress? Ochone—Ochone! Th-*a*-aves! I'll riz the nabor'ud on ye—Where's me misthress?"

Luke silently pushed the police officers aside, and taking Peggy Grud by the hand, led her forward.

"There—" he cried fixing his snake-like eye upon her, with a glance which she dared not face—"There is your Mistress!"

"Murder—Mur*der!*" cried the Parrot, rustling about in the cage above the mantel piece.

Peggy Grud looked down upon the corse, and then leaped into the very air, with a start of unfeigned horror. Uttering shriek after shriek, no longer feigned by shrewd hypocrisy, but wrung from her bosom, by the horrible sight of the ghastly corse, combined with her own guilty fears, Peggy Grud, sank in a kneeling position with her face averted from the dead body, while she tore her hair, in very madness.

"Who ses I did the murther?" she shrieked—"It's a lie! It's a lie! Who ses I did the murther? It is a lie as black as hell! Ocho—chone!"

"Yer a purty pictur' aint you?" cried Larkspur advancing from the throng of police officers—"Yer a purty thing, aint ye? You'll be in all the papers, now wont you? Oh, git out, ye ugly cripple! Ye'll have your portr'it in the Black Mail, with these verds below—"*Peggy Grud the murderer of her missus.*" And they'll have an account of yer trial in the Ledger and the Chronicle, vith full descriptions of yer relations, and yer family affairs! Oh, ye'll become a public karac*ter* ye will! I'll tell you what it is, fellers, there's none of ye can ever say, that you ever heered of Easy Larkspur bein' seized with an affecshun o' water in the eyes, but d———n them werry eyes, but if that sight doesn't beat me out! To see an ole woman murdered by an hired gal, while the werry cats, vich the ole woman, fed with her own hand, comes a-weepin' round her corpse—"

True it was that the favorites of the old lady who in the first uproar of the contest, between her and Devil-Bug, had slunk away into the nooks and crannies of the room, now stole forth from their hiding places, and came purring and moaning round the shapeless corse. They walked in the old woman's blood, picking her dress with their claws, as though to arouse her from slumber, while they looked up in the faces of the bystanders, with an expression of brute anguish, more painful to see, than the deepest agony of a human countenance, for the human countenance has a tongue to speak, while the brute can only look and mourn.

Ike, the tortoise-shell cat, and Wesley the blue-and-white cat—to give them the fanciful names, by which the old lady knew them—Nappy, the black cat with snake-like eyes, and Washy the lubberly white cat, with a sleepy look, all walked round the dead body, staining their feet in the thick blood, while with moan after moan, they picked the torn dress of the old woman, with their claws, and seemed urging her to rise.

"Genelmen aint that a sight for you?" cried Larkspur in a tone of feeling. No one replied. Luke stood beside the corpse with his head drooped over his folded arms.

"Genelmen aint that a sight for you? Here the cats and the hired gal! The old woman fed 'em all! The hired gal murders her missus—the cats mourn for the death o' their missus! Aint that a sight genelmen?"

"Ochone—Ochone!" screamed Peggy Grud—"What have I done? Jist tell me anybody, what have I done?"

"Murder, Mur-*der!*" screamed the Parrot, from his cage—"Mur-*der!*"

CHAPTER SECOND

DORA AND LUKE

"No sign of violence, no mark of murder, to tell the story of an untimely death! The victim will lay, calm and motionless, as though he had but resigned himself to a pleasant slumber! One moment his cheek glows with health—let but a drop from this phial, pass his lips, and his face, will take the hue of ashes, his heart grew cold and lifeless! The world, ha, ha, ha! The world, will wonder and stare, and the Doctor, nodding sagely all the while, will aver, by all the knowledge of his craft, that Livingstone, came to his death, through the natural result of the fatal disease, which has been gathering round his heart for years!

"I, alone, will hold the mystery of his death, locked fast among the secrets of my bosom!"

Dora Livingstone was alone. Alone in that gorgeous chamber, which Livingstone had delighted to crowd with the evidences of his wealth. Situated in a central part of his mansion, it was illumined by a splendid chandelier, whose price, told in round heaps of dollars, would have bought you a seat in Congress, or wrung Justice, from the most impartial Bench.

The light of the chandelier, subdued and softened, by thick shades of costly glass, fell around the chamber with the effect of moonlight, disclosing the satin hangings, which concealed the lofty walls, the gorgeous carpet laid along the floor, and the splendid furniture, which gave an appearance of extreme luxury to the place. The wide hearth, surmounted by a mantel, adorned with vases of alabaster, was enlivened by the glow of a cheerful wood-fire, whose gleams, now shot flashingly along the room, and now died away, into a steady and cheerful blaze. All around the walls, among the hangings of crimson satin, pictures in gorgeous frames, received the glow of the chandelier full on their canvass, every inch of which, had been made immortal by the hand of one of the Painter-Genii of the old world. Venus rising from the bath, fresh in the lustre of her charms, Apollo erect in the glory of youthful manhood, Daphne awaiting the approach of the god, Eve bending over the fountain, in whose clear waves, she saw another Eve, radiant as herself; such were a few of the figures, beaming from the pictures, hung along the walls, with the rich folds of the satin hangings falling carelessly aside from their heavy frames.

The chamber, we say, was crowded with evidences of Livingstone's wealth. On the centre-table of rich Mosaic were caskets of ebony, glittering with the jewels of Dora, the Merchant's wife; rare curiosities, prized and costly from their very variety; vases of alabaster; antique gems, rich with the fairy-sculpture of some classic Artist; and all the costly spoils which gold, that conqueror and dispoiler of Art, more unrelenting than the Goth or Corsican, had won from the galleries and cabinets of Rome and Florence. The carpet, whose gorgeous hues overspread the floor, considered by itself alone, was worth the price of a first rate statesman, as statesmen are valued in the political market; while the elegant sofa and the chairs, elaborate with Gothic work, and embroidery, turned into gold, would have bought up a dozen patriots of the common order. Altogether, the room was full of wealth, luxury, and splendor, and here it was that Dora, uncompanioned save by her own dark thoughts, had retired to arrange her plans and hasten on the fatal crime, on whose result she had perilled her soul.

But an hour returned from the Theatre, where she had shone among the magnates of the Quaker City nobility, she had thrown aside her costly robes and assumed a garb, whose loose folds, gathering gently around her queenly form, displayed her beauty to more advantage than all the silks of France, or costumes of an Imperial Court.

Seated in that article of furniture peculiarly American, a rocking chair, with her head thrown back, her eyes upturned with their lids half-closed, while her dark tresses, released from comb or braid, fell carelessly over her shoulders, the lady was enrobed in a gown of faint azure satin, whose ample developments of shape—or want of shape—

wide sleeves and swelling folds, gathered round her bust, and waist, and limbs, with a voluptuous adaptation to every outline of her faultless form.

Her arms were crossed carelessly over her bosom, while the softened light of the chandelier fell warmly over the whiteness of her small hands and rounded shoulders; snowy and roseate as alabaster, tinged by the flush of daybreak. Her feet, in all their delicate outlines, unconfined by slipper or stocking, peeped from the heavy folds of her night-robe, white as Parian marble, and quite as beautiful in their proportions as these from which Canova modelled the feet of his Venus.

Certainly a beautiful woman is the greatest wonder of God's universe! Certainly the remarkable combination of beauties, presented by her form, the outlines, rounded and flowing, whether manifested in the fulness of the bust or the faultless symmetry of the limbs; the various hues which are combined in her person, the deep black of her hair, the soft rose tint of her cheek and lips, the alabaster of her hands and neck and shoulders, the lustrous darkness of her eye, and the blackness of her brows and lashes; the magic of her walk, each limb moving in as much harmony with the general effect, as the star circling in his orbit, compares in the regularity of its motion with star; certainly, we say, these beauties and graces afford more convincing proof of God's power, than the whole universe combined!

But then, when we add to these, the attractions of her soul, that strange magnetism of her look, which enchains and fascinates, that varied intonation of voice, which can awe us in a whisper, or bring us to ruin with a word, that power to flatter, to glose a falsehood and cover the naked blackness of a lie with such a delicate surface of ivoried-fiction; when we remember that by the pressure of her hand, slight, warm and thrilling, she can lure the Preacher from his pulpit, the Statesman from his solemn thoughts, the grave Justice from his Bench; it becomes a wonder, why that most wonderful of all things, a beautiful woman, was ever permitted by the Creator to have the power of evil entrusted to her nature!

Here we have Dora Livingstone sitting in yonder rocking chair by the light of that splendid chandelier, as beautiful as God's own light, and yet, in her heart, as corrupt as the blackness of hell! Is she not beautiful? Mark the head, thrown backward, the soft flush warming over her face, the half-closed lids, the parted lips, so rich, so small, and yet so full and ripe in their redness and shape; mark the glossy blackness of her hair, sweeping down in careless clusters to her shoulders, and those very shoulders! how round their outline, how soft their surface, how bewitching that dimple, indenting itself like a living smile into the centre of each shoulder, just where the full arms are joined to the queenly bust! Ah-ha! The bust! How it heaves beneath the careless folds of the satin gown—slowly, slowly, higher and yet higher, like a wave hidden by a snow-flake!

The hands lightly crossed over that bosom, the tapering fingers, the dimples along the surface of the white skin, where the fingers, join the hand itself, the clear nails, tinged with a circle of deep red around their edges! That glimpse of a wrist and an arm, disclosed by the wide sleeve, as it falls, carelessly aside! The slender waist, its shape revealed by the voluptuous (a good word for any thing that is easy in position, swelling in outline, bewitching in general effect) folds of the satin robe! The full proportions of the lower part of her form, suggest mingled ideas of stateliness ripeness and beauty; pleasant images of white swans, smiling grandly over smooth waters, ripe peaches, heavy from their very ripeness, hanging lusciously from some bending bough; or soft daybreaks, or lovely sunsets, or still midnights, or indeed any thing, whose beauty is without comparison!

And then, the feet! Ha, ha, we have come down to the feet, and these, let me tell you, are not the most contemptible of Dora's beauties! The high instep—do smile at our minuteness—the long and narrow form, the shape of the toes, the nails, like the fingers, tinged, each of them, with a deep circlet of red!

A look at the face, again! Do not those red lips, with glimpses of the ivory teeth, stealing out upon you, from the interval of the moist vermillion, do they not, look as though they were but made for a man to kiss once, and then die? The eyes—gleaming between the half-closed lids, beaming from the shadow of the long and trembling lashes,—how beautiful they are, as veiled in a lustrous moisture, a mist-like dimness, they indicate the soul, absorbed in a reverie! The broad forehead (a thing we do not always like to see in woman) the dark eyebrows, the regularly shaped nose—Grecian with the slightest inclination, toward the aquiline—the firm, round chin—ha, ha!

Here's a beautiful woman, sitting easily in the rocking-chair, as a good wife, who has not a single bad thought should sit, and yet this beautiful woman, is already in heart a Murderess!

Already false to the Honor of her husband, she now would assail his Life! And she, so beautiful, so queenly and so like the impersonation of a pure Thought in every outline of her form! And this, was once a confiding, loving, and boasting girl; but the Canker of Ambition, has warmed itself into her Soul, the atmosphere of Sensuality, has changed her inner nature, while her outward beauties remain the same! Alas! Alas! Why did not Eve stay at home in the garden of Eden, and refrain from wandering about, she knew not whither, and plucking forbidden fruit, and listening to handsome serpents? Ever since that fatal hour, too many of her fair daughters, have not only plucked, but turned themselves into, forbidden fruit; not only listened to handsome serpents, but transformed themselves into very snakes, whose venom of sting, is but ill-recompensed by their glittering and brilliant exterior!

"No mark of violence, no sign of murder, to tell the story of an untimely death!" the thought, flashed over the mind of the wife, but did not shape itself into words—"The world, will say, he died of that fatal disease, which threatened him for years! Dora of Lyndeswold, ha, ha! Algernon, thinks he can mould me to his slightest purpose! What is the block of marble, should seize the chissel, and change places, with the Sculptor?"

Extending her hand, she lifted the small bell, from the white cloth of the table at her side. A moment, and the silvery sound of the bell, rung round the room.

The servant in Livery, presented himself at the door.

"Did you ring, Ma'am?"

"What time did Mr. Livingstone say he would return home?" exclaimed Dora, without turning her eyes, in the direction of the door, which was behind the back of her chair.

"Ha'past ten ma'am."

"It is now half-past ten." she exclaimed looking at her watch.—"You may bring in the coffee, Thomas."

"Coffee for you and Mr. Livingstone? Yes ma'am—"

Mrs. Livingstone was alone again. Raising her form languidly from the half-reclining position, in which she had lain, Dora, lifted her right hand, slowly to her very eyes, and gazed intently upon a small phial, clasped between her delicate fingers. The phial not larger, than the most delicate finger on her snowy hand, was filled with a liquid, clear as crystal, which sparkled like a star, within the glass as she raised it in the light. Wrapping her spotless handkerchief, carefully around it, as ladies are wont to do, with their smelling bottles, Dora again relapsed into her half-reclining position on the back of the rocking chair.

"A drop, fresh from the phial, mingled with any liquid is sure to kill! But it must be applied, the moment ere the victim drinks, or it is harmless! That paper of the Doctor's did me good service—thanks to the cant of the day, which educates young girls, as though they were intended for any thing else, but wives or mothers, I learned something of chymistry at Boarding school; that was before father died. To day, I have dispatched twenty servants, twenty different ways, for the various drugs, with which to prepare in liquid: suspicion, cannot lay a finger's weight upon me!"

"Coffee ma'am, for you and Mr. Livingstone, Ma'am—" said Thomas, entering with two porcelain cups—smoking with coffee—which he placed upon the small table, beside her chair. This done, Thomas, who looked as though he had been born in his grey and velvet livery, with but the power of saying yes ma'am, no ma'am, retired from the room, in the same formal manner, which had marked his entrance.

Dora relapsed into her reverie, again. A footstep sounded in the entry, leading to the chamber. Her frame, quivered with a slight start, but in an instant, she sank into the chair again, with her head thrown backward on the soft velvet cushioning. Another moment and the footstep grew nearer.

"It is he!" she muttered, and with an effort, maintained her careless, half-slumbering attitude. As she spoke, the door opened, and she heard the pressure of the footstep upon the carpet.

"My dear, you have been absent very long—" said Dora, languidly, without moving from her position.

A slight, yet deep-toned laugh, echoing behind her chair, was the only answer she received from the new-comer.

"Ha! I should know that laugh—" she cried, starting, "Luke Harvey!" she murmured as she beheld the form of the stranger—"Luke Harvey, and at his hour! That man is my evil fate!"

"Excuse this intrusion, madam—" exclaimed Luke, advancing with a slight bow—"Mr. Livingstone made an appointment to meet me at this hour. He is not in, I perceive?"

"Mr. Livingstone is not at home!" exclaimed Dora, rising, even in her dishabille, with an air of freezing politeness.

"Oh, well, well—" replied Luke, fixing his dark eyes upon her beautiful face—"Well, well, it makes no difference. I'm one of that class who can either wait or be 'put off—' "

And as he spoke, with the coolest manner in the world, he drew a chair and sate down on the opposite side of the table. Dora gazed upon him in utter surprise. With one hand she seized her dark tresses and bound them up within her comb, while with an instinctive movement, she withdrew her naked feet under the shadow of her satin night-robe.

"Ha!" cried Luke, sleepily, with a slight yawn, as he drummed on his hat with his fingers—"Ha! hum! Cool evening, ma'am!"

"*Sir*—" exclaimed Dora, as her proud form towered proudly erect—

"This is my private chamber. You can wait for Mr. Livingstone in the hall, down stairs—"

She fixed her dark eyes upon him as though she would wither him with a look.

" 'Sir!' " echoed Luke, with that sneering laugh which sometimes gave his sharp features the expression of a sneering devil—" 'Sir' to *me!* Ha, ha! Dora—too good that! '*Sir*'—ha, ha, ha!"

" 'Dora' "—echoed the Merchant's wife, in a tone of utter astonishment as though she had not heard aright—" 'Dora'—indeed! You are either mad or impertinent, sir—"

"Sit down, Dora, sit down and compose yourself!" replied Luke, still drumming on the crown of his hat—"Doesn't it strike you as extremely odd, Dora, that you should assume that freezing look and call *me Sir!* D'ye remember the little back parlor in Wood street, Dora, where you used to sit on my knee and call me, *Luke*—"

"You are insulting!" exclaimed Dora, as one burning flush of indignation brightened over her face, while her dark eyes flashed fire—"Leave the room, sir!"

" 'Luke, *dear* Luke,' you called me, and, ha, ha, ha, kissed me—"

"Leave the room!" exclaimed Dora, growing very white in the face. Her voice was husky with indignation.

"Those are fine lips of yours, Dora! Your troth was plighted to me then, Dora! Egad! What a picture you present for an artist! Fine study for a rising genius.—'The Enraged Beauty!' One night you kissed me so sweetly, Dora, so lovingly! 'Good night, Luke,' and kissed me! The next day you picked a delightful quarrel with me, and forbade your 'plighted love,' the house. Why? Because the *rich* merchant, Livingstone, had called at your mother's dwelling. Your eye was fixed upon *him*. The *poor* clerk was eclipsed! In less than six months you were Mrs. Albert Livingstone, wife of the merchant prince.—'Sir,' indeed! ha, ha, ha!"

"Mr. Livingstone shall be informed of this insult!" said Dora, in a deep low tone, that indicated the most deadly anger. She rang the bell violently, as she spoke.

"I presume you are about to order your servants to thrust me from your doors?" said Luke, his voice sinking to a whisper, as he leaned over the table, and awaited her answer.

She made no reply, but sinking in the chair, turned her face away from her former lover, and with a gesture of fierce anger, rang the bell as though her life depended on its clamor.

"Thrust *me* from the doors! 'Dear Luke,' you said, and kissed me!" Luke bent slowly down, gazing at the indignant woman through the shadow of his thick eyebrows as he spoke.—"Do you know, Dora, that

I often think of that little back parlor in Wood street? A splendid woman on my knee, her full arms around my neck, her soft whispers falling on my ears like delightful music. 'When we are married, Luke,' 'twas, thus, you often whispered, 'we'll live together, in some nice two-story house, secluded from the world. Your salary is small, Luke, and we may be very poor, but'—and then you would smile, Dora—'we have that which the wealth of the Indies cannot give, love—Luke—love!' *Then* you would kiss me! When I shut my eyes, and forgot the Present, I can feel those kisses still clinging to my lips!"

"Mr. Livingstone shall be informed of this insult, sir," exclaimed Dora, her brow darkening with rage, as with her back turned toward Luke, she clenched her hands in very anger.

"I pray you, inform Mr. Livingstone of my conduct!" whispered Luke, leaning over the table, as his hand was thrust within his bosom. —"Have me thrust from your doors, inform Mr. Livingstone of my conduct; but, but—" his voice sunk to a whisper, like the hissing of a snake—"at the same time inform him of the contents of *this note!*"

Leaning over the table, he held a letter which he had taken from his bosom, open to her gaze.

"What folly is this!" began Dora, as she glanced over her shoulder at the letter, which Luke held extended in his hand. "Ah!" she shrieked, in utter horror, as with a lightning glance she caught a view of the superscription.—"My letter to Fitz-Cowles! Oh God, I am in this man's power!"

She buried her face in her hands, while her hair, escaping from the comb, fell wildly over her neck and bosom.

"How interesting you look just now! 'Good night, dear Luke!' Will you inform Mr. Livingstone of this insult; will you order the servant to thrust me from the door?"

"Did you ring, ma'am?" exclaimed Thomas, opening the door.

Dora started from her seat, and advanced hurriedly toward the fire-place. Her brow was darkened by a fearful frown, and a big black vein marred the beauty of her forehead.

"I am in his power!" she muttered to herself.—"He can, by a single word, scatter all my schemes to the wind, and cover me with shame! What! Endure the foul tongue of public slander! Never! Ha! This man must die! I have resolved upon my course!" She turned to the servant, and exclaimed in her usual commanding tones—"Mr. Harvey will take coffee, with me to-night. The coffee, which you have placed upon the table is cold. Bring in fresh coffee, Thomas."

With a wild stare of amazement, as though he suspected all was not right, Thomas closed the door, and disappeared.

"You are a bold and desperate man," cried Dora, as she advanced toward the table, and gazed fixedly in Luke's face. "I am in your power! What would you with me?"

"I thought *that* would bring you down a peg or so!" exclaimed Luke, smiling as he rattled the letter against the table. "However, here's the coffee"—he continued, as Thomas entered, like a spirit, placed fresh cups of coffee on the table, and in an instant was gone. "Here's the coffee. Take a cup with me, Dora! D'ye remember those nice little suppers in the back parlor in Wood street?"

"Do me the favor, sir, to arrange the fire on the hearth,"—exclaimed Dora, in a tone as commanding as though she spoke to the humblest of her menials. "The room is quite cold!"

Luke smiled pleasantly, as a man is wont to smile, who indulges a child in some trifling humor, and then turning toward the fireplace, commenced arranging the huge sticks of wood upon the hearth.

A wild light flashed from Dora's dark eyes. Bending slightly forward, she held her right hand over one of the porcelain cups, and taking the cork from the small phial, she suffered a single drop to mingle with the fragrant coffee. It was the work of a moment. When Luke turned again from the fireplace, she was seated in the rocking chair, her head thrown back, as with her right hand upraised, she made a show of applying salts to her nostrils.

"Good coffee *this!*" said Luke, as he seated himself by the table. "Take a cup, Madam?"

Dora silently raised the cup which was untinctured with the contents of the phial. As she lifted it to her lips she silently watched Luke's movements, over the edge of the cup.

"Good coffee," he exclaimed, "has a pleasant fragrance!" He raised it to his lips.

A slight start quivered through Dora's frame. "He drinks!" the thought flashed over her soul—"He drinks! He is lost! In a moment he will fall from the chair a lifeless corse!"

"Good coffee, I say," exclaimed Luke, gazing quietly at Dora, over the edge of the uplifted cup. "Has a surprising fragrance, but—" he hesitated, slightly lowering the cup from his lips, "but, Dora—" and a smile of strange meaning crossed his lips.

"What mean you sir?" she exclaimed, sipping her coffee with a careless air, while her heart swelled to bursting, and her inmost soul was thrilled with the appaling interest of the scene. "What mean you, sir?"

"Fragrant coffee; but I prefer Cogniac to Mocha," said Luke, quietly placing the porcelain cup on the table, without tasting its contents.—"Ha, ha! I can make the same remark to you, that the convict made to the hangman, who did his business in such a bungling manner, that the poor fellow, with his neck in the rope, roared out a forcible reproof. I say, you wasn't quick enough with the—'*drop!*' Ha, ha! Pooh! You can't poison me, Dora! I'm not one of 'them' kind!"

Dora could feel her heart grow cold in her bosom. For a single instant she felt as though she was about to fall dead on the floor. She had but presence of mind to conceal the small phial in the handkerchief, and place it within the folds of her dress, when her very reason seemed to fail her, and pressing her hands against her burning forehead, a single exclamation escaped from her lips.

"All is lost!"

"Suppose I show the letter to your husband?" said Luke, with a quiet sneer, as he stood surveying her agony, with a silent delight.

Her bosom rose heaving from the folds of her dress, as though convulsed by the agony of death. Still her hands were pressed against her brow, while her large black eyes, dilating with a wild stare, glared fixedly in the face of her torturer.

"To-morrow, to-morrow,"—the thought came darkening over her soul—"I will be the scoff and jeer of all the fashionable circles! My name a by-word—my reputation a bauble! And more than all—more than the scoff of the world, more than my husband's hate, my plans will all be scattered in ruins! No! No! I will try my last hope with this man—he loved me once! And—how the thought of the degradation galls me—now I must kneel to him for mercy!"

"*Luke!*" she shrieked aloud, as she rose on her feet, and stood before him, a breathing picture of mortal Agony, her hands convulsively clasped, while her long dark hair, fell glistening over her shoulders—*Luke!*"

"That sounds better than 'Sir,' "—replied Luke in the same dry and biting tone.

"Spare me Luke!" she shrieked flinging herself on her knees at his feet—"Spare me Luke!"

"Ha, ha! The beauty of the Quaker City at my feet!"

He said this with his usual dry and caustic laugh, but the spectacle, began to touch the chords of his dark and mysterious nature.

Her dark hair showering over her shoulders, the loose robe floating wildly around her voluptuous form, her womanly bosom rising into view, her hands clasped, and her eyes glaring with a vacant stare, she shrieked forth, in a voice whose agony of emphasis, no words can depict—"By the memory of the love, you once felt for me, oh spare me! Mercy, Luke, in God's name, mercy!"

"That love, which wound your image round my heart, as never man's love entwined the image of mortal woman before—that love you trampled upon!" and his snake-like eye gleamed with a savage light—"Had you been but a bosom friend, and stolen my money, I would have forgiven you! Had you been my wife, and left me for dishonor, I might still have forgiven you! But girl that you were, you trampled upon a heart, that would have bled its last drop for you, you trifled with a soul, that would have dared eternal ruin for your sake! Spare you? Never!"

The cool and biting tone in which he spoke, restored Dora, to full consciousness and reason. She saw that her very soul hung in a fearful balance; and by one quick operation of her genius, she resolved to fling the weight of her charms into the scale.

"Luke—" she cried, spreading her arms toward him, as she knelt at his feet, while her eyes, swimming with well-affected passion, were fixed upon his countenance—"You once loved me Luke—you will spare me, now!"

As if by accident she suffered the folds of her night-gown to slip aside, and her white shoulder, with all its faultless symmetry of shape, lay open to the beams of the light.

Luke gazed upon her, and felt his heart relent! She knelt before him, an embodied Tempest of voluptuous loveliness. Her cheeks flushed in lively hues, her eyes, beaming passion, her long dark hair streaming down to her uncovered shoulders, glimpses of her bosom, whose womanly fullness, now grew animate with voluptuous agitation rising slowly in the light—Luke gazed upon her and thought of the olden time.

"Mercy, Luke! Mercy!"

"On one condition—" he exclaimed in a whisper, that thrilled to her very heart.

"And that is—"

He hissed a single word, in her ear, as his dark eyes, drank in the living picture of her beauty.

She started as though an adder had stung her.

"Never!" she shrieked with a glance of unfeigned indignation. "Sooner will I face the very worst! The world's scorn and my husband's hate!"

She had prepared herself, to use all the influence of her charms, to win mercy from his iron heart, but—to *sell herself for the letter!* The thought aroused all that pride, which had been the first cause of her ruin.

"This letter published, the world will call you an—*Adultress!* A pretty word, Dora!"

She quivered in every limb, as the foul word, broke on her ears. Dropping her head upon her bosom, she clasped his knees with her trembling hands. The cup of her degradation was full.

"I consent—" she murmured—"Do with me what you will!"

"The letter is yours, Dora—" he said in a husky voice—"You place yourself in my power?"

"I have sold myself to you—" her voice sunk to a whisper, almost inaudible "The price this witness of my guilt!"

Luke gathered his arms around her form as she knelt before him, and bending her head slightly backward gazed upon her face. Her eyes were dimcast and a deep crimson flush mantled over her face. She lay in his arms, motionless as a statue, yet living as a flame. Luke slowly raised her from the floor; her head dropped on his shoulder, and her bosom throbbed warmly against his breast. For a single moment, the light of passion subdued the cold and snake-like gleam of his eyes, but even in that instant, the face of the fair and unknown girl, whom he had seen that morning for the first time in his life, rose like a guardian angel before him, and with that vision, a frown darkened over his forehead, and an expression of scorn trembled on his lip.

"You place yourself in my power, Dora! Ha, ha! Here's beauty for the sight and touch—here's soft glances of the eyes, kisses of the lip, pressures of the moist hand, all for sale! And I, I, with the most beautiful woman in the Quaker City in my arms, waiting to become mine—I, with this living picture of health, loveliness and passion, in my arms proffering her lip to my kiss, her bosom to my touch—I have still the *moral* self denial, ha, ha, ha! to scorn the embraces of an—*Adultress!*"

With that mocking laugh he flung her rudely from him, and rushed from the room.

Extending her arms with a faint effort to preserve her balance, she fell insensible to the floor.

God save from the vengeance of this woman, the man who dared to put such galling scorn upon her! There she lay, all her pride and beauty brought down to the dust, there she lay, her cheeks pale as death, her lips parted, and her eyes, glaring upon the ceiling with an unconscious stare, there she lay, insensible and motionless, but the Fiend was locked within that faultless form; within the snowy whiteness of that bosom, now gleaming coldly in the light, was Hell.

CHAPTER THIRD

THE FREE BELIEVERS AND TRUE REPENTERS

" 'Genelmen, my daddy vos a scavenger and my mommy sold rags!' On my travels again, ha, ha! Let me compare notes with myself—and first of all, that scene with Dora! Don't know what in the deuce possessed me to work her up so; Livingstone merely requested me to leave a note with her, in which he stated that business would detain him at the counting-house all night. I called to leave the note, found her alone, and I suppose some devil must have inspired me, for I never planned that scene myself, no, never! A pretty mess I've got myself into, with all this planning and plotting! The old woman murdered, the Jew and Devil-Bug escaped, and all my work to do over again! Peggy Grud, however, is safe: and the 'proper authorities' have promised to leave the arrest of Devil-Bug to me; I'll manage him before to-morrow night, or my name isn't Luke! And that pale-faced girl, with the soft eyes and dark hair—Parson Pyne's daughter, is she? I'll know more about her, *too*, before I'm many hours older!"

Attired in the rags of Brick-Top, with the red hair falling over his eyes, and his face all smeared with paint and invested with huge crimson whiskers, Luke was hurrying down Third street, his hands in his pockets, and his body thrown forward, while his walk was that of a genuine loafer, being made up of an Indian's tramp when on a war-path, and a Highlander's characteristic trot; a sort of half-walk and half-run, with a slight sprinkling of a lazy lounge.

To say that Luke did not relish these excursions, for the adventure's sake alone, would be doing him rank injustice. He found as much pleasure in pursuing the thread of a difficult enterprize, which combined danger, romance, and mystery, as the most indefatigable novel-reader finds in the pages of a book like Rookwood,* where the atten-

* The author begs leave to record his humble admiration of Wm. Harrison Ainsworth, whom all the starch-and-buckram critics have been abusing so heartily for years. Rookwood is a production of which Walter Scott might have been proud. Ainsworth understands the art and theory of the *plot* of a story better than any living writer.

Among other remarkable things, uttered by an industrious compiler, named Griswold, who, with singular modesty, has taken upon himself to say who are, and who are not, the Poets of America; the following passage is one of the most remarkable—"*Mr. Cooper is less read in the United States than Harrison Ainsworth.*"

tion is, from first to last, rivetted and enchained by one passage of breathless interest succeeding another, in transitions as rapid and thrilling as the changes of some well-contested battle.

"Here's a new mystery—" muttered Luke, as he struck into a bye-street—"Mary Arlington missing and her brother in the bargain! Egad, this will be an eventful Christmas, if things keep on this way. However, my business to night is to follow in the footsteps of the illustrious Parson Pyne! In the first place, I must make for his Lecture Room—"

Passing from the bye-street into a dark alley, where the winter wind was doing a fierce concert on its own account, while the clear, cold stars shone down between the intervals of the roofs that almost met overhead; Luke presently halted under the light of a lamp which projected from the wall of an old brick building, illuminated the dingy confines of an entry, disclosed by an open door. Above the door, a large sign bore the legend, in bright yellow letters painted on a dark ground—

FREE BELIEVERS' AND TRUE REPENTERS'

LECTURE ROOM

Rev. F. A. T. Pyne—Principal Free Believer and True Repenter.

UP STAIRS. ☞

Passing over the solemn joke of '*Mister*ing' the greatest Novelist that ever gave a literary name to our country abroad, or enchained his million-readers at home, we come to the implied sneer on the genius of Ainsworth; for though it's a very dull attempt at sarcasm, still the intelligent Griswold, with that commendable *effort*, which marks all his compilations, *meant* to be very bitter by insinuating this comparison between the two men. In the first place, the *fact* about Cooper being less read than Ainsworth, is a compiler's *fact*; about as substantial, sometimes, as his title of Reverend, or his claims to the acumen of a critic or the power of a genius. In the next place, we humbly opine, that works like Rookwood and Crichton are not to be killed with a sneer, although that sneer comes from the same pen, that (with its twin-scissors) has compiled a small library of "Poetry"—"Annuals"—"Curiosities"—"Sermons"—"Cock Robins"—*illustrated*—and "Jack the Giant killers"—in cloth, with notes.

"Fat Pyne is piling on the agonies"—exclaimed Luke, as the sound of a voice, shouting out something in a very hoarse tone, came echoing from a distance—"I'll go up and get a little patent grace from Pyne: I will that!"

"Brethren and Sisters—I ask you a plain question, and I want a plain answer! We have assembled on a most interesting occasion, I might say a sublime occasion, to which all other occasions are but a mole-hill to the mighty Andes, or a gin-shop to the Palace of Nebuchadnezzar! We have met together to forward the objects of our grand Association which, as you all know, is called 'The Universal Patent Gospel Missionary Society, for the conversion of the Pope of Rome—in particular—and the suppression of Vatican Paganism—in general.' We are a-going to send the Gospel to benighted Rome! Trembling in his pontificial robes, with a Bull in one hand, and a cup o' coffee in the other, the mighty Anti-Christ shall start in his Vatican when he hears our thunder a-booming over the fragrant plains of idolatrous Italy. He shall hear our thunder, and while his knees tremble, and his eyes water, he shall ask his four-and-twenty Cardinals, as they sit revelling in oysters and wine—'Boys, what's *that!*' And they shall answer, turning white from very fear—'That's the American Patent Gospel, Pope! That's the roaring of a real Buffalo a-seekin' to fight your Bull!' And then the Pope shall ask, what *is* the American Patent Gospel? As he speaks, our answer shall thunder in his ears! Our Gospel is a patent improved Gospel; a terrifier; a scorcher; a real Locomotive-off-the-track sort of a Gospel! We hold it to be a comfortable doctrine, to abuse the Pope o' Rome afore breakfast, and after breakfast, and all day long!

We hold it to be a consoling belief, that of all the millions o' human bein's ever created by the Lord, three-fourths of them are roasting in the broad lake o' fire and brimstone, this very minnit! Our Gospel is a gospel of fire and brimstone and abuse o' the Pope o' Rome, mingled in equal quantities—about half o' one and half o' tother—that's what our Gospel is!"

Standing on his small pulpit, which looked something like a cross between a watch-box and a bath-tub, the Reverend Mr. Pyne, extending his arms, with his coat thrown back, and his portly paunch thrust forward, his broad face red as a turkey's gills, and his watery eyes starting from their sockets, thundered forth the solemn assertion yet once more—"Fire and brimstone in the morning, abuse o' the Pope o' Rome at night—Brimstone and fire at night, abuse o' the Pope o' Rome in the morning! Turn it and twist it as you will, that's what our Gospel is!"

One universal sensation spread through the lecture room like wild fire. The old women, sitting on the first benches, in big black bonnets, and long faces, groaned—positively groaned: the old gentlemen, sitting behind the old ladies, stuck their hands far down in their pockets, and groaned in chorus: while all the young men, in white cravats, and all the young ladies in straw bonnets, with flashing ribbons, vented their enthusiasm in a simultaneous cough.

The lecture room of the True Believers and True Repenters was a long and narrow apartment, with a dingy white ceiling, from which depended a rusty chandelier, and smoky walls, lone, cheerless, and desolate in its appearance, with here and there a great spot of indefinable black, looking as though the plaster had received a bruise, and immense cracks, running from ceiling to floor, like veins in the lithograph of a coal mine. At one end of this large room, was the pulpit, looking, as we have said, like a composition of a watch-box and a bath-tub; at the other end was the narrow door, and between the door and the pulpit were seated one dense mass of human beings, male and female, old and young, high and low, rich and poor, packed together, along uncomfortable benches of unpainted pine, like sardines in a tin-box. Back of the pulpit, on a green settee, were gathered some dozen gentlemen, in white cravats and sanctified faces, their hands clasped on their crossed knees, as bending earnestly forward, they listened in painful intensity to the words of Elder Pyne. Immediately in front of the pulpit, around a large table covered with green baize, in the centre of which, was an inkstand, a sheet of paper, and two quills, freshly mended, some dozen more brothers were seated on green chairs, their heads thrown backward, and their mouths wide open, as they all listened to the words of the pious Brother Pyne, with an acute earnestness quite remarkable to behold.

"*That's* what our Gospel is!" continued F. A. T. Pyne, with a final flourish—"The various committees appointed at the last meeting of our Association, will now *Re*-port!"

One of the gentlemen sitting at the back of the Rev. Pyne now arose and came to the edge of the bath-tub, with a great roll of paper in his hand. He was a short little man, with a long face, thin lips, and thick eyebrows, which well-nigh concealed his diminutive eyes.

"Brother Augustus Billygoat, from the Committee on the Pope o' Rome—" observed the Rev. Pyne, in a suggestive tone to the assemblage.

"The *Com*-mittee on the Pope o' Rome *do re*-port—" began Brother Billygoat in a voice, somewhat afflicted by a cold—"That they have examined into the Pope o' Rome, and weighed him in the balances o' th' Patent Gospel; and he is found wantin' as follers—"

A great sensation. One old woman exclaimed "tremendous!" in a tone, somewhat too loud, whereupon a brother sitting on the next seat, pinched her lovingly in the arm.

"He is found a wantin' whereas he sends out bulls; and the scriptur' don't tolerate any bulls! He's found a wantin' because he lives in a sumptuous palace called the Wattykin! We defies the whole world to find the name o' th' Wattykin in the Bible! Friends and Brethren, we of this *Com*-mittee think the day will come, and is not long a comin' when the Pope o' Rome, like Nebbykudneezir will have to go to grass, and chaw roots for his livvin'! The Watty-kin will be desolate! The owl will hoot through its walls, and the rooster crow from its towers!

"With these few brief remarks, I lays the report on the table without readin' it in full, makin' a motion at the same time, that it shall be printed in The Universal American Patent-Gospel Exposition for the instruction o' futur' ages!"

The motion was carried by acclamation. Brother Billygoat sat down amid a murmur of applause.

Another Brother rose. He was a man of the middle height, with a look of deep sanctity oozing from the parchment of his saffron skin. His eyes were, as is often the case with persons of remarkable piety, inclined to be watery and dump-ish. His voice was a low-toned persuading kind of voice slightly tinctured with a snuffle. His hands were placed behind his back, as he spoke, while his long, lank hair fell carelessly around his cheeks and over his ears.

It gave him great pleasure, he remarked, to behold this demonstration. With that he pointed emphatically at the front bench, filled with old ladies in large black bonnets. Such things as this, were calculated to expand the feelings, while they confirmed the religious sentiment. As the Editor of the Patent-Gospel Expositor, he felt proud. As a Christian, he felt delighted. As a Protestant of the Universal American Patent-Gospel School, he felt enraptured. He, too, considered it his duty to testify to the abuses of Papal Rome. Old Babylon, ought to be exposed, laid out, and cut up. Those were his sentiments. In order to carry them fully into action he would relate a painful incident.

The Captain of an American Brig, which made a voyage to Naples, one summer's day suggested to his crew and passengers, that it would be a capital idea to visit the old Pagan in his Vatican. The Crew, the Passengers, consented.

"They went to Rome—" continued the Rev. Syllaybub Scissors, as the Editor of the Patent-Gospel was styled—"They saw the old Pagan. There were ten men of the crew and twenty passengers, not counting a little boy. They all had tracts, from the Patent-Gospellers Association in their pockets. The Pope sat in his chair, with a large number of

Cardinals in attendance. It may be as well to remark, that the old Pagan keeps these cardinals as gentlemen in waiting, to bring him coffee and muffins or perhaps oysters. Well, the crew and passengers, all dressed in their best, took a view of old Anti-Christ. But mark ye, brethren and sisters, they are called upon to kiss the Pope's toe. Like Americans, like Patent-Gospellers, they refused. They refused, the ten men of the crew, the twenty passengers, and the little boy! What was the consequence of the refusal? What I say was the consequence?"

There was utter silence in the hall of the Free Believers and True Repenters. You might have heard a pin drop.

"Why Brethren and Sisters, I'll tell you!" cried Syllaybub Scissors, growing very much excited—"Those passengers, crew, captain, little boy and *all, have never been heard of since*. (Great sensation!) They went into the Vatican, it is true, but *they never came out again!* (Tremendous excitement) I have nothing further to remark, my friends, but will close with a painful fact. It is melancholy, but it is too true, that next door to the Vatican is a large manufactory for Bologna sausages. (The excitement becomes intense.) Sometime after this painful disappearance, an American gentleman, travelling through Italy for his health, saw fit to order a large amount of sausages from this very factory. Well, the sausages were sent home; the American gentleman ordered one of them to be cut. A slight obstruction opposed the passage of the knife. It was a small lump of something wrapped up pretty tight. The American gentleman with his own fingers picked up the small lump o' something from the very centre of the sausage. It was a piece of paper—he unrolled it. Brothers and sisters, it was nothing more than a fragment of a Tract issued by the Patent-Gospellers; and headed—"*A Thrust at Pagan Rome!* Brothers and sisters, each one of that lot of sausages on being opened, contained one or more of such fragments! Brothers and sisters, those ten men of the crew, those twenty passengers, that captain, and that little boy, all had Patent-Gospel tracts in their pockets when they were missed! Brothers and sisters, I will leave you to draw your own conclusions!"

The Rev. Syllaybub Scissors sate down amid a perfect hurricane of applause. What the Free Believers applauded it was difficult to tell. Whether it was the Pope of Rome, or the crew, or the passengers, or the little boy, or the sausage manufactory, or whether it was the American Gentleman, so mysteriously held in view, to this day remains a mystery.

"Missionaries, stand forth!" cried the Reverend F. A. T. Pyne, rising statelily behind his bath-tub.

Three young men, with long hair, very tow-like in hue, stuck behind their ears, and white cravats around their necks, stepped slowly forward, and took their place in front of the pulpit, crossing their hands very meekly on their breast, and casting their eyes, upon a particular nail in the floor, with a sanctity of look, that was quite edifying, even to an unconverted man.

"Abel Stump, Joshua Hoe, Benijah Baker, are you willing to go abroad to the Pope of Rome, as Missionaries sent by the Universal American Patent-Gospel Association—" exclaimed Brother Pyne, in a loud voice with his fist raised in the air, in a gesture of indignant menace.

"We *air*—" responded three faint and sickly voices.

"Do you understand your calling?" continued Brother Pyne in his most Boanergian voice—"You are to allow the Pagan no peace! You are to give him Tracts as he comes from mass, you are to present him with a fresh Bible every Sabbath; you are to hail him in the street, and tell him that in America, the Patent-Gospellers are raising a Buffalo to fight his Bull! Are you willing to defy the Inquisition in such a cause. Are you willing to defy death—are you willing to be made up in sausages, in such a cause? Are you, Brothers, I say?"

"We *air!*" responded the three faint and sickly voices.

"Here is a sight for the whole world to see!" continued the Reverend F. A. T. Pyne, his eyes dilating, while his crimson face, looked like the full moon seen through a distempered mist—"Here, standing upon the Rock of Freedom we tell the Pope of Rome, that his schemes are defeated, that his Babylon has fallen! Ha, ha! We laugh at the Pope of Rome! We tell him in tones of indignant thunder, that his grand plan of buying up the state of Missouri, in order to erect a Papal Kingdom on American soil, and let his Bulls loose, to run wild on American prairies, has fell through—been nullified—and trampled upon with the ponderous foot of the Universal Patent-Gospel Association! He would build a Vatican on the Banks of the Mississippi, would he? He'd have his Propaganda, in the State House would he? Yes, yes, he would have his College of Cardinals in Faneuil Hall, would he? He would, but he *can't!* We snap our fingers at him! Ha, ha! Let him jump Jim Crow in his Vatican at Rome if he likes, but he musn't try to build another St. Peter's on our Soil! No, no, no! Down with the Pope say I—down with the Pope say all! We'll fight his Bulls with spiritual weapons, with the Patent-Gospel bowie knife! We'll crowd our pulpits with lecturers—no matter who they are, or what they are, or whence they come from! From the prison—we welcome them! From the jail, or the galleys, or even from the rope of the gibbet—still, still, we welcome them! Are they not brothers? Co-workers with us? Let them but affirm that they once were Priests of Rome, let them but declare they are converted

Jesuits, and with all our hearts, we welcome them! But they must decry Rome! Down with Rome, down with the Pope—UP with the Bible!

"They must rake up from the ashes of the past, all the firebrands ever lighted in the flames of Hell! All the old books, which show up the atrocities of Rome, must be republished—their contents shouted from the street-corners, printed on our Patent-Gospel Press, thundered from our Pulpits—down with the Pope of Rome!

"Awake St. Bartholomew, with your blood and ashes and flame—we want you here! Awake bones of the martyrs; awake sword of the Solemn League and Covenant! Down with the Pope of Rome!

"Stir yourselves up in the good work, brothers and sisters! Let not your efforts slack! Whenever you find a deluded follower of the Pope—teach him, or her, the error of their ways! If he is a porter in your employ, or a drayman, or a common laborer—discharge him, I say, wash your hands of him, bid him *go forth!* If she is a seamstres, or a governess, or a hired girl, especially an Irish Pagan hired girl—turn her from your doors!

"Thus let Pagan Rome be met at the threshold! Awake Guy Faux, with your lanthern and faggots, awake Inquisition with your tortures, with your fiery furnace, into whose flames you cast those good Protestants, Shadrack, Meshack and Abed-Nego—awake we want you here! You must help to witness against Pagan Rome!

"Down with the Pope and his Bulls! Down with St. Peter's and the Vatican! Down with the Priests, and the Monks and the Nuns, down with the Sisters of Charity and the Orphans under their care—down with them all! Up with the Patent-Gospellers, up with the good old doctrine which John Calvin preached to Servetus from the window of his chamber, looking out into the open square of Geneva—where that same Servetus, a rank infidel, was burning—up with the good old doctrine, which proclaims fire and brimstone, the cardinal points of the belief of the good Savior Jesus! Down with the Pope—up with fire and brimstone; up with toleration; UP *with the Bible!*"

How the applause of the Free Believers and True Repenters, rose up to the ceiling like the voice of some huge monster! Thunder was mere silence in comparison! How the old ladies rose from their seats in extacy, how the old gentlemen punished the hard floor with their thick-soled boots! How meekly the three Missionaries resumed their seats, how warmly the brethren, crowding round them, crushed their fingers with very joy, and almost dragged their arms from the sockets, with intense religious feeling! But when the Reverend Pyne, resuming his seat, took from his coat pocket a large white handkerchief, and wiped the perspiration from his red round face, ah me, that was the time for the applause! A Quaker City Theatre, with Fanny Ellsler on the stage, and all the grey-haired men in the pit, never raised such a round of applause as that! Death to the old Pagan, death to the Pope of Rome! Up with fire and brimstone, up with toleration, up with the Bible!

When the excitement was somewhat subdued, a faint voice was heard echoing from a far corner of the Lecture Room, and the light of the rusty chandelier fell upon the grey hairs of an old man who trembled nervously as he spoke.

He stated, in feeble tones, that he was an American citizen; that his father had fought in the Revolution. At Monmouth, Trenton, Germantown and Brandywine, he had fought under the banner of George Washington. The old man's voice trembled as he spoke this name; and he paused for a moment to collect his thoughts.

"That's the stuff!" cried the Reverend F. A. T. Pyne—"A soldier under Washington—let us hear him!"

"Somethin' against that tarnel Pagan, no doubt!" cried an old woman, quite joyously.

"Now let the Wattykin look to itself!" murmured brother Augustus Billygoat.

"An incident for my Patent-Gospel Expositor!" meekly suggested the Rev. Syllabub Scissors.

"My father fought under Washington—" continued the old man, speaking from that distant corner of the room, in trembling tones—"And though but a mere boy, at that time, I fought with him! He died in my arms on the battle-field; his last words were, God take my soul and bless brave Washington! Therefore, brethren, I humbly think, that I have some small claims to the title of an American: my life does not, I believe, contradict the additional claim, which I make to the title of Protestant Christian!

"My friends, I ask your attention to a passing thought, which struck me while our Reverend Brother was enchaining you all with his eloquence. Is there no need of Missionaries for other purposes than the overthrowing of Pagan Rome? Do we not want Missionaries in this our good city?

"Are there no holes of vice, to be illumined by the light of God's own Gospel? Are there no poor, no sick, no needy? Would not a true physician first turn his knife to those cankering sores which gather near the heart of the patient, ere he proceeded to bind up wounds or cut off limbs? Are there no hideous moral sores to be examined and healed by the Missionary of Jesus in this our moral heart of Philadelphia, ere we cut off the limb of Pagan Rome, or bind up the wounds of idolatrous Hindoostan?

"Might not the Missionary of Jesus find room for much well-doing in our Courts, our Churches, our Streets, our Homes? Might he not stand upon the grave of old Stephen Girard (leaving the Pagan of Rome to his errors for a little while) and point to Girard College—that unfinished Monument of a foul wrong, done to ten thousand orphans—and, as he pointed, might he not call upon the God of the fatherless to protect those same orphans, who were scattered abroad through the world, in order that a Corporation might feast and riot upon old Stephen's money?

"Down with Pagan Rome by all means, but down with the Paganism of Protestant Philadelphia!

"And oh, friends, might not the true Missionary of the cross enter the thickly-carpeted chambers of some of our Reverend Pastors, and tell them, as God will tell them one day, that they are a blot upon the name of Jesus! That the seduction of female innocence is not a light crime to rest upon the souls of those who administer God's Sacrament!

"That foul-mouthed temperance in public—wine-drinking in private—the assailment of private character in the pulpit—the destruction of some poor girl's honor in the parlor—that bitter controversy—violent appeals to excited mobs, combined with insidious endeavors to create those very mobs—that these are not the characteristics of God's own Ministers, but rather the fuel with which the Devil will kindle a hell for their souls!"

They silenced the old man with a hurricane of groans.

"A Catholic!" shouted Brother Pyne—"A pagan—A Roman! Hand him over to the police!"

"To think of his impudence!" screamed an old woman—"To come here an' try to p'ison our minds! Papist!"

The old man felt himself seized by the arms, and hands and coat-tail, all at once. Brother Billygoat forced his hat over his eyes; Brother Syllabub Scissors helped to lead him out. The three Missionaries merely groaned. To the door, down stairs, into the street—old man, soldier of Washington, son of a soldier, this is your share of Patent-Gospel charity! Into the street, and into the dark with him and his lies! He belongs to Pagan Rome!

After the old man was dismissed, the Free Believers composed their minds in a hymn of pious import; being three lines to the Pope and one to the Devil, on the average, through ten long stanzas; and this finished, Brother Pyne poured forth his soul in prayer!

Prayer! Ho, Ho! Was that a fiend's laugh as he heard the mockery of that prayer ascend in tones of blasphemy to the very throne of God?

Prayer! Hurrah—hurrah! Was that the yell of all the devils gathered in the shades of death, as they heard the name of Jesus profaned, and mocked, and polluted by the hot breathings of yon round-faced hypocrite? Prayer! Is this long-drawn Anathema Maranatha, made up of curses, falsehoods and impious vulgarities, is this prayer?

Is the whispering of the young mother, over her first-born, prayer? Is the trembling supplication of the father, by the bedside of his dying daughter, uttered in husky tones with eyes blinded by tears, is this agony of a breaking heart, prayer? Are the holiest feelings of the heart, rising up from the soul to its God, in the silence of night, when earth sleeps while heaven watches its slumbers, are these warm uprisings of man's better nature, prayer? Are all these prayer, and are the whining blasphemies of yonder smooth-tongued Pander to the lust of the Bigot, are these loathsome falsehoods, linked together by a chain of Scripture phrases, are these prayer?

If this is prayer, then let us shut the Bible and cry with the madman-atheist of France—'There is no God—Death is an eternal sleep!' If this be prayer, then let us blaspheme, curse, swear, or sell our souls for a Preacher's hire—any thing but pray!

The Free Believers dispersed as soon as the howl of Brother Pyne was over. How the sisters and the brothers thronged around the Reverend Brother as, with his cloak wrapped around his portly form, he hastened from the room! What pressing of hands, what picking at his cloak, what glancing in his face! Old and young, fair and foul, red lips and grey hairs, all joined to do the Parson honor! How was his cold; had the Lord been good to him lately; had he heard from that poor, wretched, runaway daughter; was he blessed in prayer; and did he not hurt himself by studying so late at night!

Down stairs, followed by his loving congregation, Brother Pyne pursued his way, Brother Billygoat clinging to his arm, while Brother Scissors, with the three Missionaries, hung closely at his heels. The alley was reached, and in a few moments the saintly quadruple, stood in the bye-street, where a carriage waited for Brother Pyne, with a stout lusty coachman on the box, wrapped up in an unknown number of overcoats, with a broad hat flapping its broken rim over his eyes.

"Good night, sisters, good night brothers!" said Brother Pyne, in a tone of spermaceti smoothness—"Good night, my children, good night!"

The door closed, and the carriage drove off.

"He goes to his night-long studies, after the Truth!" cried Brother Scissors, wiping his nose with the cuff of his sleeve—"Let Pagan Rome look out!"

"Dear heart!" echoed an old lady—"And so he studies all night, does he! A bringin' himself to the grave with his zeal!"

"The saints and martyrs are nothing compared to Brother Pyne!" meekly exclaimed Brother Billygoat, expectorating violently on an old lady's bonnet—"Let Pagan-Rome look out for its Wattykin; that's all!"

Meanwhile the carriage, containing the Foe of Pagan Rome, dashed down the street like mad, the coachman lashing the horses into perfect fury, while a poor ragged loafer, gliding from the side walk, crept up behind the vehicle, and assumed a quiet seat all to himself, without saying a word to the holy preacher within, or the white-coated driver in front.

At the corner of a wide street, the coachman held up for a single moment. He tapped the window of the carriage with the handle of his whip.

"Vich vay?" he shouted in a deep, hoarse voice.

Down went the carriage window, and the red round face of Parson Pyne was thrust out into the full glare of the gas-lamp on the corner.

"Down town, of course, Simon—I've got to visit the sick you know—"

"In vich quarter?"

"Monk-Hall!" whispered the preacher, and then the coachman cracked his whip, the carriage window went up, and the carriage rolled off, while the poor loafer, sitting behind, chuckled merrily to himself, and whistled for very glee!

" 'My daddy was a scavenger, and my mammy sold rags!' Ha, ha, ha! Hurrah! Down with the Pope and the Wattykin! Up with the Patent-Gospel, up with Monk-Hall! Let Pagan Rome look out for itself—hurrah!"

CHAPTER FOURTH

STRANGE VISITORS IN MONK-HALL

The beams of a small lamp of rusty iron, standing on the table near the fire, gave a faint and dusky light to the Doorkeeper's den. Devil-Bug was seated beside the table, with his elbows resting on its rough oaken surface, while his hands grasped his tawny cheeks, the long finger nails sinking into the flesh like the talons of an eagle, and spotting his face with drops of blood. His teeth were fast clenched, but his lips, hung apart, shrivelled with a fixed and grotesque grin; like the smile of a fiend, frozen into marble. His thick, matted hair hung over his protuberant brow, and his solitary eye, dilated and enlarged to twice its usual size, glared steadily forward, with one fixed and unvarying gaze. The light streamed full in his face, revealing each hideous feature in stern and immovable distinctness, while the outlines of his deformed body, and the details of the den, were wrapt in a twilight shadow. In the recess on one side of the fire, sate the negro Musquito, his arms crossed, and his head sunken on his breast, while on the opposite side of the fire, his companion, Glow-worm, rested in the same attitude, and slumbered like some overgrown animal who has been gorged with food. Their common costume—the red flannel shirt and corduroy trowsers—dimly disclosed in the light seemed to increase the outlines of their herculean frames, while it gave them a wild and ruffian-like appearance.

Alone in his den, with his attendant satellites slumbering on either side, Devil-Bug sat silent, as though he was but an uncouth effigy of stone, while his fingers, digging their talon-like nails slowly in the flesh of his cheeks, gave some indications of the terrible agony which was eating through his soul. He had sate thus silent and motionless for the space of an hour, when the small door, leading into the hall of the mansion, was softly opened, and our friend Brick-Top, clad in his array of rags, came treading stealthily into the Doorkeeper's den.

He started at the sight of Devil-Bug, but in a moment advanced, and laid his hand upon the Doorkeeper's shoulder.

"You're a purty old cove, aint ye, now? To run off, and leave a feller in the lurch! The old 'ooman's dead body up stairs and the poleese below! Pack me up in a *see*-gar box, somebody, and bury me in a common for a werry infant, arter that!"

"Ha! What brings you here?" cried Devil-Bug, starting from his reverie—"Where did you leave the Jew? And the chest o' gold—hey, hey?"

"What brings me here? Business o' course! You see it aint pleasant to have the poleese inquirin' arter yer health, 'specially when an old woman's been knocked in the head, by some 'indewidooals at present unknown.' So I came to the Pawnbroker's—went down stairs and along the vault, and then up stairs again—you know the way. Here I am, and there you are, and we're both a pair o' beauties for Cherry Hill! Brick-Top and Devil-Bug—hurray!"

"Where did you leave the Jew?" said Devil-Bug with a fierce scowl as he struck his fist against the table—"And the chest o' gold—hey, hey?"

"Young man does yer mother know yer out? Venever ye meet a

werry green young genelman, as doesn't know what huckleberries is compared with persimmins, then axe him sich a question! I don't know nothin' 'bout the Jew, no more nor yesself!"

"S-h-ew!" whispered Devil-Bug with a sudden start as he motioned his companion to be silent—"S-h-ew! Don't ye see that feller a layin' on the floor with his jaw bruk and his tongue out?"

"Cussed if I do!"

"Nor the old woman, with the brains oozeing out from the holler skull?"

"Not the least circumstance!"

"S-h-ew! Don't ye hear that feller groan? Look how he wriggles there—a-twistin' and twistin' like a snake, and his tongue rollin' out all the while! And the old woman—don't ye see her? I tell you man, she's there—there—right between us on the floor; her holler skull layin' at my werry feet, and her long grey hair, dabbin' in her blood! Don't see her indeed! He! He!" and he smiled ghastily—"Why man, I tell ye, I can count the blood-drops as they fall—patter—patter—from the holler skull to the floor!"

And the solitary eye of Devil-Bug glared wildly from the shadow of his brow, while the sweat, cold and clammy, stood out on his forehead and trickled down his swarthy face.

"And not to git the chest o' doubloons arter all!" Kin ye read feller, I say kin ye read?" he exclaimed in a fierce tone, as he laid his hand on Brick-Top's arm—"Or are ye a stupid jackass as don't know nothin'?"

"Shut me up in a coal mine all my life, and make me chaw dirt for a livin'! Kin I read? I wish my daddy could hear you say that! He'd show my school bills, old chap, with a wengeance to ye!"

"Here's a package o' papers, which I picked up on the stairs o' th' widow's house. Sit down on t'other side o' th' table and read 'em to me!"

Brick-Top sate down on one side of the table, while Devil-Bug resumed his seat opposite.

"Papers!" cried Brick-Top pulling his lank red hair down over his brows—"Egad!" he muttered to himself—"The very packet entrusted to me by Livingstone this morning! The seal broken, too!"

"Read, will ye? And mind yer eye feller! If I ketch you playin' the fool with me, and readin' any stuff what isn't there, I'll make no bones of hurtin' your body so no doctors wont buy ye arter yer a corpse!"

"Talk that way to the Wolunteers, will ye? Howsomever, here goes into the doc-y-ments—"

In a low toned voice, still marked by his vagabond accent, Brick-Top began to read the contents of the package.

At first Devil-Bug leaned over the table with a look of the deepest interest, but soon the details of the package seemed to tire him, and he leaned listlessly to one side, with his eye fixed vacantly upon the ceiling. Brick-Top read on. A name attracted Devil-Bugs attention, and then a date, and an incident. He leaned over the table, his solitary eye blazing with the most intense interest.

"Look here, youssir—you aint a-foolin' me are ye? *Ellen*—did ye say!"

"The werry same," replied Brick-Top burying his face in the unrolled package. His attention also seemed rivetted to the paper and its contents, for his glittering and snake-like eye grew more brilliant in its glance, while the outlines of his countenance became fixed and compressed. Brick-Top pulled his red hair farther over his brow, until it almost concealed his eyes, and then resumed the reading of the paper.

Devil-Bug listened with every power of his soul, enchained by an overwhelming interest. His solitary eye, dilated and flashed with excitement, and the nails of his talon-like fingers were thrust into his tawny cheeks with a movement of involuntary agitation.

"*Christmas Eve?*" he echoed, repeating the words of the Manuscript as they fell from the lips of the reader—"*Christmas Eve, Eighteen hundred and twenty four?* Hallo, youssir? Is them the words?"

"The werry same!" replied Brick-Top raising the paper before his face—"Left her mother's house on that date—"

"Read on will ye? Don't ye see how I'm a quiverin'? I want to know the rest—read on!"

Brick-Top again turned his attention to the Manuscript. Devil-Bug was utterly absorbed in its details. He held his very breath, as he drank in each word, and date and incident.

"*The second child died, did it?*" he shrieked, starting wildly from his seat—"Now look here feller, if you're got the feelin's of a common human bein' don't make a fool o' me! Read it agin—be sure that it's the second child; jist be sure o' that!"

"The second child—born Christmas Eve, Eighteen hundred and twenty-four—" exclaimed Brick-Top reading from the Manuscript, while a slight tremor was observable in his voice.

"That's the date, too, that's the date!" cried Devil-Bug in a voice of the deepest agitation—"Look here feller, d'ye see that arm? The night arter she left this house, I got a sailor-chap to print this here with Injin ink."

And as he spoke, Devil-Bug bared his right arm, and thrust it forward into the full glare of the light. Brick-Top gazed upon it in surprise. On its brawny skin, in rough characters, was punctured, this brief name and date—"CHRISTMAS EVE—1825—ELLEN."

"And so ye know'd her did ye?" exclaimed Brick-Top, gazing in Devil-Bug's face with a piercing glance, while his lip trembled with some unknown emotion—"Werry singular that!"

"Know-'d her?" responded Devil-Bug in a tone of sudden anger—"Don't axe no questions feller, but read on!"

Brick-Top again resumed the Manuscript. A name, once more started Devil-Bug from his feet.

"Dick Baltzar?" he echoed—"Sure that's the name?"

"The werry same. Here it is—"*The second child, was buried by a man named Dick Baltzar, who with his wife, resided in the widow's house. The first child—*" howsomever let me read on!"

The Manuscript drew near its close. His brows woven in frown, his teeth clenched, his hands clutching his cheeks with a convulsive grasp, Devil-Bug listened to the closing words with breathless interest.

"The whole of his fortune?" echoed Devil-Bug repeating the words of the Manuscript—"Luke Harvey entrusted with the commission? Hey, hey? Is that it?"

Brick-Top nodded, but said nothing. Well was it for him, that Devil-Bug occupied with his own strange thoughts, had no eye for his companion's demeanor. A tear stole from Brick-Top's eyelid and rolled down his freckled face. His hand trembled as he grasped the Manuscript, and his lip quivered with a tremulous motion.

"Luke Harvey!" muttered Devil-Bug—"He's a wild fellow, and one of the devil's disciples who hold their meetings in this house! A purty chap to have sich a matter in his charge! He'll be here sometime to night, and I'll have a talk with him! Gi'me that paper—will ye?"

"I say, old feller, come now and uncork this mystery! Let a body know all about it—that's a conwivial old devil!"

Devil-Bug turned toward him with a lowering brow, but as he turned a knock was heard at the front door.

"Dig off—*feller!*" said Devil-Bug, with great emphasis—"'Taint for sich as you to know what quality comes to this house! Dig, I say!"

Brick-Top lounged lazily toward the doorway of the mansion-hall, while Devil-Bug, unbarring the front door, gazed through the crevices of the green blinds upon the form of the new-comer.

"Who's there?"

"Monk Baltzar—" answered an assumed and artificial voice.

"What had you for dinner to-day?" asked Devil-Bug, repeating the first part of the countersign of Monk-Hall.

"Fire and Brimstone!" answered the voice.

"Come in!" said Devil-Bug—"All right! The gal's up stairs in the room—I'll be up d'rectly!"

And as he spoke the Reverend Parson Pyne strode silently across the floor of the den, and with his face muffled in the folds of his cloak, passed through the doorway, and along the hall, and up the stairs; and in a moment disappeared into one of the rooms on the right side of the massive staircase, on the second floor of the mansion. As he disappeared, a tall figure rose upward from the darkness, which hung round the bannisters of the staircase near the floor.

"Parson, I think I've tracked you to some purpose!" said a deep-toned voice—"The girl *your* daughter and you in Monk-Hall! I'll drop Brick-Top for a little while and assume Luke Harvey again, in order to be ready for all accidents! My game is a desperate one, but I'll play it with a cool head and firm hand!"

With these words he disappeared into the door of Luke Harvey's room; and in a moment the sound of the key, turning in the lock, echoed faintly round the hall.

Meanwhile Devil-Bug, standing near the table, in the centre of his den, with his arms crossed over his breast and his right hand grasping Livingstone's mysterious packet, seemed utterly absorbed in the contemplation of the disclosures which it had revealed.

The sound of voices, mingling confusedly together, came echoing suddenly from the stairway leading to the Banquet-Room of Monk-Hall. And then a rude burst of laughter, resounded through the hall, mingled with the hurried tramp of footsteps.

"Ha, ha, ha! And so you drugged the brother with opium!" exclaimed a voice familiar to the reader—"That was an odd mistake of mine, Gus, about the fellow's name!"

"To think Silly should introduce him to you by the name of Byrnewood!" cried another voice—"And then—ha, ha, ha!—the Bridal scene! Oh Lord, that was too good, wasn't it, Gus?"

"Very good, no doubt, very good, gentlemen—" exclaimed a third voice—"But there are some jokes which cost a mint of money. I rather think suspect that this amusing adventure is one of the costly class!"

Ere the words had ceased to echo in the air, Lorrimer, followed by Petriken and Mutchins, lounged into the Doorkeeper's den. Their faces was slightly flushed by the kisses of that long-necked giant, the champagne bottle, and their entrance into Devil-Bug's private parlor, was heralded by clouds of smoke issuing from the segars which the trio carried between their lips.

"Well, boys—" cried Petriken, moving toward the door—"Let's out and have a night of it! My Western Hem. was put to press to day, and so I'm free for a fortnight! D'ye see my last Hem., Mutchins?"

"Never, except on one occasion, after a long night's carouse, when my temples were bursting with the effects of the champagne. I wanted to sleep and couldn't for the life of me. However, happening to pick up a copy of the Western Hem. with 'Autumn, a Homologue: by S. J. Petriken,' I fell into a gentle doze after the first twenty lines, and slept for thirty-eight hours, as I'm a living sinner! Is your Mag. printed near a laud'num factory, Silly?"

"Pshaw! You ought to see the last number! Two engravings, one tragic, one comic! Tragic—the death o' Cock Robin, with an illustrative piece o' poetry, by my friend Deacon Shewbrush! Comic—Nigger church on fire, with the Sheriff and Court looking on, to see that it is done in an effective manner.* Good number, that!"

"Come on, fellows!" exclaimed Lorrimer, who had been gazing quietly at Devil-Bug, as he stood unconscious of their presence—"Let us out, and make a night of it!"

As he spoke, a hand was laid upon his shoulder, and Long-haired Bess stood before him, her jet-black tresses hanging dishevelled along her white neck, while the peculiar brilliancy of her eyes, with the dark circle of discolored flesh beneath each eye, gave indications of deep and powerful agitation.

"Well, Bessie, what's the matter now? How is the girl, that is to say, how is Mary?"

"She has lain unconscious all day long, until within a few minutes past"—answered Bess, in a low toned voice—"She has now recovered her reason. She does nothing but wring her hands as she paces up and down the room; nothing but wring her hands and shriek your name. Lorrimer, you had better see this girl before you leave the house—"

"Why the fact is, Bessie, I don't see the necessity of the thing"—answered Lorrimer, moving towards the door—"Quiet her, Bessie, quiet her! I will see her to-morrow!"

"Have you a man's heart within your bosom?" said Bess, with a flashing glance of her dark eyes—"Can you refuse this request? Do what ye will with Byrnewood, but for the sake of your own self-regard, do not refuse this request! She is dishonored, Lorrimer, but who was the

* See the charge of a certain Judge, in which he instructs the Grand Jury to present a certain Hall as a nuisance, because it was threatened by a mob, and, therefore, it endangered the surrounding property. It was owned and used by Negroes for benevolent purposes. This latter fact furnishes sufficient apology for any act of outrage in a city where Pennsylvania Hall was burnt by the whole population, because the object for which it was built happened to be unpopular.

cause of her dishonor? Do not refuse to look upon the ruin which has followed your crime!"

"Not to-night, Bessie, not to-night—" cried Lorrimer, moving toward the door—"Any time but to-night; as for Byrnewood—"

"That 'ere patient is in the hands of the Doctor—" exclaimed Devil-Bug, advancing. "I give him a leetle opium to begin with; arter awhile I'll *per*-scribe somethin' more coolin'—a leetle hard steel for instance. Vonders how that 'ill vork?"

As he spoke, Lorrimer and his companions disappeared through the front door, with a loud burst of laughter.

"He is gone!" cried Bess, folding her arms across her bosom—"God of Heaven! The shriek of that ruined girl is ever in my ears, its accents of despair freezing my soul with a horror I never felt before! And the brother—"

"I tell ye, Bessie, I'll tend to him!" cried Devil-Bug, with his hideous grin—"Go up stairs an' tend to the female wictim, my dear, go along my duck. I think I hear your mammy callin' for you—"

Bess looked at him with a glance of scorn, and then her deep black eyes flashed with an expression whose awful meaning thrilled him to the very soul.

"Don't you see the corse at your side?" she shrieked, as she stood in the doorway—"Ha! Ha! Ha! There is evil in store for you, Devil-Bug, evil, I say, and doom and death! Hark! hark! Don't you hear *him*—" and she pointed to the floor—"Hark how he groans!"

And she was gone. Her wild shriek rang like a death-knell in Devil-Bug's ears.

"That gal is a born devil—" he said, in a whisper, as he wiped the cold sweat from his forehead—"Ha! There's the feller agin—his jaw broke, and his tongue lollin' out! Ha! And the old woman too; her holler skull droppin' blood on the floor! But I'll not be troubled this way much longer—" a ghastly smile crossed visage—"It seems to me I've got to wade through blood up to my neck! I'm only ancle-deep jist now—arter a while I'll swim in blood, I'll float, I tell ye I'll float. As to that Byrnewood———"

There was a knock at the door. Musquito, rising from his slumber, slowly opened the inner door and demanded the watchword of the new-comer. It was given in a faint voice, and in a moment the stranger entered the den. He was a young man with a figure somewhat below the middle heighth, whose elegance of shape and beauty of proportion, was disclosed to every advantage, as his sweeping black cloak fell carelessly back on his shoulders, its collar of fur, almost concealed by the thick ringlets of jet-black hair, which swept along the fair face of the stranger. It was, indeed, a fair face, almost effeminate in its regularity of feature, while its extreme pallor gave additional effect to the brilliancy of two large black eyes, whose glance was full of fire and expression. A small velvet cap placed jauntily on the centre of his head, amid a profusion of black curls which fell waving over his fair brow, as well as along his face and down to his neck, gave an air of saucy daring to the stranger, which won Devil-Bug's good opinion for him at first sight. His form, remarkable for its effeminate beauty of shape, was enveloped in a close-fitting black frockcoat, buttoned tightly over the breast, with its dark hue relieved by a large white shirt collar that fell aside from the fair throat of the stranger.

"Well, young slim-waist, who are ye, and what d'ye want here?" said Devil-Bug, more from his habitual taste for sarcasm than from any positive dislike to the stranger—"You're not one of the Monks, I perceive. How did ye git hold o' th' watchword?"

"Your name is Abijah K. Jones?" said the stranger, in a tone which was evidently assumed.

"'Taint that no more!" cried the Doorkeeper, with a look of mocking glee—"Devil-Bug for ever! While there's strength in these arms to strike or to kill, call me Devil-Bug and I'm your man!"

The stranger quietly seated himself beside the table, and gathering the cloak around his slender form, carelessly tossed his dark ringlets over his brow and looked in the face of Devil-Bug with a long and penetrating glance.

"Portr'it painter, I s'pose?" said Devil-Bug, with a grin—"Wants to put my phizzog in the pictur' winders."

"You know a man named Luke Harvey—" said the stranger in a deep voice widely different from the careless tone, which he had assumed at first.

"Well, I do, boss. But fust of all, who are *you!* How did ye git hold o' that watchword?"

"No matter about my name—" answered the stranger—"The watchword of Monk-Hall, was given to me by one of the Monks. To the point—You know a man named Luke Harvey. He will be in this house, by three o'clock to morrow morning. I hate him, and he must die!"

"Ha, ha, ha! You are a *han'some* copy o' Devil-Bug! Ha, ha! How your eyes sparkle, how your teeth grit agin one another! 'You hate him and he must die!' Quite short—ha, ha, ha!"

"Kill him, for me, kill him by the pistol or the knife, by fire or by the sword, any way you like, kill him this night, and I'll make a rich man of you! There is gold for you, as an earnest of your future reward."

"Right fat purse, this! How your chest swells underneath that cloak, and your eyes; one could light a *see*-gar at 'em!"

"This Luke Harvey carries a ring on the third finger of his left hand.

Its shape is peculiar, and it bears a name, engraven on the inner side. This ring was given him by his ladye-love long, long ago: he values it, as his life, and will not part with it save with his life. I will wait in a secret chamber of this house until daybreak. Bring me this ring, before the dawn of day, and I will reward you, with gold sufficient to buy you ten thousand pardons, from the hand of justice—"

"Or a seat in Congress, or a place on the Bench, among them big chaps in court! I vonders how that 'ud vork? Devil-Bug in Congress, makin' laws? Or Judge Devil-Bug—ho! ho! ho! on the bench a-sentencin' little boys to Cherry Hill for stealin' nose-wipers!"

"Do you consent?" said the stranger, gathering his cloak more closely around his form—"Is it a bargain?"

His eyes, so dark in their hue and piercing in their gaze, grew alive with a clear and flashing light, that spoke the settled resolve of a fearless soul. A deep flush mantled over his face, and his lips were firmly compressed, while, beneath the thick curls which fell over his forehead, you might discover the settled frown which darkened his brows, so regular and arching in their outline. His breath came thick and gaspingly, and you might discern the throbbings which agitated his chest, through the heavy folds of his cloak.

"Consent? Ha, ha! S'pose I should pocket this 'ere money and then laugh in your face?"

"You would lose the reward which is in store for you—" drily responded the stranger.

"That reward is about your slim-waisted body? S'pose I take it from you, and turn you from my doors with a flea in yer ears?"

"You dare not—" said the stranger, throwing his cloak back on his shoulders, and displaying a pistol in either hand—"One word of insolence, one sign of violence, and you die!"

"Pluck, good pluck! Ha, ha, ha!" laughed Devil-Bug—"Good pluck for a slim waist, good pluck for a heaving bosom, ha, ha, ha! Stranger, push aside your curls, will ye? What 'ill ye bet I can't tell your name?"

"My name!" cried the stranger, with a sudden start, as he hurriedly gathered the folds of his cloak around his handsome form. "My name—What know you of my name?"

"Your name is—" Devil-Bug began, in a slow and deliberate voice. He ended the sentence by a quick whisper which he hissed in the stranger's ears, as he leaned over the table, with his head thrown forward until it well-nigh touched the face of the listener.

But we must depict a scene which occurred one hour before this incident of our Revelations.

CHAPTER FIFTH

DORA AND FITZ-COWLES

We open this scene with a picture.—Kneeling on the carpet of a princely chamber, a man of some thirty years and more supports the insensible form of a lovely woman in his arms. The dim light of a massive chandelier illumines the scene. The dark-hued face of the man, marked by massive features, his stiff black hair descending to his neck in heavy curls, his well-proportioned form clad in a black frockcoat, all combined furnish an effective contrast to the careless loveliness of the woman, her fair-hued face turned upward to the light, her long and glossy hair, falling in tresses of jet along her shoulders white as snow, while a night-gown of azure silk, gathering round her form, so swelling, so lithe and so voluptuous in its every outline, in negligent folds falls gently aside from her neck, and reveals a glimpse of her bosom, slowly heaving into view.

A dark and ill-omened smile rests upon the lip of the man, as he surveys the beauty of the insensible woman, while a gentle flush, tinting her cheeks, and warming over her bosom, betrays her return to consciousness. The minor details of the scene, tell the story of the picture. In her extended hand, she grasps a letter, with a convulsive grasp like that of death. His hat and cane and gloves, flung carelessly on the carpet, his cloak thrown over a chair, and the door of the chamber, hanging wide open, all tell the story of his sudden entrance and his surprise. The back ground of the scene is supplied by the furniture and the crimson-hangings of the chamber, varied by pictures in massive frames, and mellowed into gentle twilight by the dim beams of the chandelier. Altogether, the picture is an effective one, worthy the genius of an artist who has a soul to feel, and a hand to execute; like Darley, for instance, whose pencil is a mine of unwrought gold.

"A lovely woman, by Jove!—" muttered Fitz-Cowles—"And a deep one! Passions like a volcano, and a soul fearless as the fiend himself! I must take care that she does not out-devil me!"

"Is *he* gone?" Dora exclaimed in a whisper, as she slowly unclosed her eyes—"Ha! Fitz-Cowles! Then you know, all?" and half-rising from her prostrate position she gazed in his face, with a look of the most intense anxiety.

"*All*—Dora?" echoed Fitz-Cowles with a look of vacant surprise—"What mean you?"

As he spoke, he gently assisted her to rise from the floor.

"Know you this letter?" she exclaimed, in a whisper, as she threw herself in the rocking-chair, and placed the letter in his hands.

"Your letter to me!" cried Fitz-Cowles, with a start of surprise—"I lost it from my pocket-book, sometime yesterday. How fortunate for us both that you found it!"

"Luke Harvey found it!" exclaimed Dora, in a slow and deliberate tone, as she leaned over the table—"And Luke Harvey holds us in his power! A single word from his lips, and our secret is known to Livingstone—"

"Luke Harvey!" exclaimed Fitz-Cowles, recovering from the stunning shock of surprise which had thrilled his very soul, as Dora made the momentous disclosure—"And he was here and threatened you, Dora?"

"Not only threatened me, but assailed me with deliberate and galling insult. It is but five minutes since he left the room. We stand upon the edge of an awful precipice, Algernon; already it crumbles beneath our feet! A word from Luke, and our plans are overshadowed by utter ruin—"

"He visits Monk-Hall to-night!" exclaimed Fitz-Cowles, with his finger to his lip, in an absent tone—"Visits Monk-Hall with our secret in his possession. A single blow, and he were silent forever!"

"That blow must be stricken!" exclaimed Dora, and a deadly light flashed from her dark eyes as she spoke. "Luke once silenced, we are safe! To-morrow morning, Livingstone and myself leave town for Hawkwood. To-morrow evening, Livingstone will have to return to town on business, and after he has set out on his return, you will arrive at Hawkwood in the secrecy of night. We can then arrange matters for our flight or otherwise—"

"My plan is a plain and a clear one. After Livingstone has set out on his return to the Quaker City, I will arrive at Hawkwood, and then, mounted on fleet steeds, with suitable disguises, we will leave the country mansion together; and riding all night overtake the New York cars near Burlington. It is then but half a day's journey to New York; and the steamer sails in the beginning of next week. This is a straightforward plan, Dora, and we would both do well to adopt it—"

"I have other plans which may essentially alter our arrangements—" said Dora, in a deep and meaning whisper, with that same deadly glance of her eyes—"However, Algernon, do not fail to meet me at Hawkwood to-morrow night. But what folly is this! While we lay plans for our flight, Luke Harvey is telling Livingstone the story of his wife's guilt and his dishonor!"

"This Harvey seems to hate you, Dora—" began Fitz-Cowles,

aloud, but he finished the sentence by a muttered whisper—"By Jove! He is on my track also! I learn from that Buzby Poodle—whom I have been forced to buy—that Harvey was dogging the Jew's heels to day! That same Luke has a spiteful black eye!"

"Hate me!" echoed Dora—"Ha, ha, ha! To tell you the truth, Fitz-Cowles, he was once a lover of mine. I rejected the poor fellow, he has exchanged his love for spite, and now would sell his soul to ruin me! He must be silenced, Fitz-Cowles?"

She leaned over the table, fixing her dark eyes with a meaning glance upon the face of her paramour. Fitz-Cowles involuntarily averted his eyes, and shaded his brow with his upraised hand. Dora gazed upon him silently and sternly for a single moment, and then laid her fair white hand upon his arm.

"He must be silenced!" she repeated in that same deep whisper.

"The Jew is *safe* by this time; I have nothing to fear from that quarter!" muttered Fitz-Cowles. "Why the fact is, Dora, I hardly think the man would have showed you this letter had he meant to betray you. He will attend the banquet in Monk-Hall to-night, and consequently cannot see Livingstone before to-morrow. By-the-bye, where is the old fellow?"

"Mr. Livingstone sent me word by the servant that matters of pressing business would detain him at the counting house all night, until the hour of our departure to-morrow morning. To be plain with you, Algernon, I do not feel safe while this man Harvey lives with the power of mischief at his control. Can you think of no plan to secure his *silence?*"

"Tut, tut! He is not worth our notice, Dora—" exclaimed Fitz-Cowles, resuming his hat and cane, and moving towards the door. "Let him take his own course. He is too pitiable a thing to cause one solitary fear. By-the-bye, you must excuse me, Dora—I left a friend waiting in the parlor down stairs. Remember, Dora, to-morrow night we meet at Hawkwood—"

"My disguise is safe in the next room," exclaimed Dora, assuming a careless and languid manner. "By-the-bye, Fitz-Cowles, how does your Club manage Monk-Hall? Are you assured of the silence of your subordinate? Now if any person who has money to clear his way can enter the mansion, I would not give a straw for the secrecy of the place—"

"Ha, ha! You women are so curious!" laughed Fitz-Cowles—"Anybody enter the Hall? Nonsense! No one can enter without the password, which is changed by the Abbot every night. Old Devil-Bug would murder the man who attempted an entrance without the secret word.

Last night I gave out the pass word for to-night. 'Fire and brimstone'—you know? Tart and expressive, Dora!"

" 'Fire and brimstone!' " echoed Dora, rising from her chair—"And this Jones, or Devil-Bug, is a desperate sort of man: is he not? Something of the cut-throat and the bravo?"

"By Jove! I should not like to tempt his cut-throat skill! But really, Dora, my friend down stairs is growing impatient. Remember, Dora—" and he made a slight bow—"Hawkwood, Dora, to-morrow night!"

He closed the door, and the merchant's wife was alone.

She stood silent and motionless, with her arms folded across her breast, while her dark hair hung clustering over the fair bosom, now rising in the light with the impulse of a dark and terrible thought. Her eyes, dark and lustrous as they were at other times, were now almost hidden by her compressed brows, while they shot forth a dead and glassy light, which indicated a mind buried in itself, as it called up its most fearful elements, to nerve it for the accomplishment of a desperate and appalling deed.

"My name whispered through all the town with epithets of scorn and contempt? In the parlor, the saloon, and the theatre? And then the daily Journals, who fatten on the garbage of private discord, will parade in their loathsome columns the disgrace of Livingstone, the guilt and degradation of his wife! My name will become another word for pollution and dishonor! Shall this be? Never—by all the energies of a soul, which has a woman's passion without her fear, *never!*

"The deed which I contemplate is most appalling! It requires a firm soul, and a heart which shrinks not at the sight of blood! It perils a world to gain a world! But what of that? A sure eye and a firm footstep may guide the traveller, unharmed, along the edge of awful chasms, which yawn to engulph him, and echo his tread with the sound of crumbling rocks! What cares he for the death that reaches forth its arms to grasp him, so that he can escape by a hair's-breadth from its clutches?

"My soul is resolved! Before the dawn of day, Dora, the Cobbler's grand-daughter—ha, ha, ha—will fear no living witness of her guilt! And to-morrow, to-morrow—Catharine De Medicis must—ha, ha, ha! —must clothe these young limbs with a widow's weeds!"

These words uttered, she pushed aside the crimson hangings, and disappeared into the next chamber, with a single exclamation.

"The disguise—" she murmured—"The disguise which Fitz-Cowles prepared for our flight, is safe in this chest!"

Meanwhile, passing down the stairs, Fitz-Cowles was saluted by his companion, who stood waiting in the hall, under the light of the hanging lamp.

"Cool my blood with a julap!" exclaimed the indomitable Major Rappahannock Mulhill, as he stood picking his teeth with a large bowie knife—"But it's too bad to keep a fellow waiting in this way! I say, Colonel, did you find old Livingstone in? No? Then you won the bet!"

"I told you not to bet, but you would!" replied Fitz-Cowles, twirling his cane with a *nonchalance* air—"You wagered a cool thousand that I would find Livingstone up stairs! How deuced foolish in you! I never saw such a fellow for betting; never, by Jove! By-the-bye, Major, there's a fire in the parlor, let's walk in and settle the bet."

"Oh, we bloods down south are awful chaps to bet, *awe*-ful!" replied Rappahannock, as his round face assumed an expression of deep solemnity—"Why Fitz, my boy, I recollect one occasion, when the head of a large family was buried—it was my father—that bets were made with all the heirs with regard to the length of the Parson's sermon! The odds ran strong on an hour and a half. Bets were freely offered, ten to one, that the Parson would not get done in two hours. I booked them all. The Parson, strong winded chap as he was, broke down after the first hour, and they handed the bets to me over the old man's grave—"

"Let us walk into the front parlor," exclaimed Fitz-Cowles, opening the door.

"But the most singular fact of all was, that we had to use the old man's coffin as a writing desk, on which to settle the amount of the various bets. The Parson waited till we had finished. One fellow was mean enough to skulk out of his bet; I licked him, and we had a row over the grave—"

"Now, Major, your bet was a thousand, was it not?" cooly interrupted Fitz-Cowles, opening his pocket book, as if to receive the money.

"We had a row over the grave. You'd hardly believe it, Colonel, but fifteen funerals sprung from that very circumstance. Why the amount of Bowie knives and pistols which were used in that fight may be estimated, when you are informed that a dev'lish enterprising blacksmith in the vicinity made horseshoes from the fragments for six months afterwards. 'The Mulhill funeral horseshoes' were all the go! Cool me with a julap, by———"

"Your bet was a thousand dollars"—said Fitz-Cowles, quite pointedly, as he displayed the pocket book in his right hand.

"Oh my dear fellow, I sha'n't have a remittance till Monday. Just make a note of it, will ye. By-the-bye, Fitz, my boy, I'll take you another bet that I don't get that remittance till Tuesday."

"All right, Major, all right," exclaimed Fitz-Cowles, concealing his chagrin with the best possible grace. "Don't think I'll take that other bet. By-the-bye, I am going to Mrs. Tulip St. Smith's *conversazione* to night. Will you go with me, Major?"

"What is to be did?" replied the Major, sticking his hands in his vest pockets—"Cock fightin' or a bear bait, or any thing o' that kind?"

"Nothing so refined. You must talk of Byron and Shelley and Mrs. Hummins or Hemans—"

"Don't know much about Byron, Colonel, but as poor Shelly—Gad! Didn't my next neighbor give him thirty-nine for runnin' off with a yellow gal? Shelly was the worst buck nigger on Jones' place!"

Fitz-Cowles' acquaintance with the literature or the literary cant of the day, was exceedingly limited, but the remark of the round-faced Mulhill was too strong for even his intellectual nerves.

"The fellow is a decided jackass!" he muttered, leading the way from the parlor—"I say Mulhill, did you ever read a book in your life?" he exclaimed, as he lifted the dead-latch of the front door—"Did you ever read so much as a Magazine?"

"Didn't I? Haven't we all them pictur' books down south? Steel plates in front, depictin' the feelin's of pussies deprived of their ma's, and nice love tales full o' grand descriptions of the way young genelmen an' ladies dies for won another, without so much as leavin' a pocket-hank'cher to tell their fate! Read the Migizines? Wot po'try, wot sentiment, wot murder, an' madness, an' mush-and-milk, for a greasy quarter! Cool me with a julap, by—!"

"Hist! Look yonder, Major!" exclaimed Fitz-Cowles, pointing to the door-steps of Livingstone's mansion, which they had but a moment left—"Who is that young fellow, standing in front of Livingstone's door? Who can it be? A fashionable hat and a sweeping mantle! Egad! He leaves the door and hurries down Fourth street! Come on, Mulhill—let's give chase!"

"Kick' me to death with crickets! And why should I give chase? Ha, ha, ha! D'ye see that paper, Curnel, d'ye see that document? Ho, ho, ho! What 'ud ye give to read it? Hurray, hurray!"

And to the utter astonishment of Fitz-Cowles, the ardent Southerner with his red round face, half-hidden by an immense shirt collar, and his portly form enveloped in a white blanket overcoat, commenced performing an irregular dance along the pavement of South Fourth street, tossing his felt hat on high with one hand, while the other grasped a slip of dingy paper, and waved it to and fro, in the winter air.

"What in the deuce do you mean? Folks will think you're crazy. What's that letter about?"

"What's it about?" echoed Mulhill, with a broad grin widening his features—"Nothin' pertikler! Jist a love letter from a g-a-l!"

CHAPTER SIXTH

DEVIL-BUG IN LOVE

"Your name is—"

As Devil-Bug leaning over the table, hissed these whispered words in the ear of the listener, his face assumed an expression of hideous glee, his lips parting with a sneering grimace, while a multitude of minute wrinkles, diverging from the corner of his eyelids, spread over his swarthy skin, in a smile of fiend-like triumph and scorn.

"My name—" echoed the stranger, drawing the folds of his cloak yet more closely around his form, while his hand with an involuntary movement swept his dark curls more thickly over his white forehead. "My name is—"

"Dora Livingstone!" whispered Devil-Bug, resting the knuckles of his iron hands upon the edge of the table. "The wife of the rich Merchant! Alone and in Monk-Hall!"

The face of the stranger became suddenly pale as death, and then the dark eyes, gleaming from beneath the mass of jet-black curls, shot forth a glance of fixed resolution.

"Beware how you whisper that name within these walls!" The voice was calm and resolute, that spoke these words. "Woman, as I am, it were not safe for you to dare my vengeance! I came here for revenge! You are the man to fulfil my settled purpose—I have asked you to commit a horrible crime—but you shall have gold for your labor. Gold sufficient to make you a rich man! This Luke Harvey must die!"

"It's quite a pleasure to hear her talk!" cried Devil-Bug, gazing upon the face of the disguised woman, with a look of gloating admiration. "To think that the creetur' with them devil's eyes is a woman, with a soft buzzim and a plump form! Ho, ho, ho! Luke Harvey *shall* die, good lady if you wish it, but the wages aint to be paid in goold."

"What mean you?" exclaimed Dora, with a look of disgust impressing the lines of her proud countenance, as she marked the expression of Devil-Bug's loathsome face.

"The goold I want good lady, is a kiss from a red lip; a little love you know, and a good deal o' fondness! That's my price. I aint to be had on any other terms. Ho, ho, ho! The han'some Merchant's wife in love with old Devil-Bug—I vonders how that 'ud vork?"

The bosom of the disguised woman rose heaving beneath the folds of her cloak, and her dark eyes flashed with fierce indignation.

"And dare you presume to hold such language with me? Another word of such insolence from your lips, and by the Heaven above me, you die!"

She sprang to her feet, and flinging the cloak from her shoulders, stood with her proud form elevated to its full stature, while her fair white hands, each held a pistol extended at arms length, in an attitude of determined menace.

"Look here Musketer, look here Glow-worm—aint that a purty sight? You're the rale pluck I tell ye, g-a-l! D'ye mean them words as a purty speech or as rale sensible tolk? D'ye see them niggers? Suppose ye fire at yer humble sarvant, d'ye think a g-a-l with yer soft bosom and smooth limbs ar' a match for sich reglar iron-boned devils as them darkies? I have seen ye afore, gal, and liked ye—Come to my terms, and I'll come to yours! A kiss for every drop o' blood I shed on your account!"

Dora started at the sight of the two negroes, nestling in the dark corners of the Doorkeeper's den.

"Oh madness, madness!" she muttered, dropping her face instinctively on her bosom, while her extended hands still grasped the pistols in their fair white fingers. "I have placed my name and reputation at the mercy of this fiend in human shape! There are witnesses to this dark interview—oh madness, madness!"

Devil-Bug quietly motioned his Negroes to leave the den. As they crept through the door leading into the mansion, he silently glided around the table, and stood at the side of the beautiful woman, whose head still rested upon her bosom.

"I like yer spirit—" he whispered, fixing his solitary eye upon her reddening face with a look of gloating admiration—"If you want to leave these doors, old Devil-Bug is not the man to stop you. But look ye, good lady, if you but say the word, Luke Harvey shall not see the sun rise to-morrow! You go up stairs, and wait till daybreak in a private room; no one shall dare to molest ye! When I bring you that 'ere ring, which Luke aint to part with except with his life, then you are to pay me, the—the—goold?"

Dora said never a word, but letting the pistols fall from her hands, she sank in the seat, and hid her face in her bosom, while the long tresses of her dark hair, escaping from beneath the velvet cap, fell showering and luxuriant over her neck and shoulders, so beautifully disguised in man's attire.

"Insulted, scorned, despised," she murmured, "And by the man I once so deeply loved! My name at his mercy, my whole fortune hanging on a chance word from his lips! Shall I pause in my career of revenge? This night and to-morrow safely passed, I am Countess of Lyndeswold. Yes, yes, Luke Harvey must die, at any price, at all hazards, must die—"

"Lady what's the use of mutterin' an' mumblin' to yerself? Is it a bargain? If it is, jist reach out yer hand, and let me kiss it—"

"Bring me the ring, and you shall revel in wealth—" whispered Dora, raising her face slowly from her bosom.

"If you'd a kept yer face hid a minnit longer, I might 'ave come to yer terms. But with the sight o' that face afore me, I'd sooner you'd come to mine! I'd sooner revel on yer lip, good lady, than to float in goold up to my eyes! Is it a bargain? Gi' us yer hand—"

Dora slowly rose from her seat. How beautiful she looked, as standing erect in her disguise, with her long dark hair, falling aside from her face, she folded her arms across her heaving bosom, and remained for a single moment, silent and motionless. The light fell softly over the outline of her form, revealing the symmetry of her limbs, so round in their faultless shape, the swelling ripeness of her bosom, heaving beneath the disguise of the closely-buttoned frockcoat, the slender waist, and the proportions of her figure, widening with beauty below the waist, and gradually narrowing again like the outline of an invented pyramid, as they approached the small and delicate feet, enclosed in tight-fitting boots, which reached mid-way to the knee. She was very beautiful, and her compressed lip, and pale forehead, darkening with a frown, gave her lovely countenance, an expression of deep and painful thought, which disclosed the mighty struggle at work within her soul.

"Gi' us yer hand!" said Devil-Bug, as he glided closer to her side.

"The ring—" was all that Dora, found strength to murmur, as with her face averted, she slowly extended her fair white hand toward the deformed wretch by her side.

"This is the goold for which I bargains—" exclaimed Devil-Bug as dropping on his knees, he applied his loathsome lips to the skin of that delicate hand—"Before daybreak you shall have the ring, and I the goold! Ha, ha! Ho, ho! Vonders how that 'ill vork?"

CHAPTER SEVENTH

PARSON PYNE AND HIS DAUGHTER

"Comfortable range of apartments," muttered the Rev. Dr. Pyne, as he entered a small chamber on the second floor. "This is my study. A nice little room, with a coal fire in the grate, a lamp on the table, a cupboard in the corner, and a bed in the other. This is what I call comfortable," he smiled pleasantly as standing with his back to the fire, and his hands under his coat-tails, he warmed his respectable person, and surveyed the room, at the same time. "This is the retreat to which the Foe of Pagan Rome retires, when the labors of the pulpit are over. Ha, ha! I am blessed with an affectionate and loving congregation. Dear people, they love me! I preached with unction to night, powerful, very powerful unction, and talking of unction, I believe I'll try a little brandy."

With that pleasant smile beaming from his red round face, that smile which won him bank-note opinions from the wealthy old women of his flock, and endeared him to the hearts of all the Patent-Gospellers, the good Doctor advanced to the cupboard, and taking a corpulent decanter from its recesses, poured himself a very tolerable glass of blushing Cogniac. Surveying the creature for a moment, with his one eye closed, and his full red lips dropped apart, the Reverend gentleman after this silent pause of thought, raised the glass to his lips with the emphatic sentiment; 'Down with the Pope of Pagan Rome; up with the Patent-Gospellers!'

"Good brandy, that," he murmured replacing the empty glass in the cupboard. "Old Swipes, one of our Elders who keeps a wine store, sent me that brandy in mistake for wine. It was intended for the use of our church on particular occasions; I use it instead of the church which does just as well."

The Reverend gentleman then seated his portly person, in the large armchair beside the fire, and taking a corpulent pocket-book from a side pocket, he displayed its contents, on his outspread knees.

"Funds are easy with us to-day," said the good man smiling as he spoke, "My wants were quite numerous this morning; to night they are amply supplied. That ten dollar note came from a good old lady, on account of a poor man, who was run over by the cars. A widow with five small children and one at the breast, will doubtless be relieved when she beholds the 'twenty', which was presented to me for her, by an aged brother of our flock. That gold-piece is for the poor man, who fell from a five-story house, with a hod on his shoulder. This five dollar note, came with a letter, which defied the Pope of Rome in very strong language. 'Down with the Pope of Pagan Rome, yours—*Shadroe*.' Shadroe is a very zealous brother; quite fiery. And here is a 'fifty,' which was tendered me for the use of an indigent young brother, about to commence the Gospel Ministry. There's somewhere near a hundred dollars in all, collected by me since breakfast this morning. A good day's work."

The Rev. F. A. T. Pyne chuckled pleasantly to himself, and winked rather viciously at the small Bible on the mantel-piece. It was a very pleasant thing to behold the fruits of his day's labor resting on his knee, in the shape of solid gold and bank notes; and our admiration of the sight is increased to a positive reverence for Dr. Pyne, when we remember that the poor man who was run over by the cars, the widow with five children and one at the breast, the man who fell from a five-story house with a hod on his shoulder, and the indigent young brother about to commence the Gospel Ministry, were all lively fictions, invented by the Foe of Pagan Rome, for the especial benefit of his two rooms and other conveniences at Monk-Hall. But this you will understand is a positive secret, and having been entrusted to us in strict confidence, must on no account go any farther.

"A little opium wont hurt me, I opine," said the good Brother taking a small paper from his pocket, which being opened, disclosed a number of smaller papers, all carefully folded in a square form, with an Apothecary's label, on the outside of each. "We temperance folks must have some little excitement after we have forsworn intemperance. When we leave off Alcohol, we indulge our systems with a little Opium. That's what I call a capital compromise."

The Brother now arose from his seat, and quietly opened a small door, leading into the adjoining chamber. A cheerful smile overspread his round face, and his watery eyes twinkled with glee. There was something very meaning in the energy with which he smacked his large red lips together.

"She sleeps!" he muttered, and then with a quiet manner and cautious footstep stole into the chamber, closing the door carefully behind him.

It was a wide and spacious chamber, with lofty ceiling and wainscotted walls. A small lamp burning on the table near the fireplace, gave a clear cold light to the hearth-side, while the other parts of the room were wrapt in shadow. Like most of the chambers of Monk-Hall, this room wore an ancient and desolate appearance. The heavy oaken wainscot of the walls, the chairs of massive mahogany, with high-backs and carved limbs, the small couch standing in one corner, with its snow-white counterpane and spotless pillow contrasting with the heavy carvings of the bed-posts of dark walnut, the faded carpet on the floor, and the elaborate wood-work above the mantel, with the coal fire smouldering in the grate below, such were the characteristics of the ancient chamber, which was rendered dark and gloomy by the absence of windows from the lofty walls. A small aperture near the ceiling not more than two feet long and one foot high, could scarcely be called a window; although it was intended to give a faint glimpse of light during the daytime.

Near the fire, a fair girl, dressed in spotless white, was sleeping as she reclined in a massive arm-chair, whose high-back thickly cushioned with dark velvet, afforded a gentle repose to her maidenly form. The light fell mildly over her countenance, disclosing its pale hues and regular features, strikingly relieved by the long black hair which half unbound fell waving over her cheek, down to her shoulders. Her hands small and delicate, and death-like as the whitest marble, were clasped in front of her person, and the light folds of the robe, which enveloped her form like a death-shroud, were softly agitated by the faint motion of her bosom, heaving gently upward as she slept.

So like a pure and holy dream was the beauty of the fair girl, as she lay sleeping quietly in the den of Monk-Hall, that Altamont Pyne, started with involuntary awe, as he gazed upon his daughter's face. Her beauty was of that peculiar cast which mingles high intellect and purity of soul with all the enticing loveliness of a fair young form, soft limbs, a delicate bosom, throbbing with the impulses of youthful blood and a lustrous black eye beaming with the undeveloped love of a stainless soul. Her form somewhat below the middle heighth, was marked by peculiar and characteristic beauties. A neck fair and round; wide shoulders, the skin as white as alabaster, and veined with delicate streaks of azure; a slender waist widening into the lower proportions of the figure, which were marked by the swelling outlines of womanly beauty, and a small foot, thrust from underneath the folds of her dress.

Her face was fair, in its hues, round in its contour, swelling in its outlines, the features regular, the brow calm and eloquent, the lips red and ripe, marked by a bewitching loveliness of shape, and the chin, firm and resolute in its expression, was varied by a laughing dimple. And yet with all this beauty, the countenance was white as marble, never animate with the flushed hues of maidenhood, save when strong emotion, called the warm blood to the swelling cheek. As she lay reclining in the arm-chair she looked for all the world, like a marble statue of an intellectual and voluptuous maiden, with all the outline and shape, which gives fascination to the face and form of beauty, without the warm hues, which tint the lips with love, and fire the cheek with passion.

"Mable is quite beautiful!" muttered the oily-faced Parson gazing upon the girl with his watery eyes distended by an expression of animal admiration. "It's most a pity to awake her! However *Brother* Devil-Bug will be here directly, with the potion. Mabel," his voice assumed its blandest whisper as he applied his mouth to the sleeper's ear. "Mabel, look up, my child!"

The maiden moved in her sleep, but did not unclose her eyes. Gathering her hand convulsively over her bosom, as the soft accents of the Reverend Pyne broke on her ear, she murmured wildly in her sleep, as though some terrible vision had dawned upon her soul.

"It is night again," she muttered in a voice scarcely audible. "I am alone. The door is locked and—oh, save me good Heaven! His footstep is on the stairs! He comes, and I, stand trembling at the approach of my father! My father, ha, ha, ha! It is night again and his hand is upon my bosom, his hot breath on my cheek. Help, oh God, help! Father, have mercy, oh have mercy! Your voice it was that taught me God's own holy truths, and now that same voice whispers pollution in my ear. Your hands first raised mine to God as we prayed together, and now father those hands—oh God! Oh God!"

"Awake my child," whispered Altamont Pyne as his red round face grew suddenly pale.

"It is night, it is night!" muttered the sleeping girl, "Back, father, I say back! God's vengeance will strike ye dead, if ye but attempt this horrible crime! Back I say, or with this lamp I will fire the window curtains, and in an instant this house, which you have forever polluted by this attempt at crime, never to be named in human ears, this house will arise to heaven in flames! Each spark of flame, a witness before God, of the horrible crime! Back I say—I will to the door—back, or I fire the house! Ha, ha! I gain the door, the entry is past and the stairs! Ha, ha! I am in the street, the night is cold and the flinty stones rend my feet, but I am saved, I am saved!"

"Mabel, awake I say!" exclaimed Brother Pyne, with an angry frown. "You should not encourage these night-mare dreams. Ugh! The girl makes me shiver, and yet her lip is ripe as a May cherry! Where is Devil-Bug with his potion?"

"Oh let me in for the sake of God!" the accents of the sleeper broke on the air in tones of agony. "The night is dark and I am cold! My feet are pierced by the flinty stones, and the winter hail and snow beats against my bosom! Open your door, oh stranger, for *he* pursues me! *He*, my father, and I fear him worse than the grave!"

"Mabel—girl, I say will you hush this nonsense!" exclaimed Parson Pyne, in an angry tone, as he shook the maiden roughly by the shoulder.

The girl slowly unclosed her eyes and gazed in his face with a bewildered stare.

"Oh do not hurt me, father," she exclaimed clasping her hands beseechingly in his face.

"Hurt ye, girl? Who talks of hurtin' ye?" exclaimed Pyne, betrayed by his excited feelings, into an harshness of dialect which spoke of the habits of his former life, when he was not precisely a saint. "What d'ye set there dreamin' about such stuff and nonsense? Haven't I provided you a home, where you might recover from the unfortunate state of mind which has possessed you of late? Dismiss that unhappy dream, my child, dismiss that unhappy dream, now and forever!"

Brother Pyne drew a chair, and sat down by his daughter's side.

"And then, father, you think it *was* a dream?" she exclaimed, with an expression of rapture warming over her face.

"To be sure I do, Mabel, to be sure I do!" said Brother Pyne, quickly. "Put your arms round my neck and kiss me, that's a good daughter."

Mabel reached forth her arms and entwined them round her father's neck. She kissed him on the cheek with her lips, now reddened with excitement, but a cold shudder ran over her form, in the very act. She shrank back into her chair as though she had been stung by a serpent. At this moment she looked very beautiful. Her swelling cheeks were flushed with sudden life, her large dark eyes beamed with soul, and her lips so bewitching in their shape, grew moist and red as rose-buds heavy with morning dew. Her brow white as alabaster and calm as death, was eloquent with the silent intensity of thought, which absorbed her soul. And aside from that fair brow swept her raven hair, falling in long and glossy tresses to her rounded shoulders, and imparting a solemn beauty to the loveliness of her countenance.

"Oh father," she murmured, "the night, *the night* when I fled from your roof. Was it all a dream?"

"To be sure it was, my dear," replied Dr. Pyne, taking his daughter's hand within his own.

"Did you not seek my chamber, did you not—oh horror, horror! My tongue cleaves to the roof of my mouth, when I endeavor to picture forth that scene in words!"

"Tush, tush, this is all nonsense!" and as he spoke the Doctor gently wound his arms around her waist. "Have I not always been a kind father to you? Have I not rented this house for your especial comfort? You see, my child, your solitary way of life has slightly, very slightly, affected your mind. A few weeks of quiet, with the change of scene afforded by this old mansion, the perusal of wholesome books, together with the cheerful conversation of your father, will bring you right again. Have your attendants brought you any refreshments, my child."

"Yes, father. An hour ago, just as I had lain down upon the bed to rest myself for a few moments, a servant entered the chamber, and set food upon the table before the fire. He did not observe me, father, but I saw him and was chilled with horror at the sight of his hideous countenance. Why do you employ such a hideous monster, father?"

"What, Brother Abijah? Oh he is a fine fellow, a Christian, my daughter, although his face is not precisely handsome. What are you thinking of now, Mabel?"

And Brother Pyne patted the palm of her fair white hand, while his arm gathered more lovingly around her waist.

"Of my mother! She has been dead long, very long, has she not, father? Many and many an hour, in the daytime, when abroad in the street, and at night when resting in bed, have I endeavoured to recall the memory of her face, or a tone of her voice, or a smile wreathing her lips, but in vain! All is dark with me, when I think of my mother."

"The fact is she died when you was a mere baby, Mabel. Think, my child, what a care you have been to your father, how he has reared you up in the Lord; how, from time to time, he has filled your young mind with the teachings of divine truth. Think of this, my child, and then think of your conduct in leaving that paternal roof which had sheltered you from childhood! Forgive this tear, Mabel, I can't help it."

The Rev. Brother Pyne was deeply affected. If ever his oily face glowed with an expression of sincere feeling it was at that moment. Mabel gazed upon him for a moment, and then flung her arms around his neck.

"Forgive me, my father, forgive me!"

"*Father!*" echoed a hoarse voice, and Devil-Bug, holding a waiter in his extended hands, glided from the doorway and advanced toward the light. "I say, Brother Pyne, here's the hot coffee which you called for, and hot cakes in the bargain."

As he spoke he advanced toward the table, and arranged the contents of the waiter upon the white cloth which he spread over its surface.

"Ho, ho, ho! So the gal puts her arms around his neck, does she? There won't be much need of the drug in that case!" he muttered to himself, as he arranged the supper equipage upon the table. " 'Father' indeed! Could I 'ave heered my own ears?"

The girl raised her head from her father's shoulder. At the same moment Devil-Bug, turning on his heel to leave the room, caught a glimpse of her face for the first time. He started backward as though he had received a death-wound in his very heart. The waiter fell clattering on the floor, and with another start backward, Devil-Bug raised his hands and gazed upon the face of the young girl. Never in his life had Devil-Bug been seized with an agitation terrible as this. His face grew white as a sheet, and his solitary eye glanced forth from its socket with one wild and absorbing gaze. Once or twice he essayed to speak, but the incoherent words died on his tongue.

"I say, brother, what's the matter?" cried Parson Pyne, gazing upon the Doorkeeper with unfeigned astonishment, "Going to have a fit, brother?"

Devil-Bug slowly advanced to the Parson's side. He reached forth his arm and laid his hand lightly on the girl's shoulder. He spoke in a voice utterly changed from his usual harsh and discordant tones.

"*Ellen!*" he said, in a low and softened voice, whose gentleness of tone presented a strange contrast to the harsh deformity of his visage. "Ellen is this you, or is it your ghost?"

Mabel gazed upon his face in silent wonder, and Parson Pyne rose angrily from his seat.

"What means this insolence?" he shouted, in a tone of blustering anger.

"Oh, nothing," replied Devil-Bug, with his usual grunting tone of voice. "Only that gal looks somethin' like a gal I used to know; that's all."

And he strode hastily toward the door.

"Devil-Bug," cried Fat Pyne, in a whisper, as he hurried after the retreating Doorkeeper. "Is the coffee drugged?"

"Yes it is, Parson," growled Devil-Bug, with his hand on the door.

"Soh, soh! All's right then. Devil-Bug you will lock all the doors after you, if you please," he added, in a whisper. "You understand? I don't want to be interrupted and mark ye, if you should hear a shriek or a groan, you needn't mind it."

"Oh, I needn't, need't I?" echoed Devil-Bug, while an expression, which Pyne had never witnessed before, stole over his deformed visage. "Parson you've got the gal all in your own power, the coffee's drugged and the doors shall be locked, and we wont mind no shrieks or groans nor other capers. But you must answer me won ques'in. That gal called you father?"

"Did she tho'?" replied Dr. Pyne, blandly. "I really didn't mind it."

"You aint her father, then?" asked Devil-Bug, with that peculiar expression deepening over his visage.

"Of course not. Except in a spiritual sense—ha, ha, ha! A *spiritual* sense, you know!"

"Ha, ha, ha!" echoed Devil-Bug, with a wild and hollow laugh.

"Ho, ho, ho!" chuckled Parson Pyne, in a quiet way, peculiar to himself. "You won't mind a shriek or a groan if you should chance to hear one?"

"Devil a mind!" replied Devil-Bug, as he stepped through the doorway. "You're a jolly cove, you are!"

And Parson Pyne caught the strange gleam of Devil-Bug's solitary eye, and laughed merrily as he closed the door, while Devil-Bug echoed his laugh with a hollow sound, more like the groan of a dying man who struggles with death and madness at the same time, than the echo of a cheerful laugh.

"He's alone with the gal!" he muttered, as he stood in the small chamber where the Parson had consoled himself with a glass of brandy. "And she called him *father!*"

That peculiar expression which had been gathering over his face, while conversing with the Parson, now manifested itself in a look of fiend-like hatred, which convulsed every line of the Doorkeeper's countenance. Sweeping his thick hair aside, he bared his protuberant brow to the light. The swarthy skin was corrugated with thick wrinkles, which stood out from his deformed forehead like knotted cords. The shrunken eye-socket seemed to sink yet farther beneath his overhanging brow, while his solitary eye, gathering a strange light, enlarged and dilated until its gleam grew like the glare of burning coals. His pointed teeth were firmly clenched together, and his lips were agitated by a hideous grimace, which gave a grotesque effect to the terrible frown of his brow and the fiend-like glare of his eye. He shook his large hands wildly on high, and clenched madly at the air with his talon fingers.

"Ho, ho, ho!" he cried, as the idea, which absorbed his soul, rose before him like an embodied thing of flesh and blood. "Ho, ho, ho! I vonders how *that* 'ill vork!"

CHAPTER EIGHTH

THE PIT OF MONK-HALL

"Look here Glow-worm, look here Musketer!" he shouted to his negroes, who sat dozing before the fire. "D'ye see that poker and that old tongs? Stick 'em in the coal fire, and heat 'em to a white heat! The poker has a sharp pint—it 'ill do, it 'ill do!"

"Yes, massa," growled Musquito, as his lips—which the reader will remember were shapen like two sides of a triangle—distended in a hideous grin. "Yes, massa, I doves put de pokar in de fi-ah!"

"An' I de tong!" exclaimed Glow-worm, his huge mouth grinning like a death's-head, as he inserted the old tongs between the bars of the grate.

"Ye'r a pair of beauties!" exclaimed Devil-Bug, gazing upon his satellites with paternal fondness. "Hell can't produce ye'r match."

Certainly they were a pair of beauties. As squatting in low stools on either side of the fire, they looked up in their master's face, their hideous visages assumed an expression of infernal glee. Give us a picture of the scene, Darley. Sharpen your pencil, and select your best piece of Bristol board. This is a study worthy of your genius. We are looking at the scene from the dark corner of the room. The light flares from yonder table, in the background, Devil-Bug stands in front of the fire; his negroes squat on either side. Musquito with his back toward us, extends his left hand and holds the iron between the bars of the grate, and looks up in his master's face, presenting to our view the profile of his hideous visage, the receding forehead, the flat nose, the opened mouth with the lips, meeting in a point near the nose and diverging toward the sharp and prominent chin. Opposite him, Glow-worm, with the light from the table falling on his broad shoulders, and the beams of the fire illumining his face, rolls his large eyes towards his master, while his rude mouth, with the teeth projecting like fangs, is distorted with a loathsome grimace, and his muscular right hand also holds the iron between the bars of the grate. And the master, Darley, paint him for us; picture old Devil-Bug. He stands between the twain, his massive face receiving on one cheek the gleam of the lamp; on its whole extent the glare of the fire. Picture his broad brow, hanging over his wide face, like the edge of a beetling cliff over a receding precipice. The eyeless socket, the glaring eye, the heavy eyebrows, the flat nose with wide nostrils, the mouth convulsed by a grotesque grimace that discloses the clenched teeth, the pointed chin, bristling with a stiff beard, the matted hair hanging aside from the face and brow in uneven locks; picture it all, Darley. If your wonderful pencil, which traverses the sheet of drawing paper with such gracefulness and such vigor linked together by taste, if this pencil, Darley, can depict a nightmare standing erect, with a hideous Dream squatting on either side, then you will have delineated Devil-Bug and his attendant negroes as they were grouped in that cozy little chamber of Monk-Hall.

"Musketer when you've heated that 'ere iron hot enough, jist go down stairs and git a few strands o' thick rope. We shall want it in this room arter awhile. And look ye, Glow-worm, keep your ears picked, will ye? If you don't I'll pick 'em with a hot fork. If you hear a cry, or a groan, or even a moan from that gal in the next room, jist run up stairs and call me! I'll be in the Walnut-Room; d'ye mind, ye black devil?"

Seizing the lamp in his right hand, Devil-Bug hurried from Monk Baltzar's ante-chamber, as it was styled, and in a moment found himself hastening along the dark corridor which traversed the second floor of the mansion.

"I like this old place!" he muttered, as he ascended the staircase of the mansion. "Here was I born, and here I've lived all my life! I never had a friend in all my born days, but these old walls have been my friends! I've talked to the brick pillars in the dead-vault; I've had many a joke with the skeleton in the Banquet-Room; and—ho, ho, ho—the trap-doors all know me, and creak for joy when they hear me comin'! Hur-ray for Monk-Hall, say I! Its the body, I'm its soul! It's full o' nooks and corners and dark places; so is my natur'! I like the old place; there aint a brick in it that I don't love like a brother! Ha, ha, ha! When I die I should feel obliged to the rowdy as 'ud set it afire! It must go with me! When I'm gone it 'ill be like a coffin without a corpse. What's the use o' th' shell when the torkle's dead?"

Devil-Bug stood on the main corridor of the third floor, which with another corridor, meeting at right angles, separated Lorrimer's rooms from the other part of the mansion. Thus you might enter the Walnut Room, through a door which opened into the corridor, near the head of the stairs; or passing along the corridor, you might pursue the gallery which ran east and west until you reached the door of Lorrimer's Drawing-Room. Passing through the drawing room, you traversed the Painted Chamber, the Rose Chamber, and then entered the Walnut Room. Next to the Walnut Room, was the Tower Room, which terminated the range of Lorrimer's apartments.

"B'lieve I'll go into the Walnut Room by this door. That fellow Byrnewood has cost me trouble enough. I'll put an end to his story, with something sharper than a trap-door or a bottle o' drugs! Vonders how that 'll vork?"

He entered the Walnut Room. The glittering floor gave back the reflection of the light which he held in his hands. The place was silent and desolate, with nothing but the bare walls, the dark ceiling and the glittering floor of polished mahogany. In the centre of the room, lay a shapeless mass which moved slowly to and fro, while Devil-Bug advanced, and as the light flashed over its outlines, resolved itself into the form of a human being.

"Ha, ha, ha! Not more than twelve hours ago, this lump o' flesh an' blood an' broadcloth was a fine young gentleman who cut all sorts o' capers in the next room. Cussed like a trooper and swore like a preacher! A little bit o' opium mixed in his drink, and here he lays, a perfect bundle o' sleep and *stoop*idity! A werry contemptible thing is human natur'!"

He flung the blaze of the light full over the face of the unconscious wretch, who lay prostrate on the floor, his knees huddled up against his chest, and his outstretched hands clutching the polished floor, with an involuntary and ineffectual grasp. Long locks of curling black hair fell streaming aside from a young face, which seemed to have grown prematurely old in the compass of a few hours. The skin was yellow and discolored, the lips wore a livid hue, and the dark eyes, glared upon the ceiling with a cold and glassy stare. A thin, clammy foam hung around the white lips, and there were spots of blood upon the cheeks and hands of the unconscious man. He had torn the flesh from his cheeks in very madness. As Devil-Bug gazed upon him, his limbs moved with a faint motion, like the last sign of departing life, and his outstretched hands grasped feebly at the smooth boards of the floor. The light flashed over his fixed eyeballs, but they gave no sign of life, no quick flashing glance that might betoken consciousness.

"Ha, ha, ha! I'll try it,!" screamed Devil-Bug with a wild shriek of laughter. "I've heard many stories about that same thing, but I never saw it done! I'm jist the man to do it, and jist in the humor to do it now!"

He knelt beside the unconscious man, and allowing the light to play over his fixed eyeballs, he applied his mouth to his ear:

"Hel-lo! Yous sir, I say look here. I am a-goin' to bury you alive! D'ye hear that? I'm a-goin' to bury you alive! God—how the feller wriggles! D'ye feel the cold clods fallin' on your breast a' ready? Ho, ho, ho! I'm a-goin' to bury you alive!"

A slight tremor, a quivering shudder passed over the frame of Byrnewood Arlington. Was he conscious of the meaning of the words whispered in his ear? God alone knows, but his limbs were agitated for a moment by a convulsive motion, and the muscles of his face worked as with a spasm.

"I'll jist go an' tell Glow-worm to watch for me in the first cellar, while I go down, down, into the lowest hole of Monk-Hall! When the gal shrieks, then Musketer must whistle, and then Glow-worm will strike the old gong, and I will hear it, although I'm so far below the ground. So far below the ground beside that man's grave in the Pit of Monk-Hall! Excuse me Sir if I keep you waitin'—" he continued making a formal bow, with his face toward the unconscious form of Byrnewood. "Excuse me Sir if I'll keep you waitin' but I'll be back d'rectly."

Placing the lamp on the glittering floor, he departed from the Walnut Room. Scarce had the sound of his footsteps ceased to echo on the air, when the curtains leading into the Rose Chamber were suddenly thrust aside, and the form of a woman with her long brown hair falling wildly on her neck, came hastening over the floor of the apartment, her hands clasped and her white dress floating loosely around her maidenly figure.

Advancing along the room, she started backward as she beheld the shapeless form, flung prostrate at her feet, and the light flashed over her face while she stood entranced by the horror of the spectacle.

"My brother, my brother!" she muttered in a low-toned voice, and then sank kneeling on the floor.

Her long brown hair fell wildly over her shoulders, and her face white as the grave-cloth was tinted in each cheek with a spot of burning red. Her eyes of clear and lustrous blue, were marked by a fixed and glassy stare, as she gazed upon the unconscious form of Byrnewood Arlington. The quivering lips reddened to a deep purple hue, the brow animated by an expression as wild as it was startling, the hand clasped tremblingly over the bosom, faintly heaving beneath the folds of the white robe, all betrayed the deep emotion, like to madness in its indications, which convulsed the soul of the ruined girl.

"Oh brother," she cried taking his hand within her arm. "You are dying and dying for me! Speak to me, Byrnewood, speak to me. Call your sister by the name you used to love so well! Oh, God!" she cried with a wild shriek as she swept the thick locks of his dark hair aside from his pale brow. "He knows me not, he knows me not!"

The eyes of the brother still glared upon the ceiling, with that same fixed and glassy stare. He betrayed no sign of consciousness or emotion. A corse, with all the outward marks of death, and yet with the soul burning brightly within, could not have presented a more ghastly spectacle.

Mary took his cold hands within her own, she kissed his wan and discolored cheeks, she besought him in low tones to rise from the sleep of death, or to give but a look or a sign of recognition. Still he lay unconscious and motionless.

As she thus bent kneeling over the unconscious form of her brother, the figure of a woman glided from the entrance of the Rose Chamber, and stood by her side. It was the form of Long-haired Bess. She gazed upon the ruin, accomplished by Lorrimer with her aid, and a shudder ran over her form, as she gazed.

"Oh Bessie, they have murdered him!" shrieked Mary gazing upward in the face of the woman, while her blue eyes, sent forth a wild and bewildered gaze. "Look—he is dying, he is dying and for my sake!"

"Hist! Mary," cried Bess veiling her eyes with her upraised hand. "Do you not hear their footsteps on the stairs? His torturers return, and we shall be discovered—"

"Oh Bessie lead me to Lorraine, for God's sake lead me! He would not suffer this wrong. There is some dark mystery I know, overshadowing, my very soul, but Lorraine is innocent! You are silent Bessie? You do not answer—"

"Mary I will lead you from the house—" said Bessie in a hasty voice as she turned her face from the light. "I will save your brother."

She hurried the ruined girl from her brother's side, as she spoke.

"He loved me Bessie, he would not harm my brother! I would as soon suspect you of a wrong as Lorraine! There is some terrible mistake Bessie, but Lorraine is innocent—"

"Great God! It makes my heart bleed to hear her talk thus!" muttered Bess leading the way into the Rose Chamber. "Every word she utters is a dagger in my heart! Ha, ha! She believes *me* innocent!"

"Let me look upon him once again!" shrieked Mary darting aside from Bess, and flinging herself upon her brother's unconscious form. "Byrnewood, oh speak to me, oh call your Mary by her name! Only a word, my brother, or a look or a glance? He does not speak, he makes no sign—not even a glance for Mary! And I am the cause of all this ruin—ha, ha, ha! I see my father and my mother—there, there they stand gazing upon the corse of their son! And they raise their hands, they curse me, with his death! Do you not see them Bessie—oh it freezes my blood, to look upon my father's grey hair, which he scatters to the winds as he asks Heaven to curse me!"

She rose to her feet, and with her blue eyes glaring at the vacant air, with her beautiful countenance, for it was beautiful even amid woe, and horror worse than death, with her fair young face, paled to the hue of ashes, she extended her arms as if to wave back the spectres who stood beside her brother's unconscious form.

"Ha! Devil-Bug returns!" exclaimed Bess silently gliding behind Mary, and gathering her form in her arms. "I'll foil him yet! Byrnewood shall yet be saved!"

Raising Mary in her arms, she bore her silently from the Walnut Room.

A moment passed and Devil-Bug stood beside his victim again.

"Come my feller—" he cried raising the unconscious form of Byrnewood upon his shoulders. "You an' me has got a little business to transact, which ought to be done in private."

Unheeding the muttered groan which escaped from Byrnewood's lips, he raised him on his shoulder, as though he had been a mere bundle of merchandize. In a moment he left the Walnut Room, and was descending the stairs, with the unconscious man on his shoulders, while his extended hand grasped the flickering lamp. With a quiet smile on his lip Devil-Bug descended the stairs, and in a few moments stood on the floor of the hall, opening into the Banquet Room. The echo of shouts mingled with laughter rung around the place. Devil-Bug grimly smiled, and passing the doorway of the Banquet Room, stole cautiously along the damp floor of the hall, and in a moment the glare of the lamp flashed over the grand stairway of stone, leading far down into the vaults of Monk-Hall.

And far, far down over massive steps of granite, with solid arches above and thick walls on either side, far, far down, with the rays of the lamp flashing over the void beneath, with a faint yet gloomy effect, like a light darting its beams along the darkness of some hideous well, Devil-Bug pursued his way, his strong right arm supporting the unconscious form of his victim flung like a bundle over his shoulder, while his distorted face grew animate with that grimace of habitual cruelty, which gave his visage the expression of an incarnate fiend, and developed all the hideous moral deformity of his nature.

Down, down over damp steps of granite, down, down! The monotinous echo of his footsteps disturbs the silence of the air, and now and then, his victim with his face hanging over the shoulders of the Doorkeeper, utters a faint moan, as he feebly clutches at the door with his hands. The stairway terminates on a wide hall with roof and floor of stone. On one side the massive door leading into the Dead-vault of Monk-Hall, on the other side another door, as high and as massive, leading into the Wine-cellar of the old mansion. At Devil-Bug's back ascends the stairway of granite; he advances along the stone floor and at his very feet descends another stairway, more dark and gloomy than the first, with clammy moisture trickling down the walls, while the light flares fitfully over a long succession of stone blocks, sinking far, far down into the bosom of earth and night. This stairway leads to the Pit of Monk-Hall.

Ha! Old Devil-Bug starts and clenches his hand, and at the very thought of that fearful cavern, sunk far beneath the earth, below the foundations of Monk-Hall.

Has the name of the place a terrible memory for your soul, Devil-Bug? Does no phantom arise before you as standing on the verge of the stairway, you gaze into the void below, does no phantom with blood-dripping hair and ghastly eyes, arise before you, and scare you back? The phantom of a murdered man with a mangled jaw sunken on the breast, a tongue lolling from his mouth, and blood-shot eyes starting from a face darkened to purple by the hand of death.

Ho, ho! What cares Devil-Bug for phantoms in his path, or white-shrouded ghosts gliding by his side! Derided and scorned by that fellow man, whom he never yet called, brother, the offcast of the world from his very birth, a walking curse and a breathing execration upon all mankind, why should old Devil-Bug fear that Phantom World, which dawns upon his solitary eye?

Ha! Ha, ha! Old Devil-Bug loves the old arches of Monk-Hall, he loves the cellars and the dens, he loves the song of the revellers in the Banquet Room, and the glee of the cut-throats in the vaults below, he loves the Skeleton-Monk like a twin-brother, but the Phantoms, ha, ha, they are at once his fear and his delight! The murdered man gliding forever by his side with the broken jaw and the starting eyes—he hails him as a thing of joy! And the murdered woman with the quivering form and hollow skull, oozing with the slowly-pattering blood—ha, ha, this phantom is one of Devil-Bug's familiar spirits.

But the Pit, the Pit of Monk-Hall, ha, ha! He shudders at the name, he starts and grows pale. The Phantom of the murdered man he can endure as he has endured for years! But to go down step by step into the lowest deep of the pest-house, to stand in the nethermost cavern of Monk-Hall, for the first time for many long years, to start with fear at the palpable presence of the bare skull and mouldering bones of the murdered man! Ho, ho! This were a hard trial, even for Devil-Bug's strong nerves and strong heart!

But down, down into the pit he will go; down, down, with the form of his intended victim on his shoulder and the lamp held firmly in his talon fingers; down, down, until the air grows thick with the breath of corruption, and the light flashes in its socket as it dies away under the pressure of an atmosphere, never yet enlivened by a single ray of God's sunlight, but rendered fatal and deathly by the decay of the human corse, as it crumbles to dust, with the worms revelling over its rottenness, and the thick night shrouding it like a pall.

Shallow pated critic with your smooth face whose syllabub insipidity is well-relieved by wiry curls of flaxen hair, soft maker of verses so utterly blank, that a single original idea never mars their consistent nothingness, penner of paragraphs so daintily perfumed with quaint phrases and stilted nonsense, we do not want you here; Pass on sweet maiden-man! Your perfumes agree but sorrily with the thick atmosphere of this darkening vault, your white-kid gloves would be soiled by a contact with the rough hands of Devil-Bug, your innocent and girlish soul would be shocked by the very idea of such a hideous cavern, hidden far below the red brick surface of broad-brimmed Quakertown. Pass by delightful trifler, with your civet-bag and your curling tongs, write syllabub forever, and pen blank verse until dotage shall make you more garrulous than now, but for the sake of Heaven, do not criticise this chapter! Our taste is different from yours. We like to look at nature and at the world, not only as they appear, but as they are! To us the study of a character like Devil-Bug's is full of interest, replete with the grotesque-sublime. The light of the torch glaring over thick walls trickling with moisture; the skeleton resting in the coffin, that crumbles away from its bones; the solitary grave hidden far down in vaults where no mourners ever weep; the terrible chaos of a heart and soul like those of Devil-Bug, the phantoms ever present with him, like nightmares bestriding the heaving chest of the Murderer—these are subjects and fancies and characters which we delight to picture, though our pen may not fulfil the quick conception of the brain. But as for you, sweet virgin-man, oh reign forever the Prince of Syllabub and Lollypop! And when you are dead, should we survive your loss, we'll raise above your grave a monument of deep regard for your memory. Darley shall do the design. A be-pantalooned girl, with a smooth face and wiry hair, sitting on a volume of travels, with a bundle of blank verse in one hand and cake-basket full of paragraphs in the other. It shall be modelled in syllabub, dear Mister-Miss, surrounded with a border of sugar plumbs, besprinkled with pendent drops of frozen treacle. The foundation of the monument shall be of gingerbread; the crest, a rampant Katy-did. The motto, in especial reference to your travels, shall be—'Here lies the Poet of Twaddle-dom, whose whole life was characterized by a pervading vein of Lollypop-itude.' This is our promise, sweet maiden-man; therefore we pri'thee pass this chapter by!*

"Ho, ho, ho!" chuckled Devil-Bug, as he stood on the verge of the granite stairway. "Here's dampness, an' darkness, an' the smell o' bones all for nothin'. Children under ten years half price! This feller on my shoulder don't move nor struggle. Vonder if he thinks o' th' jolly things we're a-goin' to do with him? Buried alive! I do vonders how that 'ill vork!"

With these words, Devil-Bug began the desent of the granite stairway. The heavy echo of his footsteps resounded upward with a dull, monotonous sound, as lighting his way with the extended lamp, he went far, far down into the darkness of the staircase. Once or twice, as the moaning sound of the wind came rushing down the passage, Devil-Bug started with involuntary surprise, and with his burthen on his shoulder, attempted to turn round, and face the enemy, whom his excited fancy had imagined pursuing his footsteps. But the unconscious man gave a faint struggle, and occupied with the effort to hold him tightly on his shoulder, Devil-Bug smiled at the moaning sound of the wind, and with his usual grimace pursued his way. Down, down, down! Was not that low pattering noise the echo of a footstep at his heels? Devil-Bug smiled grimly as the fancy crossed his mind. Down, down, down! The old archway above the staircase grows crimson with the light of the lamp, and the drops of moisture trickling along the walls, glittered like diamonds in a river's sands. Was not that faint and rustling sound the noise of a garment sweeping the stairs at his back? Half-turning, Devil-Bug gazed into the darkness above, but the

* Will the reader pardon this digression of the author? These Critics are so apt to attack an author, merely because they know him to be young, and suppose him to be friendless, that our author wanted to get the start of them when he wrote this passage. We do not know who the author means by the Prince of Lollypop; but will simply state that in our opinion, * * * * the Poet, has written some very clever things.—PRINTER'S DEVIL.

thick gloom enveloped the stairway like a pall, and his solitary eye might discern nothing but silence and night.

As Devil-Bug turned round, he tossed the body of Byrnewood rather roughly on his shoulder, and the victim uttered a deep groan of pain and agony.

" 'Oh, groan, little children groan, as the nigger wot plays on the banjo ses, but it won't help you the least circumstance!" muttered Devil-Bug, with a hideous grin, as extending the lamp in his left hand, he grasped his victim more firmly by the right, and resumed his downward way. "You see the opium settled your hash, and the safety of this 'ere Commonwealth is in danger! You must be silenced for the sake of Monk-hall, so what's the use o' cuttin' capers? Hello—wasn't that a footstep? I'm quite narvous, as the old women say! Howsomdever, 'ere's the door, the big door wot opens into the Pit of this 'ere Theater!"

He stood at the foot of the stairway before the massive door, with timbers of oak, and bands of iron. Time had rusted away the lock, and the timbers in various places, between the intervals of the iron bands, were crumbling to decay. Devil-Bug fixed his foot against one side of the door, and it fell before him with a crushing sound, whose echo swelled upward like thunder.

Another moment, and advancing over a floor of hard clay, he stood in the Pit of Monk-Hall.

It was a vast and gloomy place, all full of oaken beams, rising from the floor to the ceiling far above, with pillars of dark brick, massive and uncouth in their outlines, towering at irregular interval on every side. Where Devil-Bug stood, at the foot of the stairway, with the light of his lamp flashing fitfully around, a few prominent features of the cellar, or cavern, were perceptible. The stairway seemed to descend into the very centre of the place. On either side, the irregular light of the lamp disclosed faint glimpses of massive walls, all hideous with dark holes and obscure nooks, while the extent of the cavern was as uncertain and vague as the ghostly shadows which flitted from the hard floor to the distant ceiling far above. The floor itself was crowded with rubbish and lumber of all kinds. Innumerable heaps of broken bottles gave evidence of the revels held in Monk-Hall, in the olden time. Crumbling pieces of timber, heaps of old boards, and fragments of broken furniture, littered along the floor, around the base of the heavy pillars, and among the uprising beams of oak, might have excited a momentary curiosity in the mind less calm and philosophical than that of the Doorkeeper.

Devil-Bug, however, treated all these things as matters of course, and holding the light on high, with the unconscious Byrnewood on his shoulder, he picked his way among the heaps of rubbish and advanced along the cellar. He had not gone ten feet from the entrance when a whirring sound broke upon the stagnant air, and then the trampling of a thousand tiny feet echoed to the ceiling of the cavern. The next instant, a crowd of rats, whose immense numbers blackened the cellar for yards around, came rushing across the path of Devil-Bug, and with that same whirring noise, in a moment they were gone again. And then crawling into the strange glare of the light, from the heaps of bottles, and the piles of old lumber, came vermine and reptiles of all kind, and of every loathsome shape. Glittering house-snakes, warmed into life by the foul air of the vault, hung twining from the oaken beams, and the thick pillars were half-concealed by thick cobwebs, woven by noxious spiders, who started from their resting places, as the glare of the light flashed around the place. Devil-Bug paused in the centre of a vacant space, extending between a massive brick pillar and a rising piece of ground, which, shooting upward at the distance of a few yards, closed all the floor of the vault beyond from view. On either side were heaps of crumbling lumber and rubbish, and near the sudden elevation, thick dust, the accumulation of years of decay, had gathered ancle deep.

As Devil-Bug laid down the unconscious form of Byrnewood, placing it on the hard clay beside the lamp, which burned dimly under the pressure of the foul atmosphere, a deep yet faint and moaning sound broke on his ears. It was like the rustling of Autumn leaves driven ashore by angry waves, or like the rolling of a deep flood, swollen by a freshet, or perhaps like the far-off moaning of wind.

"Ho, ho! That's the underground stream o' water which flows beneath the foundations o' Monk-Hall, and arter rollin' onwards for a few feet, buries itself in the ground again! Ugh!" he started as if stricken by some fearful thought. "I wonder if *his* body was carried off by the waves? This piece o' ground is under the eastern range o' trap-doors. Let's see with the light—yes, yes—" he added, rising the lamp overhead. "Yes, yes! Yonder's the archway with the trap-door o' the Dead-vault cut into its bricks! He must 'ave fell somewhere about here," he stamped his foot violently on the hard clay. "But I don't see him now, with my blind side. That puzzles me. For six long years an' more that feller has laid by my side, with his jaw broke and his tongue stickin' out! Now I don't see him, and *that* does puzzle me! Cuss the thing, I forgot the spade!"

He glanced at the form of Byrnewood with a mocking laugh.

"Ha, ha! Don't be *dis*-patient young man," he exclaimed as turning away from the light he moved toward the door. "I'll have to go up stairs for a spade, but I'll be back d'rectly. 'Pon my word I will!"

He disappeared in the darkness, but in a moment stood beside his victim, holding a rusted spade in his hand.

"Reether old fashioned this," he muttered, "I forgot it was down here. You see my friend, we used it some years back to bury a gal wot died reether sudden, as one might say. It's been a standin' against yonder pillar ever since. A little bit rusty but it 'ill do!"

While Byrnewood lay prostrate along the hard clay, with the glare of the lamp flashing on his face, so wan and discolored, the blood-shot eyes starting from the lids, and the white lips failing apart with an expression of idiotic vacancy. Devil-Bug cooly proceeded to dig the grave of the unconscious though living man, chuckling merrily to himself, as sticking the spade into the earth, he paused for a moment, and spat in his hands, like a laborer preparing for his day's work.

"I've hung a man in my time on Bush-Hill, and I've killed a man, by the trap, and I've buried some few, and I've stole corpseses for the Doctors, but I never did bury a man alive! That's a fact. Not menning any harm to you but only waiting to see how it 'ill work, I'll jist lay out the grave. Oh ye begin to be sensible o' yer sitivation do ye?"

A slight convulsive tremor was visible on the lip of the victim. His outspread hands clutched faintly at the hard clay, and it was evident that he was making a desperate effort to rise on his feet.

"This 'ere clay digs hard," calmly soliloquized the Doorkeeper. "You'd like to git up, would ye? No doubt. I should if so be, I was in your place. What's yer idea-r o' grave-diggin' anyhow? Werry low business, aint it?"

Throwing the hard lumps of clay on either side, he gazed with his usual hideous grin, upon the face of Byrnewood Arlington, as like to a corpse as ever was living man. Byrnewood had relapsed into his former unconscious state, and now lay with his fixed eyes glaring steadily upon the thick darkness above. Devil-Bug proceeded with his task. Plying the spade with all the vigor of his lusty arms, he soon stood in a square pit reaching to his knees, while the heap of clay at side of the grave increased in size. Now humming a catch of some dismal gallows-bird song in his grindstone voice, now muttering gaily to himself, now filling the old vault with the echo of a deep and piercing whistle, which he emitted from his large mouth, puckered together like the end of a purse, and now glancing slily aside at the form of his victim, while that same devil's-grin distorted his inhuman face, Devil-Bug made speedy progress in his work. He soon stood up to his middle in the grave.

"Hello! What could that be? I thought I heard the sound o' somebody breathin' behind yonder pillar. Or was it you, hey? I'll be ready for you d'rectly, that I will."

He again resumed his task. As half-concealed in the grave, he bent down to his labor, a slight shudder, like the faint indication of a spasm, agitated the form of Byrnewood. Then his hand clutched suddenly against the hard clay, and in an instant, while his chest heaved with convulsive throbbings, he arose into a sitting posture, and with his long dark hair falling wildly aside from his wan and ghastly face, he gazed around the vault, with an agonized glance that betrayed a fearful consciousness of his awful situation. Devil-Bug turned from his task, and beheld his victim. He shrieked forth a horrible peal of laughter, more like the howl of a hyena, than the sound of a human laugh.

"Ho, ho! Hurray! So ye begin to diskiver yer sitivation? It's all werry good that you should know what's a-goin' to be done with you, 'specially when ye can't help yerself! How ye sit there, a-starin' round the cellar, as though you wos about to buy the primises! Pound me to death with pavin' stones, but this *is* a jolly sight!"

Laying down the spade he advanced toward Byrnewood. The half-conscious man shuddered as his torturer approached.

"Hope ye'll excuse my not havin' prayers at the grave!" he exclaimed as he laid his hands upon Byrnewood's shoulder with a hideous grin convulsing his features. "You may shudder young feller, but into that grave you've got to go, alive and kickin' by God!"

Devil-Bug swore by the name of the Almighty, and this was always a sign of deep excitement with him. His solitary eye blazed with that instinct of Cruelty, which was his Soul. Laying his hand on the shoulders of the shuddering victim, he dragged him slowly toward the grave. Byrnewood's lips parted, he essayed to speak, but the effort was vain. An incoherent sound, like that uttered by an enraged mute, was all that came from his lips.

Devil-Bug dragged along the floor and held him over the verge of the grave when a deep groan awoke the silence of the cellar. Devil-Bug started as though a dagger had entered his heart.

"It's *him*," he muttered dropping Byrnewood heavily on the floor. "It's that or'nary feller who's been hauntin' me for these six years! He always groans when any thing evil's a-goin' to happen to me. It's him, it's *him!* Ha! There he is with his jaw broke an' his tongue out, and ha! ha! There's the old woman with the blood oozin' from the edge o' her broken skull!"

Leaping over the grave, his hands outstretched and his solitary eye flashing with superhuman excitement, he receded step by step towards the elevation, which arose above the waters of the subterranean stream. The Phantoms were before him, in all their ghastliness and blood.

As he receded, another groan sounded through the vault, and entangling his feet in some object, hidden by the thick dust which had accumulated on the piece of rising ground, Devil-Bug fell heavily on his face. In a moment he rose on his knees, and was about starting to his feet again, when a yell of superhuman horror shrieked from his lips. As he fell he had tossed the thickly-gathered dust aside, and he now beheld the object which had entangled his feet. A ghastly skeleton, with the bones falling apart from each other, lay on the earth, before his very eyes. The blackened skull, with long rows of grinning teeth, the orbless sockets and the cavity of the nose, all crimsoned by the light of the lamp, touched his very hand, as he knelt upon the corner-floor. He started to his feet with a shriek, followed by another yell of horror.

"It's him, the man I pitched thro' the trap," he shouted. "Here he lays right under the trap-door, here he has laid for six long years, and now he wants to murder me! Ugh! He moves them bony fingers as if to clutch me by the throat, he grins in my face, ha, ha! He rises from the floor—his bones rattlin' against one another, and his broken jaw droppin' blood! I say you devil don't touch me, dont ye, dont——Ah!"

His soul fired with the sight of the terrible phantom, aroused into life by the spectacle of the skeleton of the murdered man, Devil-Bug retreated backwards, with his face turned towards the light, while raising his hands as high, he aroused the silence of the vault with another yell of horror. As the yell broke from his lips, he fell backward, and was lost in the grave, which he had dug for another.

No sooner had he disappeared in the pit than the form of a man sprung from one side of the brick pillar at the same moment that the figure of a woman advanced from the other side.

"Quick Bess, quick I say," shouted the man seizing the spade. "The antidote, quick, or all is lost! Apply it to Byrnewood's lips, while I keep this monster in his grave!"

Luke Harvey, his snake-like eye blazing with excitement and his slender form raised to its extreme height, stood beside the grave, while Long-haired Bess, her face flushed and her dark eyes sparkling with animation, bent over the unconscious form of Byrnewood, and applied a small phial to his clammy lips.

"Hello feller, it was you that groaned was it?" shouted Devil-Bug as his hideous face, appeared above the edge of the grave. "What in the devil d'ye mean by them sort o' capers any how?"

"You infernal monster," shouted Luke Harvey with an oath. "Make but an attempt to get out o' that grave, and I'll crush your skull with this spade! Quick Bess—the antidote! Apply it to Byrnewood's lips, and lead him from the cellar while I hold this devil at bay!"

"Joy, joy, he revives!" shouted Bess gently raising the form of Byrnewood from the floor. "The antidote has taken effect. Keep back the monster another moment Luke, and we will escape from the vault."

"Ye will, will ye?" cried Devil-Bug grasping the edge of the grave with his talon fingers. "Jist wait till I git out o' this!" His eye glared with a ferocious gleam, as placing his knees against the sides of the grave, he began to crawl from its confines.

"Back devil! You have made the grave and you shall sleep in it?" shouted Luke, as raising the spade above his head, he hurled it full against the skull of Devil-Bug. "Back devil; you have met your match this time!"

Stupified by the blow, Devil-Bug reeled back backward into the grave. Luke turned round, and beheld Byrnewood standing erect on his feet, with the arm of Long-haired Bess gathered round his waist, while her shoulder supported his head.

"Lead him from the vault, Bess!" exclaimed Luke. "In a moment old Devil-Bug will recover from the effects of the blow, and Byrnewood may again fall into his hands."

"The antidote has restored him phisical but not mental strength!" exclaimed Bess as her cheek grew deathly pale with the war of conflicting emotions. "Ha!" she muttered to herself as she disappeared into the darkness of the vault with Byrnewood walking unsteadily by her side. Ha! It was in this vault that Paul Western fell, when the trap-door sunk beneath him. Yonder his bones lay uncovered to the light; and his Murderess beholds them, and lives!"

Luke stood beside the grave holding the spade in his hands, while he gazed upon the retreating figures of Bess and Byrnewood.

"If I believed in any particular saint, I think I'd call in their aid just now! A cursed scrape I'm in again, all from my disposition to meddle in other folks affairs. There I stood, in front of my room, where I had just left my character of Brick-Top, together with the rags and the wig, when who should tap me on the shoulder but Bess! 'Byrnewood Arlington's in danger—Devil-Bug has just now borne him to the vaults of Monk-Hall,' quoth the maiden, and without stopping to tell me the particulars she hurries down stairs, like wildfire! I hurry after her—

old Devil-Bug is seen far below with a man on his shoulder, and a light in his hand—we creep along stealthy as cats, close at his heels. He enters the cellar, places the light on the floor, and commences his infernal orgies. We steal behind the brick pillar, and watch his movements. Bess tells me about the poison and the antidote; I select my time for a melo-dramatic groan, and here lies the result of that groan! Old Devil-Bug in the grave which he dug for another!"

A deep groan resounded from the depths of the grave.

"Oh, you're there, are you?" cried Luke, as his face darkened over with an expression of mingled hatred and rage. "Suppose I try your own game with you? How would you like to be buried alive?"

With a mocking sneer playing over his features, he struck the spade into the loose earth, and threw several clumps of hard clay into the grave. Another groan came echoing from the pit, and Luke turned his jest into serious earnest, by throwing one spadeful of earth after another, into the grave.

"Oh, groan by all means, it will do you good!" cried Luke, plying his spade with renewed energy. "An elderly gentleman like yourself, who whiles away his leisure time in burying folks alive, should hold himself prepared for any little contingincies like the present. How are you off for clay—eh, Devil-Bug?"

As he spoke, the spade rose and fell in his active grasp, and his face warmed with excitement. The beams of the light fell over his slender figure, and around the grave, while all beyond was impenetrable darkness. As Luke stood on the verge of the grave, occupied with the use of the spade, which he plyed so rapidly, a swarthy hand stole quietly from the edge of the pit, and moved as quietly over the hard clay, as though feeling for some object, and in an instant another hand, with talon fingers, appeared by its side. Luke did not behold these hands moving so quietly beside his very feet, but absorbed in his occupation, continued to shower the hard clods into the grave.

"Ha, ha!" he laughed, as his dark eye gleamed with excitement. "Old Devil-Bug little thought of this when he dug the grave! It was his turn awhile ago, it's my turn now, and—"

"It's my turn ag'in!" shouted a hoarse voice, and the grim face of Devil-Bug, all streaming with blood, was thrust from the edge of the grave. "There's sich a thing as playin' 'possum, young man!"

He seized Luke by the ancles, and with all the strength of his iron-sinewed arms gathered for the effort, flung him to the earth. In another instant he had leaped from the grave, and stood over the prostrate form of Luke with his iron-hand upraised, while his eye blazed with rage.

"Take that, feller!" he muttered, with a deep emphasis, as gathering all his strength for the blow, he struck Luke on the head, near the right temple. Luke saw the blow descending, and tried to ward it off, but in vain. The blow descended, and in another moment, with a faint tremor quivering through his frame, Luke lay senseless as a stone.

"Now for the ring!" cried Devil-Bug, raising the left hand of Luke in the light. "Ah-ha! Here it is; on the third finger, and a werry purty ring it is! He wouldn't part with it except with his life—ha, ha! I reether guess that he'll part with the ring and his life at wonst!"

Bending over the unconscious form of Luke, he extended his hands and fastened the talon-like fingers around his throat, with the grasp of a vice.

"I wouldn't give much for yer eyes, my feller!" he muttered, tightening the grasp of his fingers, until the face of the prostrate man grew purple, and the lids of his eyes, slowly unclosing, revealed the bloodshot eyeballs starting from their sockets. "It's my opinion you'd make a bad subject for the dissectin' table!"

A deep booming sound like distant thunder, echoed through the vaults and chambers of the mansion. Devil-Bug released his grasp on the throat of Luke and sprang to his feet. It was but the labor of a moment to seize the lamp and rush toward the door of the cellar. With his muscular right hand he raised the fallen door from its resting place, and placing it against the door-frame, as he stepped upon the first block of the granite stairway, left the vault in utter darkness.

In a moment, however, the door was pushed slowly aside, and the face of Devil-Bug, all hideous with an expression of sneering glee, appeared in the aperture, while his extended hand flung the rays of the light over the darkness of the vault.

"He lays beside the grave—ha, ha, ha—and I've got the ring! He lays alongside o' the grave, and there he'll rot, until his clothes fall, piece by piece, from his stripped bones! Ho, ho! The worms won't play all sorts o' games with his eyes? O'course not. Nor strip the flesh from his skull, nor fatten on his lips until the white teeth grin for joy? Nobody thinks o' such a thing! Ha! There goes the gong agin—I must 'tend to the wants o' Parson Pyne!"

The incarnate sneer which played over his countenance, suddenly gave place to that peculiar expression, which had agitated his visage an hour before, in the presence of Parson Pyne and his fair daughter. What was the meaning of this expression, it were difficult to tell, but it drew the eyebrows down from the protuberant forehead of Devil-Bug, until the sockets were nearly hidden by their thick and uneven hair, it compressed his wide mouth with an expression as grotesque as it was determined, while his solitary eye grew alive with a deadly and glaring light like the white heat on a bar of iron. There was revenge in that expression, and memory and love! The heart of the monster suddenly became a chaos, over whose tumultuous clouds of storms and darkness, a single ray of light, streaming from the fair distance, revealed a gentle form, with arms outstretched in mercy, and a fair face animated with a smile of love.

"Nell!" muttered Devil-Bug, between his clenched teeth. "It's werry long ago since I saw yer face—" he paused suddenly while some dim memory seemed struggling from the chaos of his soul. "I don't know much about it now, but if it is, *if it is* I say, then he shall die by inches, or there ain't no sich person as Devil-Bug!"

He closed the door of the vault, and all was darkness. Close beside the grave, cold and stiffening lay the form of Luke Harvey, with the rats, who were so soon to hold their revel on his flesh, already crawling around their prey, and snuffing their banquet in the tainted air of the vault. Close beside the grave lay the skeleton of the murdered man, mouldering to dust, in darkness and silence, as it had lain for years, and the sullen stream of the vault still rolled moaningly onward, its sluggish waves chaunting a rude death-song for the slain. The nooks and crannies of the vault took up the echo of the flood, and on all sides a low-muttered murmur, swelling to the arching roof above, seemed but the whispered tones of fiends, chuckling with glee as they spoke of the murders done in the Pit of Monk-Hall.

Meanwhile along the rough steps of granite, Long-haired Bess, supporting the head of Byrnewood on her shoulder, while her arm encircled his waist, endeavoured to lead the half-conscious man, as the distant echo of voices came muttering to her ear from the Pit of Monk-Hall, whose door lay but a few yards at her back.

He is yet unconscious," she murmured, as the head of Byrnewood pressed heavily on her shoulder. "The stairs are dark, and his footsteps are faint and trembling, but he shall yet be saved!"

And thus, in silence and suspense, she led him up the lofty stairs, until they stood on the floor of the hall in front of the Banquet Room. Here his strength seemed to fail him, but the brave woman gathered her arm yet tighter around his waist, and hurried him along the stairs leading to the first floor of Monk-Hall. Then the massive stairway of the mansion was passed, and in a few moments Bess and her charge stood in the darkness of the hall on the second floor.

"The secret door lies this way," she murmured, leading him toward the northern end of the hall. "The secret door leading to the Well

Room of Monk-Hall. A private staircase, built in the walls between the mansion and the Tower building, leads down into a narrow entry. This entry once traversed, he will stand in the Well Room, which is on the ground floor of the Tower building. A narrow door separates him from the yard. That door passed, the fence scaled, and a long alley traversed, he will gain the wide street, he will be saved! Ha! Devil-Bug approaches, I hear his footstep on the stairs!"

"My sister, my sister!" murmured Byrnewood speaking for the first time. "Ah! I have been entangled in the mazes of some horrible dream! Where am I? Whose hand is this upon my shoulder—and this darkness, what does it mean?"

"The antidote has taken full effect!" cried Bess in a tone of joy. "His strength is restored! This way sir, this way!" she continued leading him toward the secret door. "Down the private staircase, and through the small room at its foot, you will enter the yard of Monk-Hall. Scale the fence and you are saved! Quick or all is lost! Ha! Mark you the gleam of that light, flashing from the stairway along the entry. Devil-Bug approaches and all is lost!"

The light flashing up the stairway faintly illumined the hall. Byrnewood pressed his hands madly to his brow, as if in the effort to awake himself from some horrible dream. Then a sudden glow flushed over his face, and with a rude movement of his arm he flung Bess aside.

"Ha! I remember it all. My sister, and the drug. It comes like a lightning flash upon my soul! And you, you were one of the minions of the seducer! Back, back, touch me not! Your hand is as polluted as your soul!"

"Quick! Pass through the secret door, and gain the Well-Room or you are Devil-Bug's prisoner once more!"

"Leave Monk-Hall, and my sister in the power of the seducer? Never! Oh Mary my own true sister, I will save you yet! The villain shall pay for his crime with his life; your wrong shall be washed out in the blood of the seducer!"

Exerting all her strength for the effort, Bess seized him by the shoulder, and forced him through the narrow doorway.

"Quick, or all is lost!" she shrieked. "Before God I swear to rescue your sister from the foul den of Monk-Hall! Away, away!"

As she spoke the light grew more vivid along the stairway, and Devil-Bug stood on the floor of the Hall. At a glance he beheld Bess and the form of Byrnewood, as he stood in the narrow door. He hailed them with a yell, and holding the light in his hand rushed wildly forward.

"Now will you fly?" shouted Bess. "Delay one moment longer, and your life is in this monster's power! Your sister is lost forever. Away!"

"I go!" shouted Byrnewood, as his wan face, reddened with a gleam of excitement. "But I will return again, with the power to avenge my sister's wrong! Let the seducer and his minions make the most of their hour of crime! My hour will come, and my sister's wrong shall be washed out in her seducer's blood!"

Bess hurried him through the doorway, and his footsteps were heard upon the stairs. Devil-Bug stood before the tall woman, his face darkened by a hideous frown.

"Well you she-devil, so you've let that feller escape have ye?" he muttered as he approached her, with a look that boded no good.

"He has escaped, thank heaven he has escaped!" cried Bess as her dark eye fired with triumph, while her proud form towered to its full stature.

Devil-Bug made no reply, but folding his arms across his chest, with the light in one hand, he inclined his head to one side, as if in the act of listening to some far-off sound.

In a moment a crushing sound, like the peal of musquetry, came thundering up the private staircase.

"D'ye hear that?" shouted Devil-Bug as his eye flashed with an expression of malignant triumph. "D'ye hear that sound, g-a-l? Ho, ho, ho! Yer feller passes down the stairs, he passes the entry, he crosses the room, ha, ha, ha! In the centre of that room, is the old well of Monk-Hall kivered with loose boards! Yer feller tries to cross that room, ho, ho, ho! The loose boards don't give way beneath his feet? What does that crash mean? You've made a purty spot of business of this matter, I *do* declare!"

"Great God! He is lost!" cried Bess turning white as a sheet in the face. "But I will save him yet—" she cried opening the secret door. "Even yet I will foil ye, monster and devil that you are!"

"Werry likely g-a-l, werry likely," exclaimed Devil-Bug quietly interposing between her form and the door. "But jist now you'll retire to yer apartments. Arter this minnit consider yerself a pris'ner. Go home Bessie—" he continued with his habitual sneer. "Go home little g-a-l, yer mommy's got short cakes an' coffee for supper. She wants you—don't you hear her callin'?"

Bess calmly folded her arms, and while a dark frown marred the beauty of her countenance, she moved slowly toward the staircase of the mansion.

"Fine gal, that!" chuckled Devil-Bug, eyeing her retreating form. "Only she takes too much opium in her brandy, now an' then. But Bess is a screamer, when her dander is riz; a reg'lar hell-cat for all sorts o' devilment—"

Bess slowly turned her head over her shoulder, and with her eyes flashing with concentrated rage, whispered a single name.

"Paul Western!" she exclaimed with her eyes fixed on Devil-Bug's face.

"What d'ye mean by that? Hey, you she-devil?" cried Devil-Bug, advancing with a threatening gesture.

"What do I mean?" echoed Bess with a bitter sneer. "Why I mean that your account is almost full! The blood of Paul Western clings to your skirts, and—look there Devil-Bug, look there!" she exclaimed pointing to the vacant air at his back—"Do you not see his skeleton, standing at your shoulder? Look, look! The long bony fingers are grasping for your throat—"

Devil-Bug turned round with an involuntary shudder. When he looked toward the stairway again, Bess had disappeared.

"That g-a-l is a born devil!" he muttered. "Howsomdever I'll go down stairs and see if that feller is ralely done for!"

He disappeared through the private door, and for a few moments, the Hall was wrapt in darkness.

"All right, jist as if I'd done it myself!" he cried as he was again visible through the aperture of the doorway. "The boards all broke and smashed, and a heap o' clothes flutterin' and movin' near the bottom of the well!"

He laughed with ungovernable glee, but in a moment the expression of his hideous face, was shadowed by a heavy frown.

"The g-a-l," he muttered. "Here I've been foolin' my time away with trifles, when, when———"

As he spoke he entered the door of Dr. Pyne's ante-chamber.

CHAPTER NINTH

PATENT-GOSPEL GRACE

"Is it not beautiful my child? Is it not beautiful?"

As he spoke, with his knees spread very wide apart from each other, and the cup of coffee placed on one knee, the Reverend Doctor, waved the silver spoon to and fro, nodding all the while, and glancing with a curious look at the fair face of Mabel, who was seated opposite. We say curious look, because he was a good Minister, and it would not do, to call that sensual glance, gleaming through half-closed eyelids, humid with unhealthy moisture, by its proper name.

"What is beautiful?" asked Mabel, as she raised the cup of coffee to her lips.

"To think that a berry should grow in the ground," continued Alamont Pyne, glancing aside at the face of his daughter, while he beat a tattoo on the saucer with the end of the spoon. "To think that a berry should grow in the ground, and that, that simple berry, by a mysterious decree of Providence, should in the course of time, assume the appearance of a cup of coffee!"

The Rev. Dr. Pyne raised his watery eyes heavenward, but in an instant as though impelled by some strange charm, he fixed them upon the face of Mabel, with that same gloating expression of fatherly affection. *Fatherly* affection, by all means.

"Drink your coffee, my love, drink, it will do you good!" said the Rev. Pyne with an unctuous fatness of voice. "Nothing like coffee to raise your spirits, 'specially," he added in a cheerful whisper, 'Specially when it is spiced with a drug or two."

"I feel so strange, father," exclaimed Mabel passing her white hand over her brow. "There is a burning sensation on my forehead, and my eyes pain me. Oh father, can I indeed be going mad? The room is filled with strange forms, and I feel as though an invisible hand was dragging me over a frightful precipice—"

Her dark eyes suddenly assumed a wild and unearthly light. In an instant the lids seemed to have shrunken away from the eyeballs, and each eye, dilating to an unnatural size, assumed a strange lustre, rendered more apparent and striking by the utter paleness of the countenance, with a single vivid spot of red, crimsoning the centre of each swelling-cheek. Even the lips of the maiden assumed an unnatural hue. Suddenly their moist vermilion changed to a warm and unhealthy purple.

"Father, father," she cried, "I am going mad! For God's sake, save me, save me! The room sinks from beneath my feet, the air is filled with horrible phantoms, and—oh save me, save me!"

She fell back into the chair, and covered her face with her hands.

"This is the first stage of the potion," blandly whispered Dr. Pyne, as his red face, with its rubicund cheeks, flushed all over with deep crimson, assumed an expression of the most decided character. "At first she will be frightened, then she will fall into a gentle doze, and then, ah then!" He took her fair white hand within his own, and patted it playfully against his oily cheek. "No one shall hurt you my child. Your papa is with you. Go to sleep, that's a dear, Mabel."

Her form thrown back in the chair, with the limbs disposed in a careless and therefore voluptuous position. Mabel gazed at her father with a wild stare as though she did not comprehend the meaning of his words. She looked supremely beautiful, as with her dark hair, falling in heavy masses aside from her pale face, she surrendered one hand to her father, while the other rested upon the white skin of her neck, just where it began to expand into the virgin bosom.

"I gave Devil-Bug three potions, sometime ago," muttered Dr. Pyne, as he drew his chair to the side of the bewildered girl. "One kills, the other makes crazy, the third makes love; or rather disposes a sweet young girl for the exercise of that delightful sentiment."

"Father, look, look! There, at your very shoulder, stands a skeleton, winding a grave-shroud round your limbs! Oh, father, for Heaven's sake, do not suffer it to stand there with its bony fingers on your cheek."

"Ugh! The girl scares the life out of one!" cried Dr. Pyne, jumping from his chair. "Ah-ha! She begins to doze! How beautiful! That pale face, so round in its outlines, with the spot of red on each cheek, those lips—they change from purple to red again—falling slightly apart, that glimpse of a soft bosom—Ah-ha! She *does* begin to doze—"

Mabel's head dropped lightly on her shoulder, and her eyelids slowly closed. Her long dark hair fell showering over her white shoulders. Her arms sank stiffly by her side. She lay silent and motionless as though suddenly stricken by the hand of death.

The Rev. Dr. Pyne rose slowly from his seat. He smacked her lips with unctuous fervor, and then taking his watch from the fob, he strode quietly up and down the room.

"This is the second stage of the potion," he whispered, looking at the watch. "The third stage is the most delightful of all. That paleness will give place to a peach-like bloom, that stiffness of limb will be overcome by a voluptuous languor, that closed eye, when its lids again unclose, will fire with passion and flash with all the bewitching softness of a woman's love! It now wants ten minutes of twelve o'clock. At twelve, the dear child will be in my power. The care and trouble of seventeen years will be well repaid. Ah-ah! I remember; I have to preach the Anniversary Sermon of the Gospellers on Christmas night, let me think it over!"

Mabel still lay silent and unconscious, her hands dropped listlessly by her side, while her cheeks were pale and colorless as death.

"Yes, yes," soliloquized the pious Dr. Pyne, "I might touch up the Gospellers on that score! I might talk of my wonderful conversion, my sudden reform, my glorious change from darkness to light. Yes, brethren and sisters," he continued, striking an attitude as though surveying his congregation from the heighth of the pulpit. "Seventeen years ago, I was a poor miserable wretch, destitute at once of a good coat a pure knowledge of the Bible! Now brothers, now sisters, behold me, behold the wonderful reform, all accomplished by pure Patent Gospel grace! (Ha! Mabel revives! Her eyes slowly unclose and her lips fire with passion!) Seventeen years ago I was a ragged loafer, a leprous wretch, hiding in dark corners in the day, and sleeping in the gutters at night! Now brethren—and you, my dear sisters—behold the change! A change of heart and a change of linen! I walk the streets in the day, clad in fine broadcloth; at night I sleep on a bed of down, and my conscience, brothers and sisters, oh it is peaceful, calm and peaceful! Easy, quite e-a-s-y, I assure you! And this, my children—" his red round face assumed an expression of deep pathos—"is all the work Patent Gospel grace!"

Subsiding from his pulpit attitude, the good brother approached the unconscious girl. A warm glow brightened freshly over her pale face, and her dark eyes half-closed, gave forth a sparkling glance, moistened with passion. While the pious minister stood gazing upon her, with a look as pure as the glance from the bloodshot eye of a Satyr, her form relaxing from its rigidity of muscle, began to assume the flowing outlines of voluptuous beauty. She grew radiant with passion. The red lips, slightly parted, revealing the teeth like pearls, the young bosom heaving with life, the face warmed with a burning flush, and the eye, large, dark and lustrous, humid with the moisture of passion—alas for Mabel now! The potion administered by the good Doctor Pyne, had aroused her animal nature into life, and she stood disclosed, a breathing image of that voluptuousness which is at once the charm and the curse of woman.

"Come kiss your father," said Dr. Pyne, extending his arms towards the girl. "That's a good child. Kiss your papa!"

Mabel gazed upon him with wandering glance. It was evident that while her animal nature was aroused into full development, her intellectual powers were for the moment crushed, if not utterly broken. The glance which rested upon Dr. Pyne's face was humid with passion, but it was the glance of an idiot.

"The potion works like a miracle!" murmured the Parson, as his rubicund face warmed with a ruddy glow, while his watery eyes, with the veins of each pupil filled with discolored blood, stood out from their very sockets, with a look of gloating admiration. "Come and kiss your papa, Mabel! It was a good girl, that it was, and it must kiss its papa!"

Like one arising in their sleep, Mabel arose from the chair, and extending her arms, advanced to her father's side. Her footsteps trembled as she walked. Still the flush brightened in her cheek, still the glance, flashing from her dark eye, grew more soft and mellowed with the moisture of passion, still her fair young bosom rose heaving from beneath the folds of her night robe.

She extended her arms and kissed his lips.—Faugh! Those lips were gross and sensual, though they *were* a Parson's lips! She kissed his lips again, and yet again. She laid her soft cheek against his face, she encircled his neck with her round arms; he felt her tiny fingers playing with the thin locks of his hair. The Parson's face grew more crimson, and his arms gathered more closely around his daughter's waist.

"It is a good child, so it is," whispered Doctor Pyne, kissing her red lips. "And it will come and sit on papa's knee, so it will!"

He drew the fair girl to his knee, his watery eyes grew more sensual in their gaze, and his arms gathered more closely round her waist.

"What a blessed thing it is, to possess, a knowledge of medical science, however slight!" And Dr. Pyne kissed the red lips of the girl, with priest-fervor. "Here she was, an hour ago, full of intellectual energy! Now, ho, ho, her mind is laid to sleep for a little while, and all the animal portion of her nature, is aroused into active life. Quite active! A good potion that! A-h—" the good Dr. Pyne tasted the freshness of her lips again.

"Ha! Ha! Ha!" Dr. Pyne started with a sudden thrill of horror, as that maniac laugh broke on his ear.

"Ha! Ha! Ha!" The girl started to her feet, and while her swelling cheeks flushed with animation, and her dark eyes seemed to swim in liquid fire, she stood erect upon the floor, her extending hands pointing at his face, with a maniac-gesture.

"Mabel, my child—" the Dr. began, as he rose from his seat.

"Ha, Ha, Ha!" shrieked the girl, as with that same unearthly look she gazed steadily in the face of the good Parson.

"What can all this mean? Certainly the child has gone mad! Mabel, my dear, come to your pa-pa!"

Still the girl stood erect, her form raised to its full heighth, her eyes gathering new fire every instant, her cheek, blooming with unnatural freshness, while her extended hands, with the long fingers trembling in the light, pointed fixedly in his face. Oh how beautiful the picture—a vivid impersonation of beauty, mere animal loveliness, yet still bewitching loveliness, utterly deprived of intellect! The long dark hair falling over the shoulders, the erect attitude, the extended arms, and the flowing robes of snowy white, the large dark eyes, dilating every instant, and swimming in a strange light, the pale face, with the burning freshness in the centre of each cheek, the red lips and the young bosom rising faintly into view. Oh beautiful as a dream, and yet more terrible than death!

"Ha, ha, ha!"

Dr. Pyne turned pale. The laugh sounded like the shriek of his evil angel.

"Come girl no more of this!" He advanced fiercely toward the maiden. His hands were clenched, and his brow was darkened by a frown. "No more of this! Your shrieks will arouse the neighborhood. I have trifled too long?"

"Ha! Ha! Ha!" Louder and more terrible arose that shriek of maniac laughter.

"Now for the reward, for which I have waited seventeen long years!"

He seized the maiden by the shoulder, and with one rude grasp tore the night robe from her bosom. The white fragments fluttered in his hands. Another moment and his arms were around her waist: his foul lips stained her bosom with a kiss.

A wild light flashed from the eyes of the girl. Her cheek grew pale as death, and then crimson as the dawn! Her soul was struggling with her animal nature! She tossed her arms aloft, she tore her form from the embrace of the priestly villain, she tried to cover the round globes of her bosom, with outspread fingers of her fair white hands.

"Damnation!" shouted the Preacher, as his round face grew purple with rage.

"You shall not foil me this time!"

Maddened with lust and rage he advanced, he gathered the quivering waist of the girl within his vigorous arm. She struggled and writhed, and leapt from her very feet in the effort to tear herself from his grasp. He raised his clenched hand and—oh villain and dastard! He struck her to the floor! Her white bosom received the blow. Along one round and snowy globe, a dark streak of purple, burst from the skin, and stamped the traces of his violence.

She lay prostrate on the floor, her breath heaving with convulsive gasps, her form quivering like a leaf, her cheek white as marble. He knelt by her side. He, the profaner of God's sacrament, the violator of God's truth, the blasphemer of God's name! He knelt before the crazed girl, he gathered her form in his arms, he kissed her death-cold lips. One more effort, sweet Mabel! With one convulsive bound she sprang from his embrace, again sunk kneeling on the floor, and raised her hands and eyes to heaven.

"OH MOTHER," she cried in tones that would have melted the heart of the fiend in hell, "OH MOTHER, SAVE YOUR CHILD!"

And her eyes were upward cast, and her hands were outstretched as if to grasp the phantom-form, which her crazed fancy beheld floating in the darkened air.

"You cannot escape me now!" shouted Pyne in a voice grown hoarse with passion. "Mine you are by heaven, and mine by hell! Ho, ho, my beauty! You ran away from my house did you? You placed my character in jeopardy, did you? Ho, ho my beauty, we'll see who's master now!"

He rushed toward the girl. She rose from the floor, and retreated toward a dark corner of the room. Her face turned over her shoulder, her long dark hair floating down her back, the white hands clasped over her bosom, she fled widly forward; her foot became entangled in the carpet; she fell prostrate on the floor.

A gleam of malignant triumph shot from the Preacher's eyes.

"I have you at last!" he muttered as he knelt by her side. His watery eyes grew expressive with a look of gloating admiration. For a moment he gazed upon the girl in silence. She lay prostrate upon the floor, her form quivering with a slight convulsive motion, while she gazed upon his face with her large black eyes dilating in an expression of utter horror.

"Oh tremble, trem-b-l-e!" whispered the good Dr. Pyne. "It does me good to see you laying there, helpless as a baby! You may cry for help—no one will hear you! You may attempt to escape—but the doors are locked! Tremble, oh trem-b-l-e!"

The girl shuddered as the full sense of her danger broke upon her clouded reason. Still she lay prostrate on the floor, her face pale as death, while she gazed upon the Parson, in helpless terror.

"Save me mother—oh save me!" she muttered in a low whisper, as if talking to a spirit.

"Your mother can't save you now! You must come to your pa-pa, my love!" He bent down and gathered her form in his arms.

"Save me, mother," shrieked Mabel, "Oh save me mother!"

"You are mine! You are—" began the Parson in tones of exultation, when his arms suddenly relaxed their hold, and his fat form rolled senseless on the floor.

"G-a-l you called yer mother, and that call saved ye!" said a rough voice. Mabel looked up, and shrieked. Devil-Bug in all his hideous deformity stood at her side. His face was convulsed with an expression of fearful hatred, and his long talon-like fingers worked as with an epileptic spasm.

"Here Glow-worm, here Musketer," he shouted, "Drag this old porpis' into the next room!"

The negroes came stealing through the small doorway of the apartment. They seized the unconscious form of the Reverend Pyne, and bore him into the ante-chamber. Devil-Bug was alone with the fair girl.

He stooped slowly down, while she shuddered in horror, at the sight of his hideous visage. He gathered his rough arms around her tender form, he raised her from the floor. She shrieked with affright. Devil-Bug trembled from head to foot. Stepping softly over the floor, he bore her to the bed, and laid her gently on its coverlid. Mabel's dark eyes grew lustrous with terror.

Devil-Bug stepped backward from the bed. He gazed upon her face for a moment in silence. His huge mouth was fixedly compressed, and his large nostrils quivered with a nervous movement. His solitary eye glared upon the face of the girl with a fearful intensity. She was thrilled to the very heart with a strange awe.

A wild cry burst from his lips. It was like the howl of an enraged beast holding the hunters at bay. Again that cry! He rushed fiercely toward the bed. Mabel started up in involuntary affright. Devil-Bug struck his huge hands violently against his forehead, and uttered that terrific howl yet again. Then turning on his heel, he fled madly from the room.

CHAPTER TENTH

PARSON PYNE HAS A GOOD LAUGH TO HIMSELF

The portly form of Parson Pyne lay on the carpet of the ante-chamber, with a huge negro watching on either side.

Devil-Bug rushed madly into the apartment and stood beside the form of the unconscious Preacher. His solitary eye glared with all the malignity of a devil, as its glance rested upon the round and rubicund face of the Parson.

"Here, yo' niggers," he shouted; "d'ye see that couch? Strip off the bed an' the bedclothes, and lay the Parson on the sackin' bottom! That's right, that's right! Now, Musketer, tie one leg to that bed-post, and Glow-worm, d'ye hear? You tie his tother leg to the tother bed-post! Sarve his hands the same way! Ha, ha! He looks like the letter X in the primer books!"

The fat form of the parson was extended on the sacking bottom, with each leg tightly pinioned by the ancle to the bed-posts at the foot, while his extended hands were tied in the same manner, to the posts at the head of the couch. He certainly looked like a very corpulent representative of St. Andrew's cross. His round paunch stood out from the sacking bottom in painful prominence, and his large lips hanging apart, afforded an interesting anatomical view of his mouth and pallet.

"Is the poker and the tongs heated to a white heat?" grunted Devil-Bug, scowling fiercely in the faces of his negroes.

"Yes, massa," cried Glow-worm, as he raised the tongs in the light, with its point heated to a glaring white heat.

"Dis do, massa?" cried Musquito, producing the poker, whose jabbed point, also heated to a white heat, emitted a fierce and blinding glare.

"Where am I?" said Parson Pyne, faintly, as he unclosed his eyes.

"Why you see, Parson, I wanted to axe you a few questi'ns, and bein' afeer'd you wouldn't answer 'em quite easy, I jist tied yo' to that bed, and got a couple o' first rate lawyers to plead with you—"

"Lawyers?" echoed Parson Pyne. "Ha! I am tied to the bed. What d'ye mean, ye villain? Where are your lawyers?"

"Here they is, Parson!" exclaimed Devil-Bug, and the two negroes, holding the heated irons in their hands, stood by the bedside.

"Ugh!" the involuntary groan was forced from the lips of the pinioned parson. "Villain, d'ye mean to murder me?"

"No, not 'xactly. I only wants to axe ye a few questi'ns. If so be, you refuses to answer—"

"If I refuse to answer—"

"Why then I'll burn your eyes out o' your head!" replied Devil-Bug, his solitary eye flashing with concentrated hate.

Parson Pyne was silent for a moment. He looked at the huge negroes by the bedside and a cold shudder ran over his fat person.

"What are your questions?" he faintly asked.

"Is that gal in the next room your darter?" exclaimed Devil-Bug, bending his head down to receive the answer.

"She is," responded the Parson, in a firm tone.

"That's a big a lie as ye ever did tell" growled Devil-Bug. "I see we can't git no truth out o' yo' without the lawyers. Take off his shoes an' stockin's, Glow-worm!"

"Dev-i-l," muttered Parson Pyne, with a violent struggle to extricate himself from his uneasy position. "You shall dearly pay for this insolence!"

"Werry likely," responded Devil-Bug. "But for the present we'll attend to business."

As he spoke, Glow-worm flung the shoes and stockings of the Parson on the floor, and his bare feet, with the toes thrust upward, were exposed to the light.

"Tighten them cords round the ancles," muttered Devil-Bug. "Now Parson, for the last time—will yo' answer all my questi'ns in regard to that darter o' yours? And ricollec', Parson, yer not among the Patent-Gospel fellers *now!*"

Pyne made no answer, but gazed in the face of Devil-Bug with his watery eyes distended by an expression of utter amazement.

"Gi' me the iron!" exclaimed Devil-Bug, as he took the heated poker from Musquito's hands. "Now, Parson, vich eye do yo' valley most?" He held the jagged point of the iron within an inch of the Parson's right eye.

"Oh—o-oh," screamed Parson Pyne, as the heat of the iron shot a terrible pang through his very brain. "Take care, take care! You'll burn out my eye! Oh, o-h!"

"That I will!" grunted Devil-Bug, as the gaze of his solitary eye grew like the white heat of the iron. "H-i-s-s! h-i-s-s! Parson don't yo' feel the ragged pint hissing into yer eye already?" He held the iron within a half-in-inch of the Preacher's right eye.

"Oh—o-h!" roared the Parson, as his brain was penetrated by the fierce heat of the iron. "I'll answer, I'll answer! Take the iron from the room and I'll answer."

Devil-Bug grinned hideously.

"You'll answer, will ye? I guess I got yo' on the anxious bench that time! Souse them irons into that bucket o' water, niggers! Now, Parson, with regard to that darter!"

Parson Pyne glanced cautiously aside. He beheld the negroes in the act of plunging the hot irons into a bucket of water. The hissing sound emitted by the irons as they sank beneath the water broke, like the voice of a friend, on his ears.

"Go to the devil!" he shouted, in a tone of husky rage. "You may kill me, but I will not answer your questions!"

"Oh, you won't, won't you?" exclaimed Devil-Bug, as his habitual grin distorted his features. "What 'll yo' bet, Parson, that you don't answer my questions in a minute? And answer 'em laffin', too?" As he spoke he walked round to the foot of the bed, and extended his large hands until the talon fingers almost touched the soles of the Parson's feet.

"Monster, you shall pay for this!" cried the Reverend Pyne, as his fat face was distended by an expression of surprise. He evidently gazed upon the movements of Devil-Bug with some considerable wonder.

"Now, Parson, for the questi'ns! And fust o' all, I'll tell you what I know mesself. Pick yer ears, Parson! About Christmas Eve, eighteen hundred an' twenty-five, a man named Dick Baltzar, with his wife, Sarah Baltzar, hired rooms in the house o' the widder Crank, livin' in ——— street, near ——— street."

"Ha!" the involuntary cry of surprise was forced from the Parson's lips.

"Wos yo' that man, Dick Baltzar, or wos yo' not?"

"Go to the devil!" roared Parson Pyne.

"Oh, werry well, wer-r-y well!" exclaimed Devil-Bug, as he gently touched the soles of the Parson's feet with the tips of his talon fingers. "I'll tune you up, my pianey fortey, I will! Ho, ho! How d'ye feel, Parson?"

"Ha! ha! ha!" roared the Parson, with an outburst of spasmodic laughter, the result of the titillating movement of Devil-Bug's fingers along the soles of his feet. "Ha! ha! ha! Ho! ho! ho! Oh-oh-oh! Hi! hi! hi! Oh for God's sake don't—d-o-n-t! Hoo! hoo! hoo!" And the fat form of the Parson wriggled, and strained, and heaved, as with an epiletic fit.

"Ho, ho! My pianey fortey!" cried Devil-Bug, executing a flourish with his finger tips upon the delicate soles of the Parson's feet. "I'll tune you up, I will! Laugh, Parson, it 'ill do you good, laugh, I say!"

"Ha! ha! ha-a!" roared the Parson, making a desperate effort to withdraw his feet from the touch of the talon fingers. "Ho! ho! ho-o! Hi! hi! hi! Oh mer-cy! For God's sake don't ye tickle—tickle me! Hurrah! Ha! ha!"

"Ha! ha!" roared Devil-Bug, executing another flourish.

"Hah! ya-hah!" shouted Glow-worm.

"Ya-hah-ha-yah!" echoed Musquito.

"Go it my pianey fortey!" cried Devil-Bug, with a most effective flourish. "Jist see how my fingers go over these white soles! Ha! ha! Parson, you save souls; I tickles 'em! 'Gently over the stones, driver!' E-a-s-y, I say!"

"Ha! ha! ha-a-a!" roared the Parson, as he grew black in the face, while his watery eyes started from their sockets. "Ho! ho! ho! Oh, for God's sake—hoo! hoo! hoo! Don't ye tickle—ha! ha! ha! Tick-l-e, tick-l-e me! Hurrah! hi! hi! hi-i-i!"

"Wot a spektikle for the Free Believers! Ha, ha! Jist see the Parson wriggle! Wos there ever sich twistin' as that! How black he grows in the face! His eyes big as Delawar' bay oysters—ha! ha! ha! Come on my pianey fortey—I'll tune yo' up!

Yankey doo-del is the tune—"

"Ha! ha! ha!" interrupted the Parson.

"An' nothin' comes so han-dy!
As yankey doo-del doo-del do-oo—"

"Hoo! hoo! hoo!" roared Parson Pyne.

"An' yankey doo-del dan-dy!"

Screamed Devil-Bug, executing a delicate flourish on the soles of the Parson's feet.

"Ya-hah-hah," roared the negroes, holding their sides as they beheld the Preacher's agony.

Wriggling and twisting along the bed, Parson Pyne made the most superhuman efforts to extricate himself, but in vain. Still the finger tips of Devil-Bug ran softly, oh how softly along his feet, still he was forced to rend the air with unwilling laughter. Tickle, tickle, tickle! Ha! ha! ha! His face had now assumed a dark livid hue, and as his eyes hung out from their sockets, the white surface of each eyeball assumed a fearful prominence. Tickle, tic-kle, tic-kle! Ho! ho! ho! The veins stood out from his forehead like cords, and his chest heaved and swelled as though moving under the impulse of a small steam engine. Softly moved the finger-tips, oh softly, soft-ly, soft-l-y! Tic-k-le, tic-k-l-e, t-i-c-kle! Hoo! hoo! hoo!

"Oh, God! God! God!" yelled the Parson, as the tears rolled down his livid cheeks. "Mer-cy! ha! ha! ha! Ho! ho! ho! Hi! hi! hi! Mer-cy! H-o-o-o! Ah-a-a-ha-a!"

A wild unearthly shriek burst from the Parson's lips. Then he blasphemed the name of his God, then invoked all the curses of hell upon his head, and then the white foam frothed around his lips.

"Do yo' give in?" shouted Devil-Bug executing a brilliant flourish with his finger-tips.

"Ho! Ho! Ho!" roared the Parson. "Ye-s! Ye-s! Hoo! Hoo! Hoo! Curses—ha! ha! ha!—curses! D———n! Hi! Hi! Hi! Hi-i-i!"

"Did'nt I tell yo' my feller that ye'd better not perwoke me?" calmly exclaimed Devil-Bug, walking round the foot of the bed. "Now will you answer them questi'ns?"

Parson Pyne lay silent and speechless. Poor fellow! He looked quite pitiful. He lay gasping and panting for breath, while his livid cheeks and starting eyes, bore traces of the awful agony which he had endured. Had Devil-Bug continued his musical experiments a moment longer, the Patent-Gospeller's would have lost their preacher, and the devil gained a soul. As he lay there, pinioned to the bed, his starting eyes glaring vacantly around the room, he looked for all the world like a man who has been precipitated over some awful heighth; he lay so silent, so motionless, so utterly blank and speechless. Had the Pope of Pagan Rome have seen his Foe, he would have pitied him. Even the four-and-twenty cardinals would have wept. The Vatican itself, that deplorable edifice, would have shed tears. St. Peter's Church, that object of Patent-Gospel hate and scorn would have been convulsed with pity. Alas, for the Foe of Pagan Rome! To think that he, the daring and high-souled Pyne, who had stood up so often in his pulpit, and defied the Pope and the devil, who had electrified the old women with his eloquence, and convulsed whole churches-full of Gospellers with his matchless zeal, to think that he, should have been *tickled* into submission!

For ten long and weary minutes Devil-Bug awaited the recovery of the Parson. Never was whipped dog more completely cowed by the lash than was Parson Pyne by the finger-tips of old Devil-Bug.

"Was you Dick Baltzar, or was you not? Answer old porpis'!"

"I was," faintly responded the Parson.

"You rented rooms at the house o' th' Widder Crank on Christmas Eve, Eighteen hundred an' twenty-five?"

"I did."

"The widder Crank had a darter?"

"She had."

"Her name was—"

"Ellen—" faintly chirped Parson Pyne. "I'll tell you all about her. She had been seduced two years before I came to the Widow Crank's house. Her seducer, was a young merchant named Livingstone. On Christmas Eve Eighteen hundred and twenty four, she gave birth to a female child. It was called Ellen. A few days after the child was born, her mother in a fit of rage drove her from the house. The child remained with the widow Crank. It seems that Ellen and Livingstone had quarrelled soon after the birth of the child; and the mother's harshness resulted from her daughter's confession, that she was not married to her lover. For one year no intelligence whatever was heard from the daughter—"

"Ha!" shrieked Devil-Bug. "Are yo' sure o' that?"

"Why as myself and wife, only came to the Widow's House a year after Ellen had disappeared, it's hard for me to tell!" murmured the Rev. Dr. Pyne. "I never yet, have been quite certain, but that Livingstone knew of the girl's whereabouts all the while."

Devil-Bug smiled grimly to himself.

"Ho, ho!" he muttered. "Then I'm the only human bein' as knows where Ellen was during her absence from her mother's home!"

"As I said before I came to the Widow Crank's house, on Christmas

Eve Eighteen hundred and twenty *five*. That very night Ellen Crank returned home. She was in a very sad condition you see, and her mother welcomed her back with tears of joy. That very night she gave birth to another child—"

Devil-Bug leaned slowly forward, and applied his mouth to the ear to the Parson. "And that 'ere lost child, *died?*" he muttered in a whisper that thrilled the Parson to the heart.

"Livingstone always thought so," said Dr. Pyne in an evasive tone.

"No lyin' Parson! One child died that night I know! Was it the first or second?"

"It was the *first*," answered Dr. Pyne.

Devil-Bug buried his face in his hands, and the Parson heard him groan. The Negroes looked on in mute astonishment. Their master affected by any thing like a human feeling! Ha, Ha! The thought tickled them, and they chuckled quietly together.

"And the *second* child Parson, what ever becom' of it?" said Devil-Bug looking at the Preacher through the outspread fingers of his hands.

"I don't know," answered Pyne in a faint voice.

"You lie!" shrieked Devil-Bug, "You lie! You stole that child Parson, you and your wife trained it up with the idea-r of havin' a hold on Livingstone, when he came into his father's property! Don't I know ye, ye fat dog?" he rose from his seat and seized the Parson fiercely by the throat. "Yer wife died, and you turned Parson! Ho! Ho! am I right? Tell me quick or I'll choke ye!"

"You are—you are!" cried Pyne as he felt the talon-fingers of the deformed wretch gathering round his throat.

Devil-Bug started up with a wild howl, and rushed madly into the next chamber.

CHAPTER ELEVENTH

THE SAVAGE ALONE WITH THE MAIDEN

His teeth grating together, and his hands outspread, while his eye blazed with a madman's glare, he rushed toward the bed, whereon the girl was sleeping. Mabel started up in affright, and clasped her hands over her bosom, as she beheld him approach.

"Oh save me now, my God!" she shrieked and held her breath in very terror.

"Come g-a-l, come!" cried Devil-Bug as gathering his arm around her waist, he bore her quickly along the room. "Come, I say come!"

He stopped before an antique mirror of circular shape, which depended from the wainscotted walls. He placed Mabel on her feet, and rushing from her side, seized the light from the small table near the fire. In a moment he stood by her side again, and as she started backward, in utter horror of his hideous countenance, he flung the matted hair aside from his right temple.

"Look gal, look!" he cried pointing to the reflection of his loathsome countenance in the mirror. "D'ye see that red mark along my right temple? That red mark like a snake? D'ye see it, d'ye see it? That mark was born with me!"

Mabel gazed upon him with an expression of blank wonder mingled with terror.

Devil-Bug wound his rough arms round her neck, and swept her thick black tresses aside from her right temple.

"Look, look g-a-l look!" he shrieked as he pointed to the reflection of her beautiful countenance in the mirror. "I don't want you to look at them black eyes, which are like hers, nor the lips, nor the cheeks! But the right temple g-a-l—the right temple!"

Mabel involuntarily gazed within the mirror. She started back with a strange feeling of surprise as she beheld a slight, thin and discolored streak, marring the beauty of her face, near the right temple. It was a faint and delicate copy of the deep red mark near the swarthy temple of Devil-Bug.

"That was born with you g-a-l, that was born with you g-a-l!" shouted Devil-Bug. "An' you're my—yes yes you're my———"

He paused suddenly and fell on his knees. He placed the light on a chair, and then looked up into her wondering face, with his hideous countenance distorted by a strange emotion.

Then, bending to the very floor, he clung with his huge hands to the skirt of her white dress, and impressed his thick lips upon the shoe of her tiny foot. Then big tears stole from the lids of his blazing eye, and from the shrivelled socket which was destitute of an eyeball. Then his lips became fixedly compressed, and as he raised his clenched hands he uttered a yell, like the howl of an enraged hyena.

"Oh, mercy, mercy!" shrieked Mabel, gazing upon the monster at her feet in utter alarm.

Devil-Bug seized her fair white hands and looked up into her face in silence. It was a strange and fearful picture. The Savage kneeling at the feet of Innocence!

Her form, so delicate and beautiful in all its rounded proportions of maidenly loveliness, with the young bosom, bared to the light and heaving with animation, her face so pale and yet so fair to look upon, with the dark eyes of such unutterable eloquence, and the long black hair, falling along the cheeks and down to the shoulders!

His form, so rough and so uncouth, with its harsh outlines of deformity and strength, its broad chest quivering with strange emotion; his face so dark, so swarthy and so distorted, with its protuberant brow, its flat nose, and wide mouth, its eyeless socket and its solitary eye, blazing with superhuman emotion! It was a strange contrast; the Savage reared in the very centre of Quaker City civilization, kneeling at the fair and beautiful woman, wronged and injured by one of the professed Ministers of that civilization!

"Do not, do not harm me!" cried Mabel, all other feelings absorbed by the terror which she felt for the strange being at her feet.

"Harm ye?" growled Devil-Bug, as he rose from his kneeling position and forced her gently into a chair. "Gal, who is it that talks to me of harmin' ye?"

He seated himself on a chair opposite the maiden. The light, standing on another chair, flashed its beams over the outlines of their faces, so strangely contrasted to each other.

A wild hope fluttered over the heart of the maiden, as she beheld something like human feeling in the solitary eye of the monster.

"He may aid me to escape from this house!" she murmured.

"G-a-l, had ye ever a friend?" And as he spoke he took her fair white hand within his talon fingers.

"Never!" answered Mabel, as her heart warmed with a strange sympathy for the being before her. "My father has given me food, and clothes, and shelter, but I never yet looked upon the face of a human being whom I could call friend! No mother ever smiled upon me, and as for my father—oh, for God's sake do not, do not place me in his power again!"

"The g-a-l's been edicated!" muttered Devil-Bug. "You never had a friend, then? You don't remember your mother? I do, g-a-l, I do!"

"You!"

"Yes, g-a-l, I was your mother's servant, a-good many years ago. I used to kiss the very ground she stood upon. Don't mind me, my dear, if I talk a little wild. I'm a poor one-eyed devil, and nobody cares for me! But I'll be your friend g-al—I, that never yet was friend to a human bein' save one—I will be your friend!"

"You!"

"Yes, gal, me! I'm ugly as the devil—I know it! But for you, gal, for *you*, my heart feels warm! Ask me to hold my hand in that fire for your sake, jist ask me!"

He reached forth his hand toward the light as if to carry his words into action, when a spot of thick red blood crusting the swarthy skin, attracted the gaze of his solitary eye.

"Ha! It is *her* blood," he shouted, starting from his seat. "The old woman's blood! The blood of Ellen's mother! Ha! There she lays with the red blood droppin' from her holler skull! There—there—" he pointed fiercely to a vacant spot of the room. "Don't ye see her, gal? And here, gal, here, by my side, his jaw back and his tongue stickin' out, he lays—*he*, jist as he fell through the trap!"

He rushed wildly toward the door, as the terrible phantoms, in all their horror, broke anew upon his gaze.

"But I'll be yer friend, g-al!" he shouted, turning suddenly round. "I, I, old Devil-Bug will be your slave! You shall roll in wealth, g-a-l! Parson Pyne ain't yer father—not a bit o' it! Yer father has gold enough to buy ye a row o' houses! I tell ye, gal, old Devil-Bug is yer friend! The man that tries to injure ye will have a wild beast to fight—that's all!"

He rushed into the next room where Parson Pyne still lay pinioned to the sacking bottom of the bed. The Herculean negroes watched by the bedside.

"Put on this feller's shoes an' stockin's an' let him clear out!" shouted Devil-Bug. "And look ye, Parson Pyne! it 'ud be better for you to crack jokes with a hungry tiger than to dare touch that gal ag'in! Go home, Parson Pyne, and mind yer business, and put down the Pope o' Rome! The g-a-l shall go to her father, the rich merchant Livingstone! Her face is proof enough that she is Ellen's darter! And mind ye, Parson Pyne—" he cried, as he stood in the doorway, his face darkened by a scowl of rage. "If yo' ever lay a finger on that g-a-l ag'in, I'll have my revenge on you, if I have to drag you from yer pulpit! I'll have yer blood if I have to spill it in the sacrament cup!"

He closed the door and rushed madly down the stairway of Monk-Hall.

"To the vault, to the vault! An' let me think these things over! My brain feels kind o' crazy like, and my blood biles in my veins! Ha! ha! ha! Old Devil-Bug's darter shall ride in her carriage, and wear silks an' satins—that she shall!"

And as he went down to the vault of Monk-Hall, his wild and discordant laughter broke upon the air with a sound of strange and savage joy.

CHAPTER TWELFTH

THE FLIGHT FROM MONK-HALL

The negroes were alone in the ante-chamber. Glow-worm stood on one side of the fire gazing into the face of his comrade, who leaned against the mantel on the opposite side. Musquito grinned hideously as he caught the gleam of Glow-worm's eye.

"Ha-hah! Yah-hah!"

"What fo' you make dat dam noise?" asked Glow-worm, with dignified severity.

"It am so dam queer, it am!" replied the other Insect, with an additional chuckle. "So berry pertikler, dam queer!"

"Ha-yah! Yah-ha!" chuckled Glow-worm, as the idea which amused his comrade stole suddenly over his mind. "To tink o' de pa'son bein' tied to dat ah bed—yah-hah!"

"Jis like a sof' crab on he back—ha-yah!"

And the delighted gentlemen chuckled merrily together, and showed their white teeth, and held their sides until the walls of the chamber echoed with their uproarious glee.

The door leading into the hall of the second story opened suddenly, and long-haired Bess entered the chamber. Her large dark eyes flashed with a clear and brilliant expression, and her jet-black hair streaming wildly over her shoulders gave a strange relief to her deathly countenance.

"De Lor Jimminy! It am de gal!" muttered Musquito, with an expression of idiotic surprise.

"Quick, I say, quick!" exclaimed Bess, approaching the fire-place. "I want the keys of the house—old Devil-Bug is waitin' for 'em! Where are they? Quick, I say!"

"Dere dey are, missus!" exclaimed Glow-worm, with a mock bow, as he pointed to the bunch of keys resting on the small table near the light. "What de debbil yo' want 'em foh?"

Bess seized the keys and rushed into the adjoining chamber where Mabel was imprisoned.

"I say, nigga, what all dis mean?" exclaimed Glow-worm, gazing in Musquito's face.

"I 'spect dar's some fuss down sta'rs!" responded the other negro.

As he spoke, Bess re-entered the room with the form of Mabel, supported by the embrace of her right arm, while the pale face of the young girl, lit by her large and lustrious eyes of midnight blackness, wore an absent and bewildered expression.

"Come, this way, this way," whispered Bess, moving toward the door which led out into the hall. "This way and you shall be saved!"

"What foh you do dat foh?" muttered Glow-worm, fiercely, as he turned toward Long-haired Bess with a threatening look.

"Hush, h-u-s-h!" whispered Bess, as she glanced meaningly at the half-conscious face of the girl who hung on her arm. "You see, Glow-worm, there's a rumpus kicked up down stairs, and Devil-Bug wants to have the gal removed to the Tower Room. Open the door quick, and let me hurry up stairs with her. You are so stupid Glow-worm—quick, I say!"

The look which animated the face of Long-haired Bess, dispelled all the doubts which the negro had entertained. With a mechanical gesture he flung open the door.

"Now, Glow-worm, close it after me—" she said, gazing in his hideous face, while her tone was that of a confidential whisper. "And if anybody should come up here and ask after the gal, you must swear that she was never in the house."

"Yes, missus."

"Ha, ha, ha! We know how to manage these things—don't we, Glow-worm?" laughed Bess, as, standing in the doorway, she gathered her arm more closely around the waist of the girl who lay half-fainting, in her embrace. "It takes us, don't it, Musquito?"

"It jist does dat!" chuckled the negro, and Glow-worm, joining in his laugh, carefully closed the door.

Bess stood in the darkness of the hall. A smile of triumph flashed over her proud face. She felt the heart of the girl, throbbing against the hand that held her form to her side.

"The plot of the Parson and his tool shall be scattered to the winds! I will save the wronged girl, save her from the hands of her *priestly* father! This way fair girl, and we will escape together!"

"Whither are you leading me?" murmured Mabel in a bewildered tone. "Oh save me from my father! Do with me what you will, but do not hurry me to his roof again! I will work my fingers to the bone, beg in the streets, or starve, but—oh! Do not place me in his power again!"

Bess silently led the way down the stairs. Crouching on the steps, about half-way down, was the form of a woman, attired in floating robes of white.

"Mary arise; we will escape!" exclaimed Bess in a whisper. "Take my arm, and cling to me with all your strength: we will escape from Monk-Hall!"

The fair girl rose in the darkness, and clung to the arm of the fallen woman. No word escaped her lips; no sigh heaved her bosom; she was silent as the grave.

"Ha! I hear the sound of his footsteps on the lower stairs!" muttered Bess. "He is ascending from the vault of Monk-Hall. Now help me heaven! If he bears a light with him we are lost! Another moment and all will be discovered."

She pressed her hand madly to her forehead, but in a moment an exclamation of joy burst from her lips.

"Stand close against the wall on this side of the stairway; I will cover your form with this cloak?"

They crouched against the wall, as the sound of Devil-Bug's footsteps were heard on the floor of the hall below. Seizing the cloak, which she had left with Mary, while leading Mabel from the chamber above, she flung it over their figures, and stood erect against its folds, her dark dress, shrouding her form from view. The sound of Devil-Bug's footsteps were heard on the first step of the stair-case. There was barely room for him to pass, between the form of Bess and the banisters opposite. He ascended the stairs. Step by step, he ascended, his hard breathing breaking on the still air like the panting of a wild beast about to spring at the traveller's throat in the darkness of some hideous ravine. The heart of Bess fluttered in her throat. Another step, and he would be at her side. She held her breath. His foot was on the step where she stood shielding the forms of the girls from view. The light from the distant roof fell dimly over his hideous face and form, while the side of the stair-way next to the wall was enveloped in thick darkness. Bess beheld him turn—his coarse garments rustled against her dress. She placed her hand against her mouth to smother the shriek which arose to her lips. The solitary eye of Devil-Bug peered into the darkness with a fixed glare. Bess silently grasped the massive key of the front door in her right hand, and separated it from the ring which confined the bunch of keys. In the action the keys jingled together. Devil-Bug started. Bess raised the massive key in her hand—it was her determination to crush his skull with its weight, if he laid his hand upon her. Her lips were compressed, and her bosom for the moment, was motionless as marble.

"My heart's full of all sorts o' queer tantrums"—muttered Devil-Bug. "I just now thought I heered somebody breathin' on the stairs, and now I thought I heered my keys a jinglin' together! Wot a rediculus fool I am to be sure!"

He pursued his way, he passed the form of Bess, and the sound of his footsteps presently echoed from the stairs above.

Bess breathed freely again. A wild feeling of joy fluttered round her heart: She seized the trembling girls, one in each arm, nerved for the effort by a hallowed hope that now began to brighten over her soul, she gathered a fair form in each arm, and hurried down the stairs.

"The key, the key!" she shouted in a wild delirium of joy. "A moment longer and we are saved. A moment and we escape from Monk-Hall!"

Meanwhile Devil-Bug ascending the stairs, stood before the door of Monk Baltzar's ante-chamber.

"I'll see the gal once agin," he muttered. "I'll look on her purty face agin; she shall roll in gold; she shall! Old Devil-Bug's darter shall have the money—ha, ha, ha! Sich lots o' money!"

He entered the ante-chamber, and passed along without heeding Glow-worm and Musqueto who stood by the fire. Gently unclosing the door of the next apartment, he stepped within the chamber where he had left the girl. He closed the door and advanced toward the light.

"She's a-sleepin' on that bed, the darter of Ellen!" he muttered folding his arms. "Many and many's the night I've laid at Ellen's door, watchin' her while she slept, and keepin' her from harm. There was'nt never a human bein' as did'nt cuss me, except one, except *one!* That was her—Ellen—the gal whom I'd 'ave died for! And this is her darter—ha, ha, ha! And she shall ride in her carriage, and have goold pieces, thick as flies in a molasses jug."

He advanced a step nearer to the bed, his head inclined to one side, as if in the act of listening. He listened for the low, soft sound of a woman breathing in her sleep.

"She sleeps wery softly!" muttered Devil-Bug. "An' I'll go to Livingstone, an' I'll tell him the story, and I'll tear that Parson's heart from his carcase, if he dares say that she ain't the merchant's darter! I hate and cuss the whole world; the whole world hates and cusses me—but the g-a-l! I'll skulk along the street, and see her ridin' in her carriage; I'll watch in the cold winter nights and see her—all shinin' with goold and jewels—as she goes into the theatre, with the big folks round her, and the rich merchant by her side."

He drew a step nearer the bed.

"And then I'll skulk down into the pit, and hide my head, but keep a look-out on her with my one eye. When I sees the folks makin' much of her—the jewels shinin' on her dress, the bracelets round her wrists and the goold band around her white brow, then I'll stick my face in my hands an' laff! Ho, ho; ho.—*There*, I'll cry to myself—there is old Devil-Bug's darter among the grandees o' the Quaker City!"

He drooped his head on his breast, while his eye blazed, and his thick lips parted in a grotesque grin.

In a moment, however, a strange mood of thought seemed to pass over the distorted intellect of this monster.

He stood with his head drooped low on his wide chest, while his hands hung extended by his side. His solitary eye, which contracted and dilated like the eye of a tiger, grew large and lustrous. His teeth were clenched, while his thick lips receded in a convulsive grimace. He stood motionless as the aged walls of that old house, of whose wide rooms and dreary vaults he seemed the living soul.

In that moment of silence what a world of thought passed over the soul of the monster!

First came a vision of the fair woman, who had loved him. Loved the outcast of mankind, the devil in human shape! Could you have seen Devil-Bug's soul at the moment it was agitated by this memory, you would have started at the contrast, which it presented in comparison with his deformed body. For a moment the soul of Devil-Bug was *beautiful*.

Then the scorn of the world crowded upon his soul. His ignominious birth, his lonely life, the hatred was felt for him, and the loathing which he felt for man, his distorted face and deformed body. Like a black cloud it gathered upon him. Had Devil-Bug's soul assumed a tangible shape, his body in comparison, would have grown beautiful. It was terrible to note the malice of his soul flashing from the eye and trembling on his lip.

Then came one wild and wandering thought. It darted over the chaos of his mind like the long and trembling ray of a star that shines but for an instant and then is dark forever. It was a thought, brief it is true, wild and wandering, yet mighty in its very brevity of existence, and most glorious in its wandering shape, it was a thought of God. Devil-Bug for a moment felt the existence of a God. For a moment he felt that he had a Father in the Universe. He imagined an awful being, with a face of unutterable beauty, an awful being looking forth from a vast immensity of clouds and darkness, while a frown broke over his eternal brow. Devil-Bug felt that this being was his Father. He felt that he, Devil-Bug the outcast of earth, the incarnate outlaw of hell, had one friend in the wide universe; that friend his Creator. He felt in every fibre of his deformed soul that the eyes of the awful being were fixed upon him in terrible reproof, yet with a gleam of mercy breaking from their eternal lustre.

This thought was but for a moment. Like a flash of light it came, like a shadow it passed away.

Then, slowly and terribly, there came gliding to his side, the phantoms of the murdered man and woman. The man with the body distorted by death, the knees drawn up to the chest, the jaw broken and the tongue lolling out; the woman, with the blood oozing, drop by drop, from the hollow skull, while the fragment of the face, clung by the quivering neck, to the shattered and mangled body. Devil-Bug could see the old woman's flesh quiver; he could hear the sound of the dropping blood. Drop! Then a pause. Drop! Another pause. Drop, drop, drop! How red it grows as it curdles over the hard bricks of the fire place! He could see the blood-shot eyes of the man moving slowly to and fro; then the tongue blackened, and then—Ugh! That low-toned yet terrible moan!

"They are with me!" muttered Devil-Bug, wiping the cold sweat from his brow. "With me forever! But I don't see that man Harvey. I don't see his corpse.—Ugh! there he is now, layin' beside the grave, his body straightened out and his eyes glaring upward like bits of glass in the sunshine! He moves—ugh! He rises on his feet, he makes toward me! Ugh! Back I say—you're dead, yo' devil, and yo' can't frighten me!"

This was uttered in a low whisper that would have thrilled a man's blood to hear. His right arm extended while the cold sweat trickled from his brow, Devil-Bug stood immovable as a rock, while he regarded the phantom with a fixed and glassy eye.

"Back yo' devil—you're dead—ugh! Back I say—yo' can't frighten me!"

In a moment the fit subsided, and Devil-Bug gazed around with a wild shriek of laughter.

"Them things is werry delightful!" he observed, with his usual grin. "They quite refreshes a feller."

He approached the bed, and his mood changed. His child lay sleeping there; *his child!* The darkness, which shrouded the corners of the chamber, lay thick around her couch, but she was *there!* His heart beat with a strange feeling of joy as he approached the bedside, and from his heart through every vein that strange joy darted like lightning.

He extended his hand, he passed it over the bed-clothes. A shudder ran over his frame. Again he extended his hand, again passed it nervously over the white coverlid. He started backward with a cry of horror.

He stood for a moment silent and immovable. Then running from one corner of the room to another, he shrieked the name of Ellen, again and yet again, while the muscles of his face, worked as with a death-spasm.

"Ellen," he shrieked, in his frenzy confounding the mother with the child. "Where have they tuk yo'? Ellen—did I not watch yo' in the winter nights? Did I not fight for yo'? Say, Nell, was there ever sich a sarvant as old Devil-Bug? Nell—Nell! Answer me Nelly; don't play 'possum with Devil-Bug—I know you're hid somewhere; I know it! You'd not leave me.—Nell!"

Again he shrieked that name. He listened for a moment—no answer came to his call. He rushed hurriedly into the ante-chamber; he seized the negro, Musquito, by the throat with a giant's grasp.

"Tell me, yo' scoundrel, where did yo' take that gal?"

"Massa"—replied the negro, speaking with difficulty as the talon fingers encircled his throat. "Missus Bess—took de keys—and de gal—dat's all, Massa."

"Nigger, I'll have you roasted alive!" shrieked Devil-Bug, with an ominous scowl of anger. "Bess took the gal and the keys, did she? Niggers, I'll tell you what it is, if that gal escapes, I'll have your black flesh torn off with hot pincers—I'll—"

He rushed through the doorway, and was heard descending the stairs.

Meanwhile, with the fair form of a trembling woman on each arm, Bess pursued her way down stairs, and in a few moments stood at the small door of the Doorkeeper's fireroom, It hung slightly ajar. Bess gazed through the crevice, and to her utter horror, beheld two persons standing near the fire. She looked again, and recognized the portly form of the fat Parson and the well-built figure of Fitz-Cowles. They were chatting pleasantly together.

"A fine girl you say, Parson? Ha, ha! You're a sly rogue, you are! Where is she now?"

"Don't speak so loud, Fitz. She's up stairs—a lovely girl, with a soft form and red lips! Ah!"

Bess could hear the Parson smack his thick lips together, with holy fervor.

"Take care Parson, or I'll cut you out! I'll buy off old Devil-Bug and have the beauty all to myself. I know you preachers are awful sly with the womon; and the pulpit is rather celebrated for its taste in that line. My curiosity is excited, Parson—I should like to see the girl—"

"Ah-ha! Shouid you? I've had a good deal of trouble in trapping the beauty—she shan't pass out of my hands for nothing, I assure you."

There was a pause for a few minutes. Fitz-Cowles and the Parson whispered together.

Bess looked through the crevice, while the girls hung trembling on her arms, and beheld the good Parson in the act of rattling a dice-box, which Devil-Bug had left on the mantle.

"Ha, ha! The hundred dollars are mine!" chuckled the Parson.

Bess beheld Fitz-Cowles take up the dice, and rattling them for a moment in the box, fling them out upon the surface of the mantlepiece.

"And the girl is mine!" exclaimed Fitz-Cowles, with a look of triumph. "Our agreement was that the one who had the highest throw should take the money; the other should have the woman! Being a Parson, you of course had more luck with the dice than one of the laity like myself; I am content with the girl. Where is she?"

"Up stairs. My room you know?" and the Parson waved his hand toward the door.

Fitz-Cowles moved from the fireplace. In a moment the door would be flung open, and Bess, with her companions be discovered.

"Now is my time!" muttered Bess. "Girls, stay here for a single moment, and I'll save you!" She placed them in the darkness, one on either side of the doorway.

"The house is on fire!" she shrieked, as with her dark hair flung wildly over her shoulders, she rushed through the doorway and confronted the astonished Parson and the Millionaire. "Save yourselves while it is in your power! The house is in flames—away, away!"

She rushed toward the front door while they stood utterly confounded, near the fireplace. In a moment the key was in the lock, in another instant the door was flung wide open.

"Save yourselves!" shouted Bess, elevating her voice to an unnatural pitch. "The house is on fire—delay another moment and you are lost!"

"Shall we move, Fitz?"

"I guess we'd better, Parson!"

The words had scarcely passed his lips when the folds of white garments fluttered before his eyes, and two female forms, rushing from the doorway of the hall, bounded along the floor with one convulsive spring like that of the doe when environed by hunters. Mabel, herself all terror, supported the quivering form of Mary. In an instant they passed the form of Bess, as with the key in her hand, she held the front door wide open.

"Now girls," she shrieked. "Cling to my arms, and we may escape!"

With a fair girl clinging to each arm, she darted from the doorway, and was lost to view.

"It's the very girl—the one in the white dress—It's Mabel!" exclaimed Parson Pyne.

"Yes, but there were two in white dresses—" interrupted Fitz-Cowles.

"The one with long dark hair, and jet-black eyes; that was Mabel!" cried Parson Pyne, moving toward the door.

"Ha! Say you so! I'd peril a cool thousand to win her. Let's give chase. That alarm of fire was all a sham."

They moved to the door, and looked out upon the night. At a short distance down the narrow street, the white garments of Mary and Mabel waved in the light of the moon.

"I'll pursue them!" shouted Fitz-Cowles, darting down the street.

"And I'll run this way, and head them off, at the next street!" cried the Parson, moving briskly along the alley in an opposite direction. "Ten chances to one, they take the alley, which winds round and round like a boa constrictor, and at last strikes into the street, about a hundred yards ahead! Ha, ha! I can walk quietly along and head them off. Should dear little Mabel get into my hand's again———ah-ha!"

The Parson pursued his way along the street, chuckling gaily to himself. And at the very moment that Fitz-Cowles pursued the wanderers in one direction, while the Parson endeavoured to intercept them in another, the form of Devil-Bug appeared in the broad door-way of Monk-Hall.

"Ho, ho!" he cried, looking westwardly down the narrow street. "There they go, with a feller chasin' em! There's Bess—curse her! There's Lorrimer's gal, and there's Nell! Ha! They strike into the alley, which instead of going straight ahead like a reglar Phil'delphy alley, winds round the yard of Monk-Hall, and comes into the street agin about a hundred yards ahead. Ho, ho! I have it! I have it! I'll just climb the fence of the yard, and drop down into the alley back of Monk-Hall! The gal's will come trampin' down the alley for dear life—they'll see a black lump on the ground—they'll rush on thinkin' it a stone, but that black lump will rise on its feet and it will stretch out its arms and grasp 'em. Old Devil-Bug will have the child, his darter agin!"

He disappeared within the door of Monk-Hall.

The moon rose above the housetops. Monk-Hall gleamed in the silvery light like a goblin mansion. Each peak of the roof, each fantastic chimney, the massive tower and the front of black and red brick intermingled in strange contrast, were disclosed by the light of the rising moon, floating so soft and mellow from the expanse of the fathomless winter sky.

Meanwhile along the narrow street, each arm supporting the form of a half-fainting girl, Bess pursued her way, her heart filled with one fixed purpose, and her very soul nerved for the effort. The sound of footsteps struck upon her ear. She turned her head over her shoulder, and beheld Fitz-Cowles at the distance of some fifty yards. His conical hat and gold-headed cane were directly perceptible in the moonlight. But one course remained for Bess. She must strike into the narrow alley or be overtaken.

Gathering the arms of the girls more firmly within her own, Bess whispered a word of encouragement in their ears and darted around. The three forms were lost to view in the winding alley.

"'Gad! I'll have them yet!" shouted Fitz-Cowles, gaining the corner of the alley, and gazing intently upon the figures of the wanderers. "That face and those eyes are not so easily forgotten! 'Gad I'll have them yet!"

Bess turned her head over her shoulder—she saw the pursuer gaining upon her at every step.

"On Mary," she whispered. "On Mabel!" for by some strange means she had gained the name of the strange maiden. "You are running from death, and worse than death!"

Her words infused a new life into the heart of Mabel; poor Mary, too, felt a strange energy darting through her veins.

Not a word more was said, but on and onward they dashed. Over the rough stones, through the puddles of miry water, beneath the shadow of the thickly clustered houses, on and onward—a race for maiden purity, a race for woman's honor!

At every step Fitz-Cowles gained upon the wanderers. His shout of laughing derision burst upon their ears; the echo of his footsteps smote their hearts like a death-knell.

"Ha, ha!" he laughed. "My black-eyed damsel. I'll have you, by Jove, I'll have you yet!"

Bess reached a point of the winding alley, where the thickly-clustered houses, were superseded on one side, by a high board fence. Over the fence, dark indistinct and gloomy, was seen the roof of Monk-Hall, with the tower rising in the moon-beams.

As Bess reached the fence, Fitz-Cowles was within ten paces of her side. Nothing could save her now. Panting for breath, the girls clung tremblingly to her arms; their weight began to drag her down; her strength gave tokens of exhaustion.

Fitz-Cowles uttered a shout of triumph and sprang forward to grasp his victim. He did not heed the dark lump which like a blackened rock, uprose from the very centre of the pathway. The girls rushed past the blackened mass. Fitz-Cowles sprang forward to grasp them, laughing gaily in the action, when a wild yell broke on the air, mingling with his cheerful laugh, the black mass at his feet assumed the shape and form of the monster, and Devil-Bug confronted the Millionaire.

"Ho, ho, my feller. I've got yo' have I?" he shrieked with a blazing eye. "What in the devil d'ye mean by chasin' that gal?"

"Stand back or I'll cleave your skull with my cane! Stand back fellow—you're in my pay, and I'll chastise you for this insolence!"

And Fitz-Cowles brandished his gold-headed cane in the light of the moon. "You'll chastise me, will ye?" shouted Devil-Bug. "There never yet was a man as felt the weight o' this arm and lived a'terwards!"

He sprang upon Fitz-Cowles with a yell. They clenched together, they fell in the mire of the gutter, and fought like dogs, the Savage and the Millionaire!

Onward with faint and weary steps, the wanderers held their way. They reached the termination of the winding alley, where it emerged upon the narrow street, a hundred yards distant from Monk-Hall. Panting for breath and trembling in every tired limb Mabel clung nervously to the arm of Bess, while Mary, her senses whirling in strange, confusion flung the weight of her quivering form full upon the shoulder of the dark-eyed woman.

"Ha! There is a man standing at the corner of the street—we are watched!" Bess exclaimed in a whisper. "Courage, Mabel, courage Mary, you shall not be dragged to Monk-Hall again while Bess has a firm soul or a resolute arm!"

"It is my father!" whispered Mabel, trembling in every limb.

"Yes, yes, my pretty Mabel! It *is* your father!" cried the portly Parson, advancing from the shadows of the street. "Come here with me, and I'll overlook your recent misconduct; come home my dear!"

He approached the trembling girl. She clung to the arm of Bess with the energy of despair. Bess suddenly flung the maiden aside, and raised her arm on high. Each sinew was braced for a desperate effort, and the tiny fingers of her hand grasped the massive key of Monk-Hall.

"Oh do not cast me from you," shrieked Mabel.

"Come to your pa-pa, my dear," exclaimed Parson Pyne, reaching forth his hand to grasp the form of Mabel.

Her eyes flashing fire, Bess sprang forward, and struck the Parson on the forehead with the massive iron key. The blow was as sudden as it was unexpected: he reeled to one side and fell upon the pavement like a dead man.

"Now, girls, cling to my arms yet once again. Ere an hour passes over my head, I will place you in a quiet refuge, where no wrong can assail you, no dark passion mar your peace!"

"Any where Bessie, to the lowest hovel, to the abode of rags and misery and want, but for God's sake not to that home—the home which I left only last night for the mansion of Lorraine. I have had my dream, Bessie—God alone knows how terrible has been the awakening from that dream!"

As Mary spoke, her voice grew tremulous and Bess turned her face away from the gaze of the ruined girl. That wan countenance, those eyes of liquid blue dilating with a frenzied glare—the vision blasted the very eyesight of Long-haired Bess.

Mabel clung to the arm of the tall woman, and in a whisper besought her to fly from the spot.

"Let us away," she cried. "My father—" and she pointed to the portly form which cumbered the roadside. "I fear him worse than the grave."

Bess silently gathered the arms of each girl within her own, and then as the moon shone upon the wan yet beaming face with blue eyes and golden hair, on one side, and the pale countenance with dark eyes and midnight tresses, on the other, she raised her gaze to the moonlit heavens above, and for the moment her dark orbs grew lustrous with a strange eloquence.

At that moment, as standing at the corner of the gloomy street, with a ruined girl on one side a wronged maiden on the other, her face, once so beautiful, and now lovely to look upon in its very ruins, was imbued with an expression holy as that which mantles over the face of the dying mother when blessing her first born child.

Up to the throne of the pure and merciful God, from the heart of the Courtezan there ascended a vow, a holy vow! She was degraded, steeped to the very lips in pollution, cankered to the heart with loathsome vice, yet at that moment, she was a holy thing in the sight of the angels, for before the altar of Almighty God, she swore to protect the ruined Mary to the death, she vowed to guard the stainless Mabel from the shadow of a wrong. And the vow went up to God, and the moon, rising higher over the roof-tops, seemed to shed a more kindly light as if to crown that vow with an omen of success.

And the Three Sisters, the Fallen, the Betrayed and the Innocent, wandered forth, along the streets, on their gloomy way.

One, from the old State House clock, *one*. There is a wild music in the sound of that old bell. It rings like the voice of a warning spirit, when heard in the silence of night. How many have heard it in the dead hour of night, ere they laid down to die? The suicide, wan faced and heart broken, has paused on the edge of the Delaware, as the sound of that bell has for a moment, called him back to life. The poor mechanic, starving in his desolate home, has raised his head for the last time, as the old bell struck one upon his freezing ear, and then moaned and clutched the air and died. The Bank Director revelling at the sight of his gold, won from the poor by fraud to which a pirate's crimes are acts of benevolence; the jolly Bank Director counting over his sweat-wrung gold at the solemn hour of the night, has been aroused from his reveries by that awful sound, dim, booming and knell-like—the State House clock tolling ONE. Woman, fair, and young, and beautiful, sinking into the arms of shame, has started from the polluted couch as that sound broke on her ears, now fast-sealed to all the warnings of conscience. She has started, and thought of the voice of her grey-haired father, she has started and wept!

One!

The young author, with his sallow cheeks, lighted by the glare of a flickering lamp, and his threadbare coat, fluttering in rags on his wasted form; the young author sitting at his desk at the lone hour of night, while he wrestles with all the world for fame and fortune, his only weapon a rusted pen, hears that State House bell—God bless it for its memories!—striking the hour of one, and rising from his task he beholds his success painted on the very darkness which beclouds his path. Already he beholds the world at his feet, already the bloodhounds of calumniation and persecution, lie gasping in their last agonies, while his foot is on their necks. Huzza for the old State House bell, and above all other hours, huzza for the hour of one.

One!

The minister of justice, bending over the table, on whose surface the hard gold is flung ringing down by the hands of the wealthy citizen who sits smiling opposite; the hard gold which buys the life of some wealthy murderer from the gallows, or the liberty of some gilded robber from the jail, this honest minister of justice, starts and trembles as he hears the State House bell strike one!

That dull and booming sound seems to call into life the vengeance of the People, which shall one day hurl the lordly minister of the law from his proud position; already he beholds written on the walls of his chamber, in letters of flame, that black and staring word—"Corruption."

Huzza for the hour of one.

That sound, speaking from the heighths of Independence Hall, strikes over the Quaker City like the voice of God's Judgment, rousing crime from its task, mirth from its wine-cup, murder from its knife, bribery from its gold.

Huzza for the old State House bell, and above all other hours huzza for the hour of one.

Two figures were slowly wending their way along a well-known street in the District of Southwark.

"Curse the huzzy. Just look at my forehead! The marks o' that key will disfigure me for life."

"It doesn't improve your forehead much—that's a fact, Parson. But you should have seen the keelhauling that monster gave me! Egad, there isn't a bone in my body that doesn't ache!"

"How did you get off from old Devil-Bug? Eh, Fitz?"

"Palavered the old scoundrel. Made believe that I was a-going to protect the girl and all that. Deuced singular he should take such an interest in her—ain't it?"

"Quite unaccountable, as we say in the pulpit, when the morning collection is rather small. However, Fitz, I've sold the girl to you for one hundred dollars, and you shall have her."

"When, for instance?"

"By to-morrow at noon!"

"Say you so, my Parson! Place this girl in my possession by to-morrow noon, and another hundred shall be yours!"

"Give me your hand on that Fitz. There my boy it shall be done! Now Mabel my pretty chit"—he muttered to himself while his rubicund face was purple with hate; "we'll see who places the character of the reverend Pastor of a loving flock in jeopardy: we'll see who gets old monsters to defend them———the huzzy!"

"What a comfort it is," soliloquized Fitz-Cowles, "what a comfort it is to think, that the hundred dollar note which I gave the Parson was on a Sand Bank."

"Ha! Fitz. Look yonder—there they go—the three beauties. Let's give chase!"

"Agreed! Now for another race—a moment and we'll have them!"

In the distance, at the corner of the next street, the white garments of Mabel and Mary, with the dark robes of Bess fluttering between the two young forms, waved for a moment in the moonlight. In another moment the portly Pyne and the well-formed millionaire gave chase; in a moment the three women turned the corner of the next street. It required but a few seconds for Pyne and Fitz-Cowles to gain the corner of the street. They looked up and down the street—the women had disappeared. The moon was shining brightly in the heavens, and its beams illuminated the long street, which like all Philadelphia streets was laid out with all the matter-of-fact straightness of a ten-pin alley.

"Where could they have disappeared!" muttered Pyne, "there is no alley between this street and the next, and I see no signs of any other hiding place. They must have gone into some o' these houses."

"Egad! where will you find a house open at this hour? They must have sunk down plump into the bricks of the pavement."

"Ha! Here is the widow Smolby's house. Ten to one they went in this door—wait a moment, I'll knock."

Accordingly, the Reverend Doctor Pyne knocked at the door of the widow Smolby's ancient mansion. In a few moments the door receded about the width of an inch, and the glare of a light flashed out upon the side-walk.

"Is the widow Smolby in?" asked the pious Dr. Pyne, assuming his blandest tone.

"Not e'zactly, but her corpse is, if that 'ill answer"—answered a rough voice from the crevice of the door.

"Her corpse?"

"I 'spose you don't know that the widder was took bad with an attack of murder and thieves this arternoon? The crowner sot upon her, which considerin' as he's a wery fat man, was raythe an ungenteel thing for him to do."

"You did not see any thing of three young ladies in these parts, did you?" asked the zealous Dr. Pyne, in his most unctuous voice.

"Now wot a precious question that is, to wake a man up in the middle o' th' night for! Make a pin-cushion of me somebody, and hang my up agin the wall for all the old ladies to stick pins in, but if I ain't got a notion to come out there old porpis!"

With these words, the gentleman on the inside, being in somewhat of an angry mood, violently closed the door, using a familiar synonym for condemnation with some considerable emphasis.

"How much his voice sounds like that of Major Mulhill!" muttered Fitz-Cowles.

"The gal is in this house; I've not a doubt of it!" blandly remarked the Foe of Pagan Rome.

"I'll tell you what it is Monk Baltzar, I feel interested in this girl. Her dark eyes have made a decided impression on me. I never yet fancied a woman that I did not win, and so if you'll by some means or other, I don't care how, secure this girl for me by to-morrow at noon, another hundred shall be yours!"

"I'll manage it; trust me with the affair Fitz. You must know I've some small spite against this girl, and by to-morrow at noon this petticoat shall be in your power. By-the-bye, what's that object in the gutter yonder?"

"Nothing but a drunken man. Come Parson, let's stroll down the street, and arrange matters."

And as they strolled down the street talking earnestly together, the dark object in the gutter moved to and fro, and in a moment it resolved itself into the outlines of a man's figure. The Moon shone over a wan and ghastly face with glassy eyes, glaring fixedly on the blue heavens above. Around that face fell thick locks of jet black hair, all matted with the mire of the gutter and soiled with the dust of the street. And the man crawled slowly along the hard stones of the street, and then as if unable to move from weakness, he raised his face faintly in the light of the moon and looked upon the heavens and uttered a low cry. Then his head dropped upon the stones of the street, and he lay like a dead man.

The heart of Bess thrilled with despair when, after all her wanderings, all her efforts to escape from Monk-Hall, she heard the triumphant cry of the Parson and the Millionaire, as they again pursued her.

Dragging the exhausted girls with her, she rushed forward, but the strength of the three soon failed, and she was about to sink down with despair when Mabel uttered an exclamation of surprise.

"This is the widow Smolby's house from which my father dragged me twelve hours ago!" exclaimed Mabel, as she beheld the gloomy walls of the old house rising in the moonbeams.

"The widow Smolby!" muttered Bess, as though some strange memory had flashed over her brain. "Ha! We may obtain shelter here—I'll make the attempt at all events!"

She knocked at the door. It receded slightly, and a rough voice from within demanded her errand.

"Ha! Larkspur!" she exclaimed, "Is that you? Long-haired Bess asks you to give her shelter for the night—she has some important facts to disclose with regard to the late murder."

"Why, Bess, my duck, is that you?" cried Easy Larkspur, opening the door. "Two young ladies with you—oh, ho! Up to some new caper, I 'spose! Come in, my dear!"

For the first time a wild suspicion darted over the brain of Mary Arlington, that Bess was a courtezan, that she had been betrayed through her means. That thought, so wild and vague and yet so terrible, smote poor Mary to the soul. The familiar manner with which a rough looking gentleman like Easy Larkspur, greeted Bessie, first aroused this suspicion in the mind of Mary.

"Walk in ladies: walk in! You see I was jist enjoyin' a glass of whiskey punch by the fire, with a prime Hawanner! And whiskey punch, ladies, as you may have had occasion to know, is a werry good drink, an' goes down quite e-a-sy! Ladies, I'd always adwise yo' to marry a gentleman, as knows how to make good whiskey punch, but you must be keerful he don't make it too weak. Weak punch—" continued the red-faced gentleman, with an anti-total abstinence smile—"Weak punch, in my opinion, is the most despisable thing as is!"

"Larkspur, I have one word to say to you. From an accomplice of the murderer I have gained some knowledge of the murder committed in this house yesterday afternoon. This knowledge I will place in your keeping on one consideration. Give these ladies and myself shelter for the night; this is all I ask of you."

"Why you see, Bessie, I was app'inted, after the crowner's inquest had sot upon the old lady, to stay here all night, in case the thieves might take a notion to repeat their wisit. My fellers is a-sleepin' in the back room. You wouldn't like to try a leetle of this punch, would yo'? You may stay here all night; no doubt o' that! But as all the other rooms was locked up by the Ma'or, you'll have to sleep in the room where the corpse is—"

"Oh, heaven!" whispered Mabel—"Is the old lady dead?" And her dark eyes grew lustrous with fear and awe.

"Dead, my darlin', as the 'Nited States Bank!" observed Larkspur, with whiskey punch beaming from every line of his face. "And a deader thing than that I don't know; it's about the deadest thing as is; that's a fact!"

Bess silently led the girls up stairs. The same shudder thrilled through every heart as they entered the Ghost-Chamber. Two formal wax candles gave a dim light to the place. The massive bed, with its thick curtains, still stood in one corner, the high-backed chairs had been replaced in their positions against the wall; the mirror between the windows still flashed back the light of the candles. The room was the same as in the morning; the furniture still wore the same antique and ghostly air; and the portrait above the mantel, still gazed around the place with its pale and beautiful countenance, relieved by sweeping tresses of long black hair and enlivened by the gleam of lustrous dark eyes.

The Ghost-Room was the same, and yet not altogether the same. There was a crust of hardened blood congealed along the cold bricks of the fireplace; the very air seemed tainted with the smell of human blood, shed in violence and murder.

In the centre of the chamber, in the full glare of the light, rested a coffin covered with a plain cloth, and placed upon tressels of sabel wood. The glare of the light flashed over the details of the cold white shroud, the stiff hands carefully crossed over each other, the feet thrusting the death robe slightly upward, all were painfully disclosed, but the face was covered with a loose piece of snowy linen. Mangled, and shattered, and crushed, it was too fearful a sight for the eyes of the living to behold, and yet was it not tenfold more horrible to see that white cloth thrown over the face, leaving the vivid fancy to depict the loathsome reality, than to look upon the palpable reality itself? To fancy the cold blood falling drop by drop upon the bottom of the coffin, from the hollow skull!

There she lay, her gold forgotten, her blood cold and icy, her limbs stiffened as marble. And as the light flickered with an uncertain glare, and as the wind moaned through the crevices of the chamber, and as the hangings of the bed and the windows rustled heavily to and fro, while from the frame of the portrait, the face of a beautiful woman gazed sadly upon the scene, it seemed as though an awful and invisible fiend had infected the very air with a curse. That fiend was Murder; in the rustling curtains, in the moaning wind, in the flickering light, in the sad gaze of the portrait, in the spectacle of the coffin and the corse; in all these he spoke with a voice that froze the blood in its career, and stilled the heart in its beatings.

"Behold your mother!" cried Bess, in a tone of wild agitation, as seizing Mabel by the hand she pointed to the portrait. "Behold your mother! You are the child of Livingstone the merchant; this house and all its contents are yours! Yours by the will of yon murdered woman, who rests cold and icy in her coffin. Behold the face of your mother, gazing upon you in kindness and love. Kneel, Mabel, kneel, and thank your God that after the long night which has darkened your life, the day has dawned at last!"

And while Mabel stood stricken dumb with astonishment, while her brain whirled in wild confusion, and the very room seemed to reel around her, Bess turned aside and took Mary by the hand.

"Now hear the dark confession which I have to whisper to your ear," she shrieked, falling on her knees. "I was the cause of your ruin; I was the accomplice of the seducer; I took his wages; and earned them by selling myself, body and soul into his hands! I, it was, that lured you from your home, I, it was, that led you on to ruin—my soul is blackened by the full guilt of a crime than which hell can name no deed of darker horror.

"Hear this confession and hear my fixed resolve! Spurn me from you, trample on me, curse me, oh curse me, but from your side living I will never depart! You do not wish to return to your father's house. I will slave for you, work for you, beg for you! Let me wash out some portion of my crime by a life-long devotion to your service. Curse me, Mary, spit upon me, Mary, spurn me as the base thing I am, should be spurned, but I am your slave through life—my crime shall be washed out in tears of blood!"

Vain were the power of language to paint the horror which paled the face of Mary Arlington as this dark confession fell shrieking on her ear. She looked vacantly in the face of the kneeling woman, she even toyed playfully with her long dark hair, and then she gave utterance to a wild and maniac laugh.

"Lorraine," she cried, "Lorraine, ha, ha, ha! He will return at last, he will yet be mine! Lorraine! Lorraine!"

CHAPTER THIRTEENTH

THE GOLD WHICH DEVIL-BUG WON

Slowly and silently Devil-Bug ascended the staircase of Monk-Hall. The lamp which he held extended at arm's length cast a flaring light over his distorted face, now rendered tenfold more hideous by the tokens of some terrible emotion. He had bitten his upper lip until the blood trickled over his clenched teeth, down to his pointed chin. There was a glassy light in his solitary eye, and a lowering frown, full of omen, upon his protuberant brow.

Slowly and silently, with the light in his hand, he ascended the massive staircase of Monk-Hall. He uttered no word, but fearful thoughts were working at his heart. One hour ago, his heart had been softened into something like human feelings—a very child might have led the savage, and ruled him with a word. That word, a word of kindness to the child of Ellen. *Now*—they had stolen the child, they had torn the fair girl from his arms, and Devil-Bug was a savage once more. Like a black cloud arising from the stagnant waves of the Dead Sea, so the feeling of fierce malignity to all the human race, arose hideous and terrible from the depths of the monster's soul.

"Ha!" he cried, as he suddenly paused upon the stairway. "The corpse o' that man Harvey, is a-layin' beside the grave in the Pit o' Monk-Hall! I must go down and bury it. Yes, yes, snug under the airth, snug, snug I'll put it out o' sight."

He turned round and began to descend the stairway.

"I'll bury it—that I will! And as the hard clods fall on his white face, I'll laff—ho, ho, ho! I'll laff when I think o' the prize that's in store for me—the tall woman with the rale ripe lips, and jet-black eyes!"

He raised his left hand into the glare of the lamp, and then a fiendish laugh convulsed his brawny chest.

"Nobody don't see that ring on my little finger, do they? It's most too small for the finger, so I had to squeeze it on above the j'int. Does anybody see it? I wonders if the dead man 'ill see it, when I holds it to his glassy eye, and tells him about the prize it won for me!"

Again that low-toned yet horrible laugh echoed along the stairway, and Devil-Bug flung the lamp wildly on high, in the excess of his infernal glee.

"Yes, yes, I'll force his cold eyelids slowly apart, I'll rub the ring against the frozen eyeballs and I'll shout in his ear, 'Luke, my boy, you was a jolly feller when alive, and now when you're dead a ring from your finger buys *sich* a prize for Devil-Bug, *sich* a rale screamer of a prize!' First I'll bury the corpse—and then, ho, ho, ho, I'll taste the red lips o' that sweet young woman as is a-dyin' to see me up stairs!"

Laughing horribly to himself, he descended into the vault of Monk-Hall. There was a long pause of silence, and the light of the moon, streaming from the skylight in the roof, faintly illumined the winding stairway. Nearly half an hour passed, and the night began to wane toward its close, when the beams of a lamp again flashed over the stairway, and Devil-Bug came hastening upward, with a strange and peculiar expression impressing the lines of his distorted visage.

With immense strides he hurried up the stairway, flinging the hand which grasped the light merrily from side to side, while that hideous sound, like the laugh of a devil, echoed from the depths of his chest.

"It rather puzzled me," he muttered, and then chuckled gaily to himself—"Quite a riddle—a werry good riddle to be sure!" His features gleamed with an expression of infernal triumph. "Ho, ho, ho! I see how it was done, I see it all! The feller come to himself, and tried to crawl from the cellar, and not knowin' whar' he wos, he fell into the water, and wos carried off jist like a dead rat, or a cat, or any other crittur! I should 'ave like to have heered him howl when he found himself floatin' into the underground channel—ho, ho, ho!"

In his gleee he raised his left hand to his forehead and swept the thick hair aside from his eye. The ring on his finger glittered in the light.

"The sweet young lady with the red lips and the dark eyes—ha, ha! I don't think I ought to keep her waitin' any longer. The ring is on my finger, and the prize is mine! The han'some woman is bought and sold —ho, ho, ho!"

Hurrying up the stairway, Devil-Bug presently attained the hall on the second floor. In a moment he stood in front of the chamber, where Livingstone, the night before, had witnessed the guilt of his wife.

Raising the light overhead, he applied his ear to the keyhole of the door and listened with speechless intensity for a single moment.

That ghastly grimace, that flashing eye, that upraised hand with the ring glistening in the light—oh Dora, proud and fearless Dora, better death than the foul dishonor, which glares upon you from the monster's face!

The lofty chamber was full of shadows. The shadow of the lofty bed, the shadows of the high-backed chairs, the shadow of the antique dressing bureau, all thrown along the floor, by the trembling light which stood upon the small table in the centre of the gorgeous carpet. Then the fire on the wide hearth, ever and anon, would light up in a ruddy glare, flinging along the carpet, the shadow of a young and beautiful form, seated by the table of ebony. Then the curtains of the bed would rustle into the light, presenting the soft azure of their folds to the glare of the fire or the mild beams of the lamp, or the oval mirror would reflect both shadows and light with a gloomy and spectral effect, or the uncouth figures, delineated in warm colors on the rich carpet, would assume a temporary life as they basked in the glow that flashed from the fireside.

The chamber was full of sombre shadows and full of glaring flashes of light. Now the golden coronet, surmounting the canopy of the bed, glittered in the light, and the rich silken folds of purple and azure which lined the lofty walls of the chamber, were tinted with a lively glow, and again the painting above the mantel, where Venus in all her softness and beauty lay uncovered amid the rosy freshness of the rising morn, felt the gentle influence of a sudden flash from the hearth, or warmed into life, beneath the beams of the trembling lamp.

Still amid thick shadows and glaring gleams of light, along the floor was flung the shadow of a young and beautiful form.

Dora Livingstone sat beside the table, her cheek resting on her hand, while the glossy tresses of her dark hair fell clustering to her shoulders. The lovely outlines of her form were still disclosed in the close-fitting frock-coat which became her so well. The collar of the coat was thrown back and the shirt flung open at the throat, disclosed the whiteness of her snowy neck, with a glimpse of her bosom, now heaving and throbbing with tumultuous thoughts.

She was very beautiful, was that proud and scheming woman in her male disguise. The light fell warmly over her wide shoulders, so voluptuous in their outline, over the rounded fullness of her bust, over the slender gracefulness of the waist, as the close-fitting frock-coat gathered round her form with the nicety of a glove.

She was very beautiful, and yet along each cheek of her queenly countenance there flashed a spot of vivid and burning red, which betokened the feverish anxiety which absorbed the soul of the proud woman, while her dark eyes, flashing with a clear and brilliant glance, fraught with unutterable meaning, glared upon the thick shadows of the chamber with a fixed and immoveable gaze. Her brow was calm and unfrowning as that of the sleeping babe, and the emotion which absorbed her soul was manifested in the agitation of her bosom, as it swelled into the light, in the compression of her red ripe lips, in the feverish spot of burning red upon each blooming cheek.

Thus had she sat for hours more like a criminal waiting for the morn which was to bring her fair neck to the doomsman's axe, than the determined Murderess waiting for her victim.

And now, as the silence of the chamber gradually awed her soul, as the flashing gleams of light, struggling with the thick masses of shadow, imparted a spectural effect to the chamber and its costly furniture, the thoughts of the proud woman, sitting there so silently in that unwomanly disguise, dwelt on the Past and its memories.

First, like some pale and reproachful ghost sent from the grave to warn her of her guilt, arose the thought of the days when she was a pure-hearted and innocent girl.

The hand which supported her cheek trembled, and her lips grew ashy white. The face of her mother was before her, that face with its outlines broken by grief, and the large black eyes, dilated to an unnatural size by sickness and pain, arose before her for a moment in appaling distinctness.

Starting with involuntary terror, Dora's gaze was fixed upon the gorgeous bed. At the sight of that canopy with its luxuriant folds and its coronet of stars, all the blackness of her crime rushed upon the dishonored wife. There, upon that couch of shame, had she lain down the purity of a wife, to take up the dishonor of an adultress!

Dora turned her eyes away from the bed, and tried to drown the silent voices speaking forever within her, by the thought of the prize for which she had trafficked her soul. Glowing visions of pomp and power, the coronet on her brow, and the title to her name, the smile of a Queen beaming upon her face, and the glories of ancestral rank flashing all around her; glowing visions in which her grasping ambition was crowned with triumph, dawned upon her soul.

And yet, whether it was from the feverish anxiety of her long and terrible watch, or whether the future already gleamed upon her soul, mingling its revelations with the remembrances of memory, whenever she thought of the coronet which was soon to entwine her brow, it became all loathsome with crawling grave-worms, the Queen who smiled upon her, became a grinning skeleton, and all the lordly flatterers whom she had fancied kneeling at her feet, suddenly arose with the ghastliness of death painted on their faces, while around their icy limbs the death-shroud waved in drooping folds.

Dora covered her face with her hands. By one sudden effort she banished these thoughts. The echo of a footstep struck upon her ear.

She started, she turned pale, she arose to her feet.

"It is *he!*" she muttered with ashy lips, while her hands were clasped over her bosom. "It is the Murderer!"

She listened eagerly for the footstep. It approached the door of her chamber—it passed—it was but the footstep of a reveller from the Banquet Room. Dora resumed her seat and breathed freely again.

Then, leaning her cheek on her hand, she endeavored to banish all thought from her soul, while her ear drank in the slightest echo of a sound.

Worn out by feverish suspense, she fell into a brief and half-wakeful slumber, in which her soul was startled by terrible dreams. The faces of the dead were before her sealed eyes, grinning hideously in her face as if in derision of all her ambitious plans, and then a coffin, black as midnight, was borne slowly past, by hands outstretched from a lowering cloud. Then the death-stricken countenance of Luke Harvey arose from the coffin-lid and smiled upon her in scorn, while his hands tore the shroud from his limbs, and scattered the fragments in her very face. Dora started from her brief and feverish slumber, and gazed around the lonely chamber. The bed with its costly hangings arrested her eye.

"Ha!" she exclaimed, in a low whisper, as though her blood was chilled by the fear that one loud tone of her voice might arouse the dead into life, from the thick shadows of the room. "My soul is terrified by strange fears, yet I will endure it all! Skeletons have arisen and gibbered in my face, the dead long-forgotten have been with me, and a coffin has been borne before me, by hands outstretched from a lowering cloud—yet will I endure it all! Ha, ha!" her deep-toned whisper was succeeded by a wild and startling laugh. "Such a ridiculous fancy! It is quite laughable. I just now imagined that my husband might have been looking through the bed-curtains last night, while I slumbered, unconscious of his gaze—how very amusing!"

She laughed gaily, and her face brightened with an expression of careless glee.

The sound of a heavy footstep resounded in the hall without.

Dora stood as if frozen to the floor. The laugh died in her throat.

"'Tis *he!*" she murmured, in a hollow whisper.

And in a moment Devil-Bug stood before her, flinging the light aloft with his extended arm, while his features were agitated with a grin of triumph.

"Is *it* done," murmured Dora, in a whisper.

"Lady, behold the ring!" exclaimed Devil-Bug, slowly approaching the proud woman, with the ring flashing in the light. "It is done, good lady. I've got the ring; now for the *goo*ld!"

"He is dead!" exclaimed Dora, and a wild light flashed from her dark eyes. "I have triumphed!" She clasped her hands together with a convulsive gesture, and for a moment stood motionless as a statue.

"Yes, lady, he's stone dead, and the rats—jolly fellers—have already begin to crawl over his carcase." Devil-Bug advanced a step nearer the proud dame, and glared upon her with his solitary eye.

"I have triumphed! Rank and power are mine. Not an enemy in my path, nor a shadow on my future! I shall walk among the titled dames of the royal court, I shall feel a coronet pressing on my brow. To-morrow Livingstone and I depart for Hawkwood. From Hawkwood Livingstone never returns alive! In a month—ay, in one short month—" and her form rose towering to its full heighth, while her eye flashed and brightened with all the glory of the vision that burst upon her soul—"In one short month, Dora Livingstone, the Cobbler's granddaughter shall be the Lady Dora Dalveney, of Lyndeswold."

"But the *goo*ld, good lady—the *goo*ld."

The proud woman started at the sound of that harsh voice, she started and beheld the eye of Devil-Bug glaring upon her lovely face with a look of terrible meaning. His huge hands were crossed upon his breast, and with his head drooped low, he stood regarding her with a fixed gaze. That gaze spoke volumes! Better for the fair bosom of Dora to have been torn by the talons of an enraged tiger, than to have had the beauty of her proud countenance devoured by the animal fire of that steady look!

She started with involuntary surprise, she receded a single step, and then with a faint and trembling voice she addressed the savage.

"The ring," she whispered, averting her face as she reached forth her hand.

"Here it is, good lady!" And the solitary eye of Devil-Bug flashed with a glance of gloating admiration, as he extended the ring.

Dora looked steadily at the ring for a single moment.

"It was my mother's ring!" she whispered, in husky tones. "I gave it—" her voice trembled—"I gave it to him on the night when I consented to become his wife, as a pledge of my love."

These words fell trembling from her lips, and then like a flash of lightning, all her dreams of ambition passed away, and a terrible memory agitated her soul.

"I gave it to him while his eyes were fixed upon mine, and my hand trembled in his—I gave it to him, while his kiss was yet fresh upon my lips! And now—Great God! now I have murdered him!"

No words can depict the utter agony of look and emphasis which accompanied these words. Her proud form, rising in all its queenly stature, quivered from head to foot, as she held the ring extended in one hand while the other shaded her eyes from the light.

"The goold, good lady, the *goold!*"

Devil-Bug suddenly advanced, and grasping her extended arm with his talon fingers, impressed a loathsome kiss upon the fair white hand, which held the glittering ring.

She started with a look of silent disgust; she endeavored to fling the savage from her, but his talon fingers gathered more closely around her arm. His grasp was like the embrace of a vice.

"Yo' made the bargain good lady! Yo' sold yourself—black eyes, poutin' lips and all, for the ring. D'ye think I'm sich a fool as to be cheated out of my wages in this here way! Don't think sich a thing good lady! Old Devil-Bug wants the goold you promised!"

"Release me—" whispered Dora, with an ashen face, as she felt the grasp of his fingers on her arm—"Let me pass from this room and from this house, and I will reward you with gold beyond all your expectations—I will make you rich for life."

"Ho, ho, ho!" chuckled Devil-Bug. "Here's a tall woman afore me, with a look like a queen, a lip like a cherry, a cheek like a peach, and eyes like di'monds in a jew'ler's winder! She axes me to give up all this,—" he pointed to her voluptuous form—"she axes me to give up all this for goold! Redikulus!"

Dora's countenance suddenly grew lovely with all the hues of the summer dawn. Her eye dilated and sparkled with a clear and burning light. Casting her glance over Devil-Bug's shoulder, she beheld her cloak flung over the rounds of a chair. On a table, besides this chair, lay the pair of loaded pistols which she had brought with her to Monk-Hall.

"Could I but obtain them," the thought crossed her soul, like a ray of hope; "I would defy the monster to his teeth."

"Lady, there's a werry purty bloom on yer check, and there's a werry rich look in your eyes." He paused and raised her fair white hand to his loathsome lips. Then reaching forth his other arm, with his blazing eye devouring the loveliness of her face, he endeavored to encircle her form with his arm.

"I am faint," muttered Dora in a whisper, and she reached forth her hands as if to save herself from falling to the floor, while her eye closed as in a deadly swoon.

"Ho, ho, my beauty faints, does she?" muttered Devil-Bug, catching her form in his arms. "Werry purty in the beauty, that is! It's a genteel way o' sayin' she consents I 'spose."

With her head resting on his shoulder, while her bosom almost touched his face, Devil-Bug encircled her form in his arms and bore her slowly along the floor. He laid her gently down in the chair, where her cloak had been thrown.

Then stepping backward, he quietly surveyed her voluptuous form while that look of animal admiration reddened over his face.

"She lays there werry beautiful—her head thrown back a little, her eyes closed, and her red lips parted! Sich white teeth! And that form, all dressed in some gentleman's coat and pants; ho, ho, it all belongs to me! Sich a nice bosom! It looks quite purty, with the shirt collar thrown wide open about the neck! An' that's all mine!"

The swooning woman lay reclining upon the folds of the cloak, flung over the rounds of the chair, while the light streaming over the back of Devil-Bug fell mild and softened over her lovely face with the eyelids closed as if in death. Never had Dora looked so beautiful. Never had her lips been tinted with such a rose-bud freshness, never had such a lively glow bloomed from the fulness of her cheek, never had the tresses of her unbound hair, fell in such bewitching carelessness around her countenance and along her snowy neck.

She lay there like a beautiful incarnation of sleep, while the savage stood gazing upon her with a look of increasing admiration. His solitary eye grew loathsome with its expression of brute passion, while his lips were agitated by a hideous smile.

"Hello! My beauty's a comin' too! Look, she moves her head, she rests it on the table at her side, her eye-lids are openin' agin!"

In her unconscious state, Dora gently moved her arm, and as gently laid the hand upon the white cloth of the table. At the same moment her eye-lids faintly unclosed, and she gazed around with a bewildered stare.

"Soh, my beauty's had a faintin' spell all to herself," muttered Devil-Bug with a hideous chuckle, as he approached the side of the half-conscious woman. "I believe I'll taste her lips."

Laying his hand on her shoulder, he stooped slowly down, and the shadow of his face darkened her countenance. His loathsome lips well-nigh touched the ripe lips of the proud woman, when her hand moved nervously along the white cloth of the table. Nearer drew his lips, his hot breath streamed over her cheek.

"One kiss my purty beauty, only one kiss!"

With one sudden bound Dora Livingstone sprung from the chair, and when Devil-Bug looked for her again she stood in the centre of the floor, her eyes flashing fire, her long dark hair streaming wildly from her brow, while each extended hand, held a grim pistol at the monster's heart.

"Now devil, I defy you!" she exclaimed in a tone of withering scorn. "With a loaded pistol in either hand, I will fight my way from this den. Advance but a step, and I will stretch you out upon the floor a lifeless corpse!"

Devil-Bug started, and covered his face with his hands, as if utterly confounded by this sudden movement of the beautiful woman.

"Ha, ha," the scornful laugh of Dora broke on his ear. "Do I hold the blood-hound at bay? Monster, where is your courage now? Stand back and let me pass, or I fire this pistol!"

And with deadly aim she points the pistol at his brawny chest. Devil-Bug raised his face from his hands. Every harsh lineament of his countenance was convulsed with an expression of fiendish laughter.

"Ho, ho, what a sweet creetur you are to-w be-sure! Be so kind as to blow my brains out with them pistols—it 'ill quite dissap'int me if you don't. That's a good girl; oh fire away my duck! Wot a pity it is for you that them bull-dogs ain't got no balls in 'em! Ha, ha! Wot in the devil made you leave 'em down stairs with yer cloak, while I showed yo' the way up in this room? I did'nt draw out the balls—of course I did'nt! Who the devil said I did!"

Dora's face grew deathly pale. With an involuntary gesture she extended her hands—the pistols fell to the floor with a heavy deadened sound.

"All is lost!" she muttered as her hands dropped listlessly by her side.

"So it is!" cried Devil-Bug; and with the celerity of lightning he sprang forward and seized the pistols. "Ho, ho, my gal, did I fool you that time? The pistols *are* loaded, but you don't get 'em agin! No you don't, upon my word!"

"Fool that I was!" cried Dora with a flashing glance. "Oh that I had lodged the bullet in his heart!" She turned away, and pressed her red lip between her teeth until the blood started from the skin.

"Now my ducky dear, down on your knees and axe for marcy!" Devil-Bug advanced with a scowling brow, while each extended hand held a pistol toward her form. "Down on your knees, or I fire!"

"Fire!" echoed Dora, as her proud lip curved with scorn. "Fire, and I will thank you!" She folded her arms and confronted the Savage with a fearless brow.

"Pluck, reg'lar pluck!" exclaimed Devil-Bug with a stare of involuntary admiration. "But come my gal, you made the bargain an' you must stick to it! I've stood foolin' long enough. Its time to put an end to these small matters. Now for the goold!"

He dropped the pistols on the floor; with one convulsive bound like a wild beast darting on his prey, he sprang forward, and gathered his long arms around the form of the proud woman, while his rough face rested against her velvet cheek, and her lip felt the pressure of his kiss.

Starting with a shriek, she endeavored to tear her form from his embrace, but in vain. She, the proud and haughty woman with the outcast feasting on her lip and revelling on her beauty! Even in that moment of despair the thought aroused all her energies. She sprang from his embrace, her convulsive efforts for a moment loosened the grasp of his arms, but in another moment they gathered around her form with a closer pressure, and like a bird fluttering in the coils of a snake, she lay in his power and at his mercy.

She sank helplessly on her knees. Devil-Bug bent over her kneeling form, and with his arms gathered around her waist, impressed his loathsome kiss upon her pouting lips.

Nothing could save the proud beauty now. Dishonored, and by a devil in human shape! The thought filled her veins with madness; her eyes seemed all on fire with the terrible intensity of her thoughts.

His hot breath streamed over her cheek. His sneering chuckle echoed in her ears like a death-knell. His solitary eye drank in the beauty of her countenance with a look of brutal passion. Dora gathered her strength for one last struggle. Her brain throbbing with wild delirium, she shouted a name that rose to her lips, she knew not why, she shouted a name of the olden time.

"Luke!" she shrieked, tossing her arms madly on high. "Luke! Save me, oh save me!"

As if her voice had aroused the dead from the grave, the secret door slid back, and Luke Harvey stood revealed, a dim taper held in his extended hand, flashing its light over a pale face, spotted with drops of blood, and marked by a fearful gash which laid open the flesh along the right temple. His dress all torn and disordered was soiled by the earth of the grave, and his long black hair hung lank and stiffened around his face. His eye, dark, piercing and snake-like at all times, was now animated by a lustre that seemed supernatural.

There in that same doorway, which the night before had been passed by the husband in search of his guilty wife, in that same doorway stood Luke Harvey gazing upon the savage and his victim with one fixed and immoveable gaze.

"Luke save me, save me!" shrieked Dora, unconscious that the man whom she had sold to death, stood gazing upon her peril. "Luke, oh save me!"

His head bent down, Devil-Bug suddenly felt the gleam of a strange light flashing over his face. He raised his head, he beheld Luke standing silent and pale in the doorway, and then flinging Dora from him, uttered a wild howl of surprise.

"G———d d———n!" was his solitary ejaculation. "If there ain't that feller come to life agin!"

He was about to rise from his feet, when the apparition rushed forward, and seizing a pistol from the floor, struck Devil-Bug a fierce and fearful blow over the forehead.

His skull echoed the blow like a piece of metal ringing on the anvil. With a curse on his lips, Devil-Bug rose fiercely to his feet, but the pistol again descended, again that ringing sound—the monster fell heavily to the floor. He lay senseless as the oaken planks on which he rested.

Thrown prostrate along the floor, Dora arose into a kneeling position and gazed around in speechless wonder.

Tall and erect, the dim light held in his extended hand, Luke Harvey stood before her, gazing down on her face with a saddened and immoveable look. The light flashing upward gave a ghastly and fearful appearance to his pale countenance, while his blazing eye encountered hers, with a look so strange and piercing, that she was forced to avert her gaze.

"His ghost comes to reproach me!" muttered Dora in an almost inaudible yet thrilling whisper.

"Oh Dora, Dora," said a calm and deep-toned voice, rendered fearful in its very calmness, by its striking contrast with the usual sneering tones of Luke Harvey. "Oh Dora, Dora, little did I think in the times when I gathered you to my heart, and tasted the freshness of your virgin lip, and in very fondness of passion called you my own sweet wife, little did I think in those times, now gone forever, that a moment could ever come, when I would behold a scene like this! Dora, whom I once so fondly loved, thrown prostrate on the floor of this polluted chamber, her person, her honor, the price of a cold-blooded murder! Oh Dora, Dora you might have spared me *this* shame!"

The sneer had gone from Luke's tongue. He stood gazing upon the kneeling woman with a trembling voice and a look of agony. Even while he looked a scalding tear rolled down his deathly cheek.

"Your body, the price of a cold-blooded murder!" he uttered in a whisper, as his immoveable gaze was still rivetted to her countenance.

"Murder!" echoed Dora, gazing wildly in his face.

"Yes, murder, replied Luke in that same tone of unnatural calmness. "I overheard your plot Dora, overheard every word. In the darkness I stood beside the door of the room down-stairs; I saw you enter; I heard you bargaining for my blood. Oh Dora, I have felt something like a desire for revenge, whenever I thought how you trifled with my feelings and trampled on my heart, but now Dora, *now!* You are revenged upon me! Far better the knife of the assassin had cut my heart in twain, than to look upon you, in such shame as *this!*" She was indeed revenged upon him. There was agony in his look and tone, in his pale face and trembling voice, agony worse than death.

Dora was silent. She bowed her face on her bosom as she knelt at his feet, she bowed her face and veiled her eyes with her hands. The ring dropped from her finger.

Luke knelt silently by her side. He took the ring from the floor.

"This ring you gave me on the night when you first consented to be mine—" he said in that calm and deep-toned voice. "Then it was the testimonial of our love—now it is the witness of your shame!"

Dora shuddered. That voice speaking so sadly to her ear, penetrated her very heart with remorse.

She raised her face from her bosom, she gazed upon his countenance in silence. It was a strange and awful moment. The Rejected lover kneeling beside the proud woman, at once the faithless Mistress and the guilty Wife!

"Luke," she whispered in a tone strangely in contrast with her usual commanding voice. "Luke, if ever you loved me, take that pistol from the floor and place it to my forehead! I am utterly lost—death would come to me now like a welcome messenger!"

There was silence for a single moment. They gazed sadly in each others faces, while the same thought rose from each heart! Dora thought how pure and happy would have been her life, had she become the wife of Luke. Luke thought how dear and holy a thing she would have been to him as a wife—she, the fallen and dishonored.

"Curse on the fate that severed us!" he cried, wringing his hands with a mad gesture.

"There is an awful gulf between us now. I am lost, and lost forever! said Dora, as the first tears of repentance which she had ever shed, rolled down her cheeks.

"Dora, there is yet a glorious hope for you!" cried Luke as his ghastly features warmed with an expression of enthusiasm that might almost have been called holy. "Promise me that you will renounce all unhallowed love, promise me that you will from this time forth, dissolve all connection with the poor creature who has dishonored you by a foul crime, promise me that you will ever be to Livingstone a true and faithful wife; and I swear before God, to sustain you in your course, to defend you from all harm!"

Oh that tone, that look, that beseeching gesture of the rejected lover! Dora was melted to the heart.

Radiant with all the beauty of a new formed and holy resolve, she raised her heart and eyes to heaven.

"I promise!" she cried, and the tears rolled down her cheeks.

"I swear to sustain you to the death!" cried Luke, raising his hands on high.

There was silence for a single moment, and the character of the place in which they knelt, the guilt of the wife, the revenge of the lover, all were forgotten. That Resolve hovered over their hearts like the halo around the cross of a dying saint.

In a moment Luke raised her gently from the floor, and silently gathered the cloak around her disguised form. She reddened to the very roots of her hair as he placed the cap upon her head. Her ambition, her recklessness of soul alike were gone; she felt the modesty of a wife once more. She stood ready to depart, while the form of the insensible savage lay prostrate on the floor.

"In a moment, Dora, I will be with you," said Luke as he turned toward the secret door. "In a moment I will lead you from this place."

Dora was alone. Oh what a tide of tumultuous thoughts came rushing madly over her brain! As she stepped across the floor it seemed to her that she trod on air, that the present was some glorious dream from which she would soon awake to the reality of life and the pollution of crime. The tones of her former lover lingered yet upon her ear, how like the days of stainless innocence and love! Then the affection of Livingstone, his care for her slightest wish, his doting love came like a burst of sunshine on her soul. With a trembling lip and flashing eye, she wondered to herself that idle toys like the world's ambition and the love which is born of guilt, should ever have lured her from the duty of a wife, the purity of a woman.

As these thoughts flashed over her soul, Luke stood by her side again.

"Give this to your husband at the earliest opportunity," he said as he placed a sealed note in her hands. "You start for Hawkewood in the morning. For God's sake do not fail to give him this."

Dora placed the note in her bosom. Then her large eyes, dark as midnight and lustrous as the morn, encountered the glance of her former lover, and for a moment they silently gazed upon each other.

"Oh Dora, my fever of revenge is past! Till this hour I never knew how your image had wound itself into my very heart!"

"And I would have been your assassin!" Dora exclaimed, turning suddenly pale. "Oh Luke, I am too vile a thing for your slightest notice. I am—how the word chokes me—I am an *adultress!*"

"Let the past be with the past?" said Luke in a solemn tone, as taking her hands within his own he raised them on high. "Let us now in the sight of Heaven confirm our mutual vow!"

Fools that they were! As they stood there in that lonely room, hand linked in hand and eyes raised to heaven, Fate was weaving its threads of Doom around and about them; silent and stern and immutable Fate was surrounding them with its serpent-coils, while it looked upon them in scorn, and laughed in derision as its awful hand pointed to the Future! To-morrow it murmured—ha, ha—to-morrow!

And while they stood in that lonely chamber, hand linked in hand and eyes raised to Heaven, in his counting room silent and alone, the husband mixed the poison which on the morrow was to lay his guilty wife a stiffened corpse.

Bending over the table on which were scattered the various drugs which composed the fatal draught, bending over the table, with the light of the taper falling upon his death-stricken face, the husband laughed madly to himself and whispered in husky tones, "to-morrow, ha, ha, to-morrow!"

Fools that they were! To think that Fate which drives its iron wheels over hearts and thrones and graves, would turn aside in its career for them!

"Away Dora," cried Luke, "away from Monk-Hall!" They moved toward the door. The wretch thrown prostrate on the carpet, groaned.

"Ha! I forgot the keys!" cried Luke, retracing his steps. "There they are—" he bent over the form of Devil-Bug. "In a moment your escape is certain."

He led her from the room, and down the stairs. In a few moments they stood in the Doorkeeper's den. By the dim light the negroes might be discerned sleeping by the fireside.

It required but another moment for Luke to place the key in the lock, and open the massive door.

She stood in the doorway with the cloak thrown round her form and the beams of the setting moon falling on her face.

"Go, and God go with you Dora!" whispered Luke, pushing her gently from the door.

"Do you not go with me?" she whispered as she paused upon the threshold. "There is danger for you within these walls, *perchance death*."

"I have other matters to arrange," answered Luke. "I must avenge wrong and defend innocence. Go, Dora, and remember your vow!"

He pushed her gently across the threshold, he closed the door, and stood alone in the Doorkeeper's den.

The negroes still slumbered by the fireside, and the faint light of the fire illumined the face of Luke with a ghastly radiance.

He advanced toward the fire, he placed his hand hurriedly against his brow, while his eye grew animate with strange and powerful emotion.

"The world would call me a fool for acting thus," he whispered. "True, she trampled on my heart, true, she dishonored her husband, true, she bargained with the ruffian for my life, but God alone knows how the face we once loved to look upon, ever maintains a strange influence over the heart, how the voice we once loved to hear, even has a music for the soul! My brain whirls in confusion—I am weakened by the loss of blood—ah!"

Turning to regain the door which led into the mansion, he felt the strength generated by the excitement which had agitated his soul during the past hour, he felt this unnatural strength passing from him like a shadow, he stretched forth his hands in the effort to preserve his balance, but in vain!

With a cry of agony on his lips he fell helpless to the floor.

Half an hour passed, and Devil-Bug stood over the form of the prostrate man with a light in his hand. He regarded the pale face of Luke with a scowl of fierce malignity. His own distorted countenance, spotted with blood near the temples and livid in hue, assumed an expression of savage hate.

"Soh, Soh, mister, yo' helped the woman to dig off, did yo'?" he muttered, placing his foot upon the breast of the insensible man. "I've a notion to knife your wizzin'—wonders how you'd look with a small air-hole in your throat?"

He drew an old-fashioned spanish knife from the breast of his coarse garment as he spoke. The blade, long, pointed and glittering, flew open with a touch of the spring. Stooping over the form of the insensible Luke, he applied the knife to his unbared throat, and with a wild grimace destorting his features, he moved it gently along the skin.

"I on'y wants to see how near to the skin I can go, without cuttin' his wynd-pipe! Ho, ho, ho!"

There was a great deal of the philosopher in Devil-Bug. Never a doctor of all the schools, with his dissecting knife in hand and the corpse of a subject before him, could have manifested more nerve and coolness than the savage of Monk-Hall. Slowly and gently along the throat of the insensible man, he moved the glittering knife, holding its keen edge within a hair's breadth of the skin. Then as if to show that his spirits were not depressed by the solemnity of the operation, he laughed merrily to himself, and hummed the catch of some dismal song.

Suddenly his protuberent brow grew heavy with a scowl. He clenched the handle of the knife with a grasp of fierce resolution, and in a moment, the blade glittered in his upraised hand.

"I'll put an end to this," he muttered hoarsely. "I'll give him a taste o' this piece o' hardware. Crack me over the skull with the butt o' that are pistol, did he?"

For a moment the knife quivered in the air above his head, and the scowl grew darker over his brow. The next instant, as if some strange thought had suddenly taken his soul by storm, the frown cleared away and the knife fell from his hand and stuck upright in the oaken floor.

"Nell," he slowly muttered, "Yer only hope lies *here!*" He pointed to the body of the insensible Luke. "Here lies yer hope, and yer fortin' —this man can make all matters straight. He can place yo' afore the proud folks o' this town as the daughter o' Livingstone; and nobody else can do it! I'd rayther burn myself alive than to hurt a hair of his head."

Stooping to the floor, he raised Luke on his shoulder, he bore him from the den, up the stairs, and into his room. He laid the form of the insensible man upon the bed, and then rushed hurriedly from the room, and down the stairs again.

In a few moments, the lamp which he held in his hand flashed over the massive brick pillars of the dead vault.

The place was infested with a deathly chill, and the atmosphere was like the breath of a pestilence. Devil-Bug gazed calmly round the vault, as if marking the rows of coffins stored away in the nooks of the walls, or the fragments of the human skeleton scattered along the floor. Then he gazed upon the pillars of massive brick, and then shifting the light from side to side, he seemed to feel a strange pleasure in observing the heavy shadows which ran along the distant walls, or crept over the arching ceiling above.

"I'd a'most forgot it," he soloquized as he seated his deformed body on the floor. "The *doctor* sent for me last night; the one what wants me to steal dead bodies for him. I must go airly in the mornin'; he pays me well; and I likes the business. Sich a jolly business! To creep over the wall o' some grave yard in the dead o' the night, and with a spade in yer hand, to turn up the airth of a new made grave! To mash the coffin lid into small pieces with a blow o' the spade, and to drag the stiff corpse out from its restin' place, with the shroud so white and clean, spotted by the damp clay! To kiver the corpse with an old over-coat or a coffee bag, and bear it off to the doctor, with his penknife's and his daggers and his gim'lets! Hoo, hoo!" he emitted a wild imitation of the screech-owl, from his compressed teeth, "sich a jolly business!"

Then placing the lamp on the floor, and drawing the fragment of a crumbling coffin beneath his elbow, he rested his brawny cheek upon his hand, while his solitary eye glared fiercely upon the thick shadows of the vault. He sat thus for a few moments, when his senses were overpowered by slumber, and he lay there huddled in a heap along the floor, sleeping with his eye wide open.

The light flashed over his face, while the muscles worked as if under the influence of a spell, the brow was corrugated with wrinkles like thick cords, the eye flashed and sparkled and glared, the teeth were clenched together, and then around the quivering lips, the white foam began to gather like the froth on the nostrils of the dying warhorse.

The soul of Devil-Bug was passing through the mazes of a fearful dream. This it was that made his eye glare and his lips move, this it was sent the cold shudder through his sleeping form; this it was that clenched his hands and made him grasp wildly at the air. As he lay there, his soul absorbed by an awful night-mare, a world of phantoms passed before him.

The sight that he saw in his sleep, the vision that broke upon him! Was it a Revelation from the other world? Was it a Prophecy whispered to the monster's soul by the tongues of angels?

CHAPTER FOURTEENTH

DEVIL-BUG'S DREAM

When first he slept, the phantoms of his murdered victims rose before him; the man with the broken jaw and the lolling tongue, the woman with the blood falling drop by drop from the hollow skull. Then the eyes of the man started from his death-stricken face, then he could see the neck of the woman quiver as with the convulsive throes of death, and then he could hear the low-pattering sound of blood dropping from the hollow skull. The sleeper groaned in agony. The woman reached forth her skinny arms and clasped them round his neck, and applied her thin lips wet with blood to his ear, and whispered *Murder* in a tone of horrible laughter.

And the man lolled his blackening tongue—ugh! how clammy and how cold! against the face of Devil-Bug, and looked into his very soul with those blood-shot eyes, almost touching the forehead of the dreamer. Then the dream became confused and wandering. Devil-Bug was surrounded by a hazy atmosphere, with coffins floating slowly past, and the stars shining through the eyes of skulls, and the sun pouring his livid light straight downward into a wilderness of new-made graves which extended yawning and dismal over the surface of a boundless plain.

Then the sun assumed the shape of a grinning skeleton-head, and the stars went dancing through the dim atmosphere, dancing round the sun, each star gleaming through the orbless socket of a skull, and the blood-red moon went sailing by, her crescent face, rising above a huge coffin which floated through the livid air like a barque from hell. Then the sky was full of comets darting along like lightning, each comet with a long white shroud sweeping the heavens as it rushed through the air, and then sky and sun and moon and stars, were succeeded by thick and impenetrable darkness. There was a long pause, and the darkness resolved itself into shape. Devil-Bug stood in the midst of a boundless plain, covered with a darkness like that which betokens the approach of day. The whole sky was changed into one vast curtain, which hung in midnight folds across the immensity of space.

The dreamer looked upon this awful curtain in awe and wonder.

"This," cried a voice speaking shrilly from the darkness, "this is the curtain of the Theatre of Hell!" And then Devil-Bug laughed loudly to himself, as if in glee at the merry conceit.

At the very instant there arose from the dark plain, a chorus of shrieks and groans and yells of agony. It was as though the dying in some vast battlefield had suddenly, one in breath, sent their combined death-shrieks to the heavens above. Yell on yell, groan on groan continued to rend the air, and then a horrible chorus of laughter broke on the ear of the dreamer.

"This," cried the voice, this is the Orchestra of Hell!"

Then the curtain slowly rose. Up, up, the dark folds ascended; higher, higher! The theatre of hell lay bare to his view. Devil-Bug started forward, and looked upon the scene, and howled in glee!

What he then beheld may never be told to the ears of living man. Oh! horrible and ghastly, that sight of all sights the most dread! Oh, horrible and ghastly! On every wave a lost soul, on every breeze of that heated air, a groan of death! That throne rising black and lurid, from the centre of the chaos of flame—oh, picture its horror to no living ear! But the fair bosomed women, floating on those waves, are they not spared? And the babes, lifting their tiny hands on high, is there no mercy for them? And the old men, dashed against the red-hot rocks, is there no deliverance for them? Look, look! Strain your eyes, Devil-Bug, behold that sight of grandeur! That wave, ha, ha, see how it rises from the bosom of the sea, that wave of fire! How it roars around the throne, how it towers and swells! And in the fiery surf which crests its summit, look, look, there are millions of souls, shrieking for mercy! Only a drop of water, only a drop of water!

The orchestra of hell strikes up its music, and the play goes on.

Suddenly all became dark again and the dream changed.

The Last Day of the Quaker City

He stood in the wide street of a magnificent city. All around him, from lofty windows, the glare of many lights flashed out upon the winter night. Above, the clear cold sky of a calm winter twilight overarched the far extending perspective, brilliant with light and life, which marked the extent and grandeur of that wide street of a gorgeous city.

Devil-Bug looked around him, and beheld the sidewalks lined with throngs of wayfarers, some clad in purple and fine linen, some with rags fluttering around their wasted forms. Here was the lady in all the glitter of her plumes, and silks, and diamonds, and by her side the beggar child stretched forth its thin and skinny arm, asking in feeble tones, for the sake of God, some charity good lady! And the lady smiled, and uttered some laughing word to the man of fashion by her side, with his slim waist and effeminate face, she uttered a remark of careless scorn, and passed the beggar-child unheeded by. Here passing slowly onward, with a look of sanctimony, a white cravat and robes of sable, was the lordly Bishop, whose firm step and salacious eye betokened at once his arrogance and guilt; here was the man of law with his parchment book and his cold grey eye; here was the Judge with his visage of solemnity and his pocket-book crammed full with bribes, and here, hungry and lean, was the mechanic in his tattered garb, looking to the clear blue sky above, as he asked God's vengeance upon the world that robbed and starved him.

Devil-Bug rubbed his hands with glee. There was something so exhilarating to him, in the sight of all this, in the spectacle of the lofty windows stored with silks and satins, gold and jewels, enriched with the tribute of a whole world, in the animation of the sidewalk, its crowds of wayfarers, its rich and poor, its worldly and its holy men, that old Devil-Bug laughed gaily to himself and rubbed his hands in very glee.

Wandering slowly onward, he was wrapt in wonder at the magnificence which broke upon his vision, when suddenly a massive edifice rose before him, with long rows of marble columns and a massive dome breaking into the blue of the sky far overhead. Beside this gorgeous structure, which appeared to be in progress of erection, for there was scaffolding about its columns and the implements of the workmen were scattered around; beside this edifice arose a small and unpretending structure of brick, only two stories high, with its plain old-fashioned steeple rising but half-way to the summit of the marble palace. This small and unpretending structure was in ruins, the roof was torn from the steeple, the windows were concealed by rough boards, and from one corner, the bricks had been thrown down.

Devil-Bug, when he beheld this structure in ruins, while the marble palace by its side arose in such grandeur upon the clear blue sky, smiled to himself and clapped his hands boisterously together.

"This," he cried, pointing to the edifice, "this should be the old State House, and I must be in the Quaker City!"

As he spoke, a ghostly form glided from among the gay wayfarers of the sidewalk, and stood by his side, a ghostly form like a thin shape of mist with large dark eyes flashing from its shadowy face. "It is the old State House," whispered the ghostly form, in a voice that thrilled to the heart of the listener. "Yes it is old Independence Hall! The lordlings of the Quaker City have sold their father's bones for gold, they have robbed the widow and plundered the orphan, blasphemed the name of God by their pollution of his faith and church, they have turned the sweat and blood of the poor into bricks and mortar, and now as the last act of their crime, they tear down Independence Hall and raise a royal palace on its ruins!"

"What d'ye mean by that," cried Devil-Bug, fiercely. "*Royal* palace —hey? That means something about a king, don't it?"

"King!" echoed the Ghost, in a sad and sorrowful tone. "Look at those proud chariots rolling along the crowded street, look at those chariots with the horses decked in tinselled trappings and with liveried retainers riding at their sides."

"Yes, yes I see 'em," cried Devil-Bug, in his coarse way. "Them carriages with horses all rigged out like circus horses, an' with fellers ridin' along side dressed in monkey-jackets—what does it all mean, any how?"

"Those chariots are the equipages of a proud and insolent nobility, who lord it over the poor of the Quaker City! Yes, there rides a Duke, and there a Baron, and yonder a Count! This palace is intended for the residence of a king! Liberty long since fled from the Quaker City, in reality has now vanished in its very name. The spirit of the old Republic is dethroned, and they build a royal mansion over the ruins of Independence Hall!"

As the spirit spoke the blaze of lights grew more radiant, the sidewalk was thronged by gayer wayfarers, the street resounded to the echo of chariot wheels, and up to the clear sky, like the echo of Niagara, went the hum and confusion of the wide city.

"Ho, ho," laughed Devil-Bug. "So they git on quite lively, do they? Stranger, if I may axe sich a questi'n, whar is Girard College—hey?"

The eloquent eyes of the Ghost lighted up with an expression of speechless woe. "They have torn it down to build this palace with its marble!" it answered, in a tone of unutterable agony.

"And what year d'ye call this?"

"The year of our Lord one thousand nine hundred and fifty," said the Spirit, but Devil-Bug was not sure that he had heard aright. It seemed to him afterward that the Spirit had added a word to his enumeration of the time.

"And this King, whose palace is a-buildin' yonder, an' these Dukes and Lords, who are ridin' in their big carri'ges yonder, what great deeds did they ever do?"

"Cheated the poor out of their earnings, wrung the sweat from the brow of the mechanic and turned it into gold, traded away the bones of their fathers, sold Independence Square for building lots, and built this palace for a King! These are their mighty deeds!"

"It seems to me, stranger, that the King with his Dukes an' Lords aint nothin' but a pack o' swindlin' Bank d'rectors—hey? In the year eighteen forty-two, there was some fuss made about a monument to Gin'ral Washington, in Washington Square—can you tell me, stranger, whatever became of it?"

The Ghost led him silently through the archway of the ruined State House, and in a moment they stood upon Independence Square, all cumbered with heaps of marble and piles of building timber. The greater portion of the square was occupied by the royal palace, but from the western extreme a free view of the heavens might be obtained.

"Do you see that dark and gloomy building yonder?" exclaimed the Ghost, pointing in a south-western direction.

"What, that great big jail of a buildin'? Why, stranger, that stands where Washin'ton Square used to stand. What does it mean, anyhow?"

"It is indeed a gaol, built on the ground of Washington Square. Within its gloomy cells, all those brave patriots are confined, the brave men who struck the last blow for the liberty of the land, against the tyranny of this new-risen nobility. There, day after day and night after night, with the rusted iron eating into their wasted flesh—there they drag their lives away in darkness, in cold and hunger!"

"Hello! mister, isn't that a gallows I see yonder—opposite the jail? It's quite confortin' to see that old-fashioned thing alive yet!"

"It is a gallows!" said the Ghost. "And thanks to the exertions of some of the Holy Ministers of God, it is never idle! Day after day its rope is distended by the wriggling body of some murderer, day after day these merciful preachers crowd around its blackened timbers, sending the felon into the presence of his God, his ears deafened by their hallelujahs, while his stiffened hands grasp that Bible whose code is mercy to all men!"

"Hurrah!" shouted Devil-Bug. "The gallows is livin' yet! Hurrah!"

"For some years it was utterly abolished," said the Ghost.—"Murders became few in number, convicts were restored to society, redeemed from their sins, and the gaols began to echo to the solitary footsteps of the gaoler. But these good Preachers arose in the Senate, and the Pulpit and plead beseechingly for blood!"

"Hurrah for the Preachers! Them's the jockies!"

"Give us but the gibbet," they shrieked. "Only give us the gibbet and we'll reform the world! Christ said mercy was his rule, we know more about his religion than he did himself, and we cry give us blood! In the name of Moses, in the name of Paul, and John, and Peter, in the name of the Church, in the name of Christ—give us the gibbet, only give us the gibbet!"

"They said this? The jolly fellers!"

The gallows was given to them. The gibbet arose once more in the streets. Murder became a familiar thing. Crime dyed its hands in blood, and went laughing to the gibbet. The good Preachers plead for blood, and they had it!"

"Hurrah!" screamed Devil-Bug. "The gallows is livin' yet! Hurrah!" He sprang from his feet in very glee, and clapped his hands and hurrahed again.

When he again looked round the Ghost had disappeared. Retracing his steps through the archway, Devil-Bug stood on the sidewalk of the broad street again.

He passed along among the crowds of gay wayfarers, he passed many a princely equipage, many a gorgeous chariot, and here and there at the corners of the streets or among the gayest of the laughing throng, he beheld a squalid beggar crouching to the earth as he asked for bread, or a pale-faced mechanic in worn and tattered clothes, who shook his hands in impotent rage as he beheld the stare of wealth which flashed from the lofty windows as if to tantalize him with their splendor.

At last Devil-Bug stood in front of a lofty marble church which arose from the centre of a grave-yard. All around the massive church in the cold light of the stars, arose long rows of whitened tomb-stones, with here and there a lordly monument or slender obelisk, or lofty pyramid of snow white marble.

Devil-Bug looked at the church intently for a few moments, admiring its massive structure and expansive dome, when to his utter astonishment the top of a vault near the wall of the grave-yard rose suddenly upward, and through the aperture a shrouded form issued in the star-light and stood erect, lifting its hands to heaven, while the death-shroud fluttered in the air.

Suddenly the figure turned, it advanced toward Devil-Bug: he started in utter horror. A ghastly corpse with eye of leaden dimness gazing fixedly from a face yellowed by decay stood before him. And as he started in horror from each marble vault of the grave-yard, from each rising mound from beneath each pyramid and obelisk, arose the shrouded form of a corpse, and in an instant the place was white with the fluttering shrouds of the multitude of dead.

On they came, advancing slowly toward the grave-yard wall; on they came, their hands crossed over their white shrouds, their leaden eyes gazing fixedly forward, their foreheads all alive with the loathsome grave-worm. On they came gliding over the wall, on they came, a throng of the ghastly dead. While Devil-Bug started aside in horror, they glided over the grave-yard wall, they mingled with the gay throngs of the side-walk, their white shrouds fluttering amid silken gowns and velvet robes, their ghastly faces seen among gay visages, vacant with the joy of a pleasure-loving world.

Devil-Bug beheld them file along the street, one by one, a long and fearful train, he saw them pass beneath the glare of the lights, beneath the shadow of the palaces, he saw them gliding slowly around, their leaden eyes wearing that same fixed gaze, while their hands were folded on their breasts. With utter horror he discovered that the gay revellers of the street beheld them not. They walked merrily round while the arisen dead glided all around them, they smiled gaily, unconscious of the leaden eyes that were gazing so sadly in their faces, they rent the air with laughter, unheeding the rustling sound of the thousand death-shrouds that swept the fringe of their costly robes.

Oh what unutterable agony was painted upon the faces of the arisen dead, as they discovered that the living beheld them not! How their blue lips moved, yet uttered no sound, how their white hands were upraised as if in warning, while the worms went crawling round each brow.

"What does this all mean!" shouted Devil-Bug, in utter dismay. "Good folks don't you see that the dead's among you? Good lady, look there, look! There's a walkin' corpse at yer shoulder! Fine gentleman, look, look! There's a dead man at yer back! Look! the whole grave yard is emptyin' itself into the street, look, ye fools, I say look!"

He screamed and shouted as seized with an agony, whose origin he could not comprehend, he felt himself forced to declare the awful spectacle which he beheld to the ears of the pleasure-loving citizens, but he screamed and shouted in vain.

They heard him not. The lord rolling by in his gilded equipage, was unconscious of the shrouded corpse that looked in his window, the beggar in the gutter knew not that the form of a friend, long since dead, was now gazing sadly upon his misery.

Devil-Bug gazed far along the street, and to his amazement, beheld a long multitude of shrouded dead, walking beneath the flaring lights as far as eye could see, until the magnificent perspective was lost in a mass of vacant darkness.

"Good folks," shouted Devil-Bug in horror—"Hello! Don't you see yer town is alive with dead!"

"Let them alone, let them alone!" said a mild and saddened voice.

Rushing madly along the street, Devil-Bug turned hurriedly around.

The pale Ghost was at his side.

"Let them alone," it cried in that low-toned voice. "The dead arise around them, to warn them of their coming doom, yet they know them not! These are their friends, their relatives, their wives, their sisters, their brothers, risen from the grave, to warn them of their doom, but their sealed eyes behold them not!"

"Their doom!" echoed Devil-Bug. "Speak plain will ye? What d'ye mean?"

"Behold!" cried the stranger, pointing to a black cloud which arose from the blue in the western sky.

Devil-Bug looked and beheld written on the cloud, words in letters of fire, which he could not read.

"What does it mean?" he shrieked, turning to the figure at his side.

"The angel of the Judgment writes the doom of this proud city, from the heavens his hand is extended, behold the words of flame on yon glistening cloud."

WO UNTO SODOM

Devil-Bug looked upon these characters of flame and felt a strange awe penetrate his heart.

"Come," cried the Ghost, "I will show you sights that no human eye may see, I will unseal your ear to sounds that no human ear may hear!"

Devil-Bug felt himself borne upward, he felt himself hurried with the speed of wind along the crowded street.

And he was borne along from every grave-yard, he beheld the

shrouded dead arise, beheld them pour out upon the thronged side-walk, he saw them lift their hands on high, he saw them fix their leaden eyes upon the faces of the living with a look of unutterable woe. From lonely burial places, from the banks of the broad river, from the grounds of the prison, up started the shrouded dead, nay from the very bricks of the crowded pavement they rose, and joined the snow-white multitude who thronged the streets.

Devil-Bug and his guide stood at the foot of a gallows, which arose like an evil omen upon the night. The corpse of a convict hung in chains, swung heavily to and fro. As Devil-Bug looked, the convict came down from his gibbet, and clanking his chains on high, with a hideous face festering with corruption, and lighted by leaden eyes gleaming with all the malignity of hell, the felon-corpse rushed by and joined the train of the dead.

Through street after street, through avenue after avenue, Devil-Bug was borne by his ghastly guide, but every wide street, every avenue, each pathway and side-walk was crowded by throngs of laughing citizens, mingling with the multitudes of the shrouded dead.

"What does all this mean?" cried Devil-Bug to the Ghost at his side.

"This night is a festival night with the lordlings of the city. To-morrow they will hold a grand revel through the whole extent of the wide town, and to-morrow—"

The Ghost paused. It pointed to the lurid cloud over head with the letters of flame written on its darkness, and as it pointed, a sad smile stole over its lips, and it whispered,

WO UNTO SODOM

"To-morrow" shrieked the spirit, "To-morrow will be the last day of the Quaker City. The judgment comes, and they know it not."

As he spoke, he set Devil-Bug down again in front of Independence Hall. "Listen to the song of the dead!" cried the Ghost. "Hark how they sing as they mingle with the crowds of light-hearted revellers! Hark how their low-toned song breaks like a funeral hymn on the air—hark!"

And as the shrouded dead glided along, mingling unseen with the gay and living, there broke from their livid lips a fearful song, uttered in a low and moaning chaunt that arose to the heavens in notes of prayer and execration.

A single voice pealing from among the dead, moving along the street, as they sang the solemn hymn, prayed God to curse the Quaker City.

Then the whole legion of the dead shrieked in one horrible chorus, "Wo unto Sodom! Anathema Marantha!"

"Cursed be the city," cried that solitary voice, leading the supernatural choir. "Its foundations are dyed in blood. The curse of the poor man is upon it, and the curse of the orphan. The widow, with her babes starving at her breast, raises her hands and curses it in the sight of God. Wo unto Sodom!"

And the ghastly train, extending far along the streets, their stiffened hands folded upon their white shrouds, took up the cry with their livid lips and chaunted in a low yet horrible tone—

"Wo unto Sodom, wo! Anathema Marantha!"

"It has burned the Churches of the Living God. It has torn His Cross from the Altar, it has soiled His banner with dust and ashes! Even the graves of the dead it has not spared. The hands of violence have torn the bones of the dead from their graves, and flung them mockingly beneath the hoofs of the horses. Cursed be the city. Wo unto Sodom!"

"Wo unto Sodom! The hour of doom draweth nigh. The Church of the living God in ruins curses it; the Cross polluted and covered with ashes curses it; the grave torn open by the hand of violence and the bones of the dead, curse the city before the throne of God! Anathema Marantha!"

Again that solitary voice resumed its chaunt of death and wo.

"The poor man toils in want, and the rich man riots in his sweat and blood. Wo unto Sodom! The guiltless and the innocent pine in the dungeon, while the unholy judge feasts upon the price of bribery and shame. The corpse of the innocent swings upon the gibbet, and the worms crawl over its brow, while the Murderer rides in his chariot, his proud form clothed in fine linen and his guilty face decked in smiles! Accursed in the sight of God be Sodom, now and forever!"

And all along the street, from the ten thousand thousand dead, arose the response—

"Amen! Accursed in the sight of God be Sodom, now and forever! Amen and Amen. Anathema Marantha!"

And thus, in low and solemn tones, the solitary Spirit recounted the foul litany of the city's crimes, and as each hideous deed of wrong or murder fell from his livid lips; the multitude of the dead raised up their voices and shrieked, "Amen and Amen! Accursed be Sodom, now and forever! Anathema Marantha!"

The curse seemed to pierce the ear of Heaven. From the sky, shadowy forms of grandeur looked down upon the scene, and suddenly a figure of awful and majestic beauty, bent from the dim azure and waved a flaming sword across the heavens. Up to the sky like the blast of the last trumpet swelled the Anathema of the arisen dead, and from the blackness of the cloud, overhanging the city like an embodied curse, flashed the letters of doom, Wo unto Sodom!

"Accursed be the city in the sight of Nations! It has torn the flag of Freedom from the rock, and dashed it in the dust."

"Accursed be the city in the sight of God!" shrieked the voices of the dead. "Wo unto Sodom! Anathema Marantha!"

And then they raised their leaden eyes to heaven and clenched their cold white hands on high, and then their solemn chaunt was heard once more—

"Accursed be the city before the throne of God! It has torn the flag of Freedom from the rock, and trailed it in the dust. Wo unto Sodom, wo!"

And through the streets they wound, this ghastly multitude, circling among the careless crowd, their hands crossed on their breasts and their leaden eyes raised up to heaven, and far, far along each avenue they extended, one awful train of shrouded dead, moving slowly onward while around them swelled the hum and roar of the gay city holding its carnival.

And still up to the heavens arose the chaunt of the solitary voice, and still like the thunder-blast of the last trump arose the dread response, "Wo unto Sodom. Amen and Amen. Anathema Marantha!"

The scene changed. Suddenly Devil-Bug was borne upward through the air and the city passed from his view. All was night, and blackness, and silence.

He looked around again, and an exclamation of wonder burst from his lips. He stood upon the portico of a proud palace, which arose from the midst of a dark and angry river. The palace was reared upon a solitary island which broke the fury of the waves in the centre of the river. Devil-Bug looked to the west, and beyond the channel of the river, he beheld the dim and dusky outlines of the magnificent city extending north and south in one dark mass of roofs and walls, with here and there a heavy dome or towering steeple rising into the sky, while from the lurid cloud overhead a strange light was flung upon the darkness of the scene. And from that cloud, hovering in mid-heaven, that cloud so lurid, so black and dismal, from that mass of ominous darkness, flashed the red-words of flame, "Wo unto Sodom."

All around the isle burst and foamed the waves of the swollen river. The torrent was choked with masses of ice, and a rustling, heaving sound went evermore up to the heavens.

Looking to the west, Devil-Bug beheld the black outlines of the city, with the light from that fearful cloud playing upon its roofs and domes, but as he gazed upon the east, all was thick darkness, with the broad waves of the river moaning and foaming in the blackness of the night. Here and there a towering wave rose heaving into view as it caught a faint gleam of light from the cloud above the far-off city, but it suddenly sank again into the bosom of night and all was darkness, thick as chaos.

As Devil-Bug standing on the roof of the palace, gazed round in wonder, the river became the scene of a strange and awful spectacle. The waves were suddenly crowded by a fleet of coffins, tossed wildly to and fro, each coffin borne upon the surface of the waters like a boat, with the foam dashing over its dull dark outlines. And in each coffin sate a corpse, with the death-shroud enfolding its limbs and waving along the blackness of the night, while it urged its grave-boat merrily over the waters, using a thigh-bone for an oar. And at the foot of every coffin, which served for the prow of the unearthly boat, was a lurid light burning in a skull, and flinging its radiance around over the waters, over the faces of the dead and over the fluttering folds of each death-shroud. Ten thousand coffins, each bearing its boatman in the form of a shrouded corpse, floated on the surging waves of the river, ten thousand lurid lights, each flaring from the eyeless sockets of a skull, gave a terrible radiance to the scene, and the river, far as the eye could see, was crowded by this fleet of grave-boats with their shrouded oarsmen, tossing the water aside with the skeleton bone for an oar.

Devil-Bug shouted aloud in the wildness of his glee. Ha, ha! Ho, ho! There was something so merry to his fancy in the spectacle of a broad river crowded by a fleet of coffins, something so joyous in the light flaming from the orbless eyes of ten thousand skulls, something so grotesque and horrible in shrouded corpses, scattered over the surface of the river, that Devil-Bug felt a strange frenzy of glee darting through his veins; he raised his hands and shouted for very joy.

As Devil-Bug looked around in fiendish glee, a new wonder met his gaze. The fleet of coffins parted suddenly into two divisions, and each division arrayed itself as if in the order of battle. On the north, from the island to the city, over the surface of the waters extended one grim line of coffins, with a livid corpse setting upright in each coffin, and raising the skeleton bone aloft in the stiffened hand, while their white shrouds waved like banners upon the night.

On the south, with a broad path of waves between, another grim line of coffins extended from the island to the river, the white shrouds of the corpses borne aloft by the wind, while ten thousand deathly hands swung the thigh-bone wildly overhead. In front of each line of coffins burned the lights, flaring from the orbless eyes of a skull, and now as the lurid rays gave strange radiance to the scene, the faces of each corpse, the leaden eyes, the blue lips and the brow all green and clammy with decay, became fired with deadly rage, and beating the thigh-bone on the side of each coffin, the antagonist lines of the dead began to move slowly towards each other.

Then an unearthly peal of music broke upon the air—the music of the hollow skull echoing to the blow of the skeleton-bone—from side to side it swelled, it rose clanking to the heavens, it deafened the ear of night with its infernal din. Nearer and nearer to each other the opposing lines of coffins drew, faster and faster they glided over the waves, wilder and more terrible swelled the music of the skeleton-bone and the skull!

Now the opposing lines of the dead glared in each others faces. Now they raised their stiffened hands as if eager for the onset, and waved their white shrouds in the air. Now a thin line of water lay between each division of the dead. Hissing and whirling and plunging, the combatants drew near each other, with a low muttered groan, far more terrible than the loudest shout, each party hailed the approach of its opponent, and then with one deafening crash they closed together. Corpse fighting with corpse, dead throttling dead! Coffin meeting with coffin, each urged onward by the heaving waves, each crashing madly into the prow of its antagonist, while the dead arise, and leaning over the side of their death-boats, they reach forth their arms and grasp each other in the clutch of an infernal hate! Then how the fires flaring from the orbless eyes of skulls danced to and fro. Now the river grew alive with the white robes of shrouds fluttering on the air, with the gleam of lights hissing as they sank beneath the waters, with that horrible groan of the corpse as it fought with its fellow corpse!

Then how merrily the music of the skeleton-bone and the hollow skull shrieked over the waters, and mingling with the low-muttered groans of ten thousand thousand corpses, rose echoing to the heavens above! Then crash upon crash with horrible yells of laughter, the shrouded dead again urged their coffins full upon each other, and fought like living men upon a battle-field! With ghastly faces mouldering with corruption, yet fired by all the passions of life, upturned to the sky, with the waves rearing and plunging all around them, with their shrouds tossing madly on the air, while the skull-fires danced to and fro they closed together in terrible combat, and fought amidst the howling of the waters.

Another peal of the skeleton-bone and the skull, another wild burst of laughter. Like a flash of lightning the scene was changed.

The river was calm as the joy of the Saint, first awakening from the sleep of the grave into the peace of God's own sweet rest. Pure, serene, and placid. It lay like a mirror before the eyes. Yet still in the sky overhead, hung the cloud with its letters of flame,—Wo unto Sodom—still from the letters of flame a lurid light fell over the waters, now so calm and tranquil. And the dark mass of walls and roofs which marked the position of the city, with the lofty steeples and proud domes steeped in livid light, was reflected in the calm waters, like a magnificent picture, delineated by some unearthly hand.

And along the calm waters marched a long and winding Column of the dead, gliding over the bosom of the river, their stiffened feet but touching the smooth surface, while their solemn faces were upraised to the sky, and their white shrouds fell in drooping folds around their awful forms. Gliding over the waters, two abreast, a long column of the dead, their ghostly figures mirrored in the depths below, they sang a low-toned and solemn song.

Oh how its notes of awful tenderness and feeling floated on the still air, how that soft melody filled all space and breathed forth upon the universe, like a perfume from eternal flowers. Softly and gently it floated over the river, that wild and bewitching lament for the dead. Now it died sadly away until a whisper of deep and absorbing melody was all that broke upon the silence of night, then loud and louder it rose, it filled the sky, and like a chorus of angel-voices seemed to hold earth and heaven, enchained with its deathless song.

It was a lament for the dead. It was a lament for the dead who were to die on the morrow. It was a lament for young maidens, for grey-haired and helpless men, for smiling and sinless babes. All were to be mingled in the destruction of the morrow, all were to share the doom and the death of the Last Day of the guilty and idolatrous city.

The lament wept its tears of melody for them, the young and beautiful—it wept for grey-haired age—it wept for smiling innocence.

Suddenly its notes changed from sadness to joy. Joy to the captive in his cell, joy to the sick man on his couch, joy to the felon who was to die on the morrow; Joy to the poor, oh joy! Their day was come at last. The rich with their purple and fine linen had enjoyed the world long enough; now the God of the Poor would arise in his might, and crush the lordlings under the heel of his power! What cared the Poor if they too shared the ruin? Was it not triumph to see the rich and corrupt dragged down from their high places—was it not triumph worth all the deaths in hell?

Therefore the band of shrouded dead, winding over the smooth surface of the river, sang joy to the poor, joy to hunger, joy to starvation, misery and wo. Joy to ye all! Your God arises; his arm is uplifted; already the rumbling of his chariot wheels draw near! No more hunger now, no more crying for bread. No more huddling down in squalor, and want, and cold. The avenger comes--Shout ye poor, shout from your factories and work-benches, from your huts and dens of misery—shout! Hail to the Last Day of the guilty and blood-stained City!

As the last echo of the song broke on the air, the forms of the dead, their mouldering faces, and their white shrouds, faded slowly from the view, and the day began to dawn in the east. The last day of the Doomed city! Streaking the east with faint grey and then with soft crimson and then with purple and gold, the day arose upon the river and the city. Devil-Bug looked for the cloud: it was gone; gone with its letters of flame: the night with its Phantoms was over. And now the day came on, the awful day preceded by that Night of Omen and Prophecy. The Last Day of the doomed city—all hail!

The laughing waves of the river caught the red gleam of the rising sun, and the proud domes shone like masses of burnished silver, and the steeples rose glittering in the sky.

Devil-Bug beheld the sun arise in grandeur, he saw the stars fading away before the day-god, slowly and solemnly as they looked their last glance upon the beautiful earth, he gazed upon the blue sky and marked the flashes of purple and gold, warming upward to the very zenith. It was a glorious day, this last day of ten thousand years of blood and crime. The air was freshening and balmy although it was winter, and the broad river rippled in innumerable tiny waves, caught the sunbeam on its transparent surface and smiled in welcome of the rising day.

As Devil-Bug gazed around, the palace on which he stood sank suddenly beneath him. Like a rock hurled from some dizzy height it sank; one moment its towers gleamed in the light, the next instant a small, narrow and barren islet uprising from the waves, like the back of some huge ocean monster, assumed the place of the gorgeous fabric. The palace was gone, and a flood of sun-light poured over the river, where its shadow but a moment before had darkened the waves.

Devil-Bug was suddenly lifted from the isle by invisible hands and borne across the waters towards the mighty city. The waves laughing beneath him, and the clear sunshine around, he was borne slowly onward. As he glided through the air, a strange wonder met his gaze. On the surface of the river floated a solitary coffin, containing a stiffened corpse, whose white shroud and ashen face lay open to the warm gold of the sun-beams, while its fixed and leaden eyes gazed steadfastly upon the sky.

"Ha, ha!" shrieked Devil-Bug. "It's the corpse of Lorrimer—hurrah!" A strange glee animated his breast. As his loud laugh broke upon the air the corpse arose in its coffin and flung the folds of its white shroud to the winds. It tossed its arms on high and echoed the glee of the Dreamer with a ghastly laugh. Then borne onward by the tiny waves, the coffin floated down the river. A low muttered chaunt broke from the lips of the corpse, and then sitting erect with the white shroud fluttering on the winds, it went sailing merrily over the waves.

"Hurrah!" cried Devil-Bug. "It's the corpse of Lorrimer—hurrah!"

As his laugh shrieked along the winter air, the river and the coffin with its corpse rushed from his view. He stood in the streets of the wide city once again, and the awful Drama, which formed the soul of his Dream, wore on to its last scene.

The streets of the doomed city were utterly deserted. Devil-Bug wandered up and down, but gained no sight of a human face. A strange panic seemed to have laid hold of the denizens of the proud town. They kept within the shelter of their homes; the lord within his mansion, the king within his palace, the beggar within his hut. The streets were deserted by the living, and yet up and down the wide avenues glided the white bands of the countless dead. Up and down the wide avenues, evermore and unceasing, their cold white hands crossed on their breasts and their leaden eyes glaring steadily forward, glided the corpses of the night before. And the warm sunlight shone full upon their ghastly faces, upon the livid lips and the discolored cheeks. Their leaden eyes,—O! merciful God, how fixed and ghastly was their glare!—Their leaden eyes were turned to horrible gold. The loathsome worms crawling around each forehead, glistened gaily in the light, and wreathed a hideous coronet of death upon each festering brow!

Devil-Bug passed along amid these shrouded forms, he passed along unheeding their ghastly faces and their frozen looks. He had grown used to these sights of horror. He passed swiftly onward, noting the grandeur and magnificence of the streets, the temples of marble, the mansions of towering splendor, the churches with their lofty steeples and the halls of pleasure with their glittering domes.

And as he passed along he noted with strange awe a new omen of the day. The towering mansions along the wide streets were sinking slowly into the earth, slowly and almost imperceptibly, inch by inch they were sinking into the hard ground. Wherever Devil-Bug passed, this wonder met his gaze. In narrow alleys and in spacious streets, the same fearful spectacle was exhibited—the wide town was sinking slowly into the bosom of the earth.

Suddenly the streets became alive with people. From obscure huts in lonely alleys, and from lordly palaces along far vista-ing streets, from quiet dwellings and from gorgeous mansions poured the contrasted multitude. It was a gala-day in the city. It was the anniversary of the death of Freedom. The King was to be crowned, and the multitude were gathered in grand procession to swell his triumph.

Devil-Bug stood in front of the Ruins of Independence Hall. Along the wide street, as far as eye might behold, was one living sea of banners and plumes, bayonets and spears. Horses with glittering trappings and gallant riders were speeding to and fro; armed bands thronged the streets. There were chariots all glistening with cloth of gold, there were long files of liveried retainers, there were proud lords glittering in purple and jewels, and enthroned on a royal seat, perched on the summit of a splendid structure, a mimic temple borne on wheels and drawn by milk-white steeds, above the gleam of spears and the flutter of banners, sate the King. He looked to the blue heavens and smiled; it was such a glorious day! He was to be crowned again, in honor of the anniversary of his triumph. The sun-shine streamed over his dark and swarthy face; the breeze played with the ringlets of his jet-black hair.

The King glanced over the living sea and smiled again. The heaven above, was the only space that met his eyes, that was not occupied by banners and plumes, stern visages and merry faces. From the roof to the gutters on either side of the wide street, all was glitter and show. Fair forms crowded the lofty windows, and white hands flung showy scarfs upon the air. Aged matrons lifted little children, upon high, and pointing toward the throne, bade them look upon the King! White bosoms rose heaving in the sun at the sight of his stern majesty; bright eyes glanced upon him in pride. Along the roofs of the houses, along the side-walks of the street, clinging to the pillars of the uprising palace, nay, over the ruined walls of Independence Hall, gathered the dense multitude, young and old, rich and poor, gazing with fixed interest upon the triumph of their King. Purple and rags, grey-hairs and cherry lips, smiling foreheads, and wrinkled cheeks, all were mingled in strange contrast!

It was a grand day and a glorious sight—that sky of blue, that cheerful sun, that long vista of palaces and pillared mansions, that dense mass of people, that glittering array of spears, and plumes, and banners, with the proud King sitting enthroned above all.

The procession began to move. First came the music rending the air with its martial joy, the peal of bugle, the roll of drum, and the clang of cymbols! Huzza! How that cheer of the mob shrieked up to the sky! Then came the banner-knight surrounded by throngs of brave warriors, and riding on a milk-white steed. His firm arm swung aloft the Red Banner of the city, with the Crown, and his Chain emblazoned on its folds. Huzza! Another cheer from the mob, at the sight of the Crown and Chain! Then solid files of soldiers were tramping by, their bayonets gleaming in the light, their plumes waving in the air. Then came the temple drawn by milk-white steeds, and the King sitting on the throne, raised his glance to the heavens, while his proud lip curled in scorn. He despised the multitude whose necks were under his feet.

And at this moment, as his eye was fixed upon the heavens, while the proudest jewel in his Crown, shone like a meteor in the light of the sun, at his very shoulder stood a ghastly corpse, its stiffened limbs folded in a white shroud, its dull, dead eyes fixed upon his visage—the visage of the King. He saw it not. There, there upon the summit of the temple, beside his very crown it stood, but he saw it not! Its clammy visage was all alive with hideous grave-worms, and its fearful eye was gazing sadly into his own—into the proud eye of the King—but he saw it not.

Nor did the vast crowd of living men behold the dead multitude as it mingled with them, and crowded away their ranks. Nor did the soldiers tramping in pride, behold the files of dead men, marching amid the glory of their banners, all uniformed in deathly shrouds. Yes, yes, on every side gathered the legions of the shrouded dead, amid the ranks of the Procession, in the lofty windows, along the side-walks, on the roof tops, and on Independence Hall, they gathered, that band of countless dead.

Devil-Bug beheld them, he alone of all that innumerable crowd, beheld the corpses in their shrouds. He beheld them and laughed in glee. It was a sight of glory, a sight of maddening glory to the King as he looked over the soldiers—but the corpse at his side, with its dull dead leaden eyes fixed upon his face—ah, ha! he saw it not. It raises its arm, it places its stiffened hand upon the shoulder of the King. He feels no pressure of the cold, dead fingers, but looks upon the living crowd, and smiles.

Devil-Bug laughed until his sides ached again. An old and withered man standing at his side, looked up at the sound of that wild laugh, and Devil-Bug felt the glance of a cold grey eye fixed upon his face.

"Why do you laugh?" said the old man in a deep and mournful voice. "Know you not Liberty is buried to day? This is her funeral!"

Devil-Bug laughed loudly, yet again, and pointed to the Procession, with its pomp and banners.

"That's why I laugh!" he cried. "Only look at the Crown and Chain, and then look at Independence Hall—ho, ho, ho!"

The old man drew him aside into a dark corner. Under his arm, he carried a huge port-folio.

"I'm an antiquary," he said in that low-toned and mournful voice. "I gather up the relics of the past—"

"A sort o' cur'osity-monger?" suggested Devil-Bug.

"Look here!" whispered the old man. "Be careful that no one sees you, it will cost you your life. Look there!"

He placed a piece of damp cloth in the hands of Devil-Bug.

Devil-Bug gazed upon it with some interest. He unrolled it and threw its colors, alas! how faded and tarnished! he threw its colors open to the glare of the day. It was an old banner, an old banner with thirteen crimson stripes, and twenty nine white stars, emblazoned on a blue field.

"Ho, ho," chuckled Devil-Bug. "Why this is the 'Merykin Flag!' "

"That *was* the American Flag," said the grey-eyed antiquary.

"*Was?*" echoed Devil-Bug.

"*Was* the American Flag, I say! There is no America now. In yonder ruined Hall, America was born, she grew to vigorous youth, and bade fair to live to a good old age, but—alas! alas! She was massacred by her pretended friends. Priest-craft, and Slave-craft, and Traitor-craft were her murderers. And now, a poor old Antiquary has to skulk like an assassin through the street, because he has discovered a relic of the olden time, and bears it with him—this proscribed and forbidden Flag!"

The old man bowed his head.

"Ho, ho! Yonder's the purty banner, with the crown and the Chain! Hurrah!"

As Devil-Bug laughed in his frenzied glee, the old man concealed the Flag, in the port-folio under his arm, and walked silently away.

The procession came sweeping by in all its royal pomp. After the temple with its throne and King, came the sacred Clergy, in all the pride of priestly robes and godly faces. Walking four by four,—they talked eagerly together, and disputed with great force and energy upon subjects of grave import. Various banners marked their various creeds. One fat-faced parson swung aloft a banner of white with a grim gibbet pictured on its folds. Hurrah! The mob yelled in grateful applause at the sight—the gibbet and the good old gallow's law, they shouted, the gibbet and gallow's law forever!

Then came another preacher with lanthern-jaws, and an eye like a vulture's. He swung aloft a banner of sable, dark as midnight, with "Eternal Death" emblazoned in its dark surface in lively letters. Hurrah—hurrah! That mob was a pure old fashioned orthodox mob! Eternal death forever they shrieked. Eternal death in the next world, for every soul that disbelieves in our creed—and in this world, the fire and faggot for all heretics! Hurrah!

And among the dark bands of the Sacred Clergy, walked the shrouded dead, looking into the godly faces of the reverend men, with that fixed stare of their leaden eyes. There was a corpse at the side of each Doctor of Divinity, a ghastly dead man at the shoulder of each oily Priest. And they trooped on with their black robes and their banners, and then the Ministers of justice drew nigh. A glorious band. A figure of justice done in gilt upon a black ground, floated like a bird of omen above their heads. By their sides walked dark-faced miscreants, with whips and manacles in their hands; and a long line of penniless Debtors, with staved forms and wan faces brought up the rear. Hurrah—hurrah! That was a lusty cheer! A law-loving mob was this—old laws and Judges, who have an eye for their friends, they shouted, Justice with a bandage over her eyes, so thick that gold alone can make her see clear—hurrah, hurrah!

Then came the slaves of the city, white and black, marching along one mass of rags and sores and misery, huddled together; a goodly tail to the procession of the King. Chains upon each wrist and want upon each brow. Here they were, the slaves of the cotton Lord and the factory Prince; above their heads a loom of iron, rising like a gibbet in the air, and by their sides the grim overseer. Hurrah, hurrah! This is a liberal mob; it encourages manufactures. The monopolist forever, they yelled, his enterprise gives labour to the poor, hurrah, hurrah! The slaves lifted up their eyes at the sound of that tumultuous hurrah, and muttered to each other, of glad green fields, and a farmer's life, and then they clanked their chains together, and gazed at the ruins of Independence Hall.

So they went trooping by the slaves of the cotton Lord, and the factory Prince. And at their sides, and among their ranks, walked the unseen forms of the shrouded dead. For them, the manacled and the lashed, for them the Slaves of Capital and Trade, the grim faces of the dead wore a smile. Look up brothers, they muttered in their awful tones, the day of your redemption draweth near! This is the last day of your toil. The slaves heard them not, but gazing madly upon the ruins of Independence Hall, went sadly on.

Suddenly a dim faint murmur burst from the ranks of the procession. A murmur as faint and dim arose from the side-walk, from the windows, and the house-tops. Devil-Bug looked around in wonder. Every face grew suddenly white. A strange and awful fear had descended upon the hosts of the King, and the crowds of spectators. Rushing to the head of the procession, Devil-Bug looked upon the face of the King. It was ashy.

He turned to his soldiers, he turned to his subjects, he shrieked aloud in horror. And at that very moment ten thousand, thousand eyes beheld the object of the Monarch's terror. At his side stood a ghastly corpse, with worms crawling round its brow, and dull leaden eyes, animate with a horrid light, like a gleam from hell.

One shriek went up to God from that vast crowd—one shriek of horror. Every eye beheld the corpse at the side of the King, and now—oh God of judgment! Every man in all that countless crowd, beheld the form of a grim Dead Man at his side! How the shriek of horror, rushed up at the clear sky, like thunder from hell! Yes, yes, every man beheld the form of a corpse at his side, every woman saw the leaden eyes gazing upon her beauty, the very babes beheld the awful spectacle and hid their heads in their mother's bosoms, and mingled their shrill cry of horror, with the shriek of the millions.

The film had fallen from their eyes! They *knew* that the Dead walked among them. They knew that the Last Day was upon them in blackness and fear. The Priests cast aside their banners and grovelled in the dust. They shrieked for mercy to that God, whose name had been blasphemed by their every act and word. With a clanking sound ten thousand muskets and swords, and spears rolled upon the ground. The warriors too were on their knees, but they looked upon the sky not in imbicile fear, but with a stern and awful agony. Then the shrieks of the women, the wild yells of the crowd, the horrible anguish of old men, tearing their grey hair in very agony! There, there, with them, and among them, and around them, glided the forms of the Dead, with their ghastly eyes and their long white shrouds.

Above the sky was clear, the sun was radiant. Azure and serene, the heavens were undimmed by a cloud. The King looked up and folded his arms, while the cold sweat trickled down his brow, he set his stern lips together, and muttered a curse upon his God. At the very instant, from the clear sky leapt a bolt of red thunder;—the King lay on the earth a blackened corpse. Then the long line of houses began to sink into the earth, slowly, slowly, inch by inch, like ships at sea, with the waves creeping over their decks. Then from the earth burst streams of vapor, hissing and whirling as they spouted upward into the blue sky. Around each pillar of vapor, in an instant there lay a circle of blackened corpses. That steam smote the living to the heart, it withered their eye-balls; it crisped the flesh on their bones, like the bark peeling from the log before the flame.

Then from the sky so clear, so serene, leapt ten thousand bolts of red thunder, each bolt striking the earth with a fierce hissing sound, and laying the living along its path, a heap of blackened and a festering dead. Then the earth began to heave, like the ocean in a storm, and waves of solid ground rose up to the clear heavens, bearing palaces and domes, and steeples on their crests!

A storm on the land, waves of solid earth, billows crested with domes and steeples, with myriads of human beings, hanging like foam on the top of each wave and billow—huzza!

Columns of hot vapor rising from the heaving earth, ten thousand, thousand columns, winding upward to the clear blue sky, with a circle of blackened dead, thrown in one huddled mass around each hissing column—huzza, huzza! Then the shrieks, and the groans, and the low muttered thunder, echoing from the bosom of each earthly wave!

Then the fair women tossed in the air, clasping their babes in their arms, as they were dashed in fragments on the earth, the old men and the bright-eyed youth, all mingled together in the Massacre of judgment!

Devil-Bug beheld it all, and was not harmed. An invisible hand bore him on through the heaps of bleeding dead, over the waves of tossing earth, on and on, unscathed and without harm. He heard the crash of one wave, crested with temples meeting another, with the mass of human beings tossed from its summit like foam-sparkles from a brooklet's ripple, he heard the cries of despair, and over all, he beheld the smiling sky.

He felt himself borne suddenly aloft, on the crest of one long and tremendous pillow of solid earth! High above the ruin, high above the universe of that city's woe, it rose, it shot upward into the sky! It remained fixed in the air, an awful column of trembling earth, with its crumbling peak tenanted by three living beings, besides Devil-Bug.

A father, and his child, and the lover of that child. The father standing on the summit of this dizzy column, tore his grey hairs in very despair, as he beheld the city rocking to and fro at its base. The daughter clung to his knees, her long golden hair waving in the sunbeams, and her large blue eyes upturned to his face. The lover with a dark eye, gazing on the sky, and jet-black hair damp with the beaded sweat, trickling from his brow—he cowered to the earth of that fearful isle, he howled in imbecile agony! Devil-Bug looked upon the scene with a strange pleasure. There they were, perched on the summit of that dizzy column, that column of solid earth, thrown upward into the air, by the wave which had tossed them aloft, there they were, alone in that world of death.

Below them, and around them rocked the city, its temples tossed like autumn leaves by the wind, its uncounted myriads of human beings mingled in one awful massacre!

Then the earth began to crumble from the edges of the column, and far, far below, whirling first to one side and the other, the hard lumps of solid clay were tossed like wounded birds upon the breeze. The father moaned and gathered the blue-eyed girl closer to his knees, but the lover—Devil-Bug, laughed in glee as he beheld the dastard act!—the lover rose with a mad shriek, and seized the maiden in his arms.

"Down!" he cried tossing her aloft. "There is room but for one upon this isle—down!"

The old man caught him by the throat, he tore the girl from his arms, and then battling over her prostrate form, for a foothold on that dizzy column's surface, they grappled together, and fought like devils! The old man's eyes started from his withered face, and the lover seized his cheek between his teeth, and howled like a hyena rushing on a corpse! Devil-Bug beheld the scene, and yet, by some strange influence, maintained his foothold on the rock. The old man gathered the lover in his arms, he tossed him wildly aloft, he sprung from the æry isle! How their folding bodies went down through the clear air, with a sound like the whizzing of birds upon the airy! The fair girl raised herself from her prostrate position, she gazed over the edge of the crumbling column! Oh God, what an awful space lay between that column's summit and the rocking earth! She raised herself upon her feet, she tossed her golden hair upon the wind, she looked to the blue sky with outspread arms, she leaped toward the radiant sun with a wild shriek! "I come!" she cried. Then down to the heaving wreck of the city, like a dove wounded by the hunter's shaft, plunging through the still air she fell! Devil-Bug was alone upon the surface of the awful column, alone with that utterable sight, seen far below.

He raised his hands aloft, he flung them in the air with a shriek of infernal glee!

And then right over his head, dusky and black gathered the cloud of the night before, like the raven corpse of the dead. And in its awful surface was written the words of flame and a ghastly voice whispered their meaning to the air.

WO UNTO SODOM

Again like a spirit reigning over the evil which he had wrought, Devil-Bug raised his hands and laughed in glee.

"Look below," cried the ghastly voice, speaking from the still air, "look far below, and behold the wreck of the doomed city. Temples and domes, heaps of dead and piles of solid earth mingled in one awful ruin! The river burdened with blackened corpses, and the bright sky watching smilingly over all! Look and behold the Massacre of Judgments! The Sacrifice of Justice! The wrongs of ages are avenged at last! At last the voice of Blood crying from the very stones of the idolatrous city, has pierced the ear of God. Look beneath, and look upon the wreck of the Doomed City! Look below and with the angels of eternal justice, shout the amen to the litany of the city's crimes, shout Wo,

WO UNTO SODOM."

BOOK THE FOURTH

THE SECOND DAY

Ravoni the Sorcerer

CHAPTER FIRST

GOD IS JUST

The night drew near its close. From the dark azure of the sky, the cold winter stars shone down over the streets of the silent city.

At that moment, when the night had yet an hour to run, when the morning dawn was yet an hour distant, in two chambers of the slumbering town, removed from each other by the space of a mile, were progressing scenes fraught with a deep and solemn interest.

In one chamber was mystery and gloom; in the other was poverty and death. In one chamber was priestly guilt bargaining with sorcery for the downfall of purity and virtue; in the other, a ruined woman lay, while starvation and suicide stood watching by her couch.

First, we draw the veil from the chamber of the sorcerer.

It was an hour before the dawn of morning, on the night of Friday the twenty-third of December, when two figures came walking slowly and carelessly along one of the prominent streets, near the heart of the city.

A solitary lamp illumined the pavement, near the centre of a massive block of towering mansions. For a few feet around the lamp, was thrown a vivid and ruddy light, while all beyond and above, was shadow, starlight and the heavy obscurity which falls upon the night, before the dawn of day. The figures paused for a moment in the light of the lamp.

"Parson do you believe in a God?" said a voice rendered indistinct and husky with wine.

"Why to tell you the truth Fitz, I've preached about that particular belief frequently, quite frequently. So often, in fact, that I've forgotten what is my especial faith on that point."

And with a bland smile the godly Dr. Pyne gazed upon the swarthy countenance of Fitz-Cowles.

"Quite drunk," he muttered to himself with a pleasant chuckle. "Has quite a snake in his hat. A perfect viper of a snake!"

Because if you do believe in a God," returned Fitz-Cowles, endeavoring to maintain possession of a particular brick near the lamp-post. "I'd just thank you to name him! For, Parson—hear me now, you fat old dog! I swear by that God, to have the girl before another day goes over my head!"

Fitz-Cowles struck his gold-headed cane against the lamp-post, while the Parson seemed to enjoy the scene, with a vast fund of good humor.

"That was very good wine we drank in the cellar? Eh, Fitz?"

"The devil take you and the wine. I was talking of the girl."

"Oh, you was, was you? And you'd like to *have* her?"

"Don't grin that way again, Parson, or I'll knock you down. I will *have* her, eh? *have* her, before another sun goes over, over, my———"

"Hat!" suggested the Parson, with a wide grin.

"Head, curse your, head!" roared Fitz-Cowles. "Hello! what old building is this?"

Fitz-Cowles started backward toward the curb as he spoke, and placing his conical hat on the end of his cane, took a quiet though half-drunken survey of the building.

It was an old-fashioned structure, four stories in height, with a massive hall door in the center, and a multitude of windows on either side. The surface was a bright yellow. This fact, by itself, was sufficient to excite the attention of a wayfarer, for in the Quaker City, the eye is wearied by one unvarying sameness of dull red brick. The man who paints a house blue, or yellow or pink or white, or any other hue in fact, than this monotonous red, is incontinently set down by his neighbors, as slightly weak-minded or positively crazy.

In addition to this striking peculiarity, the house was marked by several other characteristics, well adapted to excite the wonder of a citizen or a stranger. The windows were numerous, but each window was small and cramped in size, with its dingy white shutters, hermetically sealed. The roof was flat, the cornices around the eves massive, and the hall door approached by a flight of time-worn marble steps. The mansion was separated from the adjoining houses by a narrow alley on either side, whose darkness the light of the lamp could not penetrate.

"That's what I call a venerable structure," exclaimed Fitz-Cowles, maintaining his position on the curb-stone, with a gentle see-saw motion. "It looks as though it were one of the town residences of that respectable old gentleman, the Wandering Jew. Dammit, Parson, what's it used for?"

Parson Pyne smiled pleasantly as he replied in an unctuous whisper. —"The uses of that house are three-fold, Fitz-Cowles. In the first place"—"Curse your first places!" You ain't in the pulpit now, old boy."

"It is a Mad-House," whispered Dr. Pyne.

"Ha!" ejaculated Fitz-Cowles with a vacant stare.

"It is a Dissecting Hall," continued the fat Parson.

"A what?" cried the drunken Millionaire.

"And it is a Sorcerer's Den!" exclaimed Pyne with deep emphasis.

"Hello!" ejaculated Fitz-Cowles. "You don't say that? And who is the Mad Doctor, the Dissector, and the Sorcerer? Is their names Smith, or Jones, or Miller?"

"Did you ever notice on Chestnut street, on a sun-shiny afternoon, a slight thin individual, rather well built, but with a stoop in his gait? He dresses in a dark cloth over-coat, rather profusely adorned with furs, and wears his hair long and lank about his shoulders? His face is yellow as a guinea, but he has an eye like a devil incarnate—do you know the man?"

Fitz-Cowles raised his gold-headed cane slowly to his lips. At that moment he presented a finished picture of drunken wisdom.

"He is called a Signior, is he not? A Signor or a Don or a Prince?" "The same. Well, this sallow-faced gentleman in the furred dress and the dark eyes, is the Mad-Doctor, the Dissector and the Sorcerer."

"It seems to me that I should like to have a little conversation with the old boy," exclaimed Fitz-Cowles, aiming a blow at a particular brick with the end of his cane. "Is he visible at this hour?"

Dr. Pyne raised his hand suddenly to his forehead. "I have it!" he muttered between his teeth. "I must get rid of this fellow without delay. Look ye, Fitz-Cowles," he exclaimed aloud. "We must part for the night. By to-morrow at noon, I will place this girl in your power. There is my hand on it! Good-night!"

And he strode hurriedly down the street.

"That's what I call *cool!*" muttered Fitz-Cowles with a drunken leer, as he strode away from the lamp in an opposite direction. "Ha—ha!" he chuckled to himself. "Has a sallow face and a devil's eye—ha, hee! Be in my power—to-morrow at noon, hurrah!"

In a moment the Millionaire was lost to view in the darkness, and the fat form of Dr. Pyne emerged from a neighboring alley, and ascended the marble steps of the old mansion.

He rang the bell in silence. There was a long and weary pause, and the sound of a key turning the lock was heard. One of the panels of the massive door receded, and a dingy black hand was thrust through the crevice. Dr. Pyne took a small piece of green paste-board from his pocket, and after glancing for an instant at the strange characters scrawled upon its surface, he placed it within the grasp of the sable hand, which immediately disappeared. There was a pause for a moment, and then the door was opened, and a negro dressed in green livery, beckoned the Parson to enter. In an instant Dr. Pyne stood at the end of a long and narrow hall, illumined by a single lamp, suspended near its centre, with its farther extreme occupied by the steps of a massive stair-way.

The negro in livery locked the door, and then folding his arms across his breast, stood before the Parson, motionless as a statue.

"Is your master in?" said Dr. Pyne.

The negro made no reply.

"D———n the nigger," muttered the Parson. "He must be addressed by his proper name, or else he will not answer. Avar*—I would see the Signior Ravoni?"

The negro Mute waved his hand toward the stair-way, and slowly led the way along the Hall. As they passed under the lamp, Dr. Pyne started with involuntary disgust. The full ugliness of the negro's face broke upon him at a glance. The Mute did not observe the start, but silently led the way up the thickly carpeted stairs, and along a dark and gloomy entry. The negro opened the door, which turned on its hinges without the slightest approach to a sound, and the Rev. Dr. Pyne entered the Den of the Signior Ravoni.

As he stepped over the threshold the door was closed, and he was alone with the Sorcerer. He looked around, and an involuntary feeling of awe gathered round his heart.

It was a spacious chamber, lined along its firm walls with thick folds of dark velvet. At one end the dreary uniformity of the velvet was broken by a massive mirror, which enclosed in a glittering frame, reached half way from the ceiling to the floor. The ceiling was painted black, and the floor concealed by a sable carpet, gave no echo to the footstep.

In front of the mirror, seated beside a table, covered with black cloth, with the light of a small lamp falling over his sallow face and dark

* Pronounced Aa-*var*, with the accent on the final syllable.

robes, the Signior Ravoni sate silent and motionless, his pale white hand tracing lines on a sheet of paper, while his head was downcast, and his long dark hair hung carelessly about his neck and shoulders.

He raised his head slowly from the manuscript, and his large dark eyes were fixed upon the face of the clergyman.

"Who is it that seeks audience with the Signior Ravoni?" he said in a deep sepulchral voice.

There was something so calm, so dignified yet spectral and unearthly in the manner and tone of this singular man, that Dr. Pyne was awed into silence for a few moments. At last shaking off the feeling of superstitious fear which began to creep over him, he advanced and laid the green card upon the table.

"This was given to me by Doctor ———" he said, naming a celebrated Surgeon of the Quaker City. "He is one of your friends and pupils. He informed me that you were skilled in the treatment of the Insane."

"You seek the advice of the Signior Ravoni?" interrupted the voice of the Signior.

"I have a daughter—" began Dr. Pyne. Ravoni motioned him to a seat, and then resting his sullen cheek upon his pale hand, he fixed the glance of his large dark eyes upon the face of the priest, and listened in silence to his story.

Their interview continued for the space of half an hour, when the Parson took the pen from the table, and wrote a few lines on a slip of paper.

"This will settle the matter," he cried with one of his Satyr-like smiles.

"Arrange this business and the money is *yours!*"

A gleam of contempt flashed from the dark eyes of Ravoni.

"It shall be done," he said as he rose from his seat.

The door was flung suddenly open and a loud laugh burst upon the air.

"Ha, ha, Doctor! I've come to steal that corpse for you," shouted a rough voice, "I've come to steal the dead body—hurray!"

Well was it for Dr. Pyne that he sank behind the table, as the sound of that voice broke on his ear!

For in the centre of the chamber, stood Devil-Bug the door-keeper of Monk-Hall, every line of his distorted countenance, quivering with a wild expression akin to madness, while his solitary eye dilated and flashed like phosphorus gleaming through the orbless socket of a skull.

"I've had *sich* dreams," he shouted, dashing the thick hair aside from his protuberant brow. "Sich dreams o' death an' hell, that I could murder a man jest now, for the wery fun o' th' thing!"

"Did yo' say I was to steal a dead body to-night, Doctor? By * * * I could steal a grave-yard of 'em!"

The expressive lip of Ravoni curled in scorn.

"Is the day drunk or crazy," he muttered, with that slight foreign accent which marked his speech. "Slave!" he cried advancing with his arm outstretched, "How dare you cross that threshold unbidden?"

His sallow face grew animate with contemptuous indignation. Every muscle of his countenance quivered; his lip trembled with scorn; his eyebrows were joined in a withering form.

A strange magnetic gleam darted from his eyes. He waved his white hand in the air with a gesture of command.

Devil-Bug endeavored to brave that look, but in vain! There was a fearful magnetic power in the glance of those large dark eyes. He felt himself drawn toward them. He felt the control of his limbs, the mastery of his immense strength passing from him like a dream.

"To your knees," whispered the deep tones of Ravoni. "To your knees, dog! Am I not your—*master*?"

The glance of those eyes was upon the monster. Impelled by an unknown influence, which darted from their unutterable lustre, Devil-Bug walked tremblingly along the floor, and crouched at the feet of Ravoni like a spaniel at the call of his master. And there clinging by each hand to the feet of Ravoni, he still fixed his gaze upon the lustre of the full dark eyes which held him prisoner. And this, when one single blow of his iron hand, might have crushed the man who stood before him into a shapeless mass of clay. It was a sublime spectacle. The triumph of an Intellect, over the Brute and the Savage!

As Devil-Bug crouched spaniel-like at the feet of the Signior Ravoni, Dr. Pyne stole from his hiding place, and slunk away from the room.

"Brave me thus but once again," whispered Ravoni, gazing steadily upon the monster at his feet, "and I will take from you the power to think or act without my consent. My will shall be yours. Your brute strength shall be mine. Yes, yes," he added in a muttered whisper, "by one fixed exertion of my brain, I can make my Will, the Soul of this mass of savage strength."

"Master," whined Devil-Bug, still crouching on the floor, "Do with me what you like! Ask me to steal dead bodies or set fire to a house, or murder a man in broad day—an' I'll do it."

Ravoni smiled and motioned Devil-Bug to rise.

Our way now leads to the chamber of want and suicide.

We return to the nameless man whom we left, sleeping on the way side stones in front of the widow Smolby's house.

It was an hour previous to the scene which we will shortly depict.

Two watchmen enveloped in thick white overcoats were taking their quiet way along the deserted street. Their conversation was fraught with that deep and absorbing interest peculiar to the conversations of sleepy watchmen.

"I say Smeldyke, wots yer opin'on o' th' Tariff?" said the watchman in a fur cap. "Don't yo' think its the cause of half the robberies a-goin'?"

"I don't know about that Worlyput," responded the other guardian of the night, whose distinguishing characteristic was an extremely picturesque relic of a hat. "It seems to me there hai'nt been nothin' like comfort since the Nasshunal Bank was destroyed. Everything's gone wrong since then. Why you may believe it not, but the wery day the news came in that the Deposits was removed, my wife makes me a present of a pair o' boys. Now that never happened to us afore, and bein' a poor man with six growin' children it was'nt a bit funny."

"What had the Nasshunal Bank to do with that?" responded the Fur Cap. "I tell you Smeldyke it's the Tariff wot makes all the mischief. Was not the Tariff the cause o' th' Florida war, where them Seminole injuns set fire to the Bahamey Banks?"

"Pooh! Don't talk to me! I tell you its the removal o' the 'Nited States Bank!"

"Don't Pooh me," responded Smeldyke. "I was n't made to be 'poohed' by a man like you. There now. An' wot have you got to say to that?"

Doubling his fists, Smeldyke advanced toward his comrade Guardian with a manner full of menace. Worlyput squared his elbows, and returned his brother guardian's look of fierce defiance. There was every prospect of a fierce encounter between those respectable functionaries, when their attention was attracted by a deep groan, proceeding from the centre of the street.

In silence they advanced to the side of the prostrate man, as he lay with his limbs flung carelessly over the rough stones of the street. His face was pressed against the earth, and his long dark hair was soiled with the dust and mire of the gutter.

"Come feller, wake up! You're a purty one to be layin' here in this state," exclaimed Smeldyke, raising the strange man on his feet.

"Yes, you're a purty feller, you are!" chimed in Worlyput. "In these days o' Washin'tonian rewivals, when they makes Congressmen out o' drunkards, and the worse drunkards they've been, the better Congressmen they makes! You're a beauty I vow!"

With these amiable words on his lips, the intelligent Smeldyke dealt the unconscious man a vigorous punch in the sides, and Worlyput paid a similar compliment to his breast and shoulders.

"What 'ave you got to say for yourself? eh?"

"Mary, I will save you, save you yet!" exclaimed the stranger, opening his eyes, and gazing wildly around. The last beams of the setting moon fell upon the discolored face of Byrnewood Arlington!

"Mary there is death in my path, but I will save you!" he shouted, springing from the grasp of the watchmen. "I will save you yet!" And with a speed that defied pursuit, he darted down the street, dashing his arms wildly overhead, and shouting madly as he was lost to view in the shadows of the street.

"Mary!" the name was borne upon the winter wind.

"Well, if that ai'nt cool!" ejaculated Smeldyke.

"I suspect Mary's his wife—the young scamp! Been ill-treatin' her, has he? I say Smel, my boy, wots your idea of the 'Nited States Bank?"

Shouting the name of his sister to the still night, his senses whirling in mad confusion, and an awful consciousness of calamity pressing upon his heart like a dead man's hand upon the breast of the living, the Brother fled along the deserted street, his flashing eyes upturned to the starlight sky, while his long black hair streamed wildly on the winter wind.

He knew not why he fled, but there was madness in his veins and fire in his heart. Invisible hands seemed leading him onward. Had some fathomless chasm yawned at his feet, he would have plunged into its darkness with a frenzied joy. The very stars of night had a voice for him. A low-toned and whispering chaunt filled the vault of heaven, and its burden was full of omen and woe.

Thus madly, with his hands grasping at phantoms, he fled along the silent streets; while time and space were lost and forgotten in his delirium.

It was after the space of half an hour, when standing motionless as stone, at the corner of a wide street, his hands solemnly upraised to the sky, and a wild oath trembling on his lips, it was at this moment when his dark eyes blazed with frenzy, that the spell passed from him, and he stood like a man aroused from a dream. He looked around in vague wonder. The effect of the Potion was gone! And with it had passed all memory of the fearful incidents of the last forty-eight hours.

He stood there, beneath the gleam of the starlit sky, and his reason was with him, but when he tried to remember an incident or even a thought of the moment previous, all was shadow and dream.

This was indeed the peculiar curse of the Potion administered by

Devil-Bug. It destroyed the memory. There are men who can never call to mind the incidents of a sight of intoxication. With these men wine is oblivion. So with the drugged potion; it might stupify a man; it might arouse him into frenzy; he might murder his best friend while under its influence, but that influence once over, he was as unconscious of the past as the dead are of the living.

"I have had a horrible dream!" muttered Byrnewood, folding his arms and stalking slowly along the pavement. "Ah! I see how it is. I have been indulging in wine! Fool that I am! To steep my soul in madness! Yes—yes—I remember, I was with Lorrimer. We drank freely. I became crazy from the effects of the wine, left my company, and here I am, wandering about the streets, like an escaped lunatic. I vow I've lost my hat—" he raised his hand to his head, "And my hair is matted and tangled. Pshaw! What a miserable fool I have been making of myself!"

He ground his teeth together with mortification and remorse.

"It was indeed a horrible dream! Mary dishonored—yes, yes, and let me remember? Who did I dream was her seducer? Was it Lorrimer? It has all escaped my memory, but it was a fearful dream. Thank God it was a dream!"

He clasped his hands in silent joy.

"Thank God, it was a dream!"

A wild sound, like the cry of a strong man in mortal agony, broke on the still night air. Byrnewood listened and looked around. He stood in front of a row of massive buildings, dwellings and warehouses, with a small frame house, arising near the centre of the square, like an image of starvation in the midst of plenty.

Again that low moaning sound startled the still air.

The door of the frame house was flung suddenly open, and the figure of a woman rushed out upon the side-walk.

"Help! Help!" she cried in the shrill tones of age. "There is murder in this house! Help! Help!"

She perceived Byrnewood, and rushed forward, and clung wildly to his arm.

"For God's sake stranger," she cried as her white hair escaping from beneath her torn cap, streamed down to her shoulders. "For God's sake stranger, this way!"

And ere he could reply she hurried into the house, clinging nervously to his arm while she urged him onward. They passed through a dark room, and in an instant stood at the foot of a narrow stairway, at the head of which, a light was streaming from an open door.

"Quick, quick, or we'll be too late," screamed the old woman, as she led the way up-stairs, her tongue and her feet clattering to one brisk tune. "You see, I'm a poor widow, and about six months ago, I let out the upper part of my house to poor Davis. He was a carpenter, and no doubt meant to do well, but troubles came thick upon him, he could not get any work, and about a month ago his wife died. Come in, Sir, or we'll be too late! Oh, my God, sich a thing in my house! And then Sir, some rascal—I wish I had the villain here—ruined his poor daughter, and so to-night, poor Davis went out and—oh my God, my God!"

They stood at the stair-way, and the light from the room flashed full in their faces. Byrnewood glanced within the room, and felt his blood grow cold.

In that chamber Starvation and Suicide watched by the death-bed of Innocence.

Ere Byrnewood enters the place of death, we must travel back some hours in our story.

Our Episode will furnish to the world a pleasing illustration of that Justice, which in the Quaker City, unbars the jail to Great Swindlers, while it sends the honest Poor Man into the grave of the Suicide.

The State House clock had just struck eight, when amid the gay crowds who thronged Chestnut street, might be discerned one poor wan-faced man, who strode sadly up and down the pavement in front of a jeweller's window. The night was bitter cold, but a tattered round-about and patched trowsers, constituted his scanty apparel. He had not been shaven for several days, and a thick beard, gave a wild appearance to his lank jaws and compressed lips. His face was pale as a mort-cloth, but his eye shone with that clear wild light that once seen, can never be forgotten. There was Famine in the unnatural gleam of that eye. His much-worn hat was thrown back from his pale forehead, and there, in the lines of that frowning brow you might read the full volume of wrong, and want, which the oppressors of this world write on the faces of the poor.

Up and down the cold pavement he strode. He looked from side to side for a glance of pity. There was no humanity in the eyes that met his gaze. Fashionable Dames going to the Opera, Merchants in broad-cloth returning from the counting-house, Bank Directors hurrying to their homes, godly preachers wending to their Churches, their faces full of sobriety and their hearts burning with enmity to the Pope of Rome: These all were there, on that crowded pavement. But pity for the Poor man, who with Famine written on his forehead and blazing from his eyes, strode up and down, in front of the Jeweller's gaudy window? Not one solitary throb!

"No bread, no fire," muttered the Mechanic as he looked to the sky with a dark scowl on his brow. "No bread, no fire for two whole days. I can bear it, but—God! My child, my child!"

With the tattered cuff of his coat sleeve he wiped away a salt tear from his cheek.

"God!" he fiercely muttered between his set teeth. Is there a God? Is he just? Then why have these people fine clothes and warm homes, when *I*, *I*, with honest hands, have no bread to eat, no fire to warm me?"

Your pardon, pious people, your pardon for the blasphemy of this starving wretch! Starvation you know is a grim sceptic, a very Infidel, a doubter and a scoffer!

"Two days without bread or fire!" he muttered and strode wearily along the street. Suddenly a half-muttered cry of delight escaped from his lips. A splendid carriage, drawn by two blood horses, with a coat of arms gleaming on its panels, met his gaze. It was the work of an instant for the Mechanic to spring up behind this carriage, while a smiling-faced elderly gentleman, sate alone by himself within. And away the horses dashed, until they reached a large mansion in one of the most aristocratic squares of the city. The smiling-faced elderly gentleman came out of the carriage, and after telling James the coachman, to be very careful of the horses, he took his night-key from his pocket, and entered the mansion.

"*He* failed three days ago," said the Mechanic, glancing at the mansion with a grim smile, as he leapt down from the coach. "The Bank of which he is President broke a fortnight since! Ha, ha!"

And with a hollow laugh he pointed to the retreating coach and then to the mansion, from whose curtained windows the blaze of lights flashed out upon the street.

"*He* is the President of the Bank that broke, and yet has his coach and horses, his house, his servants and his wines. I had six hundred dollars in that Bank, and yet have not a crust of bread to eat. I 'spose this must be what they call *justice!*"

And with that same mocking laugh he strode up the marble steps of the Bank Presidents Palace.

"I will make another effort," he whispered. "And if that fails—Ha! God will take care of my child. As for myself—ha! ha! I 'spose the over-seers of the Poor will bury me!"

The door of the Bank President's Palace was ajar. The Mechanic pushed it open and entered. A ruddy glow of light streamed through the parlor door-way into the hall. Walking boldly forward, the Mechanic paused at the door and looked in. Oh, such fine furniture, a splendid glass above the mantel, ottomans, a sofa, a gorgeous carpet, and silk curtains drooping along from the windows—magnificent furniture!

"And *he* is the President of the Broken Bank."

Mr. Job Joneson, the President of the Bank which had just failed for only one million dollars, sate writing at a table in the centre of that gorgeous parlor. He was a pleasant man, with a round face and small eyes, a short neck and a white cravat, corpulent paunch and a showy broad-cloth coat. Altogether Job Joneson, Esq. was one of your good citizens, who subscribe large sums to tract societies, and sport velvet-cushioned pews in church. He did not perceive the entrance of the Mechanic, but having taken his seat in a hurry, was making some memoranda in his note book by the light of the astral lamp.

"Twenty dollars to the Society for promoting Bible Christianity at Rome," thus he soliloquized. "Good idea, that. Be in all the Patent-Gospel papers. Two hundred dollars for jewellery; Mrs. Joneson *is* very extravagant. Fifty dollars for furniture broken by my son Robert who is now at College. Bad boy that! One thousand dollars for a piano, *grand* piano for my daughter Corinne—Ha! Hum! Who's there? What do you want?"

The Mechanic advanced, and taking off his hat, approached the table. It was a fine contrast; the unshaven Mechanic, and the Bank President; on this side of the table rags and want, on that side, broad-cloth and plenty; here a face with Famine written on its every line; there a visage redolent of venison steaks and turtle soup.

"Your business Sir?"

"Do you not know me, Mr. Joneson? I am John Davis."

"Indeed! You shingled a house for me last summer. Why you are sadly changed!"

The lip of the Mechanic trembled.

"I was a little better-looking last summer, I believe," he said, "But Mr. Joneson, I have called upon you in order to ascertain, whether there is any hope of my ever getting any portion of my money from the * * * * * Bank?"

"Not one cent!" said the Bank President, taking out his watch and playing with the seals.

"I worked very hard for that money, Mr. Joneson. I've frozen in the winter's chill, and broiled in the summer's heat for that money, Mr. Joneson."

"My dear fellow, you talk to me as if I could help it," said Mr. Joneson, gazing intently upon the motto engraven on his seal, '*Up with the Bible.*'

"And now Mr. Joneson, I am without work; my money is gone," continued John Davis, speaking in a low tone that God's angels could not listen to without tears. "My child lays at the point of death.—"

"How can I help *that*, my good fellow? I am sorry that your child is sick—but can I help it?" said the Bank President in the tone of withering politeness.

"I have neither bread nor medicine to give her," said Davis as his grey eye blazed with a strange light. "There has been no fire in her room for two days—"

"Get work," said the Bank President, in a short decided tone.

"*Where?*" And Davis extended his lean hands, while a quiet look of despair stamped every line of his countenance.

"Anywhere! Everywhere! You don't mean to say that an able-bodied man like you can't get work in this enlightened city of Philadelphia? Pshaw!"

"I have tried to get work for two long weeks, and am now without a crust of bread!" And John gazed steadily in Joneson's face.

"Well then, where's your credit? You don't mean to say that an industrious mechanic like you are, or ought to be, can't obtain credit in this enterprizing city of Philadelphia?"

"There is no imprisonment for debt," said John with a sickly smile. "No poor man gets 'trust' now-a-days."

"Well my poor fellow I am sorry for you, sorry that our Bank failed to meet its liabilities, sorry that you invested your little money in it, very sorry! But d'ye see? I have an engagement, and must go."

The corpulent Bank President rose from his seat, inserted his watch in its fob, put on his great coat, and moved toward the door.

Davis stood as if rooted to that gorgeous carpet. He made an effort to speak but his tongue produced but a hollow sound. Then his lip trembled, and his quivering fingers were pressed nervously against his breast.

"Come my fellow, I pity your case, but I can't help it. There is a meeting of the Patent-Gospel Association to-night, and I must go. You see my fellow, the Pope of Rome must be put down, and I must go an' help do it."

Davis advanced toward the corpulent Bank President.

"Look here Mr. Joneson," he said in that husky whisper, which speaks from the thin lips of want. "My hands are hardened to bone by work. Look at these fingers. D'ye see how cramped and crooked they are? Well, Mr. Joneson, for six long years have I slaved for that six hundred dollars. And why? Because I wanted to give my wife a home in our old age, because I wished to give some schoolin' to my child. This money Mr. Joneson, I placed in your hands last summer. You said you'd invest it in stock, and now, *now*, Sir, my wife has been dead a month, my child lies on her dyin' bed without bread to eat, or a drop of medicine to still a single death-pain. An' I come to you, and ask for my money, an' you tell me that *the Bank is broke!* Now Mr. Joneson, what I want to ask you is this—"

His voice trembled, and he raised his hands to his eyes for a single instant.

"Will you lend me some money to buy some wood and some bread?"

"Why Davis, really you are too hard for me," said the round-faced Joneson, moving a step nearer to the threshold. There was a supercilious curl about his fat lip, and a sleepy contempt about his leaden eyes.

"Will you," cried Davis, his voice rising into a whispered shriek, "Will you lend me *one* dollar?"

"Davis, Davis, you're too hard for me," said the Bank President, jingling the silver in his pocket with his gouty hands. "The fact is, were I to listen to all such appeals to my feelings, I would be a beggar to-morrow—"

He strode quickly over the threshold as he spoke.

"John," he cried to the servant who was passing through the hall, "If anybody calls for me, you can say that I have gone to the special meeting of the American Patent-Gospel Association. And look ye John, tell James to have the coach ready by twelve to-night: one of the Directors gives a party, and I must be there; and when *this person* goes out, you can put down the dead-latch."

Having thus spoken, the Bank President walked quietly to the front door of the mansion, and in a moment was passing along the crowded street. John Davis stood in the centre of that gorgeous parlor, silent and motionless as a figure carved out of solid rock.

"Come *Mister*, as the gentleman's gone, I 'spose you may as well tortle!" said a harsh voice. John Davis looked up, and beheld a fat-faced servant in livery, motioning him toward the front door.

Without picking his hat from the carpet, John walked slowly from the house.

Meanwhile Job Joneson, Esq. passing with a dignified waddle through the crowded street, reached the corner of Sixth and Chesnut streets, where the outline of the State House arose into the clear, cold, star-lit sky.

A hand was laid gently on his shoulder. Joneson turning quickly round, beheld a man of some thirty years, whose slovenly dress and red nose betrayed his profession. He was a tip-staff of one of the Courts of *Justice*.

"Beg pardon, Sir, your name Joneson Sir? There is a case to be tried in Court to-morrow, and you are summoned to appear as a witness. Here's the Subpœna—"

Joneson reached forth his hand to grasp the paper, when the figure of John Davis strode quietly between him and the tip-staff.

"And *I*," shrieked a voice, wild and broken, yet horrible in its slightest tones, "And *I* have a summons for you, also!" The Bank President made an involuntary start as the glare of those maniac eyes flashed upon him. "I subpœna you, *you* Job Joneson, to appear at the Bar of Almighty God before day-break to-morrow!"

And he raised one thin hand to Heaven while the other rested upon the Bank President's shoulder. Joneson shrunk from that touch—it was like hot lead on the bare skin!

"I will be *there!*" whispered Davis. "*There!*" And he waved his thin hands towards the stars. "At the Bar of God Almighty before day-break to morrow!"

The Bank President raised his hands to his eyes with an involuntary gesture. When he again looked around, the maniac was gone.

We will leave Job Joneson Esq, until the hour of daybreak on the morning of Friday the twenty-third of December.

Byrnewood Arlington stood on the threshold of the Poor Man's Chamber.

The first object that met his eyes was the body of a man flung over two chairs, with the arms dropping heavily to the floor, and the long thin fingers touching the uncarpeted boards. A miserable candle half burnt to its socket, and fixed in an old bottle, was placed upon a table rough pine. The flickering light fell over the face of the man. It was pale and livid, the lips hung apart, and the lower jaw was sunken. Byrnewood advanced and looked, and again that cold chill ran through his veins. There was a gash across the throat of the man, and his dingy shirt was spotted with curdled blood.

Byrnewood started as if to avoid the sight, when a low faint cry burst upon his ears. It was the cry of a child.

"You see," said the old woman pointing to a cradle in a dark corner of the room—"The child was born, about three weeks since, and I took care of it, while the mother was sick. Little did I know that the poor girl wanted for bread! And she a mother too!"

"*The mother?*" muttered Byrnewood as his expressive face manifested a strange agitation. "Where is she?"

"There behind you," answered the old woman.

Byrnewood suddenly turned round, and beheld a white sheet thrown over a miserable bed in one corner of the room. Beneath the folds of the sheet the outlines of a human form were perceptible. It looked like a statue of a beautiful woman, covered with a thin drapery that but half concealed it from the view. The arms lay motionless along the bed, and the feet were thrust upward, causing a slight elevation in the folds of the sheet.

Byrnewood advanced to the bedside. His face was ashy, and the sweat hung in thick beads upon his forehead.

"An' the night afore last," cried the old woman as he advanced— "Sick as she was, poor thing! She went out in the street to try and find *him*, the villain who———"

A deep groan heaving from Byrnewood's chest, made the old woman start with a strange fear.

Byrnewood advanced slowly, he knelt by the bed of death. The sheet concealed the face of the dead girl. Byrnewood reached forth his hand— the white fingers trembled like leaves in the wind.

He lifted the sheet and looked upon the face of the dead. One look was enough. With a wild howl he fell backward, and for a moment lay like a dead man on the floor. A low groan came from his lips. Then with a sudden bound he sprang to his feet—his dark eyes were rivetted to the face of the dead. Again that wild cry burst from his heaving chest; his hands were pressed madly against his forehead. He fled from the room and from the house, as though hell was yawning at his back.

The old woman stood stricken dumb with astonishment. It was some minutes before she could recover her presence of mind.

"Oh my God, my God!" she cried. "What's the use of so much misery in the world! What good does it do? oh, Lor' what am I sayin'? An' she so young an' beautiful—oh Lor', oh Lor'!"

"And how is our young patient?" said a soft and whispering voice.

The old dame turned round with a start. The Signior Ravoni stood before her, his slight form clad in a long robe or surtout of dark cloth, adorned with fur along the edges, and around the neck. The sleeves hung wide and loose, their dark fur borders, imparting a marble whiteness to the delicate hands of the Signior. A diamond pin of dazzling lustre, confined the plain black cravat which encircled his throat, while his black hair, long and lank, was surmounted by a circular cap of dark fur. His sallow face wore a calm and insinuating smile, as his dark eyes were fixed upon the countenance of the old dame with a clear impenetrable glance, that sent a shudder through every fibre of her withered frame.

"And how is our young patient?"

"Dead, oh my God, *dead!*" shrieked the old woman pointing towards the couch.

"Dead!" cried the Signior with a start. "And this sight," he whispered as his glance rested upon the form of the suicide,—"What does it mean?"

"Why you see Doctor Raven, when I went to see you the 'tother day, and begged you to come and wisit a poor girl as was sick an' had no friends—for I'd heered you was kind and charitable tho' a forriner—I did'n't know how poor Davis was, and my God!—All the time you're been comin' here—*unknown* to Davis d'ye mind? For he was poor, but proud and could'n't bear to think of havin' a Doctor 'tend on his child for *mere charity*. And so—what was I a-sayin'? Oh, why all this time Davis, has been waitin' for bread, and so to night———"

"Cut his throat in despair? And this in the pious Quaker City?" And a withering smile played around the expressive lips of the Signior. "Cut his throat because he had no bread to give his child? Can such things happen in pious and *Protestant* Philadelphia?"

"Oh my God," cried the old woman bursting into tears, "If I live a-hundred years more, I'll never forget the look which *she* gave me tonight, when she was dyin', and her words! "Missus Wilson," says she with the tears in her big blue eyes, "that crust of rye bread on the table yonder, is all that I've had to eat for twelve long hours. She was too proud to speak of it, until she was dyin'!"

"There was a noble soul locked in that lifeless form!" muttered Ravoni. "And the medicine which I gave you last night?"

"I mixed it with some gruel, which I made for her, and she drank it, but it was'n't of any use! She died an hour afterwards."

"She died an hour afterwards!" echoed Ravoni, with a meaning smile.

"She died in my arms only half an hour ago," chimed in the old dame. "An' there but five minutes ago as I was straightenin' her out on the bed, her father poor John Davis comes in, looks for an instant on the face of his child, and then—oh Lor', oh Lor'—he cuts his throat from ear to ear, and falls on two cheers as dead as a stone!"

"He is yet warm," muttered Ravoni laying his hand on the dead man's face. "There is an awful Despair written in the face of that ghastly corse! And so she died an hour after taking the medicine?"

"And sich a purty corse!" cried Mrs. Wilson, "Jist look there! Did ever ye see sich hair? So curly and long, and so like gold. Did you ever see sich a mouth?"

She lifted the sheet, and Ravoni gazed upon the countenance of the lifeless girl. Death was there in beauty. Long curling locks of golden hair, fell twining around a mild and wining countenance, with arching eyebrows, lips that smiled even in death, and a round chin, still indented with a laughing dimple. The neck was snow-white, and as the sheet was lifted slowly up, a gleam of light shone upon a fair young bosom—dainty food for the grave-worms!

Death was upon the face and the bosom in holy beauty. The veins still traced their azure lines upon the alabaster of those rounded globes; a rose-bud spot of red still bloomed upon each swelling cheek.

Ravoni folded his arms and gazed upon the corse in speechless silence. His meaning eyes dilated and flashed with a peculiar expression, and his thin lips trembled with an emotion as strange as the gleam of his eyes.

"Widow you are poor, but you have been kind to this man and his child," he said in a calm dignified whisper. "Here is money for the funeral of this poor Suicide. I myself will attend to the burial of the girl—"

The Widow was about to reply, when a confused sound like the trampling of feet over the pavement below, attracted their attention. Then came the sound of a door flung suddenly open, and then a voice resounded from the foot of the stairway.

"Hallo! Is there anybody in this house?" it cried in thick gruff tones. "Its the watchman," muttered the widow, going to the head of the stairs—"Is that you, Mister Thompson?"

"Yes, it is widow," replied the gruff voice, "but here's a man taken sick in his carriage comin' home from a party, and he wants help mighty bad—"

"You see Master made a little too free with the wine at Deacon Rogers' house," chimed in another voice. "An' consequence is, he's took bad with an appylectic fit—"

Then the sound of footsteps was heard on the stairs, and in a few moments the back of the watchmen's great coat appeared in the doorway, with the fat face of a man in livery, peering over his shoulder. Between them, was the body of the sick man. He groaned and struggled as they laid him on the floor, and turned his head from side to side, as though the death rattle was in his throat.

As his head turned from side to side, the light fell upon the round fat face of Job Joneson, the Bank President!

"Well," screamed the man in livery, "If there aint the man I turned from Master's door last night—if there he aint with his throat cut!"

The Watchman looked upon the Suicide with a start, and muttered distinctly to himself the words, "*dam—fool.*" Watchmen are great philosophers.

Meanwhile in the centre of the uncarpeted floor, his dark broadcloth coat soiled by the white foam which fell from his lips, his round face turned from glowing red to dark purple, with the distorted veins standing out from his skin, lay Job Joneson, the Bank President, moving piteously as he clutched the breast of his shirt with his gouty fingers. His eyes red and bloodshot, protruded from his face, and rolled from side to side with a pitiful stare.

"Cant you do nothin' for him nobody?" said the Man in Livery. "He's *my* master!"

"I am afraid all is over," said Ravoni stooping down over the prostrate Bank President. "However we may bleed him—"

The words had scarcely passed his lips when Joneson rose on his knees with a violent struggle.

"Where—where—" he muttered as a gurgling noise sounded in his throat—"Where—am—I—ah!" His voice rose into a horrible shriek husky with the death rattle. He beheld the ghastly face of the Suicide.

"Ah—a-h!" he groaned clutching at his throat with his gouty hands. "*At the Bar of God Almighty before daybreak to-morrow!*"

With these words on his lips, he fell—a shapeless mass of clay. He had obeyed the subpœna of the Suicide; he had gone to meet his pale Accuser before the Throne of Eternity.

God is just.

This is a truth we often hear preached, but it falls upon our ears with a hollow sound.

God is just.

Come hither, all the world, come to the chamber of Want and Suicide, and gaze upon this picture of God's Justice.

On the floor, the bare and uncarpeted floor, lay the portly form of the Bank President, beside the very chairs which supported the lean figure of the Suicide. The face of the Bank President was loathsome purple; and his bloodshot eyes hung from their sockets; the visage of the Suicide ashy pale, and there was a red gash across his throat.

The legalized Robber lay beside the wretch whom he had plundered. The well-fed Bank President who not ten hours past, had refused the starving Mechanic one solitary dollar, now lay beside the victim of his lawful fraud, like that victim, a loathsome mass of clay, on which worms would soon hold their revel.

Say, was not this the justice of God?

And the trembling light fell over the forms of the two dead men, the Summoner and the Summoned, and upon the figures of the strange group who encircled them. There was the Signior Ravoni, his sallow face wearing that meaning smile, his eyes flashing their calm impenetrable glance, while with folded arms he gazed upon the dead. The old widow, and the phlegmatic watchman, and the well-fed servant, all stood by gazing upon the scene with one common awe.

And behind the group was the bed of death, with the cold white sheet thrown over the icy form of the ruined girl.

The good and merciful God has flung between our eyes and the shadow of Eternity an awful veil, or else we might follow up to Judgment, the soul of the Bank President. We might behold the long train of orphan's ghosts who follow his soul with curses to the bar of Almighty justice, and there while the pale Suicide stalks before him, blasting his sight with a spectacle of speechless woe, we might see how the guilty wretch trembles and crouches in the presence of his God, as the wrongs of ten thousand men and women and children beggared by his fraud, come blackening upward, in palpable shapes of doom.

But let him pass to his account. There are hundreds like him, walking the streets of the Quaker City, their round fat faces wearing a pleasant smile as they think of houses and lands, torn from the honest poor by legalized robbery. Let them all pass—God is just.

The Watchman and the Man in Livery bore the dead man to his carriage.

"How cussed heavy the old chap is," muttered the Watchman, as he tumbled the mass of clay through the carriage door.

"Wonder who in the d———l 'ill pay me my wages?" cried the Man in Livery, jumping up behind the coach.

The coachman, who had been sleeping on his box, woke up from his quiet nap and asked a brief question.—

"I say John, is it a common fit, or has the old man kicked the bucket?"

"Kicked the bucket, James!"

"No!" replied the other in a tone of complacent wonder. "Cussed glad he paid me off, yesterday. W-h-oop!"

He applied the whip to the blood horses and away they dashed, bearing to his home, his wife and children, the dead body of the Bank President.

As the carriage drove away from the door, and disappeared in the distance, another vehicle came slowly along the street and halted in front of the widow's house. It was drawn by one horse, and was by no means as gorgeous in appearance as the coach of the Bank President.

There was no gaudy coat of arms emblazoned on its panels, nor did the coachman wear a livery of showy hues garnished with bright tinsel. It was a hearse, and the driver who dismounted from the box, was dressed in black, with thick folds of crape drooping over his face.

"It's near day-break," he muttered in a hoarse voice. "It's near day-break and I must be in a hurry. Werry fine coffin that!"

He pointed to the glittering coffin which the uplifted folds of the hearse exposed to view, and then disappeared into the house of the widow.

Ravoni and the old woman stood beside the bed of death.

"I will attend to the burial of the girl," said Ravoni, placing gold in the hands of the woman.

As he spoke the figure of a man, with crape drooping over his face glided between the twain, and extending his rude hands, gathered the sheet around the form of the dead girl.

"What does this mean?" cried the old woman with a haggard look. "I don't 'xactly know what to make of it?"

The man with the crape hung round his face, silently placed the body of the girl upon his shoulder, and while Ravoni confronted the old woman, strode quietly toward the doorway.

"What does it mean? Why d'ye take the body from this house?" said the old woman in the shrill peevish tones, that old women are wont to use, when slightly angered.

"Woman do you think I could harm the dead?" said Ravoni, and he bent the glance of his unfathomable eyes upon the withered face of the woman.

There was something awful in the magic of that man's look.

The arms of the old woman fell by her side, and she stood like a statue, yet with her grey eyes chained to the glance of Ravoni.

What was the power of this man? In the dark ages they would have called it Magic; in the Nineteenth century, they call it Magnetism.

"Are you satisfied?" said the Signior with a mild and insinuating smile.

"Yes, yes," gasped the old woman. "Only leave me—That's all."

The man with the corpse on his shoulder thrust aside the crape from his face. The grim visage of Devil-Bug was revealed by the beams of the trembling light.

"Curse the man," he muttered. "I b'lieve he's a born devil! I don't feel as tho' I had a will of my own any more. I don't like the way things work!"

He strode down stairs with these muttered words on his lips. As the corpse of the Mother disappeared, the Babe sleeping in the cradle awoke and uttered a faint cry.

"Here is gold for the child," said Ravoni, and then folding his arms calmly together strode from the house.

The rattling of the hearse, as it dashed along the deserted street broke on his ears.

"Ha, ha, I must prepare for the scene of *to-morrow*," he muttered. "Now for my home, now for the *Orgie of Ravoni.*"

He paused for a moment, and raised his hands to the day-break sky.

"Ye stars, beneath whose light I have walked two hundred years, tell me, shall I not live until my name is worshipped as a God among these playthings of an intellect like mine, there men who plot and plan and gather gold, and yet creep into the same dull grave at last?"

CHAPTER SECOND

THE CURSE OF THE DRUGGED POTION

The day was breaking in the east, when a pale man came trembling up the marble steps of a mansion in South Third street, and leaning against the stone pillars of the door, buried his face in his hands, while every fibre of his frame, shook with emotion.

The day was breaking, and red gleams of morning shot up into the sky, cold white clouds, sailing slowly through the heavens, caught the first kiss of sun-rise on their bosoms.

The man who leaned for support against the heavy door pillars, raised his face from his hands, after a moment of silent agony, and tossing his dark hair aside from his brow, looked fixedly at the vacant air, with set teeth and flashing eyes.

"It is all fancy, I know it, I know it! And yet there, there, floating in the dim air, I see her form,—oh! how cold and icy! The death-shroud waves round her stiffened limbs—the taint of corruption is on her cheek.—Her eyes—so dead, so lustreless—have still a gleam that burns into my soul. And I am her Murderer! Yes, yes, her *Murderer!* Her babe will live to curse my name. In her last hour she called on me—she shrieked my name with her last breath!"

He pressed his hot eye-balls against his hands, and was silent again. A terrible remorse had seized upon the soul of Byrnewood Arlington.

In that hour the poor drudge, the despised Servant Girl was forgotten.

The wronged woman, holy because trusting, innocent because loving with a pure love, that flung the world of her honor at her lover's feet, the wronged woman glided like a phantom between the seducer and the light.

A noble soul throbbed within the bosom of Byrnewood Arlington. In crushing the honor of an unprotected girl, he had only followed out the law which the Lady and Gentleman of Christian Society recognize with tacit reverence. Seduce a *rich* maiden? Wrong the daughter of a *good* family? Oh, this is horrible; it is a crime only paralleled in enormity by the blaspemy of God's name. But a poor girl, a *servant*, a domestic? Oh, no! These are fair game for the gentleman of fashionable society; upon the wrongs of such as these the fine lady looks with a light laugh and supercilious smile.

Now it was that the better soul of Byrnewood awoke within him and plead for the woman he had wronged. Could his life, at that moment have restored her to life and purity, he would have flung it on her grave with joy.

He stood at his father's door again. In the strange oblivion of soul which succeeded the drugged potion, he fancied that only a night had passed since he left his father's threshold.

The key was in the lock; he turned it, and after the lapse of a moment, he stood in the dark entry and closed the door at his back.

He advanced along the hall, while an awful presentiment flashed over his soul. Dim memories of the scenes in Monk-Hall rushed upon him.

"I will seek my sister's room," he muttered. "If she is there, then all is right, and these presentiments are but folly."

He was passing by the parlor door, when the sound of voices talking in low tones, arrested his attention. Gently opening the door, he started back in surprise, as a blaze of light rushed out upon the darkness of the hall. He entered the parlor with a softened footstep, and looked around in vague wonder. The astral lamp stood lighted on the centre-table, and the remains of a coal fire mouldered in the grate.

Two figures were seated upon the sofa, an old man and an elderly dame. They sat with their hands clasped on their knees, and their eyes fixed vacantly upon the carpet. So deep was their reverie, that they did not look up, or manifest any knowledge of the intruder's presence.

Byrnewood stood chained to the spot, by a silent horror. Scarce might he recognize his father, in the care worn old man, who sat silent and withered before him; scarce might he know his mother in the hollow-eyed old woman, whose dark hair, slightly silvered by age, fell carelessly over her shoulders.

He advanced a step, and beheld that his mother's dark eyes were red with weeping; his father's lips trembled with an incessant movement.

They looked like people who have been watching long days and weary nights by the sick-bed of some loved one, without once changing their apparel or taking an hour's repose.

Byrnewood advanced another step; they beheld him, and started to their feet with a half-muttered cry. Oh, there was a volume of Hope and Fear and Agony in that involuntary shriek!

For a moment there was silence. The father and mother gazed in the face of their son, with the same look full of horrible suspense. Byrnewood returned that look, and the three stood like statues of some unspeakable Agony.

"*Mary*"—gasped the Father, and then all further words died on his tongue. He stood with his hands extended and his lips trembling as with a spasm.

"Mary!" echoed Byrnewood. "Father there is some dark mystery here. Is she sick? Or—or—" and his lips grew white—"Or it may be that she is—*dead!* Keep me no longer in suspense; tell me the worst at once!"

"Know you not Byrnewood that your sister has been missing since the night before last?" slowly asked the old Merchant.

"The night before last!" echoed Byrnewood. "Surely father that cannot be. Last night when I left home, she was in your arms—"

"Last night?" echoed Mrs. Arlington in vague astonishment.

"Why Byrnewood you have been absent from home for the last thirty-six hours" exclaimed the Merchant sharing the wonder of his wife.

Byrnewood made no reply, but tottering to the sofa, he buried his face in his hands, and was silent for a single moment. With all the force of his Soul concentrated on one point, he endeavored to remember the events of the last thirty-six hours.

"Did I ever think of this!" cried the Father clasping his hands wildly together. "Did I ever think of this, when I toiled day after day over the desk, laboring like a slave at the galley, to build up a fortune which my children might enjoy, when I was dead and gone! Did I ever think that Mary—Mary for whom I have toiled and toiled for years—should be torn from me in this way? My God! This suspense is tenfold more horrible than death!"

"Don't you remember her light laugh as she sprang over that threshold two nights ago—'I'll be back, I'll be back to-morrow!' "

The mother paused and burst into tears. There are some things which can be written down in language, but not a Mother's Love, nor a Mother's Fear. What was Mrs. Arlington thirty-six hours ago? A blooming matron with a healthy cheek, and a dark eye, speaking affection and tenderness. What is she *now?* An old woman, with a withered cheek and a hollow eye-socket, a brain fired by a thousand mingling emotions, and a heart cankered by the gnawings of care. A mother's Love, does not manifest its tenderness in words, but in the gleam of the eye, or the smile of the lip; a Mother's Fear is written down in the wrinkled brow, the faded cheek, the eye darting unnatural light and the lip quivering with a tremulous motion, that speaks the helplessness of the agony, that is eating into the Soul.

"Father—mother," cried Byrnewood starting from his seat. "There is a strange mystery pressing on my brain! I am either the victim of an awful delusion, or else there is in store for me, for you, for us all, a Reality worse than death! Even while I speak to you, there are passing before me, shapes and forms and visions, whose mystery I dare not—oh dare not—speak to you! You know father that I love Mary, that I always loved her. You know that I would give my life for her. Trust the mystery of this matter, with me! A few hours will bring her back to this threshold in safety and honor, or confirm these horrible suspicions which are working through my brain—"

"Yet stay, Byrnewood," cried Mr. Arlington as his son moved toward the door. "Where have you been during the last thirty-six hours, where—"

"Ask me not, ask me not!" shouted Byrnewood with a start and look full of frenzy. "Ask me not for the sake of Mary, ask me not! In a few hours I will return to you—then you shall know all!"

With these words he rushed from the room. The old Merchant gazed in the face of his wife, who returned the intensity of his look in silence. Not a word was spoken, not a single cry of anguish broke from the lips of father or mother. They suffered in silence. They *endured*, while every tone of their lost daughter was ringing in their ears, while every look of her beaming face, treasured by memory, came back to haunt them like a Ghost sent from the bosom of the past, they endured and suffered in silence.

And yet in all the bitterness of their anguish not one thought came across their souls of Mary's *dishonor*. She might have been the victim of some terrible accident, she might have lost her way in the crowded city, to whose maze of streets she was a stranger, she might be dead and buried and without the knowledge of father or mother; but that the voice of Wrong had lured her from her home, that her virgin soul had been stained by *dishonor?* The thought never crossed their souls. God in his mercy, may have withheld this horrible thought from the brimming cup of their agony. It was terror enough for them to know that their child was gone; but that she was dishonored! Better than to tell them this, would it have been to pour molten lead on their quivering eyeballs!

Byrnewood rushed hurriedly up the stairway of the mansion and in a few moments entered his bedchamber. The morning dawn broke through the curtains that hung along the windows. How his heart rose to his throat as he crossed the threshold! Thirty-six hours ago he had left that chamber a free-hearted and joyous man; now he came back with an awful mystery pressing on his soul.

Advancing toward a dressing bureau, which stood between two lofty windows, Byrnewood opened a drawer, near the top, and took from thence a small casket.

This casket he opened and placing some object, which it contained within the folds of his vest, he knelt down on the floor, and raised his hands to heaven.

His face was ghastly pale. His eyes were not upraised, but they glared steadily forward, with a wild and watery stare. As he knelt you might see the muscles of his clenched hand writhe like serpents, and his white lips moved but uttered no sound.

The first red gleam of the morning sun fell on his pale forehead. Still his lips moved with that soundless motion, and the muscles of his hand still writhed beneath the skin.

It was thus for a moment. He then arose on his feet, and assuming another hat and cloak in the place of those which he had lost at Monk-Hall, he went slowly down the stairs and from the house.

It was now sunrise on the morning of Friday the twenty-third of December.

On CHRISTMAS EVE *at the hour of* SUNSET, *one of ye will die by the other's hand. The winding sheet is woven and the coffin made.*

The Prophecy rushed over the soul of Byrnewood, as he left his father's threshold. Where he had heard it, by whom it had been spoken, or when was the other person included in its wild denunciation —all was shadow and mystery to Byrnewood Arlington.

"To-morrow night is Christmas Eve," he muttered as the winter sun-beams broke over his brow, and then passed from the shadow of his father's door.

Into that door again, he did not return until the hour before Sunset on Saturday the twenty-fourth of December; the hour of Christmas Eve.

CHAPTER THIRD

"RAVONI A GOD!"

The gleam of a vivid light illumined the Audience chamber of Ravoni.

Beside the table, in the centre of that room, with its walls and floor and its ceiling of one gloomy blackness, stood a man of impressive look and manner, whose entire appearance was in strange contrast with the place.

His figure slight yet beautifully proportioned was clad in a costume, like that worn by the Chevaliers of France in the palmy days that went before the night of the Revolution. He wore a coat of lustrous dark satin.with wide skirts and sleeves hanging in easy folds around the waist. Around the collar and along the front, it was adorned with rich embroidery of gold lace, and in place of buttons, a line of diamonds, flung back the reflection of the light with a gleam like stars shining in a clear lake. His vest was of snowy whiteness; his hose of dark hues, displayed the shape of his elegantly moulded limbs; and his red-heeled shoes,* glittered with diamond buckles. His shirt bosom was of transparent whiteness, and his small white hands were relieved by the thick folds of the ruffles that fell back from his wrist.

Altogether he presented a fine specimen in his appearance and costume of one of those gorgeous gentlemen, whose presence gave life and wit to the circle of courtiers, who in the olden time clustered around the gay Kings of France.

His head and face were singularly beautiful. His complexion was a rich olive with a flush of deep vermillion warming the centre of each cheek. His eyebrows were dark and arching, his nose a delicate aquiline

* 'The red-heeled shoe' was worn by the French nobility previous to the Revolution.

with slight nostrils that quivered in scorn and dilated in anger; his mouth was small and expressive with lips of the most voluptuous ruby. The upper lip curled with a proud scorn, while the lower projected slightly, with an expression of refined voluptuousness. His chin was small, round and decided; and altogether, though somewhat large in proportion to the size of his body, his face was at once thoughtful in its every outline and delicate in every feature. His brow wide, massive and deathly pale, was well relieved by thick masses of dark hair, which fell twining in ringlets to his shoulders.

And from beneath the shadow of that pale brow, gleamed evermore the clear light of two dark eyes, whose gaze sent a strange thrill of awe into the souls of men. It was not the excessive brightness of these eyes that attracted your attention, nor their intense blackness, nor the delicate fringe of the long and quivering eye-lashes. There was a strange magnetic power in their glance; their look was a spell; their anger an awful fascination that left the gazer powerless; their love an irresistable influence that dragged the victim to shame and ruin with a smile. That terrible consciousness of soul, which men in their poverty of words, call THE WILL, gleamed calmly and fixedly from those wizard eyes.

And this gayly dressed Chevalier, standing alone in the Audience Chamber, this strange man with the striking face and the shadowy eyes—who was he?

It was the Signior Ravoni.

* "Yes, yes, I am myself once more," he muttered, striding slowly along the room. "The sallow hues of care have vanished from my cheeks; the stoop of age has fallen from my shoulders. Once more I stand attired for the festival of Ravoni! That Festival I have celebrated beside the waters of the Ganges, in the fragrant air of Ceylon, amid the snows of the polar desert, and in the boundless deserts where moulder the palaces of Montezuma!

"Two hundred years—a glorious career! Once an idle Courtier of a thoughtless king, a *Chevalier* whose very breath hung suspended on a Monarch's will—*now* I am a soul, an Intellect, a deathless Power! What playthings are these men of science! In all ages and in every clime the same! When they have won a little knowledge, they stoop

* The sentiments expressed in this chapter; are *not* the opinions of the author, but of the character, which it is his object to delineate. The author does not hold himself responsible for a single word or line. This note is made in order that all critics with weak eyes and tender consciences, may be spared the trouble of abusing the author for the opinions of one of his characters.

from their proud height to gather gold, in the gutter of a human and contemptible rivalry. I gathered knowledge, I won science from the earth, the air, the sea, from the very sky above me, but how glorious the object for which that knowledge was acquired!

"What have I won? A deathless career among things whose life is death!

"Even now my soul leaps from scene to scene of that memory which written in books men would call History!"

"When the torch of St. Bartholomew flashed through the streets of Paris—I was there! When the pikes of the Revolution glittered around the scaffold of a doomed King, and a pale-faced Priest bade the Son of St. Louis ascend to heaven; I was there!

"The proud Corsican, stood on the heighth of the Egyptian pyramid, and surveyed his hosts, scattered far and wide beneath, at once his warriors and his worshippers, while his bronzed brow lit up with a deathless ambition, and his lip curled in scorn as he gave to the air the thought of his soul, "When all the world is mine, then I will build up a religion of whose altars I shall be the God!" As these words fell from his lips, I, I the *Savan* Ravoni stood by his side.

"Where is the Corsican now? Where is Ravoni?

"And in that old Hall, where Fifty-Six stern hearted citizens gave the law to a world, down-trodden by tyrants, there, there I stood, while the pens whose very ink was Destiny, were tracing the immortal Signatures upon the scroll, which is now Eternal!

"I stood there, and saw their faces fire as the last name was written.

"Where are the Signers now? In the dust!

"Where is Ravoni? Still on his deathless career!

"I stood by the side of Washington, when he took the Oath as President of this New World, which was then the Hope of all mankind.

"Where is Washington now? And where is La Fayette and Adams and Jefferson and Hamilton?

"Ask the dust of annihilation to give back its dead?

"And what is that New World which they fondly hoped would become the Ararat on which the Ark of a World's Salvation was to find a rest at last?

"Go to her Senate Halls, and find bullies and braggarts wearing the robes once worn by men, who were gods in soul!

"A pitiful craven lurks in the Chair, where Washington once sate, the wonder of a world. Treason blasphemes the place once sanctified by Honor!*

* The reader will remember that the Era of this story is the year 1842.

"Bribery sits on the judicial bench, and a licentious mob administers justice with the Knife and the Torch. In the Pulpit crouches grim superstition preaching a God, whose mercy is one Incarnate Threat, whose benificence is written on the Grave stone of a wrecked world!

"Such is the Land of Freedom for which Washington fought and La Fayette bled!

"And where is Ravoni now? Still on his deathless career!

"Such as Ravoni have lived in all ages, in every clime! Bold Intellects who wrested from corruption the secret of undying energy. And these Intellects so various in their powers, so various in their weird histories, common Tradition has combined in one form, and called a thousand mighty Souls, by one paltry name, the Wandering Jew! Superstition must baptize a giant Truth in the waters of puerile fiction! Few of these great Intellects survive at the present day. Some have grown tired of the sameness of their being, and rushed into annihilation through the grim portals of Suicide. But few survive—Among these, lives Ravoni!

"And if this great earth must one day sink into chaos, when the gleam of her last sun illumines the summit of the last solitary mountain, reeling to its foundations, it will also the brow of Ravoni!

"I will build me up a Religion!

"There is no God. There is no Heaven. There is no Hell. At least, the belief of the million, with regard to mysteries like these, is all shadow and fable.

"I believe in a God, but my God is the Power of a Giant Will. In a Heaven, but it is that Heaven which springs from the refused cultivation of all the senses. In a Hell I believe—it is the hell of Annihilation.

"The million, led on by the herd of Priests and Drones, have seized upon these Truths of the olden Sages, and made Realities of these Fables, by which Thought spoke to the souls of men, in the ancient times.

"I will build me up a Religion. A thousand years hence looking from the brow of some tremendous mountain, I shall behold the plains below whitened by the marble domes of a mild and benificent religion; those domes shall tower in the name of a God, in the name of Ravoni!

"The rock on which all Religions have been wrecked, shall not endanger the Faith of Ravoni. Its Founder will not die! He will not like Mahommed build up a Beautiful System, and then sink into the grave, leaving his temple to the ravages of priestly liars and robbers.

"The Faith of Ravoni will be simple and beautiful. War shall be buried. Anarchy forever dethroned; all Treason against the Life of man, shall be eternally crushed. Men shall live, love and die in their peaceful beds. Priestcraft shall be no more!

"I will teach men that in the Refined cultivation of the Senses is Happiness. Not a pore on the body but may be made the Minister of some new Joy; not a throb in the veins, but may become a living Pleasure. Every outrage committed against the refinement of the Senses brings its own punishment. When Mirth sinks into Drunken Revelry man is a brute. When Love sinks into coarse Lust man is a brute and devil.

"In order to acquire an influence over the minds of men, which shall be irresistable and eternal, I will appeal to a principle rooted deep in every human heart. I will evoke the love of Mystery! I will awe and terrify by Miracles and Pageants and Shadows!

"At noonday to-morrow they will behold the First Miracle.

"Now for the Festival of Ravoni!"

The eloquent Blasphemer passed through a small door, concealed beneath the hangings as he spoke.

"Now for the Festival of Ravoni, where the Senses hold their revel, and Thought is softened and mellowed in the delirious atmosphere of Passion."

CHAPTER FOURTH

THE PRIESTESS OF RAVONI

In the course of one hour occurred three prominent Incidents of our Revelation.

The State House clock struck nine, and the carriage of the Merchant Prince stood waiting in front of his door. The coachman in grey livery, turned up with black velvet, sat on the box, and the footman attired in like costume, stood beside the carriage door which was flung wide open. The burnished harness of the dark bay horses glittered in the sunbeams, and the panels of the coach emblazoned with the Merchant's coat of arms, shone like mirrors in the light.

It was nine o'clock, and from the front door of the mansion, the merchant and his wife came forth. Attired in a splendid travelling habit of dark green cloth, which developed each queenly outline of her form, Dora hung lightly on her husband's arm, while her eyes shone with unusual lustre, and her cheeks glowed with the hues of the damask rose. As she stepped gently down the marble steps she was peerlessly beautiful. Every look, each gesture and grace of her faultless limbs and imposing countenance, bespoke the Queen, whose throne was in the hearts of all beholders.

It was observable that as the Merchant led his wife toward the carriage, his face half-buried in the shadow of a fur travelling cap, was turned away from hers, and once or twice as her gloved hand touched his arm, he shrunk with a slight but involuntary start, as if there had been pollution in the contact.

Their eyes met as they stood before the carriage door. The merchant's face was almost hidden from the sight, by his fur cap, and the upraised collar of his great coat, but his blue eyes dilated to an unnatural size, gazed in the beaming face of his wife, with a cold impenetrable look that sent a strange awe to her inmost heart.

"The day is beautiful Albert," said Dora with one of her winning smiles.

"It is indeed beautiful!" replied Livingstone as his lips parted, not with a smile, but with a spasmodic contraction of the muscles of his face. "We have seen many such beautiful days, Dora; may we live to see many more!"

There was a singular gleam in his large blue eyes, as he spoke. "Have you invited our friends to meet us at Hawkwood?" asked Dora, as she entered the carriage.

"Trust me Dora, we shall have a pleasant company at the good old place," said Livingstone in a tone of affected lightness. "Bye-the-bye my dear, you will have to travel on alone, for an hour or so. I have some business to transact, which will detain me a short time in town. I will join you on horseback in an hour."

Without waiting for her reply, he softly closed the door, and waved his hand to the coachman. The carriage whirled away over the echoing stones of the street, and Livingstone stood alone in front of his mansion.

"Let me see, let me see," he muttered pressing his hand against his forehead, "What Author is it, that tells the story of an English Lord, who world-worn and heart-sick used to amuse his leisure hours by rehearsing his own funeral? Ha, ha! There is scarcely twenty-four hours of life left to me, and yet I while them away in digging my grave, and—another grave beside my own!"

That cold spasm, which mocked a smile, played round the Merchant's lips, and he went slowly up Fourth street, in the direction of his Warehouse.

The State-House clock struck nine, and two little men were walking up and down the broad walk of Independence Square. All around them, arose the giant trees, whose massive trunks had been young sixty years ago, when the Proclamation of Independence rang from the steps of the ancient Hall. Their leafless limbs shot upward into the cold blue sky, and between their intricate branches, the white clouds might be seen, sailing slowly through the winter heavens. At one end of the walk was Walnut street, with a line of splendid buildings towering in the place of the old gaol; at the other, through the vista formed by opposing lines of trees, was seen the ancient State-House, with its steeple rising into the full glow of the sunshine.

And up and down this walk, paced two little men, engaged in an interesting conversation, as might be seen from their linked arms and rapid gestures. One little man wore a high hat and frock coat, which was buttoned so tightly around his thick body, that it gave you the idea of a mammoth Dutch pudding, stuffed and crammed until the skin was ready to burst. Beneath the skirts of this frock coat appeared a pair of legs which once seen might never be forgotten. With a thick piece of cord reaching from one calf to another, they would have described the letter A; as they rubbed together at the knees, and were separated by the space of a foot between the boots. Bury a man eighty years in a coal mine, and show him those legs after he is brought out into the light again, and show them to him, apart from the pudding body, and if he had ever seen them before, he would know them on first sight. Who could ever forget Buzby Poodle's legs?

The other little man was dressed in a grey over-coat and a shiny leather cap. That pale, square, Dresden-wax-doll-face would have been known among a thousand. Who could mistake the large oyster-colored eyes of Sylvester J. Petriken?

And there, they walked, the editor of the Daily Black Mail, and the Magazine proprietor. Poodle's face reminded you of a grimacing ape, making mouths at a magpie; Petriken's was the visage of a solemn old baboon, wrapt in deep thought. The one fattened on the garbage of the town; the other lived on stolen literature. One was a Scandal-monger, a Bravo on a small scale; the other a plagiarist; a very Jew, who lived by clipping the coin of the wide realm of Intellect. There they walked, the one living on the Murder, Suicide and Bloodshed of the town, the other thriving on the fruits of various adroit literary robberies; there they walked arm in arm, alike the boon companions of blackguards, and the loathing of all honest men; these Courtezans of the Press. Poodle was the Pander of the whole town; anybody could buy him, body and soul, for three dollars, a bottle of wine, a Bologna sausage and a few crackers; Petriken was the hireling of but one Libertine, Gustavus Lorrimer, and his price varied from a two dollar subscription to his Magazine, up to the value of a second-hand steel engraving.

"And so you see we'll have a great Magazine!" exclaimed Petriken with one of his sickly smiles. "To-morrow morning all the Intellects of the land meet at my office in order to talk the matter over. I, Sylvester J. Petriken will become the Focus of American Literature."

"Won't the name of Busby Poodle be known all over the country? Posterity shall reverence the name of Poodle, and millions yet unborn, will write on their hearts. Is'nt there somethin' in that? The name of Poodle inscribed on the pillar of Immortality, a-longside the name of Shakspeare! And then the name of Petriken!"

"Let us mingle our names together!" cried little Sylvester striking an attitude. "We will go down to posterity as Petriken *and* Poodle!"

"The *Petriken* and *the* Poodle! Huzza! A sort of Siamese-twinship of genius! *Ensemble de chose*—decidedly the cheese—as we say in Domestic French!"

The little men then shook hands, and stood erect, like proud representatives of the Out-cast Literature of the Quaker City.

Suddenly Petriken started.

"I vow there's Lorrimer and Mutchins!" he exclaimed, looking toward the State House; and ere a moment had flown, the magnificent Gus stood by his side with the round-faced Mutchins hanging on his arm.

"Ha, ha, Pet my boy, how d'ye do!" cried Lorrimer as a gleam of laughter broke over his manly visage. "Silly who is *this* fellow?" he continued arranging his moustache as he glanced at the Black Mail man with somewhat of a supercilious smile. "Who is the gentleman in the big hat and duck legs."

"He, he, he, you're quite jocular this morning!" exclaimed the little editor who had heard this a side speech. "Why, I'm Poodle Sir, Buzby Poodle of the—the Daily Black Mail!" And the little fellow advanced with a spring.

"Oh you *are* Buzby Poodle?" exclaimed Lorrimer with a glance from his half-shut eyes. "Come on Petriken, come on Mutchins; I've something to say to you. And so *that* is Poodle of the Black Mail; is it? Jove! He looks for all the world, like a monkey dressed up to dance on the top of a street organ!"

And taking the arm of each gentleman within his own, he strode down the broad walk, leaving Poodle to his own delightful meditations.

"Well," muttered Buzby, "w-e-ll if I don't cut that fellow up some day my name ain't Poodle! And as for that Petriken—damme I'll go right to the office and abuse his Western Hem. People that insult Buzby Poodle must look for a Poodle's vengeance. I'm a perfect Injin; I am!"

"Boys I've a capital joke for you," exclaimed Lorrimer, as they hurried along the broad walk. "You see Mutchins, ha, ha! It's capital, capital! And d'ye hear, Pet—by Jove man!" he cried, starting suddenly. "You are as white as a cloth in the face!"

Petriken stood transfixed to the spot by some unknown horror.

Not a word escaped his lips, but standing motionless as one of the trees along the walk, he pointed with his outstretched hand towards Walnut street.

"Look! Look!" cried Mutchins, pointing in the same direction. "There's a sight for you Lorrimer!"

Lorrimer looked toward Walnut street, and at the same moment, a cold shudder darted through his frame. He was dumb with astonishment. Could he believe his eyes? Yes, yes, there, there before him, advancing slowly and leisurely along the walk, was the form of Byrnewood Arlington! Byrnewood Arlington whom he left the night before in the hands of Devil-Bug, whom he never dreamt to behold among living men again! Lorrimer's expressive face grew pale, and, red by turns; for a moment he gasped for breath.

"Leave the matter to me," he muttered to his companions, who stood silent, "and mark ye—*deny everything*, d'ye hear?"

He had scarcely time to whisper these words to his frightened panders, when Byrnewood approached. Lorrimer started as he beheld the wild light gleaming from his dark eyes.

"I have a few words to say to you, Sir," Byrnewood begun in a low deep tone like a voice from a sepulchre.

"I beg your pardon, Sir!" cried Lorrimer with a haughty inclination of his head, "You have the advantage of me. I do not know you Sir!" And his face was wreathed in a polite and insinuating smile.

"Not know me!" echoed Byrnewood. "Was I not in your company last night?"

"Decidedly not!" And Lorrimer dropped the arms of his minions, and placed the head of his gold-mounted cane to his lips in an easy, devil-may-care manner, characteristic of a Chesnut street Lounger.

"Why Sir, Mr. Petriken here, introduced me to you; and the introduction took place at this gentleman's rooms." He pointed to the red-faced Mutchins as he spoke.

"Pet did you ever introduce this gentleman to me?" exclaimed Lorrimer with a meaning look.

"Nev-er!" faltered the white-faced pander.

And damme Sir, I never saw you in all my life Sir?" blustered Mutchins buttoning the front of his white coat in a pompous manner.

Byrnewood placed his hand to his forehead for a single instant.

"I remember the introduction;" he said in a slow deliberate tone, "I remember being in the streets with you; and beyond that all is darkness!"

"Depend upon it, Sir," exclaimed Lorrimer, laying his hand pleasantly on Byrnewood's shoulder, "You are the victim of some strange delusion. I give you my solemn word of honor that I never saw you in my life before!"

"And your name is Lorrimer?"

"Egad! you've hit it! Bye-the-bye my dear fellow, is n't that a bald eagle sailing among the clouds yonder?"

With an air of languid nonchalance he pointed upward with his cane.

"Will you give me your word of honor, that you never saw *my sister?*" exclaimed Byrnewood as the Images of Memory darted over his brain.

"*Your* sister!" echoed Lorrimer with a vacant stare. "Oh, ho! My dear fellow you're too hard for me! Upon my honor I never saw your sister, nor any member of your family, to know them by name. Your name is—"

"Arlington," responded the Brother with a steady look, "Byrnewood Arlington."

"Have heard the name, but never knew any member of the family. By Jove! That *must* be a bald eagle yonder!"

Byrnewood advanced a step nearer, and looked silently into the dark hazel eyes of Lorrimer.

"Now for the last trial!" he muttered, and then repeated in a slow and solemn voice the words of the prophecy.

" '*On Christmas Eve at the hour of sunset one of you will die by the other's hand. The winding sheet is woven and the coffin made.*' Tell me sir," he added in a voice full of emotion. "Did you never hear these words before?"

Lorrimer's cheek did not blench, nor his eye quail. He raised his cane languidly to his lips, and then replied in a careless tone—

"Never! Yet stay—I think I've read them somewhere in Dickens or Bulwer."

"Oh madness! madness!" muttered Byrnewood pressing his hand forcibly against his forehead. "I am indeed the victim of some dark delusion. Excuse me, gentlemen for this intrusion," he continued in a tremulous voice. "It is all a dream a horrible dream!"

With these words he darted down the walk, his head bent on his bosom and his eyes fixed upon the ground.

"Well, Lorrimer that was neatly done!" cried Silly Petriken, approaching the Master-Libertine who stood in the centre of the walk, gazing upon the retreating form of Byrnewood.

"You did him brown," laughed Mutchins. "But boys we must be careful—there's a devil of a stir made about this baby-face!"

Lorrimer made no reply. A strange glow brightened over his face, and his hazel eyes gazed sternly on the vacant air.

"I say Lorrimer," began Petriken, but a fierce scowl on the brow of the Libertine silenced him.

Without a word, Lorrimer strode slowly away from his companions, and passing through the State House, hurried rapidly along Chesnut street.

His manly form, his handsome face, attracted many a look, many a gaze of admiration. But that heaving of the chest, that flashing of the hazel eye! Little did the fair dames who gazed upon the handsome Libertine, dream of the Hell that raged within his bosom.

Christmas Eve, the River and the Death, glided like a warning from Eternity before his dilating eyes. Dim and shadow-like yet terrible, the VISION rushed upon his Soul.

It was nine o'clock, when a hackney coach, driven by a Negro, whose hideous face, afforded a strange contrast to his rich livery of dark green, stopped before the door of Widow Smolby's house.

A man of slight form somewhat bent with years leaped from the couch, and knocked at the door of the dreary mansion. His long dark robe, faced with furs, attracted the attention of some inquisitive neighbors, who from their doors or windows took observation of his appearance; and his sallow face, illumined by eyes of impenetrable darkness and relieved by masses of long black hair, hanging loosely about his shoulders, excited the wonder of some casual bystanders. He was evidently a strange man, as the old lady gossips have it, and his appearance, in the streets of matter-of-fact Philadelphia, robed in this picturesque costume, was a subject of more than common wonder among the intelligent shopkeepers of the place.

The door of the Widow Smolby's house was presently opened, and a thick voice demanded the object of the visitor.

"Wot's the row," said the voice as a rubicand face appeared in the doorway. "Is the President dead or has he only sent for Easy Larkspur to go on a foreign mission? What is it?"

It was evident that Easy Larkspur had been wounded in a combat with a flagon of whiskey punch. His breath was fragrant and his eyes were winking to quick music.

"I would see the young lady who sought refuge in this house, last night," exclaimed Ravoni in his commanding tone.

"You would, would you? Which young lady for instance? Bess and the Blue-eye girl went away an hour arter the old 'oman's funeral, and the Black-eyed female sits all alone up stairs a-moanin' like the north-wind thro' a key-hole. You see stranger I'm left here until the Crowner comes back—"

"The lady up stairs is the one I wish to see," replied Ravoni. "Tell her, that I bear a message from her father—"

"Jist walk up an' tell her yourself," muttered Larkspur. "Come in stranger. You ought to seen the old 'oman's funeral! It took place at sunrise, and devil a preacher was at the grave to do a prayer. Giminy! Merself and the crowner's depitty was chief mourners. Did'n't we do the groans?"

Closing the door, Larkspur led Ravoni through the front room on the first floor.

"Now sir, up two pair o' stairs in the front room you'll find the gal. And look ye! There's three or four maniac cats and a parrit, a-prowlin' about unchained. If you see 'em kick 'em for my sake! Wot I've suffered with them cats durin' the night imagination *may* conceive, but pen *can't* depict—the devils! While I was drinkin' my punch last night—*mi-a-w, spit, phiz!*—they puts into my hair, and me not sayin' a word—"

Ravoni left the gentleman in the midst of his philosophic meditations, and ascending the stairs, in a few moments, stood before the door of the front room on the third floor.

"Now for this Mad Girl," he muttered as he gently opened the door. "This Mad Girl who fancies—ha, ha, that she is not the *child* of her *father!*"

He prepared himself for the sight of a gibbering idiot, and entered the Ghost Chamber.

One step forward, and he receded, folding his arms as he gazed in silent wonder upon the unexpected vision that met his sight. In the dim light that came through the purple curtains of a window, flung open to the sunlight for the first time in seventeen years, sat a fair young girl, dressed in white, her hands clasped listlessly together, while the transparent paleness of her face, was beautifully relieved by her dark hair which hung in a thick mass along the cheek turned from the light, and then fell drooping over her shoulder. Her eyes were downcast, and the trembling eyelashes rested upon the alabaster of each cheek.

"And this is the Mad Girl!" muttered Ravoni advancing. "By my life she looks not like a living thing, but like a carved statue of some pure and holy Enthusiasm!"

Mabel raised her eyes, and gazed upon the portrait above the mantel. A soft moisture glistened in each dark eye, and a burning glow crimsoned the centre of each pale cheek.

"My mother," she muttered, and then with a start, beheld the deep eyes of the Sorcerer fixed upon her.

"Start not my child," he cried in his low and musical voice. "I come to lead you to your father!"

"To my father! Sooner than return to his doors again, would I beg my bread on the highway, sooner far sooner would I———"

"Nay, nay," interrupted Ravoni, "I speak not of the *imposter*, who has so darkly wronged you, but of your *father!*" How his musical voice lingered on that word!

True to the instructions which he had received from Pyne on the night previous, he now placed the note which the Parson had written, in the hands of the wondering girl.

"Ha!" she exclaimed, as she raised the note to the light. "It is a message from my father! 'MABEL, my own child, so long lost to me, but now forever mine, trust yourself without fear in the hands of the bearer of this note: he will lead you to your father, to—LIVINGSTONE.' Oh joy, joy! I am ready Sir!" she cried with a radiant countenance, as she extended her hands toward the Sorcerer.

"What, without hat or cloak?" said he playfully. "You love your *father* then?"

"Oh Sir, my heart beats freer at the word. Lead me, lead me to him, to my father!"

Seizing an ancient and threadbare cloak, which had once rested on the form of her mother, from a chest near the bed, she flung it over her shoulders and stood ready to depart.

A calm yet meaning smile broke over the face of Ravoni, as he led her down the stairs, and lingered around his expressive lips as he handed her into the carriage.

"And this child with the beaming face and the speaking eye is the Mad Girl," he muttered as he sprang in the carriage and closed the door. "Ho, ho! My parson, you have entrusted your treasure to the Lion's mouth!"

A muttered word in a foreign tongue was the signal to the Negro in green livery; and the coach rattled away over the rough paving stones.

Larkspur looked from the front door in mute and drunken wonder.

"Does'nt that beat pigeon-shooting? To come an' take the gal from under my wery eyes without so much as sayin' thankee! Does'nt it beat 'possum huntin'? I hope to grasshus some old nigger will take me as a 'prentice to the wood splittin' business arter that! Howsomdever," he muttered as he closed the door, "I must go and rig up as Major Rappahannock Mulhill says, and to-night—ho, ho! Won't we nab the murderer of the old woman? Bessie did'nt tell me nothin'—oh no!"

Meanwhile the carriage rolled on, while Ravoni sate gazing steadily in the beautiful face of Mabel. She felt a strange awe steal over her, as the gleam of those dark eyes seemed to look into her soul.

"And she shall be the Priestess of Ravoni!" muttered the Sorcerer.

"And I shall see my father!" cried the fair girl in a joyous tone. "At last I shall find a home!"

"*Here* you shall see your father, *here* you shall find a home!"

As Ravoni spoke the carriage stopped before the gloomy house, whose bricks were painted a dull and tasteless yellow.

With a throbbing heart, Mabel leaped from the carriage, with every vein fired by emotion, she ascended the marble steps, and as the door slowly opened, a wild cry of joy burst from her lips, and she entered the—Den of the Sorcerer.

Ravoni cast one look at the bright sun, ere he disappeared within the door, and his large eyes, dilating and burning with a lustre that was super-human, seemed to behold some gorgeous landscape, denied to all other sight.

"And she shall be the Priestess of Ravoni!"

CHAPTER FIFTH

THE DISSECTING ROOM

A tall thin man, attired in a close fitting great coat, was hurrying along Walnut street. His face, marked by thick eye-brows and an aquiline nose, and imbued with an expression of deep thought, was drooped upon his chest, and while his hands were buried in his coat pockets, he muttered to himself as he hurried along.

"Beautiful operation that would be—beautiful! To take a man's skull off, look at his brains, and then fasten it on again! Beautiful! They say it's done in Paris. Ha! Hum! Byrnewood that you? Heard anything of your sister yet? Sad thing that—your father told me all about it—sad thing!"

"It is indeed Doctor," exclaimed Byrnewood, as he took McTorniquet by the hand. "Had I but a single clue to the mystery, I would follow it to the death. But this utter darkness is worse than death itself!"

"Never mind, my boy, never mind; clear up after awhile; clear up I say!" cried the good hearted Doctor, drawing Byrnewood's arm within his own. "Bye the bye, Byrnewood did ye ever read those accounts of '*burking*' folks in London? Five men hung at once for murdering *live* people, in order to sell their bodies to the Doctors! Its my opinion that that same thing is done in this good Quaker City."

A terrible suspicion flashed over Byrnewood's soul.

"My God!" he exclaimed, "This singular disappearance of my sister —no traces of her after she left my father's house on Wednesday night— not a word or sign of her since the moment she crossed the threshold of her home! Doctor, it is a horrible thought,—" He dared not syllable forth that thought in words. *The dead body of his sister laid on the foul altar of a dissecting table!*

"Nonsense, nonsense," exclaimed the Doctor, reading Byrnewood's suspicion in his look. "Come with me my boy, I want to preach you a sermon on *Popular Credulity*. You have heard something of a man they call the Signior Ravoni?"

"I have."

"He arrived in this city almost a year ago, coming from God knows whence, and going the devil cares where. Well, this Italian or Frenchman, or Turk or Jew, no sooner puts his foot on the soil of the Quaker City, than he astonishes the Faculty; strikes Science dumb; plucks Theology by the beard, and in fact walks over everybody's notions on everything.—"

"How does he do all this?"

"That's the mystery. He walked into our Medical Halls unbidden, and proved himself a great Anatomist, a splendid Surgeon. No one has had the bravery or impudence to question him concerning his former life, because there's a cold impenetrable gleam in his eye, that few men would like to brave—"

"You spoke of his knowledge of Theology?"

"There it is again. I know several of our first Divines. This Ravoni walked into their houses, unknown and unbidden, and astonished them, *first*, by his knowledge of the theory and philosophy of the Reformation, *second*, by his daring and atrocious sophistries—"

"And the lawyers?"

"He knocks away their most elaborate arguments, constructed with all the care that a child devotes to making a baby-house out of its toys, with one clear word of practical reason, that is worth a world of legal tom-foolery. The lawyers and the judges hate him worse than poison!"

"You spoke of *Popular Credulity*, Doctor—"

"An unknown Pretender appears in the Quaker City, and lo! Everybody hastens to entrust him with their own lives, and the lives of those they love. You ask how? He gives out that he will cure the Insane, and before a day is past he has an hundred patients under his care."

"Does he cure them?"

"Ha, ha! The ugly ones he cures, and returns to their relatives with all possible despatch. But the women, and the *handsome* women, ho, ho! 'It will require *time*,' is his invariable answer. And then he has established a Lecture Room, where he gives lectures on Anatomy. Egad! our students are crazy with the fellow—"

"You said just now that he was a skilful anatomist?"

"I never saw one half as good! But I'll tell you what annoys me! This Ravoni has given out that he will reveal some important discoveries in Anatomy at the hour of ten precisely, this morning at his Lecture Room. He pretends that he has discovered some new Theory of the origin of life, which he will illustrate by the dissection of a subject. This annoys me!"

"Why?"

"Because I believe its all humbug, and the fact that our Professors seem to place some confidence in the fellow, furnishes me with a very good illustration of the popular disposition to believe in—*moonshine!*"

"You will attend the Lecture?"

"Of course. Should you like to witness a dissection of the human subject? It's quite a treat to the uninitiated. Come along with me."

The fearful suspicion which had crossed Byrnewood's mind, not many minutes past, now returned in all its vigor. The dead body of his sister on the dissecting table!

"I will go with you!" he said, and they turned into a southern street, and after the lapse of a few minutes stood before the House of Ravoni.

"We enter the Dissecting Hall by this alley," said Dr. M'Torniquet, leading the way along the narrow avenue on the east of the mansion. "Did you ever see my blood horse Harry Clay?"

Ere Byrnewood could answer this characteristic question, the Doctor pushed open a small door which was the only object that varied the massive side of the mansion, from the pavement to the roof. He then led the way up three flights of stairs, so narrow and confined, that there was barely room for one man to pass at a time, between the walls. The last of these stairs terminated in an extensive corridor, which traversed the entire width of the building, with the doors of various rooms fashioned in its walls, and a wide window at either end, giving light to the passage.

They traversed the corridor from east to west, and then stood before a door of dark mahogany.

"First we enter the Dissecting Hall," said the Doctor as he pushed open the door. Nodding to the hideous Negro, who attired in the green livery, worn by all the attendants of Ravoni, stood watching within the door. M'Torniquet led Byrnewood into the centre of the hall.

It was a long and narrow room, with a lofty ceiling and snow-white floor. It was lighted by five large windows on the western side; and two on the southern end of the room. The walls were white and bare and blank, without a solitary object to relieve their monotony of hue. Around the room, between the windows and along the walls, were placed some twenty oblong tables, each standing in the full glare of the sunlight, which poured freely over the ghastly spectacles peculiar to the place. Bending over each table was a young man, whose long hair and characteristic look of frankness and recklessness combined, betrayed the Medical Student of the Quaker City. At some of the tables were groups of two and three, talking earnestly together, knife in hand all the while, and the whole body of students wore the same dark apron reaching to the shoulders, and each arm was defended by a false sleeve of coarse muslin. And on each table, sweltering and festering in the sunlight, lay the remains of woman and child and a man. Here was a grisly trunk, there an arm, there a leg, and yonder a solitary hand occupied the attention of the Student. Rare relics of the Temple which yesterday enshrined a Soul, born of the Living God!

Here a ghastly head, placed upright, with the livid lips parted in a hideous grin, received the gay light of the sun, full on its glassy eyeballs, there a mass of flesh and sinews and bones, shone in the beams of the morning, as corruption only can shine. A Soul once shone from those eyes, a voice once spoke from those lips!

Here lay an arm, whose soft and beautiful outlines, were terminated by a small and graceful hand, and over the alabaster arm and the snowy hand, the blue taint of decay spread like a foul curse, turning loveliness into loathing. There in the full glare of the sunlight was spread a reeking trunk, lopped short below the waist, with loathsomeness and beauty combined in one horrible embrace. The head had been severed and below the purple neck two white globes, the bosom of what had once been woman, were perceptible in the light. And the Rainbow of corruption crept like a foul serpent around that bosom. For Corruption has its Rainbow; and blue and red and purple and grey and pink and orange were mingled together on that trunk in one repulsive mass of decay. And on this fair bosom hands of affection had been pressed, or sweet young children had nestled; or maybe the white skin had crimsoned to a lover's kiss!

Byrnewood passed slowly along the room, gazing around in mingled wonder and loathing, while the lively conversation of the students broke strangely on his ear.

"I say Bob, this must have been a jolly old chap!" cried a young gentleman whose snub nose harmonized with his wide mouth and cross eyes. "No doubt these lips have opened with several thousand jolly grins in their time—now look at them! Pah! How blue and livid!"

And he tossed the head of the old man down upon the table, twining his fingers in the white hairs, while his knife severed the flesh from the brow.

"Sweet girl, this was once upon a time! Many a poor devil has been dying for love of her eyes and lips. Just now she dont look altogether loveable. The eyes starting from their sockets, and the lips falling to pieces! And then the bosom, ha, ha! The Scalpel makes love to it now!"

And the sunbeams glistened upon the blade of the knife as it plyed briskly over the livid flesh.

"Wonder how many people have shaken hands with this old fellow?" muttered another student, with dark eyes and stiff lank black hair. "Just look at this hand—old and withered and hardened by toil. How these cramped fingers have clutched at the dollars and the pennies —ha, ha!"

"This woman wore a deuced pretty shoe; I'll bet a dollar she did!" exclaimed a withered little man in a bald head and gold spectacles. "Did ever you see such a foot? And the toes, and the instep, and then what an ankle! Wonder who knit her stockings!"

"He, he, he!" laughed a young Student in tow-colored hair and a pear nose. "Jist look at that—good, capital!"

He had placed the mangled body of a dead man, against the wall in a sitting posture, with the knees drawn up to the chin, and the right hand fixed between one knee and the face, with the fingers outspread and the thumb pressed upon the nose, in a gesture very much the vogue among dirty little boys, rowdies, and cabmen.

"Is'n't that the touch?" laughed the tow-haired Student. "Does'n't he say '*Cant come it!*' plain as chalk? And then that eye half shut—is'n't the wink perfect!"

"Ha, ha! Ho! Ho! Good—capital!" chorused some dozen students.

And over the livid brow of the dead man, who sat erect in this attitude of grotesque mockery, streamed the yellow sunshine coloring the leaden eyeballs and the hanging lip with hues of vivid gold.

"There," murmured Doctor M'Torniquet, who had been silent for the last few minutes, "There my boy you see the respect paid by living dust to dead ashes! Consoling sight; is'n't it?"

"Lead me from this place," muttered Byrnewood, "The air is foul with corruption; I'm in no mood to look upon scenes like these!"

"Come this way," answered M'Torniquet, "Ravoni is about to reveal his wonderful discovery in the Amphitheatre."

Opening a small door in one side of the Dissecting Room, the Doctor led Byrnewood along a dark and narrow passage, which terminated in another door. Pushing gently against this door a blaze of light streamed upon the passage, and the Doctor entered the Amphitheatre, with Byrnewood at his side.

The vivid rays of a gas light streamed down upon the square table of the Lecturer, placed near the wall in the centre of the Amphitheatre. Around and above this table rose thick tiers of benches, arranged in the form of a half circle, and ascending in easy gradation from the floor to the ceiling of the spacious room. A partition of painted board separated the table of the Lecturer from his audience, and immediately in front was the main entrance to the Amphitheatre, forming an alley in the centre of the room, with tiers of benches on either side.

The place was thronged by a dense array of spectators. Faces arose above faces, from the floor to the ceiling. Some four or five hundred students from the various Medical Schools of the Quaker City, had assembled in the Lecture Room, anxious to witness the wonderful discovery, announced by Ravoni. The singular mystery which enveloped the man, his profuse charity to all poor students who came within his notice, his enormous charges to the opulent class of medical aspirants, the large mansion which he had furnished in a style of oriental magnificence, the various strange stories which floated on the current of popular rumor in relation to his former life—all these things combined had not only excited the curiosity of the students, but of their Masters. The grave faces of Doctor and Professor were seen amid the reckless visages of long-haired sons of Virginia, and swarthy striplings from Alabama.

The devil-dare Carolinian with his unstrapped boots resting on the next bench below his seat, was companioned by the care-worn man of science with gold spectacles on his hooked nose. The lean Yankee, the round-faced Pennsylvanian, the pale and emaciated youth of Philadelphia, the blustering Hoosier from the far west, all were mingled together in that motley crowd. Ravoni had announced a great discovery in medical science; his tickets were free, his invitation general to all the faculty, and to every man and boy of the students under their care, and therefore his Lecture Room was brimming full.

Byrnewood and McTorniquet found each a vacant seat close beside the Lecturer's table. Scarce had they time to seat themselves and glance around, when the green-baize door at the head of the principal passage which divided the Lecture Room in the centre, was thrown suddenly open, and two uncouth men bearing a burden on their shoulders, came forward with hurried footsteps.

They laid their burden on the table, and every eye beheld the outlines of a corpse, as it lay with its stiffened limbs concealed in the folds of a tattered white overcoat.

A light footstep was now heard from the narrow passage, by which Byrnewood had entered, and in an instant Ravoni stood beside the table, his sallow cheeks and thoughtful brow, warming with a slight flush as the loud welcome of the audience broke like thunder on his ear.

Ravoni gazed into the faces of the two men who stood before him. Their visages would have hung them in any Christian community. Their faces had been unshaven for days, and a stiff red beard mingling with the lank red hair that covered their foreheads, gave a cut-throat look to each visage. They stood with their eyes fixed upon the floor, as though they feared to look into the face of a living man.

"From whence did you bring this subject?" said Ravoni in a low whisper.

"From the poor man's grave in the Alms-house grave-yard," answered the tallest of the Resurrectionists. "Yer honor knows there's one grave which is the prope'ty o' th' Doctors? Any body what dies in the Almshouse and hai'nt got no friends to claim him, is put into this grave, and the d——l himself may take him if he likes.

"Ven yer honer's done with that body I should like to have my great coat again," observed the short Body-stealer in a mild and polite whisper.

"We got the subject in the night, Sir, and wrapped it up in that great coat, and it hai'nt been opened since. Hope it 'ill suit yer honer?"

Ravoni waved his hands and the Body-stealers tramped out of the Lecture Room.

Every eye was now centered upon Ravoni. Some wild burst of his accustomed eloquence was anticipated, some rhapsody which mingling the sublime and the mystic, would rouse the hearts of the auditors into wonder and enthusiasm. But no word passed from his lips. In silence he proceeded to lay bare the corpse. Glancing at the case of instruments placed on one corner of the table, he slowly flung aside the tattered overcoat which enveloped the dead man.

There was an awful silence. Every eye beheld the corpse, and every heart grew cold with dread. Ravoni himself at the sight of that hideous spectacle started backward with a pale cheek and a trembling lip. Then the first awful pause of terror was past, and a murmured cry of horror shook the room.

There, there on the dissecting table, lay the corpse, its features set in death and its blue eye-balls glaring on the ceiling, but it was not the '*subject*' anticipated by Ravoni or his pupils. From head to foot, along the trunk and over each limb, that corpse was all one cankering sore, one loathsome blotch. Features on the face there were none; brow and lip and cheek were all one hideous ulcer. The eye-balls were spotted with clotted blood; the mouth a cavern of corruption; the very hair was thick with festering pollution. It was the corpse of a man who had died from that terrible of all diseases, the most infectious of all epidemics, a curse at whose name beauty shudders and grave science grows pale—the small-pox. Better to look into the plague-pit where man and woman and babe lay mingled together, one reeking mass of quick lime and gory flesh, then to have gazed upon that corpse extended on the Dissecting table before the eyes of five hundred living men!

Every man in that room felt his danger, as that ghastly sight dashed ice into his heart. Every man knew that there was infection in every breath he drew, that there was a death linked with every atom that floated in the air.

Ravoni stood silent and pale. There he stood with eternal youth in his veins but in his twelve brief hours, he might lay a foul thing of ulcers and blotches, like the corse before his eyes. For the common phases of this disease, there were remedies; but let a single infectious atom breathed from the lips of a corse like this, enter the lips of living man, and no arm under God's sky could bring relief.

To lay a corse, with no calm beauty speaking from the pale brow, no gentle smile moulding the livid lips! To lay a mass of gory flesh and stagnant blood, to decay before your last hour, to anticipate the rottenness of the grave while life yet lingers in your veins! That thought, paled even the cheek of Ravoni, and the spectators, Doctors, Student and Professor, were spell-bound with a fear worse than death.

A wild cry of horror shook the room, and then in one mass the audience rushed toward the door. It was a living picture of a panic. With one movement they swept from the benches, with one bound they sprang into the narrow passage, and then another wild cry added horror to the scene. The main door opened *into* the room, and the crowd blocked up against its panels, were helpless as a child in a tiger's cage. Still Ravoni stood silent and pale, regarding the loathsome corse with a fixed stare.

Then moving as one mass, with a force like the impulse of a battering ram, the dense throng rushed against the door, crushing all who stood near its panels until they howled in very agony, and then came another rush and another yell! There was a wild crashing sound; the door gave way; splintered into fragments it fell before the living mass, and through the opened passage, the panic-stricken crowd rushed from the place of death.

Ravoni still was beside the corse. The crowd was gone but a young man, with long black hair and a flashing eye, stood by his side. It was Byrnewood Arlington. He too had seen the crowd, he too had looked upon the corse, he too had felt some throbbings of the panic, which like a heart of terror, palpitated in the air of room, but he still stood silent and firm, tho' ashy pale. The Doctor had fled from his side with an involuntary shriek of fear, the face of the Sorcerer himself had grown pale, but the awful mystery resting like a nightmare upon the soul of Byrnewood Arlington left no room for a lesser terror.

"Thou hast a firm soul," said Ravoni in that low toned voice, which was music to the ear that heard it. "Thou hast a firm soul!"

He laid his hand on Byrnewood's shoulder as he spoke, and the magnetic ray of his eye, held the glance of the young man enchained to his own. A strange sympathy for the being before him, fluttered through Byrnewood's heart.

"Thou hast a firm soul," spoke the Sorcerer, "And by my soul, yes" he added setting his teeth together, while his eyes shone and his brow warmed with a sudden enthusiasm, "By the Soul of Ravoni thou shall be one of the Chosen; thou shalt be a Priest of the Faith!"

"The Faith?" echoed young Arlington.

"The new Faith which shall arise over the ashes of the creeds and superstitions of this day. The Faith which dwelt in the hearts of men, ere the Sword of the Jew or the Cross of the Christian or the Crescent of the Sorcerer arose on the horizon of man's soul, scattering pestilence and death, wherever they flashed or shone! That Faith, buried for long, long centuries which man in the olden time, in the world's youth of promise, loved and cherished, which raised him to godhead, and made the Universe itself his own, that Faith will we raise from the grim ruins of fable and superstition! And the old Faith, revised and re-created shall be our New Religion of hope to Man!"

The words of the Sorcerer were wild and strange, but his look and tone, were lightning and music to Byrnewood's soul. He was awed, he was fascinated. Slowly he reached forth his arm, and with his eyes fixed on the eyes of Ravoni, he seized the Sorcerer by the hand.

"*This hour shalt thou behold the dead arise!*" exclaimed Ravoni with his deep dark eyes, alive with the rays of magnetic power. "Come!"

"Ho, ho, ho!" laughed a rough voice. "The doctor and the students all skeered to death by a bundle o' small pox! Woders how that 'ill vurk?"

And hurrying from the secret passage, Devil-Bug emerged into the light, his distorted face convulsed with sneering laughter and his solitary eye twinkling in hideous glee, while his tangled hair fell thickly over his protuberant brow.

Byrnewood started at the sound of that voice; he advanced toward the savage. Devil-Bug beheld him, and turned pale.

"What!" he shouted, "Another sperrit come to ha'nt me? Ho, ho! There 'll be a miliskey muster of 'em arter a while! There—there lays the man with his jaw broke and his tongue lollin' out—there, right at my feet is the old woman with the blood a droppin' from the holler skull—but *this* feller!"

With his talon fingers extended he turned aside his head, while his frame quivered with emotion.

"I have seen you before!" cried Byrnewood laying his hand on the arm of the monster. "I have seen you, and———"

"A sperrit could'n't grip me that way!" muttered Devil-Bug, "I see how it is—he escaped from the well, tho' the boards cracked from under him and here he is with his ricollecshun destroyed by the drug!"

"I have seen you before," repeated Byrnewood in a whispered voice, inaudible to Ravoni. "Tell me, oh tell me—"

He would have demanded his sister of the savage, but a wild laugh drowned his words.

"You've seen me afore? Werry likely young man. Public charact'rs like the President and me, is to be seen most any day in the week, by sich persons as likes! And then my name young man, my name is pe*coo*liar—You know it among ten thousand—my name is *sich* a sing'lar one! It's *Jones*, young man, nothin' but *Jones!*"

"Madman!" muttered Ravoni advancing. "Do you trifle in my presence? Away—and to your watch! See that no one enters the chamber beside whose door I placed you this morning—Begone!"

Devil-Bug trembled beneath the glance of his eye, like a raven who dreads the attack of an eagle. He slunk quietly into the secret passage, and in a moment was gone.

"Come!" said Ravoni in a whisper, as he placed Byrnewood's arm within his own. "You shall behold the Miracle!"

Ten thousand thoughts whirled through Byrnewood's brain. The grief of his father and mother, the mystery which enveloped the fate of his sister, and then the sweet smiling face of that sister, with her brown hair waving along her rose-bud cheeks, all were present with him, and his soul was a chaos with uncertain gleams of light playing over the summit of tossing clouds. But the eyes of Ravoni were fixed upon him; he felt his veins fire and his heart kindle as that glare shot into his soul, like a ray of light from the eternal world.

"I go with you!" he whispered and his pale cheek glowed with a new fire, and his dark eye gathered a strange light.

CHAPTER SIXTH

THE FIRST MIRACLE OF THE NEW FAITH

The taint of corruption and the breath of incense, the shrouded form of the dead and the dark-robed figure of the Sorcerer, the commanding forehead, over-arching eyes that sent forth rays of majestic power, and the pale brows of enthusiasts lit by eyes hollow with watching, and flashing with unnatural light, these all were there, in that chamber of the New Faith.

It was a spacious chamber, circular in shape with lofty walls, and a wide ceiling, which in the centre arose into a dome. From this dome, a star of burning light flung its lustre down over the centre of the chamber, while from the dim shadows of the room, white columns of incense wound slowly upward, like the hope of a true soul gleaming through the darkness of its despair.

In the centre of that chamber all was light, while beyond, save the snowy columns of incense, all was darkness. And in the centre of the chamber, beneath the moon-like radiance of the light falling from the dome, was a strange and fearful spectacle, more like a wild dream on a picture of some olden-time tradition, than a plain and palpable reality.

An altar white as snow arose in the light, with its drapery falling in gentle folds down to the sable floor. On one side of the altar, calm and impassive stood Ravoni, gazing intently upon the faces of twenty-four young men, who sate grouped along the floor on the opposite side, their eyes enchained to his glance with a singular intensity.

These young men were Students, gleaned by Ravoni from the various medical schools, and from the haunts and nooks of the wide city. The light shone over haggard faces, high pale foreheads, well developed in the ideal organs, and white hands tremblingly grasping rolls of manuscript. There was a wild light shining from the eyes of every one of the twenty-four, a fixed glare, a feverish and unhealthy brightness. It was the meteor light of fanaticism. Their careless attire, their long hair flung loosely over each shoulder, their fixed gaze and their statue-like stillness, all betrayed the absorbing and painful interest with which they awaited the words of the Sorcerer.

And among the foremost, pale and wild as the palest and wildest of them all sate Byrnewood Arlington. He too, gazed upon the face of Ravoni with a woven brow and flashing eye. His hands were convulsively clasped upon his knees, and his under lip was pressed between his teeth.

And on the altar, lay a stiffened corpse, whose outlines were dimly seen through the folds of a white cloth, flung lightly over each icy limb. There was beauty in that corpse, and grace, for the cloth was moulded into soft folds, as though it veiled a woman's form. The feet were thrust upward, the arms folded over the chest, and the globes of the bosom rose gently in the light, even beneath their thick disguise. The face, like the form was veiled from the gaze, yet the outlines of a countenance, which death had only made more sternly beautiful, were clear and apparent.

Ravoni stood by the altar and the corpse, his slight form clad in robes of deep sable, while his long black hair fell wild and lank about his shoulders. There was an unusual expression stamped upon his face, not manifested indeed in any violent working of the muscles, or sudden contortion of the features. All was calm, and yet it was a calm full of omen. The scornful lips pressed tightly together, the nostrils quivering with a scarcely perceptible motion, the forehead, high, wide and massive, impressed with a look of conscious mind, and the eyes, dark, full and thoughtful, glaring a light that sent forth rays like a star. There was a silent intensity of thought revealed in every line of that pale countenance.

And the light from the dome streamed over the dark robes and pale brow of Ravoni, over the white cloth which revealed the outlines of the corpse, and upon the faces of the Students, who sate waiting in awed silence for the words of their master, while up from the dark corners of the room curled the white incense, strewing the air with grateful perfume, and the shadows with scarfs of snowy mist.

Ravoni gazed upon the faces of the Students, and then his lips moved, but no sound broke upon the air.

He was about to make a dread and awful experiment, not with machinery of wood or iron, or with the air or the lightning in its bosom, or with the earth or the secrets of its depths, but with something more terrible than all, the Soul of Man.

For a moment, a voice seemed whispering in his ear, a voice speaking from the Invisible world to his soul, words of strange import.

"Ravoni there is a God! Ravoni there is a God! Blaspheme not his name!"

In a low and musical tone he spoke of the New Faith, while the voice within was whispering unceasingly to his soul.

"There has been too much of God," were the first words he uttered. "There has been too much of God in all the creeds of the world! Where-ever Fanaticism has raised its fanes, there the name of God has been mouthed by the foul lips of priests.

"The Hindoo mother gives her child to the Ganges in the name of God, and the car of Juggernaut crushes its thousands, who shriek that name as they are mingled in one gory massacre!

"The torch of St. Bartholemew was lit in the name of God, the fair fields of Ireland have been soaked with the blood of her children, while that name shrieked in every musket shot! Europe has been desolated in the name of God! In a single foul and atrocious war, nine million souls went down to one bloody grave, because they did not believe with their King that the God-head centered in a paltry wafer! The name of God was shrieked by booted troopers and cowled priests over their desolate hearth-sides, over a land rich in graves and blood!

"In this fair land of the New World, the children of the Forest were hunted and butchered in the name of God! It mingled with cry of death and it shrieked in the blood-hounds yell! Helpless women and aged men were burnt by grim sectarians, who gazed upon the blackened flesh of their victims, and shouted glory to the name of God!

"In this name earth has been desolated ten thousand times and ten thousand times again. In this name home has been made a hell, the gardens of the world transformed into howling deserts, the heart of man changed into a devil! In this name blood has flown in rivers, and in this name earth has been made a pest-house, with its valleys levelled into plains, and its hills raised into mountains with the heaps of dead!

"These things have been done in the name of God! You may say that they were the work of ignorance, of superstition, of fanaticism, but still that blistering fact, stands out from the history of the world, *these crimes were done in the name of God!*

"*Now!*" and his voice rose into a tone of absorbing enthusiasm, while his white hand undulated over the corpse. "*Now!* Aye *now* the time has come, when something for *man* should be done in the name of MAN!"

A wild murmur of applause trembled from lip to lip. The dark eyes of the twenty-four enthusiasts shone with the wild light of fanaticism.

Byrnewood Arlington leaned forward with flashing eyes and parted lips while he felt his soul drawn to Ravoni by a strange yet irresistible sympathy. Ever and anon his eyes wandered to the corse, and with a shudder he withdrew his gaze from the spectacle of death. A dim suspicion crept over him, that the form of his sister lay on that altar, a lifeless corse. It was a horrible thought, and in his soul he knew it false and baseless, yet whenever he glanced upon the white cloth which shrouded the face of the dead, *it was his sister that lay there!*

"In the name of MAN and for the good of MAN shall our new Faith arise!" exclaimed Ravoni in his deep toned voice. "Yet think not that Ravoni denies God! No, no! Over the body of the dead, I preach unto you a pure and merciful God! Through all matter, through sun and sky and earth and air, he lives, the soul of the Universe! We are all beams of his light, rays of his sun; as imperishable as his own glory! To us all, he has entrusted powers, awful and sublime. Think not because these powers may never be manifested that they do not exist. They are all in us, and in us for good.

"All men from the slave to the prince, from the dull boor to the man of genius, are connected with each other by an universal sympathy, an invisible influence on which souls float and undulate like rays in the sunshiny air. This* influence or sympathy, call it what you will, is the atmosphere of souls, the life of intellects!

"Some men absorbing a larger portion of this invisible life than others, become men of genius, warriors or statesmen.

"And through the long and drear and bloody history of this world are recorded instances of mighty souls, who appeared on the earth, gifted with powers that made men worship them as Gods. These men were thoroughly imbued with the atmosphere in which the soul breathes thoughts of God-ship. These intellects were known as Saviours, Prophets, Reformers. They were distinguished by an irresistible power, which beaming from the brow or flashing from the eye, awed and subdued the souls of the million. These men demonstrated the great truth, that the AWFUL SOUL having created us, hath left us all to our own salvation or our ruin, as we shall by our deeds determine; thus we shape our own destinies; that we are the masters of our own lives; that we, by developing the mysteries implanted in our bosoms, may walk the earth superior to the clay around us, each man *a* GOD *in soul!*"

* It may be presumed that a reference is intended to the doctrine of magnetic influence, pervading all space, and linking man to man, and man to God, by the same awful and immutable power.

Vain were it to depict that outstretched hand, that flashing eye, that look and port of mystery! As one man, the twenty-four students rose to their feet, and a dark-eyed youth tossed his arms wildly on high, and muttered with white lips, "Ravoni is a God—Ravoni is a God!"

And the murmur broke over the throng in a whisper full of meaning "Ravoni is a God—Ravoni is a God!"

The light from the dome fell over the Sorcerer, the Corse and the enthusiasts, while up from the shadows of the chamber, wound the columns of snowy incense.

"As ye all may be gods, so am I a God! As ye all may look into the bosom of the Universe, and make the secrets of nature your own, train the lightnings to your will, and sweep the souls of men in adoration at your feet, so have I done!

"And you my chosen Priests will I bind together in a high and solemn Brotherhood, as the first ministers at the altars of the Faith! In silence and in mystery will we compass the wide land, selecting our converts from the mass, as we shall know them worthy of our mysteries, and adding them one by one to our holy brotherhood! No loud prayers in the tinselled church, no vapid trumpetings of our godliness from street to corners, but slowly and silently and in power will we work for the New Faith, built in the name of MAN for the good of MAN!"

Well had Ravoni chosen his converts from the young, the hopeful, the enthusiastic! His words uttered in that deep music of tone which mingling with the syllables of speech, can allure the human soul to good or evil, struck the mysterious chords of every heart. They were no longer the same men. Every face was stamped with an excitement that corded the veins on the forehead, and fired the eyes with a blaze like that which streamed from the dark orbs of Ravoni. It was a terrible picture of Fanaticism.

"We are thine!" they shouted in one voice raising their hands in the light, "We are thine!"

Byrnewood Arlington was no more himself. He stood amid that throng with an eye blazing and a hand uplifted. "We are thine!" he joined in the chorus of fanatics. "*I* am thine!" he shouted in a voice that rolled to the dome above, "*I* am thine!"

There was silence for a moment. A picture of Sorcery, Death and Fanaticism! The form of Ravoni with the uplifted hand, the throng of frenzied enthusiasts, and the still corse of the dead. On the brow of Ravoni sat calmness and grandeur, while his eye shone with a brightness all its own; the still corse, in its stern quietude presenting an emblem of rest; the fanatics crowding in a group with uplifted hands joined together, and faces quivering with emotion, while the soft light showered down upon the scene from the dome overhead, and the incense ascended evermore from the dim shadows of the chamber.

"Ye shall witness a proof of my power," exclaimed Ravoni. "You all behold the Corse laid prostrate on this altar. When the Corse arises from the sleep of death, then shall our Faith commence its reign———"

A murmur of wonder interrupted the words of the Sorcerer.

"I tell you the dead shall arise!" exclaimed Ravoni, and then in short and vivid sentences, he described the Mysteries of life and death.

As thought after thought fell from his lips, his manner grew more animated, the interest of his hearers more intense. His treatment of the subject manifested immense research combined with ingenius sophistry. Now dealing in wild rhapsody, and now giving one of his points of argument, all the clearness of a mathematical demonstration, he averred in plain terms that the dead might be raised to life. He dimly insinuated a belief in the principle of eternal youth, and then gave a cursory yet forcible glance at the long history of the search after a 'universal solvent,' which would change the baser metals into solid gold.

His hearers were wrapt, silent, and motionless. Every point of his argument stood displayed before them like a palpable thing.

"I will raise the dead before your eyes!" he exclaimed yet again, as he surveyed the faces of his auditors. "It is now within five minutes of noonday. At the hour of noon, the Corse before you shall arise!"

Then folding his arms across his breast he strode slowly up and down the floor beside the altar. Now was the moment for his face to manifest an agitation tenfold more powerful than the emotion displayed by the most enthusiastic of the students. That frowning brow beneath which the half-hidden eyeball gleamed with fixed and glassy light, that lip quivering with a tremulous motion, those white hands clutching nervously at the chest! Can it be that the Sorcerer fears the failure of his magic in this, his hour of trial.

In silent wonder the students resumed their seats, and a young man beside Byrnewood took forth his watch, and noted the seconds as they fled, with a wild and haggard eye.

A minute passed!

Byrnewood gazed vacantly upon the veiled corse, and muttered incoherently to himself. "Am I dreaming? Why does he not lift the cloth from the face of the dead?"

And then as in very fear that the lifting of the cloth might reveal his sister's face, he turned his head aside and shaded his eyes with his hand. Not a word passed from the lips of the Enthusiasts. All was silent as the grave.

The second minute passed!

Ravoni approached the corse. "Ha! He will lift the cloth at last!" muttered Byrnewood starting from his seat. The Sorcerer placed his hand beneath the veil and drew forth into the light, the fingers of an icy hand. "How dead and cold!"

Again he resumed his walk beside the altar, again the Students sank back in quivering suspense.

"Lift the shroud from the face of the dead!" gasped Byrnewood, and then as if startled by the sound of his own voice, he shuddered and grew pale.

Ravoni advanced to the Corse again. Slowly, slowly he lifted up the grave-cloth. First the face was visible, then the neck and bosom, then the body of the corse, and then the limbs. Dead, dead cold and dead! White yes as the stainless snow! Pure, aye pure as God's own light!

Why did that yell die in Byrnewood's throat? What fiend was it that choked the agony, as it gurgled up from his heaving chest? Whose hot fingers were those that burnt his eyeballs? Why might he not gaze steadily at the sight? Why did his eyes swim in fiery moisture, why did his brain burn as with a red hot iron pressing against the bare skull one moment, and the next grow icy cold?

The Students rose up in silent astonishment, in wrapt wonder.

It was the corse of a young and beautiful woman. There was a smile on the lips, a calm glory beaming from the face, around whose swelling outlines, a warm mass of golden hair curled and twined and glistened. The round arms folded on the breast, the white fingers gently clasped, and the snowy bosom with the blue threaded veins, that bosom whose fulness bespoke the mother—ah! Death was there in holy beauty. Fairer form than that, did painter never shape, sweeter limbs than those did sculptor never carve.

Yet she was dead, ah, cold and dead! And the light streamed warmly over the marble whiteness of that uncovered form, revealing beauties on which the worms were soon to riot. Over the round limbs, over the white bosom, over the beaming face the worms would crawl, marking their progress with the blue taint of decay. And Ravoni could raise this corse to life again? Mockery of mockeries!

One cry shrieked from the Students' lips.

"Raise the dead to life, Ravoni, raise the dead to life and we will worship thee!"

His arms resting on his knees, his face half veiled in his hands Byrnewood chuckled to himself with an idiot laugh.

It was not his sister; it was not Mary; that delusion had vanished. The delusion was over, but the reality was there!

In that corse Byrnewood beheld the form of Annie, the Poor Man's daughter, the Seduced, the Mother! "It is a dream," chuckled Byrnewood with an idiot laugh, "I am haunted by her corse—it is a dream!" The Student by his side picked up the watch which had fallen to the floor.

Three minutes had past!

Not a word was spoken. As motionless, as silent, as pale as the corpse itself, the students clustered round the altar.

"Ha!" suddenly whispered one enthusiast to another. "Do you mark that faint color in the cheek!"

"Silence," muttered the other student, "There is no color there! Yet, ha! Do you not see the bosom heave?"

It was all fancy. No color gave warmth to the cheek, no throb of life swelled the white bosom.

Another long and weary minute passed, each second told by the gasping breath of the awed enthusiasts. One minute alone remained!

"Restore the dead, Ravoni," muttered one of the Students, "Restore the dead or thou art false even as yon corpse is cold!"

The Sorcerer stood silently regarding the body of the dead girl. His face was fearfully calm, but his dark eyes blazed with a terrible light.

"On this miracle I peril my soul!" cried Ravoni between his set teeth.

"One half minute is all that is left thee!" whispered a dark browed student in a voice tremulous with the agony of suspense.

Ravoni extended his hand; it was white as marble, and the beaded sweat glistened along the slender fingers.

"Arise ye dead!" he muttered, and pressed his lips to the clay cold lips of the corpse.

A wild murmur of fear from the whole band of Students! A murmur and a start, and then a fearful silence.

The cheeks of the dead had warmed with rosy life, the bosom heaved, and one hand moved gently to and fro!

"Arise ye dead!" shrieked Ravoni with the cold sweat on his brow.

"Arise ye dead!"

The hand of the dead girl was slowly raised; flushes of warmth ran over the limbs; the eyelids began to unclose.

"Arise ye dead! Arise—arise! For the third time I bid thee—arise!"

One shuddering start of horror!

The body of the dead girl quivered, the bosom heaved, the limbs shook. Then a shudder ran over her frame, and with a convulsive start the body rose on one arm, the eyelids unclosed, and the blue eyes gazed wonderingly around.

"Hail, hail Ravoni, we worship thee!"

Raising himself from his idiotic stupor, as that shout burst on his ear, Byrnewood rushed through the group, he beheld the uncovered form of the girl warming with life, he saw the blue eyes gazing around with a look of wild bewilderment.

"Annie!" he shouted, and sank kneeling beside the altar. His head dropped on her bosom, his arms encircled her form. He was stiff and cold and lifeless as marble.

The fair girl gazed round upon the group, her blue eyes swimming in frenzy.

"My child," she murmured, extending her hands with a maniac smile. "Where have you taken my child?"

CHAPTER SEVENTH

RAVONI AND MABEL

It was one o'clock when a dashing carriage, with cream colored panels and a liveried driver, came rattling along the street, and halted suddenly in front of the House of Ravoni. The bay horses were all a-foam with exertion, and their harness was covered with dust. They had evidently been driven at a most unreasonable speed, and now they struck the hard stones with their fore feet, and tossing their long manes on the air, manifested their impatience by a long and quivering neigh.

The carriage door was thrown open, and Fitz-Cowles sprang out upon the pavement. He was attired in a dark travelling over-coat, copiously adorned with frogs and braid, and he still flourished his gold-headed cane in his right hand.

"Come on Parson," he exclaimed, glancing within the carriage door. "You know I must send the girl on to New York to-night—there is no time to lose. She shall accompany me to England," he muttered between his teeth. "But Dora, ha, ha, she must not know a word about it. Come on Parson!"

"Wait," responded that well-known voice from within the carriage,

"Wait till I compose my features into the proper Patent Gospel look. Now Fitz, how does that go? Saintly enough—eh?"

The good Dr. Pyne stepped from the carriage, and taking Fitz-Cowles' arm within his own, ascended the marble steps of the yellow house. He rang the bell with a godly smile; his eyes were turned up, and the corners of his mouth were turned down, while his soul seemed to be meditating upon the unfortunate state of the unconverted Hindoos.

In a moment the hideous face of Abhar was visible in the door-way.

"I would speak with the Signior Ravoni!" said Dr. Pyne, bowing to the mass of ugliness, with an air of deep deference.

The negro pointed toward the main stair-way, and then closing the front door, left Dr. Pyne and his friend to make the best of their way to the Audience Chamber of Ravoni. They ascended the stair-way and stood at the commencement of the entry on the second floor, which was dimly illumined by a small window in the southern wall. Passing along the entry, they well-nigh stumbled over a dark object, which was laid in front of a door, fashioned into the western end wall of the corridor.

"Hello, Parson, what's that?" ejaculated Fitz-Cowles. "Does the old Conjurer lay traps for a man's feet in this way?"

"Never mind—let's see to the girl," grumbled the Parson. As he spoke they entered the Audience Chamber of Ravoni. The noon-day sun came faint and dimly through the thick curtains that obscured the lofty windows. The place was full of gloom and shadow, and the thickly carpeted floor gave no echo to the footsteps of the intruders.

"I say we're alone," muttered Fitz-Cowles. "This cursed den really makes a fellow shiver—black ceiling, black curtains, black carpet—ugh! Where's the Sorcerer?"

"He will be along presently," muttered Dr. Pyne in a bland whisper. "Now Fitz, suppose we could get the little maiden away from this den without the Sorcerer's knowledge?"

"It would be vastly convenient—"

"Va-s-tly! Save all disagreeable explanations. Ha—hum! What's this?"

Approaching the western side of the Audience Chamber, his eye was fixed upon a ray of red light which streamed from a crevice in the dark curtaining. A grim smile broke over the Preacher's visage.

"Look here Fitz," he whispered. "The entrance to another room, I vow!" He slowly swung the dark curtains aside and gazed thro' the aperture, while a blaze of light streamed over his round visage and the swarthy face of his companion.

"Look *there* my boy!" chuckled Pyne with a fat parson's chuckle. Fitz-Cowles applied his gold headed cane to his lips, and muttered in a distinct tone the monosyllable, '*dam*', biting it off short, like an epicure tasting a delicious morsel.

Along the dark entry and up the dim stairway, Ravoni had led the trembling Mabel, as with her heart fluttering with a new emotion, she expected to behold her father's face and rest upon her father's bosom for the first time in her dreary life of suffering and wrong.

"I shall behold my father, at last," she said gazing over her shoulder with a soft light beaming from her dark eyes.

"Thou shalt!" answered Ravoni in a tone that trembled with emotion. "Enter this door. A little while and thou shalt rest in thy fathers' arms!"

He pushed her gently through a small door fashioned in the western wall of the corridor. Mabel looked around in wonder. She was alone. She stood in a large chamber, with a trembling light burning on a small table near its centre. The light was faint and dim, yet it served to disclose the gorgeous furniture of the place, the silken hangings falling from the lofty ceiling to the carpeted floor, the glittering mirrors, the chairs, the sofa and the dark mantel adorned with figures of spotless alabaster.

"And this is my father's home!" muttered Mabel sinking into a cushioned arm-chair beside the table in the centre of the room. She clasped her hands, and gazed silently around the place. *Her father's home!* Gorgeous furniture, crimson curtains, carpets that gave no echo to the footstep, massive mirrors and a cheerful fire burning on a wide hearth, scattering warmth and comfort round! This was a gorgeous home for thee, poor orphan, but its glory in thy sight had been nothing, were it not for the thought, that a *father's heart* throbbed within these lofty walls.

"My father's home!" she murmured again, and then fell into a waking dream, which glided away into a soft and dreamless sleep. When she awoke, some unknown hand had substituted large wax lights for the trembling lamp, and placed refreshments on the table by her side.

"Will *he* soon return?" the whisper broke from her lips, and then turning round she listened to a faint murmur that broke on her ear. It required a moment for her eye to grow accustomed to the darkness which shrouded the farther corners of the room, and then with a start she fancied she beheld two faces peering grimly upon her, through an aperture in the crimson hangings.

"It is all fancy!" she muttered turning her face away from the sight. "It cannot be my persecutor! Here at least, I am safe from his violence —"

There was the sound of a hurried footstep—Mabel started to her feet in fear, and ere she could look around, she felt the folds of the dark robe which she wore, drawn closely about her limbs, while a hoarse laugh broke on her ear.

"Ho, ho, my bird! Have I caught you? You will run away from your kind father, will you? For shame, f-o-r shame!"

Mabel looked up and beheld the red round visage of Dr. Pyne, with the swarthy countenance of a stranger, peering over his shoulder. She buried her face in her hands, while her heart grew cold with despair.

"Come my canary bird," cried Dr. Pyne gathering his arms tightly around her form. "No strugglin' no screamin'—d'ye hear?"

He wound the dark robe more closely around her form, compressing her hands and limbs, as within the embrace of a vice.

"Pretty! Bi-Jove! Pretty!" muttered Fitz-Cowles as he unwound the black silk scarf from his neck and tied it round her head and over her mouth. "You've a kind pa-pa my dear, and you've treated him quite rudely. But we'll take care of you, my love, depend upon it, we will!"

He raised her in his arms and bore her toward the entrance, while Dr. Pyne followed smilingly at his heels.

"I feel good all over!" he muttered rubbing his fat hands together. "To think of my dear daughter returning to the parental roof! Oh, goodness what a Consoler that thought is!"

"And you a poor broken-hearted father," chuckled Fitz-Cowles as he bore the maiden through the Audience Chamber.

They entered the dark entry. Mabel uttered neither sigh nor moan, nor struggled to free her limbs from the arms of Fitz-Cowles. A strange apathy of despair had chilled her soul: she yielded to her fate like the pale consumptive, who counts the few hours of existence on some dreary sick bed, while every minute crumbles away a clod from the edges of the grave.

"To the carriage," muttered Fitz-Cowles, "To the carriage, and our beauty is safe!"

The words had not passed his lips when his foot became entangled in some dark object resting along the floor; he fell forward while Dr. Pyne seized the maiden from his grasp.

"Come Fitz, we must hurry," exclaimed Pyne when he felt himself grasped by the throat and bruised violently in the back, at the same moment. Unloosing his grasp which pinioned the maiden's form, he howled in very agony.

And then two stalwart arms grasped him by the neck, and two uncivil feet tripped up his heels with the precision and regularity of clock-work. In an instant Dr. Pyne felt himself rolling down the stairs; he made an effort to stay his mad career at the first landing, but in vain! He rolled over the landing, and then down the four and thirty stairs, like a bundle of cotton, with bones in it, the Reverend preacher bumped and rolled and rolled and bumped again.

He had lain at the foot of the stairway, for the space of a moment or more, full of groans and aches, when a heavy body whizzed through the air, and the Reverend Doctor felt himself hit in the paunch by the form of a full grown man, which came bounding down the stairs with the velocity of a young colt.

"Oh my God!" groaned Pyne. "Who did that?"

"What in the d———l d'ye mean?" roared the voice of Fitz-Cowles, "what in the d———l d'ye mean by layin' here at the foot of the stairs for people to break their bones over you? Hey?"

"And what do *you* mean by comin' down stairs like a flyin' fish or a bomb shell? Curse it—there ai'nt a whole bone in me!"

At the head of the stairway in the full glare of the light streaming through the small window, stood a wild and distorted form, with thick locks of matted hair falling aside from a hideous countenance, all a-flame with an expression of super-human rage.

Fitz-Cowles and Pyne felt the glare of a solitary eye flashing down upon them, like the eye of a coiled snake darting from the orbless socket of a skull.

"Did I smash you, ye born devils?" roared the hoarse voice of Devil-Bug. "You thought you'd steal off with the gal, and then you thought the bundle o' blackness on the floor was'nt nothin'! Ho, ho! Did I trundle the Parson down stairs, and hit him in the paunch with the dandy? Ho, ho! I wonders how it verks!"

"Come Parson, we'd better go," said Fitz-Cowles. "That incarnate fiend seems to mix himself up with every-body's affairs. Come!"

"Oh, O, O-o-o! I wish he had'nt mixed *you* up with *me* so confoundedly!"

Groaning and aching, Parson Pyne followed Fitz-Cowles to his carriage.

Five minutes passed. With the cold sweat standing in thick beads on his forehead, fresh from scenes of super-human horror, Ravoni passed up the stair-way, his arms folded on his breast, and his dark eyes buried beneath the interwoven brows.

At the head of the stairway the light from the circular window streamed over a strange and impressive picture. A monster in human shape knelt on the floor, with the form of a fair and beautiful girl resting unconsciously upon his knee. His solitary eye was fixed upon her snow-white face, and his rough hands gathered her torn robe, over her alabaster bosom. Ravoni started, and then stood like some statue of wild and mysterious astonishment, gazing unperceived upon the scene.

"Yer dead gal, yer dead," muttered the Monster, and a big tear started from his eye. "And they tuk yo' from me, and stole yo' away and hid yo'—the dogs and devils! Yer dead gal, but I'll buy me sich knives and pistols to cut and slash yer enemies to pieces, that they'll wish the devil had 'em a thousand times! Oh yer dead, yer dead!"

His rough hand was passed over her smooth cheek, as if to wake her gently to life again, and then he moaned in a low and broken tone, "Yer dead gal, yes, yes, yer dead!"

Ravoni was touched by this strange spectacle. There was something in the voice, the look, the manner of the Savage, that thrilled the very heartstrings of this mysterious man.

Ascending the last step of the stairs, he touched Devil-Bug gently on the shoulder. "What does this mean?" he said in a low-toned voice.

Devil-Bug looked up with a scowl on his grim face, but it melted away before the deep glance of Ravoni's dark eyes. Had the Sorcerer indeed made *His* WILL, *the* SOUL of this Monster?

"Why yo' see," said Devil-Bug in a submissive tone, "I did'nt dream when I lay watchin' beside the door, that my pretty little Nell was the gal, either! Not a bit of it. An' while I was watchin', in comes Parson Pyne, an' a dandy with him, an, they carries off the gal, thro' the door leadin' into the Aud'ence Room; they brings her this way—the dogs! Did'nt I rise on 'em? Did'nt I pitch the Parson down stairs, with the dandy a-top of him? Ho, ho!"

"And so you know the girl?" asked Ravoni with his dark eyes fixed upon the visage of Devil-Bug.

"Know the gal?" exclaimed the Savage. "I tell you she's the child of the rich marchant; she's the daughter o' Livingstone!"

A sneering smile wreathed the lips of the Sorcerer.

"I have heard this story before. Parson Pyne told me all. The girl is a maniac. She *fancies*—d'ye mark—she *fancies* that she is the child of Livingstone."

Devil-Bug was nettled by the cold tone of Ravoni.

"Is them fancy?" he cried, drawing a pacquet of papers from his coarse garment.

"Is them papers wot proves it all, as straight as A, B, C, is *them* fancy? Let me put 'em in Livingstone's hands! Vonders how that 'ud verk?"

Ravoni leaned slowly forward, keeping the glance of his impenetrable eye fixed upon the face of the Savage.

"It is all nonsense," he said in a jeering tone, and then cooly reaching forth his hands, he took the pacquet from the grasp of Devil-Bug. "Here is gold for you, my fellow. Leave these papers with me. I shall not want you again, until to-morrow."

Devil-Bug's arms dropped by his side. The gold pieces rattled on the floor.

"Look here, Man or Devil, whatever yo' are, I'm ugly as a sarpint, and I've stole dead bodies for you, and may-be I'd murder for you, if you paid me well, but I can't take gold for them papers! This gal's life and fortin' an' name, is locked up there in that package! Give it to me, I say, and I'll be yer slave for life!"

He lifted his huge hands beseechingly, as he spoke. His rough voice was quivering and tremulous, as the tones of a child. Cold, calm and impenetrable Ravoni gazed upon him, his dark eyes gleaming with those awful rays, which were magic and power.

"Your object is gold," he slowly said. "You shall have it. The papers and the girl are mine."

He raised the fainting form of Mabel from the knee of Devil-Bug, and with his foot, thrust open the door of the western chamber.

"Begone!" he exclaimed with his hand pointing toward the stair-way. "I shall want you to-morrow—Begone slave!"

He disappeared within the room, and closed the door. Devil-Bug stricken dumb with awe and astonishment rose on his feet. He moved slowly toward the stair-way.

"And she is to be one of his nuns!" he muttered between his teeth.

"To-night she's pure as one o' God's angels—to-morrow morning she'll be foul—*foul!* There ai'nt a tru!l along, the streets fouler than this child will be! And yet I'm *his* slave! Ha, ha! He *ses* and I must *do!* Why did'nt he bid me tear my bare arm with my teeth? But to give my child to him—to *him!* To lay sich a butterfly in a spider's nest! And he'll give me gold for her—gold!"

It was awful to see the malignity of hell, gleaming from every line of that distorted countenance. The solitary eye stood out from the socket, blazing with a glaring lustre; the lips writhed and worked over the clenched teeth. And yet whenever he thought of Ravoni, a cold chill quivered through his deformed body. He could fight with a man, yes he could grapple with phantoms from the grave, but Ravoni! The deep dark eyes of the Sorcerer were forever before him, their awful rays pouring into his soul.

One word broke from his writhing lips.

"Monk-Hall!"

Yes, he would bury himself in the nooks and corners of the accursed mansion; in the dim shadows of that hall of death and crime his soul would find such comfort, as the grave-worm finds when revelling over the hollow skull. Darkness to darkness, guilt to guilt, the ghost to its haunt, the murderer to his den!

"Monk-Hall!" he muttered, and then departed from the House of Ravoni. On one side wriggled and crawled the man with the broken jaw and lolling tongue; on the other, the old woman glided, with the blood oozing from the hollow skull. The groan of the man, and the sound of the woman's pattering blood mingled together, but what were these horrors to the thought which burnt like a hot iron through his brain? *His child* in the arms of pollution and shame.

Fitz-Cowles stood beside his cream-colored carriage. The groans of the bruised Dr. Pyne came through the open door, and the bay horses struck their hoofs impatiently against the stones of the street. Fitz-Cowles stood with one foot on the carriage steps, when his brow grew dark with sudden thought. He started back upon the pavement, and stood with folded arms, and his cane raised to his lips.

"All is safe!" thus ran his wandering thoughts. "This morning I sent the 'hair trunk' and all my other baggage to New-York, under an assumed name. Public curiosity is still alive in regard to the—forgery—and yet no one suspects me! I stand clear as the day, among the Aristocracy of the Quaker City! Von Gelt is gone; no accomplice can now mutter treason with regard to his master. Dim my Creole slave, has orders to have two of the best horses to be had in this town, for love or money, ready saddled and bridled to-night, in the wood beyond Camden. With these horses Dora and I will escape from Hawkewood; bye the bye she must take care to have all her jewellery with her. I must make something by this woman must turn her fancy for a Coronet into good Fitz-Cowles' gold. All therefore is fair day with me, and what should I fear?"

"What should I fear?" he muttered aloud, and ere the words had died on his lips, a dark Presentiment crept thro' his blood. "While I stand here, this man Harvey may be laying some infernal plot to blow all my schemes in the air! That would be a pretty spectacle! As I am about to leave the city to-night, to feel an officer's finger on my shoulder, 'you are my prisoner, Sir'—ugh! I have not seen Harvey to-day—this silence annoys me! Poodle gave me a hint that Harvey was on the track of the Jew yesterday—Zounds! Could he have seen that rascal before his—*death?*"

Fitz-Cowles was troubled. His lip was compressed, and his swarthy face grew darker with a settled frown.

"Drive to my rooms, Parson," he whispered through the carriage door. "I will join you there in an hour."

The carriage door closed on a curse which broke from the Parson's lips, as his fat frame writhed beneath the agony of manifold bruises; and the vehicle rattled away along the street.

"I will go to Monk-Hall," he muttered. "I will spy out the secrets of the den, and if the Jew made any communication to Harvey before his death, I will know it ere this day is gone by. Ha! Here is that fool Mulhill!"

And with a smile on his red visage, the redoubtable Major Rappahannock Mulhill came lounging lazily along the street, twirling an enormous crooked stick in one hand, while the other was inserted in the capacious pocket of his pantaloons.

The costume of the Major, you will remember was striking and peculiar—a broad brimmed felt hat with a blue cord and tassel; a white blanket over-coat which was thrown open in front, revealing a sky-blue coat with metal buttons, a deep red velvet vest and a pair of pants made very full, and striped like bed ticking. Brimstone kid gloves and patent leather boots, completed the costume of this dashing gentleman.

"How do Curnel. Fine day," wobbled the Major lounging to the side of the Millionaire. "Cussed dull town this is! Not a man shot down in the streets to day, I vow!"

"Your humble servant, Major. May I request your services in an affair of great delicacy? I have an enemy. He has resorted to mean practices to injure me. I have determined to put him down. In order to do this, I must visit one of the vilest dens in the Quaker City. I want a friend to go with me, stand by me and fight for me. Will you be that friend?"

"Where is the den of thieves?" drawled Mulhill with a sleepy look.

"Did you ever hear of Monk-Hall?"

"There's my paw," said the classic Mulhill. "But mind ye, if there ain't a man killed I shall account the affair, low, d———d low!"

"Thanks, Major, thanks," exclaimed Fitz-Cowles taking the proffered hand. "Meet me an hour from this time, at the corner of Fifth and Chesnut Streets. Till then good bye."

"Da-day!" drawled Mulhill, "I will not fail you. A-*doo!*"

And Fitz-Cowles hurried up the street with a frown on his brow, while Mulhill lounged in an opposite direction, with a broad grin on his red visage. Fitz-Cowles placed his gold-headed cane to his lips, and muttered wildly to himself, while Mulhill drew from his pocket, a slip of paper, and rattled it against the tip of his nose with a broad grin.

"A love letter from a g-a-l!" he muttered, and then went laughing on his way.

And at the same instant, like a Ghost walking forth in the noonday sun, from the house of Ravoni, the form of Devil-Bug emerged into the light.

"Monk-Hall!" he shouted with a hideous grin, and rushed wildly down the street.

Ravoni bore the maiden into the western chamber, and laid her unconscious form, on the velvet cushions of the arm chair, beside the table. Then stepping backward, he contemplated her face with folded arms and a dilating eye. Her long dark hair fell in one thick mass around her pale countenance, and the long fringes of her eye-lashes rested upon the whiteness of her snowy cheeks. There was a sweet smile lingering on her lips; a silent thought, a calmness and a love speaking from her pallid brow.

Ravoni stood gazing upon her, and even through the sallow paint which marred the eternal manhood of his visage, you might see the warm blood glowing and brightening with deep emotion. His dark red lip grew eloquent with feeling; something full of passion, and yet holier than sensual love.

"Thou art very beautiful!" murmured Ravoni speaking in that low toned voice, which flowed like music on the air. "And thou shalt be the Priestess of the New Faith!"

Leaning gently forward he impressed a kiss upon her brow; too warm for a father's kiss, too holy for a lover's.

The maiden unclosed her eye, and murmured in a low whisper two half-audible words, "My Father!"

"Girl, thou hast no father! It is all a trick, a delusion, a show. The poor wretch who forged the note, which lured thee, to this mansion, tore thee from the arms of father and mother, when but a babe. Thy parents are long since dead, and thou art an orphan."

There was something so calm and so assured in the tones of Ravoni, that the hopes of Mabel, broke away from her soul, like the crumbling sands before the waves of Ocean. Her world was gone! And yet the utter desolation of her agony was too deep for tears. Her dark eyes flashed and dilated, and yet their glance never wandered from the eyes of Ravoni.

"Thou art an orphan!" he repeated, taking her white hand within his own, and looking through her eyes, into her soul. "In this goodly

Christian world thou hast had, never a friend. Thy life has been made the sport and plaything of a hypocrite, who would have visited thy soul, with an eternal stain. Tell me, fair girl, what are the ties that bind thee to life?"

"*Orphan!*" muttered Mabel in an absent tone.

"Yes, orphan! Another name for youth, helplessness and misery! Orphan! A thing to be trodden upon by the oppressors of this world, to be trampled by godly feet, crushed by pious hands. Look upon me, fair girl, gaze in mine eyes, and mark my words. In this great world where thou art friendless and alone, *I* will be thy friend."

"You!" murmured Mabel. "And will you not too, deceive and betray?"

"Deceive a soul like thine?" exclaimed Ravoni, with a bitter smile, "Leave that to priests and worldlings! Could *I* deceive *thee?*"

He leaned forward, and his dark eyes shone into her soul. With parted lips and gasping breath, Mabel gazed upon him, and murmured "Never! Never!" There was an irresistable power in his look, his tone, and speaking brow. She felt drawn to him, and yet it was not with passion! It seemed to her, that she could lay forever at his feet, and listen to the wild music of his tone, without a word or motion in reply.

Was the Sorcerer subduing her *Will*, with the wierd Magnetism of his spirit? In other words, was the Man of deep and powerful intellect, silently overshadowing her Soul, with his irresistable Will? Why does the maiden, pure and stainless as God's angels, hang on his look and tone with that fascination which seems more like a deep religious reverence than an earthly love?

"It is from such as thee, fair girl, that the Great Father chooses his rarest jewels! Unto such as thee, are unlocked the mysteries of the world, the sun, the sky, the air, and of that most wonderful of all creations, the human soul. Thou art an orphan, yet shalt thou breathe ir a world, unknown to grosser souls. Thine unsealed eyes shall gaze upon sights that shall fill the blood with rapture, that shall make the heart undulate on waves of music, like some angel barque, freighted with perfume, as it glides in light and song over gently-rippling waters. Thou art an orphan, and yet in thought and soul, thou shalt be, as one of the Seraphim who live in the sunshine of the Father's Presence!"

No word from Mabel's lips, not even a sigh! Already the words of the Sorcerer were bursting into fulfilment. While her wrapt eye grew glassy with fascination, while the tones of Ravoni fell on her ear, with the musical murmur of green leaves dipping gently into rippling waves, a strange panorama of beauty glided on her Soul.

First a soft and mellow light, then a cool lake environed by green hills; then from a mountain's summit, she gazed upon a gorgeous sweep of forests broken by vinyards and cities, with streams of blue water winding along grassy plains, where marble palaces arose upon the summer air. Then she trod the streets of an ancient city, where strange costumes and swarthy faces flitted by, while immortality looked down, from long lines of massive temples, sublime with the triumphs of an architecture, which was reared in the sweat and blood of millions, thro' the long lapse of ages.

Then strains of music, whose melody never stirred the chords of a harp touched by human hands, filled her soul, and from the bowers of a green isle, she gazed upon the calm expanse of ocean, with white clouds uprising from the waters into the sunny sky.

"Would'st thou behold the face of thy Mother?" the calm tones of Ravoni broke on the ear of the maiden, and like a flash, her dream or vision, call it what you will, was past and vanished.

She awoke to the consciousness of Ravoni's look and tone and brow. "My mother," she exclaimed in tremulous tones, "Oh let me look upon her—"

"Advance to yonder mirror. Let the whole force of thy Soul be centred upon thy Mother, whom thou hast never beheld with the eyes of sense; advance and gaze and thine own mother, shall stand before thee!"

Trembling through every fibre of her young form, Mabel arose. The Mirror reached half-way from the floor to the ceiling, in an interval of the crimson hangings. It was but five steps forward, and yet Mabel seemed an age in passing that trifling space. Trembling and pale, she stood before the Mirror, afraid to gaze within its glittering frame.

"Look within the Mirror," exclaimed Ravoni. "What dost thou behold?"

"I see my own form, and I see yours—" whispered Mabel.

Ravoni bent his eyes to the floor, and pressed his hand on his forehead.

"My will shall pass into her brain," he murmured. "What dost thou see now?"

"There are faint outlines as of a woman's form," slowly whispered Mabel, "There is the gleam of two dark eyes, but all beside is mist and shadow."

"Thy soul is not yet firm! Think of thy mother, think earnestly, and with thy entire soul, and lo! she will stand before thee!"

There was silence for a moment. The Sorcerer sate by the table, with his hand pressed against his brow, while Mabel stood before the Mirror, her dark eyes burning with an unnatural light.

"Joy, joy," faintly murmured Mabel, "she comes!"

And like a beam of light from the bosom of a cloud, the vision stood before her! The form of a woman, clad in light robes, with two dark eyes of unutterable beauty, beaming from a pale face, around whose outlines, fell thick tresses of raven hair. It was there for a moment, there within the Mirror and then it was gone.

"My mother, I have seen thee!" muttered Mabel, and fell fainting into the arms of Ravoni.

Her head rested upon his shoulder, and her dark hair fell waving over his arms and hands.

"There are those who search the ocean for its secrets, the air for its mysteries, who devote a long life to the properties of a flower or the qualities of a plant! Fools and madmen! Within my arms I hold a Mystery, more hallowed than all the secrets of the earth combined. Here is a fair and stainless woman, whose heart is full of truth, whose soul is all enthusiasm! On this heart will I write the teachings of Ravoni; this soul shall throb with the impulses of my Will!

"From this hour thou wilt begin to live, fair girl! This moment thou art born! And with the past, let all things that remind thee of thy former life, be buried! Thy name itself shall be forgotten in the name which I now give thee!

"I baptize thee with a kiss, and whisper the name which shall dwell on my lips in many an hour of joy, a name soft as a ripplet's murmur or a woman's sigh, when first her cheek kindles to her lovers kiss.

"Izole."

CHAPTER EIGHTH

THE DEATH OF THE WHITE OWL

An old man, leaning upon spade, stood on the brow of a gentle eminence, with the beams of the setting sun falling over his wrinkled face.

He stood in front of a massive gate, whose posts falling to decay, were in strong contrast with the solidity of a thick stone wall, which extended along the eminence, until it was lost to view in the hollows on either side.

Behind the wall arose a thick grove of pines, with the steep roofs and grey walls of an old-time mansion, dimly visible through their evergreen boughs.

In front of the aged man lay a wild and broken tract of country, plains of dreary sand, varied by sombre forests of pine, or here and there an orchard of peach trees, with the bare and desolate limbs, waving stiffly in the winter air, or a solitary farm-house rising from some bleak waste of brown earth. The distant western horizon was one dim and dreary wall of pine forest, with the broad disc of the setting sun, seen half above the dark barrier, while his level beams fell with a red lustre over the wintry landscape.

The whole tract of country, in view of the old man, who stood on the brow of the eminence, wild and dreary as it was in summer, was now rendered fearful as some night-mare dream, by the absence of the scanty foliage, which served to hide some of its most hideous features.

The setting sun-light streamed over the sides of steep ravines, sunken in the bosom of the sand wastes, like colossal graves, or along the surface of black pools of water, visible through the intervals of pine forests, or over the side of some barren hill, which shot up suddenly from the surrounding plain with its bleak sides covered, with the trunks of burnt and blasted trees.

The eye of the old man was fixed upon the road, which made one straight track through the landscape, from the distant horizon, until it terminated at the gate of the mansion. Frequently crossed by streams of water, or again rising into slight eminences, this road was all one dreary path of sand. A sight more barren can scarcely be conceived.

Within the compass of a mile from the spot where the old man stood, arose three gentle hills, and on the summit of each of these, his eye was rivetted with peculiar interest.

On the nearest hill a carriage was visible, drawn by two noble bay horses, whose harness glittered in the sun.

On the next hill, like some enormous beetle, creeping forth from its haunts, ere the day was done, a black and gloomy hearse, came rapidly onward.

On the last hill, the form of a horseman, bestriding a gallant grey steed, rose up between the eyes and the setting sun.

"Man and boy, for sixty long years, I've lived on this old place, and yet I never see'd sich a sight as that afore! For the last half hour I've watched 'em, and still they come on, the carriage fust, the hearse next, and the horseman last! An' they will drive at the same pace; the hearse keeps little over a quarter-a-mile from the carriage, and the horseman keeps the same distance from the hearse! Well, well, if that ain't the queerest sight, and reether the solemn'est, I'll never strike spade into airth agin!"

As the old man muttered this rude soliloquy, an aged woman clad in a petticoat of coarse linsey, hobbled through the gate, and took her place at his side, her grey eyes dilating with wonder as she gazed upon the road beneath.

Meanwhile the carriage, the hearse and the horse came hurriedly onward.

We will descend for a moment from our eminence at the mansion gate, and take a glance at carriage, hearse and horse.

In one corner of the thickly cushioned carriage, sate a proud and peerless woman, whose tall form enveloped in a green riding habit, was also muffled in the warm folds of a dark cloth cloak. Her hands were folded across her bosom, and her face drooped down, until her chin rested on her fingers. There was a volume of thought in her full dark eye, and a strange meaning in the steady frown which indented her queenly brow.

"To give up all, a Coronet and a title, for virtue and Livingstone! The thought is galling! and yet I have given my Oath, and it shall be!"

As these thoughts flashed over the soul of Dora Livingstone, she leaned slightly forward, and looked through the opened carriage window.

"How strange! A journey of only thirty miles, and yet it has consumed the entire day. First the carriage breaks down—it takes the servants at least three hours to repair the accident. Then at noon, I am overtaken by Albert; he tells me, that the doctor has forbidden him to ride in a close carriage, so he will follow me on horseback. Then with one delay after another, we are detained on the road, and now as the night is coming on, we approach the old domain of Hawkewood. How singular! That hearse has followed my carriage since noon-day. I know its all superstition, but still I cannot repress a shudder whenever my eye chances to fall upon that gloomy vehicle. Yes, yes," and her thoughts resumed their original channel, "I have given my oath and it shall be!"

As she fell back on her seat, her soul became engaged again in the fearful contest which had convulsed it during the entire day. Virtue and Livingstone, or a Coronet and Murder!

Meanwhile along the brow of the next hill, the hearse drawn by a dark horse, half concealed in sable trappings, came gloomily onward. The Driver a man of some forty years, with a phlegmatic countenance, sate on the box, smoking a cigar. The dark velvet hangings of the hearse, wafting slowly aside, disclosed the coffin. It was covered with rich black cloth, and the sun-beams glistened on the silver plate, inscribed with name and age of the deceased.

The driver tossed the thick weepers aside from his face, and cracked his whip and puffed his cigar, and the hearse rolled rapidly down the hill. A sharp stone, projecting from the road-side, struck against one of the wheels, and well nigh overturned the hearse in the road.

The driver stopped the horse, jumped from his seat. "I must see if that 'ere Mortality box ai'nt damaged a little!" he exclaimed, and approached the side of the hearse. The coffin was slightly moved, and leaning within the hearse, the driver proceeded to arrange it in its former position. While thus occupied, he read the inscription on the silver plate of the coffin. Thus it ran:

Dora Livingstone.

DIED, DEC., 22, 1842.

AGED 21 YEARS, 3 MONTHS AND ONE DAY.

"Couzin o' his," muttered the phlegmatic driver, pointing to the distant horseman. "Ha-hum! Died this morning 'fore daybreak; he was in a hurry to get the plate made! Queer! Howsomdever, all I've got to do, is to drive out to yander old place, put the coffin in an outhouse, without bein' seen, in order to spare the feelin's of relatives, and then drive back to town agin! 'Spect the young lady made a *felo see* of herself!"

With this soliloquy the driver jumped on the box, puffed his cigar, and with a crack of his whip, the hearse rolled down the hill.

The noble figure of the horseman and the form of the gallant grey steed which he rode, rose up in the light of the sun, from the summit of the last hill.

Pausing for a moment on the brow of the hill, the horseman bared his brow to the setting sun. The thick corded veins stood out from the bronzed skin, and the blue eyes, deep sunken beneath the dark eyebrow, glared with an unsteady and wandering light. For a single moment as the light of the sun shone over that face and brow, it presented a sight of fearful interest.

For a single moment, the muscles of the face, the veins of the forehead, the livid lips, worked and writhed, like crawling lizards. The blue eye, so strangely contrasted with the dark eyebrow, dilated until the pupil absorbed nearly the entire surface of the eyeball. It was but for a moment, and then all was calm again, but it was a calmness like sunset over the black waters of the Dead Sea.

A deep husky sound like the mingling of a death rattle with cheerful laughter, shook the broad chest of the Merchant, and then with a set smile on his lips, he gave the rein to his steed and dashed along the road.

He had not gone ten paces, when another horseman, dressed in plain black, riding a brown horse all whitened with foam, attained the summit of the hill, and shouted to Livingstone at the top of his voice.

"Hello, you sir, hello!" he cried, "Can you tell me which is the way to Hawkewood?"

Turning his head over his shoulder Livingstone gazed upon the stranger.

"Yonder building among the trees, is the place you seek," he calmly answered.

"Dev'lish glad to hear it," exclaimed the stranger, who was a man of some thirty years, with a face of no particular meaning. "Never in all my born days, have I had sich a ride as to day! You see Sir I landed at New York yesterday, from the steamship, and came post haste to Philadelphia, where I found that I'd have to ride a matter o' thirty miles before I could see the genelman I was seekin' after. Could'n't tell me Sir, whether I'd *be sure* to find Mr. Livingstone at that old place yonder?"

"My name is Livingstone," cooly responded the Merchant.

The Stranger gave a start, which he communicated to his horse by a violent twitch at the reins.

"What Albert Livingstone Esq., Philadelphia, Pennsylvania, 'Nited States o' 'Merica?" he shouted in a voice of unlimited astonishment.

"The same, Sir," replied the Merchant.

"Well, Sir, I'm a clerk of your father's lawyers—Messrs Billings, Smith, & Charmley, London. I'm a special Messenger Sir, sent over to see you. There's the package Sir, that is to say, *My Lord*—"

The excited Special Messenger had thrown himself from his horse, and hat in hand, approached the stirrups of the Merchant, holding a large pacquet, in his hand, sealed with enormous red seals.

"I guess its purport," said Livingstone with a slight smile. He took the pacquet; placed it within the breast of his overcoat, and then drew forth his pocket-book. "Here is something, for your trouble," he exclaimed handing the Special Messenger a roll of notes.

Then putting spurs to his steed, he rode forward, leaving the gentleman standing in the centre of the road; a very well executed statue of Blank Astonishment, with its hand crammed full of paper money.

In a few minutes Livingstone dashed by the hearse, and speeding rapidly forward, he reached the eminence in front of the Mansion Gate, at the same moment that his wife stepped from the carriage. Dismounting from his steed, the Merchant received the salutations of the servants.

"Welkim to Hawkewood Mister Livingstone; welkim to Hawkewood ma'am," exclaimed the old Gardener and his wife as they hobbled forward.

Mrs. Livingstone greeted the old people with a cordial bow, while the Merchant, took them each by the hand, and spoke cheerfully of the good old times, when his father was living, and he roamed the deep woods, an idle and free-hearted boy.

Livingstone now approached his wife. She stood erect in the centre of the knoll with every outline of her magnificent form, displayed to advantage by the green riding habit, which she wore.

"You have had a weary ride, my love," said Livingstone in a kind tone, as he laid his hand upon her shoulder and gazed in her beautiful face.

"Such vexatious delays!" she answered with a smile, "But do tell me Albert, where is that hearse going, that I now see, ascending the road? It has followed the carriage, the entire afternoon—"

"I had some conversation with the driver as I came along. It appears that a poor girl of good family, died suddenly in a village some ten miles beyond Hawkewood. This man is taking the coffin for her funeral, and will stop here for a few minutes to refresh his horse. He made the request of me, Dora, when I told him, that I was the owner of this place, and you know," he added with a playful smile, "I could'n't refuse. The poor fellow and his horse are *so* tired—"

As he spoke the hearse came up the hill, and while the driver sat calmly smoking his cigar, it passed through the gate and rolled away toward the outhouses of the mansion.

Dora uttered an involuntary shriek.

"Oh—the coffin!" she murmured, and turned her head away.

"It certainly looks very solemn," said Livingstone calmly, "and then the plate on the top, reflects the last rays of the sun, like a mirror."

While the merchant's horse, the carriage and the hearse, were led or driven toward the outbuildings of the mansion, Livingstone and his wife, stood on the summit of the knoll gazing in silence upon the setting sun. The aged man and woman like statures of extreme old age, leaned against the crumbling gate posts, and gazed steadily upon the beautiful form of the Merchant's wife.

"Wot a han'some couple!" muttered the old woman, "But then it's so *on*lucky that that 'ere hearse followed the carriage!"

The beams of the setting sun streamed over the proud form of the Merchant, and over the figure of his beautiful wife. Behind them lay the thick grove of pines, with the massive outlines of the old mansion, seen through the darkening boughs. In front of them, swept the wild track of broken country, now blending into one mass of darkness, under the gathering gloom of twilight, while far away, the last glimpse of the sun was stealing over the thick horizon of pine forests.

Dora gazed upon the scene, and felt a strange feeling of awe steal over her soul. Turning to Livingstone, she began an observation on the thoughtful quietude of the hour, but it died half-uttered on her lips:

"It is a solemn sun-set, Albert—" she whispered, when she caught the gleam of his calm, blue eye. There was something so unnatural, so fearful in the expression that flashed from the eyes of Livingstone, that Dora felt a thrill of horror dart through every vein.

"It is indeed a solemn sunset," answered Livingstone in a calm and even tone. "But the morning will be bright, Dora, bright my love!" He turned his head aside to conceal a frightful grimace that distorted his face.

The whirring of wings was heard in the air over-head. Livingstone and his wife looked toward the zenith, in momentary curiosity.

"It's the old white owl," exclaimed Davidson the gardener. "You know Mr. Livingstone, the white owl, that was old when you was a boy?"

"Ah—yes! I remember Davidson," began the Merchant, but his words were interrupted by a whizzing noise in the air, followed by a dull sound near his feet.

The bird, an enormous white owl, lay dead on the earth, between himself and his wife. Without a shot or blow, or wound, from a clear sky it had fallen dead. It lay with its wings out-spread, and its dying eye covered with a glassy film.

"How strange!" muttered Dora, with an attempt to smile. "I hope it is no evil omen!—"

"Come my dear," interrupted Livingstone, without bestowing a glance upon the dead bird, "The evening is cold. Let us walk toward the mansion."

She took his arm, and soon their figures were seen in the intervals of the pine trees, through the dimness of the twilight.

Old Davidson advanced along the road, and gazed upon the dead owl. His wrinkled cheek was pale as ashes: his aged dame stood by his side with quivering limbs and chattering teeth.

"Omen," muttered the old gardener in an absent tone—"Omen"—

"Why yes, don't ye ricoleck?" screeched the old woman. "That old Livingstone always took sich keer o' that owl? He always feared the prophesy that had been made some time or other, about it. He always sed that when the old White Owl of Hawkewood died, one of the Livingstones 'ud meet with a sudden death! an' there it lays, dead as a stone!"

"Stuff!" muttered the old man, and yet he stood surveying the dead owl with a look of unmingled fear. "Since you do rake up sich foolish tales why don't yo' tell 'em right? Old Livingstone always charged me to take good keer o' the White Owl's life, for 'when that bird dies,' ses he, 'one of the Livingstones will murder his best friend, or the wife of his bosom!"

As though conscious of the words uttered by the old man, the dead owl faintly fluttered its wings for a single moment. It was only the winter wind, passing through the snowy feathers.

Livingstone and his wife stood in the doorway of the old-time mansion. Around them lay thick shadows of twilight, and through a long avenue of pines, extending in gloomy perspective from the hall door toward the west they beheld the last glimpse of the expiring winter's day.

"Here my father made his home," exclaimed Livingstone, turning to his wife, as they stood on the threshold of the place. "Here, escaping from the cares of city life, he delighted to bury himself in the shadows of the dim old halls, where the first man of our race, who trod the American shores, had lived and ruled, in the state of an old English Baron—"

"Your family were noble in the old world?" asked Dora, gazing upon the sombre countenance of her husband, now half-veiled by the shadows of twilight.

"Aye, noble by the lineage of a thousand years! Broad lands and stout throngs of retainers owned their sway, when—" a bitter smile broke over his lips—"A *woman* brought dishonor and murder to our house. Under an assumed name, the last *Lord* of the race, sought the American shores, leaving his hands in the old world, to distant kinsmen. He reared this mansion, and lived and died within its walls. It is a long story, Dora, and a dark one, and when I think of my father's soul, clouded by the cankering memory of a nameless wrong, I begin to think that a hereditary taint of superstition lingers in our blood—"

"Superstition?" echoed Dora.

"Was not my father superstitious? From brooding over the crime which had dishonored our house, he came to walk in a world of his own, where every object was darkened by the memory of our traditional wrong. You'd hardly believe it, Dora, but my father indulged and cherished a wild belief, approaching in certain respects, the old doctrine of the transmigration of souls—"

A muttered exclamation of surprise escaped from Dora, as she beheld Livingstone's noble countenance fire with an expression of singular enthusiasm.

"Through the treachery of a woman, ha, ha, the *treachery* of a *woman* mark ye, the pride of our house was levelled to the dust. A wrong, terrible as it is nameless, was done to the dearest friend of my lordly ancestor. My father, either from some wild tradition which had descended to him with the memory of that wrong, or from his peculiar habits of thought, believed firmly that the spirit of this much wronged friend, hovered around our house, for its evil and its ruin. The White Owl which fell dead at our feet to night, enshrouded that spirit in its bosom. Ha, ha, such was my father's superstition! For more than an hundred years, that owl, has hovered around the roofs of Hawkewood. My father believed that within twelve hours after its death, some awful calamity would befall our house—"

"A singular superstition!" exclaimed Dora, who took a strange interest in the words of her husband. "Did the belief of your father specify the nature of the calamity?"

"What a pitiable thing is human nature!" said Livingstone with a bitter smile. "To think that a man like my father, should be the victim of such a puerile superstition! Will you credit me Dora, when I tell you, the nature of the calamity, which the death of this 'doom-bird' was to bring to our house? Ha, ha, the absurdity of the thing makes me smile!"

"The calamity—"

"Was this! '*When the White Owl of Hawkewood dies, then shall a Livingstone crimson his hands in the blood of his wife, or receive his death through her guilt and shame.*' Such is the prophecy! How absurd!"

"And in this prophecy your father held implicit faith?" asked Dora, with a pale cheek and dilating eye.

"The night grows cold, my love," said Livingstone with a manner of affectionate regard. "Let us enter the mansion. Yes, yes, my father was tinctured with this ridiculous superstition, but the greatest men, have had similar follies. Cæsar had his phantom, Napoleon his star, and ha, ha, the Heir of Hawkewood must have his Spirit, disguised as an owl!"

And as he crossed the threshold with a careless laugh, the gloomy hearse rolled past the hall door toward the gate of the mansion, its uplifted drapery disclosing the vacant space, no longer occupied by the coffin, concealed in black cloth with a glittering plate on its bosom.

BOOK THE FIFTH

THE THIRD NIGHT

The Death-Angels

It is night again, and we are once more in the Quaker City. It is the third night of our history, and from the bosom of darkness, which like a bird of omen, broods over the city, forms of mist and shadow arise; they raise their hands to the heavens, they glide along with looks of unutterable woe. Do you hear the mournful music floating on the air? Do you see the awful frown, darkening over the faces of these Death-Angels? For they are Death-Angels, sent forth to dip their raven wings in blood. It is night now, but ere the morrow breaks, these ministers of wrath, will lay down before the Throne of Fate, the souls of the slain.

One angel glides solemnly over the city, folding his awful wings above the House of Ravoni.

Another Death-Spirit spreads his wings over the broad Delaware, and points to the far sand plains, where a light, like a world on fire, rushes into the dark sky.

One spirit of doom watches over the city and the Sorcerer's house; and the other spreads his wings for the wild forest, the old-time mansion, and the plain of sand.

Again that wild music on the air!

The Death-Angels are muttering with impatience; they hunger for the blood which shall drip from their wings ere the morrow's dawn.

CHAPTER FIRST

THE OUTCASTS OF THE QUAKER CITY

The Dead-Vault of Monk-Hall was illumined by the glare of lights. In the centre of the square space, described by four massive brick pillars, stood a large table of unpainted pine, with some dozen candles, arranged along its surface, burning in candlesticks of rusted iron. Gusts of wind moaning from the dim vault, flung the light with a flaring lustre, over the massy outlines of the pillars, revealing the fragments of coffins scattered round the floor, mingled with human bones, or sending a wild uncertain ray into the far recesses of the cellar, where dismal nooks, yawned like graves, or the substantial masonry of the place, assumed a thousand strange and fantastic forms.

Beside the table, with one huge hand resting on its boards, stood the Door-keeper of Monk-Hall, his head half drooped upon his broad chest, and his solitary eye glaring down upon the oaken floor. Now and then the wind tossed his tangled hair aside from his protuberant brow, and a single vein, shooting up between the eyebrows, was revealed as it stood out from the skin, like a thick cord, or the light flared over his distorted features, giving their harsh outlines, a momentary and horrid glare.

"Devil-Bug—" he muttered in his hoarse, grating voice. "Yes—That's my name! The gal's tuk for my arms, and I'll live to gather the good red goold—Devil-Bug 'ill be a rich man afore long! To think that Jew should have been hid so snug, a night an' a day in the Tower Room! Did'nt I pump him? He offer'd to sheer the chest of gold and the papers, if I'd help him to escape to furrin parts. Ha—h-a! Bess hid him there, did she? And the old 'oman's will is in the chest—what a cussed fool I was! To murder the widder for her goold, when by her will she gives it all the 'child' of her Ellen and Marchant Livingstone, should sed child ever be found! And that child is now in the hands of the Wizard—ugh!"

Devil-Bug clasped his talon fingers together, and uttered a low groan. How the heart of the Monster clung to the child of Ellen!

"The Jew must be *done* fust of all: then the goold is mine!"

A roar of wild laughter from an adjoining cellar drowned the whispers of the Door-keeper.

"It's them!" he cried with a wild grin. "The dogs—the cut-throats—the thieves! Ho-hoo! The Jew belongs to their band—"

Again his words were lost in a wild burst of laughter, and the rude strains of the Vagabond's song, broke on the air, chanted by hoarse voices to a quick cantering measure.

THE VAGABOND'S SONG

"A jolly band of good fellows all,
Are the Outcast Monks of old Monk-Hall!
They dance, they steal, they drink, they fight
And turn the shiny day into night—"

"Chorus boys!" shouted a hoarse voice.

"Raw Mon'gahaley is the g-o!
Clink you're mugs with a jolly sound
Down in the vaults below, bel-ow!
Down in the vaults below the ground—
Hurrah, foı the brave lads, one and all
The Outcast Monks of old Monk-Hall—
Hur-rah!"

"That's the stuff!" exclaimed Devil-Bug approaching the massy door of the thieves' cellar, which fashioned of stout wood, and strengthened by bands of iron, was dimly perceptible in the light, at the distance of some twenty paces from the table.

"Come out o' this!" he shouted pulling at the bolt of the door. "Come out yo' thieves, yo' robbers, yo' devils!"

The door flew open, and the blaze of a warm hearth streamed into the Dead-Vault. Devil-Bug's amiable greeting, was answered by the thunder shout of some twenty or thirty voices.

"Hurrah, for the brave lads one and all,
The Outcast Monks of old Monk-Hall!"

And through the opened door, into the Dead-Vault there poured one breathing mass of rags and lameness, filth and crime!

Some forty or fifty vagabonds, men who had grown old in crime, women whose bloated visages belied their sex, and puny children, whose distorted faces, were stamped with cunning, came tramping through the door, and surrounded the form of Devil-Bug, who in the midst of that motley crowd, looked like a devil among his attendant imps.

These were the Outcasts of the Quaker City! In the day-time, vagabond man and woman and child, lay quiet and snug, in the underground recesses of Monk-Hall; in the night they stole forth from the secret passage thro' the pawnbroker's shop in the adjoining street, and prowled over the city, to beg, to rob, or perchance to murder.

Bleared eyes, distorted faces, shrunken limbs, these all were there. On every side was filth and rags. The rags, indeed, were a wonder. Had the heavens on some stormy day, rained rags, and our friends, the vagabonds been caught in the shower, they could not have been better furnished, with tatters, than they were now. The children's faces peeped out from a wilderness of rags; the shrunken limbs or the stout forms of the men, were muffled in rags, thick as the scales of a fish, and the bloated countenances of the women, were framed in tatters. There was not one whole garment in the entire crowd. Here was a stout burly ruffian, with the remnant of a white over-coat, appended to the sad remains of a pair of checked trowsers, there stood an unshaven loafer, in a blue roundabout with one tattered sleeve, and then came a throng of women, clad in modified remnants of petticoat night-gown and frock, ragged as an election banner after a patriotic fight.

And among this haggard crowd were women, who twenty years ago had been *belles*, in the saloons of fashion; men who had been educated by rich and aristocratic fathers, for Lawyers, Judges, Bishops and Governors! But the mass had been born in misery, Baptized by Starvation, and Confirmed at the altar of Poverty, by the good old Bishop Crime.

Here they stood the Heathens and Outcasts of the Christian Quaker City, rotting in misery and sin, while Bibles, sent by goodly missionary societies were on their way, to degraded Hindoostan; here they stood, steeped to the lips in vice, while pious preachers were hurrying over land and ocean, in order to save the souls of naked Savages of the South Sea, or rescue freezing Greenlanders of the polar waste, from the perils of eternal death.

* "Hurray for old Devil-Bug!" the shout broke from the assembled band of vagabonds.

"Hush your d———d noise!" growled Devil-Bug. "Or shall I lame two or three of you? Anybody here that would like a leg broke or a head smash'd?"

"Silence genelmen!" roared a Loafer who gloried in the name of Rusty Jake. "The Perprieter o' this establishment has the floor!"

And with a solemn bow, the ruffian arranged the solitary sleeve of his roundabout.

* In this scene the Author omits the various allusions in the '*slang*' peculiar to the vagabond tribes of the Quaker City. They have a language of their own, but its repetition in these pages, would afford no interest to the general readre.

"Silence! Silence!" chorussed the Vagabonds.

"Let the wimmen and childr'n *re*-tire," observed Devil-Bug with quiet gravity. The bloated females, and the precocious children, obeyed the motion of Devil-Bug's hand, in silence. They trooped through the door, into the next cellar. The Doorkeeper stood alone with some thirty ruffians, whose visages, would have effectively adorned the windows of a goal; they all wore the same coarse, unshaven, desperate look.

"Wot I wants to know is this," resumed Devil-Bug. "Have I been a father to ye, ye ugly devils?"

"Has *he* been a father to us!" echoed Rusty Jake turning to his comrades with a leer of astonishment. "*He* axes that 'ere quest'in! Oh my! Has'n't he been a reglar daddy to us boys?"

"Hurray for old Devil-Bug!" Shouted the Thieves, Cut-throats and Vagabonds. Devil-Bug hammered his fist on the table.

"Have n't I hid you, when the Poleese was arter you? Have n't you had plenty of grub to eat? Have I treated you to the best Monygahaley? I puts the quest'in to you! Have n't I treated you like genelmen?"

"Like Lords!" cried Rusty Jake.

"Like fightin' cocks!" exclaimed a thin-visaged Loafer, known as Slippery Elm.

"Like pigs in swill," was the classic remark of another vagabond who wore the upper portion of a great coat, "Or like a Bank D'rector treats the Judges o' th' Court wot try's him!" And Pump-Handle, as the ruffian was styled, flung up his hat in very glee.

"Hurrah for old Devil-Bug," chorussed the mass of Vagabonds.

"Genelmen, I wants to *per*-pound you a quest'in. Wot should be done with the feller, who arter all my care and trouble for his sake, and for your gineral welfare, goes and blows us to the Poleese?"

As Devil-Bug uttered these words, in a tone of quiet gravity, he presented in his person and manner, a capital burlesque of some 'Godlike' Senator,' while the vagabonds, grouped around him looked like Congressmen eager to pay their attentions to Judge Lynch.

One wild burst of execration arose from the band.

"To the d——l with him! We'll cut his throat!"

"Genelmen," resumed Devil-Bug, "This 'ere Jew, Gabr'el Von Gelt is sich a man! What shall be done with him?"

"Gabr'el Von Gelt!" muttered Rusty Jake striking an attitude. "I never thought much o' that feller! Why he was above drinkin' Monygahaley whiskey!"

"And he would'n't eat pork!"

"And he was too proud to go ragged!"

There was a great excitement. The ruffians murmured together, and their rude hands drew forth knives and pistols, from the thick concealment of their rags.

"What shall be done with him?" was the quiet demand of Devil-Bug.

The answer of Rusty Jake was terse and pointed.

"Its my opinion vich I entertains, in common these genelmen, that this 'ere Jew's wizand ought to be examined!"

He passed his hand across his throat, in a gesture at once graceful and expressive.

"Cut his throat!" was the response of the Outcasts.

"Hark! There's his footstep on the stairs," exclaimed Devil-Bug. "He's comin' down! A word with yo' fellers. I must go up stairs a minnit—don't do anything with the Jew till I get back! I'll bring you some rare Monygahaley! I must get 'em drunk afore they murder the Jew!" he muttered. "Nothin' like rum to sharpen a cut-throat's knife!"

As he disappeared in the direction of the western door of the vault, the sound of footsteps grew louder in the opposite direction.

"It's the Jew!" muttered Rusty Jake, and as he spoke a murmur of surprise ran thro' the ruffian band. A tall figure, clad from head to foot in rags, stepped from the shadow of a brick pillar and advanced toward the table. His hair and whiskers made him resemble a Walking Conflagration; they were thick, bushy and burning red. His skin was hideously freckled, and from beneath his red eyebrows, flashed the glance of two snake-like eyes, giving his face, a strange and wild expression.

"Hello, comrades!" growled Rusty Jake, "Who's this feller?"

"Vy you see," said the Stranger with a genuine vagabond snuffle, "I'm a feller bein' in distress. The poleese is arter me. I wants you to hide me, old boy. Cover me up snug, will you?"

A murmur of suspicion ran thro' the band.

"The watch-word if you please, Stranger!" asked Rusty Jake.

"O' course," calmly responded the red-haired vagabond. " '*Pork and beans is a werry good dinner*, '*specially with molasses*.' My name is Brick-Top gemmen. My daddy was a scavenger, and my mammy sold rags—"

The outcasts looked upon him in suspicious wonder, and then huddling in a group, murmured together.

"I must obtain the papers from the Jew or die!" was the whispered remark of Brick-Top as he stood beside the table. "For a night and a day I have lain, half-bruized to death, in my room up stairs. But a few moments ago disguised in these old rags, I escaped from the front door of Monk-Hall, passed thro' the pawnbroker's shop, and here I am, in the power of a band of reckless cut-throats. I must watch the course of events; the Jew is concealed somewhere, in the old mansion; I will find out his hiding place and obtain the papers, or forfeit my life—"

"You sir, it's all right" exclaimed Rusty Jake. "The 'nitiation fee if you please."

"Heaven grant that Dora may show Livingstone the note which I gave her last night!" muttered the disguised Luke. "And then Mabel—mystery accumulates on mystery! The girl is Livingstone's child, I must save her from ruin—"

"The 'nitiation fee—" growled Slippery Elm.

"There's a shiner," snuffled Luke in his Brick-Top voice. "I'll fork up reg'lar if you hide me away—I will that!"

"Hello, fellers," exclaimed Slippery Elm, "He's given Rusty Jake a rale yaller boy! Now boys, we'll have the grub and the likker—huzza!"

"I say my coves," exclaimed Rusty Jake, as fingering the gold Eagle he glanced aside at the form of Brick-Top. "Ai'nt he ragged! My stars! Why he's reg'lar nasty! What's the poleese arter you for?"

"Robbin' a market wagon," answered Brick-Top in a surly tone.

"Oh you werry contemptible individual!" exclaimed Rusty Jake, "Robbin' a market wagon! Wot a low business! Turn him out."

"Robbin' a market wagon!" echoed the band. "Ugh—quite a loafer!"

Brick-Top squared his elbows, and looked around with a threat'ning scowl.

"What the d———l you growlin' at? I've murdered my man in my time, been convicted; sentenced for it too. I'm no new hand at the bellows, I tell you!"

"That's somethin' like!" exclaimed Slippery Elm. "Good, capital!" echoed the band.

"You were sentenced were you?" quoth Rusty Jake. "How did yo' git clear?"

"Well, you're a nice 'un!" exclaimed Brick top with a sneer. "You are a precious fool! To axe me sich a questi'n! *Why the Governor pardoned me of course!*"

"Why so he did me!" cried Rusty Jake.

"And so he did me!" exclaimed Slippery Elm.

"And me!" shouted Pump-Handle.

"And me!" cried another ruffian.

"And me, by hokey!" added an unshaven vagabond.

"Hurrah for the Pardenin' Power," chorussed the rest of the band.

It was now Brick-Top's turn to ask questions.

"What were you tried for?" he exclaimed, turning to Rusty Jake.

"I had a misfortin' " responded the worthy. "I killed a man by accident. You see, it was on the highway, at night. I axed him a civil question. He replied with impudence. We had words. His wizand was perforated."

"What was your question?" growled Luke.

"Oh, nothin' pertik'ler!" meekly replied Rusty Jake. "I merely axed him for his purse, or—his life. He would'nt give the fust, so I tuk the last. But—" he added with a grin, "I found *mercy*. I was pardoned!"

"You found *money* you mean," exclaimed Brick-Top, "and what were *you* tried for?" he asked, turning to another vagabond.

"Why you see, a party of us one Sunday arternoon, had nothin' to do, so we got up a nigger riot. We have them things in Phil'delphy, once or twice a year, you know? I helped to burn a nigger church, two orphans' asylums and a school-house. And happenin' to have a pump-handle in my hand, I aksedentally hit an old nigger on the head. Konsekance wos he died. That's why they call me Pump-Handle."

"And you was tried for this little accident?"

"Yes, I was. Convicted, too. Sentenced, in the bargain. But the Judge and the jury and the lawyers, on both sides, signed a paper to the Governor. He pardoned me. But I could'nt keep my hands in the ways o' virtue, so here I am agin, hidin' from the poleese!"

Rusty Jake looked around with an expression of deep thought.

"I say fellers, why could'nt we have a Governor that 'ud *weto* the Poleese?"

"Hurray for a Governor that 'ud weto the poleese, and the Judges and the Courts!" Slippery Elm sprang from his feet with excitement as he uttered this remarkable sentiment.

Rusty Jake had been a small politician in his time. Two years past he had been an influential party man, on a limited scale. In procuring forged naturalization papers for verdant foreigners, or in swearing native paupers and thieves into the inestimable knowledge of voting, he was alike efficient and skillful.

Rusty Jake had also been a speech-maker; he had stirred up the patriotism of the people with the cry of 'Down with the Bank,' or 'up with the Bank' as the humor seized him, or as he was paid for his services, by more magnificent politicians. Rusty Jake, therefore had grown into the habit of speech-making; he could not let the present opportunity pass, without a few improving remarks.

"Genelmen, feller citizens, freemen!" he shouted, ascending the table, and gazing upon the assembled crowd of ruffians.

"Wot was it that our forefather's fit, bled and died for? Wot did they go in the cold for, without a mint-julip to make 'em jolly, or a sherry cobbler to warm their insides? Was it to have *this* item o' human rights wiped off the slate o' liberty, with the sponge o' tyranny? Was it to have the Pardenin' Power struck out o' th' Constitooshun? The id*ee* is redikulus! Why the fact is, tho' it ain't ginerally known—that the whole Revolution was on account of the Pardenin' power! Gineral Washington—as history will tell you—was put in jail, for killin' an injin' in a nigger riot down South! That old curmudgeon, George the Third, refused to pardon Gineral Washington. The Revolution, gentlemen, wos the konsekence o' that refusal! I refers you to history, gentlemen, for further pertik'lers."

* "Genelmen, feller citizens," shouted Slippery Elm, "Three cheers for the Governor, wot pardons everybody, for doin' everything, and don't axe no quest'ins! Huzzay!"

The loud hurrah of the vagabonds was interrupted by the footstep and voice of Devil-Bug, who now appeared from the shadow of a brick pillar, holding a large earthen jug in his hand.

"Will you hush that cussed noise?" he thundered in his growling voice. "Here's the Monygahaley boys. Pass it round. D'ye know fellers, that Von Gelt is comin' down stairs? Hello! Brick-Top here!"

He started as he perceived the form of his pretended accomplice.

"You see the poleese is arter me—" began Luke.

"H-u-s-h! These fellers must n't know nothin'!" muttered Devil-Bug. "That Jew Von Gelt has been betrayin' us. He must die. You must help dispatch him, and I," he muttered this sentence to himself, "Will see to you, and so git rid of both my partners! The Jew must die," he cried turning to the vagabond crew.

"How?" asked Slippery Elm.

"You see this square table? It stands upon a trap. Let the Jew set down on a bench at this side, and let one of our fellers, set down on a bench opposite. S'pose he begins to talk to the Jew, and gits him drinkin'? A single kick from the man's foot, will strike this knob, sink the trap, and send our pork-hater to the devil! D'ye see it boys?"

Rusty Jake and the other vagabonds examined the knob, which arose from the floor, near one of the massive legs of the table, with a quiet and peculiar attention.

"What 'ill become o' th' feller who sinks the trap?" asked Slippery Elm.

* The last day of the administration of a certain Governor, will long be remembered with pious reverence, by the turnkeys of the various prisons. On that day, the merciful executive, filled up the measure of his fame, by setting free a batch of convicts, thieves, burglars and murderers. In the course of six years, this truly merciful Executive granted about 700 pardons.

"You'll obs*a*-rve that the bench on which he is to set, is some inches away from the edge of the trap," exclaimed Devil-Bug, "While the bench on the other side of the table, is right in the middle o' the cons*a*rn!"

"Death to the traitor," muttered the vagabonds, as the earthen jug passed from hand to hand, "Death to the Pork-hater!"

"But who'll be the feller to stamp upon the knob?" exclaimed Devil-Bug.

"Let's pull straws for it!" cried Rusty Jake, "This is capital Monygahaley! Put a lot o' straws into a hat, and the man as has the shortest does the thing."

"Agreed, agreed!" echoed the ruffians, whose sparkling eyes, betrayed the effects of the Monongahela.

"Here's a decent hat to put the straws in," exclaimed Slippery Elm, producing a piece of dark felt, which in remote ages, might have been a hat.

"And here's the straws," cried Rusty Jake, seizing a handful of loose straws from the floor near a brick pillar, he proceeded to sever it into various pieces, with a knife which he drew from his rags. These pieces, numbering thirty-four in all, were poured into the fragment of a hat, which was placed on the end of the table.

There was a dead silence. One by one, with the same look of stolid indifference, each thief, cut-throat and robber advanced, each turned away his face as he placed his hand in the hat, and then seizing one of the straws from the mass, walked silently away.

Luke Harvey's turn came last.

"This grows interesting!" he muttered as he approached the table. "Heaven grant that the lot may fall on any one, but me! Here I am in a pretty 'pickle!' A candidate for the Honorable office of Executioner for a Jew! However, here goes—" he placed his hand in the hat—"My fate is decided one way or the other."

"Fellers measure your straws!" exclaimed Devil-Bug with quiet dignity.

They all grouped together: thirty-four rude hands, with the white hand of Luke among them, were ranged in a row; there was a pause; you could hear each man gasping for breath, and then a loud laugh broke on the air.

"Mister with the red beard, yours is the shortest!" exclaimed Devil-Bug. "The job is for you!"

For a moment Luke stood stricken dumb with a strange fear. He must either murder or be murdered! The eye of Devil-Bug was fixed upon him; all hope of escape was in vain.

"I will procure the pacquet at all hazards!" muttered Luke with set teeth. And he confirmed his resolution by a solemn Oath.

"Here comes the cripple," cried Devil-Bug. "Ho, ho" he murmured —"The chest o' gold and other leetle property is mine!"

As he spoke, a shuffling footstep was heard, and the light presently shone upon the large face and distorted body of the Jewish dwarf, Gabriel Von Gelt. He came forward with one hand resting upon his fragment of a chest, while his dark eyes glanced around with an expression full of inquiry.

"Well folksh good eveningsh!" he said blandly. "I vonders vot they means by looking plack at me?" he muttered to himself. "Folksh I shay, good eveningsh!"

The vagabonds turned away from him with evident signs of disgust.

"The fact is my friend," cried Rusty Jake with a sneer, "There's been reports of a wery injurious natur' circulatin' in these parts lately, in regard to your karacter!"

"Brick-Top wants to speak a word with you, in regard to *your escape* —" said Devil-Bug in a friendly whisper. "Don't mind these cut-throats—"

"Sit down there, if you please," said Luke in a surly tone.

Von Gelt sate down on one side of the table, while Luke seated himself opposite.

The thieves retired a few paces from the table, and Devil-Bug leaning against a brick pillar, silently observed the scene.

A trifling fact may be recorded in this place. Right over the head of the Jew, the arching ceiling descended in a point, with a substantial pulley of iron inserted in the rude plastering. The original object of this pulley was evident. A thick rope passed through the pulley, dropped down into the Pit of Monk-Hall through the trap-door, lowering or raising the hogsheads of rich old wine, which were formerly deposited in that vast cellar. At the present moment, the light from the table, shone upon a slight but strong cord which, arranged in a slip-knot right over the head of the Jew, was passed through the pulley, and along the ceiling, until it hung in loose coils around a stout iron hook, projecting from a massy brick pillar.

Devil-Bug stood beside this pillar, watching the rope, and the Jew with evident interest.

Luke Harvey leaned over the pine table, until his face well-nigh touched the countenance of Gabriel Von Gelt.

"I have ten words to say to you," he exclaimed in his natural voice. "On answer to these ten words hangs your life. Make but a start, show but a sign of emotion, and you are a dead man—"

"Fader Moses! Vat is dis!" Von Gelt's florid countenance grew pale as ashes. The slip-knot above his head began slowly to descend, as Devil-Bug touched the other end of the rope.

"Don't you see by the looks of this band, that they have resolved—"

"On what—" The slip-knot dangled in the air within three inches of the Jew's head.

"On your murder!"

"Fader Abraham!" cried Von Gelt with a start, and his dark hair brushed against the quivering rope.

"Start one step," whispered Luke, "and I will stamp upon the spring which sets *the trap* in motion! Your life is in danger: I alone can save you, I alone can rescue you from the power of these devils!"

"Den you are not von of dem?" faltered the Jew. "Supposh I betraysh you?"

"Give but a sign of such a purpose, and, ha, ha, the trap *beneath the table*, falls!"

"Hurray there you feller, with the red head," exclaimed Devil-Bug, "Finish this little business!"

"Little bushinesh!" echoed the thunder-struck Jew.

Luke leaned gently forward, and fixing his eyes on the terrified countenance of the Jew, whispered a single name:

' "*Ellis Mortimer!*" '

"Veres you hear dat name?" cried the Jew with another start.

"You were concerned in the great forgery, committed on the House of Livingstone, Harvey & Co., about a month since. You have about your person certain documents which will convict Algernon Fitz-Cowles of the forgery. Give me those documents, and the ten thousand dollars which you have about your person, are yours! As for the '*murder*,' you can turn 'State's Evidence;' it will just suit you, being a Jew. Give me the papers!"

"I vill die first!" muttered Gabriel, trembling in every limb.

"Then by heaven, I spring the trap!" Luke hissed the whisper in his ear.

"I conshents!" cried Gabriel. "Dere's de pacquet!"

Luke grasped the prize, and buried it among his rags.

"I say red-head, what are yo' up to there?" growled Devil-Bug, as he gave the rope another shake. "Be quick, I say!"

A growling murmur arose from the band of thieves. Luke saw that no time was to be lost.

"I say Gabriel, can you run or fight?" he whispered. "If you can run yonder's the door! I fight myself!"

Gabriel was rising from his feet with a look of horror and fright stamped on every line of his face, when Devil-Bug strode silently forward at his back. He extended his huge hand, and the slip-knot encircled the neck of the Jew. Gabriel felt the cord around his neck, he sprang forward in horror, and as he sprang, the massive foot of Devil-Bug was stamped upon the knob. The trap, the tables, and the candles fell, and ere a moment all was darkness. In that single moment of light and horror, Luke Harvey, starting back from the edge of the chasm, beheld a sight that he might never forget. He beheld the Jew struggling in the air, above the blackness of the void, he saw the rope which tightened round his neck at every struggle, and like some horrible vision, that large face, with red skin turning to purple and the mouth agape and the dark eyes bulging from their sockets, rushed before him! A single moment he beheld that sight, and all was darkness.

The wild yell of Devil-Bug mingled with the hurrah of the out-casts. Then a choaking groan gurgled from the darkness above the trap-door. Then the sharp sound of a rope snapping, strand by strand, and then another gurgling groan!

"He dies hard!" muttered Devil-Bug through the darkness.

A light flashed suddenly over the vault, from the western entrance. Luke looked for the corse of the Jew, quivering in the air. It was gone! The rope broken off near the ceiling, waved gently to and fro, and a dead whizzing sound came up from the depths of the pit, like the echo of a heavy body dashing into fragments against the hard earth.

While Luke's heart quivered with a strange horror, he looked toward the western entrance, and saw the huge forms of Musquito and Glow-worm advancing with torches in their hands, while two paces before them, a figure muffled in the thick folds of a sweeping black cloak rushed hurriedly onward, leading the way toward the trap. Luke knew the stranger at a glance; he looked upon him for a single moment, and then silently drew two pistols from among his rags.

"Devil-Bug you are betrayed!" shouted the stranger, as he stood in the glare of the light, beside the trap-door. "Yonder stands the traitor!"

"Ha! Fitz-Cowles!" muttered Devil-Bug, and for a moment, as a wild frown darkened over his brow, he seemed hesitating on whom to spring, Luke Harvey or the Forger.

"Seize him!" cried Fitz-Cowles as a dark scowl impressed his swarthy countenance, with the malignity of a devil. "He has betrayed your secrets and your lives!"

"Come on my civet cut!" sneered Luke, dashing aside his red wig and beard, as he stood with a pistol extended in either hand. "I'll sweeten you with a new perfume! The smell of powder!"

The thieves drew their knives and pistols, and silently circled round Luke Harvey and his antagonist. It was a striking picture. The tall form of Luke, clad in rags, standing on one side of the chasm, each hand grasping a pistol; the well-proportioned figure of Fitz-Cowles, with a cloak falling from his shoulder, on the other, his raised arm, flashing a bowie knife in the light; while at the head of the pit stood the deformed savage, Devil-Bug, with his band of outcasts, circling in the back ground. For a moment the savage held his bloodhounds in check.

"Upon him, the dog! Upon him!" shouted Devil-Bug, pointing to Luke.

With one movement the ruffian band advanced, their upraised knives glittering in the torch-light.

"I will die hard I tell you!" said Luke, with set teeth, as he placed his back against a pillar. "Come on blood-hounds! Come on, forger and knave! Lay but a hand on me, and your brains shall plaster these cellar walls!"

"Hew him down you dogs!" screamed Fitz-Cowles, hoarse with rage.

There was a quiet determination in the eyes of Luke, that for a moment held the vagabond's in awe. It was a brave sight; one man against thirty-four ruffians, with a well-dressed bravo, hallooing them on to a deed of cowardice and blood.

Forming a half-circle the thieves advanced, slowly and silently, while Devil-Bug stole behind the pillar. There was the report of a pistol, and thick clouds of smoke rolled to the ceiling of the vault.

"Ha, ha," screamed Luke, "I told you that I would die hard!" And the form of a grim vagabond lay quivering and sprawling on the verge of the chasm.

At this moment, a rough hand came gliding round the pillar; its talon fingers encircling the neck of Luke with a grasp like death, while the whole band of outcasts, rushed upon him with one sudden spring. Another instant passed! He lay on the floor, with the knives of the outcasts flashing above him, the knee of Devil-Bug on his breast, and the hands of the monster tightening round his throat.

"The peril is past!" shouted Fitz-Cowles from the other side of the chasm. "Another throw of fortune's dice, and I am saved!"

A puffy face, adorned by a curly wig, was thrust from behind the pillar at his back.

"Here's a family party, *ce la est un partie domestique*, as we say in very Domestic French! I tried to sell Fitz-Cowles to Harvey: he wouldn't buy me! So I wormed what secrets I could concerning Harvey, out of the police, and incontinently sold him to Fitz-Cowles! "WE" is always on hand when 'black mail' is to be had!"

With this half-murmured remark, little Poodle drew his bewigged head behind the pillar again.

"Why there's rather a muss here, my feller!" said a cheerful voice at the shoulder of Fitz-Cowles. The Millionaire turned, and beheld the round, visage of Major Mulhill, appearing between the wooly heads of the Negroes, who stood holding the torches at his back.

"Yes, y-e-s!" whispered Fitz-Cowles, "I've the scoundrel safe! Safe at last! Into the pit with him Devil-Bug!"

A deep groan came from Luke's lips as he felt himself slowly dragged along the floor toward the chasm.

"I vonders how *that* 'ill vork!" chuckled old Devil-Bug. Two outcasts held the feet of the pinioned man, while the others were grouped around gazing silently upon the scene.

At this moment, the torch-light flickering fitfully along the corners of the vault, gave the rude walls, the nooks, and crevices of the place a wild and fantastic appearance. For an instant, it seemed to Fitz-Cowles, that the dim shadows assumed the forms of men skulking in the darkness of the place.

Luke groaned in agony. His feet dangled over the chasm.

"Ex-cuse me, Curnel, if I admire the pattern o' your cravat," said the redoubtable Major Mulhill, fingering the dark scarf of Fitz-Cowles with a playful air. "Quite genteel! Does it fit tight round your neck?" He inserted his fingers between the cravat and the neck as he spoke.

"Take care; you'll choke me—" muttered Fitz-Cowles with a start. A bland smile broke over Mulhill's fat face.

"Now my gemmen, will you read *this!*" He tightened his grasp around the throat of the Forger, and displayed a broad slip of paper, before his very eyes. " 'It's only a love letter from a ga-l!' "

"What does this mean—" gasped Fitz-Cowles, "Hands off—" His words were drowned by a wild shriek, that quivered through the cellar.

"Seize him, seize the murderer of Paul Western!" shrieked a woman's voice, and the queenly form of Long-haired Bess stood on the verge of the chasm, her dark hair, showering aside from her pale face, and her black eye, flashing with a glance like madness.

There was a moment of terrible and confused action! Devil-Bug started up from his victim, leaving his form trembling on the verge of the pit, and with him, the vagabond band drew their knives, and turned to face the newcomer. One wild murmur of despair quivered from lip to lip! By the side of every cut-throat there stood the form of a burly police officer, at the back of Bess, along the cellar, around Fitz-

Cowles and Mulhill, circled a firm and determined band, some hundred strong, with maces and pistols in their hands.

"Fight ye devils!" screamed Devil-Bug, but the band of police suddenly advanced, surrounding the thieves, and compressing them in one mass, by the superiority of their numbers. In a moment the thieves were disarmed, and beaten to the floor with maces. Devil-Bug clenched his weaponless hands, and gnashed his teeth, in the effort to bite the feet that trampled him down, but it was in vain!

As he lay trodden beneath the feet of some dozen police officers, Luke Harvey, sprang over the chasm with one bound, and seized Fitz-Cowles by the throat. The forger was deathly pale; his under lip quivered like a dry leaf in the wind.

"Now coward, the hour of reckoning has come!" Fitz-Cowles lay on the floor, with the foot of Luke Harvey on his breast. "Do you know those papers," shrieked Luke. "Ha, ha, ha! Do you feel yourself, within the prison's walls already? Do your dapper limbs already feel the cheering warmth of the convicts dress—and then the manacles, and the lash! Ho, ho!"

"This is wot I calls a cheerin' scene," was the smiling remark of Mulhill.

The sound of a woman's voice, tremulous with remorse and agony, shrieked through the dead-vault.

"He stands before me!" shrieked Long-haired Bess, gazing with starting eyes, into the blackness of the chasm. "He stands before me, his pale face clotted with drops of blood! He wronged me, and he died —oh, God! his dying shriek rings in my ears! But he shall be avenged!"

"The gallows for me, you hell-cat!" screamed Devil-Bug, raising his head from the floor, while a fiendish grin convulsed his face. "The gallows for me; you hell-cat!" He shook his manacled hands together. "Ha, ha, hoo! Vonders how that 'ill vork!"

CHAPTER SECOND

THE OAK CHAMBER OF HAWKEWOOD

DORA LIVINGSTONE GAINS THE CORONET, FOR WHICH SHE PERILLED HER SOUL

"A fine old-time mansion, Dora!" exclaimed Livingstone as he crossed the threshold of the chamber. "That was a solemn hall thro' which we passed, with its gloomy pictures and quaint carvings in dark stone, and then the stairway Dora, with its steps of massive oak—by my life, I like this mansion of Hawkewood! It has a wild baronial look."

"And this chamber, with its old-time furniture and antiquarian appointments," exclaimed Dora with a smile, "Has it a characteristic name?"

"It is called the Oak Chamber of Hawkewood. You see, the walls are concealed by huge panels of dark oaken wainscot, and the floor is covered by an old-fashioned carpet. In yonder corner, stands a bed with dark purple hangings, and here, from this lordly hearth, the glare of a cheerful wood fire flashes round the place. I like it Dora!"

"And then this round table, of dark walnut, standing in the centre of the room, with a Gothic arm-chair on either side! Certainly the place looks like the den of some old monk, half wizard, half antiquary!"

"In that chair my father breathed his last," whispered Livingstone with a sudden sternness of tone. "And on that table words have been written, which were followed by deeds of bloodshed and horror!"

With a kind gesture he pointed to the arm-chair on one side of the round table, motioning his wife to a seat, while he sat down on the opposite side.

"We'll have a cup of coffee, before you change your travelling dress my love," said Livingstone with marked kindness of tone. "I forgot to inform you, that by a careless mistake, I dated the invitations to our friends, for to-morrow, instead of to-day. You will have to endure the solitude of this place, until the morning, when old Hawkewood will put on a face of smiles. Bye, the bye, my dear, I have despatched all the servants to town, in order that my various preparations for the Christmas festival, may be completed. Old Davidson and his wife, will wait on you, until the morrow—"

There was something so natural and commonplace in all this, that Dora forgot the strange wildness of manner, which Livingstone had once or twice manifested within the past hour; and her own dark thoughts, were for the moment, silenced by his calm tone and composed look.

"Ha, ha," cried Dora, with a laughing smile, "I can endure the solitude of Hawkewood for a single night, unless, indeed, yon bed, with its gloomy hangings, should chance to be haunted by pale ghosts or hideous dreams."

"Oh, your dreams will be sweet and undisturbed. I pledge my life for it!" said Livingstone, with a peculiar look, which escaped the eye of his wife.

There was a knocking at the door, and in a moment, the trembling form of the old gardener entered the chamber. His long and slender arms, embraced a shapeless mass of canvass, entwined with thick ropes, and looking for all the world, like the sails of a vessel, tied confusedly together.

"Squire whar shall I put this bundle?" exclaimed Davidson. "It looks amazin' big, but it taint so heavy as you'd think."

"What have we here?" exclaimed Dora, looking at her husband with a glance of wonder.

"Only the scenery for our private theatricals," said Livingstone in a careless tone. "You may as well stand it against the wall, behind the bed, Davidson. To-morrow we'll have it unpacked. And now my old boy," he added placing his hand familiarly on the gardiner's shoulder. "Tell your dame, to make one of her best cups of coffee, for myself, and Mrs. Livingstone. Don't you remember Davidson, how fond I used to be of your wife's coffee?"

"And I will say," cried the old man rubbing his hands together, "That my Hannah's *ee*-kal in the way o' makin' coffee, and right strong coffee, with good cream to make it look yallar as goold, an' a lump o' loaf sugar, do give it a taste o' sweetenin' aint to be found in these parts!"

With this remarkable tribute to Dame Hannah's abilities, the old gardiner left the room, and Livingstone and his wife were alone once more.

From the broad hearth, the crackling hickory fire, sent a ruddy glow around the room, which now obscured the light of the wax candles, standing on the round table, or again, dying suddenly away, left the place involved in comparative gloom.

Gazing steadily in the face of his wife, Livingstone sat on one side of the table, his broad chest, enveloped in a dark frock coat, presenting a fine contrast to the form of Dora, whose every outline of beauty and grace, was disclosed by the folds of her dark green travelling habit. They sat in the centre of that strange old room, with the dark wainscot of the walls, the heavy curtaining of the bed, the massive frames of the windows, looking to the east, half-concealed by sombre hangings, and the spacious outlines of the fire-place, affording the effective details of a picture, in which the form of the merchant and his wife, were the striking and central objects of attention.

The face of the merchant was deadly pale, yet an expression of immoveable calmness lingered on every feature. The massive brow, towering above the dark eyebrows, was full of silent thought, and the slight smile, playing round the expressive mouth, gave his face a mild and benignant look, which was in fearful contrast, with the discolored circles of flesh, beneath each eye, or the sunken outlines of each bronzed cheek. The eyes of Livingstone, wore a look, never to be forgotten. Large, azure and calm, they shone in a strange light, which seemed to flicker around each eyeball like rays around a lamp.

Her form flung back in the arm-chair, in a position of grace and ease, Dora's face, afforded a vivid contrast to the countenance of her husband. The dark eyes swam in a mild, melting light, the smiling cheeks were flushed with warm rich hues, the high forehead was full of soul, and the small mouth with its lips of deep voluptuous red, was curved in a winning smile.

"Dora, my wife, you are very beautiful," said Livingstone in that deep-toned voice, which sounded from the depths of his chest. "We have now been married one year. You have been to me, a faithful, true and *affectionate* wife. As a slight tribute of my love, let me place in your hands, this Christmas Gift."

He drew from his breast, a small casket of gold richly set with jewels. Dora received it with an exclamation of delight.

"A gift like this would not shame the bride of an emperor!" she murmured, as her delicate fingers enclosed the princely gift.

"That casket encloses a gift, yet more precious than the jewels that glitter on its exterior," said Livingstone as he rose from his seat. "Excuse me one moment my love, I have some trifling orders to give to Davidson. In an instant I will return with the key of the casket—"

He advanced to the door of the chamber, and passed out into the spacious landing, at the head of the stair-way. The dim beams of the stars obscured by clouds streamed through a solitary window in the southern wall, giving a faint light to the oaken floor and the massive walls. Closing the door of the Oak Chamber, Livingstone stood with his back toward the window, gazing down the dim stairway, with folded arms and compressed lips. Presently the sound of footsteps was heard; a slight tremor ran over Livingstone's powerful frame, and the next instant, the form of Davidson was seen through the dusky shadows, ascending the stairway with a waiter in his hands.

"I will take the coffee, Davidson, while you hurry down-stairs, and have my horse brought to the hall door. Business requires my immediate return to Philadelphia. Lose no time, my good fellow, but let it be done without an instant's delay."

Taking the waiter from the astonished servant, he advanced to the window, and laid it down gently on the oaken sill. In an instant the form of Davidson, was lost in the shadows of the stairway, and soon the faint echo of his footsteps sounded faintly from the hall below.

Livingstone stood in the faint light of the stars, gazing steadily on the waiter, whose dark surface was relieved, by two large cups of white porcelain, smoking with fragrant coffee.

For a moment the Merchant stood silent as the grave. His chest heaved, and his lip quivered with emotion. With a low muttered groan, he drew forth from his breast a small phial of glittering silver.

He raised it in the dim light, and the fingers which clasped it trembled like dry leaves in the storm. Then his blue eyes was fixed upon it with a gaze of horrible intensity, and a single large and scalding tear, starting from the hot eyelid, rolled slowly down his bronzed cheek.

"My wife!" he groaned, and still absorbed by an awful effort to control his reeling intellect, he stood regarding that silver phial with the same wild and intense stare.

Meanwhile, Dora sate in the arm-chair beside the table, with the golden casket resting lightly in her hand.

Her husband closed the door, and a wild expression, mingling hope and fear, love and hate, guilt and shame, brightened and darkened over the face of the wife.

Placing the casket on the table, she thrust her hands in her bosom, and while the agitation deepened over her queenly face, she displayed two objects in the light. One was the note, given to her by Luke Harvey the evening before; the other was the small phial of deadly poison, which she had prepared with such fearful secresy and care.

"On one side a Coronet beckons me, on the other stands Livingstone with love in his look and honor on his brow. Shall I choose the Coronet—then Livingstone lays a lifeless corse within this very hour! Shall I trample the Coronet under foot, and subside from all my high dreams, into a patient and gentle wife? *I* patient and gentle! Suppose Livingstone is dead, even then Fitz-Cowles' plan of immediate flight is ill-judged, worse than foolish! Livingstone once dead, I must act the disconsolate widow, walk broken hearted at his funeral, and after a decent lapse of time, inherit the vast fortune, left to me by my *affectionate* husband. My brain whirls, and I know not which to choose, the phial or the letter! The one secures the eternal secresy of Luke; the other lays a Coronet at my feet, but the price is terrible—the dead body of my husband! And then my oath, my oath—"

As the thought of that Oath, which in sight of the awful God, calling his angels to witness, with her heart filled with pure emotions, and her hands clasped in the hands of the only man she ever loved in solemn truth, as the thought of that Oath flashed over her soul, Dora half started from the chair, and uttered a low-toned shriek.

Livingstone's footstep broke on her ear, with a hurried movement she buried the letter, and the phial in her bosom. Calling a calm smile to her face, she awaited the approach of her husband.

"Here is the coffee, my dear," said Livingstone in a careless tone, as he entered, and placed the waiter on the round table. "It is a long while since I tasted coffee in this house, but I can commend old Hannah's coffee, above all other's, for its delicious flavor. Is'nt it singular my dear, that so few people in the world, know how to prepare, even tolerable coffee?"

Dora looked into the pale face of her husband with a glance of vacant wonder. If there was a thing in the world that he sincerely contemned, it was a common-place remark, on any subject at all; but the pleasures of eating and drinking, in especial. This colloquial remark on the peculiar merits of old Hannah's coffee, might well excite the wonder of the merchant's wife. There was a volume of awful meaning concealed under the trifling words and careless tone of Livingstone.

Seating himself beside the table, the Merchant raised one of the porcelain cups to his lips, and sipped its fragrant contents.

Reclining in the arm chair, her beautiful face glowing in the mild beams of the light, and her rounded limbs disposed in an attitude of careless languor, Dora followed the example of her husband, and raising the other cup to her lips, athirst from the fatigue of travel, she drank profusely of the smoking coffee.

At this moment, Livingstone's blue eyes did not glare, nor shine, nor glisten; they seemed to blaze with a glassy lustre, as deadly as light emitted from the eyes of the rattle-snake, ere it kills its victim.

"Bye the bye, my dear, I must mention a singular piece of news, which overtook me on the road to Hawkewood this evening. I have spoken to you of the noble descent of my family. I have told you that Livingstone was an assumed name, that my grand-father left the broad lands of his barony in the hands of distant kinsmen, when he sought the solitudes of the new world—"

The words of the Merchant had a strange interest for Dora. Half-starting from the chair, she listened with flashing eyes and parted lips, to the whispered tones of her husband.

"During my father's life, the last of the race of kinsmen died, leaving the old barony without a lord. My father hastened to England, and placing his claim to the lands and title, in the hands of able lawyers, awaited the result with an impatience that clung to him until his dying hour. Here was the difficulty—our Ancestor had left England, having first circulated the rumor that he was dead, and dead without an heir. He wished to bury his name, and the dishonor which the *treachery of a woman* had brought upon it, in eternal oblivion. My father's lawyers found it almost impossible to prove the identity of our ancestor, with the self-exiled Lord. That impossibility has now been overcome. While my father's ashes rest in the family vault of Hawkewood, side by side, with that ancestor, who exiled himself from his native soil, I hold in my hand the pacquet which informs the *Philadelphia* Merchant, that restored to the lands and title of his race he is now—"

"Yes, yes," muttered Dora, as her face grew ashy pale. "Speak on, for God's sake Livingstone. Yes—you are now—"

"THE LORD OF LONGFORD!" said Livingstone in a clear, deliberate tone.

Dora rose to her feet with a half muttered shriek.

"A title and in England!" she murmured, "The fulfilment of my wildest dream! *Lady of Longford*—ah! Already I behold myself the mistress of broad lands, already I move in the throng of a royal court already I feel the Coronet encircling my brow!"

"The coronet of worms," muttered Livingstone with livid lips, as the broken words of his wife, fell indistinctly on his ear. "Your broad lands—a pitiful grave, eight feet long and two feet wide!"

"Of course, Albert," said Dora, resuming her seat—"You will at once proceed to England, and assume the estates and title?"

"Both of us will undertake a journey soon, but not to England!" muttered Livingstone. "Would you advise me to give up my rights, the rights of an American citizen," he continued aloud, "for the rent-roll of an English Barony, and the empty sound of a title?"

"Your rights as an American citizen," sneered Dora, "Comprising among other inestimable priveleges, the right to count one, among a pitiful aristocracy, whose high deeds are written in the ledger of a broken bank, which chronicles the wholesale robbery of the widow and the orphan, accomplished under the solemn sanction of the—*law!* Glorious rights indeed!"

"Dora shall we look at your Christmas gift?" said the Merchant with a calm smile.

Dora's eye grew suddenly glassy. Was it from the overwhelming emotion which followed Livingstone's announcement?

"I will move among the proudest nobles of the British Court! Rank, title, power! The prophecy is fulfilled! The Boon is mine, without the Crime. How my head swims—I feel giddy—my heart—ah! I am too much affected by this joyful intelligence."

As these words fell wild and trembling from her lips, while her cheek grew crimson and ashy by turns, Livingstone sate regarding her with the same look that glares from the eye of the tiger, ere he crushes the victim at his feet.

Dora started from her seat; she pressed her hands on her forehead; the glassy film which veiled her eyes was succeeded by a wild and flashing lustre.

"Why Livingstone," she cried in a strange whisper, "The room is filled with strangers. Ha, ha," she laughed, resuming her seat again with a look of calm loveliness. "The suddenness, with which you imparted this unexpected news, has given me a violent head-ache—"

"*Down*," muttered Livingstone in a tone inaudible to his wife. "*Fiend* be *still!* A little while and I am yours!" Was he speaking to the Devil that lay couched near his heart—the Devil of Madness?

"Come, Dora, look at your Christmas Present," he exclaimed in a calm voice, as he opened the casket.

Dora leaned forward until her beautiful countenance well-nigh touched the face of her husband.

"Ha, ha," she laughed, "Why Livingstone, what child's play is this? You promise me jewels, and here is but a lock of hair—mine I do believe—enclosed within this casket."

"Two locks of hair, my wife," spoke the deep voice of Livingstone. "Yours and Fitz-Cowles'!"

"Mine and Fitz-Cowles'?" echoed Dora with a look of vacant wonder. "What mean you?"

Livingstone replied with a single word. Leaning forward, his blue eyes flashing with a glance of fearful meaning, he looked like a fiend, blasting a guilty soul with a single look.

"Monk-Hall!"

Dora looked steadily in his face, but her senses whirled in a delirium that lasted for a single moment.

"Monk-Hall?" she echoed—and her face was like death—"What means this jest?"

"Jest?" echoed Livingstone in a husky voice. "Vile adultress! Call you this a jest? Two nights ago, bending over the bed, in which you and your paramour lay, reposing in your shame, I severed these glossy locks of hair, as witnesses of your damning guilt—"

Livingstone's voice was fearfully calm, as he spoke these words.

"Is it a jest now?" the sneer quivered on his lips, and his blue eye glared with an expression of ferocious hatred.

Vain is the power of speech, to picture the horror, which convulsed the frame of proud Dora Livingstone, as this awful discovery rushed upon her soul, like an ante-post of hell.

Sinking in the chair, with her hands clasped quiveringly together, for a moment, consciousness, reason and mind, were gone.

"Am I awake, am I dreaming? My brain whirls * * * all, all discovered * * * * oh shame, eternal shame!"

Such were the unconcerned ravings that fell from her trembling lips.

"And you must die," shrieked the frenzied voice of Livingstone. "You must die! Ere the hand of this watch tells the hour of seven, you will be a lifeless corse!"

"Poisoned * * * Poisoned * * * * I see it all now!" muttered Dora with her head resting on her shoulder, and her eyes closed in a dreamy half consciousness, she lay, thrown helplessly in the chair.

"Livingstone—" she exclaimed in a low but firm voice, as slowly rising on her feet, she looked him in the face—"Livingstone—my husband—my friend—I am most guilty, but I can face death without a murmur!"

Her attitude was sublime! So weak, so trembling, so pale, and yet with that awful stoicism on her beautiful brow!

It was a terrible sight for Livingstone. For a moment he trembled from head to foot, that man of iron nerves and fearless heart. He trembled, but it was not with one relenting throb.

He rushed from her side; was gone a moment; and then stood before her once again, his tall form rising in all its majesty, while with a hand of iron fixidity, he pointed to the object at his feet.

"Look!" he cried in a voice of thunder.

Dora bent forward, she pressed her hands to her burning forehead, and the light from the hearth, flashing over her downcast face, gave a terrible glow to every convulsed feature. One look, and the shriek died on her lips.

At her feet, in the full light of the fire, lay the coffin, covered with black cloth, and with a silver plate, glittering on its bosom.

One look, and she read the Name, the Day, the Death!

"Our *private theatricals!*" muttered Livingstone with a madman's icy sneer. "This day, Madam, you *rehearsed your own funeral!* Ha, ha! Do you remember how we rode to Hawkewood? First came your carriage, then the hearse with the coffin of the *deceased*, and then the *chief mourner*, ha, ha, ha!"

Dora sank in the chair. Her hands were icy cold, and her brain was a mass of molten flame, burning through her eye-balls and her brow.

"It is fulfilled—the Coronet is on my brow, yet it is a coronet of flame! The room is filled with strangers—ah, ha! They are noble lords and dames—I tread the halls of a royal court! Flames? Who fired these queenly robes—who—

"Oh God—these hot coals upon my brain—"

Did you ever see a chained tiger glutting its fierce eyes, with the agonies of the helpless victim, whom the keeper's hand has thrust into its cage? So Livingstone sate, with his glaring eyes, fixed upon the frenzied face of his wife.

"The hand of the watch is on the hour of six; in one hour she will be a lifeless mass, over which the worms will crawl and revel! This is my revenge! No gushing blood, falling from a white bosom, tells the story of my wrong and its punishment. But the soul bleeds—yes, yes—I hear its lifedrops, falling from the ghastly wound—I feast upon its quivering agonies! The soul of my victim bleeds, ha, ha, ha!"

Pale, mute, motionless, sate fearless Dora Livingstone. Her eyes half closed, her hands gently clasped, her bosom faintly thobbing, while her soul became the victim of a thousand frenzies.

"Dora," shrieked Livingstone in the ear of the dying woman, "The hand of death is on you, but I can save you! I have an antidote to the poison which you sipped in your coffee—"

"And you will give it me!" shrieked Dora, starting from her seat and seizing him by the hand. The touch of those icy fingers thrilled him to the heart.

"Give it you?" his voice sounded as though every syllable was torn from his heart. "Three nights ago, I bent over the bed in which you lay, lapt in the arms of shame. I listened for a word of repentance, nay, I tried to catch but one lingering syllable of regret! Not a word, not a sound of penitence. You had sold yourself into shame, and shame in its most polluted shape. In that hour, woman, when my heart was breaking, when my soul was torn from thought and reason, when all the hopes of my life were gone, and but one awful prospect lay before me, a madman's cell, through whose barred windows I beheld the grave of a suicide, yawning for my corse, then woman, oh then, I coined my existence into a vow! By the majesty of God, by the doom of hell, by the awful desolation of my soul, I swore to make you feel every throb of the agony, whose fangs quivered through my heart!

"I matured my revenge in silence. I, madman that I am, through the course of two fearful days, laid every snare to trap you into the power of the man whom you had dishonored, *dishonored!* I lured you to Hawkewood, I gave you the poison. I flung your coffin at your feet, and now, while death darkens horribly over your soul, I dash you from me, scorn your prayer for mercy, glory in your last agonies, and shriek in your freezing ear, 'Dora, Dora, my love, my wife, I can save you, but I will not! I can save you, but still you must die!'

"Yes," he shrieked, fixing his white lips together. "Yes! You must die! The spirit of my race burns in my veins—"

"Livingstone," faltered Dora, with a look of perfect consciousness.

"It is hard to die—I am guilty but you will not, cannot kill me. Spare me Albert, for your own sake, oh spare me!"

She knew that she was dying. Guilt, shame, reproach, all were forgotten; all she craved was life! Could she have fallen dead on the floor, she would have hailed death without a murmur. But to count each pulsation of her freezing blood, to feel a separate agony in each throb of her bursting heart, to meet death while her brain was reeling in a delirium, that left her still conscious of her doom, oh merciful God, this was a hell, far beyond the rude fancies, with which superstition goads her crouching victims.

"Life, life," she shrieked, "Spare me Albert—*Life!*"

"Could every throb of your dying heart, take voice and form, and shriek for pity, I tell you woman, that still my answer would be, Dora you must die!"

He turned away from her, as in a voice of deliberate tone, he spoke these final words of fate.

There was silence for a moment. With the last impulse of her failing strength, Dora sprang forward, she flung her arms around his neck.

An awful convulsion distorted Livingstone's features.

"Oh God!" he groaned.

These arms—they had encircled his neck in the by-gone time of faith and peace. That bosom, heaving against his own—so it had heaved and throbbed in the days of his love. But that beautiful face, those eyes flashing supernatural lustre, that long black hair showering down over the queenly form!

Livingstone trembled; he made an effort to unwind her arms from his neck, but in vain! She kissed him, yes, with those ripe lips, which had called him husband one year ago, smiling like heaven all the while, she kissed him, and he shuddered. Her lips were like flame-coals.

"Life!" she whispered in husky tones, "Only *life!*"

Now was the awful moment. Now man of iron will, is the instant of your fate. This moment is destiny, eternity, heaven or hell, to you!

An expression of pity smiled from his livid face, but in an instant his fixed determination called an awful frown to his view.

"Woman," he shrieked, "I have sworn it. You must die!"

He dashed her from him as he spoke. Her magnificent form swayed to and fro for a moment, then with a look of terrible despair, she fell backward over her coffin, into the arm-chair.

"Ha, ha, ha!" she screamed, with a burst of maniac laughter. "Ha, ha! These are brave steeds Fitz-Cowles! Away, away! With the night we leave all danger behind. How softly the morning breaks, oh beautiful! H-u-s-h! My mother is dying. H-u-s-h! That was her last groan! Livingstone claims me as his bride, over the corse of my dead mother. Heaven will bless our nuptuals, yes, yes—Ah! How cold, how dark, how dread! We are in the death-vault now. I am not dead, yet they bury me—oh, God, oh God! Will no one burst this coffin lid—how it presses on my bosom, close, close, close! Oh for one gleam of God's light again, oh for one breath of God's free air!"

Her dark eyes rolled in their sockets, and with her white hands she dashed the tresses of her raven hair aside from her brow.

Livingstone gazed upon her, with folded arms he gazed upon the face of his wife. Paint me, the agony of a lost soul, and I will picture for you, the awful resolution, that distorted every feature of his face. The cold sweat on the brow of the dying woman, was not more clammy, than the beaded drops on the forehead of the husband.

"Oh, God!" Livingstone groaned, as a feeling of mercy, came stealing over his heart. He was *afraid* that he might relent.

Dora rose once more upon her feet. She rose in an attitude of fearful sublimity. Her tall form towering in all its beauty and pride, she dashed the dark hair from her clammy brow, she raised her hand on high, with a gesture of command. Zenobia, on her throne, with the spoils of all the nations scattered round her feet, could never have looked, more sternly beautiful.

"Livingstone," she shrieked, with that upraised hand, quivering in the air, while the cold sweat glistened in beads along her cheek and brow, "Livingstone you *must* save me! *I cannot, will not die!*"

There was an awful will beaming from that woman's face. Her lips were painfully compressed, and her dark eyes glared with a fierce light, wild as madness and as determined as death.

"*I will not die!*" she shrieked, clenching her white hands in agony and despair. Ere the words died on her lips, she fell heavily to the floor. She lay with her head pillowed on the coffin, with her limbs flung stiffly over the carpet, while her cheek was cold and pale as marble. Her lips—they had grown suddenly white—hung gently apart, and her dark eyes, glazed steadily on the ceiling. A glassy film was on each eye. She was dead. The proud and peerless Dora Livingstone lay on that floor, a lifeless corse.

"There," shrieked Livingstone, in a voice choked by despair, "There, there—is all that was my wife!"

He fell on his knees beside her coffin. At this moment, a thin stream of blood, stole from her lips, and trickled over her face and bosom, marking its progress, with a line of ghastly red. She had died within *the hour;* her mighty heart had burst its channels, and that blood, whose every pulsation was a thought, now stained the whiteness of her bosom.

The madman knelt beside his victim. For two long days, and two weary nights, he had anticipated the scene. With his reason, tottering all the while, he had prepared the accumulating agonies, with which to torture her closing hour. The journey to Hawkewood, planned with such cool deliberation, the coffin inscribed with her name, these were alike the work of a madman.

He knelt beside his victim. Was it a drop of death sweat, or a tear that trickled down her face?

Not a word passed from his lips, but while his blue eyes shone, with one fixed expression, he tore aside the robe from the breast of the corse. The light shone on her bosom, so beautiful and yet so white and cold. And over its alabaster skin, marring the beauty of the blue veins, trickled the thin stream of blood, mingling with the tears that fell from the hot eyeballs of the murderer.

The light from the table, and the warm glow from the hearth-side, streamed over the muscular form of Livingstone, kneeling beside the coffin, with the form of his dead wife resting on his arms. The contrast was full of terrible interest. His bronzed face with the livid lips and the glaring blue eyes; her pale countenance, with the parted lips, stained with blood, and the dark eyes, glassy with death. The Lord of Longford with his Lady in his arms!

"You have won your coronet, Dora, but it is of worms! You have won your empire, but it is a narrow grave! Here, here, lies all that was my wife!"

Laying her gently on the coffin, he silently arose. One look at the dead body, and he passed from the room into the darkness of the stairway. It was but a moment ere he stood in the large hall of the mansion, where a small lamp, suspended from the ceiling, flung a dismal light around.

"Davidson," he cried in hasty and impatient tones.

The withered figure of the old man emerged from a side door.

"Your horse is saddled at the door 'Squire Livingstone—"

"He calls me 'Squire," muttered Livingstone with a mocking smile. "'Squire and I am a *Lord!* Look ye Davidson, I must return to town on business. Do not *disturb* Mrs. Livingstone before morning, she is tired, and would have a *long* sleep."

Grasping the fur cap which he had worn to Hawkewood, from a side table, he strode through the hall door. In a moment, the clatter of a horse's hoofs echoed from the road leading to the mansion gate, mingled with a wild hurrah.

In the early dawn of the morning, a noble horse, with the saddle on his back, covered with dust, and the bridle thrown loosely over his neck, was seen wandering without a rider, along the public highway. It was the steed of Livingstone.

For one hour the light burned merrily in the Oak Chamber, and the cheerful glow of fire, gave warmth and comfort to the place, but the corse of the woman and the coffin, were gone from the floor, while a plate of glittering silver gleamed among the hearthside ashes.

CHAPTER THIRD

HURRAH FOR THE GALLOWS!

"This is wot I calls a werry respectable family party? Here's the whole lump of us, packed in this box of a room, together, and a jolly set we are. Ladies and gen'l'men, I hope you'll excuse my not handin' you somefin to drink, but you see my hands is fixed off han'some with these bracelets, and I can't use 'em to any advantage. And so, Mister Fitz-Cowles, you wos a forger, wos yo'—oh what a bad boy, to be a forger! sich wickedness! How d'ye feel Peggy Grud? They *do* say you'll have to swing for murderin' that old 'ooman. Ha, ha, hee! And Monk Luke here—you're a nice one, I swear! To come foolin' a wennerable old customer like me, in them rags. Hurray for the gallows and the jail, say I! Some of us will have to swing, and some of us will have to go to prissen—hurray!"

With this cheerful sentiment on his lips, Devil-Bug glanced around his den, while his solitary eye, twinkled with a mocking glee.

Lighted by the mingled beams of the lamp on the table, and the cheerful coal fire burning in the grate, the Doorkeeper's den, was tenanted by some five or six individuals, whose dress and appearance was in strong contrast.

Silent and alone on one side of the fire-place, was Fitz-Cowles, his face pressed against the manacles which imprisoned his wrists, while his feet rested on the rounds of the chair, and his knees touched his forehead. A more perfect picture of shame, mortification and hopelessness, cannot be imagined.

Forming a group on the opposite side of the fire, were the respectable worthies, Mother Nancy, Peggy Grud, and Devil-Bug. The old hag of the mansion, sate with her pinioned arms crossed over her breast, while the light shone over her withered face, every sharp feature, compressed in an expression of overwhelming spite. Peggy Grud sate swaying her body to and fro, and wringing her hands, while her Egyptian mummy face, was impressed with an expression of lugubrious solemnity. The distorted face of Devil-Bug, with the matted hair falling thick and tangled over the protuberant brow, stood out boldly in the light, while his solitary eye glared, and his wide lips quivered with a mocking sneer.

At the head of the table smoking a huge German pipe, sate our friend Major Rappahannock Mulhill, his red round face beaming with an agreeable smile, as with his half closed eyes he gazed around the place. Luke Harvey in the rags of Brick-Top, sat by his shoulder, his long dark hair falling in lank masses, aside from his marked and expressive countenance.

"You can't convict me of nothin' you can't, you can't, you *can't!*" And Mother Nancy's grey eyes rolled to and fro, like the eyes of an enraged parrot. "I'm a respectable widder, as keeps a respectable house, an' I defies you. There now!"

"Werry good," murmured Mulhill, taking the paper from his mouth. "Wot's yer idea-r o' things, Peggy dear?"

"Och, whilaloo!" moaned that respectable lady. "To think on a civil woman an' a dacent, bein' tuk up for the murder on her missus! Och—och! Will nobody take a pistil and *shot* me dead, and bury me out o' sight?"

"Wot's yer idea-r Fitz-Cowles? Did'nt I do you *ree*ther brown?"

Fitz-Cowles did not raise his head from between his manacled hands, but a deep curse, mingled with a groan, burst from his compressed lips.

"Wot's the use o' growlin' " shouted Devil-Bug with a grin. Some of us will go to prissen, and some of us 'ill be hung! Hurray! It's only a kick and a jerk, and won's as dead as a herrin'! I've hung a man in my time, I have that—"

" 'Spose you give us a leetle sarmin on that pint," calmly remarked Easy Larkspur, or Major Mulhill, as the reader likes. "We're all a-waitin' for Alderman Tallow-docket, who's to bind yo' over, and send yo' to prissin. Peggy Grud was brought out for final examination; and as I thought the Alderman 'ud like to make one job of it, I left her in this den, while I made a rush on the fellers down in the cellar. 'Spose they're all quiet enough in charge o' th' police? Fire away *Brother* Devil-Bug. Give us your experience on hangin'!"

THE HANGMAN'S GLEE

"Hurray for hangin' say I! It's only a kick an' a jerk, and a feller goes like a shot, right slap into kingdom come. It does wons heart good to look upon them two pieces o' timber, with a beam fixed cross-wise, and a rope danglin' down—hurray for hangin'!

"It war'n't more nor five years since, that I hung a man. Talk o' hangin' a dog or a cat, wot is it to hangin' a man? When I was quite a little shaver I used to hang a puppy or a pussy-cat, and I used to think it quite refreshin'. But hangin' a man? Ho-hoo! That's the ticket!

"It was a fine June morning, and I walks along one o' them dark entries in the Eastern Pennytensherry, and I walks into a cell. It was purty dark I tell you. A bit of light came through the narrer winder, an' in one corner o' the cell I sees a young man, with a white face, and curly dark hair. He was settin' in a corner, with his knees drawed up to his chin.

"Get up" ses I, "get up young man. There's business for you." He raises his head, an' he gives a kind o' start. You see I'm not werry han'some, at any time, but just then, I looked pertiklerly dev'lish. The Marshal had giv' me a yard or two ov black crape, and I'd put it round my face, with a hole cut, for my eye, to look thro' and———

"Come my feller," ses I, "There's business for you."

"I did'n't murder the Capt'n," ses he. "Before God, if it was my last word I did'n't—"

"Yo' see he'd been condemned for murderin' the Capt'in of a wessel at sea, an' there wos considerable doubt about it, but as he was a poor devil, and a stranger, the Judge and the jury, thought the best thing they could do for him wos to hang him, for *fear you* know he might'n't be able to get work the next winter.

"Come my chap," ses I, a-bindin' his hands. "I'm an ugly devil, but you need'n't be frightened, for I'm sent here by the LAW," pronouncin' the word big you know? "THE LAW, wot takes care ov everybody and can't never be bribed. Come feller."

"I bound his hands, and led him from the cell. The poor fool was mutterin' nonsense about his mother and sister all the while. In a minnit we stood under the archway o' the prissin gate. It wos werry cold and damp. A kind of chill, went thro' me when I looked at the pitiful face of the boy, for he was'n't more nor ninenteen, but that was only the cold you know? It only tuk a minnit to rig him out in a white roundabout, and then I led him out of the prissin gate.

"Hurray, wot a sight! Soldiers in gay coats and spangles, all standin' around a cart, with a pine box, an' a parson in it!

"Wot's that?" says Charley—for that wos his name—"Wot's that?"

"Oh ses I, that's the blue sky, and yander's Bush Hill, an' yander's Fairmount Water Works, and them things wot yo' hear singin' is birds and———"

"But that thing in the cart," ses he.

"That's a black bird, or rather a crow come to pray over yer dead body, boy. It's a parson, Charley. For you're to be *hung*, to day hung,

hung, d'ye hear, and these soldiers and the parson and me, is to be chief mourners at yer funeral."

I never saw sich a feller in my life! His lip was like iron, and his dark eye, firm as rivet.

"But that," ses he, pintin' to th' cart, "That box———"

"That's yer coffin," ses I, helpin' him into the cart, "Sit down an' take a cheer." He sit down on the coffin, mutterin' about his mother and sisters in some far away land, an' I seized the reins and giv' the horse a lick, and the soldiers began to march, and the wheels o' th' cart to rumble, and the parson to look solemn—hurray!

"Trum-te-trum-te-tum-tum, went the drums a-beatin' the dead march, rattle, rattle, went the wheels of the cart, and away we goes, down Schuylkill Sixth Street, toward Bush Hill.

"Charley, the poor devil, wot was a-goin' to be hung, set on th' cart a-groanin'. "My mother, my mother!" he cries, "and my sister Annie—oh God! Oh God!"

"Don't swear," ses the parson, "My werry dear young friend, don't you know its wrong to swear, and them wot does it, 'ill be burnt in th' burnin' lake———"

"Parson," ses I, turning suddenly round, "What 'ill you have for dinner to day?"

"Roast lamb with mint sauce," ses he, and then he blushed, for I'd took him all aback. I know'd he was thinkin' on his dinner all the while, and I thought I'd expose the old genelman.

"Hurray," ses I, as the cart reached the top of a little hill in the middle of the dusty street. "Hurray" ses I, "look yander my boy!"

"Charley looks up, and gives a groan. What d'ye think he saw? A great big, black, mass of people, reaching over Bush Hill, fur as the eye could see, with a gibbet rising in the middle of the crowd. The hot sun, was shinin' down upon us, and the drums went trum-te-trum, and the cart wheels went rumble rumble, and on we went, the poor devil that wos to be hung, the Parson that wos to pray over him, and *me* that wos to hang him!

"The mob seed us, and like a shot they rushed toward the cart. "There he is," ses a woman with a baby in her arms; "Where, where!" roars a man who come sixty miles a-foot to see him hung, "By G——d he'll die game," screams a gambler with a sweat cloth in one hand and a table in the tother.

"You never see'd sich a mob in all your life. All over Bush Hill, from the old Hospital, where the people used to die of yaller fever, away towards Fairmount, that crowd was scattered, hooting, yelling, swearing and screaming like devils, as they see'd the cart and the soldiers, movin' toward the gibbet.

"Keep up your spirits Charley," ses I, "The Law—" pronouncin' it big—"The LAW is a merciful old codger, is the law! There's a strong rope for you yonder, and a good stout piece o' timber—"

"As I said this, whether it was from the heat or the dust, or whether the poor crittur was ashamed to be seen in sich work, I never could 'xactly tell, but the horse fell down like *that*, and lay in the middle o' th' road, dead as a stone.

"The mob giv' a yell! I puts the coffin on my shoulder, and hooks Charlie's arm in mine, and beckons to the Parson, and the Captain giv's the word to the soldiers, and away we tramps toward the gallows.

"The Lord is merciful," whispered the Parson. "His word is peace and good will to men—"

"Then why do they hang me?" cries Charley, as he went boldly for'ard, "Oh my God—my mother, and my sister!" and then the feller begins to moan, and talk of his mammy and sister sittin' at the cottage door in England, expectin' their Charley to come back and, "Here," ses he, "Here am I goin' to be hung like a dog, like a dog," yes ses he repeatin' it, "*Like a dog!*"

"As he sed this, a white pidgeon fluttered over his head. The boy looks up, and a tear stands in his eye.

"Look here my chap," ses he to me, as I went trampin' on with the coffin on my shoulder, "Jist sich a pidgeon as that, white as snow, I gave to Annie afore I left home—"

Would you believe it? The words was n't out o' his lips when the pidgeon fell dead at his feet, in the hot dust of the road.

"The mob yelled agin! What they yelled about, I never could tell, but there's somethin' so jolly in seein' a live man, walking to a gallows, that I could'nt help joinin' in with 'em; Hurray, ses I, Hurray for the gibbet! The good old gallows law for ever an' Amen!"

"Charley did n't say a word arter that, but went up the gallow's steps without so much as a start. Was n't it a grand sight for us fellers on the platform? There was the Marshall, a fine fat faced feller; there was the Parson, in his white cravat and black clothes, there was I, Devil-Bug, the Hangman, with the crape over my face, and there was the poor devil, as wos to be hung, standin' in the midst of us all, dressed in a white roundabout, with a face like a cloth, and curly hair, dark as jet.

"Hurray," ses I, "wot a sight! Keep up yer spirits Charley. Jist look at the people, come to see yo' hung! Look at the Soldiers with their feathers and bagnets, jist look at the women, with babies in their arms, look at the gamblers, playin' thimble rig, look at the rum, my boy, in the tents yonder, and then, hurray! Look at the folks scattered all over Bush Hill, on the house tops away off yonder, and far down the streets!

Hurray, my boy, there's a big crowd come to see you die, and so wot's the use o' grumblin' about yer mother and sister, and a cussed white pidgeon?"

"The mob giv' a howl! It was near twelve o'clock, and they wanted their show.

"It wants ten minnits o' th' time," ses the Marshall, an' the Parson, comes up to Charley, and taps him on the shoulder, and ses he, "Look up, my friend. God is merciful. Let us pray!"

And then we all kneeled down, and the Parson made a short prayer about the Mercy o' God and the widders and orphans, and them deluded devils as had n't sich a good Gospel an' sich a stout Gallows. While he was prayin' I saw two gentlemen, with knowin' faces, slyly creepin' up the ladder, and lookin' over the edge o' th' platform. I know'd 'em well. I'd stole dead bodies for 'em a hundred times. They were doctors, a-waitin' for the dead body o' Charley the English boy.

The Parson cuts his prayer off short, and we all gits on our feet ag'in.

"Come Charley ses I, don't be frightened, an' I fixes the knot behind his ear. A delicate knot, it was! You know it was tied right behind the ear, so that his fall, would break his neck, like *that!* Then I felt his smooth neck, and ses I, it 'ill soon be over Charley, and you wont think anything more of yer mother, or yer sister, or that cussed white pidgeon."

"Feller," ses he, "yer honest. Here's all I have to giv' yo'. Keep it for my sake."

"An' he giv' me the striped handkercher from his neck. It was purty hot, I tell yo', but a shiver ran over me, when he did this.

"Time's up," ses the Marshall. The mob giv' a yell. The doctors waitin' for the body, comes up a step higher on the ladder, and the Parson, smacked his lips, as tho' he felt uncommon hungry.

"A glass o' water," ses Charley, in a faint way, but still as firm as a rock. A boy with blue eyes an' yaller hair, was hoisted on a man's shoulder's, from among the mob, till he was even with the platform.

"God bless yo' my boy," ses Charley, "An' may yo' never have a mother an' a sister, a-sittin' at the cottage door, a-waitin' fur yo' to come home, when yer a-hangin' in some far off land, hangin' like a dog!"

"He takes the glass o' water; he looks at it for a minnit; and then at the sky, and the sun, and the great big crowd, and the roofs of the houses filled with people. I'll never forgit that look! His eyes looked as if they was set afire, and his lower lip, worked like a bit o' twisted rope.

"I am innocent," ses he, and then, cool as you please, he pours the tumbler o' water, right down on the platform floor.

"That water will dry up, but my blood, will never dry up, from your soil, while yonder sun shines!"

"Time's up," ses the Marshall. I stuck the white cap on his forehead. I draw'd it over his eyes! Hurray! What a look he giv' as the cap, came down over his forehead. He stood in the centre o' th' platform, with the cap over his eyes an' the rope around his neck. The mob held their breath. In that big crowd, you could n't hear the sound of a human voice.

"With one kick o' my foot, I pushed away the trap. For a minnit the sun seemed dark, and the next minnit—ho, hoo! There quiverin' strugglin', twistin', was the body of a man, plungin' at the end of a rope, with his tongue—black as a hat—stickin' out from under the edge o' th' white cap—hurray!

"There was a noise like water pourin' from a jug turned up-side down, there was a plunge and a jerk and then the body o' the poor devil quivered like a leaf. The mob gave one yell, which sounded as tho' Fairmount Dam had broke loose, with a devil shoutin' from every wave! You could see a quiverin' run over the body of the boy, from head to foot. May-be he heered that yell, may-be he see'd strange sights in 'tother world! Who knows?

"For thirty minutes we kept him hanging, for thirty minutes the mob yelled and cursed and swore and hurrahed!

"But when I cut the dead body down—that was the time for fun! To see the Doctors huddle the carcase into the pine coffin, to see the Parson hurry one way, the Marshall another, to see the soldiers march off, with old Devil-Bug in their midst, guardin' him from danger!

"Ho-hoo! This individ*oo*al felt like a king, about that time!

"And then to look back and see the mob tearing the gibbet to pieces, and bearin' splinter's away in their fingers, that they might take 'em home to their families, and brag of seein' a man hung! Ho-hoo!

"That night I see'd the poor devil's dead body cut and slashed on a dissectin' table, with old doctors prowlin' about like wolves, with bits o' flesh between their fingers!

"One of 'em scraped his skull, and cleaned it like a bowl, an' put it in a case, with a label, '*This is the skull of Charles ——— the Pirate.*'

"Hurray for the gallows, say I! It's only a kick an' a jerk, and a feller goes straight to kingdom come!

* "The good old gallows law, for ever, and ever, A-men!"

"That's wot I calls a werry good story!" And Major Mulhill emitted

* The main incidents of this episode are strictly true. The Hangman, of course, is alone, responsible for the language and opinions of the story.

a succession of smoke rings from his mouth. Bray-vo! An' allow me to tell you Mister Devil-Bug that you'll have a pleasant opportunity o' puttin' it into practice yerself! Jist look at the crittur with his one eye, and his bushy head—wot a p*a*rfect fiend!"

Fitz-Cowles' half-raised his head from his manacled hands. "Come here Mulhill," he said in a husky whisper. "I've something to say to you—"

Easy Larkspur strode toward the fire-place, and in a moment, seated by the side of Fitz-Cowles, he was listening to the earnest whispers of the Forger.

"Would you like to know anything o' that g-a-l?" said Devil-Bug, approaching the side of Luke Harvey.

"The girl—Mabel—" cried Luke, raising his head from his hands. "Where is she?"

"That's the quest'in!" cooly responded Devil-Bug. "I 'spose you know she's the darter o' Livingstone? Them papers wot you read to me in this room, settled that matter. And that hell-cat Bess, told you all about it—hey?"

"Where is this girl?" asked Luke with a manner of evident interest.

"Ho-hoo! 'spose I'm goin' to tell you with these ornaments on my hands? Vonders how *that* 'ud vork? Strike off these irons, gin' me an hour's liberty, and I'll lead you to the place where you kin fight for the g-a-l—yes *fight* for her!"

Luke's face was agitated by a strange and deep emotion, that flashed from his eye, and quivered in his nostrils.

"This way Larkspur," he cried, beckoning to that worthy, and leading the way from the den into the dark hall of the mansion. By the dim light which came from the roof, far above, the forms of some thirty men, manacled and pinioned, might be discovered, thrown along the floor in various attitudes, while the sound of shouts mingled with laughter, came from the regions of the cellar.

"Them is our wictims," muttered Larkspur, as they stood in the gloom of the hall. "Them shouts is from my beaks! They're makin' reether free with the likker I tell you!"

"I wish to speak with you on a matter of deep interest," said Luke. "This Devil-Bug here, has in his keeping, a secret of the utmost importance to myself and Livingstone. That secret, we can only obtain by his liberation for the space of an hour—"

"Wot!" interrupted Larkspur with an indignant start. "Would yo' have a special Deppitty o' the Honorable Ma'or, let a prisoner slip? Have you been indulgin' in ardent sperrits or green peas, young man?"

"Wonders how *that* 'ill vork—ho, ho, hoo?" shouted a well-known voice from the Door-keeper's den.

Luke pushed open the door, and beheld Devil-Bug standing in the middle of the room, brandishing his freed arms over his head, while he danced round the hand-cuffs laying on the floor.

"Where's Fitz-Cowles, you devil?" shrieked Luke.

"Escaped! We found this feller's key on the floor—ho, ho, hoo! He unlocked my hand-cuffs, and I unlocked his'n. Look at the front door—ho, hoo! Wonders how *that* 'ill vork!"

"D———n———n!" shrieked Luke, rushing through the front door. "This villain shall not escape me thus!"

"I'm ruined, tee-totally smashed!" whined Larkspur, while his fat face assumed an expression of the most painful grief. "Oh, my grasshus, if I only had a small family of a wife and fifteen children, to excite the symp*er*thies of the public, for an unfort'nate poleese Deppitty!"

Tearing his hair, in unfeigned anguish, he rushed through the front door, leaving Devil-Bug standing in the centre of the den, while Mother Nancy and Peggy Grud sate against the wall, yelling and swinging their bodies backwards and forwards to the same lively tune.

"Now g-a-l, to drag you from the Wizard's den!" shrieked Devil-Bug, tramping through the front door. "First I must get Luke, and then, ho, hoo! She'll roll in Livingstone's wealth—*That* 'ill work just right!"

"See'd yo' iver the likes o' this?" whined Peggy Grud. "Them to git off, and not cut us loose! Whilaloo—ochone!"

"Young 'ooman, vy should I leave my rispectable dwellin'?" asked Mother Nancy with spiteful severity. "Here I've lived, and here I'll stick till I die—He, he, he-e! Did'nt I see the note which Fitz-Cowles giv' to Larkspur? He, he, h-e-e! It was a thousan' dollars I'll be bound!"

As she spoke, the room was filled by the band of police officers, who had been hurried from their revel down stairs, by the sounds of uproar, in the Door-keeper's Den.

CHAPTER FOURTH

THE CHAPEL OF JESUS

The Oak Chamber of Hawkewood yet once again!

The lights on the round table are burning fast toward their sockets, and the remains of the blazing wood fire, smoulder away the ashes of the hearth. The gold watch on the table, tells the hour of eleven. All is silent thro' the chamber, and thro' the mansion, silent and sad as the tomb.

Who gazing around this chamber, as it is now revealed, in glimmering light, might guess the nature of the awful tragedy enacted within its walls, since yon watch, marked the hour of six? The Chamber is the same, as when Livingstone and his wife first stepped over its threshold. The heavy curtains of the bed still droop from the canopy down to the floor, in thick and purple folds; the hangings of the windows toward the east, turned partly aside, still disclose the massive oaken frames; the light still shines on the faded colors of the old-fashioned carpet, and the dusky carvings of the wainscot, still receive its genial glow. The round table is still there, and on either side, are the Gothic arm-chairs, placed in the same position, as they stood, five hours ago. The coffin and the corse is gone, but amid the grey hickory ashes, glitters a bright object, like a piece of burnished silver.

All was deadly still, through the mansion, when the sound of a footstep was heard from the main stairway; it grew near and nearer, until it echoed without the chamber door. There was silence again, for a moment, and then the door flew open, and a wild haggard figure advanced toward the light.

It was Algernon Fitz-Cowles! His black hair streaming back from his uncovered brow, his dress torn and soiled with dust, his bronzed face covered with thick perspiration, while his dark eyes, rolled to and fro, with the glare of a bloodhound at bay, he advanced toward the light, and flung a glittering bowie-knife on the table.

"If they want to trap the bloodhound, they must fight for it!" he muttered in tones hoarse with rage. "Ha! On the Gulf of Mexico, in the streets of New Orleans, in the dens of Charleston, in the rookeries of Mobile, there have been men who dared my hate, and *died!* Yes, like dogs with *that* knife in their hearts! And shall I be trapped by a paltry counter-hopper, a peddler of tapes and thimbles? The *Son* of old ——— ——— is not to be scared by such mean dogs!

"Ha, ha! That was a gallant ride! Dim was faithful to me, by * * *! The river passed, two blood horses waited for me in the woods beyond Camden. 'Now hey, for Hawkewood—hurray!' says I, feeling the old blood of the Gulf, in my veins, once again. Not a hundred yards over the sandy road before my pursuers were at my heels! Mounted on good horses too, but—hurrah!

"Over the hill and thro' hollow, over brook and crag, with *their* hootings giving fresh speed to my noble horses, on, on, like a devil I flew! One by one my pursuers drop; one by one their horses fall! Hurrah! By a lucky chance, I find the way to Hawkewood; my horses are at the door, and now for Burlington! Dora promised to meet me at the door. Curse the thing, why was she not there?

"Lucky for me again—the hall door was wide open—I mount the stairs and here I am! Yes, yes, *they* must fight for it! Now for the search for Dora—ha! Livingstone's watch? She must be in the house; perchance in this very chamber."

He advanced to the bedside; a gust of cold wind pouring thro' the open door tossed the curls of his hair, and extinguished the lights on the table.

"Curse the thing!" muttered Fitz-Cowles. "The devil was in that wind! How thick these curtains are!" he exclaimed tossing the dark purple folds aside.

"Ha! A woman's form—By Heaven it is Dora!"

All was dark within the bed, but a faint gleam from the fireside, revealed the form of a queenly woman, half-concealed by the folds of the coverlid.

"Dora—Dora," softly murmured Fitz-Cowles, bending over the bed. "Ha! She is asleep. Her face is concealed by those dark curls—let me sweep them gently aside. Dora—awake—it is the hour of our flight—awake!"

Not a sound, not a murmur. He reached forth his hand, and dashing the coverlid aside, took her white hand within his own. As he did this, the withdrawn curtain, swung slowly over him, and gathered him within its folds.

"Great God! Her hand is cold as ice!" he muttered as he stood in the same darkness that enveloped the bed. "Dora, awake! Phsaw! How sound the woman sleeps? Know you not 'tis the hour of our flight—rise, Dora, and let us away!"

Sweeping the coverlid yet farther aside, he placed his hand upon her bosom, it was bare and cold as marble. Fitz-Cowles could feel the clammy sweat starting from his brow, while a horrible suspicion rushed like a thunder-bolt upon his brain.

With one grasp he tore the curtains from the bed; he started back a step, and a warm gleam from the fireside lit up the scene.

The form of Dora Livingstone, cold and white as snow, with every vestige of apparel, stript from its outlines of loveliness, lay before him. The dark hair fell around the pale face, and the glassy eyes were upturned, with a freezing stare.

"Ha-h!" screamed Fitz-Cowles, with an unearthly shriek. "The woman is dead, *dead!*"

A sudden glow from the fireside, flashed over the livid face of Fitz-Cowles, and over the form of the dead woman. For a moment those round arms, that bosom of swelling loveliness, that face of thought linked with beauty, and that form of peerless outlines, rich waving and voluptuous, looked like life, and then all was death again.

Fitz-Cowles stood stricken dumb with unutterable horror. Even in his base heart, there lurked a feeling like love, for the woman who lay before him.

"The woman is dead," he muttered, and looked up vacantly. He started back with a yell. There, there, before him, from the darkness on the opposite side of the bed, like the vision of some fiend whom his words had raised from hell, there gleamed two eyes, flashing with unutterable lustre, and there, the livid outlines of a bronzed face, stood out boldly in the fireside light.

"I am lost!" was the exclamation of the cowering wretch, and ere the words died on his lips, the tall form of Livingstone was at his side.

"Wretch!" he shrieked, with his wide chest heaving, and his muscular arms, flung madly on high—"Wretch! Behold your work—this ruin of loveliness and innocence!"

He pointed at the dead body, and then with a howl, like a tiger on the spring, he rushed upon his victim.

"You must die," he shrieked, "By the God above us, you must die!"

"Stand back," faltered Fitz-Cowles, retreating towards the fireplace. "Do not lay your hands on me. I am armed, I am—"

The words died on his lips! Livingstone's writhing fingers were round his throat, Livingstone's iron arm encircled his trembling frame. He raised him in the air, high over his head, with all the force of his muscular arms, gathered in the effort, he swung the craven aloft, and for a single moment, held him quivering there! His dark eye glaring on the hot coals, and his bronzed face one terrible frown, he dashed the forger to the floor, not with the iron strength of his arms expended in the blow, but with a contemptuous movement, as though he but crushed the reptile that bit his heel.

"Go!" he shouted, in a voice of thunder. "Go! Miscreant and swindler! You are too mean a thing for my vengeance!"

"But not for mine!" shouted a calm and determined voice, striding forward in the light. "Villain you are my—"

The bold words faltered on Luke Harvey's lips.

"Dora!" he shrieked, gazing on the dead body, as the light from the fire flashed over its pale outlines. There was a universe of horror, love and revenge, mingled in the emphasis with which he uttered that single word—"Dora!"

"Come," he fiercely shouted, turning to Fitz-Cowles, who leaned against the mantel. "This man has been wronged, this woman murdered, through your crimes! I am the Avenger of the Wrong and the Murder! Come! Here are two pistols—take your choice. One of us must die!"

"Ho, ho, hoo! Wot a pictur'! A dead 'oman, and a crazy husband, an' my friends Monk Fitz-Cowles an' Monk Luke! Things does n't seem to work right!"

His upraised hand, holding a light above his head, Devil-Bug stood in the doorway, every feature of his face distorted by a sneering grimace, and his solitary eye, full of malignant fire.

"Come!" shouted Luke, motioning Fitz-Cowles toward the door.

"I will fight you!" muttered Fitz-Cowles with a look of fiendish hate. "Aye, if it is over a table, with but an arm's length between us!"

Devil-Bug led the way toward the landing; Fitz-Cowles followed; Luke alone remained on the threshold. He cast one last look into the chamber.

"Luke, Luke," shouted a well-known voice, "One year ago, she crossed my threshold a fair young bride—and now—oh God!"

Luke beheld the form of Livingstone kneeling beside the dead body of his wife.

"Come!" he shouted, leading the way down the stairway. It required but a few moments, for the three to traverse the entire length of the corridor, on the second floor, which extended thro' half the length of the mansion, toward the south. Devil-Bug led the way, holding the light overhead, and at his back, in grim silence followed Luke and Fitz-Cowles.

They passed the doors of many rooms, but did not pause, until the corridor was terminated by a wide oaken door, that occupied its entire width.

"Here is the scene of my Sacrifice!" said Luke, pushing open the door with his foot. "Little did I ever think, when I used to roam these halls, many a day gone by, that the Chapel of Hawkewood would ever be polluted by the blood of a coward and a forger."

"*Coward* in your teeth!" shouted Fitz-Colwes, hoarse with rage. "You shall pay for this insolence with your blood!"

"Devil-Bug," said Luke, with a calmness of voice, that was evidently assumed. "Watch without this door. Watch I say, until this *affair* is finished. When one of us, appears at this door, with the dead body of the other in his arms, let that man pass! But until one is dead, let neither of us, pass from this door. Bury the dead man in the vaults of Hawkewood, and keep the secret of his death. You are a desperate man, Devil-Bug, and I can trust you, with this matter. You swear to do, as I command?"

"I do!" answered Devil-Bug, with a hideous grin. "Hurray with the fun!"

Taking the light from Devil-Bug, Luke led the way into the Chapel of Hawkewood, followed by Fitz-Cowles. The door closed behind them, as they entered the place, whose walls, would witness a scene of bloodshed and death.

It was a long and narrow room, with an oaken floor, and an arching ceiling. Not a solitary window, gave light to the place, and the only entrance, was the door through which they had passed, which opened into the centre of the room. The southern end of the room, was concealed by a large picture, which reached from wall to wall, and from the ceiling to the floor. In front of this picture arose a piece of carved statuary, painted to represent the hues of life and agony. And some few paces, in front of the image, was a small square table, covered with a mouldering white cloth. On the picture was delineated the Virgin Mary and her holy child; the statue, was an image of the expiring Redeemer, stretched on the cross, in all the agonies of superhuman suffering, yet with a godlike triumph breaking over his brow. The table, covered with white cloth, was the Altar of God, on which the vessels of the holy sacrament had lain, in many a solemn hour, while the tears of remorse and anguish sprinkled the oaken floor.

And those hard planks, around the altar, in more places than one, were worn into deep hollows. Here had Lord Walter Longford, the first proprietor of Hawkewood, knelt during the still watches of night, groaning in agony as he thought of the dishonor of his house.

"We will fight over this altar," said Luke, as he moved the table, nearer the centre of the room. "It is but just that wrongs, such as I have to avenge, should be avenged over the altar of God, in sight of his cross!"

The light was on the altar, and Luke stood with his back to the cross, his tall form, towering in all its heighth, as with the pistol in his hand, he gazed fiercely in the face of Fitz-Cowles.

"*Monk* Luke," sneered the Forger, taking his place on the opposite side, "You deserve your title! But enough of this trifling; I am waiting to chastise your impertinence. What shall be our signal?"

Luke silently took a letter from his pocket, and tore a narrow slip of paper from the outside. Then creasing this piece of paper, with his finger, he poured some few grains of powder into the hollow thus made, from a flask which he drew from his coat pocket. He rolled the paper in his hand, until it enveloped the powder, and advancing to the altar, wound it around the wick of the candle, between the flame, and the hollow which it had burned in the wax.

"When the candle burns down to that paper, and fires the powder, then let each man take care of his life!"

"Agreed," muttered Fitz-Cowles, examining the percussion cap of his pistol. "When the paper and the powder blazes, then by * * * I'll fire!"

For a single moment the antagonists, contemplated each other. There were but five paces between them. Fitz-Cowles was lividly pale, but a gleam of ferocity stamped his craven face, while from every line of Luke's countenance, from his compressed lip, and clear dark eye, there spoke the same holy resolution. He stood there, in that Chapel, as the Avenger of Wrong and Murder!

Lower and lower burnt the candle, until the flame, touched the paper which enveloped the powder. A start quivered through Fitz-Cowles' frame, but Luke's firm fingers clenched his pistol with an iron grasp.

"In a moment, I may be in—hell!" muttered Fitz-Cowles.

"Think of the dead body of your victim, think of Dora!" shrieked Luke, and the powder blazed up around the candle-wick.

There was a report; two pistols mingled their sounds together, and white columns of smoke, rolled upward to the ceiling. When that smoke cleared away, each antagonist, beheld his foe, standing unharmed, unhurt, on the opposite side of the altar. Luke's ball had grazed Fitz-Cowles' shoulder, and sunk in the wall behind; the shot of the forger, had whistled by Harvey's right temple, and splintered the face of the Image, at his back.

"Wonders how *that* 'ill work!" roared a hoarse voice, without the door.

"Now fool and coward! You have spent your shot!" muttered Fitz-Cowles, drawing a bowie knife from his bosom, and rushing toward the altar. "You have defied a man, who never yet failed, with this good knife."

His face darkened by the conflict of hideous passions, Fitz-Cowles rushed past the altar, with his brandished knife, gleaming in the light. Luke stood calm and firm, with a quiet smile playing round his thin lips. Was he resigned for his death? Fitz-Cowles prided himself on his skill with the bowie knife, as a butcher loves to boast of his dexterity in slaughtering an ox. He could cut and thrust, and parry and stab, and strike and maim—a brave man was Fitz-Cowles.

Two paces lay between the bravo, and Luke Harvey.

"Aye, dog—I have you!" shouted Fitz-Cowles with a brutal sneer.

Luke slowly raised his right arm with the pistol in his clenched hand.

"These pistols are double-barreled," he coolly said. "One of them is loaded in both barrels. You have thrown away yours: I am sorry for you! You took your choice of the pistols awhile ago; now take your chance from this barrel! Perhaps it's loaded, perhaps it is n't! Let this decide!"

Fitz-Cowles recoiled with one sudden movement, toward the altar; Luke drew the trigger, there was a stunning report and all was darkness! The ball had extinguished the candle.

A horrid oath resounded through the darkness—"You dog I have you at last!" spoke the hoarse voice of Fitz-Cowles, and then there was the sound of a hurried footstep followed by a sudden crash. All was still, aye, still as the corse beneath the coffin-lid. Luke could hear his own hard breathing; it was the only sound that disturbed the silence of the place. He could not see his hand before his eyes; the Chapel seemed suddenly filled with a darkness that was thick, dense and almost tangible.

Where was Fitz-Cowles? Luke felt a shudder creep over his frame as he fancied the bravo, slowly dragging his form, snake-like along the floor, in order to hew his victim down, by one sudden and unseen blow. Was he lurking beside the altar? Luke listened; the stillness of the place was intense and horrible.

In silence, and with softened footsteps, Luke receded backward, until his extended hands touched a cold and inanimate object. It was the Image of the dying Saviour. Gliding behind the cross, Luke crouched down, and unarmed as he was, listened for the approach of the bravo. Not a footstep nor a voice was heard; not even the sound of half-suppressed breathing.

Could his last ball have taken effect? Might not the oath and threat, with which Fitz-Cowles sprang forward, been his last? That crash was the sound of his dead body falling to the floor in the agonies of death!

"I will creep forward on my hands and knees, and satisfy myself, by the touch of his dead body!"

And on and on, and around and around he crept, ever searching for the altar, and yet still as far from the object of his search, after a lapse of half an hour, as when he first began. Have you ever found yourself, late at night in a dark room, hunting for a door, with whose position you were familiar, and which still, for long hours eluded your search? So Luke Harvey, creeping over the floor of the dark chapel, sought for the altar, beside which he expected to find the dead body of his antagonist, and yet, by some strange chance or other, he always found himself against the bare walls, or at the foot of the cross, or groping along the canvass of the picture which occupied one end of the room.

A strange awe began to seize his soul. He sat down, with his head between his knees, listening for the faintest echo of a sound, and at last fell into a wild half-waking sleep, from which he was soon aroused by a roaring noise that filled his ears like the thunder of a mighty river, breaking its way through a deep glen, where opposing mountains meet.

It may have been a few minutes, or half an hour since Luke had entered the chapel, but his strange bewilderment in the darkness and silence had confused his idea of time, and he rose on his feet like a man struggling with some hideous night-mare.

That awful roaring grew nearer and louder and more distinct; now it yelled without the very chapel walls, and sudden as a flash from the cannons mouth, the darkness passed away. One entire end of the chapel was a wall of flame; through the canvass on which was delineated the Blessed Mother and the Holy Child, long tongues of forked fire were thrust blazing into the place, and the dim colors glared in horrid light. Another instant, and the whole extent of the chapel, every nook and corner, the altar and the cross, the ceiling and the walls, were all laid bare by a sheet of streaming flame.

From the centre of the floor, right at the altar's foot uprose a grim and hideous head, with long locks of elf-like hair, waving in the red light, and a distorted face, grinning like a death's-head, fired by the glare of a rolling eye, that blazed like a coal from hot ashes. Slowly it uprose, it mocked the eye of the gazer with a loathsome grimace, like the grin of a mocking devil, and then a discordant laugh yelled through the fiery air.

We now return to Devil-Bug, whom we left watching beside the chapel door. The sound of the first fire had thundered on his ear, and uprising from his crouching position, he ran along the corridor, passed down the stairway and through the dim hall, laughing merrily to himself all the while.

The hall door was wide open, but all was silent throughout the mansion.

Devil-Bug passed the doorway, and presently found himself among the deserted garden walks, where winter had colored all objects with a hue of dead, monotonous brown, while statutes thrown down from their pedestals, and arbors crumbling to ruin, attested the decay into which Hawkewood had fallen during the life of Albert Livingstone. Through the dark pines which were scattered all around the mansion, Devil-Bug wandered listlessly on, until he stood beneath the shadow of the southern wing, where one bold mass of sombre grey stone projecting from the body of the edifice was dimly disclosed by the starlight, in vague yet ponderous outlines. From the earth on which Devil-Bug stood to the conical roof which surmounted this dependency of the main edifice, the uniformity of its dark grey stone was only broken by a solitary door opening into the garden.

"That must be the Chapel!" exclaimed Devil-Bug "and in the second story them fellers is fightin' like devils—ho, hoo! Wonders how *that* 'ill work!"

Passing round the mansion, Devil-Bug stood on the summit of a hill in its rear, which affording room for a broad walk between the edifice and its brow, sank suddenly into the glen below, where a faint gurgling sound like the echo of a brook, choked up by weeds and withered leaves, broke on the silent air. The pine trees on this side of the mansion were shrunken, blasted, and withered. Through their white branches, rising coldly in the air, the starlight fell brightly over the grey walls of the lordly structure. Devil-Bug's heavy footsteps were echoed by the crashing of the withered leaves which were gathered ankle-deep, around the trunks of the blasted trees. Striking into a rude path which descended into the darkness of the glen, Devil-Bug went slowly down, looking around upon the white trunks, rising like ghosts on every side, with a feeling of strange awe.

A wild fancy seized this strange monster. He had drawn forth a cigar, and having lighted it with the sparks from a steel and flint, falling on a piece of decayed wood, which soon presented a small yet substantial mass of fire, he knelt on the hard ground, while his hideous face was encircled in wreaths of tobacco smoke. Gathering the dry leaves into a heap around the crumbling trunk, the remnant of a fallen tree, Devil-Bug added brushwood and broken limbs to the pile, and then chuckled grimly at his work.

"It's cold as thunder," he exclaimed, indulging in a lively smile, "and I'll have a bit of fire."

He applied the burning wood to the trunk of the tree; in a moment it took fire, and ere Devil-Bug rose on his feet, the dry leaves were in a blaze.

The monster then leaped merrily up and down, executing a devil's dance in the light of the flame.

"Ho-hoo!" he shouted while every lineament of his face, every point of his figure, was changed to vivid crimson. "Ho-hoo! There they are, there, *there!* The man with the broken jaw, the 'ooman with the holler skull! There, there, a-layin' 'longside the fire, warmin' their cussed bones—uh-oo-hoo!"

As his wild shriek of unearthly laughter, was borne away by the wind, the flame crept up the limbs of a withered tree, winding like a fiery serpent around each decayed branch, until a long column of fire and smoke, shot away into the dark blue sky. There was a howling gust of wind, sweeping down into the glen, and from tree to tree, like a thing of life, the fire leapt, and gathered leaves, branches and dry limbs into its fierce embrace.

In a few moments, Devil-Bug was surrounded by a sheet of flame. With a wild howl, half delight, half terror, he rushed along the rude path, he gained the summit of the hill, and looked at the fruits of his labor. To the eastward of the mansion, far down into the glen, the whole wood was one mass of fire. Above the sky was bloody red; beneath were whirling waves of smoke, through which the forked flames, writhed like awful serpents of the air, whom some wierd spell, had rendered visible to human eye. Withered tree, reached forth its fiery arms to withered tree, the fires sent up their flaming crests to the lurid heavens, and then a mighty roar ascended on the still air, like the shriek of Pharoah's host, beneath the waters of the sea.

With every infernal emotion, playing over his chaos of a face, mingled with some gleams of human feeling, for the space of fifteen minutes, dancing, hooting yelling, or standing like a block of stone, with his arms folded over his breast, Devil-Bug watched the progress of the fire.

The whole eastern woods were now one wall of living flame. The winter wind, rushing toward the east, for a few brief moments, bore the mass of fire, in rolling waves, away toward the horizon of the rising sun.

Waves of flame and clouds of smoke, the blue sky above turned to burning red, and the earth beneath changed suddenly into an ocean of fire—ho, ho, this was a sight for Devil-Bug to gaze upon in maniac glee.

Suddenly the wind shifted, and the whole sea of flame, rushed with a roar like hell, upon the roofs of the doomed mansion.

In an instant, the roof was wrapped in a sheet of flame. Into the windows it rushed, along the eaves it poured, it whirled round the steep gables, the mansion seemed an altar of molten flame.

"I must save that feller Luke, I must save him for the sake o' th' gal," screeched Devil-Bug. "Hello! There's a window in the east o' that Chapel, the fire nears it, quick, quick old boy or all is lost!"

Half-stifled by clouds of smoke, Devil-Bug ran round to the western front of the mansion. At his back, roared and whirled the sea of flame; over his head, it tossed in burning waves.

With one glance, he saw that all hope of entrance by the hall-door was vain; he looked to the door of the southern wing: to his astonishment he found its huge panels, laid prostrate at his feet.

It was no time for thought! Rushing through the arching doorway, Devil-Bug, by the light of a sudden flash of flame, beheld the massive walls of a grave-vault with three coffins, placed at regular intervals on solid blocks of stone. He saw these coffins, and a cloud of smoke, wrapt the place in darkness. Another flash of flame, and in the centre of the vault, rising from the stone floor to the arching ceiling, he beheld the outlines of a rude ladder, placed in the aperture of a small trap-door.

"Hello! Here's fun for an old boy like me! One o' them fellers has killed th' tother in the chapel up stairs, and the door bein' locked he's he's got off, by this trap-door and ladder—ho, hoo! I must satisfy my mind! If Luke's killed all's up with the g-al! Fire away curse you, and smoke away, who keers?"

He rushed toward the ladder, he ascended its rounds, and in a moment, passing through the narrow trap-door, his sight was blinded by one quivering sheet of flame. The hot fire smote his brain, with a pang like death, he yelled in agony; and then a wild shriek of infernal laughter burst from his lips. He beheld the picture, tossed in fragments, on the sheets of flame, he beheld the Image of Jesus, turned to dazzling crimson by the blinding light, he saw the figure crouching at the foot of the cross.

"Luke," he shrieked rushing forward, "Save yerself! There's hell around us, above us, below us! Hurr-a-h! This is wot I likes—but come, my feller! Save yerself for the sake o' the gal!"

"The key!" shouted Luke, springing on his feet and pointing to the door.

"This way," exclaimed Devil-Bug. "Thro' that trap-door down th' ladder—hurray!"

"The key!" thundered Luke, with fierce gesture. "The key! Quick I say!"

"Take it, and to the devil with you!" screamed Devil-Bug, flinging the key at Luke's feet.

As though his soul hung on that instant's deeds, Luke seized the key, unlocked the door, and his form was lost in a cloud of smoke, that filled the chapel.

"Ven he gits in the middle o' th' fire and can't breathe—ho, ho! Wonders how that 'ill vork?" And with a wild laugh, Devil-Bug retreated to the trap-door.

The lonely corridor, yet free from flame but obscured by smoke, reechoed to Luke Harvey's footsteps. His heart was in his throat, as he darted onward. In an instant the stairs were gained. Thank God! They were free from the lurid flame, or stifling smoke. With one bound Luke rushed up the steps of massive oak, he stood on the landing in front of the Oak Chamber. At that very instant the glass of the eastern window, fell crashing at his feet; he was surrounded by a cloud of black and choking smoke. Stifled by the heat, he leaned against one of the posts of the Oak Chamber door, and a sudden gust of wind bore smoke and flame, out through the window in the fiery air once more.

Luke gazed into the Oak Chamber; one wild and horror stricken look, and all was smoke and flame again.

That gaze, that look of a moment—great God! Let its horror never be told to living man! Accursed be the lips that murmur it, accursed the pen that pictures it! Luke gave one look and a mass of flame rose up between him and the horrid vision; he gave one look, and his heart died within him!

Let us pray to Heaven that what he then beheld was only a fearful dream engendered by the smoke and heat!

That arm uplifted, that frown, that kneeling form, that tide of gushing blood—hush! Never, never to human ears may that sight be told. It was a dream, yes, yes, only a dream! But that scream, that shriek, gurgling from the smoke and flame—did ever human thing, ridden by the horrors of madness, fancy a shriek like that?

Only one look, and yet to see a sight, which it were blasphemy to tell. Only one look, and yet to have one's heart forever blasted by its memory!

Pursued by smoke and flame, Luke rushed down the stairway; over crackling timbers and through waves of fire he gained the hall door; as though a fiend was at his shoulder, flinging his arms aloft, he rushed through the grove of burning pines toward the mansion gate.

Three human figures stood on the rising knoll, an aged man and withered woman, but half sheltered from the night by their scanty apparel, and there holding the reins of two plunging horses in his iron hands, a grim monster, stood at their backs.

With a face like ashes, Luke sprang upon his horse. Not a word passed from his lips, but casting one vacant glance at the sea of flame, roaring around the doomed house, he dashed down the road with the speed of wind.

Not once did he look back, until five miles lay between him and the roofs of Hawkewood. From the summit of a gentle hill, he gazed backward upon the scene, and as he gazed the form of Devil-Bug, clinging like a toad to the neck of a foaming steed, was at his side.

"Ho, hoo! You're a purty feller to leave an old man and oo'man to be burnt up, ain't you now? If it had'nt been for me they'd a-been roasted, sartin' as hell is blazing yonder! Ho, hoo! I does wonder how that 'ill vork!"

He pointed to the world of flame, and his screech-owl laugh broke like a fiend's yell on the air.

It was an awful sight, awful and sublime as tho' the Book of Revelations had started into action. The entire eastern horizon was one wall of flame, dark purple, and bright red, and dazzling crimson, mingled together, with a chaos of smoke rolling up to the sky in awful folds, pile on pile to the very zenith.

Chasm and plain, orchard and farm-house, ravine and dell, lay bared to the eye in a blaze, brighter than the noon-day sun. Then the roar of the flames, like the groan of millions or the last convulsive throw of an expiring world; how it swelled in awful volume, how it shrieked through mountains of smoke, how it filled all space!

I have stood in the streets of the Quaker City, while a fierce mob, hungry for blood, howled onward, their ten thousand faces glaring in the light of a burning church, whose dome went up to Heaven in clouds of smoke and waves of fire. I have heard their yell of mocking triumph as the cross of Jesus tottered from its proud height, quivered for a moment, and then fell plunging into the abyss of flame!

But here, was neither church nor cross, nor frenzied mob. All was Solitary Desolation. Not a breath of fanaticism to fan the flame, nor yet the visage of a grim Bigot, grinning at the work of ruin.

All was fire and smoke and solitude. Far over the land, far along the wide horizon, the forests lapped in sheets of fire, sent their greeting to the sky, as though they yelled in triumph, beneath the wild career of Desolation.

"Never, never, never!" muttered Luke in a tone of whispered horror. "Never to be spoken by human lips to human ears! Only one look, and yet that sight! Oh, God—tear it from my soul, tear it from my heart, this awful memory! Better to die stretched on the rope of a gibbet, than to have this Phantom ever brooding over my soul! That frown, that uplifted hand, that kneeling form—never, never, never to living man shall it be spoken!"

He dashed the spurs in the flanks of his steed, and without once looking back on the sea of flame, sped madly onward, while the distorted form of Devil-Bug rode at his horse's heels, like some laughing Demon in pursuit of his victim.

CHAPTER FIFTH

THE TEMPLE OF RAVONI

White columns of incense, rolled in soft and curling folds, through the temple to the arching dome, from whose azure expanse, innumerable lights glittered like stars in a clear sky. The sound of a low-toned and absorbing music floated through the smoke of the incense, and the breath of flowers filled the air. Through the intervals of the snowy columns, filling that wide temple, with shapes of fantastic splendor, you might see the forms of beautiful women, moving in a gliding dance, their limbs encircled by a light and flowing drapery.

Then a wilderness of flowers, sweet as May or gorgeous as autumn, broke on your eye, with here and there a fountain of clear water, rising in the light, and sprinkling its spray drops in the air, with a murmur of rippling music. Then the columns of incense, closed upon the vision of flowers and fountain, veiling the forms of beautiful women, in its robes of snowy whiteness, while the light from the azure dome, gave a thousand hues, a thousand fairy shapes, to the wreaths of fragrant mist, as they swept through the temple, or broke among the pillars, or rolled away to the arching roof.

From the bosom of those snowy clouds, come the sound of women's feet, sweeping over the floor, to a low and soft-toned measure, while the murmur of fountains, mingled with the harp and viol, and the air grew heavy with the perfume of incense, overpowering for a moment, the fragrance of innumerable flowers.

Suddenly the columns of smoke died away, and a scene like some dream of enchantment, was laid bare to the eye.

In the centre of the place, around an altar of snow-white marble, were grouped a crowd of maidens, whose beauty was like the blushing dawn, or solemn eve, on still midnight, various, contrasted and enchanting. Between this crowd of beauty and the altar, knelt some twenty-four young men, whose thoughtful faces, and flashing eyes, were in vivid constraint, with the long white robes, that fell round their well-proportioned forms. On the other side of the altar, with a beautiful maiden by his side, stood a man of strange beauty, his light yet muscular form, clad in a tunic of black velvet, reaching to his knees, while from the floor, some few faces at his back, arose a tent with white silken curtains, waving to and fro, in the dazzling light of the dome.

Around the scene, the strange man and the maiden, the cluster of kneeling men, and the group of beautiful women, swept the twelve marble pillars of the temple, describing the circular form of the place, and supporting the roof of the white dome, from whose azure expanse, twinkled and fell, the glare of innumerable lights.

Twelve massive pillars of dark-hued marble rose from the variegated floor, to the dome above, and around each pillar, were clustered vases of solid stone, filled with rare and beautiful flowers, mingling their hues and perfume, while they rustled gently in the light. Here was the rose, from the vales of Persia, the lily from the clear waters of some Ethiopian lake, the gorgeous flower of Montezuma, from the wilds of Mexican deserts. Here too, from amid rich green leaves, the hue and shape of luscious fruit, were thrust into light, the golden orange and the yellow lime, the purple grape hanging in clusters, and the blushing peach, bending beneath the weight of its own ripeness. Fruits and flowers of every clime, ripened and bloomed around the massive pillars of that gorgeous temple.

Beyond these pillars, was a cloistered space, but dimly penetrated by the light, yet full of music and beauty. In the interval between each pillar, arose a gentle fountain of clear water, darting upward through the dim air, and falling into a basin of snow-white marble, with an almost inaudible murmur. Twelve fountains showering into the dim air, that lay beyond the pillars, mingled their murmurs and filled the temple with a soft and lulling melody, like the hum of bees, revelling amid the perfume of intoxicating flowers. And the song of birds, faint and chirping, or rich, full and gushing, came from the dimness of the cloister, blending, with the murmur of the fountains, or rising in distinct melody to the echoing dome.

His dark hair, falling to his shoulders, his brow glowing with a strange joy, his olive cheek flushed with the hues of immortal youth, Ravoni stood between the silken tent and the altar, looking with the same expression of triumph on the young face of the maiden, by his side, the kneeling enthusiasts extending along the floor, and the forms of the lovely women, clustering around in attitudes of grace and beauty.

Well might Ravoni, gaze upon these beaming faces and graceful forms, with his dark eye dilating with mingled triumph and admiration. Here were the beauties of the world, called from cottage, harem and hall. That maiden yonder, whose supple form is clad in light drapery reaching to her knees, whose dark brown cheek, blushes with the ripeness of her native skies, whose raven hair is tinged with a shade of glossy blue, whose lips are luscious red; need you ask the name of the land, from which this blossom sprung? A child of fair skies and sunny waters, a child of deep groves, fragrant with tropical fruits, a daughter of Hindoostan, whom Ravoni's hand sixteen years ago, rescued from the waters of the Ganges, while the animal mother, the murderer of her infant, stood looking on, with a smile.

That queenly woman, with the tall form, the fair skin, the dark eyes, and the rich brown hair? The child of old Virginia, entrusted by rich parents, to the care of *Doctor* Ravoni! By her side, that sweet young girl, with a form so fragile, and yet so beautiful, with a vacant blue eye, and sunny clusters of golden hair falling over a neck like a snow-flake? The warm skies of Carolina, laugh in her eye and in her smile. Here, in fine, are shapes from all the world, shapes of living, breathing, beaming loveliness! The Creole from New Orleans, with limbs of voluptuous softness, an eye, so dark, so melting, so full of passion, revenge and madness; the mild beauty of the British isle, with a skin like snow, warmed with a flash of daybreak; the warm maiden of Spain, with her olive cheek and flashing eye; the faultless forms of many a Grecian isle, and the heaving bosoms of Circassia; the cherry lips of Pennsylvania, and the blue eyes and sunny locks of Germany, these all were mingled in that crowd of loveliness and beauty.

Well might the smile of triumph wreathe the dark red lips of Ravoni! There, amid this cluster of lovely women, were the daughters of rich and haughty families, whose broad lands lay in the far scattered states of the American Union, whose magnificent mansions, lined the streets of many a town, and city, in North and South and West; in the peopled Centre and on the forest borders. They had been sent to the *Mad-Doctor* Ravoni, whose reputation for skill in all cases of Insanity, was without a parallel.

Here they were, grouped around the altar of Ravoni, mingled among the forms of his harem, alike the dupes of his will and instruments of his power, here they were, the willing slaves of his magnetic glance; but ere you drop a tear for the fate of these *patients of the Mad-Doctor*, let me raise up before your eyes, the shadow of a horrid wrong, which is done every day in this good Quaker City, and every hour in the day, under the solemn sanction of the Law.

Let me point your vision, to the grim cells of that Legal Mad-House, where a reckless Charlaton administers his brutal rule, in damp cells, littered by straw, amid the glorious panoply of chains and bolts and bars! Let me picture to you, this pitiless Quack, standing lash in hand, over the prostrate body of some insane wretch, while his band of brutal ruffians, stand ready to do his will, even though that will be slow and deliberate murder. When you have taken in the full details of the picture, when you have impressed on your mind the fact, that this Quack and his Mad-House are both the creatures of your Statute-books, that sane men have been dragged into their clutches, by designing relatives, and kept chained and lashed, until insanity came to their relief, followed by sudden death; *then* quarrel with the Mad-house of the Sorcerer! Even now as I write, there rises before me, the records of a judicial investigation, which gave to this Legal Mad-house, all the horrors of the Bastile, in its most gory hour!

The dark eyes of Ravoni were fixed upon the face of the maiden who stood by his side. It was a pale face, aye pale and white as snow, yet full of health, and beaming with a strange life. In thick masses her raven-black hair, streamed over her shoulders, while her dark eyes, had but one look, one gaze, and that was centred upon the face of Ravoni.

"Here amid the breath of flowers, the lull of fountains, and the song of birds, do I consecrate the Priestess of our New Faith! On this white brow I place the crown of flowers: may thy soul fair maiden be pure for evermore, pure and stainless as these lilies, thy heart young and warm forever as these buds of the opening rose! Arise and hail the virgin Izolé, arise and hail the Priestess of our New Faith!"

Slowly the enthusiasts arose, but not a murmur passed from their parted lips. Izolé stood before them, like a thing of air, so pure, so fair, and so serenely beautiful. Each dark eye, was fixed upon her in a look of reverence like religious worship.

Ravoni waved his hand, and the crowd of beautiful women, went, whirling over the floor, while the sound of the harp and viol, arose merrily on the air. The murmur of fountains, and the song of birds was mingled with the light tripping sound of women's feet, while the light from the dome shone over a scene of bewitching fascination. Now circling in groups of two and three, their bounding limbs, stirring the light drapery, which but faintly veiled the glory of each shape, the beauty of each heaving bosom, or again sweeping round the altar and the tent, in one breathing mass of loveliness, each fair arm, raised gently in the light, while they glided over the floor, their forms undulating to the impulse of soft and murmuring music.—They were worthy of Moslem's heaven, these women of Ravoni!

"These are the forms of Sense and Passion," exclaimed Ravoni. "They speak not, but as I will, they have no soul, but mine! This"—and his dark eye was centred on the face of Izolé—"This is a form of pure and spiritual loveliness. In this sweet form, in this mild face, beaming such unutterable love, behold the Incarnation of our Faith!"

Not a word from the Disciples; not a murmur from Izolé. They had but one eye, and that was centred on her face; her dark eyes had but one glance, and that was chained to the flashing eyes of Ravoni.

"From time to time, through every age, and in every clime, there have appeared on the earth, fair maidens, whose delicate organization, warming with life, yet full of spiritual beauty, indicates their holy mission. They endure persecution, they suffer wrong, their childhood is one bitter pang. Friendless and alone they walk the earth, while their souls are in the Future, while their thoughts dwell with indefinable longing on the hope of another world, hidden in the bosom of space. These are the chosen of God! It is unto such as these, that the AWFUL SUPREME, gently manifests his will. Look, my children, around you cluster fair and beautiful women, the light from yon dome, falls on heaving bosoms and glowing cheeks. Are these the chosen of God! Never! Creatures of Sense, their animal organization reveals their nature. But this fair creature standing by my side, this Image of pure thought whose dark eyes I now hold exchained with my glance, tell me, is she not the chosen of the Eternal? As I speak—behold—her eyes fire with Prophecy, her lips part in wonder as the prospect of the Future rushes on her soul!"

The twenty-four believers in the New Faith knelt down in silence. Grouping around them in attitudes of voluptuous grace, were the beauties of all the world, their vacant eyes fixed in wonder on the face of Ravoni. The lull of fountains, the murmur of birds, the perfume of flowers; these all were in the air.

"What see'st thou?" spoke the deep voice of Ravoni, and his dark eye shot a fixed gleam into the eyes of the Priestess.

Her form dilated, her right hand rose gently overhead, her lips parted, and with her dark eyes filled with wonder and awe, Izolé gazed on the vacant air.

"I am in a large city, whose domes arise into the blue sky. The streets are filled with free and happy people. There are no rich; there are no poor; I see neither church nor gaol, priest nor gaoler, yet—yet—all are happy!"

"This is OUR FAITH!" No rich, no poor, no priests no gaolers! Look again Izolé! What see'st thou?"

"A man has dyed his hands in murder. His victim lays at his feet, and the crowd circle round with pale faces. Hark! They whisper and point to the date on yonder edifice. '*The two hundredth year of the Independence of Man's Soul!*' 'Since then,' they whisper 'there have been but two murder's in our land.' Murder to them, is no familiar thing—"

"Do they drag the murderer to the gallows, or to the solitary cell, where madness digs its fangs into the victim's soul?"

"There are neither gaol nor gibbet in the land! Hush! Hear you that cry of madness! He begs them to slay him; he cries for the mercy of the sword or gibbet! In that city of happy people, he feels himself accursed. He rises—none lifts a hand to molest him. He shrieks—the face of his dead victim haunts him like a curse! He goes to his home—his friends and neighbors gather round him, they seek to comfort him. Hark that voice! 'Crime is a disease to be cured, not an ulcer to be cut off!' "

"See'st thou no place of worship, where prayers are made to the Eternal God?"

"Come—come—with a gentle footstep—come! Cross we this peaceful threshold! A father, a wife and little children! They sit in their own home, with the free air blowing through the windows, and God's sun shining in their faces. Here is their place of worship—Home!"

"And from whence comes this peace, this mercy, this Religion of Home?"

"Lo! we are in the streets again. Two citizens meet in the pathway; they greet each other with familiar salutations, but that silent grasp of each others hand, that mystic sign, made by each upon his forehead? What means that grasp, that sign? They are Brothers of the Secret Order of Ravoni, established two hundred years ago. The very existence of this band is deemed a fable by the mass of men, but in silence and in secrecy, by the children of the Faith, has this great peace and mercy and this Religion of Home, been brought to light!"

"This Faith—what is it?"

"Hope to Man!" exclaimed the Priestess as her hand rose in the air, and her dark eye flashed with thoughts of unutterable meaning.

"Hail Ravoni! We love thy Faith, we are Brothers of thy Order! It is a Prophecy! Hail Ravoni—hail! We worship thee!"

With a murmur of awe, the Disciples of Ravoni rose from the floor, they encircled the altar, the Master and the Maiden, and stood with uplifted hands, while the crowd of beautiful women whirled dancing around the scene, and the lull of fountains and the song of birds mingled with the cry, "Hail Ravoni—we worship thee!"

The Sorcerer turned from the band of enthusiasts, and tossed aside the hangings of the silken tent, which arose in the full light of the dome.

"Behold the arisen dead!" he exclaimed, while a murmur of surprise spread through the group. Fair and beautiful as some dream which comes over the half-waking soul, in the voluptuous softness of a summer's sunset, a maiden form lay reclining on a couch of light crimson velvet, her white robes displaying in easy folds, the womanly symmetry of her shape. Her glowing cheek rested on her full round arm, while the hand lay softly on her bosom, rising and falling with the gentle impulse of slumber. The hair which fell in flowing masses around her face, was bright, silken and glossy, like the hue of sun-beams bathing the crest of a rippling billow.

"She has arisen from death, but she still lingers in a state of Trance," said Ravoni, passing his hand gently along her forehead, while his dark eyes flashed with light, like a living flame. "Arise, maiden arise! Arise and speak to the children of the faith, the revelations made to thee, while thy soul, freed from the body, soared in the realms of Trance!"

The maiden slowly unclosed her eyes of a light and liquid azure, the Disciples clustered closer around the altar, waiting the anticipated revelation with interest and awe, while Ravoni stood gazing upon the countenance of the light-haired girl with an expression that indicated his powerful Will, concentred on a single object, with deep and absorbing intensity.

"Speak maiden," said Ravoni in his voice of low-toned music.

The murmur on the lips of the girl, mingled with the sound of footsteps resounding from either side of the temple. With one start, the Disciples of Ravoni, and the crowd of beautiful women, turned their gaze from side to side, while the forms of the intruders advanced into the glare of the light.

"Annie!" shrieked a voice, hoarse with emotion, and a young man, whose long dark hair, fell waving aside, from a pale face, stamped with the traces of an agony, like madness, came rushing from the cloister, with wild and unsteady footsteps.

The maiden reclining within the folds of the tent beheld him, she rose from the couch with a faint murmur, and as he rushed forward, through the group of enthusiasts she raised her arms aloft, and sunk senseless into his embrace.

"Ha! Our young enthusiast hath arisen from his slumber," muttered Ravoni, as he gazed upon the face of Byrnewood Arlington. "But lover and maiden, both shall minister to my Will!"

As he spoke the dome was filled with a sound like the howl of an enraged hyena. Every eye was turned toward the opposite side of the temple, and the light fell upon a deformed shape, rushing wildly over the floor, with head half-sunken between the shoulders, and long arms with fingers like talons, flung quivering in the air. That face with the wide mouth, the teeth fixedly compressed, the eyeless socket and the blazing eye—Ravoni knew it well, and knew that now was the time, for the exertion of his utmost power.

"The gal!" shrieked, the voice of Devil-Bug, as he strode rapidly toward the altar. "Wizard, give me that gal, or—or—"

His teeth churned with rage, and the white foam hung round his huge lips. He stood with heavy chest and a burning eye, gazing steadily in the face of Ravoni. The same start of fear quivered through the Disciples and the women of Ravoni. With one impulse they recoiled from the altar, leaving the Master Sorcerer to confront the monster, who stood before him.

Gently gathering his arm, around the waist of Izolé, the Priestess and the maiden, Ravoni fixed the glance of his dark eye upon the face of Devil-Bug. The Savage looked from one to the other, first on the pale face of Izolé, then in dark the countenance of the Sorcerer, he raised his arms aloft, with a cry of vengeance, he sprung forward. A murmur of horror escaped from the lips of the Disciples. Devil-Bug sprung forward, his hands quivering, and his eye flashing, but the calm dark eye of Ravoni was fixed upon him, he made an effort to overcome the witch of that burning glance, he clutched his brawny chest with his talon fingers, and then fell back recoiling on one knee.

"Gi' me the gal, Wizard, only gi' me the gal," he moaned, looking upward with a subdued and pitiful glance, "Gi' me the gal, an' I'll be your slave! I'll murder, stab and burn for yo'—I'll be yer slave for life—I'll—I'll—only gi' me the gal wizard—"

"Slave!" the sneer quivered on the thin lips of Ravoni. "Know you, that the man who treads this floor unbidden, has doomed himself to death? Begone, or from this temple' walls, you will never pass again, but as a corse!"

"Imposter!" shouted a sneering voice, at the back of Devil-Bug. "Juggler and knave! Resign this girl to me, or I will teach you the wholesome discipline, which Judge *Lynch* awards to strolling vagabonds—"

Ravoni raised his glance, and beheld the tall form of Luke Harvey, standing at the back of Devil-Bug, his dark eyes flashing and his thin lip quivering with scorn.

"Come juggler," sneered Luke, advancing, "Resign the girl to me, without delay. If you have so much as injured a hair of her head, you shall answer for it with your blood."

He extended his arms; Izolé shrunk back from his couch.

Ravoni made no reply to the sneer, and the threat, but his olive cheek flushed with deep emotion, and his black eye dilating, suddenly absorbed the space between the brow and cheek-bone, but an instant ago, occupied by the fringed eyelid. The Sorcerer presented a terrible picture of superhuman anger. The sneer died on Luke's lip; with an involuntary start, he recoiled a step backward, and stood like a man awaking from a dream.

"Izolé is free!" exclaimed Ravoni, in a tone of marked calmness,

"Why do you not advance, and claim your prize? Maiden thou wilt go with this man, wilt thou not?"

A look of deep emotion passed over Luke's face, as he gazed upon the beautiful countenance of Izolé.

"Maiden," he exclaimed, "Your father's last word, consigned you to my care! I swore a solemn oath, to guard and protect you, at the hazard of my life. Come with me. There is danger for you in this place, danger worse than death—"

As these low pleading tones fell on the ear of the maiden, Devil-Bug crawled softly along the floor, and plucking the skirt of her white robe, looked up beseechingly in her face.

"Come gal," he muttered, "You shall roll in wealth—you shall wear silks an' satins—Come gal! This feller's a wizard an' a devil leave him—"

"Go with them!" said Ravoni, and he unwound his arm from her waist.

Izolé stood alone in front of the altar. She looked around with a glance of mysterious meaning. Her eyes were veiled in a mist-like film, that gave them a wild and glassy stare. First she gazed in the face of Devil-Bug, and some memory of the past, seemed to give its light to her bewildered soul. Then her eyes encountered the gaze of Luke Harvey, and a murmur of joy, burst from her lips. She advanced toward him with a smile.

"I will go with you," she said, "Lead me to my father—" The words died suddenly on her lips. Her eyes met the glance of Ravoni—with a soft gliding motion, she swam to his arms.

"With thee!" she whispered, placing a fair hand on each shoulder, and looking up into his face. "With thee forever!"

At that moment Ravoni's face was sublime! Gazing down into the countenance of the fair young girl, whose bosom heaved against his chest, whose soft hands rested warmly on his shoulders, a smile broke over his face, and his dark eye grew radiant with delight.

"Izolé," he whispered in a voice, whose tones were music, "Chosen of God, called to the altar, whose faith is hope to man, thy name shall yet linger on the lips of millions, a sound of blessing and praise! Here from the solemn temple, here from these hearts of fire, shall go forth, a new religion, like the faith which in long past ages, gathered men, in the city and the plain, in the mountain and the dell, as brothers—children of one God, worshippers of the majesty of Eternity without tithe, or priest or fane!"

"Hail Ravoni!" shouted the band of enthusiasts, and the group of lovely women, the vacant-eyed maniacs and the voluptuous forms of

Ravoni's harem, went whirling over the floor in a bounding dance. Looking upon their Master with deep reverence, these forms of animal loveliness without soul, regarded this strange scene, but as a part of the mysterious ceremonies of Ravoni. Kneeling on the floor beside the silken tent, Byrnewood Arlington with the senseless form of Annie, gathered in his embrace, looked up in vacant wonder.

"The maiden hath chosen," said Ravoni turning to Luke with a calm smile. Devil-Bug rose silently to his feet, and stood at the back of the Sorcerer, gazing with a wild stare, in the face of Izolé, as she hung fascinated on the very look of Ravoni. The Savage placed his hand within the breast of his coarse garment, and his gaze wandered from the form of the Sorcerer, to the face of the girl.

"She hath chosen," repeated Ravoni, with that same calm smile, as he gazed on the wondering face of Luke. "She hath—"

The words were half-uttered, when looking over Luke's shoulder, into a large mirror, that hung between two columns on the opposite side of the temple, he beheld a sight that froze his blood. He beheld a huge hand, rising above his head, with a glittering knife, grasped in the clutch of talon fingers. It was aimed at the bosom of Izolé!

One look into the mirror, the glance of a single moment, and Ravoni started forward, to shield her bosom from the blow. He started forward, a hoarse laugh broke on the air, mingled with a deep groan of agony! The knife had entered the back of Ravoni, driven with all the force of a frenzied arm, it sunk into the flesh between the shoulder blades, the Sorcerer felt the keen point at his heart, he grew purple in the face and pale by turns, he quivered from head to foot, he tottered along the floor, he fell.

He fell, and lay a mass of palpitating agony, at the maiden's feet, while Devil-Bug shook his gory hands aloft, with a burst of horrid laughter.

"Gal, I've saved you, saved you! Ho-hoo!"

The band of enthusiasts stood thunder-stricken; the shriek of the women of the harem, mingled with the hollow laugh of the maniacs; Byrnewood Arlington laid the form of the insensible girl, within the folds of the tent, he started up, and gazed upon the scene.

There on the floor, quivering in the agonies of an awful soul wrestling with death, there lay the mighty man, Ravoni the Sorcerer! The wierd Sorcerer whose magic was in his look, whose sorcery was in his tone! Now his hands clutched madly at the marble floor, now his knees touched his chin, and then his head fell backward on his shoulders, his back bent inwards with mental agony, and the soles of his feet, were hidden in the thick curls of his long dark hair. Pale, purple, livid and ashy, all hues by sudden turns, the eyes starting from their sockets and the white lips clenched between his teeth, his face was too fearful to look upon, his agony too horrible for mortal man, to behold.

With one yell, the enthusiasts rushed upon the murderer; he dashed them back with his weaponless hands, answering their yell, with shrieks of fiendish laughter.

"He'd a-made a nun o' th' gal, would he? Ho-hoo! Not while old Devil-Bug had a knife to stab, or a hand to strike! There lays yer Wizard, wrigglin' like a frog, yo' dogs and fools! Where's his eye now? Where's his devilty and witchcraft—ho, hoo!"

The Orphan maiden gazed upon the quivering form of Ravoni, her eyes rolled wildly to and fro, her heart grew icy, she fell insensible into Luke Harvey's arms.

Again the Disciples of Ravoni rushed upon the murderer of their Lord, there was a struggle, and the dome gave back the echo of mingled shrieks and yells.

"Back! Touch him not!" spoke a calm deliberate voice. The enthusiasts started in wonder. Their Master with his dying form supported on one arm, raised his head, and gazed calmly over the faces of his disciples.

"I am dying," he said as a glow like life, warmed over his livid face, "but do not harm my murderer!"

It was the voice, so low-toned, so soft, so musical, that they had heard in many a by-gone hour. Tears fell from their flashing eyes, groans of anguish heaved their manly bosoms. Silently they gathered round their dying master, Luke Harvey with the form of the insensible Izolé, the Priestess and the maiden gathered in his arms, was there, amid that group of dark-eyed fanatics, and there stood Byrnewood Arlington gazing in mute awe upon the awful face of Ravoni. And there, his solitary eye blazing with a vacant horror, as he gazed upon his victim, there stood Devil-Bug, his long arms dropped listlessly by his side. In the background grouping in fear together, were the women of the harem and the maniacs of the mad-house, all alike beautiful, all alike stricken dumb with a strange horror.

"My children I am dying," he said, and for a moment his dark eyes flashed, as though he was about to speak in the calm voice of the bygone time, but his head dropped, his lip quivered, and his gaze was fixed upon the floor.

In that moment a Voice within him, spoke to his Soul, words of deep and awful interest.

"One moment of awful thought! Stern believer in Annihilation, man of immortal manhood, suddenly hurled from thy proud eminence of eternal youth, has the grave its terrors for thee? Is there a hereafter? Look, beyond the veil of time and life, look—is there another world? Thine eyes are opening upon the secrets of death, tell us, oh man of fearful will and magic look, tell us, what hopes break on thee, what visions affright or enrapture thy soul, what is the prospect of eternity? No answer, no murmur! Ask thine inmost soul?

"All black, dull, dead! Vacant space, darkness, nothingness! Darkness, darkness, darkness! A thousand whispering tongues from the midst of clouds repeat that word—darkness!

"Annihilation! Oh, God, the terrors of hell, the gnawings of eternal torture, anything but this nothingness! To die, to die like a brute of the field, to be thought and soul to-day, dust and worse than dust, reeking corruption, to-morrow!"

Such were the thoughts that shook Ravoni's soul, in that solitary moment, as he lay with his dying form resting on his bent arm, while his dark eyes glared fixedly on the floor.

"And shall I, because this awful scene of Eternal Nothingness presses on my soul, like a raven on the corse of the battle-slain, shall I play the craven, shall these lips murmur words of drivelling penitence? Never, never! It is my last hour, but my soul shall go out, in glory!"

"Lift me my children, lift me on my feet once again," he exclaimed aloud, in a calm deliberate voice. They raised him on his feet; he stood erect supported by the arms of his disciples.

"When I give the signal, then draw the knife from the wound, and let me die!" he cried, while his form became once more erect, even as the students, encircled him with their arms. His eye blazed with all its former fire, his lip curled with the proud enthusiasm of the by-gone time. He looked beautiful, even beyond the beauty of this earth. His dark hair fell waving aside from his brow, tossed gently to and fro by a cool breath of air that came from the dim cloisters. For a moment all was still, save the lull of fountains, the voice of birds, and half-suppressed breathing of living men.

"I die," said Ravoni in that voice of music, "I die but I shall live again! When I am dead, I charge ye all, take my body, and let it be burned to ashes! In my most secret chamber, you will find a cabinet of ebony. Within this cabinet is deposited a volume written by my own hand, a volume of parchment, on whose leaves are inscribed the words of the New Faith. There, you will discover the sublime truths on which the Brotherhood of Ravoni will arise! From those pages will dawn upon you, the secrets of the olden sages, which the present age in its vain unbelief, deems but tradition and fable; the secret of gold, and the secret of immortal youth. Take this dying hand, and swear to do, as with my last breath, I command—"

Hand after hand was pressed upon those icy fingers. In a few brief moments, each fanatic of the twenty-four, had taken the oath. Why does Byrnewood start, tremble and turn pale? He felt his soul drawn toward the soul of the dying man, by an irresistible influence. He too advanced, he too reached forth his hand, but ere he could grasp the hand of Ravoni, that voice of strange enthusiasm broke on the air again.

"Take the knife in thy hand," he said to a student, whose bronzed face, with brilliant dark eyes, deeply sunk beneath a massive brow, was like the incarnation of an enthusiastic soul—"When I give the signal, draw it from the wound, and let me die! When I am dead, let my body be burned. From my ashes, a New Being will arise. The Secret is written in the Volume—the secret that shall raise these ashes into life.

"Come hither, youth! *His* face was like thine, the wierd sage who first taught me the secret of Eternal Youth. His name was Vayomer Aloheim—wear thou that name forever! When I am dying, gaze in my face and inhale my last breath. My Soul shall pass into thine! Thou shalt be the second Ravoni of the Faith; I give thee my soul, with the last word I e'er shall speak!"

No more tears from the band of Disciples, no more groan of agony! All was sudden and wild enthusiasm. "Hail, Ravoni," burst that thunder shout, "Hail Ravoni, we worship thee!"

"Vayomer Aloheim draw the knife from the wound, and let me die!"

There was a pause—a terrible pause. The red knife glittered in the air; the blood gushed and poured streaming on the floor. They caught it on their white mantles, on their faces and their hands! It was *sacred*, the blood of their Founder, the blood of Ravoni.

He raised himself proudly to his full heighth; his dark eyes glared with supernatural light; with folded arms he stood erect.

"Farewell my children, Izolé farewell!"

The words lingered on his lips, as he fell dead along the marble floor.

BOOK THE SIXTH

THE THIRD DAY

Christmas Eve

Ho! From the mast-head a cry shrieks through the clouds of night.

"Land, there to the west—land!" Aye, land, after a long and stormy voyage, land after bloodshed, mystery and gloom—hurrah!

And now white doves, bearing green leaves in their beaks, glide through the air, and fruits and flowers, all from the land, float on the surface of the deep.

The morning breaks from the east, in glory and in promise. Look how the red beams glitter over the pinions of the doves, but—ha! What means this Omen? Where doves, white and snowy, floated through the air, but a moment ago, now are ravens, black and gloomy. They shriek a mournful death-note on the ear—their beaks are filled with leaves, sad, wintry, withered leaves, spotted with blood.

The fruits and flowers floating on the rippling bosom of the Ocean—where are they now? Ha, ha! On every wave a grinning corse-head with a raven picking its goary meal, from the livid brow!

Yet still that cry from the mast-head—

"Land on the western horizon—land! Hurrah!"

CHAPTER FIRST

HOME ONCE MORE

It is the hour of Christmas Eve. One short hour's travel down the wintry sky, and the sun will sink to rest. The sky is filled with floating clouds, grey, drifting and scarf-like; along the west, towers one dark and gloomy wall, with the red sunbeams, pouring over each fantastic buttress and pinnacle.

It is cold, bitter cold. It is cold bitter cold, and the hungry outcast prowls along the sidewalk, while the sleigh-bells tinkle in the street. There is a robe of snow on the ground; the old State House roof is white; the very trees, thrusting their bare arms on high, look like stalactites in some colossal cavern. Each rugged limb and tiny branch is white with snow.

To night will be eighteen hundred and forty two years since the shepherds watched near Bethlehem; to morrow is the anniversary of the Birth of Christ the Lord. To-night the city puts on its face of smiles. The poor man's hearth to-night will crackle and glow with mirth and plenty. The rich will feast, the outcast will starve or steal, the sincere Christian, whose thread-bare coat is pledge for his truth, will gather round God's altar, and watch till midnight for the coming of the Lord.

To-night the city which William Penn built in hope and honor,—whose root was planted deep in the soil of truth and peace, but whose fruits have been poison and rottenness, Riot, Arson, Murder and Wrong,—will put on its face of smiles, and drink and feast and dance and pray for six hours at least! So God Bless Christmas Eve!

"For twenty-four long hours, food has not passed these lips! For three days and nights I have been the sport of one delusion after another! My brain burns, my pulses are on fire! There is a mystery about this whole matter, an awful mystery which must be solved ere the sun goes down!"

Folding his arms across his chest, Byrnewood strode toward the parlor window, and looked out upon the wintry sky. His father, pale, wild and haggard, stood leaning against the mantel, while his mother seated on the sofa, gazed steadily forward with a vacant eye. No word passed from her lips, but with a half-audible moaning sound, she sate rocking backwards and forwards, while her hands clasped tightly together, rested on her knee. Her eyeballs were dry and hot; no tears gave tokens of the awful sorrow that was consuming her soul.

The light of the declining sun, reflected from the snow which covered the streets and house-tops, gave a wild glow to Byrnewood's face.

"Ha! Luke Harvey laid the whole atrocious plot bare to my eye! I ransacked Monk-Hall this morning, explored each nook and cranny of that infernal den, but still no tokens of Mary! Luke's suspicions, and my own point to Lorrimer as the villain, but I must be sure, aye sure! Accursed be the drug that destroyed my memory! Yet still every now and then gleams of light break on me—I can remember scenes, which the tongue grows palsied, to tell, which the heart grows cold to imagine!"

His dark eyes assumed an expression of deep and painful thought, while the sunlight fell warmly over his wrinkled visage. Wrinkled? Aye wrinkled and grown old, with the agony of three days and nights.

"Byrnewood," said the old man in a faint voice. "I shall go mad if this suspense continues much longer! Two days of agony, three sleepless nights—I can endure it no longer! God be merciful to me, but it is too much for an old man to bear!"

The sound of merry sleighbells tinkled in the street. Byrnewood's eye flashed, and his lip quivered. A handsome sleigh drawn by two blood horses, dashed by the window, and while the driver cracked his whip merrily, a young man sate lounging against the buffalo robe, while his manly cheeks glowed with excitement, and his rich brown hair, floated waving on the wind.

"I have sought him all day!" exclaimed Byrnewood, "He has avoided me! If he is guiltless he need not fear my presence; if he is guilty then God have mercy on him! I will bring him to your father, yes, yes, he shall kneel at your feet mother, he shall swear that he knows nothing of my sister Mary!"

With these words, he rushed from the room, and from the house. Old Mr. Arlington looked from the window, and saw his son, dashing along the street in pursuit of a slay, while his uncovered hair fell wildly over his shoulders.

"He?" echoed Mrs. Arlington, raising her head and speaking for the first time in an hour. "What does Byrnewood mean, my dear?"

"I know not, I know not!" cried the old man, still looking from the window. "Mary—Mary—" he murmured in a low whisper, as though his tongue loved to linger on the music of that name.

The fire burnt cheerily in the grate; its warm glow reflected to the burnished furniture, gave a look of comfort to the spacious parlor, and the marks of wealth and luxury, were scattered all around, but what were these, in comparison with the agony that was silently gnawing the hearts of the merchant and his wife? What were all the wealth of counting-house, land and rent-roll in comparison with a daughters honor?

As the Merchant Arlington stood gazing out of the window, with a vacant stare, a carriage drawn by two horses, whose harness betrayed the hackney coach, drove up to the door, and the coachman, a gentleman with stout form rendered excessively corpulent, by a small clothing store of over-coats, sprang from the box, and let down the steps. A tall lady in deep black, with a thick veil over her face, stepped from the carriage, and ascended the steps of the Merchant's mansion.

While the old man was yet wondering who the strangers could be, the parlor door was thrown open, and the form of the white haired Negro, "Lewey Gran" appeared in the door-way.

"Massa heah is a lady a-waitin' to see you bery 'tickler. De Lor' Moses! It may be somefin' 'bout de chile Mary—God in hebben bress her—who knows?"

As Lewey spoke, the tall lady entered the room, and confronted Mr. Arlington. From head to foot her form was veiled in deep black. Her cloak, and scarf were all of the same sombre hue. Her face was covered by a thick crape veil, but still the gleam of two dark eyes glanced through the dense folds, and rested on Arlington's face.

"Your name is Arlington," said the strange Lady in a low and whispering voice, "Your daughter Mary—"

Mrs. Arlington rose from her seat at that word; the Merchant listened in quivering suspense.

"Your daughter Mary," resumed the strange Lady with a huskiness of tone that indicated suppressed emotion, "Has been missing for three days—"

Not a word from the old man's lips, but his wife murmured "You bring news of Mary—Heaven bless you!"

"I will bring your child to you again!" said the stranger in a deep-toned voice.

"God bless you!" was all that passed the Mother's lips.

"She is alive?" muttered the Merchant, with a fierceness of tone that had never marked his voice before—"She is well? Unharmed—no mockery Madam, if you please, because, d'ye see our hearts are dying, dying within us! Hah! You start! Tell me is Mary living? Or do you come to raise our hopes, and when we look for our own sweet child again, to lay a corpse at our feet?"

"Have no fears for your daughter's life! I will bring your child to you on one condition—"

"Quick—name it!" gasped Arlington and his wife in the same breath.

"That you ask your daughter no questions concerning her absence from home, until her mind is sufficiently calm to answer?"

"We promise—we agree to this condition!" exclaimed the Father and Mother.

"Your daughter is without, in my carriage—" began the Lady, when her words were suddenly interrupted. Arlington sprang to the parlor door, with a sudden movement he opened it, "My child, my child!" he exclaimed, and then started backward, with an unexpected surprise.

On the very threshold of that door, stood a maiden form, veiled from head to foot in robes of deep black. Had it not been for the waving of her dress, as the wind from the front door swept through the hall, you might have fancied that a carved figure of ebony stood on that threshold.

"My home!" exclaimed a well-known voice, and the maiden advanced a single step. "My home!" There was a quiet pathos in the tone, with which this was said, that would have melted a heart of stone.

"*My home!*" she repeated again, in that same whispered tone.

"My child!" shrieked the Father and Mother, rushing toward her with outspread arms.

The maiden started back, recoiling on the threshold.

"Stand back father, stand back mother!" she shrieked in a tone of heart-broken despair. "Let me pass!" she cried, springing on her feet, and moving hurriedly toward the back parlor. "I am all unworthy of your slightest notice! I am a poor, fallen thing, father—a stained and dishonored girl mother!"

As though a bolt from heaven had splintered on his forehead, Arlington started backward. With a faint cry Mrs. Arlington gazed in the face of her daughter, and echoed her words "Dishonored, *dishonored!*"

"Oh mother," said Mary, raising her hands as if she wished to shrink from her mother's very touch, "Three days ago, I crossed your threshold, like one walking amid the scenes of a pleasant dream. Now the dream is over, and—oh, let me pass mother, let me hide my shame from your eyes of all others! Let me pass, but do not touch the polluted thing who was once your daughter!"

"Every word she utters is a dagger in my heart!" muttered the tall woman in black, as with a hurried movement, she closed the folding doors which divided the large parlor into two apartments. "Go in Mary; I'll be with you presently!"

Slowly Mary advanced to the folding doors; her footsteps were clogged and leaden. She advanced, she was about to enter the back parlor, when she turned and beheld the statue-like forms of her parents. Her father, with his grey hairs falling aside from a brow, on which agony like death was writhing; her mother, with her pale face, stricken with a horror that palsied every feature!

Mary spread her arms toward them with a wild shriek. "Father, mother, bless your child! But no—" and she sank back, recoiling from their outspread arms—"I am forever fallen! Ah—it was a short and blessed dream, followed by a terrible awakening! Here I was to return, at your feet I was to kneel, and *he*—oh Heaven—*he*, was to kneel by my side, and crave your blessing! Now father, now my mother, it is Christmas Eve, I return, but—"

Her head drooped on her bosom; low sobs choked her utterance; she went slowly through the folding doors.

"Ha!" muttered the woman in black, approaching the window, "Byrnewood and Lorrimer! The brother looks wild and pale, the Libertine wears a free and careless look. But hold—I will yet atone for my crime! I will force Lorrimer, to do this girl the small justice, of linking her name with his, in marriage. As you wish to see the mystery unravelled," she exclaimed aloud turning to the merchant and his wife, "do not, I beseech you, inform any one, not even Mary's brother, of her return home, until the lapse of fifteen minutes. Do you promise me this?"

"We do," murmured the parents, in mechanical tones.

"They come, the Seducer and the Avenger!" muttered the woman in black, and then she glided through the folding doors.

The merchant gazed silently in the face of his wife. Not a word was uttered. The agony had come at last, stunning, darkening, and overwhelming.

"Better death than dishonor!" muttered the Merchant, after the lapse of a painful pause. His blue eye was full of wild light.

A loud and cheerful laugh resounded from the hall: "Ha, ha, my dear boy, so ridiculous! It's hardly fair, 'pon honor hardly fair! To hurry a fellow from a nice little party of young bloods, who are about to go a-sleighing, all over town and country—it's *hardly* fair! And all this haste and hurry that I may give the lie, to a ridiculous fancy that has taken possession of your brain—"

The words were interrupted by the opening of the door. Byrnewood Arlington and Gustavus Lorrimer, entered the parlor arm in arm. The wild form and haggard face of Byrnewood, was in strong contrast with the easy, devil-may-care appearance of the Libertine. His gold-headed cane to his mustachoed lips, his brown hair, floating aside from his manly face in easy curls, his dark eyes dancing in careless glee, he came lounging into the parlor, and greeted the Merchant and his wife, with a deep and respectful bow.

"Why Mr. Wilwood—excuse me, is that your name? I never knew, that either you or your sister, were in existence until you accosted me in the State House yard, yesterday morning!"

"There stand my father and my mother!" said Byrnewood with suppressed emotion. "My father has not a hope, that does not hang on his daughter's life, my mother not a thought but for her peace and joy. Will you swear in their presence, that you know nothing of the place, where my sister is concealed?"

"More than that I will swear, that I never spoke to her in my life!" And humming an air from the last opera, Lorrimer lounged toward the window. "Pretty hard one that! But there's but one way to overcome their suspicions! Let me, ha, ha, put brass on my face, and oil on my tongue! I must *face* it out! That drug of Devil-Bug's had rather an effect on our friend's intellect!"

"Father," cried Byrnewood, "this strange mystery grow darker and deeper. The dream, in whose mazes, I have been wandering for days, becomes more dread and horrible, every instant. This gentleman can solve the mystery and awake me from the dream. Listen to the Oath which I now dictate to him. If he utters a false word, may the curse of a father's grey hairs, brought down to an untimely grave, rest upon him and blight him forever!"

"My son," said the old man in a husky voice, "I will listen to the end of this dark mystery."

"And I!" exclaimed the mother. "Heaven grant that the wronger of our child, may meet with the reward of his crime!"

They formed a group in the centre of that parlor. Lorrimer stood in the centre, with his back to the window; on either side, was the father and mother, with light of the declining day falling upon their withered faces.

Byrnewood stood before him, his dark eye, flashing with a fixed and unalterable glance; his cheek was like death; his lips white and ashy by turns.

"Do you swear by your hopes of salvation, that you know nothing of Mary Arlington my sister, and that you never did her wrong?"

"I do!" said the firm and bold voice of Lorrimer.

"Your face is truthful, and your voice is firm! It must have been a dream! Another test, Sir, and I have done. If you have uttered a falsehood, do you invoke upon your head that scorn of man, that doom of Heaven that ever awaits the *Perjurer!*"

He raised his hand on high, and looked fixedly in the face of Lorrimer.

For a moment, a slight fear darkened that handsome countenance, and then the clear words, resounded through the room—

"I do!"

As he spoke, the folding doors swung gently apart, and a maiden form clad in deep black, glided slowly into the room. A sudden glow from the declining sun lit up her face, as she advanced; her cheeks warmed with deep emotion, her blue eyes gazed steadily in Lorrimer's face.

"My sister!" shrieked Byrnewood, starting with surprise mingled with an awful fear. "My own sister Mary!"

It was all he could say. There was a death-like sensation at his heart; a choking feeling in his throat. Calm and immoveable stood Gustavus Lorrimer, the light from the folding doors, pouring warmly over his face. For a moment, a slight quivering movement was perceptible on his mustachoed lip, for a single instant, his brow was darkened by a convulsive frown.

"Now swear you never wronged that girl!" shrieked Byrnewood in a tone like madness.

Mary advanced; her arms were outspread, a glow of delight warmed over her face.

"*Lorraine!*" she cried in a tremulous voice.

"There," exclaimed Lorrimer, with a cool smile. "What more proof do you want? She does not even know my name!"

"*Lorraine!*" shrieked Mary, as with arms outspread, she glided towards her lover. There was a sneering smile on his face; his arms were folded, and he gazed upon the girl, with a half-shut eye.

Mary gave one look and intense look; the truth broke upon her, that she was a disowned and dishonored thing. With a faint moan, as though a falling rock had stricken her down, she fell to the floor, and lay insensible at her Seducer's feet.

"If you have uttered a falsehood or sworn to a lie," shrieked Byrnewood with a fierce and determined look, "Do you hope, that before sunset to-day, you may die a sudden and bloody death?"

"I do!" exclaimed Lorrimer, disengaging his boot, from the arm of the fainting girl, which had fallen over it. "I do!"

"Then a sudden and bloody death you shall die!" arose the shriek of a woman's voice. The folding doors were thrown open again. From the windows of the back parlor, a stream of red sunlight, poured over the scene. A tall woman, in dark robes, stood between Lorrimer and the light, her hand upraised, and her dark eyes, darting a withering look upon his handsome face. "Then a sudden and bloody death you shall die! For your words are false as hell!"

Lorrimer recoiled a single step, and a deep curse breathed from his lips. "Ha!"—Thus ran his thoughts—"Bess here? Death and confusion! But I will brazen it out! Byrnewood's memory is confused; he remembers nothing of the past!"

"Hear me, one and all," exclaimed Bess, as with her eye flashing and her hand upraised, she looked like an inspired Prophetess. "This man lured Mary Arlington from her home. Pure and innocent as she was, he wronged her! Stainless as one of God's own angels, he dishonored her form, and darkened her soul by a hideous crime! I, his instrument, his accomplice accuse him, and fling his money to which the hire of Judas were a hallowed thing, I fling the wages of my crime, at yon Perjurer's feet!"

"God of heaven!" shrieked the old man, tottering as though he had received his death-wound. "What dark confession is this?"

"Our child *dishonored!*" echoed Mrs. Arlington.

"Further concealment is in vain!" cried Lorrimer with a cool supercilious smile. "Your daughter was weak and foolish—I was but a—man!"

Byrnewood advanced, he laid his hand lightly on the Seducer's shoulder. His face was frightfully calm.

"There are but two remedies for this wrong. I give you your choice. Will you—" his voice died in his throat for a moment, and a sound like a death groan shook his chest, "Will you marry my sister?"

The old man's blue eyes shone with a fierce glance. For a moment he smothered the hate which rose to his eyes and lips.

"Marry my daughter," he shrieked, "Save her from public shame! Let an old man's grey hairs plead with you!"

No vision of Christmas Eve, the River and the Death, rose up to affright the haughty pride of the Libertine. To be forced to marry the girl, whom he had seduced—pah! He could hear the laugh of all his hollow-hearted friends, he could see the look and the taunt and the gibe of scorn levelled at his head.

"Why the fact is my friends, I'm not a marrying man," he said with withering politeness, as he moved toward the door. "This affair is quite unpleasant and—your family and mine, are quite different in their style. You are not of our 'set.' "

He said this, and rushed from the room. In a moment, ere the group in the parlor, could recover from their astonishment, the merry jingle of his sleigh-bells, broke upon their ears.

"Now for the other remedy!" shrieked Byrnewood Arlington. "Nay hold me not father—mother release my arm! I will neither eat, nor drink, nor sleep until I have washed out my sister's wrong, in this man's blood!"

CHAPTER SECOND

THE PERSONAGE

The light of the declining sun, reflected from the snow on the house-tops, poured warmly into the chamber of the Millionaire, in the fourth story of the colossal TON HOUSE. Dim, the Creole boy stood before the mirror, with his light form, clad in a neat suit of blue cloth, and a small cap placed jauntily on his head.

"De High-Golly!" he exclaimed, slapping his nether limbs, as he addressed his tutelar Deity. "Dat 'ill do! Dis chile look like a reg'lar buck! Wonder whar de debbil, Massa is? Hab n't seen him, since last night at Camden. Hows'ever dere's no use o' frettin' 'bout *him*—hah-a-whah—de debbil always takes care his own!"

Opening a drawer of the dressing bureau, the Creole drew from thence, a box of Lucifer matches and a cigar.

"De young gemmen will take a smoke," said Dim, with quiet dignity as he lit the cigar, and seating himself on one chair, placed his feet over the back of another. "Dis Habanner am prime! Get out now! Who ses dis chile aint a gemmen born? 'Look leah yo' dam-niggar brack dem boots, right off, and den or-dah coachee to bring out de carr'ge, or I'll smash yo' jaw!' Dats de talk! Now de young gemmen will read this news."

Taking a dingy yellow-grey newspaper, from a chair at his elbow, Dim began to persue its contents.

"Hello! De 'Daily Brack Mail.' 'Wonderful abduction case—Miss Arlington missing!' Wonder whar de debbil de murders is? 'Shockin' Calamity—Death of Albert Livingstone Esq., and his wife—burned alive—mansion house of Hawkewood in Jersey.'—Dats somefin' horrible—De High Golly!"

This last ejaculation, was caused by the sudden opening of the chamber door. A figure, enveloped in a blue cloak, spattered with dust and mud, approached the side of the Creole boy. Dim gave a start, and from the folds of the cloak, appeared a wan and haggard face, with stiff black hair falling, in matted locks, around its care-worn outlines.

"Massa!" cried Dim, springing from his seat.

"H-u-s-h, or I'll brain you!" muttered the hoarse voice of Fitz-Cowles. "Hush—not a word, on the peril of your life. Tell me quick—has *he* come?"

The look and tone were significant.

"Yes Massa. *He* am in his room, down sta'rs!"

Without a word, Fitz-Cowles drew the cloak over his haggard face, and rushed from the chamber.

The light of an astral lamp, standing on a table littered with books and papers, fell round a spacious chamber of the Ton House, furnished in a style of gorgeous splendor. Silken curtains along the northern window shut out the light of the declining sun, a massive mirror glittered above the mantel, pictures in showy frames adorned the walls.

Leaning against the mantel, was a man of wide chest and towering stature, clad from head to foot in deep black. The light from the table, fell over his bronzed face, throwing each determined feature, into bold and powerful relief. His dark eyes, were deep sunken, beneath a thick eyebrow, over which arose the massive outline of a towering forehead. There was a gleam in those dark eyes, like the glance of an enraged vulture, vivid, flashing and merciless. There was a world of thought written on the surface of that ponderous brow, a fearful determination in that firm mouth with its compressed lips, an iron will in the fixed outline of that bronzed cheek and massive chin.

The upper part of this man's face, the forehead relieved by dark hair, sprinkled with grey, the thick brows and the deep sunken eyes, was full of intellect and soul; the lower part, the nose with quivering nostrils, the mouth with the corners inclining slightly upwards, the massive cheek-bone and the heavy chin, was full of the animal and sensual.

Altogether that bronzed face, was a remarkable combination of the soul and the brute, high intellect that embraced the stars, and low cunning that grovelled in the gutter.

The towering height of this Personage, gave his striking face a look of commanding grandeur. As he stood there, leaning against the mantel, he reminded you, of those stained names which blacken the page of history, those corrupt Ministers, who ruled the luxurious kings of France, the stern Visconti, who with steel and poison, held a malignant sway over the destinies of Italy, or those tyrants of the ancient Rome, who endeavored to forget their humble origin, in seas of blood and crime.

"Hah!" ejaculated the Personage, fixing his eyes upon a portrait which hung opposite. " 'Man of thoughtful brow and chivalrous look' as your worshippers style their idols, what avail, has been your mind and chivalry, against my craft? Have you not risen in my path, at every point of my ambition, and have I not dragged you down, from the high pinnacle of your hopes? Ha, ha! Craft I say, *craft* was my silent and certain weapon! The mob, hah! Curses on them, eternal curses!

Why must they worship an idol like that? Have I not stooped to them, flattered them, cajoled them, aye, until my gorge rose with loathing? By the God, that rules the fate of nations, when I look over their crumbling fragment of a republic, I see rising above its ruins, the Giant Image of a Empire and a King!"

His clenched hand was raised in the air, and his vulture eye shot rays of fire. Tell me, was that the man to trust with POWER?

Then looking with a sneer into the face of the Portrait, he sate down beside the table, and the light strongly shone over his massive brow, as he glanced at the papers which littered the cloth. Here were Maps of states and kingdoms, territories and provinces; here too, were piles of letters bearing the signatures of various men, scattered all over the world; dollar worshipping merchants, scheming politicians, mighty statesmen, Lords and Ministers of Kingdoms. Here too was a letter, bearing the sign manual of a Crowned Sovereign.

"There are some men who would give their lives, to know the *secrets* which lie scattered over this table," said the Personage, with a grim smile, as he drank from a foaming pitcher, which stood beside the lamp. It was a stout old fellow, of a pitcher—that, and as it smoked and foamed, it could not have contained cold water.

"Hah! That 'juice of the rye' is somewhat strong!" exclaimed he, smacking his lips. "But I must be careful! Minds that have endured the shocks of fate, without a murmur, have gone out forever, with the indulgence of an appetite! Still that 'rye' is excellent!"

The door opened; there was a footstep; and the haggard form of Fitz-Cowles advanced toward the table.

The Personage looked upon him with a glance of cool astonishment. Twelve hours had worked a fearful change with the handsome millionaire. His cheeks were sunken; his eyes rolled wildly in their sockets; his lips were stained with blood, drawn from the skin by his compressed teeth.

"Well Sir," said the Personage, "what now?"

"Last night I was arrested for *forgery*," exclaimed Fitz-Cowles, "Forgery on the House of Livingstone, Harvey & Co., for the amount of *one hundred thousand dollars*. I escaped from the police officers; for a night and a day I have evaded their search—"

"You are guilty?" said the Personage in a quiet tone.

Fitz-Cowles assented by a nod of his head.

"What have you done with the money?"

"It is safe in New York. I sent it on, yesterday morning, directed to a fictitious name."

"Well sir, what is your business with me?" said the Personage, gazing on Fitz-Cowle's face with half-closed eyes.

"The gaol, the cell, the lash—all threaten me; you must save me!"

"Pray sir," exclaimed the Personage, with a smile of withering politeness. "May I know the nature of your claims, upon my assistance?"

"Certainly, *sir*," exclaimed Fitz-Cowles, returning his withering sneer. "For ten years past, I have received large sums of money from your hands. It was you that rescued me at New Orleans, when I was about to be tried for that little scrape on the Gulf. Thrice you saved me from imminent danger, and until last March, you paid me a regular pension of four thousand dollars a year—"

"Well, sir?" interrupted the Personage in a dry and biting tone.

"On your past *favors*, I found my present *claims!*"

"*Juan Larode*, you grow insolent!" and the Personage rising with a calm sneer on his lip, "There is the door! To the gaol, or to the devil as you like, but you gain no aid from me. Go!"

"Juan Larode!" echoed Fitz-Cowles as his eyes gleamed deadly rage. "Old man dare you insult me, with my mother's name?"

"Yes, yes," he cried, moving to the door, "I will go to gaol, I will be heralded from north to south as a Forger, but it shall be under your name, old man, as your son, as Juan———"

He gave a clear and biting enunciation to the name of the Personage.

"Bastard of a Creole slave," muttered the Personage with his eyes flashing incarnate scorn. "Dare you speak to me thus—"

"Do not put yourself in a passion, *father*," said Fitz-Cowles, resuming his seat with a hollow mocking laugh. "Here is the marriage certificate of my mother, which you gave me four years ago!"

The Personage sate down, and gazed in the face of the Forger. Eye met eye, sneer met sneer, scowl gloomed on scowl. At that moment the resemblance between the two was fearful and striking.

But that deadly fire, gleaming from those vulture eyes, that thick vein shooting up between the thick eye-brows—Fitz-Cowles quailed before that look and frown!

"A paltry *forgery!*" laughed the Personage. "Think you, Juan Larode, that had that certificate been genuine, I would have ever let it pass into your hands? When I employed you as a spy, yes, scowl as you will, as a *spy*, a *pimp* and *spy*, I wished to bind you to me, by the substantial link of legitimate relationship. I gave you that forged certificate in order that you might think yourself my *lawful* son. I knew that would not betray your *father*, ha, ha, ha," and he laughed loud and long, "Your *father!*"

Fitz-Cowle's grew white in the face. The hollow laugh of the man with the massive forehead, and vulture eye, smote his ears like a death-knell.

"Bastard!" he muttered the foul word, and buried his face in his hands.

The Personage sate looking upon him with a look of scorn.

"In the gaol, he will trouble me no more!" he muttered. "In gaol *for life!*"

Fitz-Cowles raised his brow from his hands. There was an expression of utter desolation in every line of his face.

"Sir, I will go, and to my doom," he said, in a subdued tone. "But ere I go, you will allow me to ask you one trifling question. Do you remember that package, enveloped in yellow paper, and sealed with three black seals?"

The tone of Fitz-Cowles was mild and subdued, but there was a devil's light in his eye. The face of the Personage changed color; brow and cheek became lividly pale.

"What know you of that package?" he said in a careless tone. "You never saw it but once, and then, only the seals and the envelope?"

"Good evening, *father*," said Fitz-Cowles, rising with a pleasant smile. "I'll never trouble you more!"

The Personage rose suddenly, he dragged a massive trunk from under the table, unlocked it, and opening a secret lid, drew from thence a massive package, enveloped in yellow paper and sealed with three black seals.

"Hah! It is safe!" he muttered, while Fitz-Cowles stood smiling beside the door.

"*Safe*, ha, ha, ha!" laughed the forger. That sneering laugh was full of meaning.

With a sudden movement, the Personage broke open the package, seal after seal cracked between his fingers; he unrolled the envelope and discovered, *a mass of blank paper, folded in the shape of letters!*

"Ha, ha, ha! I thought the day might come when that package would prove serviceable—'false keys' and 'false seals'—ha, ha, ha!"

The Personage bent his head slowly down to the table; his eyes sunken yet deeper in their sockets glared with fearful intensity.

"Each of those letters is worth a thousand lives! My name, my honor, will be eternally blasted by the revelation of a single letter! And then my friends, my associates—all—" he clenched his hands fixedly together, and was silent for a moment. "Come here, Juan Larode," he said in a calm and even voice.

With a fearless step Fitz-Cowles approached the table. Inclining his head slightly to one shoulder, the Personage gazed upon him with a sidelong glance. His fingers quivered tremulously, and his face wore a smile, that but faintly disguised the emotion, which branched from his heart through every vein.

"You have those papers?" he said in a quiet tone.

"I have!" answered Fitz-Cowles. "You know *father* it wouldn't be at all handsome, for you to see those documents published in the papers some bright morning as 'wonderful disclosures'—ha, ha, ha!"

That laugh died away into a groan! With one vigorous movement of his stalwart arm, the Personage gathered Fitz-Cowles within his grasp, and without rising from his seat, he dragged the Forger to his knees.

"Now," he shouted as his muscular fingers encircled the throat of the bravo, "Now, craven you must yield those papers or die!" With a look of cool determination, he tightened his grasp, until Fitz-Cowles grew purple in the face. Slowly his eyes began to start from their sockets. The Illegitimate lay helpless in the grasp of his father; struggling, quivering, gasping for breath.

"The papers—" moaned Fitz-Cowles—"I gave them to a friend—to keep for me. In case I am *imprisoned* or—or—*murdered*, this friend will despatch those letters to a *friend* of yours, ha, ha, ha! Already they are enveloped and directed to *his* address—"

With a choaking laugh he pointed to the Portrait, which hung on the wall opposite the mantel.

As though a palsy had stricken, his arm, the Personage let go his grasp.

"Get up Juan Larode," he said in a calm voice. "You shall not go to gaol. Something must be done for you!"

In less than a month Fitz-Cowles walked the streets a free man. The mysteries of the forgery, the hooks and crooks, by which that pliable old gentleman THE LAW was evaded and conciliated, are they not written in the Chronicles of the Criminal Courts?

Who was the individual, so mysteriously denominated the Personage? The documents from which this history are drawn, are dark on that point, but the reader may rest assured that *the Personage*, was either a Canadian Statesman, or a British Lord, or a *Mexican Prince!*

CHAPTER THIRD

MONK-HALL ONCE MORE

"What the devil yo' skeered about niggers?" growled Devil-Bug turning hastily to his attendants. "Aint I in my own home agin, aint I in Monk-Hall?"

"But Massa, de poleese is at de door"—muttered Musquito.

"And Massa de neighborhood is riz on us"—exclaimed Glow-worm.

The sound of a loud shout mingled with yells and groans, came thundering through the front door. Then came a sound of violent knocking, followed by a heavy crashing noise, as though stout arms were breaking the panels of the door, with billets of massive timber.

"Come niggers," said Devil-Bug, "foller me!"

Taking each of them a lamp in his hand, from the table in the centre of the Door-keeper's room, they followed Devil-Bug who silently led the way down stairs; he paused for a moment to look into the Banquet-Room. The glare of the lamps flashed upon the form of the Skeleton Monk, standing at the head of the table, scattered over with goblets and wine-glasses, the relics of the last feast of the Monks of Monk-Hall.

An expression of strange meaning came over Devil-Bug's face, as he looked around the ancient room, but not a word passed his lips. His solitary eye was unusually bright, and his wide lips placed fixedly together. Slowly and silently, he led the way down into the Dead-Vault of Monk-Hall.

"These old pillars is all the friends I ever had!" muttered Devil-Bug looking into the faces of the negroes, with a strange stare. "These old walls, and these pillars, and these ceilin's and these floors, has always been friends to me!"

The negro Glow-worm looked into Musquito's face with a vacant stare. There was something in the manner of their master, that excited their wonder.

"Look here Niggers," exclaimed Devil-Bug, "There's no use o' leavin' the corpse o' that Jew, above ground, and so I b'lieve we'll go and bury him,—hello!" he exclaimed, as his eye rested upon a massive piece of rock placed against one of the brick pillars. "I wonders *how that* 'ud vork?"

"What de debbil massa mean," asked Glow-worm.

"You see that rock's about three feet square," answered Devil-Bug. "It must a-been a piece o' th' foundation o' Monk-Hall! D'ye see yo' d———n niggars wot I mean? 'Spose you shove that rock to that trap door, and tumble it down into the pit o' Monk-Hall—don't yo' think that Jew's corpse 'ud be considerably smashed? Won't it be a sight easier than buryin' him?"

The negroes grinned hideously at each other, and a loud African guffaw resounded through the dead vault.

"Hah—a-whah! Wot a dam idea-r!"

The sound of yells and shouts, mingled with the crashing of the front door panels, came thundering down the staircase, and echoed through the vault.

"Look here niggers, that feller's body must be hid afore the poleese comes. I'll go down into the Pit and fix it right under the trap, and when I give the word, do you, let the rock fall! D'ye hear niggers?"

"Yes massa!" chorussed the Insects in a breath. Devil-Bug seized one of the lamps, and strode rapidly from the dead-vault, while the negroes bent their huge forms to the difficult task.

The light flashed over the arch of the deep stairawy, as Devil-Bug, went rapidly down into its depths.

"Queer," he muttered, "Cursed queer! I don't see *nay*ther of 'em—the man with the broken jaw, the woman with the holler skull! Ha! Here's the old Pit ag'in, with it's grave yard smell, its big pillars o' brick an' its beams of oak! Here I used to tumble about when I was a little bit of an ugly devil, here I've seen many sights that 'ud freeze most people's blood, and here—ho—hoo!"

Over crumbling piles of boards, over heaps of broken furniture, Devil-Bug went tramping through the gloomy cavern, while the rats started from their nooks, and the reptiles, twining round the stout oaken beams, glistened brightly in the lamp-beams, rendered dim and flickering by the foul air of the place.

"I must be near the centre o' th' Pit"—exclaimed Devil-Bug, when a start quivered through his frame, and a laugh, half surprise, half fear shrieked from his lips, as a whizzing sound, echoed through the air, and a herd of rats, disturbed from their loathsome meal, darted away from the light.

In the full glare of the lamp, lay the mangled remains of a human body, clothing, flesh and features, crushed into one undistinguishable mass of corruption and blood.

"Ha! Gabr'el Von Gelt you lay quiet enough, quiet as a—*lamb!*" chuckled Devil-Bug, gazing toward the roof of the vault, far above. "Ho, hoo! The crittur fell right below the trap-door, down plumb as a stone!"

As he spoke, there flashed the glare of a light, from the roof of the vault; it quivered through the air, and resting on Devil-Bug's matted hair, formed a long and bright column in the midst of darkness.

Devil-Bug spurned the body of the Jew aside, and placed the lamp on a stone, not more than two feet from the spot where he stood. The air of the vault was foul and stifling, and the lamp flickered with a faint and tremulous light. Then folding his arms, with that column of light, from the distant roof, pouring on his head, Devil-Bug stood silent and erect. His tangled hair fell waving round his face, while his compressed lips and glaring eye, indicated a deep and settled resolve. The rumbling of the rock, along the floor above, came heavily to his ear.

"Ha! The g-a-l shall roll in wealth, dress in silks an' satin's, and be a lady all her life, old Devil-Bug's daughter, with the mark o' the red snake on her right temple! It's all settled—Parson Pyne thinks she's the *first* child o' Nell, tho' he told me she was the *second*. He said so afore Luke to day—ho, hoo! Old Devil-Bug's daughter among the grandees o' th' Quaker City!"

Again that rumbling sound, from the roof far overhead, broke on his ear. The rock drew nearer to the chasm, and Devil-Bug chuckled grimly to himself.

"Hello! Niggers are yo' ready?" he shouted, at the top of his voice.

"Yes, Massa," the answer came faintly to his ear.

"Let it drop!" shrieked Devil-Bug. There was a pause.

The light shone over his face; it was agitated by a frightful smile.

"Good bye Nell," he said, and smiled.

Then a sound like a mighty building, falling to the ground, shook the cavern; it was but for an instant! There was a heavy crash, and all was darkness, save that dim column of light, streaming from the distant trap-door. A single beam struggled down through the darkness, and rested upon the rough surface of the massive rock, as it lay, sunken deep in the cavern earth.

"Hello, Massa!" came the voice of Musquito from the trap-door, "Did dat ar' smash de Jew?"

Not a word, not even a word in reply. Ha, ha, Devil-Bug was lying dormant behind some massive pillar, without a doubt, chuckling as he thought of the Jew's corpse, buried beneath the rock! He was such a jolly old boy, was Devil-Bug!

All at once, like the yell of 'fire' in the dead of night, on board a ship at sea, a wild and thundering noise, echoed from the stairway, leading down into the Pit. In a moment the cellar was filled by people, brandishing torches and clubs in their upraised hands.

"Hurray, hurray! We've trapped the murderer!" they shouted, rushing in various directions, through the wide cavern.

"Here he is, hidin' behind the stone!" cried a well-known voice, and Easy Larkspur, holding a light in one hand and a pistol in the other, advanced toward a massive rock, which uprose from the cavern earth.

"Here he is hidin' behind this rock," he cried as his face warmed with excitement, resembled the full moon in a crimson mist. "Come out o' that Mister or I'll shoot—come out I say!"

There was no answer! Devil-Bug was lying, quiet and snug, behind the rock, waiting to spring on his antagonists.

"Fellers stand by me," said Larkspur, looking round into the faces of so medozen 'Deppities o' th' Honorable Ma'or'—"I'll jist lean over the rock, and take a peep at the varmint—"

Laying his ponderous weight on the rock, the light extended in one hand, the pistol in the other, Larkspur leaned gently over the opposite side and looked down. For a single moment, he remained in this attitude, and then rose on his feet again, and looked into the visages of the officers. His face so lately burning red, was now the color of yellow clay. The cold sweat trickled down his features; his bulging eyes were full of fright and horror.

"By G———d!" he cried in a tone that filled his comrades with horror, it was so different from his usual voice, "I don't want to see a sight like that *twice* in a life-time! A body smashed beneath a big rock, an' a head stickin' out, with a face all purple, and the eye laid on the cheek, and tongue lollin' from the mouth! Ugh! Gen'elmen," he continued in a husky whisper—"Our pris'ner's escaped, an' that's a fact!"

CHAPTER FOURTH

THE MEETING OF THE BROTHER AND THE LIBERTINE

Around the blazing stove in the Oyster Cellar, were gathered a band of some twenty loungers, smoking and swearing in a breath, while Smoky Chiffin, the lord of the cavern, stood behind the bar, dealing out hot whiskey punch and other fragrant liquids, to a numerous band of customers.

"It's sleighin' time gents," cried Smoky, bustling to and fro, "Hot Whiskey Punch don't go bad. What say? Brandy? Brandy for this gemmen, John. What have for supper Sir? Venison, steak? Woodcock? Sherry wine, Sir? Bottle o' Porter, John! Fine time gents—glorious sleighin'! Never knew better!"

The cavern was all clatter, jingle, heat and smoke. Smoky Chiffin was in glorious spirits! Whether he looked at the conventual stalls, in the background, crowded with hungry citizens, or the oyster box, lined with shell-fish devotees, or the liquor bar thronged with thirsty worshippers of that jolly old Giant of a Decanter, the prospect was alike refreshing to his pocket and spirits.

Two little men, were walking up and down, the marble floor of the cellar, performing an easy promenade from the looking glass to the hot stove.

"You see Buzby, there's a deuce of a fuss made about it," said one of the little men, arranging a jaunty glazed cap, on his head. "I might give you something for your paper, I *might* I say"—And he applied a small wiry cane, that looked like a piece of grape-vine in a consumption, to his thin lips, and looked at Poodle with those Dresden wax doll eyes.

"It would make a capital article, Silly, 'Full particulars of the abduction case, by one of the friends of both families'—*allez avec un furie*', as we say in Domestic French! It would go with a rush! Come, Silly, give me all the 'rich licks' for the next Black Mail?"

"I might," responded Silly, "But d'ye see Poodle, you *rather* cut up my 'Hem.' in the Mail this morning. Just think of it—two plates, one the death of Cock Robin, 'tother a nigger church on fire, and all for the shockingly cheap rate of two dollars a-year, office, 209, Drayman's alley, upstairs—oh Poodle *that* was hardly fair!"

"Cut up your Hem?" echoed Poodle, admiring the shape of his *unique* leg, "Why just give me, the particulars of this abduction case, an' I'll give you a puff of a column-and-half! I'll swear that you're the tallest author we have, that your contributors are all too smart for their trowsers, that—"

"Will you do it up brown?" remarked Petriken quoting from the classics.

"Will I?" cried Poodle, arranging his wig. "Won't I? I'll refute all those cursed lies, which your enemies, have put in circulation, about you—"

"*Genius* has its enemies," meekly remarked Petriken, tapping his boot with his ghost of a cane. "I can't expect to be exempted from the lot of Byron, Shelly and Shufflebottom. You know Shufflebottom, don't you? He's one of my first contributors."

"I'll refute their cursed lies! They say you're fed and clothed by sich-and-sich a publisher, who pays you for doing his dirty work; that you never write, except with a copy of Byron, Bulwer, James, and a scissors a-fore you, that you creep into the good graces of all the literary men of any repute in the country, in order to befoul them with your lies and slander—they say all this, but I'll refute it, that I will, Silly!"

"Then they said, that one of my best female contributors, went to bed every night with a junk bottle of whiskey under her pillow—will you refute that?"

Ere Poodle could reply, the stout form of Easy Larkspur, arrayed in a grey overcoat, stepped between him and the little Magazine man.

He fixed his eye on the Editor of the Black Mail, with a look of supreme scorn.

"Is you the squirt wot edits the Black Mail?" he asked in a tone of quiet wonder. "Is you that little crooked-leg, snub-nosed squirt, wot they calls Poodle?"

These words were far from being complimentary. Poodle grew red in the face, and then pale as his shirt bosom. There was a dangerous look in Larkspur's bulging eyes. Poodle squinted over his shoulder, to the cellar stairs and to the door.

"Is you the werry contemptible squirt as made fun of my personal ape'rence, in your paper t'other day?" growled Larkspur, shaking his fist under Buzby's nose.

"Oh—it was n't me—it was somebody else"—stammered the little Editor.

"It wos, wos it? You small pattern of a man, you remnant of creation, you"—Larkspur grew red in the face with rage—"You *Poo*-dle!"

"Sir—indeed, you're mistaken in the person"—faltered Buzby.

"There's no use o' lyin'! You've got to be licked, an' I've got to do it!"

With these words, he coolly tweaked the unresisting Poodle by the nose, and boxed his ears with the palm of his hand. The little Editor, started toward the door, but Larkspur caught him by the wig, and as Poodle wriggled from his grasp, he held the trophy in his hand.

"Why consarn my buttons, the feller wears a wig!" cried Larkspur in deep astonishment, as he flung the mass of curly hair on the floor, where it lay, with the inside exposed to the light, like a spittoon or a dish.

A roar of laughter shook the cellar. Smokey Chiffin underwent a violent convulsion, and the gentlemen around the blazing stove indulged in a loud guffaw. Poodle stood in the centre of the floor, his *naked* head, but scantily clothed with sparsely settled hair, stiff and uncouth as a shoe brush, while Larkspur stood opposite, expectorating tobacco juice into the crown of the curly wig.

"There my feller, make fun o' my personal a'pe'rence agin," sneered Larkspur, adding a handfull of pea-nut shells to the tobacco juice. "Feller take up yer head o' hair an' travel!"

His eye was fixed upon the Editor's face. Poodle stooped to the floor, seized the wig, placed his hat under his arm, and made for the door.

"By Jove," he snivelled, as he crushed the wig, tobacco juice, pea-nut shells and all, down upon his cranium, "That is'n't the fair thing, if it is damme!"

"Come my feller give us the Domestic French for *that!*" exclaimed Easy Larkspur, "Put it down in the Black Mail, under the head of 'Atrocious outrage on the Liberty of the Press! An Editors wig pulled off, and filled with tobacco juice an' ground-nut shells!' "

These last words escaped Poodle's ear. With Editorial celerity he had vanished from the cellar.

Petriken stood gazing round the place, in vague wonder, listening with evident chagrin, to the hoarse laughter of the by-standers, as they made merriment out of Poodle's disgraceful Hegira.

There was the sound of a hurried footstep, Petriken felt a hand laid on his shoulder, and Gus Lorrimer stood by his side.

"The devil's to pay, my boy," he exclaimed in a quick and hurried whisper, "the very devil's to pay, about this girl. The family will raise the whole town on me. The Father and mother, and I dont know how many couzins, suspect me, and will doubtless take steps to give me, considerable annoyance. Silly we must leave town until the storm blows over—"

"Leave town?" echoed Silly, who had grown suddenly pale in the face. "I say Gus you must n't drop a word about my playing parson. Where will we go? Raising the devil are they? What a pity you did'n't let the girl alone?"

"Let the girl alone?" cried Lorrimer, while his eyes shone and his cheek glowed. "Phsaw! The girl was pretty, loveable! Her eye was a melting blue, her lip a delicious ruby—I like pretty and loveable girls, with blue eyes and ruby lips. Mary Arlington pleased my fancy; I wooed and won her. Now for the consequences! We must leave town till the storm is over. Come Silly—"

He turned toward the door, with a laugh on his lips, but that laugh, in an instant was changed into a muttered curse.

The Brother of Mary Arlington, stood between the Libertine and the door, his uncovered forehead pale as ashes, corrugated in a fixed frown, while his dark eyes, sunken deep beneath the brows, emitted a wild and deadly light. While his cloak fell back from his shoulder, he raised his white hand slowly in the air.

"Here in this cellar, three nights ago, you boasted of the Seduction of my sister," he said in a calm and deliberate voice, "You filled my ears with your atrocious plot; I sat listening to the story of my sister's shame while the wine cup was in my hand, the light laugh on my lip! Here in this vile retreat of the vilest dissipation, you must give me satisfaction for the wrong you have put upon me, and mine! Here my sister's honor shall be avenged, and in your blood will I wash out her shame!"

His tones were fearfully calm. While the loungers started up in wonder and Petriken slunk into a dark corner, Lorrimer stood in the centre of the cellar, gazing over Byrnewood's shoulder, upon the large mirror, which adorned one end of the Saloon.

"You must fight me," said Byrnewood, as he presented two pistols to the silent Libertine. "Take your choice of weapons!"

"Fight you," echoed Lorrimer, in an absent tone, as he stood gazing over the Brother's shoulder into the mirror. "Ha, ha, ha," he laughed turning suddenly to the Keeper of the Saloon, who was leaning over the bar, "I say Chiffin, why d'ye have such pictures in your cellar? D———n it man, do you mean to frighten *me*, by such cursed nonsense? Look there I say, look there! Who painted that broad river, with its waves turned to blood, by the last rays of the setting sun? And my head sinking between the waters, with that hand clenching my throat and that foot trampling me down to a shameful death—who has dared to paint that mockery there?"

With his outstretched hand, he pointed to the mirror, he turned his livid face from side to side, while his lip writhed and his hazel eye rolled with a maniac wildness. The hallucination was upon him in all its horror. Christmas Eve, the River and the Death, rushed on his soul in hues of doom and blood.

"You must answer for your crime on this spot," shouted Byrnewood, advancing to the Libertine. "Hah! *Coward* are you silent? Do you think to scare me from my purpose, with this silly mummery? Will no words, no scorn, rouse you to something like manhood? Then take the insult of a blow!"

With his clenched hand he struck Lorrimer on the chest, and then seized him by the throat.

The Libertine gazed at him with a vacant stare, as he cooly unwound the grasp of those writhing fingers.

"Fool," he cried, pointing to the mirror. "Look, my face in yon picture changes to yours! It is my hand that clenches your throat, it is my foot, that tramples you beneath the waters! Fight you," he continued suddenly, as the livid hues of his countenance, were succeeded by a healthy glow, "Pshaw man! Have I not wronged the Sister, why should I murder the Brother?"

With a half-mocking smile he pushed Byrnewood from his path, and rushed up the cellar steps. The Brother stood like a man in a dream, gazing around the crowd of wondering faces that looked upon him on every side, while the clear ringing sound of sleigh-bells in motion, came echoing down the cellar stairs. That sound roused him from his sudden stupor. He buried the pistols in his bosom, he rushed from the cellar.

He was in the street, but he knew it not. The cold wind broke over his uncovered brow, the beams of the setting sun glistened among the ringlets of his waving hair; he did not behold the sun, he did not feel the bitter wind. All was darkness and heat, within and without! Darkness, while Chesnut street was alive with the prancing of gallant steeds, the gliding of sleighs, the merry jingle of bells! Heat, while the winter sun shone over the State House roof, and the wide streets all white with snow, heat, that burned his brain and turned his eyes to flame!

All was darkness, yet his eye beheld that distant sleigh, drawn by two gallant steeds. Byrnewood had a vague consciousness of eyes fixed upon him, of houses rushing by him, yet still his eye was fixed upon that sleigh, upon that form, partly seen above its pannels, upon the ruddy face, turned over the shoulder, with locks of rich brown hair, tossed wildly on the wind.

This face, this form he saw, but nothing more. The face every moment, grew more distant, yet every moment, to him, the frenzied Brother, each line and feature was more plain and distinguishable.

He rushed down Chesnut street, with his arms outspread, his hair flying on the wind, his dark eyes flashing on the distance. The crowd gave way before his footsteps. Plumed belle, and soft-visaged exquisite, sober merchant, and prattling child walking by its mother's side on that pavement of beauty and fashion, started aside at his approach.

"It was a madman!" the shout rung from lip to lip.

He passed the marble columns of the massive Bank, where the hopes of thousands lie entombed, he passed a long array of glittering stores, and then his path was thronged by a crowd of ragged boys, who made the air ring with shouts and cries.

They held papers under their arms and in their hands, shouting their contents in loud and boisterous tones. For a single moment, Byrnewood listened.

"The seduction of Mary Arlington with a portr-a-i-t! Daily Black Mail—only one cent!"

The shame of his sister, paraded in the columns of a leprous sheet, the mouth-piece of the Ruffian and the Courtezan, a thing so vile, that to mention its name in a decent presence is an insult and a disgrace! The thought was fire to Byrnewood's veins.

He dashed onward, he turned the corner of Third street, his eye still fixed upon the sleigh, in a moment he stood in front of the Girard Bank, when his career was suddenly terminated. He felt his hand pressed in a manly grasp, and a friendly voice rung in his ears.

"My God, Byrnewood, what does this mean?" cried the hearty tones of Luke Harvey, "why are you rushing like a madman along the street?"

"The Seducer of my sister, *he* must die," gasped Byrnewood.

"Ha!" muttered Luke, "His sister's wrong has disturbed his reason, I must lure him from the city, or he will commit some desperate deed. "Come Byrnewood," he added aloud, "You shall have revenge! A word in your ear. Lorrimer takes the cars for Baltimore this afternoon. We will follow him."

"We will!" shrieked Byrnewood, "To the Death!"

CHAPTER FIFTH

SUNSET ON CHRISTMAS EVE

The warm glow of the setting sun, gleaming through an opening in the clouds, streamed down the hill of Walnut Street, over the wharf, and along the broad bosom of the Delaware.

Some few idlers were lounging round the doors of the hotel; here and there stood a vagrant, along the edges of the wharf, gazing indolently at the form of the retreating ferry boat, which some hundred yards from shore, was ploughing its way, through the waters of the Delaware, toward the dim shores of Jersey.

Suddenly the sun disappeared behind a cloud, and two figures came hastening down Walnut Street, rushing hurriedly through the snow, toward the wharf. In a few moments they attained the edge of the wharf, they stood upon the ferry landing, and gazed upon the retreating steamboat, while an expression of deep chagrin spread over their faces.

"Curse the thing," cried the tallest of the twain, whose manly form, was enveloped in a tight-fitting white over-coat, "We are too late for the boat!"

With an oath on his lips, he then gazed nervously along Walnut Street, and paced the wharf, with a wild and hurried footstep.

His companion, a little man, wrapped up in a large cloak, with a well-polished glazed cap on his head, also cast an eager look along Walnut Street, and then gazed at the retreating ferry boat, with a deep muttered curse.

"Gus, we're too late for the boat," he exclaimed in a hurried whisper. "Had'n't we better go up home again? I dont exactly like the idea of standing here in this public place—"

"I will leave this town to-night!" exclaimed Lorrimer, "Aye, leave the Quaker City, if I have to swim to yonder shore! Tell me, good fellow, is there no way of crossing to Camden?"

He spoke to a weather-beaten man, whose broad shoulders, and brawny chest were enveloped in a stout pea-jacket, while an old tarpaulin hat, shadowed over his sunburnt brow.

"That's the last ferry boat Mister," said the fisherman, "But I've got a boat layin' alongside the wharf, there, that would take you over in a jiffey."

"Quick—there's a dollar for you," cried Lorrimer in hurried tones, "Row us over in time for the New-York cars, and I'll make it five!"

Ere a moment passed, Petriken and the fisherman, were seated in the boat, while Lorrimer lingered on the edge of the wharf.

For a single instant he stood with his handsome form raised to its full height, while the wind played with the curls of his dark brown hair. His hazel eye, gleamed with light, while his mustachioed lip, was compressed with some deep emotion.

"Christmas Eve!" he muttered, "Farewell to the Quaker City, and farewell for many a day!"

He leaped into the boat, and seated himself, by Petriken's side, in the seat nearest the bow.

"Trim boat," cried the Fisherman, as he sat in the central seat, with an oar grasped in each sturdy hand, "Trim boat, an' I'll make the crittur fly!"

He was about, to urge the boat into the stream, when his attention was arrested by a voice from the wharf. Two persons stood soliciting a passage to the opposite shore. One was a tall Quaker, whose broad-brimmed hat shadowed a fine venerable face, while his ruddy cheeks, contrasted with his snow white hair, presented the tokens of a green old age. He was dressed in dark brown attire, shapen after the peculiar fashion of his sect, a capacious great coat, reaching to his heels, thrown open in front revealing the under coat, and voluminous waist-coat, all of the same respectable hue.

"Friend," he said in a calm even voice, "I will be much obliged to thee, for a place in thy boat, in case thou art bound for Camden?"

"And I," said a harsh and shrill voice at his side, "Will give you five dollars, if you will row me over in time for the New-York Cars—"

The person who last spoke, was clad in an over-coat of coarse grey, buttoned up to his throat, with a fur cap drawn down over his head, and a large black kerchief, tied round his cheeks and mouth. From between the upraised collar of his coat, and his dark fur cap, a few locks of snow-white hair, fell waving on the wind.

"Come on gentlemen," said the old fisherman in his bluff, hearty tones, "Jump in the boat, an' I'll spin you over like a top! Take that seat in the st*a*rn! Now then, trim boat, and away we go!"

The boat darted from the wharf, with the old fisherman seated in the centre, while Lorrimer and Petriken, occupied the front seat, and the Quaker sate beside the old man, in the stern.

For a few moments, all was silent, save the sullen dipping of the oars. One thick mass of clouds, lay over the city, and along the western horizon, a dense gloom covered the face of the waters, not a ray shone over the surface of a rippling billow, not a single golden beam, lighted on the crest of a rolling wave. Lorrimer turned his face over his shoulder, and glanced vacantly at the other occupants of the boat; there was a calm smile on the face of the quaker, but the man in the gray surtout, sate with his head drooped on his folded arms, while his long white hair lay floating on his shoulders. One eager glance at the sky, and Lorrimer gazed in the pallid face of Petriken, who sate like a statue by his side. He was about to speak to his minion, but the strange gloom, which fell from the clouds upon the waters, cast its shadow on his soul.

"It is a cold wind, my friend," said the Quaker, to the old man in the grey surtout, "A bitter cold wind. And look yonder, surely those are snow flakes, tossing in the air?"

"Yes, it is cold," was the reply of the old man by his side, as he sate with his head drooped upon his folded arms.

There was something so harsh and repulsive in the manner of this man, that the old Quaker, apparently baulked in his effort to start a conversation with him, addressed his next remark to the boatman.

"Can thee tell me friend, whether this darkness, is caused by the clouds, or is it sunset, indeed?"

"Sunset?" echoed Lorrimer, turning in his seat, and gazing over the boatman's shoulder into the Quaker's face. "Who talks of sunset? Ah—excuse, me sir," he continued, as if startled by his own abruptness, "I thought the remark was addressed to me. But tell, me my good fellow, has the sun gone down, or is this sudden darkness, but the shadow of yonder wall of clouds?"

"It wants five—p'rhaps ten minutes of sunset, young gentleman," was the answer of the boatman.

Lorrimer turned his face to the Jersey shore, with an expression, strange and doubtful in its character. True, his dark hazel eyes, gleamed with a steady glance, true, his manly cheek glowed with a ruddy hue, but there was a gloom on his brow, as vague and undefinable as the shadow resting on the bosom of the Delaware.

"Pshaw!" he muttered, "The boat creeps along with a snail's pace. Would I could feel my feet upon the solid ground again—would—Why Silly you sit there like a stone. Why don't you say something man?"

"The fact is Gus, my spirits, are rather low," returned the little man, with chattering teeth. "It's cursed cold on the river, too; that wind cuts a fellow like knives!"

There was silence in the boat again. She darted over the waves with a light careering motion, while the dipping of the oars into the sullen waters, struck the ear, with a wild and mournful sound. The dark atmosphere was whitened with falling snow flakes, which came down with a fluttering motion, and sunk into the waves, like birds, dissolving all at once into thin air.

In silence the boat approached the island which arises in the lordly Delaware. She entered the canal, which divides this bank of land in twain; the sound of the dipping oars broke on the air, mingled with the hoarse murmurs of the waves, as they dashed against the oaken planks which line the shores of the channel. Still all was gloom upon the waters, still the flakes of snow came gently down, still all was silence within the boat.

This channel was soon cleared; the city lay on the west like a black wall of houses, roofs, and mast-heads; the boat darted toward the Camden shore.

Lorrimer's head was bent on his breast. Thoughts of his home came gathering around his heart like dear hopes and sad farewells. He beheld the parlor, lighted by the Christmas Eve fire, he saw the form of his mother, the angel-face of his sister. And then the thought of Mary, the betrayed, the dishonored, came over him, grim and ghastly as a pall flung over a bed of roses.

"Would to God, we could reach the Jersey shore!" he muttered.

"My foot once on that soil, all these gloomy thoughts will banish —"

The clouds broke in the west, in glorious piles and towers and pinnacles they broke, and the red sun poured a flood of glory over the waters, as their rolling subsided to a soft and undulating motion. Every tiny wave was gold, every ripplet quivered in floods of voluptuous light.

Lorrimer glanced over his shoulder. The aged Quaker, was gazing round in calm delight, while the old man in the grey coat, still sate with his head drooped on his folded arms. With a murmur of admiration, he gazed upon the distant city, as its steeples rose in living light. The river was a sheet of floating gold; the western horizon was filled with a gorgeous world of clouds, rising pile on pile, with the light of the setting sun streaming over the spires and roof of the city, while the white snow-flakes floated in the air, like birds, whose hues were beautiful as the rays of a star.

Never had the sky looked so gorgeous, the river so lovely, the city so much like home.

With a murmur of delight, Lorrimer rose on his feet, gazing toward the west with dilating eyes.

The full glory of the sun poured over his manly form as it rose in all its towering height; it shone gladly over his face, with its handsome features, the curving lip darkened by a mustache, the glowing cheeks, the open brow, with the brown locks tossing in the air. His eyes were full of life, his brow grew radiant with the deep joy of existence, quivering through every vein. He stood the incarnation of manly glory and pride.

"Ha, ha," he muttered in a half audible tone, " 'On Christmas Eve at the hour of sun-down, one of ye, will die by the other's hand!' Ha, ha! The shadow is gone from my soul. It is Christmas Eve, and the prophecy is false!"

He gazed toward the massive edifice of the Navy Yard, and then as he stood with out-spread arms, his eye was attracted by some object, floating in the water near the boat. It was a fur cap half concealed by a mass of waving grey hair: while a syllable of wonder trembled on his lip, he turned his gaze to the boat, and the life-blood at his heart grew cold.

There, there, right before his face, at the back of the old boatman, stood a quivering form, there his eye met the gaze of a dark eye, flashing incarnate hate, there his sight was blasted by the vision of a livid face, with long dark hair, streaming wildly aside from a brow like death. The stranger, whose hair was white, had vanished. In his place towered the form of the Avenger, Byrnewood Arlington!

Lorrimer gave but a single look, and then, frozen with a strange horror, he beheld the arm extended, he saw that pale hand, he saw the pistol pointed at his heart.

"Back!" he shrieked, "You dare not murder me. The Prophecy is false—hah!"

"In the name of Mary Arlington—die!" was the awful and deliberate sentence of the Avenger.

There was the sudden report of a pistol, there was a cloud of curling blue smoke. In a moment it cleared away. His clenched hand raised stiffly in the air, his chest heaving with an awful agony, his parted lips disclosing his gnashing teeth, his hazel eyes bulging from their sockets, Lorrimer stood for a single instant, and then with a faintly-muttered name, he fell.

"Mary!" the word gurgled upward with his death groan, as he lay with his back against the hard plank of the seat, while his head sunk to the bottom of the boat. A thick stream of blood rushed from his chest, and stained the hands of the boatman; Petriken's livid face was red with the life-current of the Libertine.

With one simultaneous cry of horror, the Quaker, the boatman, and the minion, started to their feet. The boat quivered like a child's toy, on the agitated waves.

That cry of horror shook the air again!

Byrnewood Arlington knelt on the bottom of the tossing boat, the dead man's head upon his knees.

His face was the face of a maniac. Every feature quivered, every lineament trembled with a joy, more horrible than death. His black eyes, stood out from their sockets; his dark hair waved in the beams of the setting sun.

"Ha, ha!" the shout burst from his lips. "Here is blood warm, warm, aye warm and gushing! Is that the murmur of a brook, is that the whisper of a breeze, is that the song of a bird? No, no, but still it is music—that gushing of the Wronger's blood! Deeply wronged, Mary, deeply, darkly wronged! But fully avenged, Mary, aye to the last drop of his blood! Have you no music there, I would dance, yes, yes, I would dance over the Corse! Ha, ha, ha! Not the sound of the organ, that is too dark and gloomy! But the drum, the trumpet, the chorus of a full band; fill heaven and earth with joy! For in sight of God and his angels, I would dance over the corse, while a wild song of joy, fills the heavens! A song—huzza—a song! And the chorus, mark ye how it swells! Huzza!"

"This, this is the vengeance of a Brother!"

THE CONCLUSION

In a deep forest wild, a maiden form bent over a spring of clear cold water which bubbled upward from among a mass of green leaves, near the foot of a giant oak. She bent down on the velvet moss, while the green leaves of shrubbery encircling her on every side, and the thick branches of trees, meeting over-head in a canopy of verdure, made the place seem like a fairy bower of some olden story.

She bent down over the spring, not with a cup or a goblet in her hand, but with a white lily, trembling in her delicate fingers, as its petals dipped gently into the waters. Those waters, so clear, so cold, so tranquil, reflected the outlines of a fair young face, the gleam of two mild blue eyes, the graceful flow of light brown hair, tossed gently on the summer air. As she gazed into this living mirror, a single ray of sunlight fell quivering from the canopy overhead, and trembled on the bosom of the spring, while a smile stole over the maiden's face. It was a smile, but sad and mournful as a knell; it was a smile, but gloomy as a sunbeam falling over the grave of youth and beauty.

Suddenly the maiden uprose from her kneeling posture. She placed the lily on her bosom, and with a light step threaded the mazes of a winding path that led around the trunks of colossal trees, over the softly tufted moss, and beneath the shade of leafy branches. Now the strain of some wild and melancholy song burst from her lips, and now with her blue eyes upturned, she gazed vacantly upon a glimpse of the blue heavens, murmuring strange words to herself all the while. Again she bounded on her way, until dashing a mass of green leaves aside, she stood upon the brow of a gentle hill, with the summer wind playing among her dark brown tresses, while her blue eyes shone with a calm and holy delight.

A calm sheet of water, embosomed in the crest of the mountain, with banks high and rugged, clothed with forest trees, or gentle and sloping, crowned with soft and luxuriant shrubbery, a calm sheet of water, with its stainless depths resting in the smile of the summer sky, like a sleeping child beneath its mother's gaze! Such was the vision that burst on the delighted eye of the maiden, while her ears were soothed by the melody of the wood-bird's song, mingling with the murmur of a brooklet, echoing from the bosom of the shrubbery around the foot of the knoll, as it sank gently into the waters of the mountain lake.

The maiden gazed upon this scene of calm loveliness, while a mournful expression stole over her face, as though some memory of the past came sadly to her soul.

Arising from the centre of a fair garden that bloomed over the slope of a glade, declining gently to the water's brink, a cottage overshadowed by a grove of forest trees, with vines trailing round its arching windows, and winding walks leading down to the lake, broke on the maiden's eye like a vision of a happy home, reared by the hands of love in the solitude of the wilderness. The cottage, two stories in height, with arching windows and a steep, gabled roof, arose from a flowery knoll not more than a hundred yards from the spot where the maiden stood.

The faint yellow hue of the cottage walls, was in beautiful contrast, with the verdure of the vines, trailing round its windows, the deep green of the branches, waving above its roof, the brown gravelled paths of the garden or the beds of flowers scattered all around, with the sunbeams gleaming over rose and lily, as they waved gently to the summer air.

Suddenly the sound of footsteps came faintly to the maiden's ear. Turning toward the forest, she beheld two forms advancing along a wide gravelled walk, which sloped down toward the knoll, with the interwoven branches, forming a verdant arch overhead. A fair girl, supported the arm of an aged woman, whose tall form, clad in deep black, was in strong contrast, with the light figure at her side, also attired in robes of sable. They came slowly along the walk; they perceived the form of the maiden clad in light robes; in a moment they reached her side.

"We have lost our way in the forest, Miss," cried the aged lady gazing upon the beautiful face of the girl, with an expression of wonder mingled with admiration, "In company with a party of our friends, we left the valley of Wyoming this morning, with the intention of enjoying the free air of these mountains. But having missed our friends, we are forced to ask you, to direct us to the wood, which leads from the forest—"

The maiden in robes of white made no reply. Her blue eyes were enchained by the face of the maiden, who accompanied the aged lady. With slow footsteps she advanced to her side, she laid her hands gently on her shoulders, and with a wild gaze persued each feature of her beautiful countenance. She was indeed beautiful as a dream. Waving tresses of auburn hair, mingling the purple dyes of sunset with the deep black of midnight, relieved a fair countenance, whose pale brow was impressed with an expression of deep sadness, whose dark hazel eyes were full of thoughtful sorrow.

There they stood gazing in each other's faces, these two images of youth and loveliness, while the aged dame, looked from countenance to countenance, with an expression of mute wonder.

The free sunbeams and the glad summer air came through the windows of the cottage. In a small room, furnished in a style of neatness, combined with taste, sate a man in the prime of early manhood. His form was thrown listlessly in a large arm chair, while his arms were lightly folded across his chest. His high forehead, was rendered deathly pale, by the ebony blackness of his hair, which fell in thick masses down to his shoulders. His dark eyes dilating with an expression of intense thought, glared steadily in the air, while his nether lip quivered with a tremulous motion. His countenance was pale, yet it was not the pallor of disease, but of long, deep and absorbing thought. And as a stray sunbeam fell over his brow, or as his black hair, was tossed aside from his face, by an occasional breath of wind, low-muttered words broke from his lips, words fraught with many a bitter memory, or dear hope of the by-gone time.

While he sits there, in that silent room, wrapt in strange thought, we will glance at the contents of a newspaper, that lay among some books and letters, on the table by his side.

It was dated, Philadelphia, June ———

———————"Among the passengers in the steamship, Great Western, which sailed from New York, yesterday morning, was our respected townsman, Luke Harvey, Esq., of the firm of Harvey and Arlington, late Livingstone, Harvey and Co. His bride, the daughter of the late Albert Livingstone, Esq.—who with his wife, was destroyed in the conflagration of the country mansion of Hawkewood—accompanies our friend to Europe, where it is said, an immense fortune, if not a title, has fallen to her, through the due course of law. Many of our readers, will remember the romantic story of Miss Izolé Livingstone's former life. Stolen in her infancy from her father's arms, she was, after the lapse of seventeen years recognized and restored to her home, through the kind exertions of our distinguished Divine, the Rev. Dr. Pyne. The facts of the case, are briefly these—* * * * *.

———————"At an enthusiastic meeting of the American Patent Gospel Association, the thanks of a large and respectable audience, were tendered to the Rev. Dr. Pyne, for his able speech on the Iniquities of the Pope of Rome. We understood, that this worthy and eminent divine, will shortly publish in book form, a complete history of the Popes of Rome, from the earliest ages, down to the present time * * * * *.

———————"We are happy to inform our readers, that the base rumors, which some malignant enemies, have set in circulation, with regard to the reputation of our distinguished friend, Algernon Fitz-Cowles, Esq., have been effectively crushed, by an undeniable manifestation of public opinion. At a *recherche'* supper, given by the gallant Colonel, to a select party of friends, the following toast was given by Judge Singesam * * * * *.

———————"Strange rumors, float on the tide of public opinion, with regard to a new secret order, entitled the Brothers of the Sacred Urn. It is said to have been founded by the Imposter Ravoni, who after having duped our citizens, with his mad-house and other charlatanisms, has so mysteriously vanished from the city * * * * *.

———————"Peggy Grud, convicted of murder in the second degree, was yesterday pardoned, by our truly merciful Governor * * * * Mrs. Nancy Perkins, a respectable widow lady, who lives retired, in an ancient mansion, situated in the southern part of the city, was yesterday tried on a scandalous charge, originated by some designing enemies. She was acquitted by the jury, without leaving the box * * * *.

——————"The dead body of a woman was found on last Thursday, in the graveyard of L——— in this state. The corpse when discovered, was laying beside the grave of Mr. Walraven, once a highly respectable citizen of the town, but now some years deceased. The unknown female was dressed in deep black, her hair was very dark, and her face retained some tokens of former beauty. Having no friends to claim her corse, she was buried in the graveyard of the county poorhouse. * * * * *"

In an obscure corner of the paper, crowded up among a multitude of advertisements, was the following brief and expressive Postscript.

"The villain who perpetrated the wholesale forgery, on several houses in New York, Charleston and New Orleans, was arrested last night, just before our paper went to press. He was taken to New York, under care of the police, heavily ironed, in order to baulk any effort to escape. He proves to be, no less a personage than the *notorious* Algernon Fitz-Cowles, who has been displaying himself in Chesnut Street, for a year or two past. * * * * *.

We also learn, from the best authority, that one of our first clergymen has been guilty of a most daring and atrocious act of perfidy. As the case will shortly be brought to trial, we refrain from giving the particulars. Suffice to say, that the *victim* is the daughter of one of our wealthiest merchants, the heartless seducer, none other than the *Reverend Doctor F. A. T. Pyne*, author of several works on the Iniquities of the Pope, etc., etc., etc.

While the record of human weakness, wretchedness and crime, lay fluttering on the table, the head of the young man, drooped slowly down, until his face rested on his folded arms. There was a world of meaning in the steady gaze of his dilating eye, which glared beneath his woven brows.

The silence of the room, was scarcely broken by the opening of the door. A beautiful woman, advanced with a softened footstep and stole gently to the back of the chair. Her clustering hair, fell in thick tresses of gold, aside from a mild countenance, or whose fair outlines were written the tenderness of a mother, the deep and abiding love of a wife. In her extended arms, she held a sweet and laughing child, whose tiny fingers wandered playfully through the dark locks of the father's hair.

And there in that quiet parlor sate the man of the pallid brow, with his face drooped on his folded arms, wrapt in deep and terrible thought, while at the back of his chair leaning over his downcast head, was the form of a fair and lovely woman, with a laughing babe in her extended hands.

"Byrnewood!" whispered the soft voice of the wife.

He raised his head; he beheld the beaming countenance of his wife, the laughing face of his child.

"Annie!" he whispered, while a smile of pleasure, warmed over his pale face.

He rose from his seat, but that smile was gone. The dark thought was on his soul again; he turned from his wife and child toward the door of that chamber, from which he never emerged, without a flashing eye and gloomy brow.

"Oh Byrnewood, do not enter that chamber to day," said the soft pleading voice of his wife. "I have never sought to know the Secret of that dreary place, I have never crossed its threshold. But this I know, that you are always dark and gloomy, after you have spent but a moment, within its walls. Do not enter the chamber to day, Byrnewood, do not I beseech you!"

"This day Annie, for the last time!" said Byrnewood, as he took the key from his pocket and inserted it, in the lock. "After to-day, that room, shall never make me sad or gloomy."

With a melancholy smile he opened the door, passed into the chamber, and closed it again. It was a small and narrow room, with a plain carpet on the floor, a table standing in one corner, and an arching window opening on the lake. Through the half closed curtains of this window, came the warm sunshine, the cool air, and a glimpse of the clear waters, the deep forests and fragrant flowers.

In the centre of the wall opposite the door, a long curtain of dark velvet hung drooping from the ceiling to the floor. Byrnewood stood opposite this curtain, with his arms sternly folded on his breast, while a fearful agitation convulsed each lineament of his expressive countenance.

"Ha! I remember it well," he muttered, "I remember it well! There, there I stood, with the gaze of the callous mob fixed upon my face, the stern visages of the jury, and the iron countenance of the Judge, these were all before me! I stood in the presence of my fate.

"There too were the lawyers, full of craft and cunning. They had anticipated long speeches, ingenious pleas, knotty points of law—ha, ha! How I baulked them all! I remember it yet. "Plead not guilty" whispered my lawyer. I smiled in my heart. I knew his plan. He would clear me from the gibbet or the gaol, by the paltry plea of insanity! *I* insane! when my soul was firm as its own despair, when my hand was true as the weapon it grasped! "Guilty or not guilty!" whined the clerk.

" 'Guilty!' " I shouted, rising to my feet, while my lawyers, started up with dismay. 'Guilty in the sight of God! I am charged with this man's murder; I did murder him! Yes, yes, as a dog should die, he died! I had a fair and stainless sister, gentlemen, my grey-haired father had a pure and innocent daughter! On that daughter's happiness hung the life of a true-hearted mother. Yes, yes, your Honor, that daughter, was the hope and joy of three persons, a father, a mother, a brother; and each of these would have given their life for her!

" 'A libertine came; he lured this girl from her home; he perjured his soul that he might betray her! He did betray her! Betrayed, polluted, dishonored, she returned to her father's house!

" 'And think ye, that there was no Brother to avenge her wrong? Ha, ha! There *was* a brother. He pursued the libertine. He overtook the craven, in his guilty flight! Calling on the High God to nerve his arm, and send the bullet home, he shot the Libertine, as in the flush of triumphant guilt, he stood glorying in his crime. Not guilty? Ha, ha! I am guilty, I am the murderer, I shot the libertine, and would shoot him again! Now gentlemen, convict me if you can! Now your Honor, pass sentence of death upon me if you can!

" 'Here I rest my defence; on this I peril life and honor! He wronged my sister and he died!' "

"How that glad shout rung through the Court House! Not guilty! I was free!"

As this wild soliloquy trembled from his lips in broken murmurs, he tore aside the velvet drapery, and a portrait was revealed. It was the portrait of Gustavus Lorrimer! Strolling into the studio of a celebrated artist, Byrnewood had seen this picture, and having ascertained that it was a copy of a portrait, painted for Lorrimer a month before his death, he purchased it, and brought it to his mountain retreat among the wilds of Wyoming. There was the same laughing face of manly beauty, the same dark hazel eye, the scornful lip, with its dark mustache, the flowing locks of dark brown hair. There was the portrait, gleaming in the light of the sun, while the handsome Gus Lorrimer lay rotting in his grave, six feet below the glad earth, smiling in the summer sun.

The Avenger knew that he was right in the sight of God, in the execution of the fearful deed which had been death to the Libertine, but still there was one thought, never absent from his soul. At his board, on his pillow, in the walk through the wild wood or the crowded city, the face of Lorrimer was ever with him. He found an awful pleasure in contemplating the portrait of the Libertine. He had avenged his sister's wrong, but the memory of the scenes he had witnessed in Monk-Hall, in the parlor of his father's house, in the streets of the Quaker City, or on the broad river, dwelt like a shadow on his soul.

While Byrnewood Arlington stood gazing intently upon the portrait, the door slowly opened, and three figures entered the room. His reverie was deep and absorbing; he did not hear the sound of the opening door, nor the tread of footsteps. An aged dame, clad in deep black, a fair young girl in robes white as snow, and a maiden attired in sable, with auburn hair floating along each youthful cheek—these all, unknown and unperceived, stood at the brother's side.

"Ha!" he cried, with a sudden start as he perceived the intruders. "Mary have I not told you, never to cross that threshold—"

His words were drowned in the wild shriek that quivered on each lip. They beheld the portrait; they sank kneeling on the floor.

"My child!" shrieked the dame, and she clasped her hands in silent agony.

"My brother!" cried the maiden in black, and she buried her face in her bosom, while her auburn hair floated over her trembling hands.

The girl in robes of flowing white, knelt on the floor with her eyes so full of unutterable feeling, centered on the portrait, her cheek flushed with strange emotions, and her clasped hands raised on high. A single word burst from her lips, a single word, uttered in a whisper, like the sigh of a broken heart—

LORRAINE!"

THE END OF THE QUAKER CITY

Notes to the Text

P. 6 "Miller the Prophet": William Miller (1782–1849), the leader of the Adventist movement in America, began in the mid-1830s to predict the imminent destruction of the world and the second coming of Christ, who he said would arrive between March 1843 and March 1844. His prophecies generated intense nationwide excitement, manifested in some 120 preparatory camp meetings with an estimated half million in attendance.

P. 13 "Forrest": Edwin Forrest (1806–72), the stocky, athletic actor famous for his physical vigor and stentorian voice, was known as "The Ferocious Tragedian" and "The Bowery B'hoy's Delight."

P. 126 "Bulwer": Edward George Earle Bulwer-Lytton (1803–73) was a prolific British novelist, poet, reformer, and playwright.

P. 210 "Harry Clay": Henry Clay (1777–1852), a United States Senator from Kentucky, supported the tariff and the rechartering of the United States Bank and was, therefore, repugnant to Lippard. Having resigned from the Senate in March 1842 in protest of the administration of President John Tyler, he became the Whig nominee for president in 1844.

P. 260 "William Harrison Ainsworth": Ainsworth (1805–82) was a British novelist who became popular with adventure novels such as *Rookwood* (1834), *Crichton* (1837), and *Jack Sheppard* (1839).

P. 269 "Stephen Girard": The Philadelphia merchant and philanthropist Stephen Girard (1750–1831) had bequeathed some $6 million in cash and real estate for the founding of a college for impoverished white male orphans. Lippard, who associated poverty with illiteracy, was enraged by the long delay in the construction of the college, which was not completed until 1848.

PP. 281 and 298–99 "Darley": The Philadelphia illustrator Felix Octavius Carr Darley (1822–88) rose to prominence in 1842, when his sketches of the city's street life began to appear in popular periodicals. In 1843 he produced a pictorial series entitled "Scenes in Indian Life" as well as caricatures for Carey and Hart's Library of American Humorous Works. He did an illustration for the 1845 edition of *The Quaker City* (reproduced on page xlvi of this edition) and later became well known for his illustrations of Longfellow, Hawthorne, Irving, and others.

P. 423 "A pitiful craven": Lippard is referring to John Tyler (1790–1862), the tenth president of the United States. A states'-rights Whig from Virginia, Tyler was known as "His Accidency" because he became president as result of the sudden death of William Henry Harrison in 1841. Tyler, opposed by Henry Clay and other nationalist Whigs, suffered the humiliation of having his whole cabinet, with the exception of Daniel Webster, resign in protest against his administration.

P. 479 "some Godlike Senator": Lippard refers to Daniel Webster (1782–1852), the Whig Senator from Massachusetts who was secretary of state under Harrison and Tyler. Known for his grandiloquent oratorical style, Webster was anathema to Lippard because of his support of the tarriff and industrial interests. Lippard caricatured Webster as "Gabriel Godlike" in his novel *The Empire City.*

P. 558 "James": George Paine Rainsford James (1799–1860) was a British author who averaged a novel every nine months between 1825 and 1843. Among his novels were *Richelieu* (1825), *The Gypsy* (1835), and *Attila* (1837).

Bibliography

Chronological Listing of Books by Lippard

Adrian, the Neophyte. Philadelphia: I. R. and A. H. Diller, 1843. Novella.

The Battle-Day of Germantown. Philadelphia: A. H. Diller, 1843. Novella.

Herbert Tracy, or The Legend of the Black Rangers. Philadelphia: R. G. Berford, 1844. Novel.

The Ladye Annabel; or, The Doom of the Poisoner. A Romance by an Unknown Author. Philadelphia: R. G. Berford, 1844. Novel. Reissued as *The Mysteries of Florence.* Philadelphia: T. B. Peterson & Bros., 1864.

The Quaker City; or, The Monks of Monk Hall. A Romance of Philadelphia Life, Mystery, and Crime. Philadelphia: G. B. Zieber & Co., 1844–45 [issued in 10 paper-covered parts, 4 in 1844 and 6 in 1845]. Novel.

Blanche of Brandywine; or, September the Eleventh, 1777. A Romance, Combining the Poetry, Legend, and History of the Battle of Brandywine. Philadelphia: G. B. Zieber & Co., 1846. Novel.

The Nazarene; or, The Last of the Washingtons. A Revelation of Philadelphia, New York and Washington in the Year 1844. Philadelphia: G. Lippard and Co., 1846. Novel.

Legends of Mexico. Philadelphia: T. B. Peterson, 1847. Novel.

The Rose of Wissahikon; or, The Fourth of July, 1776. A Romance, Embracing the Secret History of the Declaration of Independence. Philadelphia: G. B. Zieber & Co., 1847. Novel.

Washington and His Generals; or, Legends of the Revolution. Philadelphia: G. B. Zieber & Co., 1847. Stories.

'Bel of Prairie Eden. A Romance of Mexico. Philadelphia: T. B. Peterson, 1848. Novel.

The Heart-Broken. Philadelphia: G. B. Zieber & Co., 1848. Tribute to Charles Brockden Brown.

Paul Ardenheim, The Monk of Wissahikon. Philadelphia: T. B. Peterson, 1848. Novel.

The Entranced; or, The Wanderer of Eighteen Centuries. Philadelphia: Joseph Severns and

Co., n.d. [1849]. Novel. Revised edition: *Adonai: The Pilgrim of Eternity,* in *The White Banner.* Philadelphia: G. Lippard, 1851.

The Man with the Mask; A Sequel to The Memoirs of a Preacher, a Revelation of the Church and Home. Philadelphia: Joseph Severns and Co., n.d. [1849]. Novel.

The Memoirs of a Preacher, a Revelation of the Church and the Home. Philadelphia: Joseph Severns and Company, 1849. Novel.

Washington and His Men. Philadelphia: Joseph Severns and Co., 1849. Stories.

The Empire City; or, New York by Night and Day. New York: Stringer and Townsend, 1850. Novel.

The Killers. A Narrative of Real Life in Philadelphia . . . By a Member of the Philadelphia Bar. Philadelphia: Hankinson and Bartholomew, 1850.

The White Banner. Vol. I. Philadelphia: G. Lippard, on Behalf of the Shareholders, 1851. Essays and stories.

The Midnight Queen; or, Leaves from New-York Life. New York: Garrett & Co., 1853. Stories.

Thomas Paine, Author-Soldier of the American Revolution. Philadelphia, ca. 1894. Lecture first given on 26 January 1846.

Some Other Writings by Lippard

"The Bread Crust Papers—The Duel in Camden." *Philadelphia Spirit of the Times,* March 8 through April 1, 1842. Satire by L.

"The Spermaceti Papers." *Philadelphia Citizen Soldier,* May 31 through August 26, 1843. Satire by L.

"The Walnut Coffin Papers . . . The Uprisings of the Coffin-Maker's 'Prentice." *Philadelphia Citizen Soldier,* September 20 and October 11, 1843. Satire by L.

"The Sisterhood of the Green Veil." *Philadelphia Nineteenth Century,* 1848. Story by L.

"Valedictory of the Industrial Congress." *Philadelphia Nineteenth Century,* 1848. Labor speech by L.

Eulogy of Poe by L [untitled]. *Philadelphia Quaker City,* October 20, 1849.

"It Is a Queer World." *Philadelphia Quaker City,* January 26, 1850. Eulogy of Poe by L.

Collection of Writings by Lippard

Reynolds, David S., ed. *George Lippard, Prophet of Protest: Writings of an American Radical, 1822–1854.* New York: Peter Lang, 1986.

Bibliographies of Lippard

Blanck, Jacob, comp. *Bibliography of American Literature.* 5: 405–18. New Haven: Yale University Press, 1969. Primary.

Butterfield, Roger. "A Check List of the Separately Published Works of George Lippard." *Pennsylvania Magazine of History and Biography* 79 (July 1955): 302–9. Primary.

Jackson, Joseph. "A Bibliography of the Works of George Lippard." *Pennsylvania Magazine of History and Biography* 54 (April and October 1930): 131–54, 381–83. Primary.

Reynolds, David S. *George Lippard.* 132–44. Boston: G. K. Hall, 1982. Primary and secondary.

Manuscripts and Archives

Historical Society of Pennsylvania has L's diary, some letters, "Notes on the Brotherhood of the Union," and issues of L's newspaper, the *Quaker City.* The Library Company, Philadelphia, has some early editions of L's works. Bucks County Historical Society, Pennsylvania, holds file of the *Philadelphia Citizen Soldier.* The American Antiquarian Society, Worcester, Mass., has an almost complete file of L's *Quaker City* newspaper as well as signed and important editions of L's fiction, many of his periodical writings, copies of his letters, and certain reviews of his works. Lyle Wright's microfilm series of early American fiction has most of L's novels.

Biographies and Critical Studies

1. Full-length Studies

[Bouton, John Bell.] *The Life and Choice Writings of George Lippard.* New York: H. H. Randall, 1855.

DeGrazia, Emilio. "The Life and Works of George Lippard." Ph.D. diss., Ohio State University, 1969.

Jackson, Joseph. "George Lippard: Poet of the Proletariat." Ca. 1930. Unfinished attempt at a modern biography. Manuscript in the Joseph Jackson Collection, Historical Society of Pennsylvania.

Reynolds, David S. *George Lippard.* Boston: G. K. Hall, 1982.

2. Book Sections & Articles

Bode, Carl, ed. *Anatomy of American Popular Culture, 1840–1861.* 149, 162–68. Berkeley: University of California Press, 1959.

Butterfield, Roger. "George Lippard and His Secret Brotherhood." *Pennsylvania Magazine of History and Biography* 79 (July 1955): 291–309.

Cowie, Alexander. "Monk Hall, Shame of Philadelphia." *New York Times Book Review,* October 22, 1944.

———. *The Rise of the American Novel.* 319–26, 759. New York: American Book Co., 1948.

Davis, David Brion. *Homicide in American Fiction, 1798–1860: A Study in Social Values.* 52–53, 154, 159–60, 176, 206–8, 227, 259–61, 279, 302. Ithaca: Cornell University Press, 1957.

DeGrazia, Emilio. "Edgar Allan Poe, George Lippard, and the Spermaceti and Walnut-Coffin Papers." *Papers of the Bibliographical Society of America* 66 (1972): 58–60.

———. "Poe's Devoted Democrat, George Lippard." *Poe Studies* 6 (June 1973): 6–8.

Denning, Michael. *Mechanic Accents: Dime Novels and Working-Class Culture in America.* 20, 85–117, 177. London & New York: Verso, 1987.

Ehrlich, Heyward. "The 'Mysteries' of Philadelphia: Lippard's *Quaker City* and 'Urban' Gothic." *ESQ: A Journal of the American Renaissance* 66 (1st quarter 1972): 50–65.

Fiedler, Leslie. *Love and Death in the American Novel.* 89, *passim.* Revised edition: New York: Stein & Day, 1966.

———. "The Male Novel." *Partisan Review* 37 (1970): 74–89. Revised as introduction to Fiedler's edition of *The Monks of Monk Hall*. New York: Odyssey, 1970.

Jackson, Joseph. *Encyclopedia of Philadelphia*. 3: 842–45. Harrisburg: National Historical Association, 1932.

———. "George Lippard: Misunderstood Man of Letters." *Pennsylvania Magazine of History and Biography* 54 (October 1930): 376–91.

Newfield, Christopher. "Democracy and Male Homoeroticism." *The Yale Journal of Criticism* 6, no. 2 (1993): 29–62.

Oberholtzer, Ellis P. *The Literary History of Philadelphia*. 7, 239, 251–62. Philadelphia: G. W. Jacobs, 1906.

Pollin, Burton. "More on Poe and Lippard." *Poe Studies* 7 (June 1974): 22–23.

Quinn, Arthur Hobson. *Edgar Allan Poe: A Critical Biography*. 385, *passim*. New York: Appleton-Century, 1941.

Reynolds, David S. *Beneath the American Renaissance: The Subversive Imagination in the Age of Emerson and Melville*. 87–91, *passim*. New York: Alfred A. Knopf, 1988.

———. *Faith in Fiction: The Emergence of Religious Literature in America*. 187–96, *passim*. Cambridge, Mass.: Harvard University Press, 1981.

———. Introduction to *George Lippard, Prophet of Protest: Writings of an American Radical, 1822–1854*. 1–42. New York: Peter Lang, 1986.

———. *Walt Whitman's America: A Cultural Biography*. Chapter 5. New York: Alfred A. Knopf, 1995.

Ridgely, J. V. "George Lippard's *The Quaker City:* The World of the American Porno-Gothic." *Studies in the Literary Imagination* 7 (Spring 1974): 77–94.

Seecamp, Carsten E. "The Chapter of Perfection: A Neglected Influence on George Lippard." *Pennsylvania Magazine of History and Biography* 94 (April 1970): 192–212.

Siegel, Adrienne. *The Image of the American City in Popular Literature, 1820–1870*. 78–79, *passim*. Port Washington N.Y.: Kennikat, 1981.

Slotkin, Richard. *The Fatal Environment: The Myth of the Frontier in the Age of Industrialization, 1800–1890*. 192–98. New York: Atheneum, 1985.

Stoehr, Taylor. *Hawthorne's Mad Scientists: Pseudoscience and Social Science in Nineteenth-Century Life and Letters*. Hamden, Conn.: Archon, 1978.

Stout, Janis P. *Sodoms in Eden: The City in American Fiction before 1860*. 50–54, *passim*. Westport, Conn.: Greenwood, 1976.

Thomas, Dwight Rembert. "Poe in Philadelphia, 1838–1844." Ph.D. diss., University of Pennsylvania, 1978.

Wyld, Lionel D. "George Lippard: Gothicism and Social Consciousness in the Early American Novel." *Four Quarters* 5 (1956): 6–12.

Ziff, Larzer. *Literary Democracy: The Declaration of Cultural Independence in America*. 91–107, *passim*. New York: Viking, 1981.